I0782160

THE PREY

SERIES

CARMEN ROSALES

THIRST
LUST
APPETITE

Erotic Quill Publishing, LLC
3020 NE 41st Terrace STE 9 #243
Homestead, Fl. 33033

www.carmenrosales.com

Editing by Lunar Rose Editing
Editing by Fairest Reviews Editing Services

Manufactured in the United States of America
Second Edition April 2024

ALSO BY

CARMEN ROSALES

PREFACE

In an elite Catholic university full of lies, lust, deceit, and betrayal Gia and
Jess become a pawn in a game of sexual seduction. They realize there is no
one they can trust. Everything is a lie with a church full of sinners.
Gia gets the attention of Dravin. He's after her, but he has a secret that no
one outside the Order knows about. What will Gia do when she finds out?
Give in to her desires, or be the sacrifice?
Jess is fleeing from a dark past.
The sons of Kenyan just take what they want and who they want.
They begin to feed on Jess's lust for desire. But Jess's dark past has caught up
with her. Her inner demons have decided to come out and play, but there is
something bigger at play. At night, a mystery man comes for her, and he
doesn't play by the rules.
He's the one she never saw coming.
The problem.
She doesn't know who he is.
And he isn't the only one who wants her.
There is only one way out for Gia and Jess: play the game or change the rules.

"NO MAN CHOOSES EVIL BECAUSE IT IS EVIL; HE ONLY
MISTAKES IT FOR HAPPINESS, THE GOOD HE SEEKS."

MARY SHELLEY

AUTHORS NOTE

Dear Reader,

The triggers include depression, death, suicide, acts of violence, and acts of bullying.All sex is for the enjoyment of all characters involved. Please note that this special edition contains the first three books in the series.

If you or know anyone you know that is suffering from mental health and needs help. Please call National Suicide Prevention Lifeline.

THE PREY SERIES

THIRST
LUST
APPETITE

THE **PREY** SERIES

THIRST

GIA
†

"THANK YOU," I tell the Uber driver as he gets in the white Honda after unloading my suitcases from the trunk.

The overcast grey clouds give off a gloomy vibe as I look at the Gothic cathedral-style building of Kenyan University. The building is imposing, and it is not just because it is a new school that I'm unfamiliar with. The campus pictures on the web are very different from what you see in person. On the internet, the images are photoshopped with the backdrop of a sunny day with a lot of green landscaping, but in reality, it looks a lot gloomier.

Kenyon University is an Ivy League school mainly for the rich. I had to transfer here just to finish my senior year because it was practically the only college that would accept me past the deadline. (Some crap I read online, that they need to offer equal opportunity and allow all types of students to attend. In other words, they have spots for poor people, but they can't make it obvious that they don't want underprivileged kids to attend.

Luckily for me, even though my parents recently divorced, I still had enough for most of my tuition. The rest I had to take out in loans. My parents had to sell the house in Wisconsin to finalize their divorce. My father wanted to get it over with because he had already met someone, or rather, he had someone already from what my mother accused him of in court. The only thing I could do was get out of there as fast as I could and start my own life. Now that I'm here seeing the campus up close, it really looks like a place straight out of a horror movie. I hope this wasn't a mistake, but with my parents' drama, I didn't have much of a choice.

The smell of rain is in the air as I take out my phone and pull up a picture of the map to see where my dorm is located. The place looks deserted, except for a few people walking away from the building.

Classes don't start until the day after tomorrow. I googled the campus social media page, and from what students post about daily campus life, I see that classes here can be intense. I have decided to major in economics, and I chose a Catholic school to appease my mother. My mother is a devoted Catholic and had me attending church religiously every Sunday. It is prob-ably why she lost it when she caught my father cheating and filed for divorce. She didn't want me to leave Wisconsin, but I couldn't deal with all the back and forth. I felt like I had to choose one parent over the other, and it was just too much. I was ready to go out into the world and become something rather than live with one of my parents. If I chose to move with my mom, my father would feel disappointed and if I chose my father, my mother would feel that I'm taking his side. In all honesty, I don't agree with what my father did to my mother, but I saw it coming. My father had been going less and less to church with my mother, and they were constantly arguing.

Throughout my childhood, the only religion I knew was Catholic. The opportunity to attend here for at least a year was too good to pass up. This religious college, built sometime in the 1800s, has a great business program. My hope is to land a good job and venture out on my own. Maybe I'll find someone to start a life with or at least date.

Hauling my suitcase, the wheels finally land on the smooth sidewalk that crisscrosses through the trees between the buildings on the one-thousand-acre campus. The whole place looks like a maze. I pull out my phone, and a large shadow materializes behind me. I close my eyes, hoping it is just a shadow of a tree or maybe my eyes are playing tricks on me, but it's not. My shadow suddenly speaks... he speaks.

"It's that way."

My head tilts up at the sound of the sexiest voice I have ever heard. It sounds like a guy giving an interview in a sexy drawl from a late-night podcast. My eyes slowly rake up dark denim-washed jeans to a plain white T-shirt under a motorcycle jacket. He points in the opposite direction with his hand holding a black helmet. When my eyes finally land on his face, I stop and stare like a complete idiot. His eyes—they are captivating. One is dark, like midnight, and the other is blue, like the ocean.

His eyes find mine, and he raises a brow because I'm standing there staring at him like I'm dumbstruck. The man has an exotic, beautiful face with a hard, angular jaw and a straight nose. His nose is not too big or too small; it is just...perfect. His dark hair is slicked back without a piece out of place. Everything about the way he looks is just...right.

My mind catches up with my mouth, but it's too late because he turns around without saying another word.

"I-I'm—My name is Gia." I stammer, but it's too late. He keeps walking, and I curse at myself for looking stupid. "Thank you," I call out, but he continues walking, dismissing me like he never spoke to me.

My interaction with cute guys is probably a three on a scale from one to ten. I attended the University of Wisconsin for three years. My parents were strict, wanting to keep me close to home. They even kept my curfew because I was under their roof and would respect living in their house. My father obviously didn't get the memo.

I tried to date, but my mother was a devoted Catholic and was afraid I would turn into a promiscuous whore. I gave up trying to convince her that I should date and focused on completing school amid my parents' divorce my junior year. I have no problem with getting married, but the whole saving yourself for marriage thing was ridiculous. Times are different, and just because you save your virginity for marriage doesn't guarantee you will end up living happily ever after. Look at my parents. Divorced. A bunch of bullshit if you ask me. I'm tired of living the straight and narrow. It's time I spread my wings and live life.

GIA

AFTER I MAKE it to my dorm on the third floor, I meet my new roommate, Jesse. She likes to be called Jess and, like me, is a 'normal' student who has to take out loans to be here. She doesn't come from money. She and her mom saved just enough for her off-campus expenses for four years, and she was lucky enough to get accepted. I spent the whole day unpacking and settling in and agreed to go with Jess to a popular bar close to campus the next day.

We enter a bar close to campus the next day like we agreed. Jess seems nice and offered to hang out which I can appreciate.

"So, what is it like to attend Kenyan?" I ask Jess, taking a sip from my vodka and cranberry.

She slides her curly hair away from her face and leans slightly over the wooden table in our booth in front of me. "Different. The students here are not like other students in other universities. The majority of people that go here come from wealthy families—the elite. They are rich, and most of them have no issue showing it and reminding people like us that we are broke charity cases. Basically, if you have money, you can get away with a lot of things."

Placing my drink down over the coaster, my eyes watch as the glass sweats. Drops of water slide down the cup like rain hitting a windowpane, and the coaster soaks up the drips like I'm soaking up everything she says about this place and the people who attend. She said they get away with a lot. Now, I'm curious to know what a lot entails.

"What kind of things?"

She shrugs and scrunches her nose at me. "I don't kiss and tell. What I will do though, and only because you are my roommate, is tell you who is important and who you should stay away from."

She is about to tell me when the front doors of the Babylon bar open. The light from outside filters in, creating a bright glare that makes me squint my eyes. After a few seconds, when my eyes adjust, I see seven people coming inside—one of them I recognize from yesterday.

He walks in with an air of confidence. All the women seated at the bar eye him appreciatively as he makes his way inside. My stomach twists into knots as I remember every angle of his face from the first time my eyes took him in.

His eyes are like the shallow and deep end of an ocean. The light eye is the shallow part of the clearest water and the other one is dark like the depths of the sea. His dark hair is longer on top and faded on the sides. The man is beautiful to look at. I googled mismatched eyes yesterday when I got into my dorm because I was bored trying to fall asleep. Even with my screen cracked on my phone, I was able to read about the condition and how you could be born with heterochromia, but it's rare. Just like he is rare...to me, at least. I have never seen a guy that is so beautiful. I watch his eyes sweep the room, captivating in his wake. You just can't help but notice him when he enters a room.

Jess turns around when she notices me staring at the five guys and two girls heading to the bar. I try to act like I'm watching them as a group, but in all honesty, there is only one I have eyes for. He is tall, chiseled with muscle under his black long-sleeve sweater and dark jeans.

I motion with my hand to the hot-ass guy that did me a solid by pointing me in the right direction to find the building I was looking for. "Who is he?"

Jess laughs through her nose and shakes her head. "That is Dravin Beckford, also a senior." She turns to look at me and snaps her fingers to get my attention before lowering her voice. "Stay away from him. He is one of the richest guys that attend here and a total player. He's a fuck 'em and leave 'em type of guy. The girl with white porcelain skin and straight black hair, her name is Veronica and she's a total bitch. Stay away from her. The other one with red hair is Lizzy, and she follows Veronica in everything that she does, including screwing people over. The seven of them are part of the rich, elite Kenyan crew. They can basically do what they want, when they want, and to whoever they want and get away with it."

"What do you mean?"

Her lips form a thin line. When I raise my brow, waiting for her to spill, she sighs, licks her lips, and continues. "The other four guys are just as hot but not as evil as Dravin and his two close friends. You need to watch out for Dravin, Reid, Valen, and Veronica. Veronica is like Dravin in many ways. They aren't together as a couple. They just like to compete."

"Compete? For what?"

"Who they can fuck over first. Who they can destroy for fun because they like to play mindfuck games. Based on what I have seen from my time here, word of advice: stay away from them. They are not like us. They are rich and get away with shit. Especially Veronica."

"Are you sure they aren't together?"

"Who? Dravin and Veronica?"

I nod, curious about them.

"Not that I know of. Maybe in secret. They both do the same things, except Dravin doesn't care what anyone thinks of him. Veronica cares, and she has everyone fooled. She acts like she is Mother Theresa or something, but people know the truth. They're just scared to admit it. She is a liar and, from what I have heard, a total slut but in front of everyone, she acts like a saint. So, she could be hiding things."

"They look very cozy to me," I say, nudging my head toward the group as they play pool on the other side of the bar. Dravin and Veronica are standing close together, whispering something to each other.

"I'm almost positive they aren't together. She was dating this guy named Warren."

"Who's Warren?" I ask, intrigued.

"Warren is rich and popular and an athlete. The five guys you saw enter the bar are all on the swim team. Swimming here is a big deal; the other guys they are playing pool with are also on the team. Warren was going out with Veronica until they parted ways last semester. She claims they were just giving each other a break, but according to him, he dumped her. Let's just say she didn't take it very well because it dented her ego."

"Why do you think he dumped her?"

She shrugs. "No one knows, but it seems she isn't over him. She still hangs around the guys on the swim team and since Dravin is the captain, she figures that if she stays tight with him and the others, Warren will show up and things will return to the way they were."

"Obviously, it isn't working."

"Nope. I think he is over her or just simply sick of her shit. The way she acts behind the scenes, you would think she is the devil's daughter and Dravin is the devil's son. I'm surprised the church attached to the school doesn't go up in flames when they enter for Sunday mass. Promise me you will stay away from them."

"I'm not interested in any of their games."

"Oh, and one more thing... Don't fuck any of the rich guys. They are all players and will tell you what you want to hear to get in your pants. I've watched many girls get destroyed by these guys. Don't say I didn't warn you."

I take a sip of my drink and when I place my cup down, eyes from across the pool table meet mine. They should be aimed at the ball for the winning shot, but they aren't. The light hanging over the pool table casts a glow over his face. One dark eye, one light eye, watching me like I'm the intended target. It's like Dravin wants to see inside my head. He wants to know what I'm thinking. What makes me tick.

The sound of the tip of the pool stick meeting the ball as he slides his fingers over the stick snaps me out of the trance he had me in. Averting my gaze, it lands on Jess.

"Stay away," she whispers. "He is controlling, and he loves a challenge. Once he is bored with you, he will humiliate you just for participating."

"Sounds like a standup guy. Who should I pay attention to then?"

She gives me a smirk. "Normal people who earn the things they are given and have morals. Translation, almost no one. There are a handful of scholarship students and the ones that have to pay their way through college. Some of them get corrupted and sucked in like little pets of the elite, but you will figure it out. I have faith in you. You don't seem like the type to fall into temptation," she says, giving me a wink.

I down the rest of my drink, but the watered-down mixture of cranberry and vodka is not as strong when it hits my stomach. I give her a smirk and say, "Like Dravin?"

"Yes," she answers.

My bladder decides to announce that it needs to be emptied, or I'll be swimming in the next five minutes. It will also give me time to wrap my mind around what Jess told me about Dravin and his crew of friends.

"I'm going to the bathroom, and then we can head back," I tell her.

"Alright. I'll finish my drink by the time you get back."

When I slide my pants up, the toilet automatically flushes, and I head to the sink to wash my hands. I watch as the water rinses the soap off my hands, swirling into the drain, forming little bubbles. When I turn to grab a paper towel, I'm suddenly aware that I'm not alone in the bathroom. My head turns to the left and I jolt biting back a scream.

"You scared me," I blurt.

My stomach begins to twist and buzz, and my heart begins to beat wildly inside my chest like I'm having a panic attack. Leaning against the wall in the dark, casting shadows on the dimly lit bathroom, is Dravin. His eyes sweep down my skinny jeans, his exotic eyes studying me like I'm an exhibit in a zoo.

When I find my voice, I quirk a brow. "Can I help you?"

His eyes slowly travel up until it reaches my face. "I've never seen you before. What year are you?"

"You saw me yesterday, and you pointed me toward my dorm. I'm a senior. I transferred in from Wisconsin."

"I didn't ask all that. Now tell me, do you have a boyfriend?"

"No. Do you?"

He chuckles, and my heart speeds up when I see how breathtaking he looks when he laughs. The sound coming from his beautiful face, with eyes that look like they have seen centuries of existence, makes me forget that I'm alone in the women's bathroom in a bar called the Babylon with the most intriguing man I've ever been around.

"No. Are you a lesbian?"

My brows raise in annoyance. "No," I quip, turning around to toss the brown paper towel into the waste basket.

"Nice."

When I turn back around, I sigh, disgusted. "Are you always this charming when you meet women?

"You have a nice ass. I was just pointing it out."

He moves close and I take a step back, my lower back hitting the edge of the counter. "Do you always stalk women when they go to the bathroom to check out their ass?"

"Don't get ahead of yourself. I was just coming in here to do you a favor and tell you not to listen to everything you hear. I don't appreciate people spreading rumors about me."

"What are you talking about?

My chin raises, and his gaze falls to my throat like a vampire wanting a taste of blood. His lips are inches from the side of my neck. I can smell his cologne, expensive, but refined. The type of scent that gets addicting when you first inhale. Dravin is like a drug wrapped in a blanket of temptation.

My mother would tell me that when you are trapped in temptation, you can either hop on it and ride it, or kneel, and pray it goes away. Now I understand what she meant.

His exotic eyes find mine, and I don't know which one is salvation or damnation. It is like looking into a lens of good versus evil—terrifyingly beautiful.

"Most people are morons. Don't believe everything you hear and don't knock what you haven't tried."

"I wasn't interested in trying anything."

His lips skim the skin on my neck, and it feels like lightning strikes before an impending storm, instantly making me a liar. His lips reach the lobe of my ear and the tiny hairs on my skin lift. Oh, fuck. I don't breathe. I don't move.

"Liar," he whispers.

The breath I was holding leaks from my lips. My head turns, and my lips are inches from the stubble of his cheek. He smells of bourbon, cologne, and me. His eyes feast on the exposed skin of my shoulder like he can read my thoughts. The only way I can take back control is if I deny him.

"Just because girls fall at your feet, and let you sleep with them, doesn't mean I'm one of them."

Silence stretches for a few seconds before he asks, "How do you know I sleep with them?"

I lie. "A friend texted me."

His jaw ticks, indicating I struck a nerve. "Maybe you should get to know a person before you make those types of assumptions and judge them based on gossip."

I feel like an ass and the last thing I need is to piss people like Dravin off. Who am I to judge?

"I'm sorry. I shouldn't have said that, but you can't expect me not to react when you get close to me just because you think I want you."

"Do you?"

My head tilts back to look at him. This close, I notice Dravin is way taller than me, and I'm five-foot-six. I already apologized, and he is being dramatic, but I won't throw Jess under the bus. I don't need problems with my roommate. I have only been here forty-eight hours, and the last thing I need is problems with rich people who can make my life miserable. He's probably trying to figure out if he can mess with me or mess with my head.

"Look, I said I was sorry. Let's start over. My name is Gia." I stick my hand out between us and he steps back. He stays quiet for a second. A second turns into a few more. He is probably not used to a girl acting normal and not bending over in his presence hoping he will have mercy and screw them. His hand slides into mine, and we shake.

"I'm Dravin."

I give him my best smile, but before he releases my hand, his thumb makes circular motions in the palm of my hand. My nipples harden under the cups of my bra, and I feel my mouth part. I have never felt this aroused by a guy before, but I'm quickly learning how to keep myself in check. If there are more guys like Dravin who attend here, then I'm really going to have to work on my body language and keep my thoughts to myself as much as possible.

His voice lowers into a husky tone. "Tell me, Gia. I'm curious. You are obviously not the type that would allow me to turn you around and pull those jeans over that sexy ass and take you right here from behind. Do you play with yourself?"

I glare at him, snatching my hand back. I go around him and storm out of the bathroom. Fucking asshole. This is all a game to him. He wants to see if I'll let him fuck me in a restroom of a bar, if I'm the type to give in. Like I would tell him something like that.

"It was just a question to get to know you better," he mocks as I stomp through the hallway back to the table where Jess is waiting to leave.

GIA

JESS ASKED last night if I was ok because, according to her, I came out of the bathroom flushed. More like pissed the fuck off and aroused all at the same time. The guy is totally full of himself and a total dick. What the fuck was that? I didn't tell her what happened with Dravin in the bathroom because nothing happened except that she was right: he is a player, and I need to stay away from him.

"Hi." A guy's voice says from behind me in class.

Turning around, I find a brown-haired, green-eyed Adonis staring at me with a smile on his face. I was right. All the guys around here look lethal.

Peering around, I notice he was talking to me.

"Hi," he repeats. "My name is Warren, and you are?"

Alarm bells begin to go off—more like the sound of a foghorn going off in my head, warning me not to make conversation with this guy. Jess warned me about Dravin, and look how that turned out. That means this guy is definitely in a no-fly zone. I don't need the wrath of the devil's daughter, Veronica. I just need to complete this year and graduate, and I will never have to see these people again.

Giving him a stern look, I answer. "Gia."

"Gia," he repeats. "I like it. It reminds me of Gia, the supermodel."

His attempt at flattery amuses me. He didn't say I looked like her, but because of my name, it reminded him of her. She was a beautiful model who was dealing with her demons and lived a tragic life.

"You know she was a heroin addict and died of AIDS-related complications. She turned to drugs to battle the dark side of modeling and to deal with childhood issues and relationships. It is a tragic story. I'm glad I remind you of her."

His mouth drops, leaving him with a confused expression, and I turn around. It was the only response I could think of that would make him feel uncomfortable, so he wouldn't continue talking to me.

The professor hands me the syllabus, and when I stretch my arm to pass back the stack of papers, Warren takes them but places a small piece of paper in my hand.

I take it and look down to read it.

*I didn't mean to offend you. How about I apologize with a cup of
coffee? 216-433-7898*
  Warren

The professor looks directly at me, and I have no choice but to slip the
paper into my bag.

The professor looks young for his age, or he ages well. He appears no
more than in his late thirties or early forties, wearing a dress shirt and slacks.
His hair is styled with gel, and he wears glasses. His eyes zero in on me and
my leg begins to bounce under my desk.

"I see we have a new student this year. Would you please introduce yourself to the class? Most of your peers are in the same economics major and will
be graduating alongside you. You should get to know them better."

The professor gives Warren and me a knowing look, but I dismiss it,
figuring that he saw him hand me the small piece of paper. It doesn't take a
genius to know Warren was flirting with me or trying to ask me out.

I introduce myself to the class and tell them I transferred in from
Wisconsin and what I'm majoring in.

After class, I walk outside the building and pull up the campus map on
my phone, looking for the cafeteria to grab some lunch. I was able to get a
meal plan and based on what I have heard from Jess, I'm sure the cafeteria is
empty. The rich don't eat in the cafeteria. They eat at local restaurants and
cafés every day.

"Hey." I hear Warren's voice call out.

I stop and turn around, and he stops right in front of me. "How about
that coffee?"

Shaking my head. "You don't give up, do you?"

"Not when I'm interested in something."

"Well, thank goodness I'm not a thing." I deadpan and turn away. "Good
luck, I hope it works out."

He follows quickly alongside me. "Are you always this difficult when a
guy shows an interest in getting to know you?"

"No, I just didn't come to this school for the sole purpose of hooking up.
I don't know you, and you don't know me."

"That is what the coffee invite is for--to get to know you."

"Don't you have a girlfriend or something?"

He shakes his head, his playful demeanor diminishing when I mention
the girlfriend question.

"No. I don't have a girlfriend. Not anymore. I dumped her before last
semester ended; she was a psychotic, sex-crazed, head case."

"Wow. I would have thought a girl into crazy sex would be a good thing."

"Not like that. She is on a whole other level than what I'm down with."

He keeps walking beside me, and to be honest, I still have no idea where I'm going, but he keeps following me anyway. I'm intrigued by the way he talks about the girl he broke up with. I know it's Veronica, but he doesn't give away her name. Interesting. He doesn't know I know who he is referring to since I'm new here, so I test him.

"That must have sucked. Who was she?"

"I'd rather keep that to myself. It doesn't matter; we weren't exclusive. It's over." He looks around nervously, and then his gaze lands back on mine. "Do you know where you are going?"

He doesn't want to put her out there. I guess what Jess said is true. He is afraid of Veronica's wrath. I don't want to seem rude, but then Dravin's comment about gossip and thinking the worst about people because of rumors pops into my head. He wasn't creepy or anything, and he didn't corner me in the women's restroom to seduce me.

I sigh and give him a grin. "Honestly, I was trying to see if you would get tired and give up following me, but to answer your question. I'm looking for the cafeteria to grab lunch."

His eyes rake over my simple black shirt, jeans, and docs. "How about I take you?"

My brow lifts. "Where?"

"To lunch. I want to take you out to lunch. It will be my treat."

"I don't think that is a good idea."

"Why not? There is no reason why we couldn't go to lunch as friends."

He seems harmless and it's not like I will let it get any further than eating lunch at the same place. He just happened to be there. Maybe he will give me more information on Dravin and the people he hangs around with.

For some reason, Dravin intrigues me. He comes off as an ass, but nonetheless, he has this air of confidence about him, like he doesn't care what people think. Except in the bathroom, he cared what Jess was telling me about him. Dravin cared what I thought about him and that is what got my attention. Why?

How would he know she would talk bad about him is a mystery. It bothered him that I saw him as a guy with a bad rep. Why would he care? He made it seem that it was all a test to see if I was down to have a quickie in the bathroom. Dravin looks dangerous compared to Warren. Warren seems harmless and he doesn't talk to me like Dravin does. He isn't forward with the sexual innuendos that make me drip between my thighs, imagining what color his eyes turn when he has sex. Would they stay the same, or would they darken and change colors?

"Alright, but as friends."

His lips lift in a smile. "I promise I will behave. We can go to the café two blocks away. We could walk, or would you rather we drive there?"

My lip is snagged by my bottom teeth as I ponder if we should walk or drive. I don't have a car, and that means I would have to let him drive me. I don't know him, so I go with the safer route.

"I don't have a car." My cheeks heat in embarrassment and I look behind him.

He walks closer, his book bag slung over one shoulder, and he slides his light brown hair away from his eyes. He is tall but a tad shorter than Dravin. His forearms are corded with muscle, but not like Dravin's, and I look away, mentally kicking myself for comparing Warren to Dravin. *What in the hell is wrong with me?*

Since meeting Dravin, I have been comparing all the guys that are attractive to him. He is every definition of a bad boy and has the mouth to go with it. But those eyes. His eyes are the most mysterious quality about him, both light and dark. I can't seem to stop myself from thinking about them.

Warren lowers his voice a fraction, "If you feel better walking, Gia, I'm cool with it. I understand if you don't feel comfortable having me drive you."

Feeling relieved, my shoulders sag and I let out a small breath I was holding. "Okay. I appreciate that. A walk it is, then."

"What time is your next class?" He asks, turning in the direction of the café, which is, in fact, in the opposite direction.

"In an hour and a half."

"Good, my class doesn't start until two hours from now. We have enough time to head over and back without either of us missing class."

He walks beside me. Close but not too far. He keeps a friendly distance, but I still feel guarded and on edge. He seems nice. Remembering what Jess told me and from my encounter with Dravin, I know I still have to be careful in this place. I will have to keep everyone I encounter at a safe distance.

DRAVIN

THERE IS a knock on my bedroom door. "What?" I shout back.

The knob of my door turns, and Reid, my roommate, appears in the doorway. I click the mouse and close all the windows on the screens I had open. Turning toward him, I glare at Reid.

"My bad, brother, I was letting you know you have a visitor."

"I could have knocked, and I'm not just any 'visitor.' I have a name," Veronica says, practically pushing Reid aside so she can walk inside my bedroom.

Reid rolls his eyes. He hates Veronica because he knows what she is capable of. She's almost the female version of me and rumor has it I'm most likely the son of Lucifer himself. The main difference between Veronica and I is that I have a terrible rep and have no fucks to give compared to Veronica. She has everyone except the people she has fucked over convinced she's Marsha fucking Brady.

"To what do I owe the pleasure?" I mock.

She gives me a devious smile. Which can only mean one thing, she wants to fuck or destroy someone.

She licks her lips seductively and turns her head, speaking to Reid. "Leave us," she demands.

He gives her the finger and she makes a silent motion with her hand in a fist like she is sucking a dick. "In your dreams. It will never happen. I don't fuck losers."

Reid gives her a disgusted expression. "Don't worry, I'm not interested in fucking demons."

He shuts the door with a click.

Leaning back in my gaming chair, my gaze lands on Veronica. "What do you want?"

"I need a favor."

"Whatever it is, hell no."

Veronica's favors are dangerous and risky. It will always involve fucking over someone I have no interest in fucking over, and let's face it, it's dull. Chicks and their drama don't do it for me, and Veronica is full of drama. If she doesn't get her way, she pouts and throws a tantrum like a three-year-old.

The only reason she is even allowed in my house is because we have known her since high school. Our fathers know each other and have done business together. You would think they would want to play matchmaker, but the problem with that scenario is her gold-digging mother was caught fucking my father after my mother committed suicide. Her father didn't divorce her, of course, but he started fucking whoever he wanted, even in their bed, if he wanted.

Her mother was forbidden from continuing the affair, but my father and Veronica's father continued to be friends and colleagues. It wasn't my father's fault Veronica's mother is a gold-digging whore. His words, not mine.

"I need your help, Dravin," she purrs.

Her skirt is shorter than it should be, with her fake breasts pushed together in her skimpy blouse and heels. One thing Veronica and I have never done, is fuck. I would fuck her, but she loves to try and play games. She knows I'm the puppet master. There is no game she can win with me, and she knows it. I am always in control. I need, and I crave it.

Not even my father can control me. After my mother slit her wrists and drowned in a bathtub full of water, something changed in me. I can't give control to anyone, not even God. Since my mother died, God and I have had a rocky relationship.

"Why should I help you? Not that I give a fuck what you want. There is nothing you could offer me that I want."

She walks close to me. My legs are slightly apart, and I'm facing her as she steps closer. Her hand slides up her thigh, disappearing under her short skirt, lifting it to flash me her completely see-through panties. I tilt my head to take a look at what she is offering.

Her two fingers slide beside her lower lips squishing them together.

"I'll give you something you've never had."

My dick twitches because she is touching something I've never had from her. Some people think we fuck on the down low, but that is not the truth. Not that I wouldn't mind sliding my cock inside her and giving her a ride.

She removes her hand and straddles me. She rubs herself on the crotch of my long basketball shorts and I'm rocking a semi. Veronica is a beautiful woman with a tiny waist and blonde wavy hair, but her soul is dark and evil. She isn't my type, except a fuck is still just that, a fuck.

I'm as dark and corrupted as it is, but throwing her into the mix is like the devil's children having an orgy. Not my thing.

"Come on, Dravin, do this for me? Pleeese," she coos.

She places her hands on my shoulders to whisper in my ear and continues to rub her pussy on the tip of my cock over my shorts. She is doing what she does best behind closed doors. She seduces to get what she wants.

"I'll let you stick it anywhere," she whispers. "Anywhere," she repeats.

My nostrils flare. Her lips graze my cheek, and my dick goes rock hard.

I'm a man, and a beautiful woman is straddling me and rubbing her pussy on my dick, telling me if I do want she wants, I can fuck her any way I like. But...I push her off me, and she slides off my lap, adjusting her skirt. Like I said, I crave control.

"What do you want?" I ask.

She sits on the bed with her legs open so I can get a good view of what she is offering. "I want you to do something for me. I have a problem," she says in a clipped voice.

Glancing at her pussy, I motion for her to get up and open her legs wider while she stands. She does, and I lean back on my chair and look up at her face with a stern expression, showing her that it will take a lot more convincing. I don't like to fuck girls on my bed. I dismiss them when I'm done; the last thing I want is their smell on my sheets. If she is mad I told her to get up off my bed, she doesn't say anything. Whatever she wants me to do, it must be very important to her.

"What problem? Does Warren have a small dick, and you need me to remind you what a big dick can do?"

"Ha-ha... very funny," she parrots.

"Didn't you two part ways last semester?" I ask.

"We're taking a break."

I sneer and raise a brow.

She places her hands on her hips and huffs. "Okay, he dumped me."

I motion for her to open her legs wider. This is interesting and I like to mess with her. She thinks she will get whatever she wants from me, but come to think of it, I'm bored. I want to know what she wants me to do.

I'm bored with fucking stupid college girls who get clingy and stalkerish. They think that if they give it up, and you have sex, it is a sign of commitment. It's hard to find one that just wants to fuck, and I hardly have any time to go outside off campus to wine and dine with a woman just to have sex. If I do fuck outside off campus, it's to destroy a person. Sure, I get pleasure from getting my dick wet, but I get more pleasure by destroying the person the act was intended to hurt.

She widens her stance, and I smirk, loving the control I'm having over her.

"What's wrong? You didn't swallow."

"Fuck you, Dravin."

"That's what you're offering me. Your words, not mine. Now what the fuck do you want? And you better make it fast. I'm losing my patience, and you're about to get asked to leave.

"Fine. Warren said we could be friends after he dumped me, but lately, he has been ghosting me and is all up this new girl's ass. I passed by the café, and he was having lunch with her. She is pretty with dark hair, full breasts, and full of… virtue. You can tell she is innocent. Her body language is sexy and hot but also…unintended."

"Who is this girl? Just ruin her like you do everyone that gets in your way."

"It is not that easy because Warren really likes her. It would be obvious if I did anything. It's too soon for me to bare my teeth. He looks at her the way he used to look at me, and I know he wants her." She arches her back and looks up, straightening and staring directly at me. "He wants to fuck her. Her name is Gia or something."

My eyes snap to hers when I hear that name rolling off her tongue—the new girl, the one I followed into the restroom at Babylon.

The one that I wanted to bend over to hear her scream my name while I gave her an orgasm we both would remember. The one that denied me. She's the type I can't use my charms on because someone has already poisoned her mind about me. They have told her the truth, whereas I told her a lie that wasn't true. She believed them, and not me, and I was irked. The way her jeans molded the curves of her ass and her straight hair and black manicured nails. *Gia.* Her name on my lips does something to me. I want her. I want to see the expression her face makes when I make her come. I want to taste every drop of her lust until she sees me as her God.

The image of her I play in my mind wearing a black negligée and red bottom heels while she worships my cock after fucking every hole in her body is imprinted in my mind. It's what I think about when I jerked off before I went to bed, when I fucked the blonde after class, and this morning when I jerked off in the shower.

"What about her?" I ask, keeping a straight face.

"I want you to seduce her. I want you to fuck her and then humiliate her by leaving her publicly. If Warren knows you fucked her, he will forget about her. He can't stand you, and he would never pursue her if he found out she rode your cock.

"What happens when you ride mine?"

"He won't find out because we won't tell him. I get his attention, and you get what you have been dying to have for years, and that is for you to fuck your brains out in every hole that big cock of yours can fit in." She slides her panties to the side so I can get a better view of her cunt by lifting her skirt. "You want this?" She twirls her fingers over her clit, and I sit up and watch the show.

"Maybe."

She stands between my legs with her legs open. My eyes find hers. "So, what is going to be? It's a win-win for you. You get her pussy, and then you get mine. You don't lose."

My hand slides up and I cup her pussy as I stand. She gasps as she takes a step back. "You're soaked," I tell her, my voice laced with steel inches from her lips. "I love the way you have to blackmail me to fuck me." I slide a finger over her clit, and she whimpers.

She places her hands on my muscled chest. "Dravin?"

"Yeah."

Her head tilts up to look at me, and she says, "I'm soaked because I'm imagining you fucking her."

I snatch my hand back and wipe her arousal on her blouse. "Liar. Get out," I demand in a rigid tone.

She swallows, embarrassed that I dismissed her like the whore she is, but I respect her control, just like her father. Her mother doesn't have any. In truth, Veronica has a shitty father and mother. They both expect her to be posh and perfect in the eyes of society, yet they're not.

Like my father, they sent her from the elite society of Ohio to Kenyan University to be closer to the church and accept God. Funny, they don't live by God's rules, although they expect us to follow rules that they didn't.

She opens the door of my house located on the exclusive street the campus students call Millionaire's Row. She turns around before she crosses the threshold, "Will you?"

"Fine. I'll do it."

Her lips lift like Cruella Deville from the Dalmatians. "If you can't do it, I'll ruin her another way, and the deal is off."

"I'll win. I always win."

"Good, I was starting to get worried."

"Why is that?"

"I could tell you were getting bored lately. Next thing you know, you will be fucking the nuns that come to the church from the convent to help out."

"Not my style," I quip.

She turns and walks out. "Yeah, right."

If she only knew, I'd already had my eye on Gia, but now Veronica has let me know, and so does everyone else. And that is a problem.

GIA

"EVERYONE IS TALKING about you and Warren the other day," Jess says.

My brows pinch and I place my laptop down on the bed and sit up on the twin bed in our dorm. "Everyone?"

She fixes the strap of her tank top, adjusts her breasts in her bra, and quirks her brow. "Everyone. Including Warren."

What the hell. It was just lunch. Why would he make it out more than it was? *Because he is a rich prick and Jess warned you, but you didn't listen.*

"It was lunch, and I only allowed it because he felt awkward about telling me that my name reminded him of the supermodel who died."

"The poor young woman that was hooked on heroin? The girl died of AIDS. She was gorgeous but tragic all at the same time."

"That's the one."

She snorts. "What an idiot. He really doesn't have game."

I wave my hand. "Exactly, I pointed that out to him. He realized how bad it sounded and I was trying to be nice by accepting his offer to go to lunch. It was harmless, and I didn't intend for it to look like anything other than what it was. Lunch."

She curls her legs so she sits crisscrossed on her bed. "It obviously meant more to him and everyone else who happened to be there or pass by. You better hope that Veronica is over him and on to someone else."

Great, that means I'll be public enemy number one if I'm not already.

"I'm her target now, aren't I?"

She bites her lip and scrunches her nose, the seconds ticking by as I wait silently. My anxiety is already climbing to atomic levels. She inhales, her chest inflates, and lets out an audible breath. "You're fucked bitch. No one has said anything yet. It has only been four days, and today is Friday. Let's get the fuck out of here and go to Babylon. We'll hang out, have a couple of drinks, get fucked up, and laugh. Hopefully, you can find a hot guy, smash, which means fuck by the way. The shit about Warren will be a distant memory. Word will get around that you hooked up with someone else, and all will be good."

I lay back on my firm pillow, cursing that I don't have enough money to buy the downier one I want. Hating how I got myself into this situation after

Jess clearly warned me about it. My naïve ass fell for it. But it doesn't mean that I have to screw someone just to get out of it.

"Fine, but I'm not sleeping with anyone."

She snickers, placing her hand over her mouth. "Why? You're not a virgin, are you?"

My head turns, and I gaze at her and then look up, not telling her the truth, hoping she will just drop it. Getting up, I shut down my computer and put my economics assignment away.

She gets up to begin finding something to wear. "You are, aren't you? That is why you are freaking out and are not interested in hooking up."

I slam the drawer shut, annoyed that she figured me out. "So what if I am? I just haven't found the right person to get it over with, and back where I'm from, my parents were this church-going perfect couple who had it all figured out until they divorced. It was all a bunch of bullshit packed with lies. They never let me date, gave me shit about liking boys. I figured that I would just fuck some guy and get it over with and live my life like a normal teenager. Now I'm twenty-one and still haven't done it because I just got away from their drama by coming here."

"Relax, boo. It's not that big of a deal." She grimaces her face in pity. "I take that back. Here, it is that big of a deal, especially with guys like Dravin lurking around in all his deliciousness. That guy will eat you alive. You'll probably love it, though."

"Love what?" I snap.

Her mentioning Dravin is rubbing me the wrong way. The guy is scorching hot, no doubt about that. He has this gothic bad-boy vibe I have never encountered before. The type you see or hear about in movies. His eyes are like a deadly sin waiting to devour you. *More like what's between my legs.* The thought makes me wet, and a thumping feeling pulsates from my clit. Instead of my heart beating widely, it's my clit thumping wildly, wanting God knows what. But the devil knows...Dravin knows. I have to shamefully admit that my last encounter had me playing with myself in the shower and I came twice. On my own. Thinking of...him.

"Letting Dravin Bedford fuck you and pop that cherry. Damn girl, I can't even imagine it. I haven't experienced it myself, but from what I have heard, the man has a huge dick."

"He probably paid some girl to say that or threatened her. But I thought he was off limits, and I should stay away?"

She shakes her head. "I've changed my mind. Every girl walks funny after a night with Dravin. They don't complain about it at all. They just want more, but he's a one-time rip-and-dip kind of guy. I know I told you to stay away, but you need to fuck someone who is a one-time type of guy."

I giggle. "Rip and dip? Really?"

She cackles. "Yeah, he is only with a girl once and never repeats or fucks the same chick twice." She waves her hand. "And, I have heard he never goes down on a girl. No one, I mean no one, has ever said the boy eats pussy." She shrugs. "Figured he doesn't for whatever reason."

I hold up an outfit in each hand. "Enough about goth boy. Which one?"

She points to the one on the left with the fishnets, short skirt, and grunge tee. "That one. A goth boy will dig the fishnets."

"I'm not going there to impress the poster boy for Hot Topic."

She laughs. "Oh, man. I am totally going to tell him you said that."

I laugh with her, not caring if she does or doesn't. I still haven't told her about my encounter with Dravin, and I don't plan on telling her because it doesn't matter. Dravin is a fuckboy and I'm not into fuckboys.

WE ARE SEATED in the same booth as last week, but this time, there isn't a hot bad boy playing pool with a stick watching me from across the room. "Greedy Fly" by Bush plays from the bar's jukebox, giving the place a 90s alternative rock vibe.

"I like this song," I tell Jess, nursing a vodka and cranberry.

"Me too. Is that all you ever drink?" She points to my cup.

"It's what I can handle."

A voice not belonging to Jess answers. "Not much, apparently."

Blonde locks frame a white porcelain face with painted, maroon-colored lips and tight leather pants under a white cropped top.

"To what do we owe the pleasure, Veronica?" Jess asks with a scowl.

"Oh Jess, are you still mad about that little thing from last year," she purrs.

I glance from Jess to Veronica, wondering what Veronica was talking about. "What little thing from last year?"

Jess' eyes flash with pure anger, but Veronica looks--amused. Jess glances at me, and she must notice that I'm giving Veronica my resting bitch face. Whatever went on, is not my problem. For the past week, Jess has been friendly to me and everything she has said about the people who attend Kenyan has been true. So far.

Veronica smiles at me and then leans close. She may be beautiful, but her attitude spoils it. I can't even blame Warren. Sleeping with this bitch must have been like lying in a bed of snakes. They can all bite you. You just don't know when, and it's best to crawl out while you can.

Veronica glances at me like I'm a meal, and I lean back, my upper lip curling in a snarl. "She's very pretty, Jess. I like her dark hair and just look at those lips." She lowers her voice and whispers loud enough over the music. "Ripe for sucking."

"Fuck off," I sneer.

She licks her lips seductively and backs away. The bar's front door opens, and it's already dark outside. Warren comes inside, followed by the rest of the swim team, including Dravin.

The air in the entire place changes, and that catches the evil bitch's attention. She skitters off in their direction. It is like a group of celebrities walking inside the building. All conversation seizes. You can tell because the music coming from the jukebox seems to have gotten louder.

After watching Veronica saunter toward the group of guys, my head whips toward Jess. "She's disgusting. If you don't mind me asking, what happened?" I down the rest of my drink and place the glass on the table with a clunk.

Jess swallows and takes a big gulp of her drink. "She saw I was interested in a guy, and she convinced him to have sex with me out of pity. We went on two dates, and then he agreed, but he wanted me with another girl at the same time. I liked him, and she knew that, but it didn't stop her from playing mind games. She manipulates people into getting what she wants. She feeds off it. That's why you need to stay away from Warren."

"Did you?"

"Did I what?"

"Do it?"

She takes another long gulp until she drains the glass and places it down on the table. "Yeah, I did."

"Holy shit," I mutter.

"Then he said he couldn't go out with me because I did and that he did it out of pity going on and on about some bullshit Veronica fed him about me wanting to explore my sexuality."

"What a fucking asshole."

She snorts. "I know. She fucked him right after, and he liked it a little too much. She had to threaten to publicly humiliate him if he didn't stop coming after her."

"Who is this asshole?"

"Garret. Third dick on the right talking to Dravin."

"So, everyone on the swim team is a conceited fuckboy. Got it."

She snickers. "I love that about you. You don't care and catch on quickly."

I shake my head. "Honestly, we all have stories, and we all want things. It is up to us to give or take with care. Everyone needs to rebalance at some point. If something goes bad or is not the way you envisioned it, change it and learn from it."

Jess nods. She points to my drink. "Another?"

"Yeah, something I can definitely handle so I can stay alert and watch out for crazy bitches with a complex. How about you?"

Jess throws her head back and laughs. "No, I'm good. I like you, Gia. You have a great sense of humor. Be careful with Veronica, though. She has claws, and they hurt."

"I see that. All I have heard about her are good things," I say jokingly.

The bartender puts a round of drinks on the bar and the rest of the swim team along with Veronica head out to the billiard tables. Veronica watches Warren like a hawk while she chats up Dravin like they are old friends who haven't seen each other and are catching up. It wouldn't surprise me if they were intimate. They look like they would be good together. Physically, at least. Veronica may come off as a psycho bitch when you meet her, but you cannot deny that she is beautiful. They probably should sleep together with their winning personalities.

"What can I get you?" the male bartender asks, slinging a little white towel over his shoulder while he leans on the edge of the bar.

My head turns, and the blonde, blue-eyed, young bartender smirks at me when he catches where my attention was a few moments ago.

He nudges his head toward the pool tables. "Kenyan's finest. You know them?"

I shake my head. "I would like a vodka and cranberry, please?"

"Coming right up."

My head tilts and I find Jess seated at the booth, her stare locked over at the pool tables like she is looking for someone and hasn't found them yet. She must feel me staring right at her because her eyes land on mine, and I quirk a brow, silently asking her—*Who are you looking for*?

The bartender returns with my mixed drink and slides it behind me on the bar top. When I turn my body back to the bartender to hand him my card, his gaze lands behind me, but I notice a hint of fear on his face before it quickly disappears.

"Put it on my tab. Whatever she wants."

My eyes close as Dravin's dry, stern tone filters through my skin, prickling in awareness. Electricity courses through me as he stands behind me without uttering another word. The bartender glances at me with my card in his hand.

"Charge my card, please," I counter, my eyes not wavering.

The bartender looks nervous, unsure of what to do, but one more glance at Dravin has my hopes go up in smoke. The bartender shakes his head and hands me back my card.

He gives me a smirk, but I know he is just trying to play it off because that same flash of fear I witnessed a moment ago crosses his expression. "I'm sorry, but if a guy wants to buy a girl a drink and she clearly knows him, I'm gonna have to allow it. Bar rules."

"What? Are you kidding me?" I hiss. "I don't know him." I point my thumb behind me.

His lips tip upward in a grin. "Yes, you do. It's okay."

"You heard me. Don't listen to her. Give her back the card and charge whatever drinks she has had on my tab."

Anger begins to spike through me. I turn around to find two different color eyes boring into me, a fitted Henley, and black jeans sitting low on his hips. This time, he has a thin ring pierced in his nose adding to his sex appeal. His jaw is clenched, and a muscle tics on the left side of his jaw.

His full lips look perfect, and I ache to know how they would feel on mine. Memories from our last encounter in the bathroom replay like a rerun. His scent when he was up close and the way he looked at me full of pure lust awakened a need inside me I didn't realize I possessed. His tongue peeks out, and his upper lip curls in a sexy grin, and I'm still imagining how his lips would feel against mine. Would they feel soft, hard, or smooth? His head is positioned straight ahead, but his eyes move downward without tilting his neck to watch me.

Breaking the tension between us, I ask, "Why did you insist on paying for my drinks? Do you expect me to sleep with you now?"

He chuckles, and it grates on my nerves. The guy is hot, but he gets under my skin when he mocks me.

"What is so funny?"

He leans close and tilts his head so his lips are close enough to my ear that I can feel his breath fan against my skin, making my nipples harden under my bra. I try to fight the attraction and move away, but when I step back, my back hits the bar's edge. My head turns, and his lips are inches from mine, just like last time we were in the bathroom.

"The fact that you want to sleep with me. I bet you wonder how it would feel for me to slide between your legs. It wouldn't take much, would it?"

My nostrils flare. Anger boiling in my veins. How can a guy be so beautiful and infuriating at the same time?

"You can't help it, can you? Look, I'm not interested in a fuckboy. Keep the drink or give it to some who falls for your shit," I snap, walking around him leaving him alone at the bar with my drink.

I head back over to the booth where Jess is sitting, and I can feel the heat of his stare behind me like a furnace, making my skin flush.

GIA

"**ARE** you sure you don't want me to go with you, Gia?" Jess asks with a concerned expression.

After walking away from Dravin and leaving him hanging at the bar, he returns to the pool tables. I grip the handle of my bag and tell Jess I'm leaving. I don't want to go, but I don't trust myself enough around Dravin. The plus side of this situation is that I'm not drunk or even slightly buzzed. I've only had one drink since we got here, but as soon as Dravin got close and riled me up, my brain started telling me to run. Otherwise, I'll end up letting him devour me before the night is over, or worse, he will make me pay for shunning him at the bar.

"I'm good, Jess. It's okay. I know you want to stay."

She has been staring over at the guys on the swim team but has been hesitant because she knows I don't want to hang out over there. Veronica showing up and acting like a creepy psycho bitch is enough to let me know—she doesn't approve of me. She is trying to jerk my chain to see if I rattle, but at this point in my life, I don't think anything can get to me.

Her face falls and a worried line creases her forehead. "I—"

Placing my hand on her shoulder, I give her a warm smile. "It's okay, Jess. Really. I'm going to pee and then I'm going to head back. I'll call you when I make it back to the room. It's all good."

Her shoulders slump in defeat, but her head turns, and she sighs. "Okay." She leans forward in the booth, placing her hand on the table so she can slide out. "Call me as soon as you make it."

Walking toward the restroom, I wave my hand up not looking back. "I will."

I'M LEAVING the women's restroom when I notice a back door to the bar that reads, "*EXIT.*"

I inwardly sigh, thanking my luck that I won't have to go back out to the front and risk running into Dravin or Veronica. I must admit seeing him so comfortable with her sparks something inside of me that feels a lot like jealousy, but I immediately brush it off.

I'm about to taste victory and exit the bar when the men's restroom door opens. Warren steps out, blocking my path. He reaches out and grips my upper arm to stop me from leaving.

"Hey." I stop and look at his hand and snatch my arm out of his grip. He raises his hands up in surrender. "I didn't mean to grab your arm, but you seemed upset. Is everything alright? I saw Dravin talking to you. Did he say or do anything?"

"Does it matter?"

"If he upset you, I think it does."

I don't feel like talking about it, but I promised myself to be nice and not let people think that they can get to me. "He bought me a drink and I refused."

He raises his brows, shock crossing his features.

"Dravin offered to buy you a drink?"

"Yeah, why is there a problem?"

He shakes his head. "No. Not at all." His brows pinch. "It's just that he never offers to buy a girl anything, and the fact that you refused says a lot."

"Says a lot about what?

Warren peers down the hall in the other direction like he is hoping he won't get caught by someone. He glances back at me like we are conducting a drug deal or something. What is up with these people? They are sneaky, manipulative, and weird.

"Just...stay away from Dravin. He doesn't have the best reputation."

"Are you warning me off, Dravin?"

He steps closer to me and licks his lips. "Yes, I am."

"Why? Why would you care?"

"Because you seem like a nice girl." He lowers his voice a bit. "And I like you. I know you said the other day at lunch that we were just two people taking the same class, eating at the same place, and nothing more, but... I like you."

Great. This is exactly what I am trying to avoid. The last thing I need is for Warren to be interested in me. Veronica doesn't look like she will take it very well and I don't need issues with psycho chicks who can't take rejection.

Whatever happened between those two, I want no part of it.

"Look, I'm sorry, but I have to get going. You seem very nice, but I'm not interested in any type of relationship right now."

His expression turns serious, and for a second, I think he is going to argue, but then he smiles. Not what I expected. His smile rubs me the wrong way because it feels like it hasn't sunk in that I'm not interested in him. Veronica or no Veronica, Warren is not my type. He seems like a rich snob and I'm a broke college student barely scraping by. We have nothing in common, no chemistry, and he just doesn't make me feel like--*Dravin*. Fuck. I'm comparing already. I really need to get out of here.

"Look, I gotta go. My ride is here."

He steps back and I'm relieved he doesn't follow me out the door.

"I'll see you in class, Gia. I'm glad you were here tonight," he calls out.

Once I'm outside and turn the corner of the building, I'm in the dark. The sidewalk running parallel to the building is desolate and dimly lit. I quickly walk away in case Warren decides to poke his head out and see if I really had a ride. The last thing I need is for him to follow me. The guy acted like I didn't just tell him that I'm in no way interested in him. He brushed it off like we were discussing the weather or what is on next week's study guide.

I'm crossing the street and notice that there is a shortcut through the cemetery behind the church. I have never been superstitious. I'm not scared of the dead. It's the living that one should worry about.

The gates are still open with the lock and chain hanging from the left side. The good news is there are streetlamps along the road leading inside, and I can see that the other side is open and passes by the Catholic church and into the school. It would be more of a risk to walk around on the public sidewalk than taking this route. How many people hang out at the cemetery at night anyway? Calling a cab or the campus rideshare doesn't make sense if all I have to do is cross this way.

I'm passing the tombstones and notice the names. Marie James, 1908, Heath James, 1895. I realize this cemetery is old and has been here for centuries. These people have been buried here for a very long time. Some are family plots full of people with the same last names.

I'm walking and stop when I find the name Bedford on one of them. No way. It can't be. It must be a coincidence.

> *Anastasia Julianne Bedford, loving wife and mother.*
> *Gone but never forgotten.*
> *April 13, 1981-June 13, 2018.*

Looking around, I notice she is the only one in the section alone. I also see that there aren't any flowers here. Most of the graves have flowers, except the really old ones.

I'm not sure if this person is related to Dravin or not, but he isn't the only person in the universe with Bedford as a last name. I'm sure this cemetery has been here way longer than his family has even existed. What are the chances that his family has lived here their whole life? What about his other family members? It seems as if this woman buried here has no other family. Her tombstone is full of dried leaves and spider webs.

I see there is a grave overflowing with flowers. I don't think anyone would mind if I snatched a single red rose to place on her grave. Hastily, I grab a single rose from the grave across and return, placing the red rose on the woman's grave.

I kneel and swipe the area to remove the collected, dried leaves, not caring if my hand gets dirty.

I sigh and decide to at least pay my respects. "I know you don't know me, and I don't know you, but you seemed lonely, and I thought it would be nice for you to have a rose. It seems as if no one has left you any flowers. I hope you don't mind."

"What are you doing?"

I gasp and fall on my butt at the sound of Dravin's deep voice.

I glance up, and he is standing over me with a hard-to-read expression. "What the hell, Dravin?"

He looks at the grave and then back at me as I dust myself off. "What are you doing?" he repeats, his voice stern and almost scary.

"I'm going back to my dorm. What are you the campus stalker? This is the second time you have followed me."

"I wasn't following you."

"Yeah, because people walk through cemeteries at nine o'clock at night all the time after they hang out with friends at a bar." I mock.

He snorts. "Look, just because I offered to fuck you doesn't mean I'm stalking you. Don't flatter yourself."

"Whatever, Goth boy."

"What did you call me?"

I tilt my head up and look at his handsome face. "I said... Whatever, Goth boy."

He points to himself with his thumb to his chest and chuckles. "Goth boy?" He tilts his head up to look at the sky and then his gaze lands on mine when I'm finally standing. "Seriously?"

Waving my hand over his tight body, I motion to his clothes and face. "The different color eyes, always wearing black clothes, the nose piercing. I can go on."

"The nose piercing?"

"Yeah, doesn't help the cause if that's not the look you are going for."

"I like my piercings."

Did he say piercings as in plural, meaning more than one?

"Piercings?"

He nods. "Yeah, I have more than one." He steps closer.

I swallow. "I only see one."

"Do you want to see the other two?

Like an idiot, I respond, "Yeah." I'm curious to see where the others are.

His lips form a smile, and he looks down to the crotch of his pants. He leans in and whispers, "Fuck, you have no idea how bad I want to show you."

My hands cross over my breasts. "Really?" I roll my eyes and turn around, shaking my head. "No thanks. I'm sure I can have someone on campus tell me where they are and what they look like."

"Funny," he blurts sarcastically.

He stands behind me and when I turn my head around, I just stare.

He chuckles. "Are you waiting for me to walk you home?"

My body stiffens, annoyed that he figured me out. I'm also relieved that he didn't say anything about the grave I was kneeling in front of, which means he isn't related to the lady resting there. But then he looks back at it and then looks forward.

When a few seconds pass by, and neither of us moves, he breaks the silence by walking in front of me until he faces me once again. "I'll walk you if you let me kiss you."

I bite my lip in contemplation. If he leaves, I risk walking alone and the fact that he scared me means I'll be even more jumpy, and it probably won't be him startling me the next time.

I shouldn't even be speaking to this guy. I hardly know him, and he has a horrible reputation of being flawed, dangerous, and a heartbreaker. If only he could walk me to my building without any sexual favors, all would be good.

If I take him up on his offer and he chooses to kiss me, I'll have an excuse to actually be kissed by one of the hottest guys I have ever met. Dravin is pure sin wrapped in a delicious body. His offer is dripping with temptation and I don't know if I can resist.

He lifts my chin with his finger, my body stays still, and my eyes remain glued to his handsome face. "Fine. Where?"

He doesn't answer me and walks away but slows down so I can catch up. We walk all the way to the other gate. It is darker on this side of the cemetery, and there is only a single light next to the wrought iron gates. The wind picks up, making the trees groan, and it's at that moment I'm relieved I made the right choice and let Dravin walk with me. The trees continue to sway with the wind like a symphony echoing all around me, blowing my hair away from my face.

He stops and walks to the left toward a secluded pillar where no one can see, even if they pass by. I follow him like I'm in a trance. The peaks of the church seem larger than life, imposing, eerie, and, for some reason, anything but holy.

Goosebumps begin to snake all over my flesh. I know it's not from the cool wind but from the man in front of me. My heart begins to beat in a staccato rhythm in my ear. Dravin is inches from me, and his lips are a breath away. He is so close that we can practically breathe the same air—*slow and even. Inhale, exhale.*

The anticipation of him kissing me is causing the pounding of my heart. The pounding begins to assault my body. It's like the whole world melted away. There is just him and me.

I've been kissed three times in my life, but never by someone like Dravin. I don't think I have ever met someone as mysterious and interesting as him. His eyes are focused on me, burning like sapphires defying the darkness of the other.

My lips part.

Waiting.

Waiting.

My head tilts up, wanting his lips to touch mine, wanting to experience how they will feel, but his head dips lower, and I inhale when he kisses the side of my neck and slowly grazes his teeth along my skin. His lips are firm but soft at the same time. My back arches slightly hoping he will continue to place kisses on my skin.

It feels like I have been branded by him. What is left in his wake is a tingling sensation on the skin of my neck and the awareness that my panties are wet.

If I squirm, he will notice.

If I move, he will stop.

He looks down and slides his hands under my skirt over my fishnet stockings and up to my ass. "I can smell how wet you are for me," he says huskily.

My eyes close because, of course, a guy like Dravin can sense when a woman wants him. A man like him has a sixth sense. His hands squeeze my flesh, and he pushes me against him. His cock is hard underneath his jeans which only adds to my arousal. He wants me to know how I make him feel and he wants to make sure I feel it.

"Can you?"

I should tell him to stop. I should tell him to fuck off and get his hands off my ass, but another part of me can't get enough. I want to feel what it's like to be this close to him. To breathe the same air as Dravin Bedford for just a moment. With every breath he takes, I inhale the windstorm he is creating. The feel of his hands on my flesh and his hardness pressing against my belly is like a hurricane of heat blowing over my skin. I don't want to move. I want to stay right here in the dark and feel it for a moment longer. Then, I can go back to avoiding him.

My eyes are trained on his lips, and he licks them like I'm a meal he can't wait to taste. "Yeah," he breathes. The pads of his thumbs on each side of my hips make circles, causing my clit to throb with unbearable need.

This is all new to me. It's like he casts a spell every time I look into those smoldering eyes that make him look like he is possessed by something. Something dark that collects and takes parts of whatever he wants. The only thing you can remember is...that it was him who took it, but you would give it to him just to know he has a part of you.

What he wants from me, I don't know, but if he keeps touching me, I'm not sure I'll win the fight that is warring inside me. The good versus the bad. The good is telling me to run and never look back. The bad is telling me to give in and let him take what he wants, that I will enjoy it, even if it means I'll lose myself in the process.

My body shivers against him and he pulls me closer to his chest. My breasts press against his hard muscles and his hands pull me impossibly closer. A whimper escapes my throat.

"You want me," he says, his voice vibrating against my skin. "I feel it. I can feel how bad your pussy aches for me."

Fuck. I'm not very good at hiding how my body responds. My hands find the rough concrete behind me, feeling the texture to make sure I'm not dreaming.

He leans close and chuckles near my ear. "I'm not interested in girls that seem desperate, my little Raven. If you only knew how refreshing it is to find you aren't one of them."

Pushing off the pillar with my hands, he steps back, and his palms release me. The shadows cast from the light above make his features look maniacal. Why is he calling me his little Raven?

"Why are you calling me your little Raven?"

"That is what you are to me, my little Raven."

"You do know that Ravens eat dead carcasses and are an omen of death."

He shrugs. "If you say so."

I begin to walk away because I'm not sure if I should be insulted or flattered, but I know one thing for sure: I need to get away from him right now. He is all over me one minute, setting me on fire the next, and then calling me his little Raven the next. I can hear his footsteps coming closer behind me, but I keep looking straight ahead.

"Leave me alone, Dravin. Whatever happened back there should never have happened."

His footsteps become more distant as I approach the building and run up the stairs. When I'm finally in my dorm room, I sigh in relief, making sure the lock is secured. I pull out my phone and message Jess that I made it back, but after ten minutes of staring at my phone, she never responds. She probably hooked up with whoever caught her eye at that bar.

My thoughts go back to the cemetery and my encounter with Dravin. His expression is full of pain and faith, with an air of want and need but then restraint.

The guy came out of nowhere like an apparition. At first, I thought I was seeing things and had made it all up. One minute, he was at the bar near the billiard tables, and the next, he was behind me, questioning what I was doing alone in a dimly lit cemetery.

When he touches me, my body responds. Flames heat my skin, making my heart skip a beat, and the tingling butterflies dance in my core. The dirty things he said have me wondering how it would feel to have sex with him. Will he be gentle or rough? Will he care that I'm not experienced? Will he laugh at me or reject me if he found out I'm a virgin, or would he be kind and teach me?

Even though part of me wants to find out, I just can't. Making up my mind, I'm determined to lay low and avoid Dravin Bedford at all costs.

DRAVIN

"HOW ARE you doing in school, Dravin?" my therapist, Dr. Wick, asks.

I lower myself in the seat across from her. "How's your niece doing?"

Her left eye twitches, but I give her credit for maintaining her composure. "I didn't ask that. Please stop redirecting the question," she says in a stern tone.

Her niece tried to overdose on painkillers after I fucked her. I had told her we would make it official, that we would be a couple, only to tell her the next day at a family function in front of everyone that she was delusional and should get help from a psychiatrist to treat her obsession with me.

It was my way of getting back at my father for requiring me to get therapy with Dr. Wick and having to sit there and watch her tell my father everything I said and what I had done. Obviously, patient confidentiality doesn't apply to Dr. Wick if I'm legally an adult, but if I don't get therapy, he threatens to report my other transgressions, and my plans to fuck over my father will go to shit. My father thinks I have a disorder. According to Dr. Wick, I have antisocial personality disorder (ASPD). I know she's full of shit and this is all my father's doing.

"It's going well," I respond dryly.

"Well? How about the casual sexual activity, manipulation, hostility, and deceit?"

She thinks that my environment triggers my actions. If she only knew the families that founded the university were the ones with the problem. The families date back to the 1800s, when the university was first built near the church. The church is the center of everything. It is the perfect cover-up for the lies. Like a secret society, these families forge power and wealth. My father's side of the family is one of them.

I lean forward in my chair and give her a sarcastic smirk. "I have been a good little boy, Dr. Wick. There is nothing to report and there is nothing to tell."

"I see." She flips through the file in her hand, and I notice it's mine. "Professors at the university have not reported any issues regarding your behavior, though I have to ask about your relationship with Veronica."

"What about her?"

"Were you part of a scheme to ruin her relationship with that boy she was parading around with at last year's ball? According to individuals who were there, she had a breakdown when he told her he just wanted to be friends."

"No. Why would I be?"

Veronica is the perfect daughter in everyone's eyes. If they only knew she is more fucked up than I am. Not that I consider myself to be fucked up. It's what everyone, including my father, says about me because they cannot control me.

My sole purpose in continuing this charade is to collect information. Dr. Wick gives me details that I need. Every session, I sit, listen, and redirect the questions back to her. I'm psychoanalyzing her and she doesn't even know it. All her questions are to see if she can take anything I tell her and run back and give it to my father. Not a chance. He wants to know everything before everyone. My father loves control and as one of the heads of our society, he needs it. He just goes about it the wrong way.

"Why do you feel you have to conduct yourself in the way that you do, Dravin?"

I chuckle. "Conduct myself how? I have sex. People your age consider that a problem, I don't. I fuck, Dr. Wick. I fuck a lot. It is healthy. I'm young, and if it is consensual, like with your niece, I get it done. That is not a problem. If someone pisses me off, I defend myself. I don't need to manipulate anyone. If I want something, I ask, and I usually get it. I don't force anyone to give me anything."

She knows I mean sex, and the jab about her niece is to rile her up so she ends the session. My father wants information because it's the beginning of the semester and things have been too quiet. It's unlikely for me to be quiet about the things I'm into and the things I want. Not for long, though.

"I think this session is over. We clearly have a difference of opinion. Your behavior hasn't been destructive as of late and there are no new reports."

"Am I cured, Doctor?" I mock.

"If the destructive personal behavior continues, Dravin, I'm afraid I will have to transfer you to another colleague."

"No need." I place the joint to my lips and light it with my zippo.

"There is no smoking in here, Dravin."

I blow the smoke in her face as I stand up to leave. "So you have said."

I inhale and blow more smoke in the air as I turn to leave.

"Leave, right now. And don't come back. I'll report this, and I will speak to your father." The phone rings interrupting her rant.

I'm walking out of her personal office and wink at the receptionist I fucked in the bathroom after Dr. Wick told me to wait in the waiting room before our appointment.

"Call me," she says, biting her lip.

"Dravin, that was the school," Dr. Wick calls out, but I'm already heading into the elevator, and the doors close, cutting off her annoying voice.

Fuck therapy. I don't need it and never did.

GIA
†

I'M SITTING through another lecture in my marketing class, and I just found out that Warren and some of the guys from the swim team are taking the same class. I'm hoping Warren got the message last Friday at the bar. When he turns to the side, I notice his hand is in a cast. My brows pinch into a frown.

Something must have happened over the weekend. Maybe he slipped and fell after he left the bar. He turns around, and our eyes lock, and I immediately glance away. Shit. He saw me looking in his direction.

He elbows the guy next to him and he turns around. I've never seen him before, but I notice him staring at me with a scowl. It seems he doesn't like me very much. He turns back around and faces the professor, and I shrug it off and pay attention to what the professor is lecturing about.

"Now, I'm going to call out group names so that you may exchange information for the marketing project due at the end of the term. It needs to be a social media ad campaign for any product. You will be graded on SEO, graphics, and the hook. It will make up twenty percent of your grade, so make it count."

He begins to call out student's names, and when Warren's name comes up, my stomach drops, and I suck in a breath. Let's hope he doesn't call out my name. When the professor calls another girl's name, I let out the breath I was holding relieved I dodged a bullet.

He paired him with a brunette named Jasmin. When I look over at her, she waves at Warren, and he scowls. He doesn't look very happy. He turns and glances at me once again and I guess he was hoping I would be paired with him. Too bad, buddy.

To my surprise, Warren raises his hand.

The professor pauses and looks up. "Yes, Warren?"

"Is it possible to change partners?"

The smile on Jasmin's face falls and she glares at Warren. He obviously isn't happy with the professor's choice. My hands begin to get clammy hoping that the professor is set on his choices.

"I'm sorry, Warren. Your partner for this assignment is whoever you are assigned to. There are no exceptions."

He dismisses Warren and continues to call out names. I finally look up when he says my name, but I wasn't paying attention to who he paired me with. My eyes widen when the guy who scowled at me gets elbowed by Warren and turns around, giving me a stare-down. He tilts his head and looks back at the professor when he is finished pairing up everyone in the class.

"The rest of class time can be spent exchanging information," the professor announces.

Everyone begins to move to their partners, but when my eyes land on my partner, he gets up and moves away toward the exit.

What the hell? I grab my bag and quickly run down the steps in the stadium-style auditorium. When I reach the door, I see his retreating back walking toward the exit.

"Hey!" I call out.

I didn't even catch his name. I run like a bat out of hell outside and squint from the sun's glare. Once my eyes refocus, they find him still walking away and I run to catch up with him. "Hey! Wait up!"

He stops and turns around. His eyes are dark, and once I reach him, I notice he is lean and tall. My head tilts up and he watches me, annoyed.

"What's your name again?"

He snorts. "Obviously, you weren't paying attention. It's Reid."

Shit. This must be the *"Reid"* Jess warned me about. I don't have a choice but to go through with it and have him as a partner.

"Well, Reid, I can't fail the class and we need to exchange numbers and figure this out." I pull out my phone from the back of my jeans and try to swipe to unlock it without cutting myself on the cracked screen. Shit. I'm upset, and I swiped a little too hard.

I gasp at the sharp stinging of pain. Snatching my thumb and placing it in my mouth, I hope I didn't get a piece of glass stuck inside the pad of my thumb. I suck but don't feel anything except the sharp sting.

Reid's lips form a thin line, and he grabs my phone out of my hand.

"Hey. What the hell do you think you're doing? Give me back my phone."

He ignores me and inspects the severely cracked screen. "It's fucked. You need to get a new one. It's not worth fixing the screen," he says, handing it back.

He pulls out his phone and it's the latest model iPhone.

"That costs money. Money I don't have right now, and no one is hiring until the holidays start. Even then, this place is in the middle of nowhere."

He continues looking at his phone and pulls up his text messages. "Try the library. What's your number?"

I rattle off the numbers and feel my phone buzz in my pocket.

"I'll text you my address. Meet me there at seven so we can go over the assignment."

"Alright, my name is––"

He finishes for me. "Gia, I know. Everyone...knows."

Lifting an eyebrow. "Everyone?"

"Yeah, and do yourself a favor. Stay away from––"

"Let me guess, Dravin." I interrupt him.

"I was actually going to say, Warren."

"Why not Dravin?"

I'm curious to know why he wouldn't warn away from the devil himself. The university's bad boy. Why would he warn me off Warren? Not that I don't agree with him.

His eyes scroll over me from head to toe. "You're not Dravin's type, and Warren is interested in you because everyone notices you. It will attract attention you are not capable of handling. I'm just trying to avoid a tragedy."

He means Veronica, but why would he say tragedy and not problem? Tragedy can mean death or destruction.

"Should I be worried?"

"Dravin wouldn't touch you. You are too... plain for his taste."

I'm too plain? Fuck him. I know I'm not sex on legs, but plain? I wear fishnets to a bar with a skirt. I'm not too thin or too fat. I think. I'm not fucking plain.

"I meant about Warren."

"If you're interested in Warren, run the other way. You might as well withdraw from the school and move far away because by the time she is done with you, you will wish you never set foot in this place."

We both know who he is talking about: Veronica. She can't be that bad. He turns around and dismisses me like I was just some random person asking for directions.

I have to say Reid is hot, mysterious, but a total ass. He has a terrible attitude problem. Then he insults me and tells me that I'm plain and that Dravin will not take me seriously. That I'm not his type. Fuck him. Fuck all of them.

THE UBER DROPS me off on a street that has what looks like estates or what they call mini-mansions. I recheck the address, swiping my phone with a band-aid on my thumb, and it is definitely the right place. Who lives in houses like this two blocks away from campus? There are a total of six houses on this street and all of them have imposing gates that remind me of horror films. Each gate has a different gothic design scene. Like the house in Nightmare on Elm Street, House of Haunted Hill, and even Michael Meyers' house. I know they are not all mansions, but it is the scene. The feeling. These houses are all mansions, but they also all have something in common: they all look haunted and unnerving.

This particular house has many trees that hide its imposing size. A black gate leads to the cobblestone walkway because the one leading to the driveway is locked.

A gust of wind picks up the leaves off the ground signifying the beginning of the fall and reminding me I should've worn a heavier jacket. The gate closes with a click, and my heart begins to beat gallop, as if I'm walking into an impending doom.

The house isn't ugly, but it is overwhelming. It is white with black trimmed windows and gas-lighted lamps like the ones you see in New Orleans. I walk up the two steps that lead to the black wooden double doors. I'm about to press the doorbell when it suddenly opens, and Reid appears in the doorway.

"You're five minutes late."

"Normal college people like me don't have cars or live in huge houses near campus. We have to take an Uber, and I wasn't sure if I had the right address."

"How is that my fault exactly?"

"It isn't, but you don't have to be a dick about it. I haven't done anything to you, but you treat me like shit. I'm here to work on an assignment with you, not to hang out. Stop treating me like I'm here to fix the internet and I'm late. I'm not interested in anything else, and trust me, I'm not your type."

"What is your type?"

I snort. "The fact that all you remembered from what I just said is the part that you're not my type says a lot. Don't worry about it. Can I come in or not?"

He rolls his eyes and moves to the side holding the door open so I can come inside.

The place reeks of wealth. An interior decorator touched every inch of this place. This is not some house on frat row that was decorated by a bunch of college kids.

I wait for him to usher me to the area where we will be working. He closes the front door with a thud. The inside is decorated with light birch wood floors and furnishings in different shades of grey and black. The ceiling is lined with dark wood paneling, and there is a black marble-accented fireplace with white trim. The house is lit with a soft glow, and I think his family or whoever lives here prefers it that way. The curtains are luxurious floor-to-ceiling, covering the large windows that lead to a large pool that is lit up red, giving the impression that you are swimming in a pool of blood. Charming. Dracula must live here.

The home has an old Goth look mixed with a modern touch. It is definitely an old house that has been remodeled to fit modern times but has maintained the essence of its character.

Reid walks up the grand staircase, and I try to break the tension by complimenting him on his home, even though it's not all my style, mainly the lighting and the red pool.

"You have a very nice home."

He pauses on the landing and slightly turns his head. "It isn't mine. I just moved in here because my best friend was alone, and I didn't want to live with my parents. My parents' home is behind this one."

"Who's your best friend?"

He doesn't answer my question and I guess it doesn't matter. I'm just interested in getting the layout for the assignment and then I'm leaving.

The house is quiet and has no life except for the lights and the pool. It seems that no one lives here except Reid and his best friend because there are no family pictures anywhere—not on the walls or the credenza—nothing. Whoever his best friend is, they like solitude.

Following Reid down the hallway, he stops and opens the first door to the right. It is clearly a bedroom with a computer desk. My spider senses kick in because I thought we would go to an office or a loft with a desk and chairs we could work on, but not his bedroom.

His bed is massive, and it is the kind that has four posts. My gaze falls on the dark sheets, and he notices where my attention is drawn to.

"Are you sure I'm not your type?"

"Positive," I quip.

He acts like a typical guy who's got a girl up in his room. Like every other guy in this place, he thinks I'm going to fall for his good looks. Most of the guys here can fool other girls and get them to do whatever they want. They must think I'm stupid because I didn't grow up here or come from money.

He smiles and sits at the edge of the bed facing me. I slide my bag, which carries my laptop and notebook, off my shoulder and walk over to place it on the chair in front of his desk.

"I like you, Gia. Not in that way. But—" He pauses and licks his lips. "Never mind. I'm just fucking with you. What do you have in mind for the assignment?"

My shoulders sag in relief and I let him know the ideas I have in my head on how a great marketing ad should look and what elements it should include.

"I'm just not good at the graphics part," I tell him.

"I'm good at the graphics part. I just need you to come up with the target audience and hook. I will put together the ad, SEO, graphics, and upload."

The computer on his desk is one of those gamer computers with RGB changing lights fading from one hue into another. He has a dock with various headphones, drives, and other computer-related accessories. He probably knows what he is doing and would be better at it than me since my laptop is old and on its last leg. It lags but gets the basic job done.

"Alright, fine. Sounds like a plan. What are we selling?"

He smirks. "What are you willing to sell?"

The door to his room suddenly is pushed open wider, and the last person I would have ever thought stands at the threshold, fury blazing in his eyes when he spots me standing in front of Reid.

"What the fuck are you doing in here?"

My eyes widen. "I––"

He doesn't let me finish or say anything. He grabs me firmly by the arm and pulls me out of the room into another room down the hall resembling his bedroom. He shuts the door and spins me around. My back is against the door, and he towers over me, caging me in. The corded veins over the muscles of his arms swirl under the ink of his tattoos. In the light of his room, I notice he has tattoos almost everywhere. I have never noticed them because he always wears long-sleeved sweaters or shirts. The only ones I could ever see are the ones that peek out from his neck and hands.

"Are you fucking him?"

I shake my head. "No, but it doesn't matter if I am or not. It's none of your business."

"You are in my house and everything that goes on here *is* my business."

Reid set me up. It is the only explanation as to why he failed to omit the fact that his so-called best friend is none other than Dravin Bedford. Now, I'm in his house and in his bedroom. When I take my next breath, all I smell is his cologne. Clean and fresh mixed with his tempting scent.

My chin lifts. "Look, I didn't know this was your house. Reid didn't tell me you lived here. I'm just here to work on an assignment and he is my partner. That's it. I think we were about finished. I can text him about it later."

Pushing myself off the door is no use because he doesn't budge.

"Move. I want to leave. I already told you why I was here."

His nostrils flare, but I'm not sure if it is due to anger or something else. It is hard to read his thoughts. He burns hot and cold, and I can't think around him. He confuses me. I'm angry with him one second, and the next, I want him.

"What's wrong? You don't want to see my room, my little Raven?"

"Why would I want to see where you bring your victims before you cast them aside." I nudge toward his bed. "I think I'll pass. I'm not interested in playing your games. I want to get my shit and leave. And stop calling me *your little Raven*. My name is Gia."

"To me, you are my little Raven. Get used to it. From now on, I'm calling you Raven."

Rolling my eyes, knowing there is no winning with him, I notice his massive king-sized bed, also with dark satin sheets and a grey comforter. His floors match the rest of the house, and he also has a desk but with three more screens than Reid.

His walls are bare except for three paintings I recognize. The first is Ary Scheffer's *Francesca da Rimini* painting, which shows a couple in lust. The second painting is John Collier, depicting Lilith with a snake wrapped around her body, known as a *demoness for thirst and revenge*. The third painting is of Francisco Goya's *Saturn Devouring His Son*, but if I remember correctly, the body being devoured is argued to look like a female instead of a male.

The three paintings remind me of the seven deadly sins. Why would he hang them in his bedroom? My eyes are so transfixed on the wall with the paintings that I don't notice he has stepped away, and I could easily open the door and leave.

"Which one do you like the most?" he asks in a husky voice.

My head snaps up to his like I was caught doing something I hadn't meant to be doing. My eyes fly across the paintings one more time and I honestly don't like any of them.

My head tips up. "None. I don't like any of them."

He doesn't answer. He stays silent. He doesn't move. After a few more seconds, I turn and run back to Reid's room, thankful that his door is still wide open. When I enter to retrieve my bag, he is still sitting on the edge of the bed, leaning back with his elbows on the mattress. The knowing grin he is sporting makes the hairs on the back of my neck stand up. Prick.

"Whatever sick perverted game you two are playing, count me the fuck out," I snap.

The grin planted on his face tells me it wasn't a coincidence that I was paired with him for the assignment. How they managed to pull it off, I have no idea. The professor was firm that whoever you were paired up with was set in stone, and you couldn't change partners.

Reid doesn't move except for his eyes as he watches me collect my things and leave. He doesn't respond, and the silence tells me everything I need to know.

I'm in trouble, but I don't know how or why. All I know is that I'm a target for something. I just need to figure out what that is and who I need to defend myself from.

DRAVIN

"DID VALEN CALL?" I ask Reid when I walk into his room.

Gia left like her life depended on it. I was at a loss for words when she told me she didn't like any of the paintings. When I asked other girls I've had in my room, they always chose one. Then I ask them to leave my room. I never screw them on my bed. It is always somewhere else in the house. The couch, the pool, or the kitchen. Never in my room.

She is the first girl who has ever said she doesn't like any of them. This tells me something about Gia. She is innocent and pure-hearted, and I want to dirty her with my filth. The only problem is that I want to be the only one to do it.

"Ask me what you really want to ask and get it over with."

I'm looking around his room for some type of evidence to prove that they were only discussing the assignment for their class. A class he specifically signed up for at the last minute at my request. Call it my penchant for control, but I need to ensure I win.

My eyes fly to his. "Fine. Did you touch her?"

He gives me a hard stare. "Why? So I can look like Warren and fuck up the season. Coach is already ripping him a new one. Now we need Valen to step it up because of a bad temper and what happened to his arm. No thanks, I'll pass. I like my hands and need them to jerk off, swim, and fuck. It's not worth it. Not for a girl you will end up fucking anyway. I thought she was too plain or innocent for your liking? Why are you going to all this trouble? Just fuck her like all the other chicks that come through here and get it over with."

Reid, Valen, and I are the sons of the three founding families that founded the Kenyan University. Valen is a sophomore and the youngest of us. He is insatiable. The guy fucks like he is starving in the middle of the desert.

As for me, I've never fucked a girl for more than one night. One night of sinful pleasure is all I ever want and all I ever need. Otherwise, they all get clingy and expect more. That is when we play. We hurt. We destroy. We show them what they don't mean to us. We've always done it. Every girl. Every time. Except her. Gia will never be the target of our wrath.

I give him a hard glare. "Don't touch her, Reid."

He raises his hands. "I'll keep my hands to myself. Like I said, I don't want to end up like our buddy Warren. What did he do to deserve the wrath, Dravin?"

"He touched what he wasn't supposed to touch."

"Did he know that?"

"Not my problem if he does or doesn't. She obviously isn't interested. Now, he can't touch her with a fucked-up hand."

"I wonder what your dad and therapist will say?"

"Don't give a fuck because I'm not going to therapy anymore. Never needed that crap, and my purpose for going to therapy is done."

He remains silent, knowing not to keep fishing for more information I won't give him. I trust Reid and Valen, but right now, I'm annoyed that he brought her to his room. That wasn't part of the plan. I regret treating her the way I just did. She ran out of here like the hounds of hell were right behind her.

I push off the door molding, looking at the time on my phone. "I need to go. Don't expect me back until morning."

"Where are you going?"

"To take care of my interests."

GIA†

MY EYES SNAP open from a deep sleep. Something woke me, except when I look around the room, it's still basked in darkness. My eyes try to adjust, but the only light coming into the room is from under the door leading to the main hallway.

Jess and I share a room with twin beds on each side. A desk is placed at the foot of each bed, with two nightstands in between. One thing they never updated in this school is the dorms. There are the old traditional dorms you see in older schools.

I guess they don't have many students who need them. There are only forty students on each floor of the female building, and each building is only three stories. From what Jess has told me, there are only fifteen students housed on each floor in the male building. The rest live off campus or in frat houses. My eyes look around the room, but everything is so dark. I can't see much, but I wonder what woke me from my sleep.

Jess was already in bed when I walked in from Dravin's house. My hand reaches out to my nightstand to grab my phone, and I press the button so that the light can help me see around the room. When my phone lights up, I almost scream when a hand shoots out and covers my mouth.

My eyes widen in pure fear, but my fear begins to dissipate as I look into eyes that have been appearing in my dreams, along with a familiar scent that I quickly realize is filling my senses. His lips move silently, telling me to keep quiet. My head nods, not knowing what to do. Should I scream? My body makes up my mind for me because my nipples harden when his gaze drops to my soft cotton tank. He can see right through the fabric because of the bright light coming from my phone. When his gaze lingers, my nipples further betray me. When he takes my phone from my hand, the light shows his mouth turning into a frown, and he drops his hand from my mouth. He inspects the phone that looks like a mirror of broken glass. Some of the numbers and apps look smeared and unreadable.

He grips my wrist gently and notices the band-aid on my thumb. He unwraps it and I recoil my hand from his grasp.

"What are you doing here?" I whisper.

He doesn't respond and just watches me. He stares into my eyes and slides his fingers over my wrist again. The light on my phone shuts off, and we are once again enveloped in darkness.

He moves, and I can hear the rustling of clothing. Another light brightens my side of the room, and I see his hand holding his phone. He lifts my hand again and turns it over to inspect my thumb.

"What––

He places a finger on my mouth and mouths silently for me to be quiet. What is he doing here? Why is he here?

He shakes his head when he notices the cut on my thumb, and I know he can tell it's from the severely cracked screen of my phone. He places my phone back on my nightstand and motions for me to move over.

I shake my head, but he ignores me and lifts my comforter. My eyes dart to where Jess is sound asleep, and the light from Dravin's phone goes off and then back on. My gaze finds his, and he pushes me gently so I can give him room on the small twin bed.

My heart begins to beat, and my hands start to sweat. Dravin is in my dorm room after hours and is crawling into my bed. My head tilts up and he raises an eyebrow expectantly. Taking a deep breath, I move over to give him room and slide my hard, firm pillow over trying to fluff it up frustratingly. He grabs the pillow and throws it toward the foot of the bed, and I throw my hands up. *What the hell?*

He removes his shirt and I'm relieved the light from his phone turns off and the room darkens. If I see what he looks like with his shirt off, I don't know how I will be able to handle myself looking at him. He slides in next to me like we are a couple, and we have done this countless times. Like he is my boyfriend, and he sneaks in after hours all the time.

I'm sitting up and I'm stunned. My mind hasn't entirely caught up to the fact that Dravin is here and he is not leaving. My head turns and my eyes are trying to adjust to the darkness so I can look at his face. He moves, and it seems like he raises his arm, and I assume it's so I can lay on his chest.

My heart is racing, beating like it's going to rip out of my chest because I have never been in a bed with a guy before. I'm attracted to Dravin, but I don't know him. The only thing I know is that he is mysterious, a player, and ridiculously gorgeous.

"Relax, Raven. I'm not here to hurt you. Now go to sleep," he whispers so low I almost can't hear what he is saying.

I swallow, unsure of what to do. Should I get up and wake Jess and kick him out, or should I lay down and go to sleep on his naked chest and smile to myself that I have the hottest guy on campus wanting me to fall asleep next to him?

For once, I stop thinking and just do what my heart wants. I lay down and snuggle against his warm body with smooth skin and hard ripped muscle. My eyes close and I inhale the scent of his skin. I imagine that he is mine, and I am his. My skin vibrates everywhere he touches, and I mentally count all the places our bodies touch.

My lips curl into a smile. I'm not sure if this is real or if I'm dreaming. I just let myself feel and listen. His chest rises and falls. I know he is not asleep but still listening and waiting. My head tilts up to see if I can see the expression on his face. I want to figure out what he wants and why he is here. I try, but it's no use; it's dark, and my eyes are growing heavy. His breathing is steady and even. His body is warm and comforting. But I know he is awake.

Waiting.

Waiting for me.

Giving up, I turn my face, letting my cheek feel the smoothness of his chest. His fingers gently brush the hair from my face. It is so quiet, yet it's so loud. The beating of his heart thumps wildly but begins to slow down and my eyes drift closed. Listening to the beat of his heart and smelling the scent of his skin begins to lull me into sleep. I'm memorizing this moment because, right now, it is the only place I want to be. In Dravin Bedford's arms.

GIA

MY ALARM GOES OFF, but my eyes remain closed. My mind begins to wake up, and then memories of last night come flooding back like a tidal wave. I bolt up from the bed and notice I'm alone. My eyes open, and I look around, wondering if it was all a dream and I imagined it. My alarm keeps going off on my phone and I silence it by pressing the side button.

Getting up from the bed, I look over, and everything appears like it was before I went to bed. I look over at Jess's bed. She must have gone to class because it is empty, and I notice her bed is made.

I shake my head. "It must have been a dream," I mutter.

After taking a shower and getting dressed, I head out of Drury Hall, where my dorm is located, and walk over to the main building for my math class. When I walk in, I take a seat in the far corner of the last row. I usually sit in the front in all my classes, but at Kenyan, with the type of college students that go here, I need to pay attention to not only the class but also the people around me. The back is where I can do both.

Something is not right about some of the people that go here. I just can't figure out what it is. Everyone looks at you like they know something you don't, and they will make sure you are the last one to find out and by the time you do, it's too late.

The professor walks in and introduces himself as Professor Walker. He looks middle-aged, but he's slightly built. His clothes are the same as most male professors—dress shirt, slacks, and loafers. He continues to introduce himself while he passes out the syllabus, and my mind tunes him out, going back to memories of last night. I'm still wondering if I made it all up or if Dravin is like Edward Cullen and shows up in girls' rooms unannounced in the dark of night. If it was real, how the hell did he get in? If it wasn't real, then I needed my head examined.

"Hey."

My head whips to my right and I see a guy giving me a smile. "Hi," I say and quickly look back to the front of the room. From the corner of my eye, I watch him as he continues to look at me with a wide grin. He knows I am looking at him even if my head is facing forward. I begin to tap my pen on my notebook. He has brown hair and brown eyes. He is good looking, like most of the guys I have seen around here. He's probably on the swim team. He has the same ripped body under a fitted shirt and pants slung low over his hips. His long legs are stretched out in front of him, and he keeps tapping his thumb on the desk.

He leans closer and whispers, "My name is Valen. You must be Gia."

My eyes widen. "How do you know my name?" I ask above a whisper.

He licks his lips and gives me a playful smirk. "A little bird told me."

Is this guy for real? Is this a joke? Smartass.

"You know it's not polite to keep secrets."

He smiles. "Who said I'm keeping secrets?"

"What do you want?" I snap.

I know I'm being a bitch, but I'm tired of the games.

"Relax. I just wanted to meet you since we are in the same class. I'm a sophomore, but I'm really good at math."

I suck at math, and I'm totally being a bitch right now, but the way he talks and the way he teases is both sweet and dark all at the same time. He said he is really good at math and is a sophomore taking calculus. Impressive. However, there is definitely more to him being in this class and sitting next to me. I can just feel it.

I'm feeling bad about the way I snapped at him just now. I'm moody and don't know who I can trust, but I can't think everyone who talks to me is out to get me. After forty minutes of silence, I sigh. "Look, I'm sorry I snapped at you."

"It's cool. I know I sounded a little weird, but I wanted to see for myself if the rumors were true."

"What rumors?"

He stays silent, and I think he isn't going to answer me. Whatever. There are ten minutes left in the class, and the professor is writing our first assignment on the board and telling us to get the required book for the class—a book I have not purchased yet.

"You are free to go," the professor says.

I collect my things and move to stand, making my way toward the exit. I pull out my phone to check the time, even though the last digit is a little blurry.

Once I'm out in the hallway, Valen comes up next to me. "You're even more beautiful up close," he says softly. He points toward the shattered screen of my phone. You need to get that replaced."

I pause, and he walks away without saying another word.

I'm even more beautiful up close?

I'm looking at my phone, smiling to myself, not believing I was paid a compliment. I'm pulling up the map on my phone, and I'm focusing on the shattered pieces to find out where the bookstore and the library are located. I can't replace my phone because I need the money I have for my books. Especially the math book. It is either the book or the phone, and I need the book or I'll fail the class. I remember Reid telling me to try the library, so that's where I head to first.

After I meet with the librarian, I have the biggest smile on my face. I was offered a job that would work around my schedule. Plus, since I work at the school, all my non-covered tuition is covered. Like my books. I will be reimbursed for any non-covered tuition expenses for this semester. All I have to do is pay for my food off-campus. The rest of the money can stay in my account. No more ramen noodles for me, and I can replace my phone.

When I get the chance, I have to thank Reid for pointing me in the right direction. The guy is an ass, but he saved mine. I'm walking across campus to Drury Hall. When I walk into my dorm, I stop. My mouth must be hanging open because my throat goes dry.

There is a small bag sitting on my bed with a sticky note stuck on it. I take a seat on my bed, pull the string to undo the ribbon, and look inside the bag. I pull out the white box with an Apple symbol on it. It is the latest smartphone, and the sticky note reads.

"Even in the dark, I fell right into you...and we fit perfectly."
Dravin

It was real. I didn't make it up. He was here. In my bed. And he held me... without his shirt on. I keep reading the sticky note over and over but put it away before Jess makes it back. Holding the white box with a brand-new phone inside, I realize I can't accept the gift. As much as I need it, I can't. It is too much, and now that I am able to replace mine, I can't accept it. I'm not sure if this is his way to get me to sleep with him, if he really likes me, or if he's just being nice, but the sneaking in, the phone, and the poetic note... He's getting to me, and I can't stop the feelings I'm having no matter how hard I try.

The door opens, and Jess walks in and sees me holding the unopened box in my hand.

"Hey, you got a new phone," she says, pointing at the box in my hand. "Whoa, that looks expensive."

I shake my head. "I didn't buy it. It was a gift."

She raises her brows. "Someone with deep pockets must really like you."

I lick my lips and ask her, "Hey, Jess. Did you wake up and leave the door unlocked last night after I went to bed? Did you hear anyone come in?"

I know I'm a chicken shit and should just ask her outright if she let Dravin in or if she knew he was here last night this morning."

She pinches her brows and shakes her head. "Um, no. I didn't hear you come in last night, but you were sleeping like the dead this morning. I made noise, but you didn't even stir. I'm surprised you woke up and made it to class."

Shit. How did he get in?

"Why? Is everything ok?"

I decide to tell her in case he does it again. I'm not sure if it was a one-time thing or not. Maybe he is testing me, or maybe he has done this with other girls, and she can tell me not to fall for it.

"He was here last night," I blurt.

I run my fingers through my hair and look at her. She's staring at me like I just spoke to her in a different language.

"I'm sorry. Who was here last night?"

I roll my eyes. "Dravin."

"Dravin?"

"Yes, Dravin. He showed up last night like Edward Cullen from Twilight and slept with me in my bed. It was creepy and hot all at the same time. Does he do that to get girls to screw him or something? Does he buy them shit he thinks they need?"

She blows out a breath. "Are you telling me he snuck in, fell asleep with you in the bed all night, and then surprised you by buying you a phone?"

"Yes," I say forcefully.

She walks around, pacing the room. After the fourth time going back and forth like she is doing suicides, she looks at me. "That is not like him, and I have never heard of Dravin buying anyone shit or sleeping in a bed with a female unless it's to fuck, and from what I have heard, never in his bed. Maybe he was hoping you would give it up."

"While you were asleep ten feet away? No way."

"You would be surprised what I have seen and heard around here."

"Like?"

"Like orgies and threesomes. It's not uncommon in college from stories you hear. It's just that these guys take it to a whole other level, and it has nothing to do with dating or liking a girl. They play games. Games that involve breaking hearts and questioning what is real and what isn't."

Is she serious? I have heard stories about frat parties and college kids getting out of control, but what she is mentioning is a whole other level of fucked up.

"Jess, what you are saying doesn't sound that far off in the sense of a bunch of college kids breaking girls' hearts and sleeping with whoever they can. It does happen."

"Not when they do it for fun and don't care about the consequences.

They don't care if you are in love with a boyfriend out of state or if you put up a giant iron wall. They will make sure to break you."

"Who's *they*?"

"The three sons come from the families that started this school, and the other kids their families deem." She makes air quotation marks. "Their circle of business friends and colleagues."

"Who are the three sons?"

"Dravin, Reid, and Valen."

My heart drops when the names rolling off her tongue are the three guys I have already encountered. Dravin showing up everywhere, Reid being my partner on an assignment, and Valen attending my math class. I start making shit up in my head. It can't be a coincidence. Can it?

"You've already met the other two, haven't you?"

I tell her how I have run into them. She nods, listening intently, though I can tell her head is spinning. The only thing I don't tell her is what he wrote on the sticky note.

"So, look. When there is an attractive girl, they see her as—" She trails off.

"What? They see her as—"

"A conquest. A game. A pawn like in a chess game. In this case, it looks like Dravin is the one who wants you the most for whatever reason. The only thing that is off, is him showing up here and buying you anything. He doesn't need to ever go to those lengths to sleep with a girl."

"Got it," I quip.

I kind of figured it was all bullshit. But hearing out loud that you are getting played... stings. The sticky note that is written by his hand is an ink of lies burning a hole in my bag. I want it to go up in flames. I would have preferred last night to be a dream. A glimpse created by my imagination. I realize that his words and gifts are like magic. And everyone knows that magic is a form of deception.

Anger begins to filter inside me. I snatch the bag off my bed and slide the phone inside it.

"What are you doing?" Jess asks me, her eyes going wide.

I hold the bag up by the strings. Two fingers curled under the handles. "What does it look like? I'm giving it back. He can shove the phone up the pin-sized hole of his dick."

Jess burst out laughing. "Fuck him. Just keep it."

"No," I deadpan, shaking my head. "No."

I get up and slide the bag inside my oversized school bag, gripping the sticky note and crushing it in my palm. I let it go so it can fall on top, swing the straps of my bag over my shoulder, and walk toward the door.

"Woah, woah. Where are you going?"

My hand is on the knob of the door, and I turn my head around. "Where does it look like I'm going—to Dravin's house."

"You're serious."

"Yes."

She gets up and throws a shirt over her tank top and slides her feet into her Vans. "I'm going with you for moral support. You can't go into the lion's den alone."

DRAVIN

"HAVE YOU FUCKED HER YET," Veronica asks as I hold my cell phone to my ear.

"I'm working on it."

She chuckles. "Losing your touch, Dravin," she drawls. "I never thought she would make you work for it. She isn't falling easily for your charms. Come to think of it, I should just have asked... Valen to do it and given it up to him instead. Reid and I don't get along very well."

My nostrils flare at her taunts. I don't lose, and I'm sure as hell not letting Valen touch her or... anyone. They have been warned not to get in the way until I'm done with her. All of us have an agreement. No fly zone until we say, or we are done with whoever we have our eye on. It usually takes no more than two weeks, but this is taking longer than I had initially thought.

"He's mad at you because you don't play by the rules."

"You're right, I don't. I break them. Let's face it. You don't follow them either. So there is that."

"Why are you calling me?"

"Because you're taking too long. I'm getting impatient."

I chuckle. "What's wrong, Veronica? Are you dying to ride my cock? You sound a little...desperate."

"Oh, please. You didn't think you could even go through with it. That little, small-town, emo bitch is not going to give it up that easily. She probably won't when she hears how you treat every piece of ass that has come your way." She sighs. "I hate to be the bearer of bad news, but I think you're losing this one. I'm just going to have to take care of her my way."

"You did enough with her roommate. She has probably told her what you did by now. They seem like they get along quite well. Reid is still pissed you went behind his back and set Jess up with Garret."

"Oh, please. Reid is a terrible loser. He is just mad that Garret and that other twit Melissa tasted her pootie before he had a chance."

Yeah, then you fucked him out of spite to make sure he wouldn't fall for the girl. Reid wanted her to himself for whatever reason, but Veronica the bitch wanted to play. Now everyone knows both Melissa and Jess play for both sides of the field. Veronica sent censored pictures to almost everyone on campus and made sure Garret told everyone Jess was a bad lay.

Everyone sees him in a different light because he has two chicks at once.

He boasted about it in front of Reid, but he shrugged it off like he didn't give a shit. But I know better; Reid doesn't like people to get in the way of his plans. His plan was to seduce Jess and fuck her every way he wanted before anyone else could. She attacked Gia, so now I'm going to get her where it hurts her the most.

"Whatever, how's Warren treating you?"

I know he is still avoiding her like the plague. He has been going around saying that the girl he was dating is a sex-crazed basket case. There is nothing that she can do that will change his mind. The guy's mind is already made up about her, but to a disturbed bitch like Veronica, I'll keep that to myself. If I tell her, she will go on the warpath. I don't have time to deal with spoiled little rich brats like Veronica. My father and then her father will want me to clean her mess up. Not happening. It is better to avoid it altogether and hope she finds new Prey and forgets about Warren dismissing her.

She huffs on the phone. "Very funny, like you don't know."

I chuckle. Jasmin decided to giggle at that exact moment. My head whips around. Jasmin is on her knees on the sundeck of the pool, giving both Valen and Reid blow jobs. While I'm outside walking by the edge.

"Is that who I think it is giggling? Don't tell me you didn't participate."

"Nah, Reid and Valen wanted to play."

Jasmin takes Valen and Reid's cocks into her mouth, taking turns deep-throating them as they grunt and each of them has a hand fisting in her hair. Veronica wanted to make sure Jasmin was taken care of since we were the ones to pair her with Warren.

"Nah, she isn't my type. Too easy. She didn't even make it interesting."

"You're a sick bastard. Do you know that?"

I'm watching as Jasmin slides her mouth up and down Valen, then Reid, and back again. She slides her fingers down and plays with herself, and I sit watching the show.

She pulls Reid's cock out of her mouth. "He's watching me," she says.

"He likes to watch sometimes."

"He doesn't want to join?"

"Hey, Dravin, we got a thirsty one," Valen calls out, tilting his head like he can't believe Jasmin is down to suck all three of our cocks. "I kinda like her."

Her eyes look up and she smiles at his praise.

"I'm good right here," I tell them.

I'm not interested in having Jasmin suck me off. This definitely has Veronica written all over it. She made sure Jasmin was up for it.

"What did you do?" I ask Veronica.

"Making sure she doesn't suck the wrong cock or, in this case...cocks."

"How do you know she hasn't already?"

She means Warren. According to Reid, Jasmin has been partnered with Warren and he made sure it happened that way. It is his way of playing games. He knew Veronica would want us to take care of Jasmin. She had little hearts in her eyes when she was partnered with Warren. Reid said Warren was hoping to be partnered with Gia. He was boasting about how lucky Reid was that he was close to the girl no one has been able to fuck.

"Don't worry. I know." She snickers in that annoying way she does. "It's just added protection. Reid or Valen will boast about it in the locker room after practice."

"Whatever. Is that all?"

She makes a noise like she is stretching. "Yes," she purrs. "Make sure you guys clean up the stains of your sins." She laughs and I hang up.

"Crazy, bitch," I mutter.

I grab the towel and dry myself after the swim I had before I answered the phone. Jasmin has decided to show Reid and Valen how deep her throat is. I pick up my shirt to head inside, ignoring the noises and grunts coming out of the three on my pool deck. Then I suddenly realize that Jasmin is boring and takes too long to please.

GIA

"HAVE YOU BEEN HERE BEFORE?" I ask Jess, closing the door of her Honda.

She parks on the side of the street, and I'm thankful she decided to tag along and save me the cost of an Uber.

She shakes her head as we head to the open gate that leads to the walkway. "No. Never. I have heard of the street the three sons of the founding families live on, just like everyone else, but I have never actually been to any of their houses. They usually hang out at the bar or at the frat houses."

We walk side by side until we reach the massive door. The sun is beginning to set, leaving the sky with streaks of purple and grey and the air is getting cooler. It will be just another week before the temperatures begin to drop. Right now, it gets hot during the day and cooler at night. The leaves on the trees are starting to turn a shade of brown and fall off leaving the sticks of the branches like swirling veins.

I grip my bag to my side, making sure the strap doesn't slide off my shoulder. "Thanks for coming," I tell her.

"Trust me. I want to see the look on his smug face when you give it back. I couldn't let you come here alone when you are so pissed. I would be too if I knew what I know now. These guys have a motive for everything. Everything has a purpose, and they Prey on girl's feelings. At the same time, you can't blame them. I mean, who wouldn't want the attention of a hot guy or the chance to sleep with them. Some girls don't even care how they're treated as long as they can have a chance."

I figure what she is saying is the truth. It seems that way, and guys like Dravin are skillful manipulators. You get sucked in by their words and forget that you are just another name in a long list, and before you know it, you're giving yourself up too easily. The war between emotion and reason, like the line between love and hate, becomes blurred. In the end, all that is left is hate because your pride has silenced you into tears.

I don't knock. I just turn the handle of the massive door and watch it open. Nervousness coursing through my veins. My hands shake as I think about the confrontation that must ensue, but Dravin leaves me with little choice, and right now, I couldn't care less if he isn't expecting me. I came to return the so-called gift and note but haven't thought about what I am going to say when I see him or how he will react to me being in his house again. Will he be happy or pissed?

Jess follows me as we walk down the hallway. Everything is the same as the last time I was here, except there is movement behind the kitchen island leading out to the pool. The sun is setting behind the massive windows as the shadows of four people come into the dimly lit house.

The girl partnered with Warren in my marketing class makes an appearance, fumbling with her fingers to tie the straps of the bottom and the top of her bikini. The two pieces of fabric covering her nipples hang loose over her small breasts. It's obvious she was recently naked.

Jess pauses right beside me as Dravin comes inside, pulling a t-shirt over his flawless body and hiding the swirls of ink on his chest and torso. My heart begins to pound not in want or need, but in anger. Anger because of the lies spilled in ink left on a piece of paper. Anger because the girl he chose to be with at this moment is not me. I shouldn't be feeling this way, but I do.

Two more figures come into the light. Reid and Valen appear, and the puzzle pieces fit perfectly. Everything Jess has said rings inside my head like my alarm waking me up every morning. I'm thrown back into reality from the darkness of my dreams.

Reid has his swim trunks slung low on his ripped frame, and so does Valen, a younger version of the three with a similar build. They are heart-throbs with perfect faces and bodies who steal hearts like thieves in the night, leaving behind tears in their wake.

"What are you two doing here?" Reid is the first to ask, his voice hard and sharp.

He is clearly unhappy that we have shown up and entered the house unannounced.

I finally swallow and find my voice. Jess is frozen in place, shooting lethal daggers at Jasmin. She smirks at us with a knowing smile, adjusting her swimsuit like she is the luckiest girl on the face of the earth, and we just discovered her secret.

Jasmin's lips turn up into a smile laced with sarcasm. "You're the girl in my marketing class." Her eyes land on Jess. "Aren't you the girl that slept with Garret? I'm really sorry about what happened. He shouldn't have outed you like that."

What a bitch.

At first, I was feeling sorry for her, but now I hope they make a point of ruining this girl. She probably just had a threesome and now is redirecting her vitriol by pointing out what happened with Jess.

"I didn't come to see you." I nudge my chin and lift it toward a silent Dravin. I came to see him."

My eyes land on Dravin and his expression is hard. His light eye twitches slightly. He is obviously annoyed that I'm here, so I decide to make this quick.

"This is going to be interesting," Valen says, crossing his arms over his ripped chest.

"Good. I was hoping it wasn't about school," Reid chimes in.

Valen raises an eyebrow to Jasmin. "You can see yourself out."

Her face falls and I smile. "Hey, Jasmin." I make a motion to the corner of her mouth." You might want to wipe the corner of your mouth. Your desperation...It's dripping."

She glares at me as she grips her bag. She shimmies into her shorts and forcefully slides her sweater over her head. Valen chuckles when she glowers at me, and Jess huffs her way toward the front door.

"Thanks for stopping by," Valen calls out after her.

Reid glares at Jess as he moves toward the stairs. "What the hell is she doing here?"

"I came with her, but don't worry, we're not interested in staying," Jess retorts.

"Good because no one invited you two. Especially... you. I'm not interested in being around someone else's scraps," Reid snaps.

Jess's nostrils flare, and I know he is talking about her falling from grace with Garret. It is messed up that he throws it in her face when he has probably done worse.

"Funny, you were interested in hearing all about it before," Jess volleys back.

Reid's lips curl into a snarl while climbing the stairs. "What's wrong, Jess? Jealous."

Jess snorts and claps her hands together. "Yeah, because you are such a fantasy. Just what a girl dreams about—a guy that has stuck his dick in more holes than a drill. Please."

Valen bellows in laughter at their back-and-forth while Dravin is still standing motionless on the other side of the marble island in the kitchen. It's like he didn't hear the banter between Jess and Reid or even Valen telling Jasmin to leave. He is standing like a spectator, watching everything unfold, with not an ounce of emotion on his face.

He watches me with his arms hanging by his sides. My heart begins to beat in my chest harder than it should. I'm suddenly aware of every breath and swallow I take. The phone he gifted me and the note sit like bombs in my bag. We just stare at each other, and my eyes gaze into his like I'm looking out a window. One eye is like the sunrise, and the other is like the sunset. Light and dark. Night and day.

Every time he is in a room, I'm aware of him. It doesn't matter if it's full or empty, I feel his presence. It is always him I remember and the only one I cannot forget. He continues to watch me as I walk forward and slide the strap of my oversized bag off my shoulder. I take out the gift bag and place it on the counter. My head tilts up, and I swear he flinches. I slide my hand over the scrunched sticky note and slowly lift my hand in a fist and open it over the bag. His eyes follow the small piece of paper as it rolls over the side of the gift bag until it lands on the counter.

Our eyes meet and no one speaks. From the corner of my eye, I see Valen and Jess leave the kitchen and walk toward the living room, leaving us alone.

My tongue slides over the front of my teeth while my mind is trying to find the right words to say. The right words that need to hide the way I'm feeling about him screwing someone today when last night he had his arms wrapped around me like a blanket. Then the anger takes over because he must think I'm just some stupid girl from the middle of nowhere that he can take advantage of.

He moves forward, looks at the crumbled note, and meets my eyes. My eyes get glassy, and I get emotional because, for one moment, I wanted to believe it was real.

That he wanted to be in my bed.

That he cared that I needed a new phone and knew I couldn't afford one.

That it pained him to see that I cut myself on the broken glass on the screen.

That he meant those words on that piece of paper.

The devil must exist because, otherwise, someone couldn't be so beautiful and so cruel at the same time.

I keep my voice low. "I know you must think I'm stupid or that I'm some girl who can easily be taken advantage of, but I'm not. I don't need you to buy me anything. I don't want anything from you. I would rather cut my fingers off than accept something from someone who lies and deceives people."

A slow smile creeps up his face before he answers. "Did I ask you to sleep with me last night? His eyes drift up at the ceiling as if lost in thought. "Did I? Did I ask you to sleep with me this morning?"

"I'm not like that tramp that just left here, or any other girl you secretly screw around with. Your looks and tattoos and mysterious charm don't impress me."

He leans on the counter and acts impervious to my rudeness. "Calm down, Raven. I'm just trying to be your friend. Sure, I find you attractive, and I like you, but I didn't mean to buy you a new phone so I could get something out of you. You needed it. It was a friendly gesture. I know I came on to you, but it is what I'm used to, and you've already expressed to me that you are not the type of girl who just sleeps with a guy who gives you the right attention." He points to the bag. "Take the phone."

"No."

"Take it. How else am I to call you without worrying you'll slit your finger when you answer?"

"Why would you call me?"

He shrugs. "I don't know. Maybe I want to ask you to go with me somewhere as friends. Maybe I could take you where you need to go if Jess is unavailable. I noticed you don't have a car. Things like that. We can hang out."

I find this side of Dravin really weird. Is he for real, or is he trying too hard?

"You don't have to go through all this trouble, you know. I'm not going to sleep with you, so you can quit while you're ahead and save yourself time."

"I'm serious, Raven."

My brows shoot up. "Why are you being so nice to me, and why do you keep calling me Raven?"

I begin to fidget with my hair, running my fingers through the long, dark strands. I'm curious to know why he keeps calling me Raven.

"Did you know ravens mate for life? They represent prophecy and insight. They are highly intelligent, and they eat anything they want. They can survive in the face of danger and are considered spirit animals. They date back centuries. Most people think they are a bad omen, but that could be further from the truth. Seeing one is actually good luck. Ravens are beautiful birds with black wings just like your hair."

"You think all those things about me?"

He nods. "Yes, I do." He walks around the island and leans close. "There are a lot of things I think about that remind me of you, and there are a lot of things I want to know about you, too."

His face is a few inches from mine, and I can smell the scent of pool water mixed with his cologne. His dark hair is spiked up and wet. His nose piercing is still in, and his eyes are tracing my lips.

His lips lean close, and I swear he can hear my pulse beating in my neck. "I didn't sleep with Jasmin. I never touched her. She wasn't here for me," he whispers.

I can't breathe. The fanning of his breath on my skin raises goosebumps over my flesh. The hairs on the back of my neck stand up like he is a magnet pulling them. It's like he has me in a trance when he pulls away and stands up to look down at me. His eyes caress my face. The only thing I can hear or feel is the sound of us breathing.

"I have to get back. Jess is waiting for me in the living room, and she's my ride."

"Oh, right." He turns toward the counter and slides the box out of the bag. His other hand reaches and takes the note, smoothing the paper I scrunched up in my hand.

He hands it to me slowly. "Please accept it. I know you have heard things about me, and most of them are true, but not all. They come from people who don't really know me."

Feeling a tad guilty that I accused him of screwing Jasmin, I take the box and slide it into my bag. He hands me the note. "I meant what I wrote."

He sticks his hand out for me to shake. "Friends?"

I sigh dramatically and slide my hands into his. "Friends," I say softly.

His eyes light up and he grins. He clears his throat. "I'll walk you out."

"Ok."

We walk down the hallway, and I can hear soft laughter and Jess's giggle from the living room. She is seated really close to Valen, and her eyebrows rise when she sees Dravin behind me. "Ready?" she asks.

I glimpse from the tiny smirk on Valen's face to Dravin. "Yeah."

When we reach the front door, Dravin softly grips my wrist, halting me. I turn my head and look at him. "My number is written inside the box of the phone. Call me to let me know you guys got home safe?"

Jess's eyes go wide like saucers. I don't think she has ever seen Dravin act this way with anyone before.

"Okay, I will. Bye...and thank you."

He leans close and gives me a soft kiss on the cheek that warms me on the inside. It is a friendly peck, but to me, it feels more intimate. It feels like the beginning of something I can't describe. I came here to throw a gift in his face and tell him to forget me. I'm leaving with the memory of his words and promise of friendship and a lot of feelings that I can't even begin to process.

DRAVIN

CLOSING MY LOCKER DOOR, I see a set of eyes belonging to Warren. My annoyance rises to unsafe levels because I'm questioning everything regarding Gia. The reasons I'm pursuing her are blurring into uncharted territory. At first, it was because I refuse to lose and love a challenge. I like to win. Especially when Gia is something I am interested in anyway. I have been drawn to her since the first time I laid eyes on her. The fact that I can get to this prick is a bonus.

There is just something about Warren even looking at Gia that rubs me the wrong way. I'm not used to being jealous of a girl, but for some reason, I want to hurt every guy who looks at her. When it comes to Warren, it would take a sexed-crazed basket case like Veronica to scare him off or someone like me.

"You ready?" he asks.

"I'm always ready."

I'm the best on the team. As a senior, I have been offered a spot on the international team. I have the stats, the athleticism, and the drive. I practice every day, and that's why I prefer to live alone in my own house. I allowed Reid to move in because his father pressures him about taking over the family business. The pressure affects his swimming, which isn't good for any of us.

The three of us, Valen, Reid, and myself, have overambitious fathers who are driven by money and power. They groom us to maintain powerful relationships and tell us that when the time comes, we will choose a wife out of convenience. The only problem is that your moral lines become blurred when you're thrust into an environment like that. Everything becomes physical satisfaction. Your emotions are only sacrificed if you lose, so you learn to never lose.

I'm walking out to the pool, ready to compete and win. I want to see the look on her face when she sees me at my best. There is only one thing I care about—the only thing my father didn't take away from me—my love for competitive swimming. "Hey, when I walked in, I saw Gia sitting in the stands."

I pause and notice Reid and Valen pass by, overhearing the dickface in front of me. "What about her?"

He uses his fingers on his good hand to adjust the band of his swim shorts that are on his skinny, lean frame. He shrugs and gives me a smirk. "I heard you two are just friends."

"And your point? You need another reminder with your other hand?

"Hey, let's go. Coach is waiting for us, and if we head out too late, we will be swimming laps until we throw up," Valen chimes in. trying to diffuse the annoyance that must be written on my face at the mention of Gia being my friend.

Warren's eyes widen. Now he knows why I pushed him hard enough to fall and break his arm at swim practice. He thought it was because I was annoyed that he elbowed me by mistake when he was horsing around with another guy on our team. He knows it's about Gia, and I might just have to wipe that smug look off his face.

"Look. I don't know what your deal is, but I do know that she isn't the type of girl you are used to having fawn all over your dick. I am just wondering if your intentions are of the good variety. I don't want the same thing to happen to her, just like it happened to her roommate Jess. Veronica has a mean streak, but I'm sure you already know that, and I like Gia. She seems like a really nice girl. I would hate for something to happen to her by associating herself with the wrong people."

My lip curls. "Are you telling me to stay away from Gia?" I step closer, my fist clenching, my knuckles turning white. The strap of my goggles crushes against my palm. "Let me guess, you're the type of guy that would treat her right. A skinny prick with a small dick and a trust fund."

He steps back. Fucking coward. He knows I will slam his face against the door just to see his nose splatter all over the place.

"We'll see, Bedford. It isn't like you to make friends with the new girls who come through here who won't fuck you. Especially the kind that live in the dorms. I wonder what your father would think?"

I lunge at him, but Reid grabs my hand and pulls me back. "He isn't worth it, Dravin," Reid says softly.

Warren chuckles as he walks away. "You did always have a bad temper, Bedford. Relax, it's not like she will last anyway. Sooner or later, she will be riding someone's cock." He shrugs. "They all fall Prey to our charm and good looks eventually. It's who can get it first—that's the fun part. Sucks for you she friend-zoned your ass."

"Piece of shit," Valen spits. "I hate that motherfucker. He's lucky his father is in our circle. If not, I'd be the first one to drown his ass."

I shrug out of Reid's hold. "That makes the three of us. Make sure he stays away from Gia. The last thing we need is Veronica on her, too."

"How about Jess?" Reid asks.

"I'll let you deal with her since you two get along so well."

"Come on, let's go give them a show. I hate Ohio State. The girls have a lousy head, and the guys on the team think they can beat us every year," Valen says.

"You need to chill, Valen. Your dick is gonna fall off."

"You're just jealous that I'm getting more pussy than you are right now because you have a hard-on for your little Raven. What can I say? I have an appetite, I like pussy."

I shake my head, knowing he is just being the way he is. He's the youngest one out of the three of us with the biggest appetite for screwing whatever catches his eye, but make no mistake, Valen is dangerous in his own way. He just respects me and sees me like the big brother he never had. He won't touch what's mine. Someday when he finds his, he will understand.

GIA†

I FOLLOW Jess to an open spot in the stands. The smell of chlorine swirls around us in the enclosed Kenyan pool center. There is hardly a seat available. This is one of the top sports at the university.

"Are you ready to see the guys in all their delicious glory?" Jess teases.

"I have never been to a swim meet before."

"You're kidding?"

"Nope. My parents are churchgoers. They aren't into sports. I chose Kenyan because my mother thinks I'm following God."

She snickers. "It's that bad, huh?"

"How else was I to convince both of them after their divorce to let me move to another state."

"No shit. That is crazy. If they only knew this place has nothing but sinners."

"Yeah, I used to think they went to church because they lived this pious life, but it was all a lie. Look at my dad. He cheated on my mother, and then she asked to divorce him. Where was God?"

"Tell me about it. This was the only place that I could get a scholarship besides Ohio State. I wanted a better education at an Ivy League school. My mother had me young and worked at a bar. My father split before I was born, and it was just me and my mom and all the random boyfriends throughout the years. I'm trailer trash where I come from. At least my mom isn't a drug addict or anything. We're just poor."

I nod. Listening to her story makes mine look like rainbows and unicorns. At least I know who my dad is, and I lived in a stable home until after I reached adulthood. I don't come from money, and my parents lived paycheck to paycheck. The only thing they lied about was how they really felt about each other. They hid it well by going to church twice a week to cover up the truth. I know now that most people, even my parents, are liars.

People begin to clap as both teams come out of the locker room for the competition to begin. The Olympic-sized pool has a total of eight lanes and is divided into two sections. My eyes seek Kenyan's swim team, and I immediately see the only reason I'm here, Dravin. I admire his flat stomach, double-wide shoulders, and well-defined biceps under his tattoos. The way his swim shorts stick like a second skin makes my thighs press together. His thick dark hair is still dry, and he hasn't put on his swim cap yet. He is sexy as hell.

A girl on the women's swim team saunters up to him and a pang of jealousy hits me when he smiles at her. The smile she gives him in return has me determined to look away and find anything else to concentrate on. I instantly regret my decision because the last person I want to see is smirking my way and waving his free hand while the other is enclosed in a white cast. Warren.

I try to look away, but he keeps waving at me. "Great," Jess mumbles.

I glance at her, and next to her is a pissed-off Veronica glaring at Warren. I rip my eyes away and land on the blonde with porcelain skin. Her gaze is boring into me like she wants to rip my heart and eyes out.

She gives me a sarcastic smirk, but I play it off. "I think he's trying to get your attention," I tell her.

She looks over and aims her best smile at Warren. His change in demeanor and the way his face hardens says it all to everyone watching. It wasn't her attention he was trying to get.

"Well played," Jess whispers as Veronica gets up.

At least he won't be looking over here. I hope she sits below us so he won't be tempted to get my attention again. Luck is on my side, and she sits in his direct line of vision to where Jess and I are seated.

I glance over at where Dravin was standing and my heart sinks. The beautiful female swimmer is back and laughing at something he said despite his serious face. His dark lashes make him look like he is wearing eyeliner. He is just so gorgeous to look at. It is like God or maybe the devil took his time when creating Dravin.

His eyes find where I'm seated in the stands, and we stare at each other. The girl is rambling off about something, but his eyes are trained on me. He doesn't wave or smile. I wave at him slightly, but he just stares and something dark passes over him. Something dangerous, and I realize it was a mistake coming here. I thought it was what he wanted. He asked me to come because he wanted to be my friend, but something has changed.

His expression is dark. Both eyes are almost the same shade, if that's even possible. He forcefully plasters a smile on his face and looks at the girl with her perfect body in a one-piece swimsuit. His gaze lands on her breasts and he smiles at her.

Having had enough, I get up. My emotions are all over the place. I have never felt jealousy before, so this is all new to me. I should have never agreed to be his anything. This is stupid, and I should take everyone's advice and stay far away from him.

"Where are you going?" Jess asks, a concerned look on her face.

"I'm leaving. It was a mistake for me to come here," I tell her.

She looks up with wide eyes and then glances over at Dravin and then back at me. He is still standing near the girl, and she touches him on his muscled chest. He doesn't make a move for her to remove her hand. He leans close and whispers something in her ear and her cheeks smolder.

"That's Warren's sister. She always flirts with Dravin or Reid. Even if her brother doesn't' approve, you can't blame the girl for trying," Jess says.

This isn't going to make me feel any better about the whole situation.

I grab my bag and move before the meeting starts and people hunker down in their seats. "You can stay. I don't think he needs me to be here for moral support. He has enough fans." I look over and spot Veronica, with her eyes still focused on Warren and his expression of pure hatred while he watches Dravin and his sister chatting it up. "I think I should go."

"Are you sure?"

I nod. "I'm sure. I'll be in the library. Find me there when you're done here, and we can go and get something to eat. I start my job there on Monday, and I need to get a feel for where everything is."

She nods. "Okay, I'll see you in a bit."

I'M WALKING through the door of the library, and it feels old. Ancient. It smells of books and construction paper. I always thought certain books smelled just like construction paper. Especially the cream-colored interior of some of the books I've read. I love to open them up and smell them before I begin. When Reid mentioned working at the library, it was like a blessing in disguise. I notice there are statues of gargoyles in the library and vines on the ceiling on dark gold baroque paper. The desk is dark wood with stained glass, lighting the area in a colored glow. It's dark but lit in all the right places.

I glance at the checkout desk and notice a young guy with straight brown hair and amber eyes. He is nice-looking, I would say, in an Abercrombie kind of way.

"Hi, you're the new girl. You start Monday, right?" A young, handsome guy in ripped jeans says, seated in the front.

I look around and notice we are the only people in here. I guess the library on campus is not a popular place on Fridays.

I slide my hair behind my ear and clear my throat. "Yeah, I'm the new girl."

He moves his brown hair away from his face. His amber eyes meet mine. "That's great. I am glad they finally hired someone. There aren't many students who attend Kenyan who need a job. Most of them don't ever need to work, much less attend school."

"I see. I guess that makes sense."

He smiles, and his expression is warm and airy. He seems pleasant.

"Have you worked here long?" I ask him.

He moves around the desk, and I notice his ripped jeans and lean build. I'm not surprised. All the guys who attend here have good looks and killer smiles. With money or without, it doesn't matter. It's like they picked all good-looking students out of high school and threw them all into one elite university.

"Since, last year. I got in on an academic scholarship during my freshman year. I needed a job, and the perk of this one is that you get your other expenses covered. My mother lost her job at the end of my sophomore year."

"That must have been hard. Where are you from?"

"Small town in Kansas. You?"

"Wisconsin."

"I guess I don't feel so bad not being from a big city now that you're here."

I give him a grin. It's refreshing to find someone normal for once. So far, Jess is the only normal person I've met. Everyone else avoids me or gives me side glances like they are waiting for something to happen. I just don't know what that something is.

"I didn't catch your name."

"Gia."

"Is that short for something?"

I smile. He is the first person who has asked. "It's short for Gianna."

"That's a pretty name. I like both versions of it." He whips his hair from the side of his face. "My name is Marc, by the way." He shifts forward and gestures to the bookshelves. "Since you are already here, I'll give you the grand tour. I thought you would be at the swim meet to watch the sons of Kenyan."

I pause and furrow my brows. "Who?"

"The sons of Kenyan." He rolls his eyes and stretches his arms, making his T-shirt ride up, showing a flat stomach. "I'm sorry. I have been sitting for a while reading up for my poetry class on Monday."

"You're taking poetry? It's an elective. It didn't start the first week of the semester because the professor couldn't make it."

His eyes smile. "How do you know about that? Are you taking that class, too?"

I nod. "Yeah. It is a solid choice for me. I like reading poetry and prose."

"Same. It's not common for guys to like it, but I do. To answer your question, the sons of Kenyan are three guys on the swim team: Dravin, Reid, and Valen. Their families founded the university and built it around the Catholic Church of Kenyan. I'm sure you have heard of them by now."

"Yeah, unfortunately, I have two of them in my classes so far. I've just never heard of them being called the sons of Kenyan before. Reid in marketing and Valen in Calculus. To make matters worse, I have Reid as my partner for an upcoming marketing project."

"I feel bad for you. I wonder how they manage to have time for school with all the girls they go through."

I stiffen because that means Dravin is also part of the *"they"* he is referring to, but I have decided to get over that jerk. He is definitely playing with me. The way he dismissed me at the swim meet moments ago by openly flirting and gawking at another girl like I didn't even exist... stung. Why can't he be friendly and outgoing like Marc?

I'm glad Marc shows me around the library so I know where everything is located. As we walk down every aisle, he points out things I need to know in every section. The computers, the system for checking books out, and how to process everything are seamless. Even if the library looks like it's a hundred years old, it is equipped with the latest technology.

"Here." He hands me a thick, leather-bound book. It's the history of Kenyan University. Read up on it. It will make sense of everything. You just have to read between the lines," he says in a serious tone.

It's like he is trying to tell me something without telling me. Like he is talking in a secret code.

"Okay," I say, taking the heavy book in my hand. "Hey, what about the church?" I ask curiously.

He stops and leans against the front desk. He takes a deep breath, like he is choosing his words carefully. "The church seems just like every Catholic church that has its mass on Sundays and confession. But there have been stories since it was built, even before the university was built around it."

I'm intrigued by the university, the church, and the fact that Dravin is one of the sons of Kenyans.

Marc lowers his voice, and I find it strange, but I'm so curious I overlook his nervous behavior. It's like he doesn't want anyone to know he is telling me anything about its history. "Supposedly, the church was built and is used by a secret society of rich and powerful men. Men who are in politics, who come from influential families with power and money. They use the church as a meeting ground to discuss what they needed to do to control their businesses, people, and the government. There are members of this group, and they are all men. Their women are chosen by their pedigree and lineage. Marriages of convenience and never of love. They have to produce an heir. Male or female, it doesn't matter. The members are allowed to sin but would use the church as a cover-up. It is a church but not a real church."

"What do you mean allowed to sin?"

He swallows, and I tilt my head and watch as he looks to the door and then back at me. He checks his phone for the time and continues. "Did you read the bible when you were a kid or go to church?"

"Yeah," I answer quietly.

He closes his eyes like he is telling me something he shouldn't. "Supposedly, they don't follow the word of God but manipulate it. Like an eye for an eye, you kill someone, but in theory, killing is a sin.

I nod, my heart drumming wildly. "You think that they still do it? That the families that founded this place use it as a cover-up?"

He swipes his hair off his face again. "Maybe? There is the fact that the three sons of the families that founded this place are hound dogs who fuck selected girls that come through here. Their fathers aren't the faithful kind, if you know what I mean. None of them are. Some of the students here are part of their family's circle, whether it is business or alliance in some way. That can't be coincidence."

I let out a slow breath and raise my eyebrows. "Wow, Marc. That sounds—"

"Crazy?"

I nod and answer, "Yeah."

The door swings open and Jess comes in and I smile. "Hey."

She glances at Marc. "Hey. I see you found a friend," she says with a knowing smile.

"Marc, this is Jess, and Jess, this is Marc. He works in the library and was nice enough to show me around."

"Hi, Marc. It's nice meeting you. I'm sorry, but I came to whisk my roommate away to hang out at a party the swim team is heading to."

He glances at me and smiles. "I see. Well, it was nice meeting you, Gianna."

I'm holding the book in my hand, but I prefer to read it while I'm here, so I hold it out for him. "Look, I would like to leave this here and read it in between my shifts. Maybe you can tell me which chapter would be more interesting. You have told me so much about the history already."

He shifts uncomfortably and glances at Jess. "Okay, I can do that," he says, placing the book away in a particular spot. Can we exchange numbers?"

"Sure," I tell him, then rattle off my number. He enters it on his phone and sends me a quick text."

It chimes, but I don't open it, knowing it is just his number. I decide to save his contact information after I leave.

GTA

"HE SEEMS NICE. I love the way he calls you Gianna instead of Gia," Jess says.

We make it to our dorm, and she changes clothes while I stare at the too-small closet, wondering what I'm going to wear to this so-called party.

"Yeah, he seems nice." I glance at her. "Did you know Dravin, Reid, and Valen are known as the sons of Kenyan?"

Jess is applying makeup, sitting on her bed with her compact mirror open. "I heard about it from someone in class during my freshman year, but it's like no one dares to say it out loud. Like it's taboo or something, but yeah, I have heard that along with all the other shit that they do."

My interest is piqued by Mars mentioning the eye for an eye and that killing is a sin. What other things do they do? "Like, what other shit do they do?"

"Remember, Fuck girls, break their hearts. Fuck more girls, ruin their reputations, intimidate, deceive, and fuck people up when they want to and get away with it. Let's not forget the people that are in their so-called clique. Rich people. They also play the part of their little pets. I mean, they get away with everything."

"Did they really hurt you, Jess?"

I feel bad that people look at her weirdly when she is not looking. When I leave and she stays, I don't think it's because she is meeting someone. I think she is just watching and waiting. Like she is waiting for the ball to drop or something. I think what they did affected her more than she lets on.

She lowers her eyeliner pencil and compact mirror. The pained look on her face breaks something inside of me.

"Yeah, they posted pictures of me asleep with Garrett and the other girl but blurred out my face. Everyone knows it was me, though. They titled it "She plays both sides," and everyone whispers how I am so desperate that I will agree to be with anyone."

I shake my head. "Bastards. But why?"

Her shoulders rise and fall. "I don't know." Her voice cracks on the last part. She tries to wipe away a stray tear and pats her chick to avoid smudging her make-up.

"I'm so sorry, Jess."

"I almost left. I didn't want to come back. She laughs, but it's her way of calming herself and preventing her from breaking down into tears. It's like she is trying to hold herself together. Like a dam holding back all the tears from rushing forth. "Just, be careful. After seeing what Dravin did today, ignoring you and flirting in front of you after he asked you to come to the meet. I know he said you'd just be friends and he could screw around like he always does, but to ignore you when you were saying hello. Everyone saw it."

She looks at the flowers and the card Dravin sent me. "I don't want you to go through what I did. I don't want you to fall victim to their games." She lowers her voice. "I think it would be wise to just forget about them, Gia. I think you shouldn't take anything from Dravin or anyone in his circle."

I turn and look inside the closet. "So, who is going to be at this party?"

"The swim team from our school and all their followers, and I heard guys from Ohio State will be there. Why?"

I angle my head. "Let's hang out with Ohio State then. Why should we pay attention to Kenyan boys anyway? Fuck them and their stupid cliques."

Jess smiles. "I like it. What are you going to wear?"

WE PULL up to a house on the other side of town. It is big but nothing compared to Dravin and the houses on his street. This house is your regular upper-class type of residence.

"Whose place is this?" I ask Jess.

"One of the guys who got into Kenyan because his parents donated enough money to the university to build the pool center is Nick. He swims for Ohio State, though, but his parents love Kenyan. I guess to keep the peace every time we have a meeting, he throws a party at his house. I've only been here once before."

"Really?"

She closes the door to her car and locks it. "Yeah, it's where I met Reid for the first time."

"How did that go?"

"It went well. I walked in on him while he was screwing a girl on the sink in the bathroom."

"Classy."

"I know. It's what Reid does, classy shit."

We walk up the porch of the house. "You look great in the little black dress with the jacket. Pantyhose and Docs are a nice touch."

I look down. "Thanks, so do you."

Jess is wearing dangerously ripped jeans and a cropped fuzzy sweater.

Although it is still warm enough to wear a dress, you still need a jacket when it's nightfall.

We walk in, and Nirvana is blaring through the speakers. People are drinking, smoking, and dancing. They all eye us curiously as we pass through. I silence my phone at Dravin's fourth text. After I threw away the card and roses, I decided not to answer him...ever.

I glance down at my phone while Jess is tugging me along.

Dravin: I'm sorry about the swim meet.

Dravin: Can we talk?

Dravin: I said I was sorry.

Dravin: Raven?

I then look at another text and it was the one Marc sent.

Marc: I'm glad to have met you, Gianna. Don't end up hurt like your friend.

"Tell me about it," I mumble.

We reach the kitchen, and she hands me a sealed fruity wine cooler and I open the twist top and take a pull. The fruity concoction goes down my throat, chasing away the feelings and replacing them with reason. Do not fall for Dravin Bedford's shit or any of his so-called friends.

From the corner of my eye, I see a beer pong game being played and a crowd of people gathered around it. I can hear cheers and laughter when the crowd screams to chug it.

"Come on, Bedford, you can do better than that! You suck, just like Warren's sister. She sucked your dick after the meet and made the walk of shame." A guy with blonde shoulder-length hair says, laughing.

I lean against the corner of the wall and swallow the rest of the wine cooler to calm the jealousy and anger radiating like an impending storm in my veins. How quickly he forgets that he invited me to cheer for him while he blatantly ignored me in front of everyone all for a blow job.

Jess stands next to me and watches the game. "What a shocker. Dick." Jess drawls sarcastically.

I walk over and grab another wine cooler, open the top, and tip it back to take another chug. Jess's eyes widen at how fast I'm drinking. "I think you might want to slow down on those. They can creep up on you."

"I can handle it."

She lifts a penciled eyebrow. "I know you're pissed, but that's the way he is, and there is nothing or no one that will change him. He doesn't know the meaning of friendship."

"Who are we talking about?" A deep voice says behind us.

I jump and when I look, I find myself getting lost in Dravin's gaze. He moves and grabs the wine cooler out of my grasp. I try to get it back from him, but he is so tall that he can hold it high in the air out of reach.

"Give it to me," I snap.

"No. You've had enough."

He takes the bottle and slides the tip in his mouth and sucks where my lips were seconds ago. He doesn't take a sip or a pull from it but simply sucks the tip of the bottle. His tongue slides over the circle of the rim. He sucks on his lips like he is savoring a hard candy.

It is the sexiest thing I have ever seen. It almost makes me forget how he treated me and what I heard he did with Warren's sister. Almost.

"What are you doing?"

"Saving you from drinking yourself stupid." He lowers his arm with the bottle and passes it to Valen, who tosses it in the trash. His lips lower to my ear. His cologne is probably called *Sinner* for how good it smells. "You wouldn't want to be tipsy or drunk around a guy like me, Raven. Friend or not, I wouldn't know how to stop if you told me you wanted me. I just tasted your sweet lips and I want more. I want to be the bottle you wrap that pretty mouth of yours around."

My head angles, and my cold, hard stare meets his, mine mixed with hurt and anger. "I think it's a little crowded and I don't like to share. It leaves a bad taste in my mouth. I'm sure you can ask Warren's sister, she's familiar with your flavor." I pull away and he flinches.

He didn't think I would find out. He must see the hurt in my eyes because he looks down, shielding his eyes from me. For one moment, I think he feels ashamed but then I think of the card he wrote and the flowers.

How quickly something ends before it even begins, even if it was a so-called friendship he was offering. If it was a lie, at least I was lucky enough to come out with my pride.

I step back, and he is still looking down, and his eyes slowly caress my body all the way until I see his face because I refuse to gaze into his eyes. "Find some other girl who falls for your shit. I've told you before, I'm not one of them. Kindly, fuck off."

I turn around to find Jess, but she is nowhere to be found. I decide I will call her from outside. I grab another wine cooler from the ice bucket and make my way outside.

GIA
†

I MAKE it to the side of the house that is half-lit. There is no one around, so I quickly fish out my phone from my pocket to text Jess. The screen lights up, and I get a text.

Dravin: Look up

My head whips up, and I look to my right. A sleek black sedan is waiting by the curb. Dravin is standing at the corner of the house, watching me. His jeans fit him like a cover model, hugging him in all the right places. He has on a black jacket, and his straight black hair shines even in the dark. He walks lithely over the grass that's crunching under his designer boots. The man can pull off the Gothic grudge look flawlessly.

He makes his way over to me. "Look at me," he demands.

I glare at him. My eyes must reflect the way I'm feeling.

"It's not what you think. Please, don't drink that." He points to the bottle. "Not out of anger or hurt because of something I have done. I never meant to hurt you, Raven. Come with me? I want to take you somewhere. Just you and me." He points to my phone. "Tell her you have a ride home. She is safe in there. No one will hurt her again, I promise."

"Why should I trust you? You are the last person I should trust. Especially with Jess."

He slides his hand through his hair, causing his bicep to flex. His build reminds me of Adam Peaty; all ripped but with more tattoos on his skin. He just got a blow job from that tramp and then he talks to me like I'm supposed to just forget her. I know I'm overreacting about the blow job thing. I shouldn't care. He offered friendship, and I agreed. He isn't my boyfriend or anything close, but the problem is that I wish he was boyfriend material. Maybe I just need to calm down and take him for what he is; it's nothing serious.

"It wasn't us that did that to your roommate. It was people she shouldn't have trusted. I had nothing to do with that, and it won't happen again."

"Why should I believe you?"

"I don't have anything to offer that would make you believe me other than my word. I would never tell you I could do something I couldn't. You just have to trust me."

I text Jess while he is standing there.

Gia: Are you ok?

Jess: Yes. I'm okay. I'm talking to Valen.

Gia: I'm heading out. I will meet you at the dorm later. Text me when you leave and don't drink and drive.

Jess: Valen barred me from the kitchen, only water.

I look up and find eyes clear as a blue sky and obsidian black watching me type in my phone. "Satisfied?" he asks.

I nod, and he waves his hand toward the car. A driver has the door open and is waiting for us to get in. What college student has a personal driver? How rich is Dravin Bedford? I must be tipsy, because I just agreed to take a ride with the devil.

He waits for me to slide in the back of the sedan. Black leather touches the backs of my thighs, encased in black lace pantyhose. The privacy window is up, and my head turns to look at Dravin sliding inside the car.

A minute passes, and the car lunges forward. The tension inside the car begins to build and all of a sudden it feels hot. I slide my jacket off, and I'm left in the tiny black dress that has ridden up my thighs.

His eyes follow my movements inside the car and darken when they reach my thighs. Awareness creeps inside every nerve under my skin, yearning and wanting to touch and taste this man sitting beside me. I try to hide the reaction he causes in me with a single flick of his gaze or the way his beautiful eyes tell me things without him saying a word.

He makes me want to lay back and spread my body out as a sacrifice. I want to let him do whatever he wants, whenever he pleases.

The car has dark tinted windows that you can hardly see out of, especially at night. I'm trying to distract myself and figure out where we are when it suddenly stops.

The door is opened, and I see that we are in front of his house.

"What are we doing here?"

He knows what I really want to ask is why did you bring me to your house?

"I want to spend time getting to know you. Preferably, alone."

I exit out of the car and follow him up the walkway. He opens the door electronically with his thumbprint on a black screen I never noticed was there. Impressive. We walk in, and the first thing I notice is that he pulls out his phone and changes the color of the pool from red to deep blue.

"I think you prefer it to be this color?"

How did he know that? I guess I'm not good at hiding my expressions when I don't like something. Or maybe he sees my thoughts in my eyes the same way I feel like I can read his sometimes.

My eyes find his. "How did you know?"

"I pay attention to a lot of things."

He takes my jacket and places it on the island, then grabs my hand and leads me outside. "What are we doing out here?"

He ignores my question and takes his jacket off and lifts his shirt over his head and I suck in a breath at the ripple of muscle as he moves his arms. His chest is bare except for the hard lines of his muscles and ink swirling in different shades and colors. His jeans come off next, and he is left in his snug-fitting black boxers that don't leave much to the imagination.

The temperature has dropped, but he doesn't shiver. It is like he is used to the cold being out here next to the pool.

We stand staring at each other. I'm memorizing every inch of his chiseled body while he stands there, allowing me to get my fill. He doesn't smirk or give me any indication that I'm inflating his ego. He just silently lets me admire him. I want to touch him and feel his skin beneath my fingers. He is so...complicated. He has an achingly beautiful darkness, but under all that darkness is a pain. An unbearable pain that I can tell he is trying to shed from somewhere so deep, it is almost haunting.

His hands reach out and touch the hollow space on my neck. His thumb slides gently like a soft rose against my skin feeling the rapid beat of my pulse. My head tilts so I can see his wrist, and I see tiny scars that he most likely inflicted on himself. They are hidden underneath his wrist tattoos, but I see them.

My lips reach his wrist. I close my eyes and place a kiss to where the faint scars are shining under the single yellow light illuminating us in the back-yard. I bear witness to the scars of his pain. They are long and vertical but deep enough that it must have hurt.

"That must have hurt," I whisper, a tear escaping the corner of my eye and falling down my cheek.

"I'm so sorry."

He cups my cheek with his open palm and wipes my tears with his thumb. He doesn't respond, but his actions are enough to tell me that Dravin is haunted by a deep pain. A loss so profound that it scares me because it makes me question everything I have heard about him. When Dravin is alone with me, I see a side of him so opposite of the man everyone talks about at school.

My eyes blur when I open them and find his own reflected at me like a mirror. He leans down and slowly pulls my dress up over my head. I'm left in only my bra, panties, pantyhose, and Docs. He kneels and removes my shoes. He tilts his head up silently, asking for permission before sliding my pantyhose off, leaving me in my black bra and lace panties.

I don't know why I let him bring me here and why I'm practically naked alone in his house by the pool. But I do know that I want to be here. I want to be near him. He's a mystery that calls to me. A mystery I want to unravel.

He grips my wrist and leads me to the sundeck at the edge of the pool. The water is glowing deep blue, and I expect it to be cold, but when my foot feels the water, it is warm like the water from a cozy bath—not too hot but not cold enough to cause me to shiver.

My body is tingling in anticipation when he entwines his fingers through mine. When we finally are at the edge, he slides in without releasing my hand. The water is at his waist, and I sit at the edge of the pool's sun deck until the water just covers my panties. He nudges my legs apart and he glides forward so my thighs are around his hips.

His forehead rests between my breasts and I slide my fingers through his dark hair.

"I want to kiss you right now, Raven. But I don't want you to think I brought you here to take advantage of you. I just wanted to share with you where I'm at peace. The water is where I feel like I'm at home. It has been my favorite place ever since I was five. My mother was afraid I would drown, so she hired a swimming instructor to teach me how to swim. It was the first time I felt alive. Truly alive. I was at peace. I swam every day after that. My mother made sure I had an indoor pool where I could swim year-round."

He raises his head and I look at him. "I love poetry. My parents were this happy couple when I was a kid, and I loved the idea of falling in love. Except when they divorced, I learned it was all a lie. I was so heartbroken that my dad cheated on my mother, and she filed for divorce. I stopped writing after that. My mother was a devoted Catholic who brought me to church every Sunday, even if I didn't want to go. I had this grand idea of love and what it was supposed to be like. Because of that idea, I would write. The words would come pouring out of me.

It was like I could speak to the dead by expressing my innermost feelings. If I were in love or sad. All my thoughts could be paired down into a single sentence or maybe three; it didn't matter. What mattered was that somewhere, someday, someone would read them. Even if I were dead, I believed that others would be able to see it no matter what. Like the bible was written for people who believed in the word of God on Earth, it was written so people could hear his message, but I wanted my own message to be heard."

"Do you believe in God?" he asks quietly.

"I believe in faith. I believe you have to have faith in something."

"Do you?"

"No. I don't."

"How about love?

He shakes his head. "I was taught love is a weakness. It makes you vulnerable, and that is when you lose." He raises his head and places his hands on the edge of the deck beside my outer thighs. "I don't like to lose."

I lean back, holding myself with the palms of my hands facing down on the concrete of the sundeck. The water reaches above my wrists, and I can feel the tips of my hair getting wet as I lean back. "Have you ever been in love?" I ask him.

He shakes his head. "Have you?"

"No," I say.

I'm being honest with him. This is a side of Dravin I would have never thought to see. I know deep inside, this is the side I prefer. The one I can see for myself and not what people tell me I should expect. They say he is dangerous and tell me I should steer clear, but I have yet to see what they mean about him being dangerous; the only danger he could be is to my heart. I can see he is mysterious and private. One thing I have noticed, though, is that no one stops him. He does what he wants, when he wants.

"Good, otherwise you're no use to me."

What? What does he mean by that?

Before I can ask him, he pushes back, creating a wave in the pool and the sound of water soothing me as he begins to swim laps. I can see his muscles moving underwater against the glow of the pool. I didn't get to see him swim earlier, and I have to say that Dravin's swimming is pure perfection. Every stroke of his arms is perfect, like blades cutting through the water. He makes it back, flips under, and pushes off again five more times. When he finally stops, I notice one thing. He isn't even out of breath.

He comes up out of the water and reaches out his hand so I can take it. I slide my hand in his and he smoothly lifts me so I can stand.

He tugs me gently so I am close enough to admire the way the drops of water slide down his hard muscles like water falling over hard glass. I shiver against the cold because the bottom half of me is wet, and the tips of my hair are causing the tiny hairs on my back to stand. He hands me a towel from the towel warmer, and I am instantly enveloped in warmth.

Trying to break the awkward silence, I ask, "What do you do during the winter when it's snowing? How do you swim?"

He turns his head while he is drying himself. "I practice on campus. It is open year-round, and they heat the pool during winter."

I wonder why he wants to live alone. I know Reid moved in with him, but I have the feeling that it was Reid's choice and not Dravin's. I can't help myself. I want to know more about him.

"Why do you live alone? I see that you are mostly alone all the time."

"I don't have many friends and prefer to keep the ones I trust close."

"You mean Reid and Valen?"

He nods. "I have known them almost my whole life. They are the only people I trust." He turns around when we get to the foot of the stairs. I pause, keeping the huge towel wrapped around my body, and subconsciously realize I left my clothes outside when I followed him. "If you ever find that I'm not around, you can trust them. They won't hurt you."

Why would anyone try to hurt me? What he is saying doesn't make sense. I haven't done anything to anyone. He turns around and begins to climb the stairs, but I stay and don't follow. I'm not sure I want to follow or what it would mean if I did. I'm wrapped in a warm towel with only my panties and bra.

When he senses that I'm not following, he stops but doesn't turn around, as if it is costing him the opportunity to say his next words. It is as if he is uncertain if what is going to happen next is the right choice.

I decide for him. "I need to go get my clothes and I will be on my way."

He bows his head. "You don't need them, Raven. I promise to not do anything you don't want me to. I want you to stay. I *need* you to stay."

I bite my lip, not knowing if this is the right move. One voice in my head is telling me I should run. Then another voice is telling me to succumb. Resisting him is futile. I know I will give him what he wants, even if what he wants right now is me. There is nothing anyone can do to stop him. He is everywhere. There is no escaping him, and I would be lying if I told myself I didn't want to stay and find out what it was like to be with him. He has a magmatism that draws you in, like right now, as I place one foot on the steps and then the next sealing my fate. Deep down, I know that after tonight, I will never be the same. There is no one like him. I will want him for the rest of my life, even if I can only have a tiny piece of him. A little piece of Dravin is better than having nothing at all.

GIA

I FOLLOW him into his room and see the massive bed. Its carved bed frame with intricate swirls looks like it's a table of sacrifice for the pleasures that will take place. My thighs clench and wetness pools between my legs and it's not because I was sitting in a pool.

Once I'm inside, he closes the door and locks it. His eyes find mine, but he stays silent. I'm standing still as a statue, gripping the towel like it's going to save me from whatever he has planned. He moves to the left of his enormous room. There are two double doors he opens that lead to a bathroom with a massive tub and a shower. The entire room is a black marble with swirls of grey-like veins over the glossy surface.

The accents are shiny gold with glass that encases the shower. My eyes find the black free-standing porcelain bathtub, and I notice it has never been used. The plastic is still on the knobs from when it was installed.

"You've never used it?"

He knows I mean the bathtub, seeing as I'm standing right next to it, fascinated by the beautiful knobs and accented white rocks underneath.

He shakes his head. "No," he answers curtly, like the topic is not up for discussion. His eyes darken with pain as he looks at me standing next to it. I want to know more about that look, but I'm afraid to ask.

He motions for me to walk closer to the shower then presses buttons on an electronic screen and the water shoots out like rain from the ceiling. When I walk closer, I notice one wall is all rocks and water is cascading down like a waterfall.

"This is gorgeous."

It really is. I never thought a bathroom could be so enchanting. Just seeing it is an experience.

He opens the glass door and walks over and tugs my hand so it will slip and release the towel. It falls in a heap on the floor at my feet between us, His eyes slowly scroll over my body. My nipples harden under my black bra and my heart beats so loudly I'm sure he can hear it. I have never been naked in front of a man before.

My lips part and my eyes close. I feel the steam coming out of the hot shower all around me and the sound of water hitting the marble like rain.

"Dravin," I whisper.

"Yes, Raven."

My eyes are still closed because I can't believe I'm here, half-naked, alone with him in his bathroom. "Why do you want me to stay with you?"

"I told you. I need you, and I know deep down you need me, too."

He slides the straps of my bra down one shoulder then the next. My nipples are on the edge of the thin fabric as I keep my eyes closed. I know if I open them, I will see in his eyes what he is feeling, and it terrifies me because I don't know if I can handle it. I don't want to run. I want to feel.

I can feel his fingers on my back, and with expert deftness, he releases the clasp of my bra. It falls to the floor like a ribbon that has been cut. He steps closer and I feel the tingle of his breath as he slides his fingers under the band of my panties, over my hips, and down my thighs. I finally open my eyes and fling them with my foot to the side.

I'm naked as the day I was born, thankful I decided to shave everything before the party. His eyes travel over every part of me. When they land on mine, I look to the left and see our reflection in the mirror fogged with steam.

In one swoop, he removes his boxers, and his massive hard cock is bobbing between us. I glance down and he smirks since I can see his other two piercings on the head. The tip glistens with precum, and my eyes travel above, noticing he shaves... everywhere.

He reaches out his hand, linking it with mine, and walks us over to the shower until we are under the spray. My eyes blink as the water falls over us like we are in the middle of a storm. A storm we are creating that will be brutal and beautiful all at the same time. I feel it. Already...right now. I know I could love him. But we both know that he cannot love. It is in his eyes, a darkness that forbids it. He's stunning and terrifying, and I want to experience every part of him, even if he breaks me.

He places body wash in his hands and slowly slides his fingers over my skin. I can feel his hands burning my flesh leaving ashes in its wake. I will never forget this moment, his touch, and the way he is memorizing the feel of my skin and every curve of my body.

His eyes caress my face while his hands caress my skin. "Your skin is so soft," he says. But I knew it would be. Just like I knew you would be this beautiful, this pure."

My body responds by allowing him to wash me everywhere. His fingers touch every part of my body, and it's like he is touching every part of my soul. No other man has touched me like this, and I'll always remember the feeling—the feeling of falling in love for the first time.

He doesn't say much, but the few words that escape his lips hold so much meaning. It is a gift for me to have his attention when his words are this beautiful, because words are his gift.

When he is done with my body, he lathers shampoo in my hair, and I almost gasp from the pleasure. It feels so intimate. I never thought a man could make love to a woman just with his hands. He rinses the soap from my dark strands, and I take his soap and rub my hands over the hardness of his muscles.

I glide my fingers over the lines of the ink on his skin and he watches me. The water sliding down his straight black hair like a river over his chest muscles. My nipples are achingly close to his torso and my cheeks smolder when my hand dips low near his cock.

It hardens in response to my fingers near its length. His hands guide mine and the smooth velvet under my fingers brings a whimper from my throat. His cock is hard, thick, and long. It's beautiful.

"You are gorgeous," I blurt.

He grins and tilts his head like he is studying me while I touch him. I stroke his length and a hiss escapes his lips.

"If you keep doing that, beautiful, I won't last much longer."

I stop and release him, embarrassment flooding me. I bite my lip and peer up. I was caught up in the fascination of his body, not thinking that I was actually jerking him off.

My eyes lower in embarrassment but he lifts my chin with his finger. He leans close and blocks the spray of water. My eyes lift, and it's like the storm that was brewing within him breaks loose, and he takes my lips in a scorching hot kiss. A gasp tears from my throat and my spine tingles like electricity surging through me straight to the area between my legs. My hands slide up his neck until they are wrapped around him, and I press my body as close as I can to his, hoping we can stay fused together.

He lifts me and holds me gently against the marble. I'm so lost in the scent of him as his tongue explores my mouth. I swear I can hear a low growl escape his throat. It's like he's the predator, and he has finally found his Prey.

Our mouths battle the storm of our tongues, our mingled breaths, in a delicious harmony. I have never had a kiss so powerful and all consuming. Nothing can compare to what I feel when I'm with Dravin.

Dravin's touch and kiss is not like a hot sex scene from an erotica novel. Pure lust and all-consuming need. It's different. It's consuming. It's possessive. His warm tongue slowly slides up from the base of my neck, until his lips meet mine again. I suck his top lip and then his bottom like I can't get enough of him. I can still taste him when we finally pull away to breathe.

He sets me back down on the floor and slides his hand over my thigh and lifts my leg over his hip. His fingers find the slit between the folds of my pussy and I whimper. His fingers find my clit and he softly rubs me.

"Oh my God," I say breathlessly.

"I'll be anything you want, Raven." He gently slides his finger inside, and

I arch my back. "Is this okay? If you want me to stop, I will. I'll never hurt you."

My heart melts at his words, and I whisper, "It's ok. I want you, Dravin."

His mouth is at that curve of my neck. "That's what I'm afraid of," he rasps.

Before I can think about the meaning of his words, he begins his assault.

I moan when he slips a finger inside me and rubs my clit with his thumb in a delicious rhythm making my climax build and my nipples harden. He lowers his head and takes my nipple between his lips. My body responds, and I arch my back, but he holds me in place. I'm at his mercy while he slides his fingers in and out.

"You're so tight, baby. I can feel you squeezing my fingers. Look at me," he rasps.

Our eyes meet, and what I see is a beautiful storm—a battle between good and bad, light and dark. It's just like before, except this time, it's all for me. I don't know how he can make me feel safe and frightened all at once. It is like he is two distinctive people wrapped in one.

"You make me feel so good, Dravin. Don't stop," I plead.

He keeps sliding his fingers in and out and I know I'm not going to last. I want him to keep touching me like this forever. He doesn't relent and I shutter.

He growls in his throat. "Come, my Raven. Let me see how you break for me."

His name escapes my lips in a breathless whisper as I come. "Dravin."

GIA
†

THE LIGHT FILTERS in through the window, waking me from my sleep. My eyes open, and I squint at the bright light coming from the sun. For a minute, I thought last night was a dream but when my eyes regain their focus, it all comes back. The pool, the shower, and the way Dravin kissed me when he made me come on his fingers.

My hand reaches out, and I notice his side is empty. The satin sheets are cold and when I lift my head, I see that I'm in Dravin's room, alone.

"It wasn't a dream," I mumble.

My eyes find the wall with the paintings I like so much, and I'm shocked to find them missing. Odd. Why would he take them down?

My head turns and I notice there is a note and a single black rose on the pillow.

I lift the rose and close my eyes to smell the flowery scent.

I refuse to exhale. Not until I have your dreams and the taste of your breath on my lips.
Dravin

I reread the words, and my heart sings even though I'm scared. I'm scared because I'm in love with a dark, broken man—a gorgeous man who has captured my soul with every glance of his beautiful eyes.

I raise the sheet from the bed, and I notice I'm naked underneath. I look around and don't see my clothes, but I see a black box with a red ribbon at the foot of the bed.

I crawl over on my hands and knees, careful to keep the satin sheet over my breasts in case the door opens.

It reads, *"It's for you, Open it."*

I smile, untie the ribbon, and open the lid of the oversized box. I gasp when I see a complete Phillip Plein outfit. It looks like the dress I wore last night, except it is an expensive version made of gorgeous, soft fabric. I look down and notice there are boots to match.

I grab the box and head into the bathroom, where I see something dangling from my throat. I lean closer to the mirror and see it is a black ribbon choker necklace with a Raven adorned with black diamonds.

I stare at the girl in the mirror, and I smile. It isn't like me to accept such lavish gifts, but I want to feel like this is real and that Dravin is mine and I am his.

I want to know what it feels like to be in love with someone like him. He was honest last night in telling me he sees love as a weakness, and maybe he is right, but this feels right. At least, to me, it does. I can have enough love for us both until he gives in to his feelings or decides to get rid of me.

I wash up and find a new toothbrush. "He thinks of everything," I mutter.

I wonder how many girls he brings home and does the same things for. How many girls have been standing here in this very bathroom wondering the same thing? I realize I'm one of them, but the only difference is, I know I'm temporary. I have no hopes for it to ever be more than what it is. Well, I do have hopes, but I'm trying very hard to be realistic. I'm trying to guard my heart. This infatuation that will probably end up in vexation.

I MAKE my way down the stairs and hear voices from the kitchen.

"I don't know who he has up there. He never brings girls to his room," Valen whispers.

I listen and smile to myself at the words every girl wants to hear. I am the only girl who got to spend the night with Dravin in his room, which made my initial thought in the bathroom regarding all the girls before me all wrong. No one has seen the side of Dravin that I got to experience last night and this morning.

My footsteps make a sound on the steps and both Reid and Valen look over with smirks on their faces.

"Now we know who he has holed up there," Valen says.

He quickly fixes me a plate with eggs and bacon and places it in front of the stool. "Here you are, milady," he says with a smile.

"Thank you."

"My pleasure. I'm glad I made extra."

Reid slaps him upside the head. "You made extra in hopes of seeing who he had up there."

I put my hand over my mouth to keep myself from laughing. "It's all good, thanks anyway."

I look around, searching for any sign of Dravin, but I see that we are the only three in the kitchen. I'm about to open my mouth.

"He left," Reid says. He gives me a sorry expression.

I shrug my shoulder because I expected Dravin to do the disappearing act in the morning. The good news is that I haven't slept with him in the true sense. I still have that if he disappears on my already.

"Don't look at me like that," I tell Reid. "I'm not doing the walk of shame."

Valen laughs. "Yeah, right. Are you telling me right now that you didn't have sex last night with the infamous Dravin Bedford?"

"If you are asking if I rode his cock the answer is no."

Valen shakes his head and Reid looks at me like I'm a dragon with three heads.

"You are telling us he let you sleep in his bed and stay the night and he didn't smash?"

"Is that hard to believe?" I ask.

"This is Dravin. I'm surprised you're in this house." He points his finger up and down. "Nice clothes, by the way."

I peer down and smooth the dress. "I know," I say, stepping down the remaining stairs, taking a seat, and digging the fork in the eggs. "I didn't buy them. He did."

They both raise their brows and lean on the marble island and watch me eat. They both keep staring at me. After a few seconds, I put the fork down. "What?"

Reid is the first to answer. "Do you have a magical pussy?"

I snicker. "No."

"She does," Valen teases. "She really does. I'm mad now."

"Why?"

His tone gets serious, and I see his demeanor change. I lean back on the stool. I look at Reid, and he seems unaffected by Valen's serious expression.

Valen's eyes turn dark. A darkness I have never seen, and he tilts his head. "I would have loved to have a taste."

My head whips to Reid, but he says nothing. Dravin told me I could trust them when he wasn't here but now, I'm not so sure. The hair on the back of my neck rises, and my appetite suddenly vanishes. Valen just went from zero to creepy in one second flat. What. The. Fuck?

My hands begin to shake nervously as I slide my hair behind my ear. "I-I think I need to get going. Jess must be worried sick about me."

"She's still in bed," Reid deadpans.

"What?"

Reid looks up toward the second floor and then back at me with a knowing smile. "Garret is a distant memory."

Valen licks his lips, and the message is clear. They fucked Jess last night. They. As in, both of them.

Damn it, Jess.

My worried expression tells them I'm not happy about it. Jess is my roommate, and I can safely say my friend—not my best friend, but my friend.

"It's ok, Gia. We were gentle," Valen says.

"Fuck you. Both of you," I snap.

"If Dravin allows it, that can always be arranged. We love new pussy," Valen drawls.

"Chill, Valen," Reid warns.

I rip my eyes from Valen and realize that he is just playing around.

I slide off the stool and look for my jacket that has my phone and wallet. "He didn't mean it," Reid says, walking after me.

"I'm sorry, Gia. I was messing around. Jess is sleeping upstairs if you want to go wake her. I pause because if I leave, that will mean I leave her with these two assholes. I don't know how she feels about them or if she is really ok.

"Relax, Gia. She's ok. I would never let anything happen to her," Reid says quietly.

I raise my chin. "I need to see her."

He turns around and leads me to the stairs. I glare at Valen, wiping the smirk from his face, and raise my middle finger.

"Anytime, baby."

"Quit it, Valen. Dravin is going to kick your ass for upsetting her."

"Whatever," he mutters.

"Valen doesn't take anything seriously. You will get used to his moods."

"I have a feeling I won't," I quip.

He stops in front of his door and angles his head like he is talking to the wood floor. "She's tired. We had her up all night."

I hold my breath when he opens the door. Jess is sprawled on her back, with the sheet covering only her breasts and the apex of her thighs. She must sense that someone is in the room because she stretches and rises on her elbows.

Her eyes focus on Reid, and when she sees me, they widen. She looks down and licks her lips. Her eyes lock on Reid standing in front of me, but I can't see his expression.

"Hey," she says to me.

"Get dressed. She's waiting for you to leave," he says dryly.

Asshole. He just slept with her and is dismissing her like she is a piece of meat left on a plate he doesn't want to eat anymore.

"Come on. Let's go. Our time is up here."

She nods and grips the sheet tighter, avoiding looking at Reid. My stomach clenches for her. I feel sorry for Jess. He simply dismissed her like she was nothing. Dravin's disappearance isn't any better. He just left a note and gift as an excuse for his absence, but he didn't promise me anything, and I was willing to participate the whole night. I shouldn't feel a tang bit disappointed, but I do.

GIA

I MAKE my way out of the library and Marc gives me a smile as he walks out the opposite door toward his class.

"Hey, how was your weekend? Are you ready for poetry today?"

We didn't discuss what happened after Jess and I made it home yesterday. We were easily persuaded to hang out with the dubbed sons of Kenyan. I was with one, and she was with the other two. How they managed to steer the night into having us to themselves is a wonder all in itself.

We went about our business, finishing schoolwork, doing laundry, and even going to pick up something to eat at the cafe. The topic of them was never brought up. It was like it never happened.

"It was good, how was yours?"

He gives me a grin. "I visited my parents and had dinner."

I instantly feel a pang of longing. I remember when my parents were together and we would have Sunday brunch together, but come to think of it, the last three years, I remember a strained feeling at the table. I also remember my father excusing himself to go to the bathroom—a lot. Now I know it was because he was seeing someone else behind my mother's back. All the signs were there, but my mother and I never picked up on them.

"That must have been really nice."

"Maybe, you could— "

A large shadow comes up from the corner of my eye. "No. She can't." Dravin's voice says in an icy tone.

Marc's eyes widen with a stricken look on his face. He looks from me to Dravin.

"Hi," I squeak.

My eyes travel over his black jacket and stonewashed denim jeans. All I can think about is his mouth-watering hard chest. I remember rubbing soap over his skin and watching it glide off with the spray of water.

I must be ogling him because he gives me a grin and says, "Eyes up here, beautiful."

My cheeks flush at being caught red-handed, and my eyes meet his stormy ones. One minute, they are annoyed; the next, they are calm and collected.

I don't know what to say, but I have recovered from embarrassing myself further. I wave my hand at Marc. "Marc, this is Dravin. Dr—"

Marc interrupts me, "I know. Everyone knows who he is, Gianna."

Marc sounds irritated, but I don't know why. His boyish charm vanished the moment Dravin showed up.

"I'm gonna get to class," I tell them.

I don't have time for guys who treat me like crap. One disappears after a night with me and the other gives me attitude when all I was doing was trying to be nice. I get that Dravin was a tad rude answering for me, but Marc didn't have to take it out on me.

"I'll walk you," Dravin says in a clipped tone.

Marc steps back and looks at Dravin with disdain. He clearly doesn't like him.

"I would be careful if I were you," Dravin warns Marc. "Consider yourself warned."

"Why?" I ask, clearly annoyed.

He passes by Marc while they size each other up. Dravin is more muscular, but they are both the same height. "Because he wants to fuck you. He just has a different approach."

My eyes widen and Marc's lip curls. "She isn't some plaything."

Marc's eyes seek me out. "He's going to hurt you, Gianna. He and his little clique do it to all the girls who come through here, who don't know what they're about. It's all a game to them. You and every girl that—"

Dravin suddenly grabs him by the throat and slams Marc against the wall. "Keep running your mouth, and you will see what happens," Dravin growls.

Marc grips Dravin's hand that is wrapped around his throat, trying to gasp for air.

"Dravin! Let him go," I demand.

People walking by look over but don't stop. It's like they know better than to interfere. When I see one of the faces of passersby, all I see is fear. They are afraid of Dravin.

"Dravin, please."

He releases him, and Marc gasps for air in a coughing fit. "You choked me, you fucking psycho. You need to go back to that shrink of yours."

Shrink? Dravin has a mental problem? I mean, besides his solitude, the weird pictures he took down in his room, the hot and cold, and the temper. I could safely say he is a little off but psycho. He wouldn't be on the swim team or in this school. *He has money, and money gets you a free pass.*

Dravin walks back and shoves him. "I'll deal with you later." He grabs me by the arm, and I shrug him off.

"You can't just attack people because they say things about you. What is wrong with you? You could have really hurt him."

"Don't listen to everything you hear."

I place my hands on my hips under my oversized knitted sweater. "Why? Because it's closer to the truth?"

"Because listening to other people can get you thinking the wrong shit, and the next thing you know, you're taking the wrong side."

"His side is the wrong side, and yours isn't. Why do I have to pick a side? I'm on my side."

"So am I. Let's go."

He walks toward my class, and when we get there, I walk through the door and notice he follows me inside. I take a seat and he sits in the one right above me."

I look up. He thumbs his nose piercing, and his eyes widen sarcastically. "What?"

"What are you doing? "

"What does it look like? I'm sitting in class."

A group of girls walk in, and they notice him. One gives him a wink, and the other three give him knowing smiles. He tilts his head and looks at me and then at the blonde.

I turn around, rolling my eyes. "Let me guess, they're not scholarship students and they don't live in the dorms."

He leans forward. "You're catching on."

Something dawns on me. I think about Marc and what he said. When he walks into the class a few moments later, his neck is red from where Dravin almost choked the life out of him. His accusations repeatedly play in my head, and I remember what Jess said. The limited number of people in the dorms. How she told me certain people are part of Dravin, Reid, and Valen's group. Why are the less fortunate exploited and people like Veronica aren't? It is like two sides, the predators and the...Prey.

The professor walks in and smiles at everyone, but when his eyes land on mine, he has this strange look. It's the same look Valen had when he––

Wait, wait. I am missing something, or I'm missing nothing at all. It is all right here. I look around and pick out the rich guys, who all give me side glances. They look at me like Valen did the day after my night with Dravin. Dravin looked at me the same way when he tried to come on to me in the bathroom––and the cemetery.

I turn my head, and the chessboard pieces begin to fall in place. Suddenly, I realize that I'm one of them.

I'm a pawn.

I'm one of the...Prey.

Dravin's words out in the hallway, right before walking in, are coming back to me on repeat. *He wants to fuck you. He just has a different approach.*

Valen's words in the kitchen and Reid's talk about Jess being in bed after sleeping with both of them. Then everything comes full circle, or maybe semi-circle. Oh, My. God. I close my eyes. My only answer to the thoughts in my head is...why?

A voice is saying something, yet I can't make it out.

"Miss Taylor. Miss Taylor?"

I shake my head, snapping my mind out of its funk. My eyes find Professor Whitmore looking at me, and I notice the blank stares aimed at me from everyone around the room.

"Yes," I croak.

"I'm glad to have gotten your attention. I was making sure you were present in my class. I––"

He glances behind me and stops mid-sentence. I have the feeling the look Dravin is giving him must be the reason. The guy has the power to silence people with a single glance. The professor's face strangely looks like a cross between surprise and fear.

The professor's eyes land on me once again. "I'm sorry. I was just trying to make sure you were with us."

I sink further in my chair. This is college, not high school. How much power does Dravin have that even the professors get tongue-tied? Normally, in a prestigious school like this, no one can sway a professor. It is their class, and they conduct it based on the rules the college sets forth, but apparently, those rules don't apply—at least, not with Dravin present.

The class moved along, and the only thing I was assigned was a journal, where we had to write a few lines of poetry to get familiar with prose. Basically, we put what we felt on paper, and he will randomly select someone to read and discuss it. Then, I will study the works of other great poets, my favorite being Edward Allen Poe.

DRAVIN
†

I'M CLOSING my poetry journal when my phone rings on my desk in my room. I look at the screen, and Veronica's name flashes at me like a warning beacon.

I take a deep breath and answer the phone. "What?"

"I see you're taking this bet a little bit too personally. Not that I'm complaining, but I'm shocked at how long it's taking you to break her."

"There wasn't a time limit, and he isn't fucking her, so you should be happy. Let it go. You got what you wanted."

She sighs. The breath making a horrible loud noise through the phone. "So far. Except he isn't paying attention to me and still thinks he has a chance. You are moving too slow for my taste. One would think you are wooing her or something. You're not catching feelings for her, are you?"

"What makes you say that?" I ask, leaning in my chair.

"I don't know. Maybe it's the fact that you are temperamental when it comes to her—protective even. I don't think I didn't hear about your explosive rage on poor Marc in the hallway."

"What about it?"

She laughs like a villain in a Disney movie. "Oh, come now. It's obvious, Dravin. You're afraid to lose and even more afraid someone else might beat you to her."

"Leave it alone, Veronica."

"I think I won't." I can hear her pout over the phone.

It is just like Veronica to take things up a notch. She can't stand someone else getting attention. If her father wasn't who he was, I would have eliminated her a long time ago. Not only is she unstable, but her penchant for vengeance is a liability only her father overlooks.

"I think you need to rethink your intentions concerning Gia."

"Are you threatening me?"

"Maybe," I answer.

"I don't do well with threats. I thought you wanted me, Dravin. Did she change your mind when she showed you her tight pootie?"

"Jealous."

"As if. I'm not jealous. I could have fucked you a long, long time ago. It would be a shame though for her to find out she is just a game. A little pawn in a game in which she means nothing to you. You'll fuck her and get me in the process."

"Fuck you, Veronica."

She's trying to get to me through Gia, and I'm afraid she probably can.

She chuckles. "Oh, don't worry, Dravin. I'm planning on it."

Anger takes over, and I growl, "Leave her alone, Veronica."

"Oh, I'm so scared. What will your father think when he finds out you're threatening me over a low-class broke piece of ass? Are you afraid you finally met the one girl who can bring the infamous Dravin Bedford to his knees? I'm going to enjoy watching when she finally realizes that everything is all a lie and that she is just another pawn in the little games we all play with the less fortunate."

I hang up before I throw my cell phone across the room. "Stupid cunt," I mumble.

I should have told her to fuck off when she came to me, but now things have changed.This isn't about a bet anymore. I don't think this was ever about Warren and him dismissing her. She wants to break Gianna because of the attention she has and the fact that she can make me lose all sense of purpose when I'm around her. I have never lost because of a girl. But Gianna is different; she is gorgeous and has a body that was created with care and purpose. Her purpose is to make every man lose his mind if he is allowed the gift of glancing underneath her clothes. I got that glance, and here I am, losing my mind. Her innocence draws me to her. She won't drop to her knees for a man. She makes him fall to his knees first and beg. The taste of her is addicting. She is fast becoming an addiction of mine. I tasted her mouth, and now I want all of her.

I have never had to wait to have sex with a girl. I have never had to try. I could have taken it further in the shower, but something told me she would have stopped if it got too far, and I didn't want our first time to be in the bathroom. I know she is into me, but I also know she feels that it would mean nothing. She has no idea how wrong she is. It doesn't matter how many diamonds, custom necklaces, clothes, or black roses I buy her, it's not the way to get her. I want her body, but I also want more. I want all of her. I'm just afraid I'm going to break her in the process.

My eyes close and one of my last conversations with my mother comes back to me. A memory that I have savored since her tragic passing. It was the beginning of my junior year in high school after she found my father screwing the maid in their bedroom. My father taught me that love was a weakness that should never be a factor in my life. He said that he wasn't cheating on my mother and that she knew the terms of their marriage. He could screw whoever he wanted, and she could do the same. But my mother never did. She fell in love with my father, and the pain I saw her in broke me every day. It made me realize that my father was right when it came to love. It was a weakness that cost my mother her life. I just wondered what made her do it. What pushed her over the edge?

"You will meet a girl one day, Dravin. She will be different than all the others. Whole and pure-hearted. She will come to you like a Raven. It will all make sense when you meet her. She will call to you like no other. Protect her, and she will guide you. She will teach you things I cannot and your father is incapable of. Everything will make sense to you. What the meaning of life is. There will be only one like her. When you feel lost, she will be there. Don't ever take her for granted, and you must protect her because if anyone finds out that she means more to you than all the others, they will destroy her or, worse, take her away from you. Always remember, she is not like the others.

"How do you know all of this?" I ask.

"Because it happened to me, and I didn't listen. I took him for granted. I tried to love your father, but he deceived me, and I don't want it to happen to you, Dravin. Follow the order, but don't let it turn you into something that makes you a monster."

"Okay, mom. I promise."

"I will always love you, Dravin."

"I love you too, mom. Always."

GIA
†

"YES, Mom. I promise to go to church."

I roll my eyes. My mother always makes sure I go to church. I find it boring, but I respect the word of God. Most of the time. I was kind of upset at him because everything I believed in with my parents was a lie. You would think that people who attend church for quite some time and preach the word of God wouldn't be liars. I'm more of a see-it-to-believe-it kind of girl.

In the end, all I have seen is lies. Some of the biggest sinners are inside the church, not out of it. It is like they are trying to cover up their sins by attending. I find that just because a person attends church, doesn't mean they are more holy than those who don't attend church. On the contrary, they can be just as evil.

"Are you coming home for Thanksgiving?"

She means to her apartment. That is all she could afford after she divorced my father. My father stayed in Wisconsin and decided to buy a nice big house with his younger girlfriend. I mean, she is only seven years older than me, making her twenty-eight to my father's forty-five.

"I have to go to dads. I told you this."

"I know. He told me I could join you, but I think it would be rather awkward for me to be there with him and her."

I know she is referring to Stephanie, my father's girlfriend, aka Side Piece, who has now become the official girlfriend.

"I know this is hard, Mom, but—"

"Are you bringing anyone? Have you met someone?"

I shake my head even though I know she can't see me. "No—I mean yes. I—"

"Which is it? Yes or no?"

"I don't know mom. It's complicated."

"Well, if he can't see how amazing you are, then he isn't worth your time. Does he go to church?"

I have had enough. "Mom, I have to go."

I hang up, instantly regretting hanging up on her, and take my little purse to let myself out the door of my dorm. I had to hang up on her before I said something and hurt her feelings or admit the sole reason I decided to move out of state was to get away from the drama and the whole I need to go to church to make me a better person thing. I refuse to listen to her preach anymore about staying a virgin until I find the right church-going guy and get married.

My mother has this old-fashioned mentality that works great in some ways, but let's face it: we live in a modern era where men and women have casual sex. Love and marriage are not always part of the equation.

I walk toward the church to ease my guilt for hanging up on my mother but make a detour toward the cemetery. I haven't been by the grave since that first night, and I am kind of hoping someone left her flowers. I enter the gate and there is someone selling flowers that is about to pack up and leave for the day.

"Excuse me? Could you sell me one?"

I reach into my pocket for ten dollars and stick my hand out to the older woman.

She nods and holds out the bucket of different flowers, and I select the red roses for some reason—for love. I think when you die and someone takes the time to visit you, it is out of love and respect.

Even though I never knew the woman, it would be a nice gesture to place a bouquet of red roses on her grave. I remember the date of her birth on the marble headstone, and she died young.

After taking the money, she hands me the roses and leaves without a second glance. I head over to the grave with the flowers and notice that the single flower I had placed there the first time has already dried and wilted.

I look around and realize I'm the only one in the old cemetery. I kneel and brush the old flower away, wishing I had brought a bottle of water so I could have cleaned it. I scan the area, and my eyes land on an empty, clear container.

I look to see if there is a water spigot. I remember back home, in some of the cemeteries, they placed a water spigot so people could water the flowers or clean the headstones. Placing the flowers near the grave, I find the container, fill it with water, and return to clean the area the best I can. I see the little brass cup made for the flowers, fill it with water, and place the stems of the roses in without getting pinched by the thorns.

"Hi. It's me again. I hope you don't mind I cleaned up the place." I laugh to myself. "I brought you flowers. I hope that's ok."

I can't believe I'm talking to a dead person's grave that I don't even know.

I sit down, and for the next hour, I tell her what I couldn't tell my mother. I tell her about my parents and why I came here. I tell her about Jess and Dravin. I even told her how creeped out I was about what Valen said, but then I told her he was probably joking. It is like I trust this dead person even though they probably can't hear me and won't be able to talk back to me. Maybe that's why it feels so safe. There is no judgement. I couldn't go to confession about this stuff. The priest is a living person, and I just don't feel comfortable telling him my innermost sinful thoughts about a guy I'm crazy about but should stay away from. Far away.

"I don't know how to act around him. After Jess and I left his house, he didn't call. Then we saw each other in class and didn't call after that and I am too much of a coward to text him. I don't know if I should or even if I could. I figure his silence means that whatever we shared was just that, a one-time thing. He asked me if I could stay, and I did and that was the end of it."

I take a deep breath. I notice the sun is setting, and purple hues are beginning to fade in the sky. After sitting for almost two hours, I get up and stretch my limbs. The wind picks up, and I shiver, closing my jacket to keep me warm.

I make my way out of the cemetery and walk toward the church I haven't been to since I arrived.

I pull on the old handle, and the wooden door creaks when it opens. I smell flowers and candles. I look to my left and see three candles lit. I decide to light one for Jess, my mother, my father, the lady in the cemetery, and Dravin.

The bell inside the church chimes, signaling that it's already six in the evening. I look at the beautiful wood carvings. I look to my left and see the priest, and he nods. He isn't old, but he's not too young either, maybe in his early forties.

"Hello, welcome," he says.

"Hello. Do you have time for—"

He interrupts me. "For you, of course." He knows I want to confess, but I find his answer odd. He nods and gets inside the wooden box.

I tell him about my call with my mother without going into detail, but he asks if I truly regret what I said and what I consider a sin under the eyes of God.

I can't answer and stay quiet. I change the subject and shift to my mother and how I lied about coming here. He tells me to ask God for forgiveness and to accept him. It is the most unusual confession I have ever had because this man doesn't seem like a priest. It is weird, and I know it is the last time I will come unless I decide to go to mass. I know different churches interpret things differently, and so do the priests, but this is weird.

A chill runs down my spine. It's like I feel my inner self warning me, telling me to leave and not to come here again. It's like this church isn't real but a mirage for something. Then, Marc's story about church and families. I get up to leave quickly and the priest notices that I'm nervous.

"Are you leaving so soon?" His eyes are black and blank, like he doesn't have a moral bone in his body. I suddenly feel like I told him things I shouldn't have.

"It's getting late."

"He's waiting for you," he says.

"What?"

"God."

I release the breath I was holding. He adjusts his collar like it burns him. I don't like him for some reason. Something is off about this church... about this whole place.

"Oh, right. Well. I'll pray in my room."

"You can pray right now. Right here." He points to where the statue of Jesus is crucified on the cross with its ancient wood carvings and beautiful intricate detail under the lights and stained-glass windows. The church is old and gorgeous. It is one of the most beautiful churches I have been inside of. I wish the people inside it matched the details of the church.

I wrap my jacket tighter around my body like a suit of armor. "I really must get going."

"If you must. If you need me, you know where to find me," he says.

And that right there is my cue to leave. "I gotta go."

His smile doesn't reach his eyes and it's like the devil himself is inside this church. I need to get the hell out of here. I'm already thinking about hell even while I'm inside a church that should make you feel safe and holy.

I practically run out the wooden door. The wind is whipping my hair and all I can hear is the sound of the trees swaying and groaning. The sky is almost black, and I hurry toward my dorm building. An eerie feeling keeps telling me to run. Something is not right about this place, or maybe I'm just paranoid. I check my phone and still haven't heard from Dravin since class. I have a missed text from Jess, though.

> Jess: Are you coming to the dorm? I've been waiting. Is everything ok?

I'm usually in my dorm room around this time. I haven't had dinner because I lost track of time at the cemetery, and then my guilt over the way I hung up on my mother led me to the church.

> Gia: I'll be right there.

> Jess: Ok.

DRAVIN

I WALK into the church and notice almost an entire row of candles are lit. I'm walking further when I hear voices and giggling coming from the offices in the back.

I find the door closed and don't bother knocking. When it opens, I see a girl dressed as a nun, but what she is doing is nothing that an ordinary nun would be doing to a priest. Sucking and gurgling sounds can be heard as he bobs her head up and down in his lap. Getting a blow job dressed as a priest by a woman dressed as a nun, inside a church. That takes balls. I have seen fucked up shit in my day, but this is downright sinful.

Father Jacobs, as he prefers to be called, hasn't noticed me standing there because he is concentrating on his flaccid dick being sucked by a woman that doesn't understand the concept.

"Watch your teeth," he says. "I'm not going to say it again," he tells her in a hard tone.

"I'm sorry," she says.

"Get up," I tell her, my tone hard as ice.

"I need to talk to you, Jacobs. Hurry up and get out of here. Now," I demand.

The girl's eyes widen. "Dravin," she says with a worried look. She gets up and wipes her mouth, and I almost throw up in mine. I look away while both of them get it together. When I see they are clothed, I turn my head and face them again.

"Get out. My father and the others will be here shortly. Where is the real priest?"

"He isn't here. You know he is old and can't be here as long or stay late," Jacobs responds.

"Fine, whatever. I need to talk to you," I tell him.

"Is it about the girl?"

"You know it is," I growl.

When the fake nun, known as Tiffany, leaves, I make sure the door is closed and I stand in front of it while Jacobs swallows and looks around like someone is going to pop out and rescue him.

"She came to confession, and she told me about her mom. She also told me about a guy she met in school."

"What about him?"

He adjusts his collar. "The normal attraction kind, but was more worried about how she hung up on her mom and the lie about coming to church."

"And?"

"Her mother. She must have a strenuous relationship with her mother and felt guilty for how she treated her today on the phone. Her parents are divorced."

"Did she give you a name when she told you about the guy?"

He shakes his head. "No. But it seemed she felt unsure and guilty about whatever happened between them. I asked her if she was ready to ask for forgiveness and she couldn't respond."

My nostrils flare. "Is that all?"

"Y-yes. Did I do something wrong?"

"Not yet, but I don't appreciate the way she left here running like she saw the devil inside the church. What else did you tell her?"

His eyes widen, and I know he was probably being a creepy bastard, but one thing is for sure: He did me a favor by making her not want to set foot inside this church.

"T-that God is waiting for her."

I step forward. "He is. It's just not the God she thinks."

He steps back and his brow begins to sweat. Jacobs is a grimy bastard, but he is here to make sure no one walks into the church when the order is here having their secret meetings.

There are voices coming from outside the door.

"I think they are already here, Dravin."

I dismiss him and walk out to face the members of the order.

I WALK OUT, and all the members take their seats in the pews. My father, along with Valen and Reid's fathers, take the places in the front like they are preaching the word of God. The most ruthless men are in this room. These meetings date back generations and are conducted in secret. They talk about a different order. Sins committed and how they should be punished under their rules. The rules being simple. If you go against their business dealings, you're out. An eye for an eye, if needed. They are all a bunch of ruthless liars who take wives for alliance purposes.

For centuries, these meetings were held by the three founding families. Reid's father, Valen's father, and my father, James Bedford. Warren is seated to the right and gives me a smirk that I return with a scowl. Fucking prick.

My father is the first to speak. "It has come to my attention that my son."

He looks at me standing in the middle because I'm a smug bastard who refuses to sit. No one says anything because they don't want to be in one of the graves near the 1900s section of the cemetery. I'm not a good man. I'm the monster my mother tried to warn me about becoming. It's too late for me, but it's not too late for my Raven. She is all that matters right now.

"Dravin has lashed out at one of our own because of a girl. One of the Prey."

The Prey are the ones we've accepted that are not part of the order. The ones that don't have a father who is a member. We hunt them, play with them, and decide to let them pass when we see fit. The ones that make it, make the Forbes list and find good paying jobs. If they don't follow our rules and keep our secrets, they get eliminated. They die.

All the member's children attend Kenyan to ensure they follow the order. They learn to curb their appetites enough to not get caught. We fuck, we play, we kill if needed, but we are a secret alliance. Politicians, presidents, mayors, and governors are all in our pockets.

Centuries of wealth are passed down among the generations to unify us and make the order the strongest organization in the world. Money, power, and alliance are the mission of the order. You are either part of it through blood, married into it, or pledged by a higher member—meaning one of the three founders. Our women are chosen to breed, not for love. They have to come from wealthy families, of course, and be part of the order.

Faithfulness is not required, and love is not part of the union. But loyalty must be given, or they die. There are no women who make decisions in the order, only men. The women are protected by the man they choose to marry. If he allows it, then it can be done. If they go against the rules, they die. It is all straightforward.

The ones we consider the Prey eventually come to the church, and they confess. They try to pray to God for their transgressions and sins.

"My son felt he had to defend a girl's honor." He means I broke one of the member's son's hands, who is on the swim team, and it raises questions about my so-called instability since my mother's death. Or, as I like to put it, suicide.

"She is Prey."

My father's dark obsidian eyes, just like my right one, look to Warren."

"What do you have to say, Warren?"

"It is nothing but a misunderstanding. He obviously wants her and can't take the fact that she was interested in me first. It is nothing."

My father gives me an evil smirk. "We don't fight over Prey. We share if needed."

"He was with Veronica. I'm sure he needs time to rethink his decision."

Warren's face turns red, as if he is about to explode at the mention of

Veronica. I was hoping they would make him marry the headcase, spiteful bitch.

My father smirks, and uneasiness slides down my spine. "I heard about the deal you made with her. She is loyal to the order, and if asked, she'd tell us what we need to know. I didn't think you would be interested in Veronica yourself. You do need to take a wife before you graduate."

My lip curls sardonically. "I don't want her." Warren smiles and I want to kill him, and I think I just might. Fuck what anyone thinks. I will soon take my spot at the top anyway. "Not interested."

Veronica's father is seated three rows down and huffs and glares at me and Warren. No one wants to marry his crazy, sex-crazed daughter. I'm sure she has fucked half the school.

"Well, you must marry. All of you. Before your senior year is over."

The sons of the members are all seated. Reid is glaring at Garret. Valen is sitting like he could care less because he is the youngest of all of us. He has time to play. He just likes to play too much, and I'll be the first to teach him manners. Garret is not so bad but just got caught up with Veronica and her games.

The others must follow the order and whatever the three of us say, both on campus and off.

"I don't want you guys attacking each other unless it is voted on here."

Fat chance. Those rules don't apply to the sons of three families.

"What about this girl?"

My head snaps up and I roll my shoulders back. "What about her?"

"Is she a problem?"

"She's mine."

The room shifts and Warren's head snaps. "He hasn't had her, no one has."

"Not true."

My father raises his eyebrows at my declaration. I have never staked a claim on a Prey before. Everyone turns to face me, some members with their mouths parted.

"How so?"

"I fucked her."

Warren's nostrils flare and Valen coughs.

His eyes meet mine and I give him a stern glare. If he says otherwise, he knows I will rip him apart. If you stake your claim on a Prey, she's yours, and no one can touch her unless she wants it or you allow it.

This is the only way I can save her. The guys at school want her. I can smell it dripping in the church. The guys here are salivating. They feed off something or someone they cannot have. When men have a lot of money and are born rich, they get bored. Throw in a bunch of college kids with hard-ons into the mix, and you've got yourself a serious problem—especially ones who can get away with anything and are raised under the rules of the order.

No one will question me because they have yet to find a woman that would deny me. On the contrary, I have a problem trying to keep them from wanting more.

"Alright, since you've no doubt already tasted her. I guess the fun is over, or it has just begun."

My eyes find Warren, and his look is crystal clear. He wants Gia bad enough that he will overlook the fact that I've supposedly had her. Veronica was right about Warren. He has a hard-on for Gianna.

The topic ends regarding Gia and moves to other business issues: takeovers and mergers, who the major players are, and who is a liability to the order. It goes on for the next hour, and when the gauntlet is thrown, it is time to make my way out.

GIA†

"YOU WERE AT THE CEMETERY?" Jess asks.

"Yeah, and then I went inside the church. Have you been?" I ask.

I wonder if she has met the creepy priest.

"I went once but have never gone again." She lowers her eyes and glances away. "I stopped going right before starting college."

Something must have happened to her for her to stop going or, worse, stop believing.

My phone buzzes on my nightstand, and I see it's a message from Dravin.

I'm surprised he texted me when I swipe up to read the message.

Dravin: Are you in your room?

Gia: Yes. Why?

Dravin: Open the door.

I look up, and there is a knock on the door.

"Who could that be?" Jess asks.

I get up from the bed and smooth my long, dark hair. I'm still dressed in black leggings, thick socks, and a sweater. The only thing I took off was my cold-weather jacket.

I hold up my phone. "It's Dravin."

She quirks a brow and gives me a wide grin. "Look at you getting cozy with the bad boy of Kenyan."

I wave her off and open the door. Standing just outside in the hallway is a sinfully dressed Dravin. His eyes hold me hostage while I scroll over his fitted sweater under his jacket, which makes his double-wide shoulders look massive. He is so tall, and his angular jaw is defined. His eyelashes are so dark that you have to look closely to make sure he isn't wearing mascara. My eyes trail over his dark pants, which are a cross between jeans and slacks.

He rakes his fingers through his straight, dark hair. "Hi."

"Hi," I respond.

He licks his lips. "Do you want to go get something to eat?"

I smile and my heart begins to beat rapidly in my chest. "Are you asking me out on a date?"

"No."

My stomach sinks at how quickly he responds. Like I'm not good enough to go on a date with.

"Oh."

"I would have to be dating you to ask you that and everyone knows I don't date. I'm asking you if you want to get something to eat."

I flinch at how easily he can forget everything we've shared. How he thinks he can show up and I'm supposed to be honored that he is asking me to go anywhere with him. "I'm not that hungry, and I have a lot of home-work," I say, trying to salvage my pride when it comes to him.

He furrows his brow and I raise mine just like Jess did a moment ago. "Is that all? Because I have to get back to studying."

He looks around me and he knows I wasn't studying. I don't have my books out, and my bed is made. His eyes land back on mine. "I'm sorry. I know that came out wrong. I just––I'm not good at this sort of thing, alright? Please come with me? I want to eat with you."

I rub my lips together and contemplate whether I should or shouldn't go. Dravin blows hot and cold, though I shouldn't be so rude.

He didn't promise me anything, I remind myself.

"Alright. Let me put my boots on. Give me a minute."

His lips curl into a small smile. "Ok," he says. He leans in the room and turns to see a wide-eyed Jess. "Reid will stop by in fifteen," he tells her. "To make sure you're not alone."

I pinch my brows and glance at Jess, who just nods silently. I give her a smile and she starts to run her fingers through her curls. I inwardly grin because she is worried about how she will look when Reid shows up. I hope he likes her in a real sense and isn't taking advantage of her vulnerability. I like Jess, even though I think she comes from a fucked-up place. She really hasn't gone into detail, but you can tell something awful haunts her. She is just trying to purge it from her system. I can only hope a guy like Reid is the answer to her trouble and he doesn't hurt her more than she has been hurt by people in her past.

"I'm sorry about how I acted back there," Dravin says once we are in the back of the sedan that I notice is a Rolls Royce. I'm not familiar with cars driven by the wealthy, but there is just nothing like it. Once you have been in something this nice, you feel you have to know what it is. It also tells me that Dravin is beyond the normal lines of being a rich college kid from a rich family. This is considered wealth. Old wealth. The driven around kind of wealth you see in movies or on TV.

"I get it. I know you aren't used to being this nice around a girl."

"How would you know?" he teases.

"Someone texted me."

He laughs, and it's still the most contagious sound I have ever heard. I never knew that a man's laugh could be considered beautiful. Everything about Dravin is beautiful, even his darkness.

He chuckles low in his throat, a deep vibration that calls to me. "You've got jokes," he says.

"I'm terrible at jokes, how about you?"

He gives me a side glance, "I'm more of a direct kind of guy."

"I figured you would say that."

"Why is that?"

"I don't know. The way people fear you. They don't question anything you say or do."

"Is that so?"

"Oh, yeah. I've noticed."

He slides down on the seat, stretching his long, muscular legs. "What else have you noticed?"

My breathing picks up, and I'm suddenly aware of him and the way his voice gets deeper. "The way you look at me."

He shifts in the seat and presses a button to the privacy screen and my heart skips a beat while it slides upward separating us from the driver. His fingers slide into my hair behind my ear. "How do I look at you, Raven?"

"L-like you've been waiting for me," I stammer.

He angles his head on the headrest like he is looking at the sky. Then he closes his eyes like he is thinking carefully about what he is going to say next.

At that exact moment, the car stops moving, and I can hear the driver's side door open. He straightens his head. "We're here," he says instead.

I peer out the window at a small restaurant just outside of town. The driver opens the door and Dravin gets out first and holds out his hand. I slide my fingers in his warm palm like a blanket protecting me from the cold chill outside.

The small restaurant looks like a bar with pool tables. It is a local fanfare, not at capacity but not empty either.

We are shown to a booth, and instead of him sitting across from me, he sits right next to me like we are a couple. The waitress comes to take our order, and her eyes widen when she sees Dravin. Her eyes find mine and she stares at the way Dravin's arm is stretched out behind me on the booth. If I moved an inch closer to him, I could feel the heat of his hard body. My stomach flutters and it is not from hunger. This happens to me every time I'm near him. I can't stop it. I can't control it.

The waitress is older and must know who Dravin is because she looks at him like someone she's seen before. "Hello, Mr. Bedford. Is this your girlfriend?"

"She belongs to me, and that's all you need to know."

"Of course, she does," she sasses, then turns to me. "What can I getcha, honey?"

"A grilled cheese and coke, please."

"One grilled cheese and coke coming right up."

She juts her hip out. "And you?" she asks Dravin, tapping her pen on the pad in her hand. The waitress is clearly annoyed with him, yet he doesn't correct or warn her like I have seen him do the others. He's just quiet. It seems she doesn't like his answer regarding me.

"I'll have what she's having," he finally says.

She glances at me and then at his arm draped over the back of the booth. "This is new," she says, walking away.

"I guess you come here often."

I'm not trying to sound like a jealous high schooler, but it is plain as day that he has brought other girls here with him. However, based on our waitress's reaction, I don't think that he usually sits this close or drapes his arms behind the booth.

"I'll be honest, I have."

I appreciate his honesty, but the butterflies quickly die a slow death in my stomach, replaced by shame for allowing myself to feel anything for Dravin. He is way out of my league, and I've come to realize this is the side of him that I have a problem with—a side of him that won't work for my poor heart.

"I understand."

I do understand now that I mean nothing to him. I'm a poor girl from Wisconsin, running from her divorced parents, trying to make something of myself in the real world. And all I ended up doing was falling for a guy who sees me as nothing but another girl he can say he fooled around with in college.

After ten minutes of silence, the food comes, but my appetite is gone. He begins to eat, but I push the food around my plate like a little kid, so it looks like I ate enough.

I think he feels the tension and stops eating, placing his cup of soda on the table.

He lowers his head and takes a deep breath. "I don't know what to say when people ask if you're my girlfriend. I have never had one before. I-I don't want to hurt you. I'm sorry." He turns in the booth to face me and cups the side of my cheek with his clean hand. His lips are inching closer, and I close my eyes.

He brushes his lips gently over mine and says, "All I know is that you belong to me. It is what I feel and what I know."

I whimper softly when his tongue darts and licks the seam of my lips. My lips part, and I can feel his breath on my lips. My eyes remain shut for fear if I open them, the moment will be ruined, and he will stop.

I hear a throat clear and my eyes open to find the waitress standing near our table. "I can see that you do belong to him. This is a first."

She leans close to the table, acting like he is not right there listening to what she is going to say. "I always knew there would be one to make him do crazy shit he normally wouldn't." She gives me a wink. "So, you're the one."

Dravin smirks. "Stop scaring her, Dorothy."

"Oh, I'm not. Your momma would have loved to see this, God rest her soul. She's gorgeous, Dravin. You did good this time. Not like those other hussies you parade around with. I like this one."

"I like this one, too," he says, taking a sip from the straw.

"From the looks of it, I bet you do."

"Give him hell, sweetheart. Make him work for it."

Dravin chuckles. "Oh, she does. Trust me, she's worth it."

My heart sings at his praise and I feel warm all over again.

He nods his head to my plate. "Eat."

I take a bite of the sandwich and smile at Dorothy."

"That a girl. I like that you order real food. You're not some rabbit eating skinny twig a second away from becoming anemic."

I like Dorothy. She reminds me of a wise grandmother. She doesn't look too old but she can easily be borderline grandmother material. If she isn't, she will be one day.

When she walks away, I ask, "She knew your mother?"

I feel him stiffen slightly at the mention of his mother, but he nods. "Yeah, my mother and I would come here twice a week when my father had business to attend to."

"You were close?"

"Very close. I was closer to my mother than my father. He hated it in some way because he wanted me to follow in his footsteps. He knew I was going to anyway. He required it of me. He just didn't like my mother's depression. She suffered from it for a long time."

I nod. "If you don't mind me asking, how did she die?"

"She committed suicide. I found her in the tub in a pool of blood."

My stomach drops and the mood dimmed at the mention of something so tragic. It is like the life has been sucked out of the restaurant.

"I'm sorry. I can't imagine what that was like."

Then a thought occurs to me and before I stop myself, I blurt, "Is your mother buried in the cemetery?"

He wipes his mouth with the napkin and places it over his plate. "Yes."

Oh my God. I have been talking to his mother about everything. About him. I think I knew deep down that she was his mother or related. Her last name is the same, but she is buried alone in an old cemetery, and he doesn't bring her flowers.

No one brings her flowers.

"Why didn't you tell me that night in the cemetery?"

"Because I didn't want you to know why I was there."

"I accused you of stalking me."

"And I corrected you, but you didn't want to believe me."

"I'm sorry.

"Don't be. And thank you."

I lick my lips and fidget with the napkin in my hand. I lower my head. "For what exactly?"

"For sitting with her and for buying her flowers. No one has ever done that for her besides me."

My eyes find his and all I see is pain. A deep pain that tears at your soul. Not just because he lost his mother so tragically but because no one visits her grave. His father never loved his mother. He doesn't go there to visit her. Her own husband doesn't bring her flowers. My heart bleeds for his mother. I can only imagine loving your son, knowing that your husband and his father never loved you. It would take a very strong woman to have dealt with that pain.

"She must have been a very strong woman. And she must have loved you very much."

He nods and my heart continues to break. It all makes sense. The way he is withdrawn. The reason he chooses to live alone. The pain I see in the depths of his eyes and the fact that he was taught not to believe in love. What I don't understand is, what kind of monster teaches his son not to believe in love. But I know the answer. The type of monster to have driven his wife to a depression so deep she felt she had no choice but to commit suicide.

He motions for Dorothy and settles the bill. She gives me a wink and I grin in response. The silence stretches between us like a rubber band about to snap. I don't know what to say or do next because his neck muscles are tense, and he has this tic in his jaw like he is at war with something.

"Let's go. I have to get you back," he says.

On the way back inside the luxurious car, there is a center console wedged between us, and I make the decision to comfort him. The cabin is quiet, and I look at the privacy screen, but it remains closed. He scrolls through his phone, and "Ghost" by Badflower plays on the speakers. I take my jacket off and I straddle his lap. He slides his hands under my sweater slowly up my shirt and I take his lips between mine and suck the top then the bottom. I slide my hands over his chest, my fingers tracing the dips of his stiff muscles.

I feel the hardness of his erection between my legs, and I gasp at how hard he is for me. His cock is like a hot metal searing me through his pants. He lowers his head and pulls my bra hard enough so that my nipple escapes the cup. He takes it into his mouth, sucking, causing electricity to snake all over my body. My clit throbs seeking a release only he knows how to give me. I grind my hips rubbing myself over his cock in a rhythm that has a hiss escaping his breath as it fans my swollen nipple.

He grips my hips, and my fingers slide in his thick dark hair, his face eye level with my chest. He looks up, and I can feel his pain radiating from him, and I'll do anything to soak it up and take it away. I grab his wrist, the one with the scar that he made trying to end his life like his mom. I kiss along the scars, small kisses, sliding my tongue up and down the wound like it is leaking blood. Tattoos hide the evidence of his agony, but not from me. The deep scar from a cut inflicted out of pain. Proof that even monsters hurt in the darkness of their hell.

The car stops, and I know the driver will open the door any second. My head angles closer to give him a kiss. As soon as the driver opens the door, I rip my lips from his, grab my jacket, and slide off his thighs, leaving him inside the car with his chest rising and falling. I run as quickly as I can with the cold whipping me in the face. The burn of the frigid air cooling my burning cheeks until I'm safely inside my dorm. My eyes scan Jess's bed, and for once, I'm glad that it is empty and I'm alone.

I look down as my phone buzzes.

Dravin: Are you safely inside your room?"

Gia: Yes.

I stare at my phone screen, hoping he will text me. Hoping he will tell me to come back outside or that he is at my door. After ten minutes, I give up and lay on my bed staring at the ceiling, my lips curling into a smile because I know deep down that I mean more to Dravin than any other girl he has ever been with.

DRAVIN
†

GIA IS FAR from being plain, but she isn't the type that would lift her skirt in the bathroom of a bar and get fucked against the bathroom stall by yours truly. I'm usually a good judge of character, but with her, I've got it all wrong. Every time I'm with her, I want to bend her over and fuck her hard, but then, something stops me. It feels wrong to treat her that way. I shouldn't care, but I do.

She's like fresh blood in a pool full of vampires. She screams innocence. Her soft skin and the smell of her arousal make my blood boil in a heat that goes straight to my cock. If I slide into her, I know I will take her hard. I'll take her hard the first time, then the second and the third. When I'm almost done on the fourth round, I'll go slow and gentle until she feels she can't take it anymore, until she's begging me for mercy. Begging me to never stop.

I look over at my mother's grave, cleaned by my Raven, with a bouquet of red roses. The roses of love. It is like she knew since the first time I saw her put a rose on my mother's grave that my mother died due to the love that was missing from the man who was supposed to love her and protect her. It is like she knew my mother loved red roses. All my father did was show my mother how much he didn't love her, and it killed her. My father thinks her suicide was because she was weak. He told me that is a prime example of how love makes you weak. Because it destroys you. But really, he destroyed her, not love. It was not having love that killed my mother.

It happened during my senior year of high school, right after I turned eighteen. My father knew she did it deliberately when I became a legal adult because everything that was hers, she left to me as her sole beneficiary. They overlooked the blood, and her wrist slit vertically. They overlooked the fact that she tried to commit suicide. She knew what she was doing but actually died from drowning in the tub. My father had it covered up and had reported to everyone that she slipped, hit her head, and drowned.

Why had she done it? A broken heart. The lack of love from my father. She didn't leave a letter. All she left me was money and lots of it. My mother came from a wealthy, predominant family, as required to be married to a founding member of the order.

There isn't much family on either side. My parents were only children, but they made sure to carry out the tradition.

My father places a lot of demands and pressure on me, but the truth is, since my mother left me close to a billion dollars, I've rebelled. I don't need him or the order.

GIA

I CHECK my phone for the eighth time hoping to see a text from Dravin. After the ninth time, I check the time and it is after eleven in the morning. It is cold outside. I shower and get dressed. I notice that Jess never made it home last night but she sent the only text I woke up to this morning telling me that she was ok. I guess she had fun last night.

Determined to talk to Dravin, I order an Uber to go to his house. I know I'm acting like a crazy chick starving for attention, but I want answers. I want to know if we are friends or if we are more. I want to know why he blows hot and cold. One minute, he wants me, and the second he gets a dose of me, he ghosts me until he needs another small dose of me and it starts all over again. The mixed signals. The way he opened up about the death of his mother is a subject I know he doesn't talk to anyone about. So why me? Why does he trust me with his pain? Why hasn't he tried to seduce me like he did before and ask me for sex? It is like he is holding back all of a sudden.

He let me go in the shower and in the car last night. He didn't go after me. I feel like I'm going out of my mind. I shouldn't want him, but I do. I want to feel him completely inside me. I want my body to melt with his. I want to show him that there is love where there is pain. I want him to be my first.

My index finger tingles when I press the button of the doorbell to his imposing house. I hear the sound of footsteps coming toward the front door. The door opens, and a shirtless Dravin is at the door in all his glory. Tattoos over hard muscles rippling with every breath he takes. His biceps flex as he bends his arm to hold the door open.

"I need to talk to you," I say quickly.

He moves so I can come inside. I barge my way through his house to the living room, noticing the fireplace is lit, and it is suddenly too warm. I take off my jacket, gloves, and scarf. I remove my sweater, and I'm left in just my tank top.

His eyes smolder when he notices I'm not wearing a bra. My chest rises and falls from the effort of removing my clothes too fast and the worry about what I'm going to say.

"Why didn't you come up? Why didn't you call this morning? Why do you blow hot and cold with me?"

He quirks a brow. "Is that why you came here? To question me? I thought you weren't the type to get fucked in a bathroom or against the pillar in a cemetery? He steps closer. "Because we both know that is what would have happened if you would have said yes."

My nostrils flare in annoyance. "How about the pool or the shower or the car? We both know you don't bring girls in your room or in your shower."

He leans close, his lips inches from mine. "Are you trying to tell me you wanted me to fuck you in my shower and in my pool?"

"You asked if it was ok and I said I wanted you. So, what are we? Friends, lovers—" I trail off.

His eyes are doing that thing again, battling. He tilts his head, and his eyes darken. I should just leave; this was a mistake. Like when you prep yourself for a confrontation, only when you are actually there do you realize you were overthinking things.

"I don't believe in love and we both know I'm not friends with girls. Last night was all you."

My heart clenches in my chest, and a sinking feeling from his rejection pulls me down. He doesn't want me. He is right; this is all me and my fantasy. I want someone who is emotionally unavailable. "I gotta go."

I turn to leave before I break down in front of him, before he sees how I feel about him and how much I have fallen for him.

"Gia," he growls.

I stop, my body tensing. I close my eyes, the want for him running through my veins. The need to finally have him. I turn around and run into his arms. He catches me. My legs wrap around his waist as his lips crash with mine. Our tongues battling, pulling, coming apart, again and again. My arms wrap around his neck like a vine. He walks to the front of the fireplace on the plush carpet and lays me down, peeling every piece of clothing off my body until I'm naked, with him between my legs. He looks down at me, and I'm lost in his ocean depths, as if I were walking from the shore to the unknown.

His tongue licks the valley between my breasts up to the base of my throat, up over my chin to my mouth. His mouth brushes over mine and his tongue licks my bottom lip then my tongue. My hips lift, seeking his warmth. He kisses my jaw and neck, and I slide my hands up his back, feeling the muscles ripple beneath my fingers.

I shiver and look down between my legs and then I tense. He glances up and licks his lips. His brows are pinched, and it dawns on him that I'm inexperienced.

"Is this your first time?" he asks hoarsely.

My eyes find his and I bite my lip. "Yes."

He raises himself with one hand and looks down between my legs and then slowly back up. "Are you sure you want it to be me?"

I nod and he gets up and removes his sweats. He walks over and comes back, tearing the wrapper of the condom with his teeth, and places it over his hard cock with his piercing and angry veins. His face is close to my neck, and he turns his head and whispers in my ear. "You tell me if you want me to stop, ok?"

"Okay," I say softly, almost above a whisper.

My head tilts up and I close my eyes when he sees that I'm ready by placing two fingers inside me. He stretches me and I clench. He keeps repeating the motion over and over again until I'm dripping. I can feel the drops of my arousal as it drips to the back of my ass. He slides in one finger, finger fucking me, and the noise mixes with the crackling of the fire. Like the burning flames right next to me, I'm burning to feel him inside of me. He settles between my legs, and the head of his cock enters me, slowly breaching my tight folds. The air charges all around us as he slides in inch by inch. He pulls out slowly and I can tell he is holding back from the way he tenses. His elbows are on each side of my head, and he is holding both of my hands.

"Don't look away from me," he whispers.

He pushes in again, and I gasp when he breaks my barrier. He stills inside me, and I try to not close my eyes at the pain. "I'm sorry," he says tenderly, kissing my forehead, but the pain gradually goes away and is replaced by need. My clit pulses and he can feel it because he moves inside me, picking up the pace.

I moan his name. "Dravin."

I arch my back and he sucks one nipple and then the other. My body begins to glisten with sweat. His sweat drips in between us and mixes with my arousal.

"More," I plead.

My legs open wider and he responds by grinding into me. "You're so beautiful," he says. "Perfect."

I grind my hips seeking more and he fucks me. He begins to fuck me so good. I feel the piercings on his cock, rubbing, and I gasp.

"More, Dravin. Please."

He grips my thighs and begins to pound into me. My breasts bounce with each forceful thrust.

"Oh, God. Yes," I say on a moan.

His lips lift with a smile. My climax builds and builds until he thrusts one last time. "I'm coming, Dravin. Oh, God. I'm coming. My pussy grips his cock and I can feel him grunt and lose himself.

"Gia," he groans while his cock spasms spilling inside the condom. He stills for a minute and stares into my eyes.

My lips part, and when I lift my head to seek his lips, he pulls away, his eyes darkening like a curtain masking the windows of his soul. He pulls out and gets up, leaving me on the rug. I cover my naked breasts and turn to see him walk into the kitchen. I sit up, embarrassed he left me there. When I think he's going to come back, he doesn't. He stops at the stairs, and my heart hollows out. Tears begin spilling down my cheeks.

He wouldn't. I shake my head. Not like this. My lower lip trembles. He doesn't even glance at me. He faces the staircase while my heart breaks into a million pieces. Then, he begins to head toward his room.

"There's a bathroom next to the front door. "You can see yourself out."

My heart drops. The tears begin to flow like the blood leaking from between my thighs. I gaze down at the mess and my eyes widen in horror at the stain on the rug. Not caring, I get up on shaky legs and look around to find my clothes. I sniff, my eyes blinded by the tears that won't stop. I pull my underwear over my thighs like a band-aid covering a gaping wound, not wanting to be here a second longer. I grab my phone and look at it like a bomb waiting to detonate.

I wipe my cheeks and look up at the stairs, hoping this is a joke or that he will change his mind, but my shoulders jump when I hear his door close with a thud. I go to the kitchen and clean the rug the best I can, angry tears scarring my cheeks, but I give up because no matter how much I scrub, the rug is stained and ruined, just like me.

THE WATER FLOWS DOWN my body, washing the memory of him away. The same way he slipped through my fingers. I knew deep down that this was my fate, but stubbornly, I wanted to see if I could fix his broken parts. I wanted to show him that it's possible for someone to love you even if you're damaged. But I was wrong. I gave myself to him willingly, and I know at heart this isn't the end of my suffering. Like a predator that has finally lured and captured his Prey, wounding them until all that is left is the pain that will soon take over. This is where my pain begins. Instead of being protected, I was hunted and now I must pay for being naïve.

For trusting the beautiful words on a card. The simple gift of a rose. Hoping that it came from a place deep in his soul. I let myself be lured into the lies. It is funny how there are no flaws when there's hope. There wasn't a single flaw in his words, but I guess that is what makes a great liar—a great deceiver. And I played right into it. I missed all the signs. All I can do is learn from it. I learned what love feels like and it took him breaking me to understand it. Every touch, every kiss, every breath felt like a lettered kiss. His eyes warned me of the beautiful storm that was coming. Deep down, I knew, but I let my heart lead me where I shouldn't have gone. Now, all that is left are the broken pieces—the pieces I will pick up. I will toss the parts away that remind me of him because that is all I can do to save me from myself.

DRAVIN
†

THE DOORBELL RINGS, and I check the camera to see who is at the door. I rake my fingers through my hair. I haven't slept in forty-eight hours. It has been two days since Raven left. Even if what happened was cruel, it would be worse to tell her the truth. The truth of who I am and how she was a bet to begin with. She doesn't need someone like me in her life. She deserves to graduate from here and find someone to share her life with. Someone that isn't fucked up. I tried to fight it, but I knew if she wanted me, I wouldn't deny her. I backed out like a pussy in the shower and then in the car. I have tried, but I couldn't deny her. She is like a priceless vase that I have destroyed.

I open the door and look at the box. I pick it up and check to see if it is addressed to anyone. Except there are no labels or names written anywhere. Once I place it on the counter, I open it and feel the knife rip through me—gutting me.

The clothes, the card, and even the phone I gifted my Raven are neatly placed in the box. I grip the phone and press the button to power it on, but it is completely erased. I drop it inside the box like it burned my hand. I fish out my phone and try to dial her number, but it's disconnected. I keep trying, but the same dial tone pops up. I tell myself it's for the best.

It is the best scenario, but I know deep down it's a lie.

My Raven is gone.

GTA
†

I CHANGED my number and got a basic phone. Nothing like the one Dravin got me, but an older model. It was all I could afford, and I decided to venture on my own and get it under my name, ultimately changing my number. My mother and father were upset, but I told them eventually, I needed to get a new number and save them from having to split the bill. I immediately blocked Dravin's number. Everything happens for a reason, and I wanted to make sure that if Dravin got my number, he couldn't get through to me.

The best way to get over someone or something is to remove all memories of them from your life and try to replace them with better ones. Ones that put a smile on your face. I went to the cemetery after I got the phone and I cried on his mother's grave. I needed to cry to someone, and I knew that my own mother would not understand. She would think some occult possessed me or something, and I refuse to be the type of daughter who always shuns her mother and hangs up on her.

"Hey, are you ok?" Marc asks me in the library.

I plaster a fake smile. "Yeah, why?"

His lips form a thin line. "You haven't seen it, have you."

I tilt my head from where I'm sitting at the check-out desk.

"Seen what?"

"Jess probably hasn't seen it, or I'm sure she would have shown you."

Getting annoyed. I swallow and roll my eyes. "Marc, what are you talking about?"

He pulls out his phone and hands it to me. I take it, and it opens to the school social page, where there is a chat open.

> Lizzy: Did you hear that Dravin won the bet that he could fuck the new girl. He obviously won. Veronica was appalled that the virgin ruined his rug. We all know Dravin Bedford never fucks a girl in his bed.

My eyes widen when I see a clear picture of the soiled rug I tried to clean up. It was ruined, and I wanted to get out of there as quickly as possible to shower in the dorm and away from Dravin. Heat radiates through my neck and cheeks as it hits home. I was a bet.

Tears well up in my eyes, but what did I expect? This is Dravin, and everyone warned me, including Marc. I was a fucking bet. It all makes sense. The bathroom, the cemetery, the pretty notes, the flowers. It wasn't just a lie, but a game, and I was the pawn.

I read the next line.

Melissa: There is only one girl he has never been able to sleep with that he desperately wants, and it's Veronica. Everyone knows that. They're perfect for each other. The perfect challenge. She is perfect in the eyes of everyone.

"I'm sorry, Gianna. I tried to warn you, but that's what he does. What they all do. You're not the first."

My teeth snag my bottom lip to keep it from trembling. The chat says the new girl, but that is how they keep from getting in trouble. There are no names, except everyone on campus knows I'm the new girl.

I hand the phone back, and now I know how Jess must have felt, but this is ten times worse because I fell for him.

"Are you ok? Gianna. I'm so sorry."

I look up at Marc, and he must see how hurt I feel, but I keep a straight face and lie. "I'm fine. It's not like he was my boyfriend or anything."

My eyes blink and his mouth pulls into a frown. "Do you want me to get you anything?"

I shake my head. "I just want to be alone right now," I tell him in a shaky breath.

"I'm here for you, Gia. If you need anything or someone to talk to... I'm here."

"Thank you. I need to get going or I'm going to be late for poetry."

I walk into the class, and the professor is already there, and he gives me a curt nod. I ignore all the knowing glances cast my way. I even ignore the whispers and the snickers. I won't let it get to me. This is my fault, and I only have myself to blame. I raise my chin and sit in a seat in the far corner of the auditorium-style room. I noticed on the first day that it was always empty, giving me an aerial view of the entire class and preventing anyone from sitting behind me.

When the class is about to begin, Dravin walks in. It's funny when you are hurting and the person who hurt you is in the same room. All the hateful words you conjure in your head pause, and when you try to find the flaws in their appearance, you can't. It proves that you still have feelings for them. It proves—I still have feelings for Dravin.

He finds a seat and faces forward. I'm not sure if he knows I'm here or not, but it doesn't matter because his attention is on the girl who waved at him the first day. Marc walks in and his eyes scan the room until they land on mine. He gives me a grin and a wave.

I'm frozen in my seat because heads begin to turn my way, and I want to curse him for causing unwanted attention. I lower my head and wave at him like nothing is amiss, like my heart isn't breaking, as I watch Dravin look over at me and then at Marc like he could care less.

"Everyone is here," The professor announces. "I will call on a few of you to read a page from your journals." His eyes scan the room, and I lower my head, letting my hair slide forward like a black curtain. I hope and pray he doesn't call on me. "Gianna."

FML. I look up and ignore the eyes cast my way. I flip the pages of my journal until I reach the last entry.

"I look in the mirror.

All my pieces are shattered.

I look closer and I wonder if my soul is on the other side.

I look inside me and I'm empty, full of lies and betrayal.

All I do is bleed and bleed.

Am I that insignificant?

Am I the sacrifice?

The soft-spoken words written as the ink dries, whispering death on poisoned lips.

I'm alone as you are no more.

My wings will heal, and I will fly away--never to be seen again."

The room goes deathly silent. You could hear a pin drop. I look up and refuse to look over at Dravin. I will never look into his eyes ever again.

"Raven?" I hear his soft-spoken voice, but I don't look, and I don't answer. It is like he is a ghost. An imaginary shadow I made up in my mind and in my head. Even if he haunts me in my dreams, I refuse to acknowledge him when I'm awake.

"Look at me," Dravin demands quietly.

There is this thing about ghosts I read somewhere. You don't have to acknowledge them when you don't want to. In this case, Dravin Bedford has become my ghost. Like the Raven, here one minute and gone the next.

THE NEXT THREE weeks are all the same—school, dorm, and sleep. Repeat. I ignore the black roses on my bed every week and throw them out. I ignore the unknown text messages.

Unknown: It's me. Dravin

Unknown: Are you ok?

Unknown: I'm sorry.

Unknown: You looked pretty in class today.

Unknown: Please answer me.

Every week is the same string of messages. I ignore all of them the same way he ignored me after I gave myself to him and he threw me away.

"Is it him again?" Jess says from across the room.

"Yeah," I answer, staring up at the ceiling. "I block the number and he figures out a way to call me from another one. It's the same thing every week."

"Did he say he was sorry?"

"Yeah, but I don't care. He got what he wanted and won the bet. I don't get what his problem is? I have left him alone."

"I think that's it, though." She turns on her side, and I do the same, so we are face to face across the room on our small beds. "No one has ever ignored Dravin before. He isn't used to it."

"He needs to get used to it because I don't want to see him ever again."

"I get it. You don't have to say anymore," she sighs. "Do you want to go get a couple of drinks at the Babylon? You've been cooped up in this room every day. You're going to turn into a moth pretty soon."

I give her a grin.

"Come on. Maybe you can talk to a cute guy and forget all about him."

I lay back down and close my eyes. "That's the thing. There isn't a guy who can compete with Dravin."

She giggles. "True, but you're going to have to make an exception sooner or later. Forget about him. What he did to you was next level of fucked up even for me. You gave him your virginity, and he exploited it like a trophy. He could have just told you he wasn't interested and moved on."

"I don't think he really liked being with me. He wouldn't look at me after. It was like I disgusted him." My eyes well up in tears. "I let him screw me on a rug like a dog. My first time wasn't even on a bed. He didn't even ask if I was ok after." I say hoarsely, my voice breaking.

"He doesn't deserve you, Gianna. I know a guy that looks like Dravin makes a girl want to try and mold him into this good guy, but the truth is, he just isn't capable, and nothing or no one will change him. Especially the sons of Kenyan. They take. They don't give. You can't lose yourself because you decided to take the risk."

I slam my hands to my side, turn my head, and face her once more. "Alright, I'll go. Let's get out of here."

She smiles, "Atta girl."

GIA
†

WE SLIDE into the booth at Babylon. It's a Friday night, and the place is full of college students. I avoid looking at the billiard tables because that's where Dravin and the swim team love to hang out.

I'm facing away from the pool tables, and I glance at Jess, who is looking behind me. "Well, don't turn around because he is there, and he is pissed. He is having words with Veronica and her white skin is red like a tomato."

"I could care less. She can have him, and he can have her."

I know it's a lie, but sooner or later, I have to get over Dravin. I have to accept that I got played like a violin. The stares and smirks aimed my way have calmed down, but I still get the feeling I'm being watched—Preyed upon.

Two young guys in Ohio State hoodies stop by our table. One guy smiles at me, and the other at Jess. "Evening ladies. Are you two here with anyone?"

I look at Jess and she winks at me with a smile. "We're just having a couple drinks after a long week."

The good-looking one, the one who looks like a young James Dean, holds out his hand. "I'm Kyle, and this is Dillon. We figured you ladies needed company. It's a shame you two are seated over here by yourselves while the rest of the guys from your school hang out with the groupies."

"How do you know we don't attend Ohio State?"

He slides in next to me and places the beer in his hand next to my vodka and cranberry. Dillon slides in and takes a seat next to Jess and smiles.

"We know this because we would have noticed you two."

His eyes gleam with laughter and I smile. "Of course, you would say that."

A dark shadow looms and the hairs on my neck stand up. Kyle peers over and Dravin, Reid, and Valen are standing near the end of the table. "You're in my seat," Dravin says in an icy tone directed at Kyle.

Kyle looks at me. "I think you're mistaken." He turns his head and whispers in my ear. "What's your name?"

I give him a grin, avoiding looking at Dravin, and tell him, "Gia."

"Gia and her friend didn't walk in with you, and she would have told me if she had been with you when I asked." He points behind him to the pool tables. "You three were engrossed in your game of pool with your girls over there."

Dravin's lip snarls. "Get up, or I'll throw you out."

Kyle smirks. "Oh, yeah. I know who you are."

"The three sons of Kenyan. The order. We know all about you and your organization. Don't think for a second people don't know who you guys are. We also know that these girls aren't part of your little circle and are fair game," Dillion chimes in.

The order? What the fuck is the order. Jess glances at me and then at Reid. Reid's fists are clenched, and Valen is grinning like the Joker, ready for a fight.

"I suggest you run along before you disappear," Reid says in a hard tone, referring to Kyle and Dillion.

"Stop it," I snap. "Leave us alone. We have left you alone. You got what you wanted."

"No," Dravin quips.

He grabs Kyle by the neck and pulls him forcefully, and like a rag doll, he slides him off the booth and drops him onto the ground.

"What the fuck, Dravin? Stop it."

I get up and I'm in his face. His eyes are lethal and full of darkness. He is breathing hard. "No."

"Yes." I pause and lift my chin defiantly. "I don't want you." He flinches. "You got what you wanted from me. Now, fuck off. I have left you alone. I don't want anything from you. I'm not your friend; I'm not your girlfriend or your fuck buddy. I'm nothing to you," I seethe. I look over at Veronica and her cronies. I point to her. "He's all yours, Veronica. You can bet on that."

Dravin shakes his head. "No. Don't say that. You don't know what you're saying." His jaw is tight. "Raven, please."

I walk closer and ignore the need to crush him to me. I ignore the smell of his hypnotizing scent and the way his shirt is melted on his muscled frame. I ignore the shameless want pooling between my thighs. "I don't want you. I'd rather be someone's whore than be with you."

He clenches his teeth. "Don't say that."

"Why, because it's honest? At least I know what I'm in for. I won't be a bet or a joke. I will be their whore. Because with you, I was less than that."

He tries to lift his hand to touch my face, and I step back. The tears burning behind my eyes that I refuse to let fall. I look down where Kyle is rubbing the back of his neck.

"Are you ok?" I ask.

He didn't deserve for Dravin to toss him from the booth like that. He didn't do anything wrong except try to make me smile. I move to the side and Dravin's hand shoots out to grab me.

I snap my arm back. "Don't touch me. I've spent hours scrubbing you off my skin."

"Damn," Valen mutters.

Dravin's eye twitches. For a second, I see guilt, but then a functioning part of my brain tells me a guy like Dravin is incapable of the emotion.

"Let's go, Jess. It was a mistake coming here," I say, walking back.

Jess gets up and Reid follows her movements with a sneer. "We're taking you home."

"No," Jess says.

"Yes," Dravin says, moving forward.

Jess and I walk out of the bar, and I'm surprised no one stops them from following us.

When we make it outside, we see a black SUV parked out front, its driver waiting with the door open.

"Get in. It isn't safe."

"What are you talking about?"

"Get in! Jesus, woman. Get inside the car."

I get in with Jess, Valen, and Reid."

"They don't know, Dravin. She doesn't know."

"Know about what?" I ask, clearly annoyed. I rub my hands together from the cold.

Dravin slides his hands over mine and I tear them away. "Don't touch me, asshole."

"I will touch what belongs to me."

I laugh sarcastically. "Yeah, in your dreams. Set the water to cold. You're going to need the cold shower."

Valen chuckles, scratching his brow. "You really hit me in the face for what I said to her that day in the kitchen, when she hates you," Valen tells Dravin.

Dravin hit Valen? For what he said to me? How did he know what he said that day?"

"You deserved it. I thought you and Reid probably told him." I tell him.

"We didn't tell him shit. I figured you did." Valen says.

I throw my hands up. "I don't talk to him much. Plus, I don't think he cares. He shouldn't matter."

"It matters," Dravin chimes in, looking out the window.

I roll my eyes. "Could have fooled me."

The SUV stops, and I realize we are not in the dorm but at Dravin's house. My head whips to him. "Take me home."

He looks at me. "You are home."

He gets out. Reid ushers Jess inside without a word, Valen trailing behind him.

I climb out of the SUV, stomping into the house and out of the cold weather. I walk into the living room and remove my jacket because I'm hot and I don't like to sweat. I'm also pissed off.

"So where this time? The couch, maybe, or the dining room table?"

"Knock it off, Raven."

He takes his jacket off and removes his sweatshirt. His muscles ripple under his black tank top. I take a step back to keep me from wanting to run my fingers down his arms.

I look around and notice he replaced the rug. Then I lick my lips and get closer.

"Want me to ruin the new one?"

He looks over at where I'm pointing to the new rug. His eyes harden and he walks me back to the wall. "You want to push me. I'm sorry for what happened. It was Veronica who got in here and took the picture of the rug. I did tell everyone that I slept with you so they would back off. I was claiming you. Protecting you."

"Claiming me? What am I an object?"

"No, you're Prey."

He grabs my hand and pulls me up the stairs until we end up in his room.

I gasp. "What?"

He walks over and moves the mouse so that his screens turn on, takes a seat in his chair, and motions for me to move forward.

He moves his finger like a hook and pats his thigh. "Sit. I have to show you something."

"Why? I can stand right here. I'm not blind."

He runs his fingers through his dark hair and blows a puff of air out of his cheeks.

"Fine." He gets up.

I back up toward the door nervously. When I'm close enough to the door, I can hear Jess moaning. My eyes find his and they freeze. We can hear her moaning while Reid is fucking her. Valen is groaning while she must be sucking him off. My pussy gets wet, and I feel it dripping between my thighs. My nipples strain under my long-sleeved sweater.

"Get on the bed," he demands. "Take off your pants and open your legs."

"No."

He walks closer. "I can smell how much you want me, Raven. I want to taste you."

Holy fucking Christ. My pussy throbs just thinking about his tongue and what it would feel like. He gets closer, lifting my chin as he angles his head so his lips are a breath away from mine. "I want to taste that sweet pussy. Tell me you don't want to feel my tongue fuck your sweet cunt, Raven. I can smell how wet you are for me." He licks my closed lips.

It is the most erotic and filthy thing I have ever heard or felt. "Why?" Why are you doing this to me?"

His eyes darken. "Because, I want more. I can't let you go, Raven." He slides his hand and cups my pussy over my leggings and flicks his finger over the seam where my pussy splits. "You feel this pussy." I nod my head slowly, my eyes half open. "It is mine. I will break you and then put you back together and break you again. It doesn't matter how many times I break you because when I put you back together, we will fit perfectly."

He slides his hand inside the band of my leggings and swipes his finger between my slit. A whimper escapes from my lips and he licks my lips after the sound escapes. "I taste it, Raven. I can taste the need." His finger runs the nub of my clit and it throbs. "I can feel it."

He slides his finger through my pussy. I'm hot and drenched between my legs.

"So wet. So pretty," he whispers.

My heart is beating...hard. I stop hearing Jess moan and can only hear the sound of his breath and the beating of my heart.

He removes his hand and slides my pants off along with my boots. He lifts the hem of my sweater, removing it in one swoop. My clothes pool on the floor. I'm left in my lace bra. He slides the straps down until the tops of my nipples peak but doesn't remove it.

He licks one nipple and then the other. "Dravin," I gasp.

He chuckles. "Get on my bed and open your legs so I can see that pussy and how much it wants me to suck it dry."

I sit on the bed and open my legs. My cheeks heat at how vulnerable I feel. He removes his tank top, and his muscles flex and move, causing me to clench my thighs.

"You want me to suck your pussy?" He walks closer until his face is inches from my center. He licks his lips and studies the throbbing of my clit. His eyes flick to my face as I hold myself up on my elbows, watching him.

My hair is fanned over his bed as he kneels between my legs waiting for my answer. "I'll lick, and if you tell me to stop. I will."

"Okay."

He lowers his lips and licks. I lift my ass seeking his tongue when it retracts. He groans and I moan on contact. He quirks a brow. "More?"

"Yes," I say, breathlessly.

He smiles and slides his tongue inside my pussy and fucks me with it. He licks and sucks and twirls as I moan.

"Dravin," I call out. "Mmm, Dravin."

"That's it, my Raven. Call my name, baby," he rasps against my clit. I grind on his face, and he uses the tip of his nose to swipe my clit, and the tingles cause my pussy to pulse all over his face and lips, and I scream. I can't take what he is doing. I lay flat on my back and he pushes his face deeper. He groans against me. He licks his lips and stands.

He flips me so that I'm on all fours and eats my pussy from behind, sucking my puckered hole, and I turn my head and watch as he fucks me with his tongue.

"Oh. My. God."

"That's right, baby. I'm your God. This pussy is mine. I'm going to fuck you and suck this pussy until you can't scream my name anymore."

Oh my god. My body feels alive, and I need him to fill me. I raise my head, and the words that have been stuck in my throat slide out of my lips. "Dravin?"

"Yes, baby."

"Please."

He kneels on the bed, and I feel the mattress dip from his weight. He lowers his pants, and I feel his cock rubbing against my thigh. He knows I want him inside me. I can't help myself. I want him to erase all the hurt. I want him to tell me it was a cruel joke or something other than the gut-wrenching feeling of him hurting me the way he did.

He slides the head of his cock inside, and then he pounds into me. He fucks me and fucks me, and I break like he promised. I explode from the orgasm that rips right through me. The slapping of skin and the moans escape my lips as I come. "Dravin," I gasp.

"I know, Raven." He slams into me and hot cum swirls inside me, filling me. Branding me. His cock pulses inside and I arch my back so he can fill the deepest part of me. His grip on my hips is firm as he holds me still until he is spent.

He pulls out slowly, and he slides his hand around my waist up my torso pulling my back against his chest. His mouth is in the crook of my neck. "I'm never letting you go," he whispers.

I close my eyes, turn my head, and place my lips on the side of his head to breathe in his scent. "Then don't," I respond.

He turns me to pick me up like a bride and carry me to the bathroom. He places me in the shower and turns on the water. It is so different than the first time we had sex. He's different. My eyes follow his movement, and I watch as he makes sure the water is at the right temperature before turning on the rain shower. He grabs my hand, pulls me toward his chest, and rests his chin over my head. "I'm sorry. There is a good reason. I promise. I thought I was doing the right thing, but I wasn't. I was hurting you. I was hurting us."

I don't know what he means. He regrets what he did, but why does he keep saying there is a reason—a reason to keep me safe? I don't get it.

He washes me just like the first time. Except this time, he sits me down in front of the vanity and brushes my hair. He then blow-dries my hair until it's smooth and flowing down my back. He gives me a grin, which I see when I look at his handsome face in the mirror. It is the most intimate thing to have a man blow-dry your hair.

He moves out of the bathroom and returns with a silk robe. "I bought this for you. I hope you like it. He pulls it off the hanger and holds it open so I can slide my arms through the sleeves.

He grabs my hand, kisses my fingers, and closes his eyes like he is afraid I'll disappear. My feelings for him are all over the place. One minute, he makes my heart soar, and the next, I'm afraid. I'm afraid he will finish breaking me and I won't survive.

"Come, I need to show you something."

I nod, and he sits me on his lap in front of his massive computer. He tells me about The Order, how it all began, how the university is built around the church, all the things he shouldn't do, why he claimed me, and why he did what he did.

"I did make a bet with Veronica, but I don't want her. I didn't know you. I never thought you would be this amazing person, that you would be my Raven. I'm sorry for everything, Gia. Please. I need you to understand that I'm part of this, and there are people who don't have good intentions."

"Like everyone."

"Yes. Like everyone."

"So what now? I'm considered Prey or whatever. What does that mean for me?'

"A Prey can choose who she wants to be with. It's not like when you're married. Once you're married, the man chooses how he wants to lead his marriage. Faithful or unfaithful, she doesn't have a choice."

I swallow and look at Kenyan's history, his family tree, and the major players—basically, the major players controlling the economy.

"What happens if they don't follow the rules?"

He looks at the computer screen and leans his cheek on my side. "They die."

My eyes widen. "They what?"

"They die, Gia. The Order decides when and how to get rid of them."

"Have you?"

He nods, "Yeah."

He knows I'm asking him if he has killed people. If he has had to. I close my eyes and shiver.

"Are you cold?"

"No. I'm scared, Dravin. I'm scared for you, and I'm scared for everyone."

I hear a knock at the door. "Are you two done bumping uglies or what?" Valen teases through the door.

Dravin rolls his eyes. "What am I going to do with that knucklehead."

"Punch him in the face again to make the other side even."

"Not a bad idea."

He taps me on the thigh. A signal for me to get up. I tie my robe around me to make sure I don't flash my naked flesh to Valen as Dravin yanks the door open and Valen almost falls inside.

He laughs, but Dravin doesn't laugh with him. "What do you want?"

Valen's eyes gleam with amusement when they land on me in my robe. "You kissed and made up." He gives me a wink.

I roll my eyes, crossing my arms over my chest. "What?"

He shakes his head. "Nothing. I can see it."

"See what?" Dravin growls.

He smirks at Dravin. "How madly in love she is with you."

I avert my gaze because I thought I could keep my feelings hidden from everyone. I tried to hide it, but Valen could see it.

"Dravin's eyes caress me and then turn dark when they land on Valen. "Your point," Dravin snaps.

"I just thought you should know," Valen answers. "It's written all over her face every time she looks at you. You better do something about that. Or...they will."

Now that I know what he means, another thought pops into my head. Jess.

"Does Jess know?" I ask both of them.

"She knows enough now—not like what I just told you, but enough. She is safe from the others for now."

"He means as long as we keep fucking her," Valen drawls with a knowing gleam in his eyes.

We, meaning both Reid and Valen. I wonder how Reid feels about that, but then again, it's not my business as long as Jess is safe and happy.

GIA

IT IS THANKSGIVING BREAK. Jess went to her family's dinner, and I had to fly out to meet my dad in his new house with his new girlfriend. My mother is already there. I'm dreading being in the middle of this awkward dinner and can't wait to leave and I haven't even arrived.

Dravin has been the sweetest and most amazing in bed. He hasn't let me go back to the dorm. He wants me in his house, preferably in his bed. We sit and do our homework together, watch movies, and binge on TV shows like a real couple. I haven't brought up the order, the rules, or even our relationship at this point. He made sure all pictures and comments about what happened were removed.

The argument I saw him having with Veronica was about her sneaking into his house and being a psycho bitch, posting that about me on the school's social media.

The Uber drops me off at my father's now larger home. This is the first time I will meet his girlfriend and my stomach is in knots. I look up at the medium-sized home with a three-car garage and notice it's much newer than the home I grew up in.

When I approach the walkway, the white front door opens, and my father appears.

"Hi, sweetheart. I'm glad you could make it. Your mom is inside with Carolyn." My father greets me.

I place a small smile on my face because what daughter wants to spend Thanksgiving with his father's new girlfriend that he cheated on your mother with. Oh, and my mother, too. This sucks.

"Hi, dad." I greet him in return, giving him a hug.

I walk inside the warm house, the smell of turkey and homemade pie in the air. I can hear voices coming from the kitchen. One I recognize as my mother, and the other must be Carolyn. Another voice is of a man.

"Oh, Carolyn wants you to meet a friend of hers from work. He is about your age and couldn't' spend Thanksgiving with his family."

I smell a setup. My father has been worried about me dating because my mother had me raised in a bubble practically my whole life. I'm not sure she would approve of the way I have given myself to a broken man who is part of one of the richest organizations in the world. If my parents only knew I'm attending a school full of sinners.

"I'll take your suitcase upstairs and put it in the spare room."

"Alright," I tell him, removing my scarf, gloves, and jacket.

I told Dravin I was having Thanksgiving dinner with my parents, but I didn't know how to ask him if he wanted to come or if that was something I was supposed to ask. I hate labeling what we have because it is so complicated. Sex is the only thing not complicated between us, but I have hope. You can't help who you fall in love with. I just hope he feels the same way. He said he was going to visit his father, so I held my tongue, but I didn't have the courage to ask him to come with me. In all honesty, I was a little worried he would tell me no.

I walk into the kitchen, and I raise my top an inch above my breast because the guy who is watching from the corner has his eyes aimed right at my chest instead of my face. His brown eyes scroll over me like he is undressing me.

"You must be, Gia," he says, walking over. He has sandy blonde hair, his dress shirt rolled over his forearms, and khaki slacks. He looks like he just got off work and didn't have time to change.

My mother, Laurie, gives me a small smile and looks over at a petite woman with brown hair and a big smile. "You must be, Gia. She comes up and gives me a kiss and I stiffen.

"Hello, everyone." I nod toward my head. "Mom."

"We are so glad you could make it. How's college life treating you? Your dad told me that you were attending Kenyan. That is very impressive."

"Yeah, wow. Very impressive. What are you studying? My name is Colin, by the way. He holds out his hand." I give him a normal handshake. "Gia. I'm studying economics."

"Very, cool."

Economics is not cool, but whatever. I guess Colin is just trying to be nice.

"How about church." My mother chimes in.

"Laurie." My father walks into the kitchen. "We discussed this. No church comments while Gia is here. This is her senior year and she is on her own living on campus at an elite university. I'm sure there are better topics than church to talk about. She has gone to church with you every Sunday since she was practically born." He chastises my mother.

"Fine," she says in a clipped tone, giving me a wry smile. I'm sorry."

"Don't be sorry, Mom. I went to confession and attended."

She gives me a beaming smile. If she only knew the priest wasn't a real priest and real sinners are the ones that go every week.

I feel bad my father embarrassed her, but I can't say I'm not glad. Everything about my mother is regarding church. She has this thing with it. She should have just joined a convent and devoted herself to God. She would have been happier, in my opinion.

I clear my throat. "Do you need me to help with anything?"

Carolyn shakes her head. "Oh, no. I've got everything under control." She gives me a wine glass with some white wine. "You go with Colin to the living room and chat for a while.

Colin takes that as an excuse and grabs a beer. He waves his hand for me to go first. "Ladies first."

I walk ahead of him praying he isn't checking out my ass. I take a seat in the living room and notice that my father has pictures of him and Carolyn everywhere. I even notice one they took together while he was still married to my mother. Prick.

"Is this your first time meeting Carolyn?"

I'm annoyed because he damn well knows the obvious.

"Why don't you ask me something that isn't stupid."

I know I'm being a bitch, but come on, first, he undresses me with his eyes without even knowing my name, then he asks me stupid questions he already knows the answers to.

He places his beer on the coffee table. "Alright? I know you don't have an official boyfriend or anything. How about you go out with me tomorrow? I want to ask you out on a date. How does that sound?"

I'm about to turn him down when the doorbell rings. I look over at the front door. "Are we expecting company?"

"Not that I'm aware of. I work with Carolyn, and she didn't mention anyone else stopping by."

My father opens the door and I hear the voice from the last person I expected. Dravin. I stand and watch as my father's eyes widen at an impeccably dressed Dravin with perfectly tailored slacks and a black dress shirt with a grey embedded pattern under a long overcoat. His hair is neatly trimmed. His driver comes into the foyer and drops off three designer suitcases.

I tighten my hold on my wine glass. He greets my father and shakes his hand.

Carolyn's voice can be heard from the dining table. "Dinner is ready, everyone," she calls out.

"Honey, I think you need to set up for one more."

My mouth goes dry when Dravin looks up. He turns his head when the driver hands him two bouquets of flowers—one of black roses and the other of different colors.

"Thank you," he murmurs to the driver. Then he says something, and the driver says, "Of course, it will be delivered, Mr. Bedford."

My father raises his eyebrows, turns to me, and tilts his head toward Dravin. My father looks over at me and mouths, "Wow," silently.

"Who is that?" Colin asks, his voice low.

Dravin walks further down the hallway in my direction. "I hope you don't mind me showing up beautiful, but I missed you already."

Oh my God. He is just perfect. My mouth breaks into a smile. "Never," I answer him softly.

He hands me the black roses and I place my nose inside and smell them. He leans in right when my mother and Carolyn walk in to see who showed up taking my lips in a passionate kiss. His hand cups the side of my cheek and I melt into his embrace not caring if we have an audience.

"Oh, my," Carolyn whispers.

"Jesus," my mother says.

My father clears his throat.

"Everyone. This is Dravin. Gianna's boyfriend from school."

My eyes find his and he leans. "Is that ok?"

I nod my head vigorously my eyes turning glassy. "Oh, yes."

His eyes move away from me and land on a speechless Colin. "Hello, I'm Dravin, Gianna's boyfriend. And you are?"

"Colin," he says.

Dravin gives Colin a once over then looks him square in the eyes. Dravin has two inches on Colin and has a bigger build. He gives Colin a *she's mine* stare down.

I fidget with the hem of my top and Dravin's eyes trail over the slight swell of my breasts. "Are you trying to spoil my dinner, gorgeous," he teases.

My face heats and I look over at my mother. "Mother, this is Dravin."

"I see that, sweetheart." She turns to me. Now I know what to call him: boyfriend. "You attend Kenyan also?"

"Yes, ma'am."

"Oh, please call me Laurie."

"Alright, Laurie. Yes, I attend Kenyan with R-Gianna." He clears his throat. "Forgive me, but I tend to call Gianna my Raven."

"You are so well-mannered, young man," my father says.

"Thank you."

Carolyn claps her hands. Well, dinner is served and welcome, Dravin. I'm thrilled you could make it. I notice she gives Colin a sad smile. I knew it. It was a setup. That was why he was quick to ask me out and why he looked at me like I was dinner. Let's just hope he behaves.

Everyone takes a seat. Colin tries to sit next to me, but Dravin moves quickly and raises an eyebrow. "I think your seat is over there." He points across to the other table.

Dravin removes his coat and unbuttons the first two of his dress shirt and rolls up his sleeves.

"Eyes over here, honey," my father says to Carolyn, whose eyes widen in embarrassment.

My mother raises her eyes and scans Dravin's arms and neck, no doubt inspecting all the ink. Even Colin notices and looks nervous.

I rub my lips together because it is rather intimidating. Dravin is not a small man, and with all the tattoos, it can be overwhelming if you're not used to them.

Carolyn smiles and waves a fork in Dravin's direction. "Are those everywhere? Don't they hurt?" she asks. I almost choke on my wine.

Dravin looks at me to make sure I'm not choking. When he is sure, he turns to Carolyn.

"You mean my tattoos. Is that what you're asking."

"Yeah. I'm sure her mother is wondering the same thing. Right, Laurie?"

She licks her lips and gives me a small smile. "I—

Dravin interrupts her. "They are." He looks over at me and licks his lips seductively. "Gianna knows where they all are."

"Oh my," my mother says softly.

My eyes find my father, but he keeps opening his mouth and closing it.

"Gianna, how are the dorms? Is everything okay?" My father finally asks.

He hasn't called or visited, so I wonder why he cares. I tense and place my fork more forcefully than necessary in my turkey, showing how I feel about the matter.

"I remember when I was in college three years ago, it was the luck of the draw who you got as a roommate. You're lucky you only have one year left," Colin says before I can answer.

My eyes lift and Dravin meets my gaze. He turns and his attention lands on my father. "She doesn't have to worry about living in the dorms or her tuition."

"Oh, and why is that?"

"Because I have made sure it's covered, and she doesn't have to share a dorm room."

"Where are you staying, sweetheart," my father asks me.

I swallow the food in my mouth forcefully.

"I'm staying with Dravin."

My mother drops her fork. "Excuse me?"

My eyes land on my mother's appalled face as she looks at me and then to Dravin and back.

Colin leans back and smiles. "As roommates?" he interjects.

Dravin takes a sip of his wine and bobbles his head from side to side. "If you call her sleeping in my bed roommates, then yeah, I guess we're room-mates," he says with a smile.

"Gianna!" my mother screeches.

I roll my eyes slightly. "Yes, mom."

"How dare you?"

Carolyn looks at my father and then to me. "Laurie, relax. You are over-reacting. She is a grown adult, and she can date and do...other stuff."

"She is well taken care of."

"Yeah, in your bed," she snaps.

"Mother," I scold.

Dravin scratches his brow with his forefinger. "I'm sorry, but it makes sense. Gia told me how you feel about the church and your religious views."

"What happens when you're bored of her, huh? Where will she go?"

My stomach clenches because my mother has a point. What happens when he gets bored of me and wants someone else? I lower my gaze and fidget with my hands under the table. This is not how I expected Thanks-giving to go.

"I assure you she doesn't have to worry about that."

"What will you do for money?"

Colin snorts because he figures Dravin lives in a small apartment, barely making it by like most typical college students.

"What do you do for money, son? You seem really sure of yourself. Colin understands the struggle. He owns the brokerage firm Carolyn works for and how hard it is to get started when you graduate college. How hard it can be to stable enough."

"Daddy, please."

"Honey, give him a break," Carolyn tells my father.

Dravin pinches his nose, and I know he must be annoyed by everyone.

"I have and make enough."

"What is your last name, son? Let's start there. Who are your parents?"

"My name is Dravin Bedford. My mother is dead, and my father is very much alive. I'm one of the three founding sons of Kenyan."

My father's eyes widen, and Colin almost drops the mashed potatoes. "You mean to tell me I have a billionaire's son or maybe a billionaire sitting at my dining room table?"

"Yes, sir. That is accurate."

"Y-you're a Bedford," My father stutters.

"I'm well aware. Like I said, Gianna lives with me on my estate off campus and she has her tuition paid for in full."

"Holy shit," Colin whispers. "You're like one of the richest families dating back generations.

If they only knew he was part of the most dangerous and corrupt organization ever. He's part of The Order and eventually one of its main three. Now, he's my boyfriend, and he wants me for himself.

My teeth scrape my bottom lip, but Dravin places his thumb to keep me from committing damage. "Easy there, gorgeous. I wouldn't want those pretty lips to sting."

Colin puffs his chest out. "Could I get a picture taken with you?"

"As long as Gianna is next to me," Dravin shrugs his shoulders and gives him a predatory smile. Why not?" Dravin leans closer over the table. "Keep your eyes on my girl, and all will be good."

Colin blinks multiple times, like something is stuck in his eyes. "I-I'm sorry. I-I didn't know."

Dravin points with his wine glass in his hand toward Colin's nervous face. "That's your only warning," he says on a chuckle.

Is Dravin jealous? Dravin's hand slides under the table, and he places it possessively over my thigh and gently squeezes it.

"Honey, you have that boy wrapped around your finger," Carolyn says, as if Dravin didn't just threaten Colin.

GIA
†

I WAS SURPRISED my mother and father didn't object when Dravin placed his bags in the guest bedroom. One of the bags he brought was full of designer clothes he purchased for me, with the option to return anything I didn't like. He wanted me to have new clothes to wear for my trip to see my parents.

Where this version of Dravin came from, I have no idea, but I want him to stay with me forever.

"Are you ready?" Dravin asks.

I check myself in the mirror for the tenth time. I am wearing a black wool dress with sheer black pantyhose and an overcoat with matching leather boots. I decided to wear my hair down and light makeup. Dravin is wearing his overcoat since the temperatures have dropped significantly. He looks handsome in his all-black suit standing behind me. We look striking together. Together. I love the sound of that. His eyes hold me through the mirror.

"There is no emptiness or lies inside of you. Your soul is not on the other side, but *with* mine. Always."

He kisses me on my cheek and murmurs, "You're forever mine."

My stomach flutters and I turn and tell him, "I love you."

He smiles. "I know."

He doesn't return the same words. I'm not sure if I should feel sad or happy. I close my eyes and he squeezes my hand.

"Let's go. My father is waiting."

We are having dinner with his father, and I'm nervous. Extremely so. I wonder what he will think of me. Am I good enough? I'm also curious as to why he came all this way to have dinner after Thanksgiving and not during.

The sports car that was delivered to my father's house is something straight out of a magazine. The doors lift up, and I'm instantly surrounded by warmth. He has the car warmed up.

"Thank you."

"My pleasure."

The restaurant is a nice venue in the city. It is discreet, expensive, but small. I have the feeling the restaurant was chosen, so this could be a small affair.

We are ushered to a table where a man with a medium-sized build and eyes dark as night is seated. He looks like Dravin but slightly older. He is still handsome for his age. I could see myself with Dravin in the future. It gives me a glimpse of how he would look when he is his father's age. Still as handsome. You can tell by the way the waiter keeps giving him appreciative looks. The other patrons glance over at Dravin and me with curious stares as we make our way to the table.

"Why are they staring," I whisper to Dravin.

"Because you're beautiful, Raven."

Mr. Bedford watches Dravin remove my coat and tilts his head, studying me.

"She's gorgeous, son. I can see why you picked her." He turns to me. "Please, have a seat, Gianna."

Dravin holds out my chair and I carefully take a seat then watch him sit to my right. "Thank you for the invitation."

"My pleasure. You're here so we can discuss your relationship with my son."

I stiffen and my eyes lift to meet Dravin's hard ones. He obviously doesn't agree with his father, but I want to know what this is about. Is he warning me off? Is he trying to tell me I'm not good enough because I don't have money or come from a wealthy family?

"Okay," I say softly, placing my hands on my lap. My appetite quickly vanishing.

"I know you are aware of how things are done, but my son brought a stipulation to my attention. I can only allow it if you agree. You have to be willing."

Dravin is quiet and he leans back in his chair. Waiting.

The waiter brings food we never ordered, but it all looks delicious. Dravin begins to eat like this is a normal conversation. I'm not sure if this is customary when his father is present, but the self-assured guy from yesterday is gone at the dinner table. He is this silent spectator, not voicing a word.

"Willing to what?"

Mr. Bedford's eyes darken like a man possessed by something evil.

"Breed."

My eyes snap to Dravin.

My nostrils flare. Did he just say what I think he did? Breed? I'm not cattle.

"He means have my child," Dravin says softly. My heart softens and my anger slowly lifts.

My brows pinch, and I realize that he hasn't been using condoms anymore when we have sex, and I'm not on the pill yet. I went to the doctor to get it, but I need to wait until after my next cycle to start. Dear God. Is he? He wouldn't?

"When the time is right and when I'm ready. I can see Dravin and I having a baby someday," I answer.

"My son has to marry before he graduates, and you are his choice. The only way a girl from your side can be with him is if you fall pregnant. Once the child is born, then you can get married. When you marry, all the rules will apply as if you were married in an alliance.

He means because I'm considered Prey, they have to make sure I can give him an heir to keep the order going. If not, he has to marry someone else.

"If I don't."

"Then he keeps fucking you until he is done with you, but he will marry who he needs to marry. You can always be his mistress. It isn't uncommon, and faithfulness isn't required in our relationships, whether we are married or not. This is a chance to change your life. You will want for nothing. The decision is up to you."

My head whips to Dravin. He lowers his gaze. "Is that what you've been trying to do? Get me pregnant?"

He doesn't flinch when he answers. "Yes."

"Why?"

"Because you're mine."

GTA

I DIDN'T SPEAK to Dravin after having the most strenuous dinner with the father of the man I have fallen in love with, who can also flip on me and make me miserable for the rest of my life. He wants me to breed like a cow right after graduating college and be married to a man who doesn't have to be faithful if he doesn't feel like it.

"I'm sorry, Raven," he says after I walk out of the bathroom, getting ready for school.

"Sorry?"

"Yes, I'm sorry. I don't know how else to keep you."

"Keep me." I snort. "I'm not a dog or a bird you can put in a cage, Dravin. I know you are part of this secret cult thing, but how am I supposed to accept it? No matter what I decide, I'm doomed to a life of hell."

"How is it a life of hell if we're together?"

"Because how will I know you won't cheat on me? How will I know you are faithful when you don't have to be? It's a life of slavery."

"You sound like—" He trails off.

"I sound like what?"

He takes a deep breath and looks up at the ceiling. "You sound like my mother did when she was alive."

I stop moving and peer over at his pained expression. I don't know what to do—choose him or not choose him. He can say everything is great, but once I'm tied to him, I lose all ability to do what I want. My child is then thrust into this society of sinners. Is that what I want? Is that what is good for me? For us?"

I walk up to him and wrap my arms around his waist. His arms wrap around me, and I'm swallowed inside his embrace. I lean my forehead against his hard torso.

"What would you want?" I gaze up at him. "What do you truly want?"

"I want you."

"You have me."

"I want you to have my child. I want you to be mine."

"I'm scared. I'm so scared."

He swallows and looks down at me. "I know.

I sigh, "What if I can't get pregnant?"

"You were just checked. Don't take the pill, please."

He went with me to the clinic to get on birth control. I didn't want to ruin our relationship with an unplanned pregnancy, but I never thought that he was actually checking to see if I could have children. I should be upset, but I understand why he did it. He was trying to find a way to keep me in his situation. For there to be an us.

I huff. "Easy for you to say. You're not looked upon like cattle."

He laughs and it's the most welcoming sound.

"The last thing I think about when I look at you is cattle," he rasps.

My lips seek his, and we kiss until I'm almost late to class.

I walk toward the cafeteria. I still have the meal plan from the beginning of the semester, so I make my way over. Maybe I'll get lucky, and it will be empty. I'm walking in, and I find Jess with Valen, but there is no sign of Reid.

"Hey. What's he doing here?" I point to Valen.

Jess swallows the bite of what appears to be a sandwich. "Hi. Um, Valen was just sitting with me."

He places both elbows on the table. "What's wrong? I can't sit with Jess now."

I take a seat next to Jess. "I didn't mean for it to sound like that. It's just that you're usually with Reid."

What I was trying to say is that I thought Reid was into Jess and not Valen. He seems the playboy type, not the serious type. He's a sophomore with two years to mess around and live carefree as a college boy. I know Jess has had sex with both, and that is her business, but she's my friend and I'm still going to look out for her. She's Prey, and people have already taken advantage of her.

"It's ok, Gia. Valen was just leaving."

He lowers his elbows and leans across the table toward Jess and lowers his voice. "Think about it." He gives her a wink. "See you later."

He gets up and looks down at me, wearing his fitted shirt and jacket. Valen is a very attractive guy, and girls break their necks to get a glimpse every time he passes by the same way he breaks their hearts.

"You're a good friend, Gia. She's lucky to have you. Just so we're clear, I kinda like Jess."

My eyebrows shoot up. Did he just say he's interested in Jess? My head leans in, and I try to rile him up the same way he always does to me. I bump my shoulder against Jess. "A lot of people like Jess. She's hot."

His nostrils flare. Like Dravin, he loves a challenge, and if he truly likes Jess, this is my way to make sure he treats her right. I know the rules, thanks to Dravin, and he knows it. He knows I have to make a decision regarding Dravin and our future. I can easily be part of The Order if I want, and not just by being with a regular member. I will be at the top as the future wife of one of the founding members.

When Valen walks away with a scowl on his face, I turn to Jess and ask, "What was that all about?"

"Valen being Valen. Don't worry about it. He plays around a lot. It's hard to tell when he is being playful or serious."

"What does Reid say about the way he acts around you?"

She takes a bite of her chips, and you can hear the crunch when she crushes them with her teeth. She's thinking about her answer, or maybe she just isn't sure.

"I don't know, and honestly, I don't trust guys. Especially guys from this school. Dravin is the exception because he cares about you. He moves you into his house. He treats you like a princess. I could go on. The man is batshit crazy, head over heels. I'm not sure I'll ever have that."

"I don't know what to say to you other than that you have a choice, Jess. Believe it or not, we do."

She slides another chip in her mouth. The annoying crunch bouncing in my ears. "My choice is to not give in to any of them. I've been treated like shit before, and I won't do that again, ever."

"What do you mean?" My stomach clenches in worry. "Did someone hurt you, Jess?"

She laughs but not the kind of laugh that makes anything that was said funny. "Let's just say I have trust issues. The whole thing with Garret put the nail in the coffin. I'm in college and will have fun like every other college kid my age. I know some don't agree with the things I've supposedly done, but I have my reasons, just like they do. Emotion is not part of it, and I'm ok with that. If they think they're emotionally unattainable, then they don't know the meaning of the word."

When she says they, I know she means the guys who are part of The Order. Maybe she can find a nice guy like Marc or someone who isn't part of The Order—someone who goes to a different school or something.

"How about dating someone from Ohio State, like that guy Dillion? He seemed nice."

She snorts. "Reid almost killed him. I don't want to be the cause of some poor guy disappearing."

Cold dread snakes up my spine because I know they are capable of it. Just because I haven't seen it, doesn't mean it can't happen.

I slide my hair to one shoulder and let out a frustrated breath. "Fine, I get it, but promise me you will be careful. I mean... screw what anyone thinks. Just be careful."

She drapes an arm around me and smiles. "I know you're just looking out for me, and I think you're an amazing person." I smile, but it is wiped off my face when Warren saunters in and stops at the table where we are seated.

"Hey there, gorgeous." He sits down next to me, and I notice his cast is off.

"What do you want?" I snap.

He raises his hands up in mock surrender. "I was just being nice. I have never been anything but nice to you."

True, but he gives me creepy vibes almost all the time. He always looks around like someone is going to pop out and catch him doing something he isn't supposed to.

"Why are you here?" I ask.

He glances at Jess and then at me. "To give you a heads up." He nudges his head toward the doors leading to the hallway on campus. "See for yourself."

Then he gets up and walks away.

Jess's eyes follow me as I get up and make my way to the hallway, pausing when I see a girl placing her hands on Dravin's chest and giggling. His face is emotionless, but he doesn't do anything to move her hands from where they are planted. My eyes sting and my throat feels like it closes with the searing pain. My vision narrows like I'm going in and out of a tunnel. My mother's words at Thanksgiving instantly hit a deep part of me that I refused to consider a possibility because I wished that what we had was strong enough for him to be different.

Will I always have to wonder?

What if he gets bored and tired of me? I will be trapped with no way out. My eyes begin to fill, and my nose gets clogged with unshed tears.

The brunette fondling my boyfriend must be a member because she isn't in the dorms, and I've never seen her in the cafeteria or anywhere the Prey usually hang out. Her clothes are definitely upscale, and she has a perfect figure. I'm sure she is a better fit to be with someone like Dravin. She leans up to say something close, but he turns his head to listen. When he turns to get away, he stops when he sees me standing by the door leading to the cafeteria. He swallows and then looks at the girl who has a triumphant smirk planted on her face.

"Please don't let me interrupt," I say, turning and walking away.

"Raven!" Dravin calls out. "It's not what it looks like."

"I'm sure. It seemed like a lot what it did. I was standing there for a hot minute. Look, I gotta go," I tell him.

He grabs my hand. "No. Please. Let me explain."

I pull my hand out of his grasp. "Explain what?" I snap. "That it was a mistake. That it's not what it looks like. Let me guess: She was lost, and she happened to find her hand on your chest after something funny you said. Wait...let me guess, you've slept with her already. I bet my life on it."

His eyes dim, and I know I hit the nail on the head. He's fucked her. It doesn't matter. If it's not her, it will be another and another. Then I'll turn into one of those jealous psychos that can't cope. I'll be a nag which will result in him doing the one thing he is notorious for doing, screwing whoever he pleases. Either way, same result.

"I'm sorry. I know I have a past, but that was nothing. I don't want her."

I snort. "Well, it sure as hell looked like you wanted her." My eyes lock on his and he grimaces when he sees how hurt I am. I have to set aside my love for someone who has never told me he loved me. I have to set aside the attraction. I can't think about his gorgeous face, his perfect body, and the way he makes me feel when I'm in his arms.

All the times I dream of happily ever after.

All the times I picture the child or children we could have together.

I wonder all the time what it would be like to be by his side or married to someone like him.

It would take a split second for him to destroy it.

Like a ruined castle crumbling to the ground, I'm at the bottom with my heart in my hands, praying to be saved.

"Raven, please look at me."

My eyes find his, one light and one dark. I decide. I decide what is best for both of us. I would rather he be a stranger and me a memory, than be cut open and bleeding for the rest of my life.

"I'm sorry, Dravin. I can't. I'm so sorry."

"No, please, baby. I'll make it right. We can go home, right now. We can talk about this. I promised I wouldn't."

He promised he wouldn't be unfaithful, but my father vowed the same thing to my mother, and look at how well that turned out.

I laugh ironically. "Yeah, I can tell. What would happen if it was the other way around, huh? The shoe on the other foot."

He clenches his teeth, and his hands turn into fists. "There would be a body to be buried."

"Huh, I guess I should go and get a spot in the 1918 section, or should it be in the late 1800s."

He raises his chin. "That could be arranged if that's what it takes."

I snicker. "I don't think there will be enough space in the cemetery to bury all the bodies."

He gets closer, and his fingers touch the tips of my hair, curling it around his thumb. "I'm not giving up on us. I won't."

"I don't know. I just need time. This is all too much right now, Dravin."

DRAVIN
†

I'M WALKING down the hallway when I spot Jess. She slows down and I quirk a brow.

"What?"

She takes a deep breath because she knows I'm on edge. My Raven is distant, and she is closed off. That stupid girl, I can't even remember her name, was trying to get me to screw her or test my loyalty to Gia. Some people can't fathom my love being for her and only her.

It is a hard decision to give up everything to be with someone like me, who is part of a secret society with rules we only follow.

"I just think you should know that it appears that the whole scenario that played out in the cafeteria was a setup to get Gia to break it off with you."

I begin grinding my teeth because whoever is behind it, is dead. No question.

"I'm listening."

"Warren came to us when we were sitting at the cafeteria and acted like he was being a friend and looking out for her best interests. He told her to go see what was happening outside. It just so happened it was at the exact moment whatever her name is, was chatting you up."

"It was a setup so she would break it off with me. Then she would be vulnerable, and he can swoop in and be her hero."

I curl my lip in anger. My left eye begins to twitch because he's done. Order or no order. She's mine. No one gets to hurt her emotionally or physically. She means that much to me.

"Yeah, I think that sums it all up. I also wanted to warn you about him." My eyes follow the way she fidgets, and a nagging feeling snakes up my spine.

"About... It's ok. You can tell me."

"I-I don't like the way he looks at her. I know it doesn't make sense, and no one picks up on it, but I do. I just want her safe, but Warren is...Warren."

"I see. I'll take care of it. If you need anything, you can come to me, and if you don't feel comfortable with me, Reid, or Valen, tell Gia, and she will come to me."

She swallows nervously and averts her gaze to the wall. When someone has been in pain for so long, they can see it in others, and in Jess's world, there is plenty of it.

"Okay," she whispers.

I sidestep and walk past her into my favorite class because it's with my Raven and I can write about her.

My eyes meet hers, and I smile, yet it falls because she seems defeated. One of the girls I have slept with gives me an appreciative once-over. I roll my eyes and make my way to Gia.

"You look better every time I see you, Dravin," she purrs.

I ignore her and see Gia's eyes flash in anger at her. I instantly regret every woman I have slept with before Gia. I hate that I cause her to feel uncomfortable. I look over to Rebecca and then Gia and say loudly enough for everyone to hear.

"I may have slept with many women, but I've only taken *one* to my bed, and that is the only place that matters. You are the only woman that matters. They are my past, but you are my present and will always be my future."

My Raven looks up with a slight grin on her lips and tears in her eyes. I give her a wink and take a seat right next to her.

The professor walks in, and class begins. After thirty minutes of a lecture on literature, he faces the class behind his podium.

"If you don't mind, Mr. Bedford, I believe you are one of the few I haven't called upon to read your latest entry."

I pull out my notebook and flip it to the last page and read.

I am lost like the forgotten footprints in the snow. Yet, you stand like the fire against the cold. Like a dark Raven bringing light, guiding me to you so I can hear the silent whispers of your soul.

"Very deep. Very deep." He glances at Gia, just like everyone else in the class. "You must be his Raven."

"She is," I say quietly.

The professor's eyes land on me, giving me a curt nod. "Understood."

He knows what it means. That she is mine in every sense. I know it, The Order knows it, my father knows it. Even Rebecca lowers her gaze. They know that in this moment and from now on, Gia is untouchable. I have claimed my Prey.

GIA

"WHAT'S WRONG?" Jess asks me. We are back at the dorm after a full day of classes.

"I need to talk to you. I need to talk to someone, but I don't know who to talk to."

Jess gets up and gives me a hug, wrapping her arms around me. "What's wrong? Gia, tell me. Did something happen? Did someone hurt you?"

"Yes, to the first and no to the second," I sniff.

"What's wrong?"

My eyes close and tears escape running down my cheeks. "I'm pregnant," I blurt in her shirt, making a wet spot.

"What?"

I raise my head and sniff. "I'm pregnant."

"Shit," she mutters.

She sits down on the edge of her bed and holds her curls tight on top of her head. "Yeah, I get it. Double fuck." She lifts her legs, crisscrossing them, and pats the bed so I can sit beside her.

I sit and rub my face with my forearm. "What am I going to do?"

"First off, are you sure? These things can be false positives, you know."

I pull the paper out of my coat pocket and hold it up. It is from the clinic.

"Blood doesn't lie. I started the pill, but I was too late. I wanted to give myself time but didn't think, so now I'm done."

"Done? No way. You have the hottest guy on campus who is crazy in love with you. He's a little off and intimidating but rich as fuck, and you have his kid growing inside you. It's a win-win in my book."

"Yeah, you forget that he is one of the sons of The Order."

"Yeah. I get it, but––"

I interrupt her. "It means I have to marry him, and he controls my life. If he wants to cheat on me, he can, and I can't do shit about it. He can do whatever he wants. I could be his slave and I wouldn't have a choice. They have everything at their disposal. Even if I move to Greece to escape them, I'm sure they have a member there, too. They're like the fucking Illuminati."

"That's a myth, by the way."

I raise my hands and place them on my head. "Yeah, but these people aren't, Jess."

She lowers my hands and places them on my lap. I wipe my face with a tissue she picks up from the tissue box. I sniff and take a deep breath to calm my nerves down. I've been feeling emotional and crappy. I have mood swings and the smell of certain colognes make me gag—except Dravin's. His scent calms me down, if anything. It is like the child growing inside me recognizes him and knows.

"You need to tell him, Gia. He needs to know."

"I know, but I'm afraid."

"Don't be. He will be happy."

"But I have a feeling the others won't be. Like, Veronica."

Jess snorts. "I'll handle that bitch. Trust me. She has bigger things to worry about."

"How's that?"

"That's another story."

There is a knock at our door, and I try to quickly compose myself while she opens it. When she opens the door wider to see who is standing there, I sigh in relief. It's Reid.

"Hi," he greets Jess. He peers in from the doorway and sees me. I give him a watery smile. "Hey, partner."

His eyes narrow because he sees me crying. "Tell me," he says in a stern tone.

"It's nothing."

He points and looks at Jess. "Tell me," he repeats.

"She pregnant," Jess blurts.

I lay flat on the bed with a thud. "Thanks a lot, blabbermouth. Now he's going to run back to the fort and tell the puppet master."

Reid walks over and looks down at me with a knowing grin. There is something different about the way he is staring at me. My heart beats wildly like when a cat catches the mouse or the tiger pins down the gazelle. He tilts his head and looks down at my stomach, then picks up the paper I have clutched in my hand and reads it. His eyes scroll through the test results. He chuckles like in a horror movie, and Jess looks at him like, *what the fuck.*

His dark eyes meet mine, and he says, "Welcome to the Order."

THE PREY

SERIES

Lust
LUST

GIA

I'M en route to Dravin's house. When Reid found out I was pregnant, he made me feel very uneasy. The emotion that crossed his face as he saw me crying sent shivers down my spine—the kind of shivers you feel when watching a scary movie, and you can imagine what the starring characters are going through.

Reid walked closer, watching my tear-stained cheeks, and then he smiled sinisterly and gave me the expression of a man hiding a secret about the future. Like a predator that hasn't shown its true colors, and it's too late to walk away after you're caught in a cage.

So, I assume they all take their prey seriously. Dravin explained to me the ways in which the Order exerts its influence to achieve its goals. The basics of it all, yet I know there is more. He was just brushing the surface.

When I open the door to leave the building, a blast of icy air rushes in, and I wrap my winter coat more tightly about me. Temperatures are dropping, and the thought of my unborn child causes tears of unease to form in the back of my eyes. Where have I gone wrong? You'd think a guy like Dravin would try his hardest to prevent me from falling pregnant so soon. I know it's also my fault for not taking the proper precautions, even if he is what I want for my future. You can't help yourself when you fall in love. It blinds you when you're trapped in the feeling. That person is all you think about. He becomes the first thing you think about when you wake up and the last person you think about when you fall asleep. They become everything. They consume every waking moment. He consumes every waking moment.

To this day, I still remember what Dravin's dad had to say about raising a child that belonged to Dravin, but I didn't think he meant right now. When he said, "after graduation," I assumed he meant somewhere in the far future.

To be honest, at first, I thought a guy like Dravin would lose interest in a girl like me. I love the flowers, the letters, and the sex. What girl wouldn't? Obviously, from the attention he gets around here, I'm not the only one who would have fallen for him or has fallen for him.

I'm scrolling through my phone to order a ride-share when I hear the rumble of a motorcycle getting closer. I look up, and it's a black-and-red sports bike coming toward me, the exhaust causing a small cloud of smoke against the cold air. The rider is wearing all-black gear, including the helmet and visor. My heart begins to race as the rider revs the engine.

I raise my shoulders at the piercing sound as it assaults my ears. The leaves that have fallen from the trees are scattered around from the force of air emitted from the exhaust. The biker is riding on the walkway, not caring if it leads into the building.

After a few seconds, the rider cuts the engine and I take a step back, not knowing who is riding the powerful bike. Rather than going back inside the building to safety, I stand there frozen, not moving. Wondering whose face is under the helmet. His body is completely covered, not giving anything away, and I can't help but be curious.

After careful inspection, I found that the bike resembles a professional racing motorcycle—the kind you see on TV in Europe. Since the rider's face is obscured by the helmet, I have no idea who he is, but based on the sartorial choice of jacket and trousers, which are tailored to fit over wide shoulders and powerful thighs, it is obvious that the rider is male.

I take a deep breath and try to shift away from where I am staring at the unknown rider, but my legs are immobilized. I ignore the chill in the air as I watch the guy place his feet on each side of the motorcycle between his knees, then remove his gloves. As I release my breath and gaze down at the tattoos on his knuckles, I recognize the tattoos across the skin of his hands when he pulls the last covered finger. *Dravin.*

"What are you doing here? I was just about to go to your house."

He takes off his helmet, his hair tousled, but he doesn't care. In fact, he probably wouldn't care if it were sticking up in a funny manner. Dravin always looks amazing, no matter what he wears or how he wears it. Some people are just lucky that way.

He looks directly at me, and his attitude is gloomy and impenetrable. An odd feeling snakes up my spine. There are times he acts differently around me. He is quiet, reserved, like he is watching me, studying me. I'm not always sure he's the one who's been sending me letters and flowers. It's as if he were two distinct people in one package. He baffles me. As much as he piques my interest, he terrifies me. Sometimes.

"Are you sure about that?" he asks.

I nod. "Yeah, where else would I be headed to?"

He holds his helmet and gives me a side grin and chuckles, folding his arms over the gas tank of the bike and turning his head in my direction.

"What's so funny? I need to talk to you. It's important."

I want to snap at him, but I know it won't help him listen to what I have to say any better. It's unclear how he'll react to the news. How angry will he be? Disappointed? Tell me to go fuck myself. Be happy.

"What do you need to tell me that you're running off at sundown alone looking for me at my house without calling anyone to take you?" he scolds.

"What I have to tell you cannot wait," I retort.

The trembling spreads to my hands, and I release a puff of air through pursed lips, mimicking the appearance of smoke.

My hands keep trembling, and he picks up on it. A tense shiver can fool him into thinking it's the weather outside, but the truth is that I'm rather anxious.

What's the best way for me to break the news that I'm expecting? I did the math and won't start showing until after graduation, which is why I really don't want anyone to know about it.

Because it would officially initiate me into the Order, I had no intention of informing him until at least a month later. In case I miscarry. I read that first-time pregnancies could result in miscarriages.

Initially, I was hesitant to be with him because he belonged to the Order, but then I remembered the baby. It's too late. I'm too late to make that kind of decision—not because of the baby, but because I love him. I'm in love with him. There is only one way to move, and that is forward... with him.

"Get on," he says in a stern tone.

"What?" I ask, shaking my head. He can't be serious. I have never been on a motorcycle before. I shouldn't because of my condition, but it's not like I can blurt it out right here, right now.

"You heard me. Come here." He waves at me with his helmet so that I can step closer.

When I walk up, his eyes roam over my jacket. "Zip that up, and let me place the helmet over your head," he instructs.

"I don't know how to ride, and I don't think I should," I say instead. I can't tell him right now, in front of the dorm hall.

Watching him on his motorcycle reminded me of the day I first arrived at Kenyan and saw him for the first time. He was holding a helmet while pointing me in the right direction. It was apparent he rode a motorcycle, but the helmet he was holding at the time was different.

After I zip up my winter jacket like he instructed, he places the helmet over my head and fastens the chin strap. The helmet is a bit loose, but he fixes the problem and opens the visor so I can see his eyes: one light and one dark.

He motions with his fingers to the right side of the bike. "You see the pegs?"

I nod, breathing in the scent of his cologne coming from the pads inside the helmet. His voice sounds muffled because of the helmet padding against my ear, and I take a deep breath and listen to his instructions. You would think it would smell of sweat, but it smells of ocean breeze and him.

"You place one foot on each side and you wrap your hands around my waist and do not let go," He instructs. "Make sure you keep your hands on tight, alright?"

"Okay," I say, loud enough so my voice doesn't sound muffled.

Once he puts his gloves back on and fires the engine, revving the gas, the sound is more bearable with the helmet on. I place my right foot on the peg and hold on to his shoulder, swinging my leg over the back seat until I'm fully seated.

He slides his leather gloved hands over my fingers that are locked over his leather jacket at his waist.

He caresses them, and I like the feeling of being this close to him wrapped around his body. My spine is tingling with anxious anticipation when he turns the key in the ignition and starts up the bike.

As soon as I hear the click of the clutch, I brace myself since he is shifting gears on the motorcycle. Shortly after he sets foot on the road, I open my eyes and see the road underneath us, like the massive belt of a running machine.

The asphalt on the road is going at a breakneck pace. He's not reckless, but traveling 50 mph on a motorbike is different from doing so in a vehicle. Every one of your senses is amplified, and you feel every gust of wind and bump on the road. The only things that count are your emotions and the events occurring around you at the moment. I can simultaneously hear the machine whirring between my legs and feel the firmness of his muscles as I lean against his back. As if there is no separation between us. Danger right below but safe above having him in my arms.

After ten minutes, I glance to my left and see that we are no longer on the street where Dravin lives. He takes a corner into a street I'm not familiar with, but I can see immediately that the homes there are grander and more spacious. Partially obscured by tall gates and high walls.

A greater sense of foreboding as we pass each gate. These residences are more like estates, complete with massive gates and tall hedges on all sides.

Trees moan and swing as they shed their leaves. My jacket isn't protecting me from the wind's icy sting, and I don't feel Dravin tensing up or shivering in the chilly wind. Therefore, his suit must be designed for this kind of weather.

I'm relieved when the black iron gate swings open toward him as he slows down. He waits until there is enough room for the bike to pass through without having to wait for it to completely open. The sting of the chill is quickly getting to me.

A dark-gray stone walk leads to double doors of a house that gleams gold from their windows. The outside wall sconces give forth the same warm light as the inside ones, but they are powered not by bulbs but by fire. To my right are six black garage doors.

After the left garage door is entirely open, there are seven more bikes in a row, different brands and models, their beautiful paint jobs glistening beneath the glow of the garage lights.

He taps my leg, which I take to be a signal to get off, and then he extends his arm out, palm up, to help me maintain my balance as I swing my leg over.

Once I am on solid ground, he drives the bike forward and parks it inside, moving the kickstand with the heel of his boot. My eyes look around the massive house, taking it all in.

Once the engine is switched off, the stillness engulfs me. The silence mixed with a small ringing in my ears from the loud bike. He walks over to where he left me standing, the sound of his boots over the cobblestone driveway, watching me fumbling with the chin strap.

His gloves are removed, and his warm fingers glide over mine, and he undoes the strap. He squeezes his fingers over my freezing hands and his lips curl down into a grimace.

He quickly lifts the helmet off my head, and my hands fly to pat down the strands that stick up. I run my fingers over the long tresses of my hair, noticing they are slightly knotted from the ride over, but not too bad.

I'm about to ask him whose house this is, when his voice floats back over from placing his helmet on a shelf in the garage. "Let's get you inside. It's getting too cold out here."

"Where are we?" I ask.

He looks around, and his countenance is unsure. For some reason, I can't quite place it. Something seems odd with his attitude. In some ways, it is him, but in others, it isn't. To me, he still looks the same. He has the same gait but a very different demeanor.

The Dravin standing before me is not the Dravin I know; he seems possessed. In my opinion, this is not the same Dravin I fell in love with. This is a rare side of him I've only seen a few times, but trying to get to know him better, I didn't give it much thought. I constructed the reason for his actions in my mind as him coming to grips with the evil that lurks within him. There is clearly something sinister inside him, if I had any doubts before. Something about him appears threatening. Dangerous.

Looking at his brighter left eye, I see that the right one is as dark as a storm at sea. It reminds me of the moment before a thunderstorm breaks out when the first black clouds roll in and the lightning strikes the water. Illuminating the dark depths.

He leans in toward me, his gaze fixed on mine. "You said you were on your way to my house." He points to the entrance. "This is my house."

Incredulity makes me raise an eyebrow. *What the fuck?*

My throat clears and my chin goes up. "You know the house I was talking about. Stop attempting to screw with my mind; I have no idea how many homes you have. You should have said something if you're in a grumpy mood; then I wouldn't have gone with you when I could have gone back to my room."

His face breaks out in a broad smile. I feel him come closer until his lips are almost brushing mine. He examines my top lip before moving on to the rest of my face and then my jacket.

He's on the cusp now of bringing our lips together; I need only to sway a centimeter for our lips to connect. Damn him. He makes me weak. When I'm with him, I totally lose my sense of reason.

"You know what I meant, Dravin," I whisper.

The tip of his tongue peeks out of his mouth. He tilts his head like he is going to devour my lips in a single kiss, but he doesn't. "You're right. I am in a mood, but it has to do with me not being inside of you. I want you on my bed with your legs spread out while I decide which way I'm going to fuck you with my tongue and then how I'm going to feed my dick to your pussy."

The movement of his thumb causes my chest to rise and fall. My thighs clench, trying to catch the drip of my arousal as it slides down my thighs while the cool air fans the heat breaking out all over my skin.

His thumb pulls my bottom lip, exposing my teeth. "Such a pretty mouth. There is nothing I want more than to keep you in my bed."

"I am in your bed. I practically live in your bed."

I'm more in his bed at his house than my own dorm room. Sometimes, I miss Jess, but then Dravin is inside me, filling me. Making me forget that I'm in college and that it's my senior year. It's like my future doesn't exist. Only the present. When I'm with Dravin, nothing else matters except us.

"This is my father's house."

He brought me here. Why?

"Why?" I ask.

He knows that I'm asking why he brought me to his parents' house.

His thumb slides across my bottom lip. "Why not?" he counters.

I shiver with eagerness. He brought me here to sleep with him in his bed at this house, but I didn't come with him to have sex. I came to tell him that I'm pregnant.

JESS

SHORTLY AFTER GIA LEFT, Reid was texting on his phone, possibly alerting Dravin that she was on her way. From the moment we met, Gia has been one of my closest friends. In truth, my only friend.

I'm from a boring tiny town in Ohio where the only exciting event is the football game. It's uncommon for girls who live on the outskirts of town in trailers to have any close friends. Well, the good kind. The type of friends that don't get into trouble.

Living in a trailer park, those types of friends don't exist. Why? They've earned a bad reputation as people who aren't deserving of reverence. Unless you have money. Then everyone is your friend.

The child who lives in a trailer with her single mother receives little notice from the outside world. Most people automatically assume that someone who lives in a trailer park is either a drug user themselves or the child of someone who is. Once that child grows up, it doesn't mean they won't look at you differently or feel sorry for you. It just means you're just part of the cycle, and it starts all over again.

"Are you coming later?" Reid asks as he looks at my nightstand, acting like he is interested in anything I keep there.

He turns his head to the side, watching me as I sit on the bed cross-legged like a lion, ready to pounce.

When he asks whether I plan to drop by later, he means for sex. Sorry to be the bearer of bad news, but the answer is no. I had sex with Reid twice and once with Valen, all in the same room, albeit never at the same time.

I have my limits. My reasons for wanting it, but then I have my guilt. The only way I am able to cope with it is to separate emotion from sex.

It was a hard lesson to learn, but after high school and what I went through with the boy I had a crush on since eighth grade, I'm viewed as less than worthy.

Listening to Gia and what she had to say about the secret society called the Order and what Dravin told her, I was intrigued but also scared.

They consider us outsiders. *Prey.* Gia has nothing to worry about because she has the attention of one of the sons of Kenyan, and he will destroy anyone who touches her or breathes the wrong way in her direction.

She has people who care about her in her corner, including me. Reid and

Valen are obviously close to Dravin, and they take care of who they consider to be their own. And right now, that includes Gia.

As for me, these people can try to break me, but they haven't figured out I'm already fucked up and broken. Sex is just a way for me to forget what they did to me back home.

What falling for a guy without thinking can cost you, but he showed me what I meant to him. How they all saw me. How everyone that finds out where I came from will see me. They will judge me. They will hurt me. They will try to destroy me. And now, prey on me.

I notice Reid pretending to be interested in going through my stuff. It's as if you're pretending to be interested in what you're looking at by caressing it and stroking it again, but your attention is elsewhere. My favorite string bracelet, which he is caressing without realizing it, is usually hidden from view.

It was the first friendship bracelet I made, hoping to find a friend when I was twelve. I had enough materials to make two, but no takers. I was planning to give one to Gia since we have stuck together and we get along.

I watch him as he holds and stretches it and I reach out to snatch it from his grasp before he ruins it. After I tell him that I'm not interested in his offer. Who knows how he will react? I'm not afraid of Reid or anyone who goes to Kenyan. I've already met with evil. I know how it deceives. How it dances.

How it takes.

How it feeds.

"I don't think that is a good idea."

His eyes flock to mine like two dark orbs pinning me to my bed. He tilts his head, raising his brows in surprise. I don't think anyone has denied Reid before.

"Why?" he asks.

I lick my lips nervously, turning the black string of the bracelet with my fingers. Rubbing it with the pads of my thumbs. The silence, beginning to stretch like an invisible band between us, is ready to snap.

"I'm not going to have sex with you. I'm not interested in complicating things."

His nostrils flare and he yanks the bracelet from my fingers, making me flinch. When I try to reach for it, he leans close until our eyes are on the same level. When I think he is going to give me back the bracelet, his lip curls in a menacing smile.

My heart sinks when he lifts the bracelet with one hand and takes his fingers from his other and pulls it, snapping it in half. I blink back at the sudden rise of tears.

His look is stern and unyielding. The two pieces of thread fall from his fingers like something filthy you want to get off your hands. I hold back the wrath that is boiling to the surface of my skin, ready to spill from my mouth. I know to him it's trivial—a stupid piece of string made by a twelve-year-old.

It isn't the kind you find in a store or even in a market. But to me, it means more. Like a diamond tennis bracelet. Something I feel proud of because I made it. Something no one could take away from me.

He leans close. His tone is deep and ominous. "You're right. Come to think of it. Garret was right. You are a bad lay."

He leaves the room without turning around to look back. I feel like he's trying to cut me in two with his words. To hurt me. But all they do is remind me that he isn't different from the rest. He sees me as nothing.

Unworthy.

Easy to destroy.

It's what they all think of me. I'm just used to it.

GIA

I FOLLOW him through the door of his parents' home. A place he has never taken me aback, until now. I find it odd that he hasn't taken me here before. The times I have met up with him or slept over, it is always at his house one block over.

My intention was to tell him at his house where we would have privacy. Away from prying ears, like his father or any other staff, they must have been working here because there is no way they do not have any staff on hand. This place is enormous. Like an old museum. There is elaborately carved wood paneling on half of the walls. High windows. As I peer through the thick scarlet drapes, I take note of the five ornate chandeliers that hang low from the ceiling, each omitting a warm glow like candles that make it clear that the Bedfords are fond of low lighting. There's a spooky air of darkness and silence about it.

A piano sits to the right of the main window, which looks out over the front lawn and the enormous fountain guarded by a gargoyle. Gee, not only would it be a fun addition to your Halloween decorations, but it also gives off an air of eerie presence. It's as though vampires have made their home here—something out of a vampire and werewolves novel. The house smells like wood, expensive carpet, and rich bergamot.

Dravin ascends the grand staircase, which is carpeted in the middle by a red runner and has dark wood steps on the sides. The railings are of the same color with gargoyles on the ends. I'm thankful he makes it easy for me to keep up by going at a slower clip.

Once we reach the landing, there is a long hallway that splits to the left and right, creating two separate wings. At the end, there is a large stained-glass window with a distinct symbol similar to the one on campus. It appears centuries old and is not something you can easily do. He walks past three doors on each side, with lighted sconces in between each room casting a glow.

He finally stops in front of a huge solid wood door and turns the antique handle, swinging the wood door open with a slight creaking sound. He walks in, removing his jacket and I take two steps forward and follow him inside.

This room is very different than his own personal home. It has a king-size bed, but its decor is more classic and even ancient. When he walks in, and I come in a little closer, I can see that the shelves on each side of the wooden desk are stacked with books. The books look like they have been here for quite some time. Like they are first editions and not copies you buy in a local bookstore. Some have leather binding and cream paper that have seen countless hands smoothing the pages. I had no idea he was a reader or even enjoyed books. From our one-on-one conversations, I assumed he was primarily interested in computers.

As he takes off his jacket and lays it on the bed, removing his tee, I take a deep breath, watching the motion of his body. The rippling effect in his abdominal muscles, resembling the powerful strength of an animal in action, makes me aware of him.

He faces me shirtless, staring at me while I do the same to him, but my eyes are everywhere except his face. Memorizing every dip and groove of his muscles under taught skin, the countless lines and shading of his tattoos.

"I want to talk," I say.

His expression is severe, not in fury but in desire. He has given me this look before, right before he asks me to come to bed so he can touch me. Kiss me. Fuck me.

"Later," he quips.

"It's important," I counter.

"I know, but right now, there is something more important I must do first."

My eyes dart to the left and then to the right looking around his room. The intricate dark wallpaper, the dark wood floors with red carpet under the imposing wood bed with satin sheets.

Unfamiliar.

Cold.

Distant.

His passionate eyes connect with mine, and he strides forward intently like a predator. I take a few steps back until I feel the cold, hard wall near the doorway behind me.

"What are you doing?" I ask nervously.

He would never harm me, yet the expression in his eyes is different. Calculating. When his nose brushes up against my cheek, I get a whiff of his scent. A hint of leather and motorcycle in his cologne. Manly. Intoxicating.

His lips graze the flesh on my lower cheek, jaw, and neck until he reaches the place directly beneath my ear that prompts all my nerve endings to rise on alert. Goose bumps spread on my skin like an avalanche effect, causing my bra to feel tight over my breasts. He reaches and unzips my jacket with skillful fingers, pulling it over my shoulders without taking his lips from my skin.

My heart is pounding in my chest. My lower belly flutters and I don't know if it's because I subconsciously know there is a baby growing inside me or if it's him causing havoc over my body.

He pins me against the wall and slips my jacket down my arms. Having him so near causes a thumping and a lulling in my chest in a rhythm I can't control. It's intense, and my core starts to pool in need, awakening all my senses.

"Do you remember, Gia? Our first time," he rasps.

I close my eyes, remembering the day I sought him out. Mad at him for ignoring me. Mad at him because he was talking to another girl who wasn't me. I ran into his arms and let him have me in front of the fireplace.

I nod and whisper, "Yes. I remember."

When his lips brush the skin just below my right ear, I gasp and maybe even whimper. I feel a tightening in my thighs, consumed by everything, his very presence, from the scent of wood in his room to the tenderness of his kisses to the graze of his teeth on my skin, is entirely seductive.

"You remember how full you were when I was pounding your pretty pussy? How much I loved it when you told me to go deeper, breaking that pussy in."

Oh god. When I close my eyes, I can still feel the sensation of him fucking me so hard that day, I let out a low groan. It only hurt for a few seconds and then he made it feel good right after. He never talks about that day in front of the fireplace. Maybe it's because of the way he acted after. It was both so good and so fucked up.

"Yes," I whisper, wanting him inside me again.

"Did you like it, baby? Do you want me inside you again?"

"I need to tell you something," I say on a moan, trying to tell him what I came to say, but I want him. I want him inside me.

"You can tell me after you spread your legs for me. I want you in my bed." He leans into me, pinning me. His lips hovering over mine. He wraps his hand over my neck. His thumb pressing over my pulse. "In this bed. I don't want to take you soft," he rasps. "I don't want to take you hard."

Fuck. He slides two fingers inside my pants, feeling my wet slit with the pads of his fingers. I moan, arching my back and rubbing myself on them in want. In need.

"I want to take you deep. Deep inside you, so you can remember me."

"I do remember you," I say on a whimper, getting confused. "Always."

He hooks one finger inside my wet folds and captures my lips with his and I'm lost. My purpose all but forgotten and the only thing that is left is the need to feel him inside me. He kisses me deep, stroking his tongue inside my mouth, taking all my breaths, exploring my need for him. Consuming me all over again. We break apart. We come together. Over and over, but it's not enough.

When he finally pulls away, our foreheads are still pressed together, and our breaths are mixed like we're breathing the same air. "I need to be inside you, Gia," he says on a breathless whisper.

He stands back and watches as I take off my shirt, pants, and shoes until I'm left wearing just my lace underwear. Rather than just undoing his pants, he takes off every piece of clothing till he stands nude in front of me. When my eyes flick to his cock, it's standing at attention to the point of leaking. A drop of precum crests on the tip, almost dripping on the wood floor. My tongue snakes out on my lower lip, wanting to be the one to taste the drop of his cum.

Dropping to my knees, I look up while my hand wraps around his thick shaft. I stroke him from root to tip so the bead of cum lands on my fingers, coating my hand to use it as a balm so I can stroke him.

He spreads his hand on the wall to hold himself while he watches me lick my lips and take him inside my mouth on a moan. I have never given him a blow job because I didn't know how, but I secretly watched porn online. When the moment was right, I wanted to pleasure him like he does to me when we are alone in his room.

He groans when I take him deeper, savoring the sweet, salty taste of him. "Jesus."

His other hand slides behind the back of my head while I take him as deep as I can go. His thumb caresses my jaw as tears begin to pool from my eyes.

His lips part, but his bottom lip is pinched between his teeth. "Such a pretty mouth."

Dravin's cock is thick and long and has a slight curve that I love. His piercings roll on my tongue as I slide back and forth, feeling the metal and smooth skin.

The salty taste of him on my tongue explodes as he grunts, fucking my mouth. "Yeah, baby. Just like that. Take it."

I gasp when he speeds up, going deeper with each thrust in my mouth. My eyes dart up and tears stream down my face with each thrust.

His eyes meet mine, as his bottom lip is still snagged between his teeth. The look of pleasure across his face spurs me on, moving faster, but he pulls out right before he comes.

My tongue licks my lips and his eyes darken. He lifts me gently so I can stand, and then he carries me like a bride to the bed. "I need to be inside you," he growls.

My arms wrap around his neck, my cheek resting on his chest, and I breathe him in. He lays me down on the thick, deep-red comforter, pulling the corner so all that is left is the cool red satin sheet.

He lays me gently like a sacred offering, settling between my legs so that my thighs are spread wide. He flicks his finger over the lace of my panties, twirling the fabric and tugging it tight over my skin and ripping it clean off.

He stares at my sex, licking his lips. "Is this for me?" he asks.

I nod, wanting to reach my arms out so I can touch the muscles on his abs and chest. His eyes flick over me slowly until they land on my face. He moves forward, placing the palm of his hand to hold himself up on the mattress while he spreads my dark, long hair over his pillows.

"I love your dark hair over my red sheets and pillows. It's beautiful."

My lips lift in a smile at the compliment. He fists his cock and reaches over to the nightstand and pulls the drawer to grab a condom. I frown because three days ago he didn't use one. What changed? He doesn't know that I'm pregnant but either way, a condom at this point is pointless. I didn't even have time to start birth control after going to the doctor, but he wanted me not to take them.

He doesn't let me ponder it further. He slides the condom on and slides inside me fast, deep as he can go, and I gasp, holding his shoulders like I'm trying to catch my breath.

He closes his eyes and stills inside me. "You're so tight."

I tilt my head up on the pillow and slide my hands down his arms. When his eyes open, I stare, lost inside their depths at the feel of him inside of me. Filling me. Full of him.

"You're so big," I say on a breathless whisper.

He grins. "Say that again."

I smile and he hovers over me, his lips over mine, waiting for me to repeat the words. "You're so big," I repeat.

He slides out and then goes deeper, taking my lips between his and plunging his tongue in my mouth, twirling it with mine.

He fucks my mouth with his tongue at the same time his cock plunges deep inside of me, making my orgasm climb. The slaps of our skin echo inside his room while I moan and he groans with each thrust.

He breaks the kiss and looks down at where we are joined. The shaft of his cock rubbing on my clit as he moves in and out. He goes in deeper like he promised. So deep I feel like I'm going to break apart.

"Dravin," I gasp.

He grips my hips and fucks me in a rhythm. The wet sounds we make as his cock drives into me fill the room, like wet slaps on wet skin. I lift my hips off the mattress and he meets me with every thrust. My tits bounce with every stroke, with every pounding assault, until my orgasm reaches its peak, and I scream his name.

"Dravin! I'm coming."

"I know," he says. His cock swells and with one last thrust, he slams into me, spilling inside the condom. "This pussy is mine, too."

My eyebrows rise in confusion. "What?"

What does he mean? He isn't making sense. He slides out of me and ties the condom and moves off the bed to dispose of it, walking through double doors leading to what must be the bathroom. I sit up on the bed and pull the sheet over my breasts, waiting for him to come back in the room.

He strides toward me as he reenters the room, confident with his cock firmly up in the air.

He kneels on the side of the bed and pulls the sheet away from my body. "Don't cover up from me. I want to see you. All of you. Every time I come for you, you spread those pretty thighs for me. Understood?"

I flinch at his cold tone. Why is he acting this way with me? What have I done? I hear my phone go off. He looks down at my jacket, where my phone's ringtone is relentlessly vibrating with the sound. A series of text messages follow, one right after another.

The back of his skull snaps up. The quirk of his brow rises in mock surprise. "Hmm. I wonder who that could be?" He slides off the bed and walks over.

"Give me my phone, Dravin," I snap in a hard tone.

The abrupt change in his attitude toward me has irritated and upset me. Everything about the situation since he picked me up in front of the dorm building has been off. There seems to be a shift. Taking me to his father's home, having sex in this room. His tone just now. The things he's said.

At first, I shrugged it off at him being in one of his moods and then me trying to tell him that I'm pregnant. I would never deny him. If he needs me, then I'm there. I love him. I love the child growing inside of me. He does get moody sometimes, but this is over the top. A cold fear begins to crawl up my spine. He finds my phone yet makes no move to give it to me.

"Give me my phone," I demand.

He tilts his head, and his smile makes my stomach drop. "No. I want to see who keeps blowing up your phone."

He begins to scroll through it, and anger at him invading my privacy has me scrambling off the bed and charging over to where he stands, not caring that I'm naked.

I reach for my phone, and he lifts it away from my grasp and sticks his other arm out to hold me back. I huff and move to the side, reaching out, but it's useless. He is taller and stronger. He slides his thumb, scrolling through the messages with a wicked smile.

"What the hell, Dravin!" I shout.

He lowers his hand and gives me the phone. I take it and see what has him smiling at me like the cat that got the cream. I scroll through the messages and look at him with a frown.

The messages are from him.

> Dravin: Hey, where are you? I was at your dorm and Jess said you left for my house.

> Dravin: Raven?

> Dravin: Why aren't you answering me? I keep calling you.

> Dravin: I'm home and you're not here.

> Dravin: Are you ok? Call me back. Text me. I need to know that you are ok. Please, Raven. I'm worried.

I look up, completely at a loss for words. Confused. My hands shake because I don't know what is going on. Is this a dream? Am I hallucinating? Is he crazy?

He walks over to his jacket, slides his phone out and places his phone to his ear. He watches me as he talks to whomever he calls. "I have your little bird," he says, licking his lips. "I must say. She tastes just as good as the first time I popped her little cherry. You did good."

He smiles at me and then hangs up, ending the call and throwing the phone on the bed.

GIA†

INHALING DEEPLY, I approach him, my nostrils flaring. "Is this some kind of sick joke?"

There's a hardness to his gaze, and I feel a mixture of anger and helplessness at my inability to make sense of the situation. Something is wrong, but I can't figure out what.

"Get back on the bed," he says sternly.

"Fuck you," I seethe.

"Then get on the bed, and I'll show you how to fuck." He leans closer. "How to really fuck. You like it when I fuck you dirty. I can see it on your face and in the way your pussy takes my cock. Nice and deep. Your pretty nipples, begging me to flick my tongue over them while I break you in."

As he approaches, I back up. Tears burn the backs of my eyes like acid, making me feel cornered and defenseless.

He lowers his voice. "I bet your pussy is begging for it right now. The want and need leaking from that tight cunt down your thighs. Whatever happens in the next five minutes, just remember, I will always be here to lick your sin."

I'm scared and so turned on. He slides his fingers between my thighs and I whimper when he feels my cum leaking.

He drops to his knees and I turn my head as he nuzzles his face on my pussy, sucking and licking the cum that has dripped down my thighs.

"Hmm. Like I said, dirty. Just how I like it."

On instinct, my hand slaps him, hard, across his face, but he just laughs. My hand stings in pain at how hard I slapped him, but he only chuckles.

"Get off me."

"I'm not on you."

He stands and his face is dripping with my cum sliding down his chin. He rushes toward me before I have a chance to move away and rubs it on my face. The smell of me smeared on my neck and cheek. Bastard.

He laughs. "Like I said, I'll always be here to lick your sin. To taste you. To fuck you."

The door to his room opens with a slam, and my head turns to see who entered, and my knees give out. They buckle, but he keeps me from falling, lifting and carrying me to the bed.

I scoot up until I reach the headboard, gripping the sheet to cover my body and take deep breaths in shock. In fear.

I point at the two men in front of me with a shaking finger.

He stands and the look of rage that crosses his face mirrors the other. "What have you done!"

"T-there are two of you," I stammer, and blinding hot tears slide down my face as I try to gulp in air.

I sniff, closing and opening my eyes, hoping it's a trick of the light or my mind. Maybe I'm crazy. I close my eyes and then open them again, but it's still the same. Two men identical in every way are standing in front of me. They're twins.

"Dravin?"

"Yes," they both say at the same time.

My hand slides over my hair, trying to find something to touch. It's real. They're twins. Oh my god. I have slept with both of them. Realization dawns. I'm pregnant, and I don't know which one is the father. They lied.

I look up with tears sliding down my face and they are both standing at the foot of the bed.

"I'm pregnant," I blurt.

One of them smiles and then the other. The Dravin I had just sex with gets dressed. You would think the other would be upset, but he isn't. This must be normal for them. They sleep with the same women. I bet they don't even know there are two of them. I wonder who else knows besides his father. All I know is that they all lied to me.

I watch them, trying to find a way to tell them apart, but I can't. They're the same. The tattoos. Eyes. Hair. They even dress the same, but they can act differently. I just saw how the one I just slept with treated me. Different.

I don't know which one is the father, but the first thing that came to my mind was to tell them the result of their sick, twisted game. I'm pregnant. It's all I know right now.

"I'm sorry, Raven."

My eyes pop open, and I speak to the Dravin, who just came in. "I'm not your fucking Raven. Don't you dare call me that. You lied. Both of you. I just... want to get out of here."

"I'm afraid that isn't possible. If you are pregnant, which I'm assuming you really are and found out recently, you belong to us now. I know we lied to you, but you need to understand some things. Rule—"

I interrupt him, fueled by a rage that I can't control. "I don't give a fuck about your twisted sick rules. You can't make me do shit. I feel disgusted and used. I hate you. This isn't love or want. This is sick and twisted and—"

"You will learn to accept it," Dravin interrupts.

"You will learn to accept us because there is not one without the other. We are both the same physically in every way. We both have the same name but spelled differently. One with an *i* and one with an *e* before the last letter in our first name. The baby isn't mine," the other twin adds.

My head begins spinning, piecing things together. So, Dravin is the father. The other one isn't. How would he know?

I throw my hands up and the sheet falls to my waist before I realize it's too late. Shit. I'm so mad.

Both of their eyes land on my breasts. I try to cover myself and they both try to look away. I know they have both seen me naked and made me come more than once, but still.

"And I'm supposed to accept this. I'm supposed to swallow the fact that you two lied to me while fucking me. What now? You pimp me out?"

Both of them whip their heads at me in sync, and it's as if they are clones. They have the same face, tattoos, even their cocks are pierced the same way. There is no way to know which one is which.

Draven pinches his nose, and I can easily see what I just said annoys him. Well, that's too fucking bad. They are both assholes.

Draven lifts his head and is the first one to speak. He places his arm on Dravin. "I'll tell her. It's better if it comes from me."

"Please. Spit it out. How bad could it get? I'm pregnant by a man who shares me with his twin brother for fun."

Dravin winces and his expression looks torn, but that's too bad. He could have been honest with me. They are both crazy, and the one I just slept with is probably even crazier by the way he talked to me a few minutes ago.

"You will marry my older brother. He gets to marry, and I don't. It disrupts the Order because we are one of the three founding families. It's been one of the rules since the beginning. There could only be one to carry it out. I don't marry, but I get other perks."

I cross my hands protectively. "Like what?" I say sarcastically.

"You. I also get you. You will have all of our children. Only you. You get to have us both. Married to one but not to the other. Unless one of us dies. If one of us dies, you have to marry the other. Either way, you get us both."

I shake my head. "That's sick. Why would you share me? What would you tell our children?"

"It isn't. It's what we both have agreed on since we were old enough to understand. Our children will understand there is only one mother. One woman."

"But if I'm married, I have no right to expect you to be faithful."

I can't believe I'm even arguing about this. I'm going insane. Have them both?

"True. But it won't be that way. We both want you." He looks down at my stomach. "Obviously, we do. We can't wait to see you swollen with our babies. No one on the outside who isn't part of the Order would know which one is with you. It's all within the Order. No one will question anything, or they will die," Draven says.

I laugh sarcastically and point my finger between both of them. "So what? I bed-hop?" I shrug my shoulders and raise my chin. "I make a schedule so you can come to my bed at night? Is there a way I can tell you two apart?"

I swallow nervously when Draven walks forward on the side of the bed to my right and Dravin to my left. My heart starts to beat faster, wondering what they are going to show me. If there is a way, how can both of them be so alike in every way? There isn't a piercing or tattoo on one that isn't on the other. If there is, I haven't noticed.

I'm sitting naked under the sheet in the middle of the bed, and for the first time with Dravin, I'm scared. They both see me tense and one brother gazes at the other.

"Don't be scared," Dravin says.

I lower my head, and my fists squeeze the sheet. I need to get out of here, leave, and think. This is all too much.

Tears fall down my cheeks like a faucet that keeps dripping and there is no way to fix it. "I want to leave," I say softly.

"Don't leave," Draven says.

I look to my right at the face I thought was his brother's. "It was you, wasn't it? The first time."

I know it was him and not Dravin. There is a way to tell them apart, and it's when you let them fuck you. They treat their woman differently in bed. When they touch you—it's different. One is pure sex, and the other is pure lust. One twin is darker than the other. Dirtier than the other.

"Yes," he says, not denying it.

He looks at his brother on the other side of the bed. "I had you first, and I took your innocence. I should have stopped you that day, but that isn't who I am. I couldn't say no because I was going to have you either way."

My eyes dart to his face, pure anger rising. He is so sure of himself.

"At the time, and even today, you might have had me. But I mistook you for your brother. Every moan and scream was for him and never for you," I seethe.

Draven flinches and hardens his jaw at my words, like the slap in the face I gave him earlier, but I can tell that my words cut him deep.

My head whips to Dravin and I swallow the bile of anger coming on from my stomach from his lies and betrayal.

"Don't cry," he says.

How can I not? He's a liar, and I fell for it—all of it. I swallowed the bet with Veronica and the other stuff, but this is my life. I still have a choice, and I'm making it.

"I'm not marrying you. I don't want anything from you."

He shakes his head. "You don't know what you're saying."

I snort, wiping my face. I sniff and lift my head, looking up at the wood paneling on the ceiling in a room that I thought was his and I laugh at my stupidity. Jess warned me. She fucking warned me. I believed all the bullshit he spilled. The flowers. The letters. It was all a trap. His father's words suddenly haunt me. *Breed.*

My eyes settle on him as he tries to reach for me and I move out of his grasp. "You touch me, and I'll scream," I warn him.

His hand falls and the expression that crosses his face is full of remorse.

"I don't want to be with you. Either of you. I want to be left alone. Please, let me get my clothes so I can go home."

"You can't tell anyone you're pregnant," Dravin says.

I laugh sarcastically. "Do you think after what I just learned I would want to tell anyone my baby is from you? I hate you both."

Draven leans close to the bed. "You can't run from us, Gianna. You belong to us, and you will always belong to us."

I shake my head. "I have a choice, and I'm making it. My choice is to be alone. You two have had your fun. Now go fuck around and prey on some other girl who falls for your shit."

Dravin storms off, leaving the room and slamming the door on his way out. Draven turns his head, gazing at me, his eyes roaming all over my body, sending a shiver up my spine.

"He cares about you, and he is happy when he is with you. Don't take that away from him."

"Is he happy knowing that ten minutes ago, your cock was inside me? Does that make him happy? Does it make him happy that he trapped me and lied to me?"

"He will do anything to have you. If it makes me happy, then yes. As long as it's me and no one else. No one touches you except us." His eyes darken, and I see the evil that lurks inside him. "No one, Gia. I'm the one that gets his hands dirty if someone touches you. Your moans and screams are for us."

"You mean you kill them," I retort.

"If it comes to that, then yes. But for you, I'll do worse. My brother has to carry out the Bedford name as the head of the Order. I'm just the backup. It is why I can't marry anyone unless I have to marry you. I can sleep with whoever I want, and I don't have the responsibility that will fall upon my brother when the time comes. I just have to make sure I stand in for him when needed."

"How long?"

He knows I mean,*how long have you been doing this?* He walks over and collects my clothes sans panties from the floor. My panties are on the bed, torn to pieces. I grab my bra, pants, and sweater. I reach to grab the shredded fabric off the bed, but he is quicker and snatches them from the bed. I fall on my back, looking up at the ceiling.

He leans over the bed in my line of vision, holding the fabric in front of me but out of reach. "These are mine."

"They're torn."

He tilts his head. "And?"

"They're trash."

He gives me a side grin. "Not to me," he remarks, stuffing them in his pocket.

"You get off on your victim's panties?"

"Who said I have victims? Not of the female variety. Do you know how many girls would kill to be where you are right now?"

I continue to dress, sliding my pants up my thighs, making sure they are on correctly. My eyes find his when I slide my sweater over my head and glide my fingers through my hair. Cocky much?

"Let me guess, hundreds," I mock, scooting off his big bed. "I must have been number four hundred and ninety-nine."

My feet land on the carpet on the side of the bed and I make my way to place my feet inside my shoes, grabbing the jacket, needing to get the hell out of there.

When I grab my phone, he chuckles. "Funny. Actually, six hundred and twenty-two."

Great, I have a number. I guess I set myself up for that one. I turn to leave, but he grabs my wrist, tugging me to him.

Clenching my teeth, I lift my chin. "Let me go, Draven."

"I will, but I need to ask you something. My brother hates himself right now, but he will get over it, or maybe he won't. He can be moody."

"I don't care how he feels. He is a liar, and so are you," I say through gritted teeth. "Like I said, you had your fun. I have a responsibility to plan for and choices to make."

"Like what? You don't have to worry about anything for the rest of your life. You will want for nothing."

"How about love, trust, honesty?"

He pulls me tighter, and I cringe. He bends his head close with a tic in his jaw. "You don't have to fear me. The only thing you have to worry about is when I come for you. And I will come for you, Gianna. I will take pleasure in your body and I will make sure you like it. Where I come from and in the real world, what you're asking for are complicated emotions that don't exist. What does exist is sex, lust, lies, betrayal, and greed. My brother and I are guilty of all of that. I know you're upset, and I get it. But don't think you have power because you carry a Bedford in your belly because you don't." He lowers his voice above a whisper and my legs begin to tremble. "I know Reid, Valen, and Jess know about your pregnancy. I know everything. What you say and when. So be careful, and don't piss me off."

I lift my chin. "Or what?" I challenge.

He bares his teeth. "I will make sure you hurt. There are other types of pain, Gianna. I would never physically hurt you, but make no mistake, I will make you hurt."

"Fuck you."

"I already did, and now I'm losing my patience. I need you to leave. Six hundred and twenty-three is waiting to take me down her throat."

"You're disgusting."

"No, I'm telling you to get the fuck out. I'm done with you. I want a woman who knows what she is doing in bed. I'm wondering how the hell my brother got you pregnant. I figured he would have taught you a few things by now. You need to learn how to pleasure a man and the way things are going, I need someone else to meet my needs."

My lower lip trembles. I don't know why, but his words sting. They shouldn't, but they do. My eyes swim with tears that I refuse to let fall. I rub my lips together to not break in front of him and silently nod, stepping back.

I grip my phone in my hand and scroll to the app, ordering an Uber to pick me up outside his gate.

I was floating in a cloud, thinking that the news of my pregnancy would be my biggest worry. I thought he was Dravin when he came on his motorcycle, but he knew. They all knew. I thought the looks I was receiving from people who are part of the Order were because I had Dravin's attention, but it was bigger than that. This is over. Whatever we had—is over. They broke me. He broke me. They deceived me. I'm trapped.

JESS

I HEAR our dorm room door swing open and Gia comes inside crying. Fear claws inside my belly. Something happened.

"What happened?"

In my arms, she sniffs and cries. I hold her close, rocking her gently back and forth, exactly like my mother used to do for me when I was a victim of bullying at school and had to come home to lick my wounds. Holding her close and without speaking to her, I move her black hair off her face.

After twenty minutes of rocking her slowly while seated on my bed, I whisper, "Shh. It's okay, Gia. Tell me when you are ready. Tell me what happened. What did he do?"

I know this has to do with Dravin. I don't want to push her, but she shouldn't be crying this way. She's pregnant.

She wipes her face and takes a deep breath, her sobs racking her body. When she sees the tears streaking my cheeks, she bursts into sobs and tells me everything.

After she's done, I take a moment to ultimately make sense of what she is telling me.

"There's two of them?" I pause. "Motherfuckers."

She nods, grabbing a tissue from her nightstand and blowing her nose. "Yeah, I know. I've been sleeping with identical twin brothers."

"There is no way of telling them apart?"

She shakes her head. "There is only one way."

I raise my brows, trying to figure it out myself. I don't even know if I've seen the other one.

Intrigued about the whole thing, I ask, "How?"

"When they have sex. It's different. The way they treat you."

I point at her as realization dawns. "Your first time. It was with the evil fucked-up one?"

That's what we dubbed Draven with an *E*. The evil twin or, rather, the crazier one. But in all honesty, they're both fucked up.

"Yes. Thinking about it, when I was feeling like a used whore, I remember that there were two times he used a condom."

"When was the second time?"

She looks up and then averts her eyes. "Today." When she found out, she thought it was Dravin with the me being—hypothetically, the nicer one.

I raise my hand, indicating she doesn't have to give me details. "Gotcha."

She tells me everything he said to her, and I sigh, running my fingers through my hair, squeezing tight on the strands to get a grip on my anger for her and releasing my hair that I straightened with my flat iron.

"Fuck them. Just finish your senior year. You won't even be showing until you graduate, anyway. You can find a good job, and I will help you. I always wanted to learn how to be a mom. I would be honored to be Auntie Jess."

She laughs through her tears, trying to wipe her red nose with another tissue. "Auntie Jess. I like it," she says with a smile.

"You don't need them. Forget about them. We will keep quiet and no one has to know. You don't have to marry anyone. Hey, and about screwing both of them, at least they look alike, and you can't forget their names."

We both stare at each other for a second and burst out laughing. Making light of a fucked-up situation.

"Thank you."

"For what?"

She angles her head and balls the soiled tissue with another one as she tosses it in the trash. "For making me feel better. For being my friend. I don't know how you could make light of all this."

I think about the things I have gone through back home and the only different thing is that she thought it was one brother when it was the other, but at least it was consensual.

She wasn't forced at the last minute and they didn't hurt her. Maybe emotionally, but not physically. These guys enjoy playing mind games and are maybe capable of killing people. Definitely on another level of fucked up, but they aren't rapists, and they don't beat up women. Not from what I have seen; they just like to screw around.

The only thing that is really messed up is that Gia is pregnant and after knowing what she knows, I don't think she is sold on the idea. I know I wouldn't be either bringing a kid into their world.

Look at Dravin and his twin brother. Then I think about Reid and Valen. Let's not go so far, being that Veronica is on a whole other level of fucked up.

"Because that is your power," I tell her, resting my head on the palm of my hand with my elbow on the bed. "If you show indifference, it drives people crazy because they see that they couldn't break you. Even if you care, don't show it because they feed off it. They feed off the fear of emotion. It will be hard at first, but then, like everything else, it will become normal. In their world, hurting people and not caring about how it made them feel is normal to them. If you let it eat you up, it will destroy you."

"It hurts," she says softly, closing her eyes.

"I never said it didn't, but you can't let them see that it hurts. Because if you do, if you let them see the part of you that is damaged, that's when they ruin you."

"What do we do now?"

I told her about Reid and Valen and how Reid asked me to go to Dravin's to sleep with him, which probably included Valen.

I turned him down, and he broke my bracelet. I slipped when I showed emotion when I saw he touched it.

He saw that it meant something to me. And when I said something that hurt his pride, denying him what he wanted, he broke it because he knew it would hurt me in some way. But what he didn't realize was that I had made another one—one he didn't know existed.

"We keep our distance and graduate. They keep secrets and have gotten what they wanted, so they will soon tire of our indifference and move on to the other Prey." I make silent quotations and meet her eyes across the room while we face each other. "They say they don't care, right? That they get what they want and who they want."

She nods.

"Then neither will we. We won't give a shit because we get to choose. We just have to make sure it's not part of the Order to survive."

DRAVEN

"YOU COULD HAVE WAITED until I was ready to tell her," my brother snarls.

He walks in front of the fireplace in his living room like a caged animal, walking back and forth in front of the fire. The glow in the background illuminates the walls, casting a shadow of his features like my own when I'm upset. I could have waited until he told her, but I couldn't resist when I saw her waiting outside her dorm room, scrolling through her phone. I sometimes pass by her dorm to see if I can get a glimpse of her. It probably makes me a stalker, but I can't help it. She's gorgeous. Her face, the softness of her skin, her tight pussy when I stretch her open, filling her.

When I saw her alone, the only thing I could think of was the urge to take her for a little while. To have her all to myself. It was the same feeling I felt when she came barging into Dravin's house when I was there because my father was fucking the housekeeper on the dining room table.

I couldn't stomach seeing his bare ass as he pumped in the girl spread-eagled on the wooden table while she faked her moans. What girls will do to snag a rich guy.

When Gia came and saw me, of course, she didn't know it was me or that Dravin had an identical twin. She came at me with a furious expression, nervously questioning my actions at the swim meet. It was me that she saw talking to Warren's sister.

My brother needed me to fuck with Warren's head. What better way than to have his sister choke on my cock? Since Warren is a member of the Order, they know we're twins, but she thought she'd scored the older twin. The one destined to be a star. The collegiate athlete and star swimmer. One of the three sons to take over the Order. I'm not jealous of my brother. I could have attended Kenyan, but I'm better at dealing with things my way.

She kept waving at me, and I brushed her off. I was there to help my big brother make a point, not entertain his current interest.

I thought the way she kept rambling when she showed up unannounced was funny. I found it amusing, but I also noticed the curve of her ass and the bow of her pretty mouth.

When she paused before walking out of the front door and then ran back into my arms, I couldn't resist her. I wanted to know what she tasted like. I wanted to know what was so special about her. Why my brother was so taken with her. I wanted a taste of her sweet pussy. I also wondered what it would be like to fuck her, knowing my brother was interested even though, deep down, he couldn't get mad at me.

Besides, if she chose him, I would have a taste of her anyway, or I would have pursued her to get it. It was too easy and I didn't stop her. She was willing and I wanted her. Was it wrong? Maybe.

When I asked if she was a virgin and she said yes, I couldn't resist. I wanted to be her first. Her soft kisses, soft skin, and her legs wrapped around me. I wanted her like my next breath, and I knew at that exact moment that I would do anything to have her.

To be her first was a bonus. My brother was falling for a girl no other man had ever touched and the simple fact lit something inside me that I recognized as possession. If she married my brother, then I would be the man who took the most precious thing from her. Something he could never have. Her innocence. Now, she knows it was me, and the asshole in me loves the fact that she would never forget me even though she thought I was him.

"It's done," I quip.

He stops and glares at me. "It's done," he mocks. "Do you know what you have done? She won't even look at me."

I roll my eyes, waving my hand from where I'm seated on the white cream couch. "She'll get over it. She's pregnant. Where would she go?"

He shakes his head at me like I'm an idiot. "You don't know her like I do."

I snort. "I know her the same way you do."

He pauses and angles his head. "Oh yeah? You think you know Gia. Why? Because you fucked her when she thought it was me?"

My teeth grind together at his jab. He knows what she said bothered me. We both knew she would never want me if she knew the truth before I slept with her.

But maybe that's why I did it. I was jealous when I saw the way she smiled at me, thinking I was him. The way her body responded when she let me take her how I wanted. The way her eyes filled with desire when she had my cock in her mouth. Her soft lips wrapped around the shaft of my dick.

I was jealous, and I wanted her to know it was me and not him that could make her come. That I could make her dripping wet just as much, if not more. When she blurted that she was pregnant, I looked at her flat stomach and secretly wished the child that was growing in there was mine because I put it there. I couldn't wait until she had my brother's child. So I could fill her with mine.

I lied to her, telling her I needed her to leave because I was going to fuck someone else. That she was inexperienced and couldn't satisfy me. I wanted to hurt her like she hurt me and took the coward's way out like a pussy.

I lay my head back on the oversized pillows, letting the jab slide. Arguing about Gia was not getting us anywhere. I was already getting a headache listening to him babble.

Compared to my brother Dravin, I'm colder. Unemotional. Except with her. She didn't deserve what we did, but my father wanted it that way. It was to ensure my brother got what he wanted. He wanted her even if he wasn't wholly in love with her. He was infatuated with her. I think it was more the fact that she didn't give in to anyone but him. When they sat me down and told me his decision, I didn't argue because I secretly wanted her. I wanted to be able to fuck her when I wanted and how I wanted. With her willing, of course.

I take a deep breath and give him a possible solution to his funk. It will also rectify this little ache I have for her. There is only one way to diminish her little power over us.

"She isn't going anywhere, Dravin. Go fuck some other chick and get your mind off of it like you always do."

My phone vibrates and I slide it from my front jeans pocket and open the message to see it's from Reid.

> Reid: Hey, Bedford. Party over at Jeremy's. Members only. Bring Dravin. I think he would like his dick stroked.

I slide my phone in my pocket and my eyes dart to my brother, watching the flames of the fire, lost in his thoughts. "Party at Jeremy's. Members only. Let's go."

He grips his phone, watching me get up as I stand and grab my jacket. "Didn't she say she didn't want you or me? She made a choice. Now, let's show her that her choices have consequences. She knows the rules. What's done is done. We can't go back in time."

His eyes, just like my own, find mine and he nods. "Fine. You're right. I can't lose my head over her or anyone. But I'm still pissed off at you."

Reaching the door and pulling it open with my keys and phone in hand, I turn to him, following me. "You'll get over it when the next chick is on her knees worshiping your cock like you're a god."

I just hope it works for the both of us.

GIA
†

I'M IN ECONOMICS CLASS, and my eyes sting from crying all weekend. I'm all emotional behind closed doors, but I have to keep a straight face. Whispers from girls have been following me everywhere as they cup their hands over their mouths, giggling like we're back in high school.

I don't know what I missed, but I think it's because they haven't seen me lately with Dravin or the other one when he makes an appearance. Jess and I spent the night researching the mysterious twin, Draven.

We found out that he doesn't even attend Kenyan. He probably shows up when his brother doesn't feel like coming to class or when he has something to do.

The members of the Order look the other way if they realize it's Draven instead of his brother, but I think they just can't tell them apart. You really can't. His parents thought this out very well or maybe his father. All their lives, they have been raised to be alike. To serve a purpose. They live like clones of each other. Disguising themselves as the same person. The same name but spelled differently. The same tattoos, piercings, hairstyle. They probably have the same habits, and they even dress the same. Not exactly, but the same style.

It's why I couldn't pick up on it, even if I suspected.

My stomach clenches, and I'm not sure if it's because I'm pregnant or the giggles and smirks directed my way while the professor lectures. I'm scanning all the people seated in the class below me since the classroom has stadium-style seating, which allows a good view of people scrolling through their phones and messaging each other.

My phone vibrates against the desk in front of me, and a message from an unknown number comes through. I unlock my phone and see that there is a video message.

When I pick up my phone, I lower it in my lap, making sure the volume is all the way down in case there is audio that can be heard. I look up, and make sure the professor's back is turned as he writes on the board and read the text on the bottom of the blurred cover photo of the video before I press play.

Anonymous: That was quick. She must have been a bad lay. It was too good to be true anyway. You know how Dravin is once he gets his fill. Poor girl. She probably thought she was special or some shit. I wonder what poem he will write about for the next girl. Or maybe it was his twin brother? #Prey #doublethefun

After reading the words, I frown. My stomach clenches, and my hands begin to get clammy at what I might find. My thumb hovers over the screen, and then I finally press play.

I purse my lips and let out a shaky breath. I watch, and my eyes quickly fill with tears at seeing two young women sitting on Dravin and Draven's laps, making out with their hands all over them. I feel the tears cresting to fall down my cheeks. They go down on their knees and start sucking them off from all sides while the twins grab each girl by the back of their heads as they watch their lips wrap around their cocks. Not wanting to witness this further, I stop the video, knowing it would just make me feel sick. Bastards.

Another text from Jess comes through.

Jess: If you get a video via text, please don't open it.

Too late. I know Jess was trying to warn me so I wouldn't have to see it. At least I know why they are whispering and giggling. My nose burns on the inside, trying to keep the tears from running down. I'm trying to hold in the need to sniff so no one notices that I'm about to cry. If they hear it, they will know I saw it, and the whispers and stares won't stop. It's better they assume I saw it and don't care. We're broken up.

I send her back a text and notice my fingers are now shaking.

> Gia: Thanks, but it's too late. I already did. I saw it.

> Jess: I'm so sorry, Gia. But remember, no emotion. That's what they want. It's what they need.

Determined to not let it get to me, I put my phone away and ignore the stares. When class ends, I gather my things, fumbling nervously, but I manage. I think about what they did, knowing it would get back to me. It's fucked up, but I figure you should expect fucked-up things from fucked-up people. It's up to me to not let it get to me. I should have known better, but sometimes you have to own the shit you get yourself into. Life isn't a fairy tale you make up in your head or read in a book.

Things happen.

People use you.

They try to break you. But one thing I have learned is that's the nature of the beast. Evil doesn't die. It morphs throughout time.

GIA †

AFTER A WEEK OF HELL, during which I avoided everything and everyone associated with Dravin, I visited his mother's grave at the cemetery off-campus and laid a solitary red rose over her grave. I wanted to escape from my dorm room and find somewhere quiet where no one would stare or make faces at me. I can only imagine what Jess went through before I arrived.

As the sun dips below the horizon, the sky takes on a warm orange hue against the deepening clouds. Surprisingly, I have not heard from Dravin. I expected his brother to give me the silent treatment, but not Dravin. Reid and Valen are avoiding me, but it isn't like we hung out all the time, and we aren't friends. It just feels weird because they don't talk to me like before. No funny comments or nods when they see me in the quad or cafeteria. It is like nothing happened, and we have never met. Dravin avoids me. No more black roses or letters. No text messages wondering where I went after class or if I wanted to spend the night with him at his house. He hasn't asked how I'm feeling.

When I checked with the professor, he said Reid turned in the assignment and that nothing further was required before winter break since it's the end of the semester. The only person I can talk to is Jess. Aside from going to class or the library, she assures me she has no problem staying in the room with me.

It's embarrassing that I'd rather stay in my room and mope than face them at Babylon or around campus after class. Whenever possible, I stay away from the cafeteria and other crowded areas on campus. I'm not really that hungry anyway and the smell of certain foods makes me feel queasy. I know I've lost weight, but I have read that it can be expected in the first trimester. I've been putting off going to the doctor because it is still early. I will after winter break since most doctors are on vacation for the holidays.

My mother has called me a few times to see how I'm doing. I don't tell her that I'm pregnant, but her words from Thanksgiving dinner ring true when I think about what she said about Dravin. I hate lying to her about my situation, but she would never understand.

However, I did tell her that Dravin and I broke up. I told her we just got ahead of ourselves and wanted to go in different directions. I felt mature in telling her that, but in truth, it is a lot more complicated than that.

"Hi," I say, sitting down with my back against the tombstone, my legs crossed over the other.

My shiny boots glitter like a compact mirror against the setting sun, knowing that any minute, the old bell from the church will ring, indicating that it's six in the evening.

"Funny how I thought I was talking to you about one son, but honestly, your other son appeared once or twice. Maybe more than that. It must have been difficult raising two boys that way. I think you're very brave. I'm not sure of your situation or how you must have felt, but that must have been... hard." I look down and my fingers begin to pick the weeds around the marble, tearing out the ugly strands and pulling up specks of dirt over my black leggings. "I'm pregnant," I whisper softly, a tear sliding down my cheeks. "I thought you should know."

After five minutes of crying, my tears begin to dry up after the bell rings. The leaves blow in the wind. Earthy scents mingle with the chill as night falls. The sky changes colors to a darker hue. The warmth of the sun disappears and the cold begins to set in. Pulling myself up by the tombstone's edge, I wipe the dirt from my hands and leggings. As I stand by the grave and look down, I say my last goodbyes.

When I'm almost to the left entrance, I hesitate. I don't know how I know, but it's Dravin. I can feel his presence. I can feel the shift of energy around me. The danger but safety radiates off of him, like meeting an apex predator and not knowing if he will attack or let you go. I know it's him because this is a place where we have met before. A place where we have shared moments. Moments that were confusing, but they were ours. A place we know if we wait long enough, we will find each other.

He walks closer out of the shadows cast by the pillar against the setting of the sun. His eyes follow my footsteps as I walk through the gate. There are no smiles or words to be said. Only uncertainty. I pass by him with my head bowed and his hands reach out to grip my wrist like a hot iron searing my skin.

His fingers feel like butterflies brushing over my skin. My eyes gently go up to meet his. As he gently raises my chin with his finger, a tear escapes my eye, and I turn my head away from him. All I see are the memories of the lies, the hurt, the betrayal, and the video. How quickly he could move on and forget about me.

"I'm sorry, Gia. Whatever you decide to do. Whatever your decision is, I'll accept it. I'm not going to make you suffer anymore because of me and what I did to you." He looks at his mother's grave for a few seconds. Then his eyes meet mine. "I want you to live your life away from here after you graduate. I'm going to stay away from you, and I'll make sure you have everything you need. My brother will do the same. You're free, Gia.

Anything you or the baby need, all you have to do is ask me, and it will be provided."

I snort, wiping my nose and face with the sleeve of my jacket. "That's the solution to everything, isn't it? Throwing money at it so it will go away." I snatch my wrist out of his grasp and his eyes darken.

The Dravin I fell in love with is gone, and in his place is this monster they all fear on campus. The hard lines of his jaw tighten as he grinds his teeth. "It's all I can do right now. I'm trying to make it right."

I nod sarcastically. "Okay. Anything else?"

He moves closer, his lip curling as he lowers his voice. "Yeah, there is one last thing. Don't visit my mother's grave anymore. You're not a Bedford. If you're feeling bad or need anything, you call me, but that's it. And stay away from my brother. It's your only warning."

I shrink back from his words. I try to convince myself that this is for the best. He has no use for me, and the Order has no interest in me if I don't agree to their rules. Now that I'm pregnant, he wants me out of his life and he probably regrets it, but there's nothing he can do about it. Because I can only do things on his or their terms. I knew deep down that he would come to his senses. He doesn't love me. He never did. It was all based on lust.

"Why did you lie? Why did you not tell me you had an identical brother and that I might mistake him for you.?"

He steps back and looks over my shoulder as though considering what to say next. After a few seconds, his gaze shifts to mine and in a harsh tone, he says, "I don't have to explain myself to you. This is what is best for you—for me. You're not cut out for this life. I have to fulfill my family's obligations. Things you would never understand. The only responsibility I have concerning you is the child you carry. I made a mistake, and for that, I'm sorry, Gia. My crush on you clouded my judgment, and I foolishly believed that you were the one for me. I was wrong."

His words feel like poison burning in the pit of my stomach. My heart begins to fold in on itself, mixing with the poison drifting inside of me, killing the beat in my heart that was just for him.

As the temperature outside drops, he tucks his hands under his jacket, and I take it all in. The words, the pain, the lies, and the heartbreak.

I read somewhere that your first love is the love that teaches you the most. It's not when you give your heart away; it's the moment they do something to crush your heart. It's in those moments that the learning really begins. In a split second, it occurs. It's their way of showing you what you mean to them. In my case, I mean nothing. I was considered a little more than a pawn in a bigger game—a bigger plan.

At first, I just wanted to know what it was like for a moment to be with someone like him. Then, I wanted more. I wanted to know what it would feel like to fall in love with someone like him—the good-looking bad boy on campus who noticed me.

I didn't think.

I fell in love.

I fell pregnant.

And it was all a game.

The only thing that is real is that he doesn't feel the same way I do. The pain of his words, mixed with the all-consuming love I have for him, slowly builds into hate.

Tears well up in my eyes, but I won't cry in front of him. I'll save that for when I'm alone. He fucked me, knowing I'd fucked his brother, knowing I could fall pregnant, and said nothing. They played me and now I'm the sacrifice. If he doesn't want me now, what happens when I give birth to his child? What happens to me? What happens to our child?

My hands ball into fists under the sleeves of my jacket. My back is to the gate, but before I sidestep around him, I want just one doubt in my mind answered.

"What happens when I have the baby? What will happen to me and them when they're born? When you take a wife and have to produce heirs? You could at least have the decency to tell me what I should expect."

His jaw hardens a fraction, but then he relaxes and scratches his chin, looking down at my front, landing on my stomach and then rising slowly. "It's not uncommon to have children and not be married, Gia. I will take a wife and have children with someone worthy of being my wife. One that accepts everything. That child will bear my name and continue my family's legacy. As for you and our child, you will be taken care of and provided for, but the baby cannot have my last name. He or she will not be a Bedford."

He walks closer, and my eyes blur as tears begin to crest on my lashes. His face becomes blurry, like a mirage in a dream, but this is real. He is the ruthless monster they say he is. I tense at his expression, hard and cold, aimed directly at me. I never thought he would be like this after everything, crushing me. He leans forward and lowers his voice. "And neither will you."

My hand lifts, brushing the back of my neck as the meaning of his words slice me wide open and I feel the metal that is hanging from my neck. The necklace he gave me had the raven on it. It begins to burn and weigh heavily against my skin and my chest. I lift my other hand and swiftly unclasp the lock.

From where he is standing, he must think I'm fixing my hair, but one thing I do have left is my pride. I can't beat him by not showing emotion from his words, but I'll learn. He can knock me to my knees, but my strength will bring me back up and every time he is near me, I'll remember how I fell.

My fingers grip the necklace as it slides away from my neck like a heavy brick in my hand. His forehead pinches for a moment and his mouth parts like he is about to say something but stays motionless.

My arm reaches out, the raven dangling under my fist. "You can have this back, along with my feelings, my love, my shame, and my tears. Maybe you can give it to the bitches you fuck, the vulture you are, waiting to catch your next Prey."

I walk closer and open my hand, releasing it to the ground. He watches silently, his breaths coming in and out. The puff of air from the cold is visible from the glow of the lamp by the church.

I lower my voice as he stares at the diamond-encrusted raven on the ground, "Or better yet, maybe you could share it with your brother, and both of you can choke on it. I don't want you to take care of me, I don't want you near me, and I don't need anything from you. I'm dead to you. Once I graduate, I'll leave here, and you never have to see or hear from me again."

I step back and turn, walking back to my dorm room, not caring if he picks up the necklace or if he is watching me. All I hear is the sound of my feet on the concrete pavement mixed with the groaning of the trees as they sway from the wind like they're whispering secrets. He doesn't call me back or stop me. I may be a pawn in everyone's eyes. However, there is one thing I learned from playing chess with an elderly man when I used to volunteer at a group home back in Wisconsin. He once told me *a well-placed pawn is more powerful than a king.*

DRAVEN

I'M SITTING in my dad's study, checking through his company's books. In the meantime, while my brother has been away at school and busy with his cybersecurity shit, I'm living in his house. I've been assisting my father with his international acquisitions and business dealings. I seem to have an uncanny ability to locate things, as well as a sixth sense for choosing the best course of action. I seem to have been endowed with a sixth instinct for recognizing a bluff and calling it.

Someday, my brother will join in, but he works in technology and I interact with international leaders behind the scenes. You can't believe everything you see on TV. Families who founded nations are the ones who have the most influence and money, and they are the ones who control the government. Secret hands feed the investors who fund governments, politicians, and the world's largest enterprises. As a matter of fact, we're one of them. There is no one we don't have in our pocket and no one we can't place there if we need to.

My phone buzzes on top of the antique wooden desk that has been in my family for centuries. I look to see it is a text from my brother.

Dravin: It's done.

Draven: It's for the best.

Dravin: Not for me.

Draven: We can't force her into this life. Look what happened to mom. She didn't take to it very well.

My mother committed suicide, and it was Dravin who found her in a pool of blood in the tub. She was battling depression and my father didn't help. He didn't care about my mother after she had us. It was like there was no use for her. She did what he wanted. She produced an heir, but in her case, she produced identical twins.

Dravin: That was different, and you know it.

Draven: You're right, it was, and this is a lot for someone like her. She's innocent, and we've fucked with her enough. The only thing we can do now is protect her. Her not accepting all of this makes her not only a pawn but a target.

Dravin: I hurt her. I said things to her I can't take back.

Draven: So did I. Remember, I had her first.

Dravin: She wasn't yours to take.

Draven: That's what you get when you play with your food.

Dravin: She fell in love with me, not you, asshole.

We keep going at it about her. About who would get her first, but I won. Well, sort of. She hates us both. More me than him. She fell in love with my brother, and maybe that is what set me off; I wanted it to be me. It didn't matter how I felt about her. I wanted her poems, her whispers, and the fire that burned in her eyes when I slid inside her to be for me too. She may have fallen in love with him, but I want her more than anyone. He's worried that he hurt her. He had her love, and what hurt me the most was that I never stood a chance. I also wanted a chance, but I didn't get it, and now I never will.

Draven: Stop rubbing it in, asshole. She hates us both. All we can do is protect her and play the part. No one can find out she is pregnant.

Dravin: I made sure Reid and Valen will keep an eye on her roommate Jess. In case they try to get to Gia through her.

Reid and Valen are the other heirs belonging to the founding families of Kenyan. Most people think there are three, but there are really four. I'm plan *B*. I'm the hidden piece, the ace card up the Bedford sleeve. I'm the insurance policy in case my brother fails or is killed. The irony is that I'm my father's favorite, and Dravin was my mother's.

My mother took more to Dravin when she was alive. She had difficulty agreeing to my father's demands and how he raised us. It was fucked up growing up. I had to watch my mother spiral while my father forced us to live our lives like two clones. Everything we did had to be the same. We were even taught to talk and walk alike. Because I was born seconds after, I can't marry. I can have children if I want, but my father never told my mother it had to be from the future Mrs. Bedford. My brother's wife. Why? Because the Order dictated it since we were the first family and because I wasn't supposed to be born. It's better than death, my mother would say when I found out. Your father and I wouldn't allow it if it came to that.

My mother would talk about a woman who would come into our lives like a Raven. The Raven will accept it and learn to love you both, she would say. I didn't believe her like my brother Dravin did. I thought it was all bullshit, and now there is a Raven, but she only fell in love with one and not the other. The other being me. She also didn't accept.

Some people think the president is the first family, but not in our world. In our world, you're born into it. Like the Queen of England, only one can rule. The rest of the members are the monarchy. There is no election when it comes to the founding families, only bloodlines. Bloodlines that control the world. The rest is a smoke screen. A cover to show the world and make them think they have a right, a voice, but in truth, the Order is the right, and we are the voice. Money makes the world go round, and there is nothing truer than it being the root of all evil.

My phone rings, snapping me out of my thoughts. I pick up my phone and see that it's Veronica. I roll my eyes and answer.

"What?" I snap.

Veronica only wants one thing, my dick, or fuck with someone and ruin them. Her little obsession with Warren was a blessing in disguise, but her crazy ass scared him off.

"Is that any way to treat one of the best fucks you ever had in your life?"

"I hardly remember. I have had many."

"You're such an asshole, Bedford. I thought Dravin was a prick, but you are a whole bag of dicks all on your own."

"My dick isn't interested in you, so what do you want?"

I can hear her tapping in the background. She does that when she isn't getting the reaction she hoped. I fucked her three years ago and it was the biggest mistake. She wanted my brother too, but he couldn't stand her, and I didn't blame him. She takes things too far and wants to be the master in control, only when she doesn't get her way, she snaps.

Veronica is beautiful but demented all at the same time. My brother calls her Marsha fucking Brady because that is who she wants to be like, but to me, she is more like the chick from the movie *Fatal Attraction*.

If her father only knew his little Marsha likes to play for the other team. She's addicted to sex and likes to mix her food too, eating everything in one bowl at the same time.

"I thought you should know. Your little stunt at the party has sent a message to the vultures." She chuckles. "This is going to be so much fun. I heard she found out about your little lie, but to me, that means your brother has a dick as big as yours."

"Of course, that is all you think about, Veronica. Are you finished?"

"No, but I want to warn you," she purrs and then lowers her voice. "They all want her now."

I lean back in my father's office chair and look out the window at the perfectly manicured lawn sprinkled with snow from last night, wondering what Gia is doing right now. "So, what's changed?"

"And here I thought you were the smart twin that figures shit out before the rest. She must hate you now, so—you two are out of the game. You two are like the extra game pieces not used. The ones you place back in the box."

My left eye twitches from the anger snaking up my neck like a rash, making the vein on my temple throb. If anyone touches her, Order or no Order, I'll kill them. The only one allowed to touch a hair on her head is my twin brother, and only if she allows it.

Veronica is attempting to provoke me and get under my skin since Gianna has achieved what no one else has: the undivided attention of the Bedford twins. The rumor that we've stopped wanting her has reached her ears, and she wants to know whether it's true.

One thing she doesn't know is that a Bedford is growing inside her, and she won't be easily swayed into falling for anyone else. There is only one other man she has slept with while pregnant, and that man is me, even if I know deep down she wouldn't have done it had she known. It's fucked up. It's dark and twisted, but that's how I am: dark. And I love the taste of sin. Her body is my sacramental bread, and the taste of her pussy is like fine wine. Gianna belongs to Dravin, but she is also mine. Even if she thinks we don't want her.

Taking a deep breath, not wanting to let her hear my annoyance, I calm myself and warn her, "Be careful, Veronica. You wouldn't want me to tell Daddy and everyone else the truth about your little sexcapades and addiction to cock and pussy." I hear her intake of breath over the phone, but I keep going. "Don't worry about your little Warren. We made sure she won't be interested, but if you think you can toy with her, you can go ahead and try. But, I assure you. You will be disappointed."

"Are you threatening me, Bedford?"

I grip my phone, holding myself back. "No. I'm warning you. You can try, but I guarantee you will not like the outcome. She isn't like the others that have come through here, but of course, you already knew that with the way we loved the taste of her."

"If she was so great, then why throw her back into the pit?"

I chuckle, playing it off. "Because all good things come to an end. You know how it goes. We get bored and we all move on."

I have to make it seem we don't care because if you show interest in something or, in this case, someone, people will do anything to get it. They will do just about anything just to have her, even if they will discard her like damaged goods when they're done with her after she signs an NDA. All Prey have to sign one once they graduate. If they violate it, they die.

JESS

WHAT AN ASSHOLE. Gia told me about her last encounter with Dravin, what he said to her, and how she handled it. She stands at the end of her bed, zipping up her suitcase, ready to leave for winter break even though it is still two weeks away. She is going with her mom instead of her dad back to an apartment her mother rented in Wisconsin.

"Forget about him. Like I said, I'm here if you need any help."

She turns her head and gives me a small smile. "Thank you, Jess. That means a lot. I'm not sure how I'm going to tell my mom. She will be forced to tell my dad, and then my dad will want to kill Dravin. Dravin will respond by telling my dad off, and it will be a mess. What if he threatens my dad?"

I take a deep breath, realizing how hard this must be for her. It's not only a difficult thing to go back home and tell your churchgoing mother that your ex-billionaire boyfriend knocked you up but wants to keep you a secret and doesn't want to acknowledge his own kid has to be the biggest blow of all.

If it wasn't for who Dravin is and his crazier twin brother, I would want to wring his neck myself, but we both know what he is capable of. It's better to lie low and learn from your mistakes. Play along until you reach the other side like a maze. You learn where not to go every time you hit a dead end until you finally reach the way out.

"Where are you headed?" she asks.

"I need to visit my mom. I didn't go during Thanksgiving break."

"Where did you go, if you don't mind me asking?"

I chew on the corner of my lip, embarrassed and feeling guilty about not going back to spend it with my mom, but I didn't want to face anyone back home. I wasn't ready. I didn't want to risk seeing people from back home. People I'm trying to run away from. My mother doesn't know what happened to me because what was the point of telling her what they did to me? No one is going to listen to a single mom from the trailer park who they think is a drug addict or alcoholic.

Especially about a daughter no one gives a shit about except her. I love my mother too much to put her through that. Ultimately, it won't change what they did or the nightmares. The only way I have been able to cope is to find pleasure in sex like a Band-Aid to a bleeding wound.

"I stayed here."

She gives me a doleful expression. "I'm not going to ask why because you have your reasons, and I don't want to pry unless you want to tell me, but you could have gone with me. I know I should've asked. I'm sorry."

I wave my hand. "Don't be sorry. I'm used to not showing up anyway. It's just me and my mom, and she usually works at the diner to make extra money, but she called and asked me to come this year." I shrug, looking at her. "I think she's afraid I'll run off and forget about her. She sounded sad over the phone."

"That must have been hard."

I nod, nudging my chin toward her. "Not as hard as what you're going through right now with Dravin. To be honest, I want to kill him for doing this to you."

She lets out a slow, shaky breath and looks down at her nails, which have chipped black nail polish that was once glossy and perfect. "I have to move on and forget about him. I know it will be hard, but it's something I have to do. I was stupid and didn't think. My lack of experience with guys is most likely to blame. I wasn't ready for someone like Dravin."

"No one is ready for someone like Dravin."

My heart clenches for her as a tear rolls down her cheek. "I should have been on the pill and not fallen for his lies. I thought it was real when I went to his father's house and his brother was there. He's a real piece of work," she says on a nervous laugh.

I give her a wry smile that turns into a smirk and try to cheer her up. "So, how was it?"

Her eyes lift to mine. "How was what?"

"Draven with an *E*," I say, emphasizing the *E* so that she understands which brother I'm asking about. "Who's better?"

She lifts her face up to the ceiling and snickers. "I can't believe you just asked me that."

I quirk a brow, waiting silently for her answer. She slides her fingers in her hair until they are close to the roots and closes her eyes. "He's..." She trails off.

I get more comfortable on the bed as she tries to open up about how she felt about him, not knowing another brother looked and acted exactly the same. I have a feeling that the members of the Order aren't so sure which one is which half the time.

Holding my head with my hand as I lie down on the mattress, I ask, "How is he? Better? Worse?"

Her eyes find mine, and she says something I didn't expect. "That's the thing. That is the only way I could tell them apart. I couldn't at first, but now that I know, that's the difference. He's dirtier and crazier, and he has this way of making you accept the way he treats you. His brother is passionate and all-consuming, but this one is the dirty version. The one that makes every dirty fantasy you ever thought of come true. The one God warns you about when you think of lust and temptation. It's hard to understand because Dravin is like that, but his twin is crazier on a whole other level of fucked up. If the Dravin I fell for is Samael from the Bible, then his brother Draven is Lucifer himself. He is dark and the very definition of sin. You can see it when you look at him, but at the same time, he comes off as the one that is sent to kill the devil himself."

"He was that good, huh?" I tease.

She smiles. "In a different way. Yeah. He is the one that you don't feel guilty about for acting out the dirtiest things that have crossed your mind because he isn't the one that you marry or introduce to your parents because you are afraid of what they might say. He's the one that you hide under your bed. The one that no one expects to be hidden in your closet. Now, his brother is the one you give your heart and soul to, and the other is the one you give your body to. But if he wants your heart or any part of you, his brother wouldn't object to letting him share that part. You can't belong to one and not the other. My problem is that it goes against everything I was brought up on. Like keeping a deep secret from everyone, but you don't really want to."

"Wow," I say, looking at her and shaking my head. "I wouldn't know how to handle that. I get it. It's fucked up, but deliciously so. To have them both."

She nods and says, "It's dangerous, Jess. It's the scariest feeling that all this time I thought it was one man while he knew the other was filling in for him. Physically, the same in every way. They talk and feel the same, but once he touches you, you lose yourself. There was no way I would have figured it out unless they told me, and it wasn't the Dravin that I fell in love with that did. It was him. The brother that didn't flinch when he found out that he was fucking his pregnant brother's girl. He liked it, Jess. It was nothing to him. To both of them. Where does love fit in all that?"

I avert my gaze because I can't answer her. After the want comes the need. After the need comes the lust for desire. After the desire comes love, then betrayal and heartbreak, followed by shame. I've lived that feeling every day since that night before graduation. How a guy can use your love and dirty it in the cruelest way. To prey on it and then try to defile and destroy you like you're nothing.

"There is nothing I can say but to go with what you feel, Gia. We all have our demons. You just have to do what feels right. What works to keep them at bay so you can function. Your head must feel like a war zone right now, but you will find a way to fight it. To make sense of it." I shrug. "It's all I can say. It's all I know when shit is so fucked up."

"What do you mean?"

"Feel, Gia. Go with what feels right and fuck everyone else. Don't let them mess with you. Learn how to take and only give to those who deserve it."

She needs to stop worrying about everyone else and worry about herself. I have learned that through pain, the only thing that is left is the ashes of what consumed you. Every waking moment you spend worrying about the demons that plague you at night is consumed with anger, shame, regret, and, most of all, the ones you know that caused it. They roam free while you are chained in the darkness of the hell they created.

DRAVEN

IT'S the last week of classes before winter break. I stand in the dark corridor and watch Gia walk out of her class. The door swings open as college students file out, making their way down the hallway. I notice some girls my brother and I have fucked give her knowing smirks while she looks down, scrolling through her phone. She is probably used to it by now.

Does it bother me? No.

Should I care? No.

Why? Because it's not about me but about Dravin, and the evil asshole in me wants her to secretly pay for shunning him. Denying him is the same as denying me. The only difference in this situation is that she's pregnant with my brother's kid when the entire purpose was for her to have our children.

It sounds fucked up in normal society, but we are not from a normal society. We are born and bred in a fucked up world, part of an evil organization that controls the world. The rules don't apply to us. We must do what is necessary to continue our legacy and our purpose. Gia was part of that purpose until she wasn't. With money comes sacrifices, not that Gianna was a sacrifice. She was a gift. A gift she took away. She felt like a Christmas gift on Christmas morning, all wrapped up in pretty paper with a shiny bow with your name on it, hoping that when you opened it, it was what you secretly wished for and finally would taste victory. But when you opened it, tearing off the paper, all you got was an empty box and a piece of paper telling you better off next time because you cheated and lied.

She has no idea I'm watching––more like stalking her, but who cares? I care about her, just like Dravin does. It's a foreign concept to me, but with her, it just isn't. It makes sense. Everything with this girl does. We dirtied her and involved her in our world, but we couldn't resist. I couldn't resist. We want her. I want her. As the saying goes, the more someone resists, the more you want them.

Her dark hair is like a curtain of silk parted in the middle just the way I like, so I can see her beautiful face and perfect brows when I'm inside her, and she is looking up at me like I'm her God, and she is praying for me to take her to heaven. But the only place I know is the way to hell. The burning flames I create when you cross the gate of the underworld. The underworld of sex, lust, and every dirty fucking fantasy a cock and pussy can make. Heaven is for white picket fences, husbands mowing the grass on Sundays after boring vanilla sex, and wives taking their kids to play dates with other moms from the PTA.

Not me.

Not us.

Not the Bedford men.

We create our own heaven in hell. A place where no one can touch what we consider ours. In this case, we want her. We want to wake up in heaven and fuck her on the breakfast table while the eggs Benedict are served on our plates.

Our lawn is immaculate because there is no way we would waste a Sunday cutting shit that will grow back anyway and just pay someone else to do it when we would rather eat our girl's pussy after her third orgasm. On. The. Fucking. Table. She is our breakfast, lunch, dinner, and dessert. Our kids are being bathed, dressed, and fed in the West Wing because mommy needs her breakfast too, and sausage is always on the menu.

She walks by me, and I take a step back so she can't see me. She'll probably mistake me for my brother, anyway. I'm stalking her because she needs to eat, and we have not seen her in the cafeteria or the little café across campus. It's too cold to walk, and she doesn't take an Uber anywhere and has chosen to eat from vending machines on campus.

I noticed the last time she was spread on my bed, and I was fucking her when she thought I was my twin. She looked thinner, but I would not point it out when thoughts in my brain were left on hold because my dick had better plans. Now that the bomb dropped, and we know it's because she is pregnant, Dravin and I decided that even though he broke it off with her for safety reasons and the fact that she can't handle what is really required for her to be with him, that we would keep an eye on her without her knowing. We take turns most of the time.

We have heard nothing on campus except our phones blowing up from the female population attending Kenyan, supposedly finding God by confessing in the church from the Order wanting to fuck, and the snarky comments about Gia not making the cut with Dravin. At least we know, with her condition, she won't be heading to any of the frat parties to get shit-faced or find a rebound fuck when she is pregnant. The typical shit women do when trying to get over the guy who lied to them and now told them they were a mistake.

The campus door opens as she pushes the metal bar, and I follow her, ignoring the knowing glances and flirtatious stares aimed my way by Jessica and Audrey. Two girls I fucked before Gia arrived. Their fathers are older members of the Order and are plausible options in marrying within to control and keep the alliances going. After Gia, they are nothing in my eyes.

Her dark hair, I remember and prefer to be on my bed sprawled out against my red sheet, whips in the breeze. The bite in the air against my exposed skin.

She stops, and so do I. The smell of the cold mixed with the electricity between us. She senses me the same way I feel her in a room or any place within proximity.

I step forward, hoping to smell her fruity scent, but she turns around, eyes narrowing as they take me in, roaming over my clothes, hoping because praying is worthless. Praying would be on my hands and knees, wanting her to choose to be a Mrs. Bedford and belong to me. To us. Asking God for one woman to belong to two men that are brothers. Her heart she can give to my brother. But she has to be willing. Hope is all that I have left. I can take the rest, but I want something more meaningful: her soul.

"Why are you following me?"

I walk up to her, looking down into her beautiful eyes, her glossy lips parted. Her cheeks were pink from the cold. The need to just take her lips in mine, eating at me. I have to slide my hands in the front pocket of my jeans to avoid taking her face in my hands and devouring her right there and fuck with what she wants.

"I'm here to take you to eat."

"I'm not hungry."

My eyes dart to her waist, knowing that her breakfast was a multigrain bar. Getting annoyed with her isn't what I want, so I try a different approach.

"We need to ensure you are eating, and we haven't seen you in the cafeteria lately."

She gives a look of annoyance. "On top of telling me I was a mistake and throwing me under the bed like a secret, you don't want anyone to know you're following me? You don't even go here. Keeping tabs on what I eat and where I am. Creepy much."

I grin. She knows which Bedford she is speaking to. Smart girl.

"How do you know I'm not your ex-boyfriend?"

She shakes her head. "As much as it was fun for you to trick me into thinking I was fucking one of you, I am not that stupid. The Bedford that attends Kenyan was wearing something different fifteen minutes ago when he purposely ignored my existence and gave two shits what I ate while chatting up a blonde in the hallway. Unless he likes to change his clothes for every class or has special powers, I'm guessing you are Draven, who lives in the haunted mansion."

I give her a wide grin and a quirk of my eyebrow. "Haunted mansion? It's really not haunted. It's old and historical, but not haunted." She gives me a cute eye roll. You need to eat, and I want to take you."

She lets out a puff of air from those lips I want to reacquaint with my cock. "Fine."

I open the passenger door to my Audi RS7, ensuring the heated seats and heater are on. She slides in after I take her bag and place it in the back seat. I make my way to the driver's seat and slide in, powering up the car.

"Where are you taking me?"

"A diner out of town?"

She stiffens, and my stomach clenches because, knowing my brother, he would take her to the same diner our mother would take us. She took Dravin there more than she did me because I was always with my father. I was the chosen wild card he loved to have close to him like a sidekick.

As I drive toward the diner, the sun shines in the clear blue sky. He took her to the diner, which just won't do. If she went with him, then she would go with me. It shouldn't matter, but her problem is more with Dravin than with me. Yeah, I should have told her she was fucking me and that I was her boyfriend's twin creeping between her sheets disguised as her boyfriend, but I'm not the good guy. I'm the villain. And the villain takes what he wants.

I catch her watching me from the corner of my eye, and she is probably trying to figure out how we look so alike or trying to tell us apart. No one can. The only person who could was my mother. My father could tell based on my brother's hateful behavior because of how my father treated her after she gave birth to the Bedford heirs. And now she is dead.

"You can't."

"I can't what. What are you talking about?"

"You're trying to tell us apart. I'm trying to save you the trouble and the stares that will make me think you want something else."

She snorts. "Trust me. I don't want something else. I already had enough, and I have proof. You can't blame me for trying to tell you two apart. Like a normal person, I like to know who I'm talking to."

I pull into the diner's parking lot, place the car in park, and turn to face her. "Does it matter if I'm him or me? When you didn't know I existed, could you tell?"

She presses the button to turn off the heater and the seats, and I smile inwardly because that means she is flustered, and I'm getting to her. I want her to tell me what she thinks of me; I also lied to her, just like Dravin did, about us being identical, but I want to know. I need to know.

She moistens her lips with the tip of her tongue and my cock twitches. I don't know how to keep my hands to myself much longer. She is right there, and my cock is right here. The space between us is killing me. Pure. Fucking. Torture.

She is my warmth in the winter, my blanket on lonely nights when I feel cold and now there is nothing but cold sheets and meaningless dreams. She was the one who could fill those dreams.

I'm her first, and who doesn't love to be first? I will always be the one she will remember now that she knows the truth.

"I could. I could tell there was something off when it was you. Because when it was you, you took. You didn't ask. You weren't soft. You didn't whisper sweet words in my ear." I roll my eyes. "You were distant, but now I know why. I was just a conquest for you. A curiosity. An itch you wanted to scratch. Now I'm the rash you want to get rid of."

If she only knew that wasn't the case. If she only knew that if I was the one she loved and told me I love you, those would be the days I lived and the days she didn't, like right now, those would be the days I died. A slow, painful death. But she is right about me not being soft. I didn't whisper in her ear things guys whisper to the woman they are falling in love with. Because at the time, I wasn't in love with her, and now, I don't know if I am or not. I just know I can't stay away from her. I don't know what love is. I have never experienced the emotion like Dravin has with her. I never saw it with my parents. I never had those feelings with anyone.

"I don't want to get rid of you. If I did, you wouldn't be the first woman I have taken out to lunch because guys like me don't do that shit. Guys like me are the ones whose fathers wait behind the door with a shotgun when I pick up their daughter for a date, knowing it's to go fuck in a parked car and then drop them off without a kiss goodnight. I'm not soft. You already know that I do not write poems. I slide my fingers through my dark hair, trying to tell her how I'm feeling without sounding like a pussy whipped prick. "I want to be the tip of the bottle you bring to your lips," I say, sliding the pad of my thumb over her bottom lip, knowing it's confusing the shit out of her but not giving a fuck. "I'm everything Dravin isn't. You wish he was. And whatever you want me to be that I'm not, he is."

She closes her eyes, and I know I'm fucking up the plan. I'm fucking up everything we agreed to do with her, but I can't let her think I don't want her. I know she saw the video of those girls and us, and everything got out of hand. The lies we spun like they were gold. We thought we could show her we were unaffected when there was no way she could accept us because of what we did, but all we did was fail her. We showed her she didn't matter when it was the opposite. She's everything. Placed on this earth for us. Only us.

She opens her eyes and angles her head, and I see in the depth of her eyes that we robbed her of the love she felt in her heart for my brother. My brother ripped her apart with his words; what I said to her was like kicking a wounded animal.

"Let's go eat," I tell her, changing the subject and wishing I could say to her I'm sorry. I already went through the loss of my mother. I hoped I could keep her, but keeping her would mean forcing her into a world where she would be unhappy. Losing Gianna would be like watching a burning building full of newborns; you can't come back from something like that. She isn't a wild animal you want to tame by keeping her hidden in your room, hoping to domesticate it when it will do exactly what nature intended, and that is to be free in its natural habitat.

We take a booth facing each other in the back corner of the diner. I can't sit next to her like my brother would. He brought her here, but I am not him. I'll slide my hand down her pants and finger her cunt while she scans the menu, knowing the only thing she would want would be my cock, and that option is not on the menu but right next to her.

Dorothy comes to our table to take our order. She gives me the once-over and then glances at Gia, smiling. "I was wondering when you two would be back. What can I get you to drink?"

Dorothy places the two-sided plastic menus on the table in front of us while I lean back in the shiny red booth, making a noise when my jeans rub against the cheap vinyl, raising an eyebrow. I lean forward, placing my forearms on the white table, the diamonds of my Cartier watch catching the light, and lower my voice above a whisper. "It's our first time."

Dorothy lifts her eyes to me as it slowly dawns on her I'm the dark, evil twin. The one that doesn't bring girls to eat at the diner. Ever.

She looks at Gia like she is afraid of her being alone with me, even in a public space. My reputation proceeds with me. The fucked-up twin that does dirty shit, and everyone looks the other way, but what they don't know is that my brother is just as fucked up as I am, if not more. I'm just the fallout guy. The one that takes the blame to ensure the older twin carries out the duty of the Bedford name.

Gia lifts her head from scanning the menu and orders water and a burger. Atta girl. I'm glad she isn't the rabbit-eating girl who sticks to salad so she won't get fat. Some people think salad is for the rich. Ordered by the rich. If they only knew poor people invented the salad. It was created from leftovers. I saw a documentary about a lady saving a million dollars by making her own candle wax for light, flushing the toilet once a week, walking everywhere she went, and can you guess what she ate every day: salad. She grew it in her own backyard and ate like she was a rabbit. Living poor so she could save to be a millionaire. Like I said, poor people.

"I'll have the same and a chocolate shake." Dorothy writes it down on her pad but lifts her eyes to me with a curious expression. She knew my mother very well and knew my brother was the one she saw the most. She must feel empowered because she knows which twin is seated at her table, and in her mind, she must be wondering why I'm having lunch with my brother's girl. Newsflash, Dorothy: She was mine when she was his.

"How's your dad?" Dorothy asks.

"He's good."

"And your brother?"

She wants to get to the point. She wants to be nosey, and what do you give a person who wants to be nosey? The truth they are afraid to hear.

"He's fine, Dorothy. Don't worry, sweetheart." Adding a wink. "Gia is test-driving us both. She is trying to see which one drives better, or maybe she wants to keep us... both," I say to her flustered face, going from ashen to red like a mood ring.

I glance at Gia, and her mouth drops open. My eyes tell her to close it before I find a good use for it, and it's not to eat the burger she ordered. She does.

My eyes zero in on her pouty, plump lips, which I'm dying to taste when they close, and I'm interrupted by my fantasy of pouring the chocolate shake all over her body so I can drink it, knowing it would taste better by my phone vibrating.

I lean back, pull out the phone, and glance at the screen to see my older twin's name flashing from a text next to a face that looks exactly like mine. It's like looking in a mirror and watching yourself calling yourself.

> Dravin: What the fuck are you doing?

> Draven: Making sure your baby momma is feeding your kid.

> Dravin: That is my job, asshole. Not yours.

> Draven: I'm taking care of our interests while you were too engrossed in the blonde in the hallway. Gia's words, not mine. I'm sure she is also tired of hearing all the girls giggling and whispering shit about her behind her back. I did what you didn't do. Make sure she is eating. The last time I had her underneath me, I noticed she was on the thin side, and I haven't seen her in the cafeteria, probably, so she doesn't have to hear the little voices traveling about how you dumped her and moved on. Get over it. I'm with her, and I'm feeding her.

> Dravin: You're playing with fire, Draven.

> Draven: No. I'm lighting the fire and doing what I do best, watching it catch. It's the best part. Oh, and when her lips part, imagining them on my cock when she looks at me like she is right now.

> Dravin: Where are you with my girl?

Draven: Having our first lunch date at the diner.

"Is everything alright?"

I set my phone down on the table and look at her gorgeous face framed by her dark silky hair that I miss on my bed. I wonder if she will let me kiss her.

"Everything is fine."

She nods and averts her eyes, looking around at the people sitting and conversing.

"How are you feeling?"

She knows I mean the pregnancy. Even if I'm ruthless and selfish, or maybe I'm the type of guy that doesn't give a fuck, but with Gianna, I do. A lot. I care. She bites the corner of her lip. I notice she does it when she's nervous.

"I get sick some mornings, and others I get hungry, but Jess is always there with crackers, or when she has an early class, she leaves me a bottle of water and a snack so my stomach can settle in the morning. If I smell something like fish or eggs. Even certain perfumes and colognes make me nauseous."

Fucking hell, Dravin. You're not there for any of it. She is doing this alone. I want to kill my brother right now. I get he had to break it off with her, but it's not his responsibility to her. Her roommate Jess takes better care of her than he does. Watching in the hallways like a creep isn't cutting it. We don't have experience with pregnant chicks, but he could do the same thing I'm doing. Asking her. All he had to do was ask.

"Does Dravin know?" I wave my hand toward her. "About the nausea and needing help in the mornings."

I already know the answer, but I want her to tell me. I want her to give me the fuel so I can punch my brother in the fucking face.

I wait as her pretty eyes look up, hurt and glassy. Her face turns white and then to a shade of green like a cartoon. She slaps her hand over her face to cover her nose and mouth.

A server passes by, and the smell is definitely fried, and I think it's fucking fish. My nostrils flare in anger, not at her but at the plate of food with a dead brown fried fishlike carcass. Its eyes are sunken in its head, staring at the man that would consume him because a grilled cheese was too sophisticated for this asshole.

I look over while the smug bastard sitting in the booth across from us places a napkin on his chest, ready to tuck it in his collar like a fucking toddler getting prepared for his two o'clock feeding. His glasses fog from the steam of the offending plate with the offending odor, causing my girl to struggle with keeping whatever she had left in her stomach, keeping the little being trying to grow inside her from getting fed. Anger courses through my veins like a volcano while my lip curls into a snarl. What is mine comes first, and this asshole squeezes lemon over the offending animal like it's a delicacy.

I slide from the booth just as Dorothy places our plates on the table. She must see the look on my face because her eyebrows raise to her hairline when she sees what has me pissed the fuck off. The twerp looks up as he sees me standing over him.

"C-can I help you?"

My hand grabs him by the collar, and I lower my face when he looks at me with wide eyes. "Throw it out, or I'll throw you out with the Goddamn fish. It stinks, and my girl can't stand the smell. If she can't eat, I'll make sure you can never eat and need to be fed by straw and will have to pee and shit in a bag for the rest of your life."

My head turns like a serial killer in a movie toward Dorothy. "Throw it out. No fish or eggs to be served anywhere near Gianna."

She nods like a bobblehead and quickly grabs the plate. "I'm sorry. I didn't know, Draven. You know I would never–" She trails off.

"It's ok, Draven. Please let him go. He didn't know. Dorothy didn't know." It's just like Gianna to be their savior when she tries to steady her stomach by taking gulps of air.

I let the piece of shit go, not caring if he did. That he would have a meal and enjoy it while she was miserable set me off. I grab the plate and walk over to the front door. The bell on top of the door rings as I push it open and fling the plate with the fucking fish in the road, watching the plate shatter and the fish slide on the blacktop with satisfaction.

I walk back inside, and everyone in the diner has their mouth open. "Go get your fucking fish," I growl to the dork with the napkin as a bib.

Dorothy looks at me with her arms crossed over her chest, shaking her head, trying to contain her laughter. "The trash was over there, you know."

"The smell would still bother her, you know," I mock. I open my wallet, slide two twenties, and hand it over to Dorothy. "For the fish."

Dorothy shakes her head. "Keep it. I'll get him something else." I nod, and she walks away, and I decide to place the money on the table to add it to the bill for her tip.

"Did you really have to do that?" Gia asks.

"I'll do anything to make you comfortable. I would never let another person eat while you're hungry or sick, especially knowing what they are eating makes you feel sick." I nudge my head toward the plate in front of her. "Now eat, Raven. And tell me what you crave."

And she does. Between bites, she tells me everything she craves and everything she can and can't eat. I file this information away in my memory to ensure food is delivered to her wherever she is and whatever she wants. I ask her questions about her first appointment, knowing it's after the winter break.

My brother did the same, but I wanted to keep the conversation going. I want to know her more deeply, not just sexually but mentally. I have found that Gianna is smart and sheltered. My brother was right. She is innocent. She doesn't know about murder and corruption. The crazy part is that she hasn't seen evil. My brother and I are evil. She is eating at the table with evil, fucked evil, and will breed the next generation of evil. God created the most beautiful angel (the devil), but he also made Gia.

My savior and my brother's angel because without her, we are lost. If she only knew how important she is to us. How wanted she is. I never thought I could fall for a woman. How deep I'm falling under her spell.

She takes a bite and a sip of water and cleans her pouty lips with a white napkin. "Thank you. I thought I could never eat without feeling queasy."

My chest swells with her gratitude. I loved that I did something good for her, even though I would have killed him for eating the fish—hung him by the throat. She wouldn't have liked the outcome, but I took the best route possible. Gia makes me a better person—a better man.

Gianna will be the only woman who will have my children. If my brother married someone else and had children with another woman, it wouldn't matter because the only babies Gianna will give birth to are our Bedford.

"What are you thinking about?" she asks, snapping out of my thoughts and placing the burger I just ate on the plate.

I swallow and meet her gaze. "How I'm going to keep you?"

DRAVIN

IT'S dark in her dorm room as I sit and watch her sleep. I miss her dark hair on my pillow. I miss her soft skin, and I miss how her leg wrapped around mine like a vine when she fell asleep in my arms.

I have had no one in my bed since her, and I don't think I could or ever would after her. The scent she left on my sheets and pillow has since faded. I waited until it was unsanitary to have the housekeeper from my childhood home come and wash the sheets. She would shake her head and mumble for me to just tell her how I felt. But I can't.

The worst part is hurting the person you love while trying to protect them. Gia is not from a prominent family and is considered Prey. The members will try to get to her. They will try to talk to her or fuck her, but she will deny them for obvious reasons. I don't trust members of the Order. This is why my brother Draven and I created the consortium.

Discreet selected members that are part of the Order that we can trust. Thirty selected members to ensure our legacies are not threatened by others who wish to eliminate us for control. It is always about power. Religion is used to instill morals in humanity. Without morals or a sense of preservation of humanity, there will be mass chaos, murder, and pandemonium in society.

The catholic church built on this land has allowed the Order to survive using the church as a sacred meeting spot for world leaders. Who would question anyone going to church? No one.

They instilled it in the Constitution as our right and freedom to practice a person's beliefs—the perfect cover-up.

My eyes flick to Jess sleeping in the other bed opposite Gia as she turns her body to face the wall, relieved that she hasn't woken up. I came to drop off a wool coat and knee-high leather boots for Gia so she could keep warm while walking across campus. I protect what is mine, and she will always be mine. I inhale, smelling the jacket she left on the chair, which is much too thin for my taste. Her scent is intoxicating, making my cock harden in my black sweats. I have been watching her sleep almost every night since I had to break it off with her. I need to be close to her, even if she hates me.

When Draven took her to the diner, my brother's words got under my skin. She thinks I don't care about her when she is the most important thing in my life. She and our baby.

I need to make sure she is safe. She didn't want me after I lied to her about my twin. I couldn't tell her when I knew she would leave me without giving us a chance if she found out. That blew up in my face because she didn't want to marry me, and I couldn't force her. I also cannot risk her denying me in front of the others and letting them know she is pregnant. She would be a target, and some members would find it going against the rules of the Order.

If a Prey is involved with a member and she falls pregnant, the pregnancy is terminated, or she can marry by choice under strict circumstances. She has to choose, and if anyone speculates it's forced, it violates the Order, and they will vote for her to be eliminated. That can't happen. We won't let it.

I place the note on the winter coat neatly placed on her desk. I slide my hands into the pockets of my matching black hoodie, feeling the metal skeleton key with my fingers. The key works on all the doors in the dorm and the school. It is how I get in and out of the buildings with no one noticing. I have never been a person to stalk someone and thought guys that stalk girls are creeps. I'm one of those people because of my feelings for her. I have to make sure she is okay.

My brother told me she gets sick and hasn't been eating when she smells something that doesn't agree with her. I'm not fond of fried fish, either. He cares about her and feels just as guilty for lying and keeping the truth about us being twins, about him disguising himself as me when she saw him. It is his fault for not coming clean, but mine for going along with it. I guess you do crazy things when you want something bad enough. We both got caught up. One lie bled into the other and another until we had a string of lies that hid the truth.

Her finding out the truth was mixed with the fear of losing her. Losing her is something I can't live with, and the fact that my brother didn't stick to the plan and reached out to her proves that he can't accept it either.

I stand over her, admiring her plump bottom lip, slightly larger than the top. Her lips part every time she is in a deep sleep. Her thin white tank is molded to her perky breast. The outline of her nipples is visible through the thin fabric.

I want to cover her with the thick blanket by her waist and watch her a little longer. I love to memorize her face so I don't forget what she looks like or if I find something I didn't see the last time.

I gently grip the blanket with my fingers and slide it up to cover her body without waking her. I'm tempted to brush my lips against hers, but if I do, she will wake up, and I don't want her to know that I come in here to watch her sleep. There are things she doesn't understand, and I refuse to force her into a life so she can end up, like my mother, depressed. It is her choice; we must respect it, and I will ensure she is safe. I'll do what my father chose not to do with my mother: put her first.

I have already made sure they deliver her meals to her dorm and decided it was time for me to leave. I let myself out quietly, making sure the door was locked.

Someone is walking toward me as I make my way down the hallway. I pause and notice the hooded figure dressed all in black and cross my hands over my chest. What the fuck is he doing here?

"What are you doing here, Garret?"

He pushes the black hood off his head. His dirty blonde hair spiked up from the effort. "I came to see how she is doing?"

I quirk a brow. "Who?"

Garret is your typical member of the Order but also a person the Kenyan sons have found to trust. Garret isn't a bad guy. He fucked up with Jess letting Victoria have her fun with Melissa, and it all turned to shit for the poor girl. The way he talks about Jess is messed up, and I guess he doesn't care about her, but I find it intriguing that he talks about his time with her. He is putting a lot of effort into talking about a girl he supposedly gives two shits about. Reid and Valen have no complaints. If anything, they like her in all the right ways.

"Jess." His green eyes lower to his black books and then land on mine. "I came to see if she was okay. I have checked up on her twice a month since freshman year."

I cross my arms over my chest and lean my shoulder against the wall. "Now, why would you do that, and does she know?"

He slides his gloved hand inside his black sweats. "Nah, she doesn't know. I want to make sure she is alright."

"Why do you care? Why go through all the trouble? You keep the rumor mill flowing about her. The reason I'm questioning you is because of Gia."

He pinches his forehead in confusion. "Didn't you two break up? I mean, it was kind of fucked up. She didn't know she was fucking Draven, thinking it was you."

"Not your problem, but ours. It doesn't change the fact that I love her and will ensure she is okay even if she doesn't want to accept it. Whatever games you play with Jess, make sure it doesn't affect Gia. They are close."

Garret is close to us and knows what is required of us when our senior year is up. He is lucky he doesn't have that problem. There is time for him to choose who he wants. He just has to abide by his parent's businesses. He can fuck and play all he wants.

He lets out an audible breath. "I wouldn't let anything happen to Jess or Gia. You have my word on that, brother. Everything is not what it seems, and like you, we have to do things to ensure the people we care about are safe from others who have too much power for their own good."

I nod, and we fist bump. "You fell for her, didn't you?"

He lifts the corner of his mouth. "Something like that." He snaps his fingers and points at me. "Don't believe everything you hear?"

"You got that, right?" I walk away and then, stop, and turn back. "Garret?"

He pauses and turns around. "Yeah?"

"Don't wake my girl up," I warn.

JESS

MY EYES ARE heavy from sleep, but I sense someone hovering over me. Am I dreaming? Is it Gia? Is she okay?

I open my eyes and blink repeatedly. *Garret.* I'm about to scream, but the palm of his hand clamps over my mouth, preventing me from screaming.

"Shh... It's me. I'm not going to hurt you. I swear," he whispers.

My eyes widen, and they dart over to the other side of the room. I sag in relief that Gia is sound asleep and okay.

I shake my head, trying to figure out why he is here and trying to scare the shit out of me. Is this a cruel, sick joke? Hasn't he done enough?

My nostrils flare, and I'm relieved I can still breathe with how hard his hand is over my mouth. His head tilts, scanning my thin t-shirt, and his gaze pauses over my chest when he notices I'm not wearing a bra. I try to squirm, but he holds my body and head in place. Not so hard that it hurts, but enough so that it doesn't allow me to move my head or speak.

He leans in close to my right ear and whispers softly, "I came to see you."

The scent of his spicy cologne that I once loved my freshman year when he kissed me for the first time invading me. I wanted a real kiss and tried to forget what happened back home my senior year. I thought an elite catholic college was a step in the right direction. I soon discovered the path was a gateway into a hell I was never prepared for.

He was my first lesson in how evil the people walking Kenyan halls really are too vulnerable people like me. How much control and influence do they have on people who are not part of their circle?

I shake my head and shrug my shoulders. The light from the top window casts a glow from the moonlight over his features, his smooth face and hard jaw.

His hands slide down my stomach, and he finds the band of my shorts. What is he doing?

"I'm going to touch you. I want to show you not to listen to everything you hear."

I close my eyes. My heart is hammering inside my chest. Why? I have so many questions. Why did he trick me into wanting him so much and letting Veronica and Melissa do what they did when all I wanted was him? I liked Garret and was falling for him at the time. He was perfect. He walked me to class and said all the right things.

Garret is attractive with a lean build and the boy next door's complexion mixed with a bad-boy vibe. He hurt me and continues to hurt me with what he says about me. Going against them is pointless, and I have learned to ignore it.

But it was all a lie, and he used me. I was vulnerable, but he didn't know that. He didn't know what I had just gone through. No one did.

I close my thighs to keep his fingers from reaching the heat between my legs. His lips find that place behind my ear, and he places a warm kiss on that spot that raises the tiny hairs on my skin like an awakening of something dormant inside me.

"I bet you are wet. Sooo... Wet. Do you remember how wet you were that night?" I shake my head because I still can't answer. "I regretted what I did when I felt you gripping my cock. Having them there with us." He slides two fingers on the top of my slit, rubbing me. "Ruining what you were giving me."

My eyes find his green ones. His straight nose rubs the side of my cheek. My thighs widen slightly, and I can hear his breathing pick up. I don't know what to do. I'm confused, but I want to feel.

"You are so pretty, Jess. Do you know how beautiful you really are?" I avert my gaze and stare at a black dot on the wall I made with my shoe when I first moved into the dorm room. I stare at it like it can guide me on what to do with him.

"Look at me," he demands.

My eyes find him, and I can see the inner turmoil mixed with lust. He wants to fuck me. It's plain as day.

"I'm sorry about Veronica and Melissa. But I'm not sorry for wanting you. I know you hate me for what I did and what I have said." He rubs his finger over the top part of my clit, causing blood to rush from my head to the apex of my thighs. "I want you to take me to the showers in this place and hate fuck me. I know about Reid and Valen, and I'm not happy."

Too bad, asshole. I slept with them because they made me forget about my past. I felt free, and they made me feel good, physically.

I roll my eyes, and his lips lift in a smirk. "You like to get me upset, huh?" He rubs faster, and my neck arches. My legs open slightly, giving him more access. I'm wet. Really wet. "That's my girl." He smiles. "Be my little bad girl. Show me how much you hate me, Jess."

THE SPRAY of the hot shower falls over our bodies. Garret has me pinned on the shower wall, the cold tiles warming up from the heat of my back. I wrap my legs around his waist, and his eyes lock on mine. He places the palm of his hand near my head and pushes me against the tiles as he puts the tip of his condom-clad cock near my entrance.

"I'm gonna fuck you hard, princess. I want you to ride my cock like you hate me. Or maybe you really do hate me. But that's the best part, the part you'll love the most when I make you come so good, making you forget whatever you're trying to forget."

My eyes widen. It's like he knows my darkest secret—the one I have yet to share intimately with anyone.

"You don't have to tell me," he says, while sliding into my pussy deep with a groan. I gasp at the burning sensation that is welcomed with pleasure.

He stills so I can adjust to his size, and I grip his firm, muscular arms with my hands. "Ready, princess."

"Yes," I say in a hiss.

He moves hard and fast like he is in a race. Fuck. I moan loudly, and he slaps his hand over my mouth. "Shh... I don't want this to end with someone coming inside to see how much I like you wrapped around me. I don't want our little secret to come out."

I turn my head roughly so I can speak. "Fuck you."

He grips my mouth with his fingers and places a hard kiss on my mouth. "I'm planning on it. Whenever you want, I can come over and slide into this tight cunt." He bites my lip softly. "I want to see how much this pussy comes from your hate towards me."

He slams his lips over mine and pumps savagely inside me. My tits bounce from his forceful thrust and I grind on his cock and arch my back.

"Fuck yeah. Damn, this pussy is so good."

The slaps of wet skin echo in the female dorm showers. The sound of the water falling like rain on the tiles. His hand wraps around my neck, squeezing tight but letting me still breathe. His other hand is gripping my ass as he slams into me repeatedly.

He fucks me hard, and I grind harder. A delicious burn can be felt from the tips of my aching nipples to the swollen bud of my clit as he rubs against me with every thrust.

I moan softly, my climax climbing to its peak. My lips find his, and his tongue slides inside my mouth in sloppy, wet kisses. If this is a hate fuck, I want to keep hating him if it feels this good. I don't know why I let him, but I need the release. I need to stop letting him get to me.

"I'm bad a fuck, remember?"

He chuckles. "Yeah, you're so bad. I'm fucking you in the female showers in the dorm at two in the morning. If you only knew, Jess."

He pumps faster, and I can't take it. My eyes roll back in my skull as my orgasm slams into me in a thousand pieces. I grind on his cock, and I can feel it swell.

"Come, princess. Come all over my cock," he says, dipping his head and sucking my nipple. It makes me come more, and I swear I see stars.

He pulls out, lowering my legs from around his waist, and steadies me. "Turn around."

"What?"

"I said, turn around. I'm not done. We're not done."

I turn around, and he slaps my ass. "What the fuck, Garret."

"Hold on to the tiles with your palms and bend over."

"Why?" I ask.

"Because you want to forget."

I hate that he knows that part about me. It's like he knows I was secretly using him.

I was secretly using them.

They don't know from what or who.

GIA

WHILE SITTING IN THE BOOTH, I tilt my body forward. "Remind me again, why are we even here?"

Jess is sitting across from me at the Babylon bar off campus. I placed my hand over the beautiful wool coat Dravin left me last night with a pair of black designer boots that probably cost more than someone's monthly salary.

It's the most beautiful coat I have ever worn. I placed it on the booth's far side so it wouldn't get ruined, remembering the note that read:

Gia,
I will always keep you and the baby warm.
Love,
Dravin

Jess leans close, nursing her beer. Her fingers tinker with the neck of the bottle as the suds bubble with the movement. "Because you need to get out and stop hiding. We both do."

I bring the plastic cup of water and take a sip of the straw. "I'm not hiding." She lifts her lips, knowing I'm full of shit.

I am hiding. I'm still determining how I will react if I see Dravin after the note he left. I didn't want to accept it, but I knew I would. I needed a better coat, and the boots kept me warm when walking around campus in the cold.

Jess looks up at me when the echoing sound of the pool stick striking the ball draws her attention.

Her expression turns serious. I turn my head to see what, or better yet, who, has her attention.

Garret is playing pool with three other guys from the swim team. My eyes dart around the pool table, and my heart squeezes. The twins are standing to the left, watching the game. I still can't tell them apart, but I can tell if I'm around them long enough. *If they allow it.*

I turn to face Jess, and her gaze lands on mine. "What's wrong?"

She shakes her head. "Nothing."

"It's not nothing. Is it Garret?"

She picks up her beer and takes a pull. The sleeves of her black sweater slide up her arms. There is something she isn't telling me. I'm unsure of what she wants to say to me, but I'm here for her. Her lips form a thin line, and she sighs.

"I slept with Garret last night."

My eyes widen, and I pick up the red plastic cup and take big gulps from the straw. "Okay."

I am trying to figure out why or how. She must hate him for what he put her through, the rumors, and how he treated her.

She gives me a guilty expression. "I know you must think--" She trails off.

"I think nothing." I snort. "I'm the last person to judge you right now."

She snickers. "It was a hate fuck."

I chuckle. "A what?"

"A "hate fuck" is what he labeled it. His words."

I raise my brows. "A hate fuck?"

"I don't know why I did it, but I did."

"It felt good," I tell her, waving my hand. "To let it out."

She smiles and laughs through her nose. "Yeah." Then her face falls, and that guilty expression sets in. "I don't want you to think of me as the type of girl that does things like that."

I lean forward, lowering my voice, "It's not like you haven't slept with him before, Jess. It doesn't mean you are any less than anyone who attends here. They have sex with random people and move on to the next."

I know first-hand how easily they can move on. How much it hurts to be treated like nothing because you didn't agree with what they wanted. To accept.

"I guess." She smiles warmly. "Thank you, Gia."

I tilt my head. "Anytime."

"You liked the coat."

My head angles up, and one of the twins is standing at the end of the booth. His eyes are fixed on the coat by the seat next to me. It must be Dravin since he was the one who left it in my room.

I have yet to notice him sneaking into my room. I used to love it when he would come in the middle of the night. I secretly wished he would keep coming. It means he cares, but the fact that I'm pregnant must be the only reason—the reason I need to stay warm. It's who I'm carrying inside me that matters—his child.

"I nod. Thank you," I say curtly.

He taps his finger on the table, and I watch the ink on his hand move. The tension is thick, like a needle about to prick our bubble.

Jess licks her lips and clears her throat. The rest of the swim team and Draven show up, crowding the booth.

My hands sweat, and my throat suddenly becomes dry. My stomach clenches when Garret leans forward.

"Are you ready for round two?"

My eyes find Jess, and she looks at Garret with a smirk. "I thought I was horrible. The worst you have ever had." He winces. "That was a one-off. I'm sure you can find someone better to meet your expectations."

The guys on the swim team raise their brows, and Dravin looks away.

"Yeah, I get it," Garret says, walking away.

I move to slide out, and Draven quirks a brow. "Leaving so soon."

"Yeah, I wouldn't want to be in the way of your brother's hunt for a better replacement." His head whips over at me, hearing my last words. "Thanks for the coat and boots," I say, as I stand, grabbing the wool coat and sliding my arms through it while Jess slips out of the booth.

"You don't have to thank me, and I'm not looking."

He means he is not looking for his future wife around campus, but it doesn't mean it will not happen. He will, and I know my fate. How easily can I be replaced?

I raise my chin. "You weren't looking while getting your cock sucked off at the party?"

Draven's left eye twitches. It probably bothers him I pointed that out. How could I not? I can't forget what I saw. Since they clarified who I was speaking to by how they answered me, I feel empowered to tell which twin I'm talking to now, what I think, or how I feel.

"I'm sure they kept you both warm." I slide my tongue over my teeth and look down at my designer boots, trying to push the hurt I feel down to my stomach. His words from the cemetery and the video going viral around campus. The tears I silently cried every night. "I'm glad I got a sneak peek of how life would have been if I agreed to be with you both. You just made it easier for me."

I move toward the back exit, following Jess. Dravin's hand shoots out, gripping me by the arm. My head whips up, ignoring what his touch does to me or the leather jacket, which gives off the scent of his clean ocean smell. "Easier for what?"

My eyes are glassy, and the light is bright in the dimly lit bar. The tears are welling up in the back of my eyes at how much he hurt me. How they both hurt me and my love for him.

"How easily you could lie to me. How easy it was for you to hurt me." I lean close and look up at his stormy eyes. "How easy it was to replace me. I hope she was worth it."

"It isn't what you think. We didn't–"

I interrupt Draven. "I know what I saw and what everyone saw. It's exactly what everyone thinks. Now please, leave me alone." I say through clenched teeth, walking out into the cool late afternoon. Jess is holding my arm while she guides me across the street toward campus. The tears I was holding slide down my cheeks.

"I'm sorry, Gia," Jess says. "I'm sorry for taking you there. We need time. We just need time."

I thought I was ready to face him. Face them. She is right. Winter break is just around the corner, and I need time to check my feelings and emotions. My hormones are out of whack. One day, I feel sorry for myself, and then the next, I feel angry. In all honesty, my heart is breaking because I know the truth deep down. I want them. Both of them. I just can't get over his words and what they did in the video.

GIA
†

AFTER THE END OF CLASSES, I stand outside in the cold as the remaining students give me knowing glances about my recent split with Dravin. Thankful that I don't feel nauseous, I ignore the smirks and murmurs that pass behind me and focus on the life developing inside of me.

It's something I receive when I first wake up in the morning, along with the extra crackers that Jess usually puts on my nightstand. She held my hair each time the dry heaving sent me to the bathroom, and she was there when the tears started falling. Because I don't have much of an appetite in the evenings, I managed to shed a few more pounds.

Walking over to get something in my stomach before it sets in again, I decide to enter the café that I tagged along with Warren at the beginning of the year. I hope they have banana nut bread and maybe a hot chocolate.

I don't want to drink coffee in my condition, and I want to do everything right even if I have done everything wrong getting pregnant by a man who doesn't want to acknowledge my baby by name, but I'll survive. I'll give my baby the love he or she deserves. I have enough inside of me for both of us.

The bell of the door rings behind me right before I'm next to place my order.

"Hey."

I glance around to find Warren standing behind me, and I have to question why he is even on campus. Only students from the dorms remain, waiting for rides, and to my knowledge, Warren does not reside in the dorms since he is a member of the Order.

When I turn around, I notice that he must have entered the café by himself, just as everyone else was getting ready to go.

"Hey."

"You're leaving to see your family tomorrow?" he asks.

I nod. "Yep."

"That will be $12.75," the clerk says.

Jesus, for nut bread and hot chocolate? I slide my hand in my jacket to give him my bank card, which has only two hundred dollars to my name. I'm going to have to find a job to save for my little one. I refuse to ask or involve Dravin in any way, even if he offered, but the meal service he has coming by for me and Jess is a Godsend.

"I got it," Warren swiftly interrupts, handing him his card. "Charge for both, please."

"Oh, that's okay. That's nice of you, Warren, but I got it."

"No," he says sternly. The clerk looks at him and then at me, but the change in Warren's expression gives me a chill down my spine. The clerk swipes the card, and the receipt slides out.

I turn to him and give him a fake smile. "You didn't have to do that."

"I want to."

"I could have paid for it."

"It's no big deal, Gia. I wanted to pay for it. By the way, how come you didn't drink coffee? I remember you telling me you liked the macchiato. What changed?"

My eyes dart around the coffee shop, and I realize only three people are inside, and two of them work behind the counter. Shit.

My eyes land on his face, and his staring at me gives me the creeps. It's like he is waiting for me to admit something he already knows, but there is no way he could know that I'm pregnant. I'm alone in a coffee shop and there are no other customers. I must be paranoid.

I raise my shoulders. "Getting in the Christmas spirit with a hot chocolate."

He smiles at me like a clown. There is something off about Warren. He seems nice, but there is just something that doesn't add up.

Walking near the window, I find a seat to drink my hot chocolate and eat my banana nut bread. I expect Warren to leave after he picks up his order, but I see him talking to the barista in a hushed tone. He pauses his conversation and then looks over.

For some reason, a wave of fear begins crawling up my spine. They nod to each other, and he turns to leave, but instead of heading to the exit, he plops himself in front of me.

"I hope you don't mind."

I do mind. I don't trust you, and you give me creepy vibes. Except I can't tell him that. I have to play it cool and maintain my distance. I didn't want him buying me anything, though I also didn't want to argue.

I blow on the surface of the cup, cooling it down enough to take a sip, trying to get a sip so I can get warm.

"So. Where are you headed?"

"Wisconsin," I answer.

He already knew that, but that is all he is getting from me. The first time we were here, he asked where I was from. I should have known better and lied, but it's too late now. He smiles in that creepy, knowing way. Then he slouches in his chair and looks over his shoulder like he is paranoid someone will catch him or something.

He watches me while licking his lower lip. His gaze stays on me while I drink my hot cocoa, his eyes dilating and then closing. It reminds me of the scene in Snow White and the Seven Dwarfs when Snow White bit into the apple.

I blink rapidly, shaking my head out of the crazy thought. Being pregnant makes you self-aware of everything around you. I guess it's because you're trying to protect something precious inside of you. You don't want anyone to hurt that special someone that you love the most in the world.

I inwardly smile, thinking how crazy it is that you love someone so much and haven't even met them. You haven't smelled or felt their skin or looked into their eyes, but you already know deep down inside they are your everything.

"I'm glad I ran into you, Gia. I know it might be premature, but I wanted to see if you wanted to go out sometime."

My stomach clenches into knots. I slide the piece of nut bread out of the paper bag, trying to find something to do with my hands. I suddenly want to swallow the piece of bread and down the hot chocolate so I can get out of here and back to the safety of my dorm room.

I take a bite and swallow, hoping he will take the hint to drop it, but luck isn't on my side. My eyes lift to his, and I lick my lips because I have pieces of food. I hate the way his eyes follow the movement. It makes my stomach churn, except I do have to make it clear to him I'm not interested in him.

He leans forward. "Not all of us that go here are assholes, Gia. Dravin and his brother are just that, assholes. At least we only have to deal with one asshole because the other one makes random visits when he is bored. I'm sure you have realized they are twins by now."

Hoping he changes the subject and doesn't press, I follow along. "Yeah. It doesn't matter anymore though, we're just friends."

He chuckles, placing his forearms on the edge of the wooden table and giving me a smirk. "There is no such thing unless you're still fucking them. Are you?"

"Am I what?" I quip, getting annoyed. He has balls, but I'm not falling for his shit.

"Fucking him or... them."

I lean forward, my appetite quickly vanishing. "I don't have to answer, and I think this conversation is over. Don't come at me again, Warren."

"Or what?" he challenges. "You're getting all defensive because I'm simply stating a fact. The Bedford twins don't have friends that are female unless they are fucking them, and from what I have seen and heard, you don't strike me to be the type to share your man with other women. He has obviously moved on, and I don't mean that in a bad way, Gia. However, I do think you deserve better than someone who plays with women like the strings on a guitar." He lowers his voice. "Do you honestly think Dravin hasn't written a little poem for anyone else? Do you think you're the only one?"

Warren is probably pointing it out so he can sway me. I already know the things he is telling me and how much it hurts me, but I can't bash Dravin with his child growing inside of me. Like it or not, I have to be civil.

The safest thing to say when someone mentions him is that we are friends. I can't say he is my enemy because he woke up and realized he doesn't want me anymore and that I was a mistake. I can't change how he feels, and he told me how he felt. I can't make him love me or be a father if that isn't what he wants. He wants to find a wife, except that person isn't me. I'm not what he wants anymore.

"I'm not stupid, Warren. He broke it off with me, and I'm handling it just fine. I'm not the first. I don't have to explain myself to you or anyone."

"Then go out with me. If you're fine, let me take you out."

I shake my head and let him down gently. "I'm sorry, Warren, but I'm not interested in you. I think you're nice." *Lie.* "But I don't like you like that. Going out with you won't change that."

His eyes narrow and his upper lip curls. Then he smiles, even though it doesn't reach his eyes and I know he must be upset, but I really don't like him. There is no connection. Every time I'm around him, I feel unsafe. The guy gives me the fucking creeps.

"I'll give you time."

What? Didn't I just tell him that I'm not interested?

I rise from my seat, move my chair back, and collect my bag. When he approaches me like that, alarm bells start going off in my head. When he leans in for a whisper, he licks his lips, and my stomach knots up in disgust. "You're the one I want, Gia. I will have you, and I'll make you enjoy it, so you may as well get accustomed to the notion."

When his tongue nips at my ear, I move to smack him, but he ducks out of the way and laughs. "Fuck off and stay away from me, you fucking psycho."

He laughs. "I'm the psycho? Baby, you were fucking the campus psycho and look at how that turned out. If anything, I'm doing you a favor. Saving your reputation and all that. I can make it good for you. All you have to do is spread those pretty legs, and I'll show you how to scream."

I move to get away from him and pull out my phone from my jacket to call Jess. My first thought was to call Dravin, but he has made it clear that I should only contact him if I need something related to my condition, not my problems. He made sure I was looked at as Prey. I have to learn to deal with psychos like Warren. I'm on my own now. This just proved it.

Me: Jess, I need you. Where are you?

I sense Warren behind me, and my body stiffens on high alert. Fear crawls over my skin. My whole being goes into fight-or-flight mode, and my skin tingles with dread.

When I shut my eyes, I try to will him away.

"See you around, beautiful," he whispers near my ear, making me want to swat him away like a Nat buzzing near me.

My phone buzzes, and I look at the message, a wave of relief going through me

Jess: I'm in the dorm. Where are you?

Me: Café. Can you come and meet me here? I'll explain later.

The doorbell chimes and he pushes the door with his back. "Who are you calling?" He laughs. "He doesn't give a shit about you. You were just a fuck like all the rest, Gia." His eyes slide down my body, making me want to throw up. "You can run, but you can't hide. I like the chase, and I always get what I want. I'll make sure you like it."

"Fuck you," I sneer.

"I'm planning on it, whether you like it or not. I'll slide in and take it."

My chest begins to rise and fall as I grip my cell phone, and then he turns and leaves out the door. When he disappears into the night, I'm afraid to walk closer in case he tries to grab me.

My head turns to the last two people working behind the counter cleaning up for the night, acting like they didn't see or hear half the things he said.

The guy that he was talking to looks up at me. "We'll be closing in five minutes."

Asshole. He heard, and he is basically telling me to leave. I peer down at my phone, silently begging Jess to show up. It's cold out there and dark. I'm afraid of the things he said he would do to me, but who can I tell if not Jess?. He's right about Dravin, he doesn't want me and is done with me. Tears sting my eyes and I look out the window, hoping she shows up before they kick me out. I could call the police, but then I remember what Dravin said. They're all in their pocket, and I'll just make it worse.

I begin to feel dizzy, coughing it up to the fear Warren brought forth. My stomach rumbles and I close my eyes. Relax, Gia. He let you know his intentions. He laid it all out like the fucking creep he is. I wonder why Veronica is obsessed with him. She's probably just as fucked up as he is.

I look at the guy behind the counter. He glances at his watch and then looks at me, quirking a brow. Fucking prick. I grip my jacket and make sure I'm all zipped up.

After a minute, I see Jess's hair while she practically sprints to the front door with a frown. She pulls the door and the bell chimes.

"What's wrong?" she asks.

I look to the guy with a knowing smile, and I snap. "I know you heard what he said. You're just as sick as he is."

He stands there with an evil grin like the girl in the movie *Smile,* not saying anything. I back away while Jess holds open the door.

Right when the door almost closes, he says, "Bye, Gia." I never told him my name. He heard. He heard everything, and he was in on it.

I grip her arm and pull her along with me as I speed walk toward the building. "I'll tell you once we are inside. It's not safe with that fucking creep lurking out here."

JESS

"HE SAID THAT?" I ask once we are inside our dorm.

"Yes," she says, and my heart squeezes for her. She's scared, pregnant, and feels all alone.

"Call him."

She knows I'm referring to Dravin. She should tell him what that creep said to her. How he basically told her he was going to rape her. Memories from my past begin playing in my head like a picture book, but I close my eyes and rub them with the pads of my thumbs.

"I'm not his problem anymore, and from what I have learned about girls like us, we don't matter. That much is clear. Jess, I think you should head out." She lets out a nervous sigh. "I think we should both head out."

"When? Where?" I ask.

"Tonight," she says, "We should head out tonight. Everyone has practically left. The few here, like us, are on their own with no witnesses. It isn't safe for me. We should go home, and when we come back, always be around people. Don't go out on your own."

She has a point. The way that guy in the café acted and what Warren said to her must have scared her.

"Alright. Let's see if we can change our flights to leave tonight, and we'll split the Uber ride to the airport."

She looks up from grabbing her suitcase with a smile. "Really?"

"Yeah," I tell her. "We will meet up when we get back to the airport so you don't show up here alone."

She runs and gives me a hug. "Thank you. You're the only one that has been nice to me here."

"You are, too. We have each other, and it won't be long. We'll graduate and leave this place, but we will always be friends, and I'll help you. I promise, Gia," I say, as we both pull back and laugh and cry at the same time, wiping the tears leaking out of our eyes.

It was the first time I felt good in a while. The first person I could call a friend.

GIA
✝

I'M SWEATING and shaking when the aircraft touches down. With nothing left in my stomach, I go to the restroom for the third time and dry heave since everything is already out. My eyes well up with tears, and I feel them trickling down my cheeks. I'm nauseous and cold all over. I couldn't get my bag from the overhead compartment, especially because my hands were sweating so much.

My mother texted me when I landed, only my hands were so clammy, and I was shaking in my seat so badly that I couldn't reach for my phone. I barely made it to the restroom at the airport.

I flush the toilet, almost falling on the side between the stalls. I wonder why I feel so weak. I feel sweaty and wet. When I look between my thighs, I see blood soaking the floor, and I scream. "HEEEELP ME PLEASE!" I scream.

Everything fades in and out and then everything goes black.

Dravin

I OPEN the door to the main building of the dorm. I have this cold feeling in the pit of my stomach. I haven't seen or heard from her since the day in the bar. I thought by giving her space it would be better for her. I acquired her bank information from financial aid and wired her money into her account. Since my family founded the school, it wasn't hard. Nothing is really out of my reach being a Bedford.

Considering what I said and how I treated her, I can't say I blame her for not calling. I don't know what to do to make her happy anymore.

My brother wants her. I see it in the way he looks at her. I know the feeling, the want, the desire, and the lust that goes through his mind when he looks at her because I feel the same way. We want to consume her. To own her. And keep her forever.

If this is the only way to keep her, then so be it. I will take care of her and watch her with my child in secret. For my eyes only. Under my protection. My biggest fear is when I look at the empty tub in my bathroom, I see her in there, dead like my mother.

My mother, Anastasia, took her life in the bathtub, filling it with water and then blood because she couldn't deal with my father. She couldn't deal with what was expected of her, how her sons were supposed to grow up. What was expected of us and the role she had to play. She lost faith in us, in herself. And most of all, she died sad, alone, and heartbroken. I don't want Gia to suffer the same fate.

I walk down the silent hallway to the door and open it with the skeleton key. The door swings open and I see that both beds are made. I walk over and check her bed and her drawers, noticing most of her things are missing. I pick up one of her shirts and hold it close to my nose to breathe in her sweet scent.

I pull my phone out of my pocket and call her cell phone, but it goes straight to voice mail. I try again and again.

"Fuck!" I scream.

I call Reid and he answers. "Yeah."

"Where are they?"

"I don't know. I tried to call Jess, but she didn't answer."

"Why? What did you do now?"

"Nothing. I was an asshole to her, and she blew me off the other day."

"What did you do, Reid?"

I know he can be a temperamental bastard when he doesn't get his way. He acts out and acts like a total dick.

"I broke the little bracelet she had on her nightstand. It looked like a guy gave it to her, and it was sentimental or some shit. I tore it to pieces and said some fucked-up shit."

"Fix it," I say through clenched teeth. "This doesn't help in any way. They're not here."

"Stalker."

"Hater."

"Why don't you fix your own shit before you get on my case? That is no way to treat the mother of your child. Even if you don't want her. I'm sure everyone is sniffling around."

"She's pregnant. She isn't going to fall into anyone else's bed anytime soon. Only mine."

"Or Draven."

"Fuck you."

"Nah, not my thing. I wouldn't mind watching you three, though. That would be hot."

"I knew you'd love to watch my cock in action."

"Go home and jerk off to the scent of her panties you must have stuffed somewhere, you dick. And wait until she comes back. She must have gone back home to visit family."

"I'll call you back," I tell him, ending the call.

I open my contacts and dial. The sound of the phone rings in the silence of the room. "Hello."

"Find her," I say dryly.

GIA
†

A DISTANT BEEPING sound wakes me from the deepest sleep. Wherever it's coming from, it just keeps on beeping. My thoughts are cloudy and hazy. My head hurts, and I can feel it cracking. It feels like an axe has slashed my forehead, and it's about to open.

"Gianna?" I hear my mother's voice. "Gianna," she says again, calling my name. My eyes flutter, and I squint at the bright white light.

"Gianna?" she calls out again.

"Mom," I croak, grimacing at the feeling in my throat. It feels like sandpaper.

"Oh, thank God. I'll get the doctor."

My eyes adjust and I try to lift my hands, except they feel like concrete bricks. Once my eyes adjust, I look around and then I remember. I blacked out.

I try to sit up, but then there is a blonde nurse by my side. "Relax, Gianna. You have to be careful and take it slow."

I look down as she motions to my hand with an IV and then the sound of the curtain being drawn back.

A man with a lab coat appears with my mother right by his side. He unwraps his stethoscope from around his neck.

"Gianna," he says, looking at the monitor where I'm hooked up, measuring my vitals. "My name is Dr. Grayson," he looks at my mother and then back at me. "Is it okay to speak freely in front of your mother?"

I nod, closing my eyes. "Yes."

It's not the ideal way I imagined her finding out I'm pregnant, but I don't want them to send her away. The memory of how I must have gotten here comes back. The blood, my body shutting down, and then blacking out on the bathroom floor at the airport.

"How are you feeling? When the EMTs brought you in, you were in bad shape."

I stay silent. My pulse rate accelerates, and my eyes widen. The alarm starts to sound from the monitors. The nurse turns off the machine, and the tears spill because I can see it. He doesn't have to say it.

"I'm sorry, but you had a miscarriage," the doctor says.

A sob escapes my throat and I shake my head. "My baby. I lost my baby."

"I'm sorry, Gianna, it was early, and there was just too much blood. We ran some tests. I'm afraid you were poisoned. Listeria or some type of food poisoning you ate. It can cause a miscarriage in early pregnancy. We treated you with antibiotics, and after a careful examination, you are still able to have children in the future. In early pregnancy, you must be careful with where and what you eat. Unsafe handling of food can cause a significant amount of bacteria. You were fortunate, young lady. Like I said, you lost a lot of blood. We had to give you a transfusion and IV fluids."

My gaze flicks to my mother and her hand is covering her mouth. The doctor listens and examines me while I lock eyes with her. The loss I'm feeling—the shame and anger for not taking better care of myself.

When the doctor and nurses leave, my mother walks up to me near the side of the bed. "Was it his?" she asks softly.

I nod. "Yeah."

"Where is he?"

I shrug my shoulders as tears run down my cheeks to my chin. "I don't know," I sniff.

"He knows?"

I look away toward the door. "Yes."

"And?"

"He doesn't want me," I mutter. It's all I can say. I can't tell her the whole truth. She would be disappointed in me if she wasn't already.

She wipes her hands across my cheeks and lifts my chin to meet her eyes.

"Then he doesn't deserve you. I'm not going to judge you about what happened. What you are going through is hard, and I'm not going to sit here and give you shit about it."

My eyes widen at hearing her curse. My mother never curses.

"I raised you in this bubble because I wanted what was best for you and tried to instill this image of the perfect family when, in all reality, it doesn't exist. It could, but for us, it didn't. There is no such thing as a perfect family. We all have skeletons we leave in the dark, hoping no one realizes they are there. I was wrong for forcing you to think you had to abide by this ideology."

"It's okay, Mom. I know why you did it. You didn't want me to end up being a girl with no morals. You wanted me to be the good girl who waits until she is married to have sex. To be the perfect wife. To have a career, a house, and a family."

She leans down and wipes my tears. "Now I'm telling you to do whatever makes you feel good. Whatever calls to you, do it. Do things I never did but always wanted to do. I was scared that it was going against my faith."

"What are you saying?"

"Explore your sexuality, and don't let a man make you feel worthless. Don't settle for less because you think that is all you are worth. Live. Have sex. Enjoy life. If you get pregnant and the father isn't around, so what? You won't be the first or the last. I'm sorry about the baby, Gia. You can still have children, but this time, make sure that person is worth it and at least respects you."

"I wanted the baby, Mom." I sob. "I wanted it with everything that I am, even if he didn't."

She wraps her arms around me. "It was early, and you didn't have the support you needed. I feel ashamed as your mother because you didn't feel comfortable reaching out. I would have helped you. I would have spoken to your father."

I shake my head, my eyes widening in horror. "Please don't tell him." I look up, sniffling. "Please," I plead. "Tell him we broke up and that I'm back in the dorm with Jess, and I'm fine. Don't tell him this, please. I was alone. I was bleeding on a bathroom floor, and I was so scared."

"Shh... I know, baby," she says, her voice cracking. I know my mother is crying with me, for me, and for the first time, I feel stronger than ever. With loss comes pain, but it also strengthens you.

There is a knock on the door and we both look up. Eyes that plague my dreams find me. They look at the monitors and the blood bag that was hooked up to the IV pole. His eyes dart around the room and my mother stiffens beside me.

"I think you need to leave," my mother says in a hard tone. She points to the door behind him. "How dare you. Get out."

He gives my mom the cold shoulder while I attempt to identify which of the brothers is standing in front of me. He's putting the phone up to his ear with his shoulder and his head is cocked to one side.

The Phillip Plein logo shimmers in the fluorescent light as it clings to the form of his fitted jacket. His black pants hang low on his hips as he disregards my mother.

She drops her hand and holds my hand in support. Seeing this side of my mother warms my heart. She has my back. I don't know how he found me, and I don't care.

"This is Bedford. I need a private room, now. I want a team sent to the fourth floor." He pauses. "Well, now you know. Send me everything."

He hangs up and walks closer to the foot of the bed. He glances at my mother. "I need a moment alone with her."

"No, you don't. You don't have any right."

He looks at me and says, "I have every right, and I'm not going to say it again. I need a moment alone with her." He looks around the room. "She will be moved from here."

"Oh, so you think by showing up here, you can snap your fingers, and everyone jumps?"

He gives her a devilish smile. "That's right. Everyone will jump."

My mother walks up to him, and I get nervous about how he watches her, arching a brow. "Where were you when she was bleeding on the floor of a dirty bathroom in the airport? She almost died. Where were you, huh? You don't deserve my Gianna. She doesn't need your filth."

"I'm sorry for what happened," he responds.

"*I'm sorry* doesn't bring her baby back," she snaps and walks outside.

When he stares into my eyes, it seems like he's in pain. I shift out of his reach as he tries to touch me. "Don't touch me, please. I don't know who..." I trail off.

He knows I can't tell them apart and my mother doesn't know that they're identical twin brothers. He slides his hand into his pocket and pulls out a black velvet box. It's flat and has an engraving in gold on the top.

"I'm not here to upset you."

"I don't want you here. I want you to leave me alone."

"I will—we will. I just have to give you something first. It's for your protection, and don't ever take it off." A serious expression crosses his face, his eyes look dark and there is a sadness to them.

He opens the lid and slides a necklace out, which is very different from the Raven I was gifted but gave back.

"What is it?"

"Most people call it a necklace."

"Very funny, Drav," I retort.

He smiles. He holds it up and there is a symbol over a circular coin and a bird attached. The bird is black with diamonds on a gold chain glittering in the light. It's beautiful.

"My mother would call me that. It was her way of letting us know she could tell us apart. She would tell me that only a mother would know how to tell her twin sons apart. Besides her, you're the only person that has ever said it."

He holds the necklace close so I can see it better in the light. "This is the symbol of the Order. When it is recognized, they will know. *They*. Only the founding three families have these specifically made. One for each son. This one is mine and now yours." He leans close and whispers in my ear, "I'm the bad twin. The evil one. The crow."

I place my hand over my flat stomach, knowing it's empty. My baby's father didn't make an appearance. Instead, his brother showed up. He slides the necklace around my neck and secures it, and I let him.

I glance up and see tears running down his cheeks, making my eyes well up with emotion. "I'm sorry, Gianna. I'm so sorry."

He places a strand of hair behind my ear and kisses my cheek. "I want you to know that this is going to crush him, baby. Everything beautiful in his life dies, and you are the only thing he has left."

He turns my chin to look at him, and tears are flowing like a river down my cheeks at my loss. *Our* loss. My emotions are everywhere, feeling lost and confused.

Dravin said he didn't want me. He said that I was a mistake. His words repeat in my head like a broken record. I should be mad at both of them, but Draven is here.

The pads of his thumbs wipe my cheeks. He grabs my fingers and leans in so that I can run them up his neck and feel the tattoo that is so similar to the crow pendant on my necklace. I rub it softly and his eyes darken.

"I'm the only one who has this. He has something else that he will show you." He lowers his voice. "That's one way to tell us apart and the other you already know, when we are deep inside you, claiming you." I suck in a breath, and he continues, "I don't expect you to accept me, and he doesn't expect you to accept him, but it doesn't matter, Gianna. You will always be taken care of because, in my eyes, you were already mine."

A man quickly enters the room with a clipboard flanked by four men in black suits. "Mr. Bedford, I apologize for the confusion. She will be moved to a private suite and her mother will also be accommodated. Is there anything else you may require to make Miss Taylor's stay more comfortable? She will have around-the-clock care until she is discharged."

Draven straightens, and the nurse that enters eyes him appreciatively. I give her a stern glare.

"I need all her medical reports sent to me. Her account, and everything else, are to be billed to me," he instructs and then points to the nurse. "I also don't want her attending to Gianna."

My head angles up to glance at Draven, but I can't see his face. I know he noticed me stiffening, or maybe he knows the nurse and the way she is looking at him in front of me after I just lost a baby doesn't sit well with him.

She's practically undressing him with her eyes, ready to pounce. I know that it would happen on campus, but here, after what I went through, I can't help but be grateful.

"Of course," the man says, and then one of the men in a dark suit escorts her out. "I'll send a replacement."

"Make sure he isn't male," Draven adds.

One thing they both are when they want to be is possessive. I'm weak and vulnerable, and something about what just happened to me and how I ended up here doesn't sit well with me. There could have been many things I ate that could have been contaminated, but I haven't eaten anything except what was given to me by the delivery service and a few items from the vending machine on campus.

The man with the clipboard smiles warmly at me. "You're a very lucky young lady."

He looks over at Draven. "He was in the airport when they found you. He was the one who called to have you brought in immediately. We had to stabilize you first, and you ended up here, but we had no idea..." He trails off. His eyes move a centimeter lower, spotting the necklace, and then he smiles. "Ah... I see it now."

"She left it at home and didn't realize I had it with me the whole time," Draven says.

After being placed in the most luxurious private room, like Draven instructed, there was an older nurse who was very careful in tending to me. I need a shower, but my mother was sent home and said she'd be back. My thoughts are drifting to the talk we had about me exploring my sexuality and looking out for myself, not allowing anyone to push me around or hurt me again. He can hurt me once, but it taught me to know what the sting feels like. I now recognize it. Losing my baby will make me stronger, and I know what I want. I want love, hope, faith, and family, and I want to be happy. But most of all, I want to feel wanted.

DRAVIN

IT WAS hard acting like my brother around her, but we did it all the time, and I had to see her. I'm the last person she would want to see if she knew it was me. There was too much I said that hurt her.

Leaving her there was the hardest thing I had to do. I left because I needed to be alone to break down and cry. It was the second time in my life I have given in to the emotion—the death of my mother and now the loss of my child. I had them run more tests before she was discharged to make sure someone hadn't tried to kill her, but I know deep down, it wasn't a coincidence.

Is it wrong to lie to her? Of course. I know I did the same thing. I acted like I was my brother. She was calmer, even though my brother was a dick to her, but coming from him, it was more forgivable than it was coming from me.

She thinks I haven't been around, but I have. I have turned into a stalker because of her. Her stalker. When I heard her scream in the bathroom at the airport, it felt like my heart and gut were being ripped open. I found her bleeding and lying on the floor. She didn't look well, and I thought it was the nausea that is common in early pregnancy.

At home, on my computer, I have been drowning myself with information about being a first-time parent. I would never abandon her. If she only knew, I could never have a child with someone else. I had to lie to her to protect her. She isn't my wife, and I can't force her to accept me and my brother. I can't force her to accept the life that will be thrust upon her by being Mrs. Bedford.

My phone rings and I look at the screen. It's my brother, so I answer, "Yeah."

"How is she? I want to see her, but then she is going to tell me to fuck off when she thinks I'm you."

I'm sitting in the back of the car with the divider up so the driver doesn't hear my conversation with my twin. I'm making lazy circles over my pants as I tell him what is weighing on my mind.

"Come here, and let's surprise her."

"I don't think that is a good idea."

"When did you start becoming a pussy?"

"Since the girl we both want and can't have because you have fucked with her in a way she can't wrap her head around. Since she had sex with two identical-looking people when she thought she was in love with only one. Now, what are you thinking?"

I sniff because I've been crying about the baby. Every time I think about it, I want to kill someone. Mainly myself for being careless with her. My relationship with God is sinking at the moment—the loss of my mother, a child, and her love.

I know it was early in her pregnancy, and it can happen, but why me? Why does fucked-up shit happen like that? I get that I'm not a good person because I have done fucked-up shit, but her? Why her?

What the hell did she do to deserve the loss of her baby? Our baby. The pain she was in, she could've died if I wasn't there. If I hadn't gone to her dorm room, they told me she was on a plane to see her mother.

"I'm checking to see if there have been any reports of food poisoning on campus, and so far, there aren't any. She has been eating the food we have delivered for her and Jess," he says.

"Someone tried to kill her," I blurt, my hand shaking in rage.

"Who?"

"It could be anyone that doesn't like us, and we have a fucking list a mile long. Whoever it is, knows that she was pregnant. So that narrows down to someone on campus, and it's within the Order. We have to think about who could have known and who would want to hurt or try to kill her. Once we find out who it is, I'm not going to stop, and I'm not going to wait for a fucking meeting at the church, so you tell our father that the rules don't apply when it comes to Gia. Not when it comes to her life. My unborn child's life."

"If you don't kill the motherfucker, then I will. Either way, the result will be the same. Gianna comes first. Always. Your room is ready for when she arrives back on campus. I will let our father know."

"Yeah, tell him to keep his fucking escapades around the house to his room, or I'll eat my breakfast at the dining table like a good boy."

Meaning, I'll eat my girl's pussy on the dining table, and I'll make sure to make him feel uncomfortable watching his son's ass as I fuck her freely every chance I get.

"That's if she'll let you."

I smile. "Is that a challenge, little brother?"

I can't see him smile back, but I can hear it in his voice. "Challenge accepted. It's going to be fun being you."

I snort. "Don't get used to it."

"Why?"

"Because I saw her first," I say, disconnecting the call before he can respond.

GIA

I GET up from the luxurious bed in a private room in a hotel that the hospital uses for procedures I have read about in brochures and plastic surgery offices. Rich and famous people use specific hotels with private staff and security to cater to the wealthy.

After a long day, I go to the rain shower next to my room, where the dark tiles gleam in stark contrast to the centrally placed light. In the shower, tiny teak shelves are stocked with high-end shampoos and body washes and a teak seat against one wall for sitting while you wash.

To stop the bleeding, I slip down the hospital underwear I was provided and hit the button to turn on the water. It feels like getting a heavy period, the doctor said, and it will pass in a few days. My chest hurts from throwing up so much, yet I feel somewhat stronger than I did yesterday. Assuming I eat well and drink enough fluids over the next several days to restore my strength, I should feel like myself again in a few days.

I was dehydrated and had anemia. I wasn't that far along, but I still felt the cramping and I was in pain. My body begins to shake from being in bed for the past forty-eight hours. I'm in need of a proper shower.

Drav—I smile to myself at being able to tell them apart. When they switch on me like they do, at least I can figure out who did and said what.

I'm figuring out that I have these weird feelings for both of them now. Even if Dravin lied and hurt me with his words, I have a feeling there is a bigger picture at play. The tears I saw Drav shed showed me that the baby and I meant a lot more than Dravin said we did.

What he said confused me, but it was like something inside both of them died. To them, the little being inside me belonged to one, but it also belonged to the other.

I have heard of twins sharing such a strong bond that they share everything. They get used to sharing. They are so equally identical and more so if they were raised that way. I find it bizarre but hot all at the same time.

There were nights I cried and nights I imagined having them both, but they belonged to me and only me. What I did to one, I made sure to give to the other, and in return, they did the same. One night, it was with Dravin, and the other night, it was with Draven.

The IV made my left hand sore. The warm water falls like rain over my head as I wash my hair with shaky hands. The steam rises like fog under the single spotlight in the shower, and then I hear a noise and jolt.

After wiping my eyes to remove the accumulated water on my lashes, I turn around.

Slowly, my gaze travels down to the shower's threshold, where it lands on two sets of feet. My dreams and the real world are both haunted by them. Their presence engulfs everything I think about. It's all connected. They're connected—the way they make me feel. Hate, love, and darkness collide like I'm the sweetest sacrifice.

My eyes train on their necks, and it's like I'm seeing them in a new light. They even share the colors of their eyes. It's powerful when all their attention is on you.

They stare, running their eyes over my body as the water sluices down my curves. Both of their cocks are hard and imposing as they step forward. The water sprays as it hits their bodies, carved like perfect concrete sculptures.

The water wets their hair as one grabs the body wash, and I can see the tattoo of the crow and the other of a wolf in the light. I don't know how I didn't see them before, or maybe they're recent, but they're surrounded by other symbols and markings inked on their skin.

When they turn, the light moves like shadows casting figures, but then I see them as their fingers trail down my cheek, one on the left and the other to my right. The tattoo of a Raven. One near the crow and the other near the wolf. On the bottom, it reads: *We pray for her love evermore.*

"How are you feeling, gorgeous?" Drav says as the suds of the body wash slide down my breasts.

My eyes flick to Dravin, and his eyes turn dark. His nostrils flare, but then I notice his eyes are red-rimmed. His head tilts to look at my stomach and then slowly slides up to my face. He walks closer, but I move closer to Drav, remembering the hurt of his words. His eyes flick to Drav with a glare aimed at his twin.

He shakes his head slowly, then grips my face in both hands and kisses me. My lips are closed, but he forces them open with his tongue, sliding it over my teeth.

"I'm sorry," he says softly while he trails his fingers over my belly. I look down, our foreheads touching as a little trail of blood slides down my thighs.

"I'm bleeding," is all I manage to say.

They both look down at the same time and see a small trail of blood mixing with water down the drain.

"Shit," Drav says with a sniffle.

They are both crying silent tears, and I give them this moment—a moment to mourn our loss, the three of us. They both wash me carefully, not too rough but with gentle strokes over my skin as the rain shower head pours over our skin. We stand under the spray, with the spotlight illuminating the dimly lit bathroom.

They wash my hair, body, and toes while they both kiss my belly. Heat pools between my legs as they inch closer to the apex of my thighs.

Drav's hand stills near my slit and Dravin watches the expression on my face to see if it's okay to wash me there.

"I think it's best if you do it. We don't want to hurt you," Drav says.

I nod in agreement. Dravin hands me the body wash, and I raise my hand to the spray, wetting the palm of my hand and squinting as I reach down to gently wash myself. I watch them and notice the smoldering gaze aimed at my hand as the tension begins to increase.

"So beautiful," Dravin whispers, but the memory of the text with the video slows my movements, and I turn around, giving them my back.

"I wasn't beautiful when they sent me the text of you and those girls."

I meant Dravin, but I recognize that I wasn't just jealous because of one. I was jealous of both of those girls touching them. I close my eyes and feel the sting of tears burning my eyes.

The loss, pain, and humiliation I felt in that moment. Then, the moment after, when he told me I was a mistake and unworthy. That he wouldn't acknowledge his child and that he would marry someone else. Have children that would be considered his.

The fog in my mind clears and I look down, ashamed of myself for letting them hurt me. Guilt for allowing myself to be used, for allowing them to be here with me. A sob creeps up my throat. Fresh tears slide down my cheeks, and suddenly, the shower becomes stifling.

"We didn't sleep with them."

I whirl around and meet both of their stares, but I lock mine on Dravin because his brother wasn't the one I was in love with. He doesn't owe me any loyalty. What he did was fucked up, but I was pregnant with Dravin's child. He didn't know at first.

"I'm going to let it slide for Drav, but for you, I can't because whoever that girl was, sure as hell had your cock in her mouth. You weren't thinking about me then or how I would feel about it, but it doesn't matter anymore because you're free of me. I'm not pregnant anymore," I say, widening my stance. "You have proof. I'm not your responsibility. The mistake was taken care of, Dravin."

He flinches like I slapped him. My eyes find Drav. "Thank you for the private room and the nice shower. I'm sure I'm not the only woman you have given the same privilege to, and you're right; the girl in the video was better than me. She sucked you off like a champ. That part you did do, right?"

I look up at the bathroom and my surroundings like it's the first time, and that I haven't been standing here feeling numb since I suffered food poisoning and a miscarriage at the same time.

"I'm sorry I hurt you. If I could take it all back, I would. We took things too far and were reckless," Drav says with a sigh.

My chin lifts and our eyes lock. "Me too. I should have listened when everyone told me to stay away from you." My gaze shifts to Dravin. "Especially you. You two are great at deceiving people and are so alike you even treat women the same. When I think of you two, I feel like I'm nothing." I lick my lips and hug myself, suddenly feeling cold. "I would like to go to my mother's and spend the holidays with her, please," I say quietly.

Dravin steps out and hands me a towel for my hair and a fluffy white robe. "Of course."

I hate having to let them go, but I need to. It's the hardest thing to let go of something you love. I can't keep throwing what happened in their faces. I need to move on. I need to let go.

JESS

WE ARE BACK from winter break, and Gia is quiet as she skims over the menu at a bar we decided to try out on the outskirts of Kenyan. We wanted to stay away from campus and the Babylon bar. It's a new semester with new classes and we have decided to lie low.

"Have you heard from them?" I ask Gia while I'm scanning the menu, still deciding between the club or the meatloaf.

"Nope. They dropped me off at my mother's, and they left but made sure to leave two men in suits to follow me and camp outside my mother's apartment."

I raise my brows. "Why would they think you need security?"

She lets out a breath. "I have no fucking idea. All I know is that I need to concentrate on graduating, have fun, and forget about them and what happened. It is in the past now, but I have to move on. It's over."

I lower my voice and ask, "Have you seen Warren lurking around?"

She shakes her head. "Not since that day at the café when he creeped me out."

"Did you tell them?" I ask, lowering the menu, my eyes locking with hers. "What he said to you."

She shakes her head. "No. Dravin isn't my boyfriend. Why would he care? I'll just report him if he says or does anything else."

I'm about to say something when two guys wearing Ohio State hoodies stop by our booth.

"Hi. We were wondering if you ladies would like some company?"

I look up, and the guy to the left looks at me. His blond friend has his eyes locked on Gia.

I give the guy on my left a playful smile. "Is that what you guys do? You go to diners and pick up girls by asking if you can join them?"

He laughs nervously, sliding his dark hair out of his eyes. "No. Just you two. We've never seen you two around here before. You ladies in school?" he asks, then looks at Gia. His eyes land back on me, waiting for me to respond.

"Yeah," I answer, pointing to his hoodie. "But we don't attend Ohio State, though."

The blond one turns his gaze on me, but then it's back on Gia. "What school do you attend, beautiful? Please tell me you don't have a boyfriend somewhere?" he asks Gia.

She licks her lip nervously and then glances at him. "Kenyan. We attend Kenyan, and no, I don't have a boyfriend. Not anymore."

The blond guy holds his hand out and sits at the edge of the booth next to her. "I'm Dalton, and this is my teammate and best friend, Tate. Since you two lovely ladies aren't seeing anyone, we would love to take you out. How about us four next Saturday night? We can meet up at a local bar. Food, drinks, dancing."

Gia's eyes find mine with uncertainty. Is it too soon? Should we say yes? I can see all her questions cross her face, silently asking me how we should answer. Accept or don't accept.

My need to forget what happened back home claws my insides, and I smile coyly while making my decision. "What time Saturday?"

"We can meet up at six," Dalton says.

"Perfect."

We exchange phone numbers, and he sends me directions to the bar we are supposed to meet at on Saturday. I guess you could call it a date, even if it's just to meet up somewhere. To be honest, I just want to forget what happened back home.

When people ask me how my winter break was, flashes of unwanted kisses and grunts fill my head. Tears burn my eyes, and the sense of feeling dirty and the need to scrub my skin overwhelms me. I hate myself, but before the disappointment sets in, I remember my mother's smile full of relief that she can pay her rent, gas, electric, and car insurance all in the same month. That she doesn't have to go down to the local church at six a.m. to pick up free groceries from donations.

When she told me the sacrifices parents make for their children are worth it, I was eight; I didn't understand what she meant. But I understand now as a grown woman. The sacrifices you make for the people you love most in your life are the ones that count. It's part of surviving, even if you begin to lose yourself. But losing yourself doesn't mean you gave up; it just means you'll rise a different person.

GIA

"ARE YOU SURE I LOOK OKAY?" I ask Jess, pulling the top that is one inch away from spilling my breasts. My dark hair is ironed straight, and I'm wearing black patent leather pants that I found in a boutique store we went to earlier today. I was surprised when I checked my bank account, which had a deposit from Bedford Holdings for fifty thousand dollars. I subtracted the difference I'd had previously and made my purchase.

I know Dravin is trying to keep his word and must be feeling guilty, but I'm going to try and move on. When I got back from my mother's house, Jess thought it would be good to get out the first weekend back. The bleeding stopped, and I had no more cramping.

My eyes scan the room through the reflection of the mirror, and I see Jess dabbing her neck again with some foundation to cover up the marks on her skin. I know they weren't there before. They look like marks someone gives you when they want to hurt you.

She looks at me through the mirror's reflection. "You look hot, babe. Just make sure you're ready because when he sees you in that outfit, I'm not sure he is going to just hold your hand," she says playfully.

A blush creeps up my neck at the thought of someone touching me because they really like me and not because they want to use me for some sick game. My mother's words from when I was in the hospital play in my head.

When she dropped me off at the airport, she reminded me to live and to do what feels right. Explore and find what makes you happy, and that is what I'm going to do. I'm tired of feeling guilty and afraid..

"Are you going to tell me what happened?" Her hands pause from dabbing the concealer with the beauty blender across her neck.

Her eyes lock on mine, and a sadness crosses her expression. Something bad happened to her when she went home.

I turn around and walk closer to her and lower my voice. "You could tell me, Jess. I saw the bruises, and I didn't want to pressure you into telling me, but I want to know if there is a way I can help. A way to make that face you're making go away. You're my only friend."

She nods and her eyes get glassy. Her hands begin to fidget and her lips purse as she lets out a breath, closing her eyes. My heart starts to beat faster because I know what she is about to tell me is going to make me hurt.

She dabs her fingers over her neck on the faded marks. "Well, you know I didn't get these because a boy loves me back home."

I visibly swallow and work my way over to her side of the bed and I give her a hug, smelling her perfume. "Tell me," I whisper.

"It's ugly, Gia."

"All I have felt lately is ugly," I say softly. "Unwanted. Used. And I'm fucking sick of it."

She knows about the miscarriage and what happened over the break. She was sad, and we both cried for hours when I broke down and told her.

She takes a deep breath and begins. "I used to like this boy back in high school. His name is Michael. He was the typical rich boy who had it all. Cars, looks, money, and a killer smile. It was like the devil created him just to fuck with me. Word got around that the trailer trash was at the top of her class liked him, and he asked me out. I felt like I was on cloud nine. I got accepted to come here, and I was being asked out by the hottest guy in school my senior year right before prom. I hadn't lost my virginity because I was secretly hoping that one day it would be him."

She gives a shaky laugh and a sniff, trying to not let her mascara run, dabbing her finger under her eye, and looks up for a second and continues. "Anyway. I was invited to this party in his neighborhood, and I thought the popular crowd was finally accepting me because he noticed me. I dressed up and I went. He was there with his friends. We talked and he was so nice. He did all the right things the entire night, and I was giddy. He knew he had me and I wasn't going anywhere. He told me I was beautiful and that he liked me but didn't know how to approach me because I was quiet. He said he didn't care where I lived or the rumors about me and my mother because we lived in a trailer."

She closes her eyes as I listen to her story. It's like she is reliving something awful every day, and my heart prepares for the blow that I sense is coming.

"He spiked my drink, and they took me to a room. Michael and his friends... they raped me."

My stomach clenches and I blink back the tears. "Did you tell anyone?"

She shakes her head. "For what? No one would believe me. I got tested, and thank God I was on birth control, but I came out clean. I didn't go to prom for obvious reasons and kept to myself. I didn't have money for a dress anyway. It's what I told myself to cope. That is why I didn't want to go back home. I hated to leave my mom, but I have a plan to get a degree and a good job and take my mom out of there, and we can start a new life. A good life."

"When you went back. Was it him that did this to you?"

She nods slowly and I want to go with her and kill the bastard. How dare he. That piece of shit. Then I think of what she said about Garret and what they did with the video. Her behavior with Reid and Valen. She's trying to pick up the pieces. To feel wanted by someone. To forget.

"Does your mom know?"

"No. I couldn't do that when the asshole's father bought the diner across the road. When I went back, she told me she applied there for work, and they turned her down, and to top it off, the owner where she works cut her hours. She didn't want me to worry, but she was struggling. She asked for a raise, and he denied her. It was so she would call me and for me to show up."

"He was there, wasn't he? Waiting like the sick bastard he is baiting you with your mother."

"Yeah, he got what he wanted. He made sure to throw a hundred bucks on my lap after zipping up his pants," she says with a shaky laugh, but it's so that she doesn't break down and cry. "Then Reid called me from a blocked number, telling me I was fun. After I scrubbed my skin raw in the shower, that's all I was worth."

I stay quiet and give her a minute. Her eyes land on mine, tortured and full of hurt and shame. "I just want to forget, Gia. I want to forget what I had to do to put a smile on my mother's face when she came in telling me they hired her. I hate the person I have become."

"Don't say that," I tell her, caressing her hair, which took forty-five minutes to straighten. It's silky and soft. "It's what they want you to become, and you're not that. You're better than they are. They have to blackmail you to get it, but you know what? They may think they have gotten the best of you, but they haven't. They will never have your love, your mind, or your loyalty. Don't let them break what is left of you."

Her voice cracks on a whisper, "I just want to forget. I don't want the memory of his hands on my skin. His tongue on my lips. I want that feeling to go away."

"Then do what you need to do to forget."

She moves to her nightstand and takes a string of condoms out, and hands me two, slipping the rest into her bag. Her eyes lift. "This is the only way I know how."

I get why she wanted to go out with the hockey players who approached us at the booth. They were both good-looking and seemed like regular college guys. Not the kind that would live in a Gothic mansion with secrets and evil twin brothers who are part of a secret society with rules.

WE ARRIVE in Jess's car, parking on the side of the bar. Dravin texted me twice on the way here, but I left it as delivered. I don't have time for him right now.

The last three weeks after the hospital, I have kept it curt via text message. He asks me how I'm feeling and if I need anything, but I just tell him that I'm okay and fine. I don't engage in conversation with him. Draven has texted me the same, asking the same questions as his brother. I wonder if they do anything different besides the tattoo markings or the way they have sex.

I clench my thighs, thinking about them and the way they introduced sex to me. I had no experience before them and everything I do know, it's because of both of them. After everything, I love to hate them and hate to love them.

When I think of them, I think of hot sex, pain, hurt, shame, and guilt. Tonight, I hope to move on from all that with someone who can show me a good time.

We both slam the car doors shut and I smile. "Ready?" she asks.

"Yeah. Let's go for it. Remember to keep your drink in hand, and let's stick to beer."

"Good idea."

We make our way to the entrance, and music filters through the door as we open it. The bouncer nods as we come in, taking our coats off.

We notice Dalton and Tate waving at us from a booth in the back. The place has dark gray interior brick walls, a bar in the center, and booths and tables flanked on the sides. Flat-screen TVs hang from the walls at different angles. Some people are dancing from the lit jukebox to the right.

I smile and give them a small wave when Tate stands from the booth, waiting for us to reach them. His eyes take me in from top to bottom and then back up again with a smile.

"Hi," I say, greeting them both.

"Glad you two could make it," Dalton says.

"Thank you for the invite," Jess responds, scanning the bar and the people around us. Ohio State banners and the years of their wins in football, hockey, and even swimming decorate the walls, but there have been very few in the last four years, and I know it's because of the sons of Kenyan. Reid, Dravin, and now Valen. I wouldn't even put it past Draven making an appearance just to fuck with them.

"Of course. You look beautiful," Dalton says, his blond hair sticking up in that messy way that looks sexy. "I love the pants. You have that dark vibe that I like."

I bet he does. He has that hockey frat boy vibe that seems normal, but to be honest, I'm missing my goth boy. Maybe even his twin. I shake my head and forget that I'm supposed to forget about them.

"Thank you."

Tate's eyes keep dipping low to where Jess's heart-shaped mesh top holds her breasts over a black tube top underneath. He slides his dark, straight hair to the side so that it doesn't cover his eyes and he can get a better view.

"So, what would you ladies like to drink?" Tate asks.

"A blonde and a Guinness," I answer.

Jess smiles at my inside joke, and I try to hold in my laughter. I said it to lighten her mood.

After five minutes, the beers arrive. I take the Guinness, and she takes the blonde ale.

"You guys like to switch?" Tate asks, playfully taking a pull from his beer.

Guess who picked up on the joke? Nothing escapes guys nowadays. I tip the bottle and take a pull, and I feel froggy. Some things happen, and they change people. It certainly changed me, and I'm all for it.

"What's the point in switching?" I say, sliding the beer to Jess, taking hers, tipping it back, the taste of her beer mixing with mine while both of their eyebrows lift in surprise. When I set the bottle down on the table and she takes a sip and does the same, I finish saying, "When you can just share."

"Sharing is sexy," Jess pipes up, teasing them.

"So is watching," a deep voice snaking up my spine, belonging to Draven, says as he comes into view by sliding himself next to me on the booth. I notice the tattoo.

I'm sitting between Draven and Dalton, and the hairs on the back of my neck stand. My eyes flick to Jess as she stiffens.

Reid and Valen lean over the back of the booth, and I don't know how we didn't see them come in or why they are here.

Reid curves his lips in a knowing smile as he looks at Dalton and then at Tate, my heart beating wildly in my chest. "You boys like to watch?" Reid asks with an evil grin.

"Depends on what we are watching. Aren't you three on the wrong side of town?" Dalton fires back.

Valen chuckles and leans forward so his lips are close to Jess's ear. He says softly, over the sound of "Mudshovel" by Staind playing in the background, "Did you hear, Jess? They like to watch."

Draven leans forward, the scent of his exotic cologne hits my nose, and his voice turns hard as he looks at Dalton. "We own the town. You're just visiting."

Tate looks at Draven in challenge. "I know who you guys are. You're the sons of Kenyan."

Reid blows smoke in the air from his vape, the tinge of marijuana from the oil permeating the air around us in a cloud. He turns his face, and his lips are near Jess's left cheek. "You're having fun without me, baby?"

Tate's eyes flash in annoyance, and he answers for her, "She was until you showed up."

"Is that so?" Reid says, his nose near her cheek and his lips near her ear. "There is only one way to find out."

His hand disappears under the table, and I see Jess's eyes fill with desire as she bites her bottom lip. After a second, his hand appears above the table and he holds two fingers up to his tongue, flicking the piercing on his lip and showing them to Tate. "Dry as the desert."

Valen leans in again near Jess's ear and says, "That's no fun. Is it?"

Jess's eyes flick to Tate. His nostrils flare and Draven leans forward. "Didn't you just say you liked to watch?"

Fuck this. I slide the beer bottles out of the way and lean across the table toward Jess. Her eyes widen, but she doesn't pull away when I plant my lips on hers and she holds my face in her hands.

Our tongues taste and twirl, the taste of our beer mixing together. We hear intakes of breath around us from the guys. I don't like girls, and I'm sure she feels the same, but I can't stand what they are doing. If they want a show, then we'll give them one, but on our terms, not theirs.

"That's so hot," I hear Dalton's voice behind me.

Strong hands grip my waist, pulling me back down on the bench seat of the booth, and I turn my head and see Draven's stern expression mixed with desire. "No," he says.

I lick my lips from her taste and whip my head toward Reid, his eyes on my tongue as it snakes my bottom lip, and I say, "She's having fun now. I bet she's wet like Florida."

Tate bellows in laughter, taking a pull of his beer and angles the top of the beer bottle toward me. "I like her."

"She's not yours to like," Draven fires back.

He leans forward, cocky as hell, and he doesn't seem to realize the danger they are both in sitting here with us. "Funny, she told us she doesn't have a boyfriend. So that means she's not yours to like."

Draven chuckles and places an elbow on the wooden table with his hand near my cheek. He then places a strand of hair behind my ear, causing a trail of nerves to ignite on my skin. He says, "I'm not a boy, and I'm definitely not her friend."

"She isn't married. That much is obvious. There isn't much left. Then what are you?"

Reid takes another drag, passing it to Valen as they both smile, waiting for Draven to reply. He isn't even my ex-boyfriend, but his twin brother that I ended up fucking, but he doesn't need to know all that.

I watch Valen take a drag of the marijuana pen. The smoke from the vape twirling around the light hanging in the middle of the booth, the tension getting thick. The silence stretches and the music playing fades into the background.

Draven's eyes flick to Tate, hard and threatening, "I'm her fucking god."

Draven slides his hand over my thigh possessively and heat pools between my thighs. I try to clench them together, but his grip tightens.

Tate leans back in the booth with a sly grin. "Funny, but yet she's here with him." He nudges his chin toward Dalton, goading him.

Draven chuckles like it doesn't matter what he says. He will always have the upper hand. "Yeah, but she's so fucking bored. She's kissing her best friend when she would rather be sitting on my cock as I make her pray for me to make her come. You two little hockey boys run along and go play with your sticks. We've come to collect what belongs to us," Draven says, getting up, and so does Reid, taking Jess by the arm.

Valen slides over the booth, plants his feet, and walks out like he is balancing himself on a balance beam. He hops off. He turns around and gives me a mischievous smile. "Let's go, Gia. Let's go have some real fun."

DRAVIN
†

THE MEN WORKING for me have been following Gia and Jess everywhere they go, whether they're taking shifts at practice or having our meetings. It's a new semester, and we made sure to keep our distance from them. All I know is that she is in danger, and so is Jess. I saw the bruising on her neck if Reid or Valen didn't, but I'll let them handle it.

I have my hands full with Gianna. I've written so many letters to her but haven't had the courage to leave them on her bed where she can wake up to find them.

We pile in the matte-black SUV, and I let Valen drive while I sit in the back and act like my twin brother so she doesn't run away from me.

Acting like Draven around Gia takes some patience because she knows me intimately. I've seen her watching me. She is studying my quirks and if he is around, she will study his. She isn't stupid, but I never thought of her being anything but intelligent. She's smart and sexy. I have to up my game, or I'll lose her forever. Her seeking out another man that isn't me is driving me insane.

Seeing her next to that asshole in the bar had me wanting to yank her out of there and pummel his face until I split it in two. The way his eyes were glued to her breasts and thighs. Those pants had my cock straining to be released; I wanted to bend her over and sink into her.

I lean into her while she sits next to me, our thighs touching. "You must be feeling better. Are you trying to escape me so I can chase you?"

Her head angles toward me. "I thought guys like you don't chase. It wasn't the fact that I was here. It was who I was with that bothered you. I never thought you were the jealous type."

I give her a side grin. "I'm not jealous."

"I can tell. *I'm her fucking god*," she mocks. "Real smooth, Goth boy. I wouldn't be surprised if you turned green next to me."

The smile on my face falls. My stomach clenches. Does she know I'm me and not Draven? Shit. She called me Goth Boy. Has she called him that?

I turn her chin toward me, and I watch as her pink tongue licks her glossy lips. She must have applied lip gloss at some point and the image of that glossy mess all over my cock has a tingle snaking up my spine.

I arch my eyebrow. "Goth Boy?"

She snickers, and so does Reid. "Where are you taking us?" Jess asks.

"To a party," Reid chimes in.

"What kind of party?" Jess asks.

"Members-only type of party," Valen says, looking through the rearview mirror.

"What kind of party is it? We aren't members," Gia points out.

"If you come with us, then you're allowed in. The rules are..." I trail off.

My eyes follow the wetness of her lips. My thumb touches her bottom lip, pulling it down slightly, feeling the stickiness and I chuckle. "There are no rules. We... are the rules."

Her breathing is slow and shallow, but I can see the desire pooling in her eyes. The clenching of her thighs. My Raven wants to get fucked. She's ready. My eyes trail down to her top, partially hidden by her jacket. I bet her nipples are straining, and I know she isn't wearing a bra.

When she leaned over and kissed Jess, I was green with envy. Jess was tasting what was mine and her pussy was wet for her. My Raven wants to break the rules, but I want to be the one she breaks the rules with.

I lean close, and my lips brush her neck and rasp against her skin, "Tell me, Gia. Do you think about me when you play with your pussy? Or do you think about him?" I place a small peck against her neck, and she squirms.

I know she wants me, but I want to make sure she wants not just one. I'm okay if she wants us both, but if it's one of us, it has to be me. "Or... maybe you think of us both."

Her head turns, and our eyes lock while the car moves over bumps in the road toward Garrett's house. The younger members of the Order are throwing the party there. I'm not sure how Jess will feel about it when she finds out, but I have faith in Reid and Valen. I don't want to ruin their night.

"How did you know we were there?" Gia asks.

"We've had you followed for your safety," I say, peppering a kiss on her cheek.

I notice she is still wearing the necklace I gave her. It is usually reserved for the sons of the founding families or their wives. She's mine in my eyes, and there will never be another. It's her or nothing.

The car slows down two miles from campus and proceeds through a gate that opens. A guy in a suit exits the security booth Garret's family has on their estate. He sees Valen and nods to proceed through.

The mansion comes into view, dark and gray. Expensive cars line the driveway, with drivers sitting inside waiting until the members leave for the night.

"Wow," Jess says from the seat next to Gia.

The lights glow against the dark pillars with a tinge of red. It's cold, but the party is indoors with an indoor pool.

Music filters through the house as we step inside. The staff takes her jacket off her shoulders. Her skin flushes at the warmth of the changing temperature. Valen leads with Reid, and Jess follows in front of Gia.

I'm walking behind her when she slows down and asks softly, "Where's Dravin?"

I want to say I'm right behind you, and I'll never leave you, but I can't—not yet. Instead, I say, "He's inside by the pool with the others. He's expecting you."

Draven is dying to see her, but I keep that bit to myself. He's been grumpy all week because she refuses to stay in the main house. I have offered, but she repeatedly turns me down. I don't think she's comfortable in the main house. I prefer to be at my house in my bed, but that is my own fault.

The indoor pool comes into view, and she stops as she takes in the scene. Candles dimly lit. The steam from the heated pool comes from the surface of the water. Women are swimming topless, laughing, and drinking. Servers with trays walking around serving champagne and hors d'oeuvres.

There are private cabanas with lounge chairs that have sheer curtains, but you can see people fucking. Moans filter through the music, "More Human Than Human" by White Zombie plays.

She looks at me. "Is this—?" She swallows, looking as one of the girls considered Prey rides one of the guys on the swim team that is part of the Order. Her tits bouncing as he pumps into her from below.

"Yes. It's all consensual. Prey choose who they want. Parents know we need to let off steam, or we will do it out there, and they can't have that."

She knows what I mean. She chooses. Girls are dancing in the pool. Some I have had sex with smile coyly at me, hoping they'll get lucky with a Bedford. Fat chance.

She turns and faces me, her head lifting so our eyes lock. "Cold" by Breaking Benjamin plays as my hands slide over her arms, and she watches me touch her. My brother Draven comes up behind her, shirtless and in his Versace board shorts. Flashy bastard.

Her head tips up, and her lips curl into a sexy smile. My chest flips inside out. He grips her by the neck gently as his mouth crashes down on her lips, and I slide her top down an inch, making her breasts spill out as I feast on one nipple and then the other. Her pink nipples are begging for my tongue.

A gasp escapes from her lips, and I remove my shirt, her neck straining and exposed while she kisses Draven. I remove the rest, not giving a fuck who is watching. The three of us crash into the warm pool water. Hands gripping and touching, removing clothes.

Her groans mix with mine as we desperately seek to be inside her, like an empty cup waiting to be filled. We go at it like two predators devouring our Prey, but it's the other way around. She's the predator, and we are her Prey.

She's ours, and she knows it, and so does everyone here. Untouchable.

Her pants come off next and the black lace thong is left, but my brother shakes his head no. We leave it on. We will work around it.

I bend my legs and slide into her wet heat first and she arches her back. My brother's tongue is on her breasts as I pump into her from behind. She gasps as I slide my tongue, licking her neck.

"Mine," I growl.

"Don't forget. I'm right here," my brother says.

She smirks and holds onto his shoulders.

I slow down inside of her and Veronica saunters up. "Damn. She's beautiful."

"Fuck off," I warn.

"I didn't come for her. I came for the one who fucks me."

Gia stiffens and my eyes flick to my brother. Fuck. This bitch.

My brother turns his head, and Gia turns her face away.

I grip her waist. "She is looking for Draven," I whisper in her ear. Knowing she thinks it's me. Veronica can only tell us apart because I moved out of the main house. She's pissed that Gia has us both right now.

"Then go to her," Gia responds.

"I can't."

"Why?" she asks through clenched teeth.

"Because I'm not the one who's fucked her."

As my confession dawns, my dick swells inside her as I pump into her, the water making waves and the steam so thick it's making us sweat. From where we are, you can't see people across the long pool.

"Drav," she says, a moan escaping her lips.

"I've been here next to you." *Thrust.* "Watching you." *Thrust.* "Always."

I pump into her. I know she is on birth control, and I haven't stuck my cock in anyone since. The blow job was only for show. Pulled out and sent the girl packing. No one is like her.

Her pussy clenches around my cock and Draven's gaze looks at Veronica watching us. "I'm busy with my girl. Fuck off," he tells Veronica.

Her lip curls and she snarls, "She's his girl."

"I shared a womb with him for nine months. She's mine just as much as his." His eyes trail over her perfect tits, licking her torso while she gets fucked.

Gia's moans mix with my grunts. "Can I come inside you, baby?" I ask.

"I'm on the pill," she gasps, and I know she's about to come. I pull out and flip her around so that my brother has his turn. This will only happen occasionally, us at the same time. I want my time with her alone uninterrupted. I'm sure Draven does too, but he can't have another if he chooses her.

The way he slides into her to the hilt, balls deep, making her lift off the pool floor, I don't think he plans to have another woman. He pumps into her savagely and her eyes roll back in her skull. Fuck.

I take her lips with mine, and she grips my cock in her hand and starts to jerk me off. Her eyes land on mine, and the look on her face as she comes has me about to bust. I grit my teeth, holding on. My brother comes in her, and she dips her head underwater and we both look down as she wets her hair coming back up. Her fingers run up my torso.

"Put it in the other side," she whispers.

Jesus. I close my eyes, wiping my face. I turn her around and the tip of my cock nudges her puckered hole. She gasps and my brother begins to play with her as I slide in inch by inch. The pressure from the water easing me inside of her.

"Deeper, Drav," she says.

I close my eyes and look down at her ass backed up against me. My hands slide on her hips, and I push in all the way.

She moans. "Yes. More. Yes."

"Fuck, she's there," Draven says with his hand on her clit.

Her hands are on his shoulders, gripping him in a vise as I pound her ass, biting my lip as my orgasm crests and I finally spill into her tight ass. "This ass and pussy are ours, baby. No one fucks them but us."

She nods and mewls. "Yes. I'm... coming."

Draven dips his fingers, sliding inside, and I feel her pussy contract even from my cock deep inside her ass.

"I feel so full."

"You're always going to feel full, baby," I tell her.

I slide out of her and kiss the side of her neck, smelling her sweet scent, hoping this is what she truly wants because it's what I want. Her.

JESS

AFTER CHANGING our flights and saying our goodbyes, we planned our return flights to arrive forty minutes apart on the same day the next week. The Uber driver pulls onto the road leading to the trailer park where my mother lives. As much as she tries to work, she cannot save enough to move out on her own.

I'm hoping when I graduate, I can change all that. I want to take my mother out of here. She deserves better and has sacrificed so much for me. She's never cared what people think of her living in the trailer park. Like always, they assume shit that isn't true.

As the vehicle leaves the trailer park, dust and smoke billow from its rear bumper. The heat and age have turned the bottom of the trailer's once-white door a dingy yellow. I drape the strap of my duffel bag over my shoulder and step toward the small concrete steps.

Inhaling deeply, I glance across at the nearby parking spot with one car and know she's home. When I would get home from school, I always knocked twice. She always worked the schedule that got her home in time to have supper ready for me every night. I would be surprised if she had kept the same shift since I left for Ohio. I'm about to double-knock, but the door swings open, and I see my mother's eyes widen and hear her squeal in excitement.

"Jesse!"

"Surprise, Mom," I say, waving my hands out wide.

"Get in here. Oh my god. You made it!"

I walk up the last steps of the shaky wood that leads between the concrete to the front door. Once inside, it smells like Dollar Store air freshener and old carpet. My mother could never make enough to change it because she saved every last dime she made to send me to college.

I embrace her tightly, shutting my eyes to keep the tears away. She's clearly working double shifts; I see the tired lines around her eyes. "How are you, Momma?"

"Oh, honey. I'm doing great now that you're here," she whispers as I hug her tight. She smells like the peach cobbler she always bakes at the diner. It's their signature favorite because she makes it.

"I miss you," I whisper back.

God, I missed her. It's been almost four years since I last saw her, and I'm only keeping in touch via phone.

We break apart and I close the front door, walking farther inside the small two-bedroom trailer. It is old but clean and doesn't smell like stale cigarettes, like the neighbor's next door, where my mother would tell me to drop off leftovers.

"I'm going to make you something to eat, and then I have to leave for my shift, but you could drop me off and keep the car if you want."

I smile. I'll drive her just so she can relax, and I'll pick her up until I leave —anything to make her life a little easier. I tell her, "I'd love to take you, Mom. How's work and the diner?"

"It's okay. I guess. Jim cut my hours last week, but I've been saving. I'll be fine."

Shit. That means she's struggling while I'm at school, not worrying about rent or utilities. She didn't tell me, so I wouldn't worry. She knows I would drop out if I knew. She's all I have.

"I'm almost done, Mom. I can get a job on weekends if you need help. Did Jim give you a raise yet, at least?"

She shakes her head, setting two plates on the small, chipped counter. "He was, but business hasn't been going well since the bar opened across the road."

Not comprehending, I furrow my brows. "What bar?"

She slides mayo on each slice of bread. "Michael and his father opened a biker bar, and it has affected Jim's diner. I tried to apply for extra shifts, but..." She trails off.

I stiffen hearing his name, and she looks at me. "I'm sorry, Jesse, I forgot. Jesus, I'm sorry."

"It's okay."

I swallow, knowing why he wouldn't hire her. Michael was the guy I fell for in high school. The one I lost my virginity to, or better yet, he took it by spiking my drink at a party. He thought it would be fun since I was out of it. His friends thought so, too. She doesn't know what really happened and probably thinks it's because we live in a trailer.

JESS

I DROP OFF MY MOM, and my stomach drops when I see Michael in a late-model Mustang across the street. He gets out and looks over when he sees my mother. The sound of the creaking door of her old Oldsmobile slamming shut.

He walks across the street, looking both ways. My hands shake because I want to run him over. Over the last three years, I have thought of so many ways to make him pay.

My mother, not knowing what would happen or what seeing him in the flesh was doing to me, greeted him. "Hey there, Michael."

He watches me with a brilliant gleam in his eye like he's struck gold. "Hey there, Mom. I didn't know you were bringing my Christmas present early. I've missed her so much. I hope she can forgive me. We went out, and I said something I shouldn't have, but we were younger, and I think we have matured since then," he says with his smug smile.

Bastard.

"She surprised me! I didn't know my Jesse was visiting."

Through the open window on the driver's side, he glances up and smirks before fixing his gaze on my thighs. Even though my mom's air conditioner is broken, we seldom need to use it since the weather is usually cool. My legs, covered in wool leggings I found in a consignment store, were warming up thanks to the vents blowing hot air on my thighs.

"Did she now?"

It's really annoying that he continues talking to her and staring at me. I despise him. He needs to be locked up, him and his friends, for what they did to me, but nobody would believe me. In this town, he has the police in his pocket. Around here, he'd be treated like a prince, while I'd be the lowlife trying to take advantage of Michael Levine's celebrity status. The Levine family owns half of the town, and if they see a business, like Jim's restaurant, doing well, they will set up shop and attempt to steal their customers. They will make it appear as if they are helping the community, but they are just trying to make a quick buck off of Jim's success.

He looks over at my mother from the roof of the car, and I see that he's gotten bigger and stronger. I wonder how I fell for someone like him. His leather jacket over his fitted sweater and black jeans. He isn't unattractive, but he's a predator. A manipulator.

"I heard you applied for a shift at the bar. I'll talk to my father and Jess. We will come up with something," he says with a gleam in his eyes.

Motherfucker. He turned her down to get what he wanted. Me to come around or contact him. To plead with him for his father to give my mother work because he knows that we are broke. He doesn't know where I went exactly, he just knows I was accepted to a college in another state.

"Oh, don't you worry. Jess and I always work something out. Don't trouble yourself." She bends down and looks at me through the open window of the passenger side. "I'll see you in a couple of hours, sweetie," she says as she walks away, her pride not allowing her to ask for any favors.

He waits until she's inside, and he lowers his head. "Take a drive with me. It will be in your best interest, Jess."

"No."

He angles his head, making his handsome face look ugly every second I watch him look at me. "Now, don't make this difficult. You want your mommy to have a job, right? Then do as you're told."

I look at my mother through the diner window, knowing she is worried deep inside about how she is going to pay rent and utilities, car insurance, and food. I'm sure she's been saving up and that my being here will prompt her to run out and buy me a Christmas present—a Christmas present we both can't afford.

My fingers are shaking, but I recognize what he wants. He wants what every other man I've ever met has wanted from me: my body. Unlike other situations, I really don't have a say when it comes to Michael. He will make me pay through my mom, and he will take whatever he wants anyway. My mom puts on a fake grin for a couple who just walked in, but I know she's dying of exhaustion on the inside as I watch her.

My head snaps up to see Michael open the door, which swings open like the devil welcoming me to hell. I swallow the bile that creeps up my throat. The ball in my throat tightens as he waits for me to slide out.

"Come on, Jess. I know you miss me the way I miss you."

The engine rumbles as Michael maneuvers the car in an abandoned warehouse on the other side of town. He finds a secluded area in the dark and parks the car. He glances over at me, leans back, and unbuckles his pants, and I hold back the tears that threaten to spill.

"I'll make sure your mom has a job. All you have to do is take care of me once in a while. It's all I want. I'll show up, you open your legs and give me that sweet cunt of yours, and all is good."

"And if I don't? What are you going to do? Drug me? Rape me like you did before?" I quip.

"Don't act like you didn't want to fuck me. Girls like you always want the rich guy. I made it easy for you. We all had fun. "

"I said *no*."

"Then you fell back, and when I touched you, you opened up and let me slide into that tight cunt."

"You bastard," I snarl. "Drugging me until I'm almost unconscious. That's called rape."

"Who the fuck cares? No one cares about you except your trailer trash mother. Your daddy doesn't even want you."

My teeth are clenched so hard in my mouth that I can hear them grind together. He lowers his head while he palms his cock, making me want to throw up.

"Do as I say, or your mom suffers. Do what I say, and she'll have a job with a raise. You won't have to worry about her. She will make her chump change and live happily ever after in her trailer. Worry free. I'll even give her a little extra for Christmas and a bonus for your trouble tonight."

"Fuck you, Michael. I hate you."

"I know. That's what makes it so good. I get what I want, you leave, I want more, and then you leave again. You think you're smarter than me because you're away at school in some college you managed to get into? You don't have a pot to piss in. You will never have a pot to piss in unless you sell what you have between your legs because that is all anyone will want from you. Now, be a good girl and give me what I want, and I'll give you what you need. You can't run from me, Jess. I know where you go to college. It's not in another state. It's here in Ohio, right? Some Ivy League Catholic university that admits poor trailer park trash like you just to look good on paper."

He chuckles and leans closer, whispering, "Are you trying to find God?" His hot breath fans my cheek, and I want to fold inside myself. He slides his fingers across my cheek, and I flinch.

"Stop it."

He grips my neck hard, knowing it will leave a mark for resisting, pushing me to where his cock is. I close my eyes and know this is my fate. *I'm doing this for my mother*, I tell myself. My demon has come to collect, and all I can do is be the sacrifice. There is no way something evil didn't create Michael. It makes me wonder if there really is a God because, right now, all I see is hell.

JESS

I SCRUB myself in the tiny shower in my mother's trailer until I'm red like a lobster. I can still smell his cologne on my skin like the first time. It's strange how some guys' scents are more appealing than others. Reid's scent is heavenly, and so is Valen's.

When they touched me, the memory of Michael faded. It was like a bad dream that could be easily forgotten, but now it's vivid. It's real, and he is blackmailing me with my mom, and I know he can make her suffer. Except I don't have a way to get her out of this situation until I graduate. I would have to tell her everything, and I couldn't do that to her.

We live in a small town in Ohio near a small road that leads to the trailer park called Cedar Lake. There isn't even a lake, and I always wondered why they decided to call it that. There are old trailers with old AC units hanging off and some stuck with duct tape. The majority of the guys who hang out here are either on meth or sell meth.

Guys like Michael were a girl's dream guy back in high school until I saw his true colors. He can make any girl feel special and lure her in like a fish on a hook. He had me fooled with the nice guy act. I thought he actually liked me, but all he wanted was a quick lay, and anyway, he got it. Willing or unwilling. To a guy like Michael, the word no doesn't exist in his vocabulary.

He wants me as his paid whore and will use my mother to get it. I lean back, tired, my throat raw from crying, silently wishing he would have just drugged me again. At least I felt numb and could only remember bits and pieces.

I hear the slam of the main door of the trailer, indicating my mother must be home. I left the car and keys with her at the diner when I left with Michael. I closed my eyes, trying to figure out how I could face her. I'm offi-cially a paid whore. I slept with a guy so my mother could get a higher-paying job, or she would lose the one she had.

Jim decided to cut her hours because Michael forced him to do it so my mother would reach out to me. Michael knows how much my mother means to me. Back in high school, he made sure I fell for his charm, and I sang like a canary. I told him about my wishes and dreams and who the most important person in my life was. My mother.

"Jesse, are you almost done? I have some wonderful news. We have to celebrate," she says with happiness pouring out of her voice.

I know, Mom. I know, I say to myself, closing my eyes. *You will have enough money and a solid job as long as I sleep with the boss's son whenever he wants. I can do this. I'll graduate, and then I can take you away from here.* I promise myself.

My phone dings, and I turn off the water and slide the plastic green shower curtain my mother bought at the local dollar store. There are some cool things you can find in those little stores.

I wrap the towel around my stinging body, raw from scrubbing. There is only one way I have been able to cope after that night when Michael and his friends did what they did to me. Have sex with someone I'm at least attracted to.

It replaces a bad memory with a better one. I could imagine someone I actually like instead of remembering the one who haunts me. I hate his name, his smell, and the way his hands feel on me.

It's funny how you can daydream about a guy for so long, and then when he shows up and proves how nasty he can be, you doubt your judgment. I threw up as soon as he dropped me off. I was disgusted and hated myself for what I had to do.

The irony is that you don't want to be labeled as a trailer trash whore, so you try to avoid it but end up becoming one. I can't be a simple girl who just happened to have been raised in a trailer.

It didn't matter if I graduated at the top of my class, helped my mother instead of going out with my so-called friends, or waited for the right boy to come along and sleep with him. It only got me to be the thing I despised the most. The one thing I didn't want to become. A woman who sleeps with a guy for money.

I look at the hundred-dollar bill near the sink like it's a serpent. Michael threw it in my lap right after he was done with me. My bonus, he said. I'm worth a hundred dollars and a bottle of shame.

I look at the text messages and my heart drops. Oh my god, Gia.

I lift my cheap pay-by-the-minute cell phone to my ear as it rings.

"Hello," Gia says, her voice croaking.

"Tell me."

I sit on the old, ugly, worn carpet at the foot of the single bed in my old room and cry over what happened to her after I hung up. Dravin, or Drav, as she now calls them so she can finally tell them apart, is there with her. One of them followed her, thank God, and was able to call for help in time. She could have died. Whatever the deal is with the Bedford twins and Gia, it's a great mystery. One minute, they want her; the next, they don't.

My phone rings from an unknown number. I furrow my brows and answer the call. "Hello?"

"You don't know how to call and say goodbye?"

I close my eyes. Reid.

"What do you want?" I ask.

"What do you?" he counters.

Of course, the typical guy only sees me as a piece of meat. "Look, I already told you. I'm not interested in being your fuck buddy."

"Oh, you're Valen's now?"

"Last time I checked, I don't belong to anyone. I'm not your whore that you pass around. Find some other Prey on campus to meet your twisted needs."

"I have, but they're all boring."

I snort. "And I'm so much fun, right?"

"Of course, you're fun. It's why I'm calling."

I look at the cheap mirror hanging on the wall and notice I have bruises on my neck from Michael when he gripped me in the car. My fingers trace the handprint of his fingers over my skin as I look at myself, not recognizing what I see. I'm not the girl I thought I was. I'm a cheap nothing. I can't escape my fate. I tried to find a higher education and ended up back to where I started. This is what they all want. What people in this town expect.

"I'm sure to you I'm just fun," I volley back in a rough tone.

"Hey, are you okay?"

"I'm fine. Why wouldn't I be? You just made me an offer. A girl like me should feel honored. She should be grateful she is receiving a blocked call from you for sex. You know—that way she won't call you back when you're done with her. I'm sooo lucky. So, what do you think my going rate is?"

"What the fuck are you talking about? You think I would pay you for sex?" He scoffs. "If you need money, just ask. I have plenty. So how much do you need, Jess?"

I hang up. He calls back, but I press the power button on my phone to turn it off. The numbness is taking over. *I know, Reid. You just want to have fun. The last thing I want is your money.*

I've never been asked out on a date. Back in high school, I didn't have money for a prom dress. Even though I wanted to leave here so badly, I couldn't wait until the year was over so I could start college. I wanted to start fresh. I didn't want to return here unless it was to pick up my mom and move somewhere else. I wanted a new beginning. A better life away from the scumbags and naysayers.

REID

JESS IS DISTANT, and I'm trying to keep my emotions in check. I don't lose my head for a girl. Ever. Especially Prey. There is just something about her. Something that calls me to her. The fucked-up parts of me. The first time I fucked her, I wanted to take her home and keep her there locked up until I fucked her out of my system.

I love her hair. It can be wavy, curly, or straight. She looks hot any way she styles it. It's like a man has many options with her. A fantasy. But fantasies are not real. I can see her weakness, her darkness, and the monster inside me feeds off it because it releases her body in the most delicious ways.

She's fucking something out of her, and I'm here to take it. So is Valen, but he's young and loves to mess around with free pussy. Enjoy it, kid. Once you're a senior, your parents throw down the gauntlet, and the rules you heard of are thrown into the mix for you to follow. The Order. The wife. Killing whoever needs to die. The deceit, lies, and betrayal come into play, and if you aren't ready, it will break you.

Jess can see her best friend getting deliciously fucked by the Bedford twins through the mist from the heat of the pool. Lucky girl. But, honestly, I think they're the lucky ones to have such a nice piece of ass, and despite everything they've done to her, she's still wrapped under their spell. Dravin won't let her out of his sight after what happened. He's like a stalker. She could have died, and she doesn't deserve to die. She's just Prey. A girl just like the one next to me, watching how her friend moans in pleasure as her men make her feel like she is the only woman. In their eyes, she is the only thing that matters. She is their future.

I come up behind Jess and press her to tell me how she got the bruises on her neck. "Are you going to tell me what happened?" I ask as I slide her pretty hair to see the faint markings on her neck.

"I fell."

My hand makes a fist. That's what every woman says when a man hits her. My teeth grind together, and my jaw hardens, and I want to shake the name of the fucker who did it out of her.

"You know, that's what all the women say after a man beats them. It's cliché. You might as well say." I lower my voice. "The fucker hit me, but I can't tell you who. I'm afraid or I liked it."

Her eyes snap to mine in anger. Of course, no woman likes that, but I had to say something to get her attention. It was for effect. I would never hurt a woman.

Valen flanks her other side. "Hot, isn't it? It's beautiful to watch when two men love a woman so much. They're in their own world. Nothing matters more than pleasuring her. Making her feel wanted and needed. They will do anything for her love."

"How do you know that?" she asks, ignoring me and what I asked.

"You see it in her eyes. It's there. The love she has inside her, and they want it. They just have to come to terms with it."

"Terms?" she asks.

Valen is a sentimental jerk. He knows emotion when he sees it, even if he doesn't possess it himself. He is like a machine. You switch him on and off. That's it. It's easy and uncomplicated.

One thing I have noticed is that he talks to her more than he ever talks to other women. He's dirty in bed, and she likes it for some reason. It's like he is throwing dirt over something she is hiding. I just have to find out what it is, and I love a good mystery. I like hunting and killing, too. Let's hope it's both. I like to get my hands dirty from time to time. And for her, I think I'm going to enjoy whoever I have to fuck up.

"Why did you meet those pricks at the bar?" I ask, snapping her attention back to me. I don't want to talk about the twins and the woman they have claimed as their own.

"I wanted to go out and needed a change of pace," she says uncomfortably.

"Why not with me? Why not with us?" I ask.

The silence stretches as she shifts from one foot to the other. I stand in front of her, and she has to look at me.

"You don't want to tell us what happened to your neck. So why the hockey pricks from Ohio State? What do they have that we don't, except small dicks and ugly faces."

She snorts. "They weren't ugly."

"They were ugly," Valen chimes in. "That fucking dork with the Justin Bieber haircut sitting next to you, he kept leering at your tits every five seconds. He was lucky I didn't crush his fucking skull against the lamp."

Valen makes a mocking motion every two minutes, flicking his hair out of his eyes. "Fucker looked like he had Tourette's syndrome. At first, I felt bad, and then he opened his mouth and I realized he didn't have it."

She laughs, and I smile, watching her. "Tell me. Why him? I would have let it slide if it was Valen."

Valen pushes me playfully on the arm. "If it were me, she'd be bent over moaning my name by now. While you watched."

I slide my finger under her chin, ignoring his attempts to piss me off. "Why?"

Her expression is torn, and I watch as she pinches her brows in a frown. "I wanted to go out with a guy. I've never done that before."

"What do you mean you've never gone out with a guy before? You're out with us," I tell her.

"She means on a date, dick. She's never been out on a date."

She looks away, but now I'm curious. "That wasn't a date. It was two girls showing up at a bar to meet two guys. That's not what I think you had in mind."

Her head whips toward me, and she crosses her arms over that sexy mesh top she's wearing. "Maybe I just wanted to fuck and not have to look at his face again."

Valen snorts. "I knew it. You were down to fuck."

I'm pissed. She was going to spread those pretty legs for that smug asshole. I am the only one she should be spreading those legs for, so I can feel that wet cunt.

"Let's go," I demand.

"I'm not going anywhere with you. I'm here because of Gia. I know how shaky things are between her and Dravin or the other one with the same name." She lifts her hand toward them fucking her friend. "The twins," she corrects.

Sometimes, I can't tell them apart except for their attitude and demeanor. It's almost as if they don't want you to know which is which. The show they are putting on here is to show the members of the Order that she belongs to them. It has a purpose. Everything we do has a purpose—a darker motive.

Veronica walks up with a pissed-off expression. Her eyes darting to where the Bedford twins are fucking Gianna. Draven must have turned her down. She could never have the fun Gia is having right now. Veronica and her sex addiction can be too much for some people. Her gaze lands on Jess and she licks her lips.

What the fuck?

JESS

THE SONS of Kenyan showing up at the bar messed up my plans. I wanted to have casual sex so I could forget. I woke up this morning with the scent of Michael in my nose and the feel of his rough hands on my skin and sprang up, feeling like I needed air. That I was suffocating. It woke up Gia, but she just turned on her side and watched me calm down; so I turned over and gave her my back. She asked if I was okay, and I assured her I was fine.

"Just a bad dream," I told her. I like that about her. She doesn't press. She listens and doesn't judge. The kiss at the bar shocked me, but she did it so that I wouldn't feel cornered. It was hot. I'll give her that.

Reid's interrogation is getting to me. I'm not telling him shit. I don't trust his kind and all he does is play games. That is what all the guys in Kenyan do... play mind games, and I'm tired of losing. I'm tired of feeling guilty.

Veronica leans in close. "You want to play?" she asks, her eyes undressing me, but she knows I like men and only had her touch me once with Garret. Melissa did most of the work on her, but I remember when I looked down, my legs spread open, she was the one sucking my clit, cleaning me up.

I didn't think anything of it because I was trying to please Garret and give him what he wanted, and at the same time, I was trying to forget what had happened back home. But now I think Veronica likes women more than she likes men.

I'm not sure where Warren fits in, but that is her issue, not mine. As long as she stays away from Gia, I don't care what she does.

My eyes follow her as she slides her manicured nail down her arm. "Pretty please," she coos.

"She's definitely one that won't look at your face in the morning," Reid says in a derisive tone.

My eyes snap to him with his smug smile, slick mouth, and sexy body. He's an asshole. But a fine asshole. I'll give him that.

Valen is the lighter version, with a darker appetite. His hair isn't as dark, and his body is leaner than Reid's. I haven't had the pleasure of exploring that tongue piercing yet and have only had the pleasure of the one on his lip. Brief kisses and flicks over my nipples are as far as I have been acquainted with it.

The second time we had sex, it was quick, and I fell asleep in his bed soon after. I was shy and couldn't believe what I had done, but he took it away. He took away the feeling. The feeling on my skin. The one I'm trying to get rid of now. Both of them did. Valen and Reid. They have so far been the only ones.

Valen shakes his head at Reid and takes my hand.

"What are you doing?" I ask Valen as he tugs me toward a dark hallway.

"Shutting him up."

He opens the door to a private room that looks like a room set up for massages. There are tables and couches. There are curved chairs in deep red velvet and teal colors, but to the right, there is one curved red chair that looks more like a chaise.

Valen looks over at it and then back at me. He lifts the hem of my shirt over my head and begins to remove all my clothes, leaving me topless and in my red thong.

He looks down at the color and smirks. "It was like fate brought you to this moment. A moment where I'm going to fuck you. I'm going to fuck you so good, Jess."

Veronica enters, and my head turns. I watch as she stares at us. Valen is fully clothed, and I'm clad in only my thong and standing in front of him. I feel comfortable with Valen and Reid. Veronica is a wild card, but I don't feel threatened with Valen or Reid nearby because they wouldn't let anyone physically hurt me.

Valen lifts his head and I'm a lot shorter than he is, so he can see over my head at Veronica. "This is all for her. If you're interested in a fuck, you're in the wrong room."

She snorts. "I'm here for her, not you. She likes me," Veronica says, like I'm not here.

"I'm not fucking you," he snaps.

"I don't want you to. I want to pleasure her."

"Fine, if she wants to, but you only get to clean her when I'm finished." He leans down and whispers, "Are you on the pill?"

My pussy throbs at the way his breath fans my ear. Valen is fun and crazy, and he always makes sure I come before he does. I'm not sure what he has in mind right now, but I want to feel good. I want him to take it away. I want Michael's memory to go away. I know it's temporary because he will show up to collect my body as payment soon, but this is better than what I had to endure.

Veronica's gaze lingers on my breasts and then moves down to the apex of my thighs. "I'll clean her up. I love the way she tastes. If she lets me, of course." Her eyes land on mine. "Rules are rules. Prey chooses."

Fuck. If I turn her down. She will make me pay somehow. She loves to mess with people's heads, but I think she has an agenda, and I don't know what it is yet. I can see it. She hides something.

"Fine, but no fingers."

She walks closer to me while Valen is behind me. His warmth was like a warm curtain against my skin. "I wasn't planning on using them. I want my tongue on your pussy." Her eyes trail over my body. "Maybe other places, too. You know I love to suck," she says, making an emphasis on the *K*.

Valen picks me up from behind and places me on the chaise. The smooth velvet on my skin keeps me warm while the cool air teases my nipples.

He moves between my thighs as he pulls down the zipper of his dark jeans and slides them off, followed by his boxers. He removes his shirt, his lean muscles rippling from the effort. His tattoos snake up his torso, then down to his washboard abs. His hair is sticking out in all directions with that messy look that I find attractive. He quirks his lip the way he does, showing a glimpse of his straight white teeth.

I widen my legs and he slides his index finger over my slit. I'm so wet his finger is coated with my arousal as I watch him slide his fingers in his mouth and suck them clean with a beam in his eye.

"Are you ready for me?" he asks.

"Can't you tell," I volley back.

Veronica walks closer, but then the door opens with a slam and in walks Reid. Valen turns his head with his hard cock in his hand as he strokes it up and down. "Someone is upset," he says softly, raising his eyebrows up and down.

"What the fuck is she doing here?" Reid growls.

"She wants me," I hear Veronica tell him.

Reid stomps over, looks at me with my legs wide open for Valen like an offering, and then glares at Veronica. "Playtime is over. Get out."

She opens her mouth, but Reid points to the door. "Get out!" he roars.

She scrambles and leaves without looking back, out the door like her ass is on fire.

Reid points to Valen. "Put your dick away and get dressed," he demands.

"What the fuck, dude. What is your deal?"

I get up and cover myself with my hands.

"It's a little too late for that," he says sarcastically.

Anger courses through me, but his next words are like guilt clawing at my skin, making me feel worse about what I was about to do. What I was about to let happen.

He bends down and collects my clothes from the pile on the floor as Valen glares at him. "You are not a whore."

"No one is treating her like that."

Reid straightens, handing me my clothes. "You were about to. You had her in here with that psycho bitch like she was some prostitute. Just because she had sex with you, Valen, doesn't mean she's a cheap lay you can run a train on."

"Yeah, like you treat her any better."

Reid snorts. "I've treated her better than those assholes out there."

His gaze lands on mine when I slide the mesh part of my top over my head. He walks over and hauls me up by my arm.

"What the fuck is your problem?" I hiss.

"*You* are my problem," he seethes. "You want to fuck for whatever reason, fine. But not here, and not with that bitch in the room."

My chest aches as guilt begins to seep in. I feel mortified. He's right, but he doesn't know what I deal with or have to deal with. He doesn't know what I'm trying to forget, what I have to hide, or how I have to survive.

This is all fun and games to them.

JESS

"WHERE ARE WE GOING?" I ask Reid.

Valen left with Gia and the twins, who gave him a ride back to Dravin's house to pick up his car.

He stays silent as he maneuvers the car that he had in the garage at Dravin's home. It is a sleek black sports car I have never seen before. While I wait for him to respond, I hug myself for warmth.

"Are you cold?" he asks.

"A little."

He pushes the button, and my seat begins to warm. Then he says, "I'm taking you somewhere."

"Okay," I say, looking out the window.

I'm tired of arguing with him. He can be so dry and cold. He's moody, but sometimes I like that because when he is angry, it means he cares. For some reason, he cared about me back there. He cared that I was in that room, and even though I trusted Valen, he didn't like the idea of Veronica.

My finger reaches out and rubs the red stitching on the black leather interior of his car. He gazes briefly at my hand, and I yank it back into my lap like I was caught doing something I shouldn't.

"Sorry," I mumble, embarrassed that I was caught admiring his car like I just came to Earth from another planet and had never sat in one before.

The truth is, I have never sat in a car like this before. It is truly a work of art. Inside, it looks like a spaceship. The car is matte black, like the SUV we rode to the party, with a black interior, a fancy screen, and red stitching.

"It's okay. I'm not mad. You can touch it."

I look up at the roof of the car. The smell of expensive leather touching every part of my body. Even the carpet feels nice. I feel bad that I'm touching it with my black boots. "What kind of car is this?" I ask.

He turns his head briefly. "An Aston Martin DBS."

"It's beautiful. It's way better than what I drive or ever had growing up. My mother's car doesn't even have AC, and my car hardly turns on some-times. I really should go back and get it."

I pause when he doesn't say anything. He remains quiet and looks straight ahead, gripping the steering wheel. Shit. Why do I always ramble when I'm nervous? I shouldn't have said that. He wouldn't be interested in the car I drive or the life I had growing up.

"Don't worry about your car." He leans forward, sliding his cell phone out, and opens his music app. "It's taken care of. I had someone get it."

He did ask me for my keys right before we left in the SUV, when we were at the bar nearby. I guess that means I should shut the hell up if he is going to play music.

He presses play on his phone, and because it's connected to his car, the sounds of Breaking Benjamin's "The Diary of Jane" play through the car's sound system. I look down and grip the strands of my hair that are turning wavy, sometimes wishing that I had straight hair.

After fifteen minutes, we pull into the valet of a five-star hotel surrounded by trees and, from its appearance, very private. There are gas sconces that are lit with a firepit in the center instead of a fountain. He rolls the car forward and places it in park.

The valet rushes over and opens the door. "Welcome, Mr. Riordrick. They are expecting you and your guest."

"Thank you," I hear him tell the valet driver. I see his jean-clad legs pause. As my door opens, he turns around, and I can hear him say over the roof of the car, "I've got it."

The door is pushed closed, and I'm sitting in the seat. He doesn't even want the other valet to open the door. Weird.

I see Reid look at me from the front of the car as he makes his way to the other side. His eyes find mine, and they are black as night. His bottom lashes are so thick that they almost seem lined with black eyeliner.

The door pops open, and he sticks out his hand so I can take it. I slip my hand against his warm, gloved palm and slide out. The door closes behind me, and I look up at the grand entrance of the hotel that is in the middle of nowhere. The fire in the center lights up the entrance, with wood doors handled by two doormen flanking both sides and allowing people to enter and exit.

"Where are we?" I ask, my breath coming out like fog.

"My hotel."

My eyebrows rise as he gently tugs me forward to enter the lobby with its dark red carpet and gold accents accented with dark wood. I feel like I'm in the Neri Hotel in Barcelona, which I saw on the travel website while researching a school project.

Every luxury hotel has a concierge and a check-in counter. Not that I have ever stayed in one, but I have seen them in movies. The closest thing to a building I have stayed in is Kenyan and a motel when my mother couldn't pay the light bill. It was one of those hourly motels, but at least we slept for four hours and had a hot shower. Whatever she paid, it was worth it.

He walks up, and the older woman with her gold-plated name tag that reads Shelley warmly greets Reid. "Hello, Mr. Riordrick. Your room is ready," she says, sliding a room key across the desk. "Will you be requiring anything further?"

"No," he answers softly, picking up the key card and holding it up. "Thank you, Shelley. Was your holiday bonus this year enough for the grandkids?"

Her expression warms, and my heart skips a beat. I've never thought of Reid as being thoughtful, but you can tell by the interactions with the employees when we arrive that they hold him in high regard. He also nods and greets everyone by their first name.

He is quiet most of the time but has a mean dark streak that I find appealing because he directs it when needed. This is the side of Reid that I find most attractive, and I secretly wish he was always like this. What he did back there with Valen made me angry and relieved all at once. He was protective and pulled me out of there when I was at my lowest.

Valen is young and doesn't take things seriously but loves to have fun. The few times I have been around Valen, he has had this carefree lifestyle and loves to push the limit and live on the edge. No consequences. No judgment.

Reid guides me by my hand, and to my surprise, no one looks at me like I don't belong. No one is looking at me like I'm worthless or poor, but my joy is short-lived when I see a woman enter the elevator wearing a long coat over a short red dress and suede cream-colored boots to midthigh. She looks like she just stepped out of a Vogue photo shoot. Her hair is mid-length and chestnut in color, and she has green eyes. The woman is drop-dead gorgeous and pauses midstride when she notices Reid.

"Miss me?" she says coyly.

He grins. "Not tonight, Tara. I have company."

She doesn't even look in my direction. It's like I don't exist, and he makes no move to introduce me as his friend, but then again, why would he? He brought me here to have sex and nothing else. I'm no one. I'm just considered Prey. Used and discarded. So I tell myself I'll use him right back so I can forget about my demons for a while until I have to face them again, or him, the one who keeps coming back for me. Michael. This is just a temporary reprieve.

"Well, later then." She steps closer, sliding her palms over his chest and a pang of jealousy hits me in my solar plexus. I try to move my hand out of his grip, but he squeezes, wrapping his fingers tighter, keeping me from removing my hand.

I don't know why he won't release me. Tara looks over at me with amused annoyance. Like I'm gum on the bottom of her boots, and she can't wait to get rid of it, and I feel like telling her he's mine. That she can go fuck off and freeze her ass outside while I warm him up upstairs.

I don't know what has come over me. He isn't nice to me most of the time, except when he's fucking me. He isn't rough but demanding, like a guy possessed with need and knows what he wants. He doesn't snuggle me or spoon me after. He doesn't caress me or give me tender kisses the way girls fantasize about sex with the right guy.

To Reid, sex is like a transaction. Once it's over, he leaves, and it's never mentioned. Sometimes, you even wonder if it ever happened. He is so quiet, and he doesn't talk about himself. Which works for me because I don't have much to say about myself. It's not like he would care what I have to say about myself anyway. He isn't interested in me in that way, and at times, I wonder if he even likes me.

Right now, this is a reminder. A reminder that I don't mean shit. I might as well be invisible next to him. Then my mind wanders to what Gia said about people in the Order. Members conduct business, and everything is filtered through the higher members, which is like a hierarchy of needs.

Business connections, meetings, parties, alliances, and, of course, private parties that involve sex. And hotels owned by founding members in the middle of nowhere, with no one knowing what happens inside.

Reid looks down at his chest, where her palms are firmly planted, while her eyes, full of promise, gaze up at him. I manage to yank my hand from his grip and rub my wrist.

I roll my eyes. "I'll just go sit in the lobby while you two catch up. You guys are clearly having a moment."

I walk away, while Tara snickers, and find a spot near the fireplace in the lobby. A man is sitting reading a document from a folder and looks up.

"He let you go already?" he asks with a grin.

I stroll over to the man dressed in slacks and a crisp dress shirt opened at the throat. "Excuse me?"

He grins, looking at me, and his eyes flick to Reid talking to Tara. Only he has stepped back so that her hands fall off his chest. I can't hear what is being said, and at this point, I don't care. My sole goal is to forget and avoid falling asleep, where my memories will take over and send me spiraling into self-destruction and misery.

The man doesn't look old but like a wealthy stockbroker who belongs in New York. His gray eyes look at me, full of promises he probably doesn't keep. I watch as he places his hand on his phone, his biceps flexing under the crisp fabric from the movement while he watches me. Did he just flex so I would notice him?

Ignoring him, I slide my phone out of the pocket of my jacket to see how far I am from campus, kicking myself for leaving with them instead of Gia and me following them in my car.

He leans forward, rests his forearms on his knees as he looks behind me, tilting his head to study me, and says, "She has nothing on you. Just because you don't have money or wear pretty things doesn't mean you're less beautiful. It just makes you flawless. The natural ability to look that stunning no matter what you wear, now that is true elegance."

Did he just say I'm beautiful? Prettier than Tara? That's not possible, this guy is just preying on the fact that I'm vulnerable.

"Who are you, and what are you talking about?"

He chuckles, wiping his mouth with his hand. "I'm the hated cousin. I run things sometimes until Reid graduates. I was surprised to see him walk in with you, but now that I can get a better look, I see why."

His cousin. I don't see a resemblance, but why would he lie? Compared to everyone that walks through here, I stick out. In a poor way, people stick out.

"I guess you have me all figured out."

He smiles. "It isn't common to see Prey from Kenyan come through here. I'm surprised he brought you to his hotel. He's never done that."

"If this is an attempt to get me to stay because you saw me scroll through my Uber app, it's not helping. Look, I know I don't belong, and to people like you, I don't mean anything, and I'm okay with that. Where I come from, I don't mean much to people, and I know where I stand. I'm not part of the happy ending in my fairy tale, I'm the tragedy."

He leans back, his right elbow on the arm of the chair, two fingers over his lips as if lost in thought as he watches me. "Let's play a game," he says.

"Why would I want to play a game with you?"

He gives me a dark, knowing smile that curves his top lip. "Because it will get you what you want, and I want to teach my cousin a lesson."

I'm intrigued. How would he know what I want? After scrolling through my poor excuse of an old-model smartphone while flipping through my thoughts, my gaze lands on him.

"How do you know what I want?"

"You stated that you knew exactly where you stood. If that's the case, then there is only one reason you walked in here with him, and it's not to sleep. It's to fuck."

My pulse is going haywire from my heart beating so fast, a mixture of anger and annoyance. I guess someone like him, being part of the Order and if he is indeed related to Reid, would know that. In their eyes, it would be obvious why I was brought here or chose to come here, but it's a different matter altogether when someone points it out. It becomes real. If he noticed, then so did everyone else.

I don't look behind me to see if Reid is done talking to Tara. I don't want to witness her touching him or him smiling back. If I see it, I'm not sure I'll be able to stop myself from walking over there and dragging him to the elevator to get away from her. I shouldn't care. He isn't mine, but I can't help the way I feel. Maybe it's because I want him to take away the memory of Michael touching me. Maybe I want to use him the way he wants to use me. Maybe it's because I find him the most attractive. I like that he is discreet. I like that he is quiet. I like when he touches me and doesn't expect anything after. He goes back to ignoring me like I don't exist, and it works for me in my current situation. I have two options right now. Play their game and get what I want, or leave and let the memory of Michael haunt me when I fall asleep.

My gaze returns from the screen of my phone to his gray eyes staring at me. "What do you have in mind?"

"This is going to be fun."

"I'm sure it is."

"My name is Alaric Riodrick."

I quirk my eyebrow. "Alaric?"

He smiles. "Say it again, gorgeous."

He wants to play games, but I'm not easily played. I don't know him, and all I know is it's obvious he doesn't get along with his cousin. I'm just annoyed with the way Reid treated me just now.

"No."

"Fine."

He flicks his eyes to his right, where there is a bar. The bartender is cleaning a glass, holding it up to the light to ensure that all the spots are gone before placing it on the black mat and preparing a cocktail.

"Have a drink with me, but first, hand me your phone," he says, standing up.

I look up as he stands above me. "What do you need my phone for?"

He looks at the phone in my hand and bends down so that his eyes lock on mine. "So I can call you. Have dinner. Fuck. Whatever you want." He glances up and lowers his voice. "There isn't much time before he starts looking for you. He shouldn't let something so intriguing and beautiful go."

I move to stand, causing him to straighten and step back. He is almost a foot taller than me and very handsome. Not the type of guy I usually find attractive, but handsome all the same. I like Reid's dark hair and body full of ink, but most of all, I like his darkness.

Alaric peers down and takes my phone from my hands. "Come with me to the bar."

I nod, and we walk side by side until we reach two barstools and take a seat. "What would you like? You can have anything you want. It's on me."

The bartender glances up at me, waiting for me to ask for what I want. I take a deep breath and scan the bottles behind him, lit up by the neon lights behind the shelves. There is a mirror, and I can see Reid in a heated discussion with Tara. At least she isn't touching him, and he isn't smiling.

I'm trying to find something to order that doesn't sound like I'm immature or an idiot and settle on the first thing that comes to mind. "A black vodka ghost martini."

The bartender raises his left eyebrow and his lips curve in a grin. "Excellent choice."

"I'll have a merlot," Alaric tells him.

"Right away, sir."

I shift slightly to my right while the bartender mixes my drink and pours Alaric his wine.

"Wine?" I ask.

He is entering his number into my phone, and for some reason, I let him. I'm not going to call him, and I don't care if he calls me or not. I'm not going to have sex with him. This is all a game to him, and I don't trust him.

"I don't look like a wine guy?"

"You seem more like a gin and tonic type of guy."

The bartender places my drink in front of me and does the same to Alaric with his glass of wine.

I grasp the stem of the martini glass and take a sip. The flavor and alcohol explode on my tongue, followed by the slight burn of the alcohol, warming me up on the inside.

"So, where are you staying? Dorm?"

"Yes," I answer. "But you already knew that. It's where we all usually stay."

He places his wineglass down on the bar counter and licks his bottom lip. "Actually, I would have thought you were staying with Reid."

I snort, shaking my head. "You mean in Dravin's Gothic mansion? Highly unlikely. Reid doesn't strike me as the type to have a woman stay with him."

"Have you?"

I angle my head, confused. "Have I what?"

"Slept in his bed."

A blush begins to creep up my neck. I did more than just sleep in his bed. I did stay the night, but he asked me to leave the next morning. It stung, though I understood. It was just sex, and he served my purpose.

The dreams. The nightmares since the day it first happened. It was the first time I could sleep without having a nightmare or that feeling you get when you wake up after being drugged and see blood and sperm coating your thighs.

Sometimes I wake up and I remember the same sting. The pain I felt between my thighs that day was still there the next morning. The way Michael laughed the following Monday at school when he told me I wanted it and he gave it to me. They all did.

I swallow down the memories and meet Alaric's knowing grin, no different than any other guy I have encountered. They all want one thing, and that is to use my body. To them, the rest of me doesn't matter. I'll never matter to these types of people. Men with privilege, money, and connections who feel they are above all others. Manipulative and selfish. To me, they are all the same. Except Valen. I can't say he hasn't been truthful with me.

I rub my lips together, grab the martini glass, and drink it all at once, hoping the burn will melt the feeling and what's left of my emotions. The sound of me placing the now empty martini glass on the bar with a clink of glass meeting wood. The fire in my belly gives me the liquid courage I need to answer what he wants to hear. I feel brave, not caring. He can ask and find out anyway. Why hide it?

"Yeah. I slept in his bed. Reid and his friend took turns with me all night. Isn't that what you want to hear? With people like you, that's all I'm good for. It shouldn't matter, so why are you asking?"

He looks at me with a surprised expression and raises his eyebrows. I know I'm being a bitch, but he's being a nosy prick, and I'm annoyed.

"I apologize for upsetting you. I didn't mean it to sound that way."

"Whatever," I mumble.

"Would you like another one, miss?" the bartender asks with a soft expression. He probably heard every word, but I'm sure he hears a lot of things working as a bartender. My mother would sometimes come home and tell me town gossip she overheard waiting tables at Jimmy's diner.

"I'm good. Thank you."

He nods, looking over at Alaric with a hard expression while he watches Reid. One drink is all I'm having. I don't mind a buzz, but I'm not close to campus, and I'm in a room full of potential predators. There is only one I feel comfortable with, and he isn't paying attention to me. The hairs on the back of my neck stand up like a magnet. I can feel his presence consuming me by the minute, and I know he is behind me because I see Alaric stiffen.

Awareness creeps down my spine and the rumble of his voice slides between my thighs. "Never fails, Alaric. I'm not surprised. You were always interested in what was mine, and you always wanted to play with and borrow my things without asking."

My eyes land on Reid. His expression is murderous, cold, and very angry. The glare aimed at Alaric is laced with pure hatred. These two clearly hate each other, and it is the type of hate that is built up over the years. What has me squirming in my seat is him pointing out that I'm his. I should feel giddy, but how he says it also makes me think he sees me like an object. A toy you play with and put back in the toy box with the others.

Alaric looks at me and then at him with a smug grin, taking his wineglass and tilting it slightly so that his lips meet the rim. He takes a sip of the wine and places it next to my empty glass as if pointing out that he is interrupting our conversation.

"I was just entertaining your guest. You obviously were engrossed in your chat with your ex-flame. I was trying to help you out since you were rude and left her there waiting for you. I saw she was about to order a ride and convinced her to have a drink with me. You should be thanking me, little cousin."

Reid's fists clench at his sides and then he turns his head and glares at me. His eyes flick to my empty glass next to Alaric's.

Reid signals for the bartender, and he says in an even tone, "Her drink is charged to my tab. Understood?"

"Yes, Mr. Riordrick," the bartender responds.

Reid gets up in Alaric's face in a stare-off. His jaw is clenched. His teeth are grinding, sounding like they're ready to snap. He is so angry at Alaric, and I wish I knew why.

His nostrils flare, and people walking by stare briefly but swiftly look away. "Go near her, and I'll kill you," he growls.

He grabs my hand and almost yanks me off the barstool.

"What the hell, Reid?"

"Shut up," he snarls.

I try to give him resistance without causing a scene as he practically drags me through the lobby, but he's stronger, and the anger coming off him in waves is making me tread cautiously on how to deal with him right now.

He slides the key card near what seems like a private elevator and the doors open. He practically drags me in the car first and cages me inside so I don't walk out.

"What is your fucking problem?" I snap.

The doors close behind him, and I'm trapped inside the elevator with Reid, and the look of fury in his eyes has me shrinking back, turning my head with a grimace.

He backs me up against the back side of the elevator and reaches with his index finger to hold the elevator. Fuck. His face is inches from my cheek, and he is breathing like he has just finished running a marathon, but it's from anger and not exertion. He isn't even breaking a sweat; he is just pissed.

He opens my jacket and feels my breast over my mesh top. My nipples harden under the thin tube top and my thighs clench.

"You need cock that bad?" he asks against my cheek. His lips snake roughly over my skin down to my neck, and he licks the spot over the yellow bruise on my neck. "Huh? Is this what you want? For me to fuck you? You can't wait, can you?"

His hands slide down my torso to the band of my skirt, and he glides his fingers under the hem of my panties to feel how wet I am and cups my soaked pussy. "You're so fucking wet it's pathetic."

My cheeks heat in embarrassment at how turned on I am. I'm so wet for him; I'm drenched. The way he touches me with rough hands but with gentle fingers is confusing. He knows how much to push me before it's too much, and I feel like he's going to break me. The things he says to me while he's inside me are dirty and cold, but it makes me feel alive.

I want it.

I want him.

It's a secret.

My secret. But I'm good at keeping secrets hidden. No one has to know how much I want him.

He undoes his pants and slides his hard cock out, stroking it with his hands between his legs while he watches me. "Take off your jacket."

I look up and notice a camera in the corner of the elevator. "There're cameras," I say.

"I know," he says, his lip curling and his voice barely above a whisper. "That's the point. I want them to see how desperate you are for my cock because you can't wait. You'll go with anyone to get fucked, won't you?"

"Fuck you," I snarl.

"Baby, I'm going to fuck you so hard you won't be able to stand when I'm done. I'll make sure to ruin you."

I turn my face, my lips inches from his, and I meet his dark gaze in a challenge. "Then what the fuck are you waiting for? Do your worst. Finish breaking me."

His eyes flick up like a serial killer before he commits a murder. Something flashes in his eyes, although I can't decipher what it is. I want him to take it away. I pray in my head for him to please kill the memory that haunts me. He's my reprieve before reaching insanity. I want him to fuck it out of me.

He growls and pushes my winter jacket down my shoulders. The camera is long forgotten. He rips my top and slides my skirt roughly down my body. I'm hoping he doesn't see the bruises between my thighs. The lighting was brighter than the dimly lit room I was in with Valen.

The tearing of clothing mixed with the tearing of the wrapper of the condom assaults my ears. The palm above my head lies flat on the wood paneling on the elevator as he holds himself while he slides the condom over the head of his cock. The angry veins running down his shaft, almost too big for me and looking like it's about to burst, have me closing my eyes and getting ready for its onslaught.

Reid fucks like an animal devouring its prey, ripping it limb from limb as it feasts. "Open your legs so I can fuck that tight cunt, or I'm going to ram it in there."

I raise my head and open my legs, my neck arched. My breasts are exposed and I'm completely naked except for my thigh-high pantyhose and black boots.

The tip of his cock is at my entrance and in one hard thrust, he rams his cock inside me, causing me to gasp at the delicious burn. He lifts my legs and wraps them around his waist. "If I catch you around another man that I don't approve of, I'm going to make you pay, Jess. I'm going to fuck you so hard I'll ruin you for anyone else. The only cock you will be begging for is mine."

"How about Valen?" I tease. "What if all I want is his cock, his tongue, inside me?"

In truth, I like his cock, but I would never admit it to him. I would never give a man power over me like that again. I'll never tell them how I feel. I fell for a man once, and he broke me. All they do is take from me.

My body.

My innocence.

My heart.

They break everything. Reid's promise of him trying to ruin me should have me running for the nearest exit. But what he doesn't know is I'm broken. I'm already ruined. It's too late. There is no turning back for a girl like me. His sex is a Band-Aid for the wound left by another. There will be more. I just have to hold on until it's over. The pain will go away and leave scars, but I'll still have the smile from a mother's heart. The only light I'll have in the darkness left inside me is when they leave me picking up the pieces.

REID

I'M THRUSTING into her while her legs are wrapped around my waist. I know I'm giving security a show, but I can't take it anymore. I want her. Since the first time I laid eyes on her. I almost told Draven to fuck off when he said to watch over her at the party. Valen saw the same opportunity, and I didn't want to show him I was interested because I was never interested in a girl. To me, they are all the same—a wet hole to stick my dick in and get my fix.

Prey is all the same to me. Poor girls coming to a prestigious school for an opportunity. When they see a rich guy on campus, it's a dollar sign in their eyes, and Jess is no different. She was practically drooling over my car. Gold diggers waiting for a payday. I almost felt bad when she told me her mom's car back home didn't have AC and that her piece-of-shit car doesn't start sometimes. Almost.

I have never lived a day without luxury. I was born into it. It's not my fault she was dealt a fucked-up hand, but that is not my problem, it's hers.

"Yes," she moans.

I continue to savagely pump into her, making her pay for being spread out in front of Valen and another hard thrust for her having a drink with my asshole cousin, who will only fuck her like a savage. He's brutal with the women he fucks. Some come out screaming after he is done with them. I was doing the right thing. She doesn't know the danger she was in by letting him get too close.

The Order doesn't care how many women he does it to. He chooses the most vulnerable ones with no money and no connections, and if they open their mouths or report him, he will kill them and bury them somewhere. He's done it before when he went to Kenyan.

I'm thrusting deep inside her, playing different scenarios in my head of other ways to punish her for her stupidity. I keep pumping into her, and I can't help myself. I place my hand over her mouth to keep her from moaning too loud. Security knows not to interfere and to call maintenance about the elevator.

"Shut up and take it like the whore you are."

I know it sounds fucked up to call her a whore, but that is what she was acting like. Like a bitch in heat needing a hard cock. She wants dick, I'll gladly give it to her.

Her eyes flash in anger, and I know that calling her that bothered her. Good. Maybe next time, she won't act so desperate. I check her mouth, making sure she can breathe. I'm an asshole, but I don't want to kill her. I just want to hurt her a little.

Her pussy begins to clench on my dick, and I know she is close. She's grinding her hips, seeking more, and I meet her thrusts. I slide my hand down her mouth to her throat. Her lips are slightly parted, flushed, and red, waiting to be sucked. I look down at her perfect breasts, bouncing up and down with every thrust I pump into her. Fuck, she's beautiful. She's perfect. Too bad. She's considered Prey. Good for only one thing, to be fucked and used. I was surprised she didn't have a boyfriend somewhere. But I'm sure there aren't any good wealthy prospects where she comes from.

I saw her get jealous when Tara walked over, wanting to jump on my cock. Her father and my father are business associates, and I don't have a good relationship with my own father. That is why I moved in with Dravin. He understands my frustration. We have to take over when the time comes and find a wife.

My father wants me to marry as required by the Order, to take a wife and be one of the founding members. One of the prodigal sons of Kenyan. They want me to marry within the Order. Preferably, Tara. And as tempting as she seems in bed, I can't stand her. I hate her laugh, her smell, and her cunt. It doesn't wrap around my cock like the girl I'm currently fucking in the elevator who's about to come.

My cock swells, and I'm holding on for dear life, not wanting to come before her, but I can't, and anyway, fuck her. She wanted dick; she got dick. She took too long.

"Please, more. Don't stop," she pleads.

"Too bad. I'm not your boyfriend. You're just a wet hole."

Her body goes slack, and she averts her eyes. My words hurt. She tries to slide down my hips, but I pump one last time, emptying myself into the condom.

She won't give me her eyes as I come so good and hard. She tries to hold herself without touching me, and I know I fucked up. I pushed her too far. I said something I can't take back.

"Are you done?" she asks without looking at me.

Fuck. What did I just do? Why do I feel so fucking guilty?

I look down as I slide out of her and tie the condom. She looks down, picks up her clothes from the floor, and slips her skirt over her legs. Her panties are in shreds. She looks at her unsalvageable shirt and balls it all together, slipping on her jacket and zipping it up all the way to her neck, almost choking herself.

I get dressed and press the button so the elevator can climb up to the floor of my suite. She stands silently, watching the numbers change with each floor the elevator passes on the way up.

I shouldn't care about the way I treated her. I should tell her that I'm sorry. I should, but I don't. I can't. I'm not that guy.

When the elevator reaches my floor, the door opens, and I step out, expecting her to follow me to my room. I stop and look behind me with a frown, noticing she hasn't exited the elevator.

"Thank you, you were great," I hear her say as the doors close, leaving me alone in the hallway.

Fuck. I march over to the elevator and press the button, then swipe my card on the card reader repeatedly, but I'm too late. I look up and see the elevator descending to the lobby.

I messed up.

I pushed her too far.

And I know she will never look at me again. I don't know what she meant about thanking me or telling me I was great. I wasn't great. I was horrible. I acted like a total asshole. I shouldn't care about what I did or how I made her feel, but somehow, now I do.

VALEN

FUCKING REID. He took her away from me. It was wrong to bring her to the back room and have my way with her, but I get why he was upset. We were at Garret's house with Veronica. I'm not sure if it was because of that or because I was about to have sex with her. I allowed Veronica inside and didn't tell her to fuck off because I didn't want Veronica to target Jess.

She didn't deserve what they did, but the children of Kenyan love to play games and break people. She's Prey, and we give them opportunities after graduation, so they should pay the price, and if not, they die. To everyone, she's no one, but to me, she's different. I see it in her eyes—the tortured pain of someone wronged by people.

It's the same look I've seen when I've had to kill. The look right before you die. Acceptance of your fate. She thinks this is it. She believes that being Prey is her fate, but she's wrong.

I drive back to Garret's house after picking up my BMW at Dravin's. Draven and Gia went up to the house to continue their night of fucking.

I didn't want to interrupt or hear them. Reid disappeared with Jess, and if he treated her like shit, I'll kill him. Not really kill him, but I'll break his face. He has this love-hate thing for Jess, and I think he has it all wrong for her.

I walk back into his house toward the pool where I last saw him. Garret is seated on a lounge chair with Jasmin sucking him off, bobbing her head like a chicken.

"Yo, Garret," I call out.

His head looks up over Jasmin, attempting to deep throat his cock but failing miserably.

"What the fuck, man? I'm busy."

The party died out, and now there are only a few guys from the swim team fucking random girls.

"She sucks anyway, ask Reid."

"Fuck off."

I walk up with the perfect opportunity. I pull my fist back and punch him in the mouth. He falls back from the impact of the blow to his mouth. The sting on my knuckles causes me to shake my hand.

Jasmin shrieks, covering her small breasts with her hands and my eyes land on Garret, who is covering his mouth with both hands while howling in pain, blood is dripping down his chin from his busted lip as he sprawls on the floor with his pathetic excuse of a dick out.

I pick him up off the floor by his hair. "W-what the fuck did you do that for?" he grunts in pain and asks.

I grip his hair hard, almost tearing it out of his scalp. "Ahh! The fuck, Valen!" Garret bawls as he howls in agony.

I bend down close so he can hear every word. "I'll come back and finish you off if you ever go near Jess or spread rumors about how your pathetic excuse for a cock fucked her. Got it!"

"Come on, man," he cries, spitting blood on the floor. The pool water mixed with the blood flowing like a crimson river down the floor from his mouth. "She's Prey. It was all orchestrated by Veronica."

"I get that you're a little shit, but you're such a pussy that you have to keep telling everyone about her and how she fucks in bed. Leave her the fuck alone. Stop spreading shit about her. This is your only warning, or I'll tell Veronica the truth about how you love Jess," I warn, shoving him roughly when I release his hair. "Don't play yourself, Garret."

I watch him, satisfied that I split his mouth open, walking backward toward the exit.

"Why? You fucking her?" he spits.

I laugh. "Maybe."

I'd never out Jess like that, but I love fucking with his head. What I do in bed with her is my business. No one needs to know. Especially a jerk like him. If he cared so much about Jess, he could have said no or warned Jess about Veronica.

I slow my steps as I watch him get up, almost slipping on the wet floor in the process of trying to pull his shorts back on. "I'll fucking kill you."

I snort. "Try it, bitch. I'm right here," I say, holding my hands out.

When I see him bluffing and not making a move, I point my finger at him. "Stay away from her, and don't let me catch you talking about her. You've done enough," I warn, turning away before I take the piece of shit and drown him in his own pool.

We were at Babylon two weeks ago and he was drunk. He started talking about Jess, and I wanted to kill him right then and there over the pool table. But what he said caught me off guard. He started slurring and saying the opposite about her.

Sometimes, when people are drunk, they tell the truth. My teammate on the swim team nodded, confirming that what Garrett was saying wasn't a lie. He wants Jess. Veronica manipulated him and Melissa to get to her.

Garrett had been interested in Jess since the beginning of her freshman year. He would follow her and sweet-talk her before I started Kenyan. I overheard about it when I started my sophomore year. He told her he wanted her to be his girlfriend, but it was supposedly all a lie.

He caught feelings and played it off that it was Veronica he wanted. In his drunken stupor, he stated that he did not want Veronica to go after Jess and hurt her in order for her to save face. He confessed that Veronica liked Jess in bed. I understand that Veronica is a sex-crazed bitch, but it still bothers me. They took it too far with her. I get that she's hot as fuck, but now I'm involved, and I don't like the fact that he won't drop it.

He was jealous that they touched her and angry with Jess for the wrong reasons. He was falling for her, but it was too late. The damage was done, and she wants nothing to do with Garret.

He's a salty asshole and wants to hurt her because she rejected him for the right reasons. I can't say I blame Jess. The reason I'm here is that I have a problem with it all, or maybe I'm falling down the Jess rabbit hole. I like her. I like the way she tastes. The smell of her pussy. I shouldn't want her that much, but I do. I want her a little too much.

JESS

I'M IN THE SHOWER, scrubbing myself in self-loathing with my loofah, but at the same time, I like that Reid was the last one to touch me. I just hate his words and how he called me a whore. I wasn't going to sleep with his cousin. He pulled me out of my jealous thoughts about the scenario playing out with Tara and him. It was self-preservation. I didn't want him to know it bothered me, because then he would know I liked him more than just for sex.

He didn't let me come. The way he did it reminded me of Michael. At first, I thought it was no big deal, but then disappointment and disgust crept in. When I saw him put on his clothes and not care what he said or how he treated me, I didn't want to be in his presence a second longer.

I wanted to get away from him. I hated that I liked him more than I should have. It brought memories of the past. The feelings and emotions that got me to that room in the party. The way you crush on a guy you like way too much, and they use it to lure you in with a false pretense. Exploitation of your emotions in order to break you. To use you. To take advantage of your feelings as an excuse to rape you.

I was craving for Reid to touch me, but the way he did tonight only reminded me of the man I was trying to forget. He said the same things Michael said to me. I was weak for him, and I hated myself for it.

Tonight, Reid reminded me of Michael.

I close my eyes as the hot spray from the shower head in the communal shower bathes my skin, rinsing the soap off my body.

Since I got into the dorm, I knew I would be alone, but the room was dark and empty. Gia is with her twins tonight, and I can't blame her. Those men are crazy, but they worship her even if they fight to hide it. I expected a blocked call from Reid after I abruptly left, but when I checked my phone, there were no missed calls, just a text from Gia saying she was at Drayin's house. I wasn't surprised Reid hadn't called to see if I was okay or if I arrived safely, like I secretly wished he would. He got what he wanted, and whatever that was didn't include the real me or my feelings.

I'm afraid to go to sleep. I have to admit that to myself and decide to take my time in the shower while everyone on the floor is asleep. I slide the pads of my thumb and index finger over my eyelids to wipe away the water and turn around to give my hair a thorough rinse when I sense a shadow looming and a scream crawls up my throat.

A hand is placed over my mouth. My heart is beating in pure fear, but when my eyes widen, I calm myself. Valen.

"Shh, it's me. I'm sorry, but I didn't mean to startle you," he says, sliding his hand off my mouth.

"Are you out of your mind?" I whisper-yell.

His upper lip curls in a small grin. "Maybe."

My eyes travel down, and I notice he is completely naked. Yes, definitely insane to be naked in the women's shower.

"How did you get past security?"

He chuckles softly and whispers in my ear as I slide under the warm shower spray. "Do you not know who I am, Jess?"

Right. One of the sons of Kenyan. He can do whatever the fuck he wants, and they will just look the other way.

"Yes, I think I do. A crazy guy breaking into the girls' shower wholly naked in the middle of the night."

"You weren't in your room. I figured you would be here since I was the one who took care of your car," he says, looking down at my naked breasts pushed up on the pecs of his lean muscles with pure lust in his eyes. "I wanted to see if you wanted to finish what we started since we were rudely interrupted."

He brushes his nose with mine and the drops of water slide down onto my chest, creating small goose bumps on my skin. "Where did he take you, huh?"

He means Reid. I guess since they are very close and didn't mind sharing me that one time, I guess it's safe to answer him.

"To his hotel."

He caresses his firm lips over mine; his lighter eyes and blonder hair are a strong contrast to Reid's. "Why are you here and not there?"

I pull away slightly, but not too much, so I don't bump my head against the tile behind me. His forehead pinches, and his expression is laced with confusion. No, not confusion, but worry.

"Did he hurt you, Jess?"

I shake my head, not wanting to talk about it. It's not like I matter to him in that way. I don't belong to Valen, and he isn't mine. He's young and fun to be around, with a hint of an edge of darkness. He probably would laugh in my face.

"He didn't hurt me physically. It just didn't feel right with him. Alright." I swallow the lump that is crawling slowly up my throat. "He called me things I didn't like while we were..." I trail off on the last part.

The sound of the water from the shower falling over our bodies like a rain cloud sliding into the drain. The silence stretches longer and tighter, causing his expression to tighten.

"What did he say to you while you were with him? What did he call you?" he asks in a severe tone.

He means while Reid and I were having sex. My eyes fill with tears, and I hope he can't see them, and if he does, I'll blame them on the water from the shower.

I bite my lip and look down between us. His cock is semi-hard against smooth skin filled with scripture tattoos all over his body. I take a deep, shaky breath and tell him what bothered me the most.

"He said I was so wet that I was pathetic, and he also called me a whore. There are other things, like the camera in the elevator where we were." I shrug, a watery smile on my lips. "It doesn't matter. I just couldn't stay there," I tell him, meeting his eyes. "I don't want to see him again. He reminded me of things I want to forget."

"And the bruises on your neck. How did those get there?"

I shake my head and avert my gaze. "I can't tell you that. Please, don't ask that of me," I say softly, a single tear sliding down my cheek like a knife slicing my skin.

He slides his finger from my belly button up my torso to my breast, making my nipples strain for his attention. He doesn't press me for answers and appears relieved for some reason, as if a heavy weight has been lifted from his chest. His eyes follow the movement of his fingers until he stops on the hollow part of my throat.

"I almost didn't let him take you out of there, but I see it wasn't the time or place. I'm sorry Veronica was there, and I should have known better. Sometimes, I don't think; I just want to feel."

"What do you want to feel?" I ask on a gasp when his other hand grips my waist, bringing me flush to his groin.

"Me, inside of you. I want to taste you. I want to fuck you."

My hands rest on his chest, over taut muscle and ink. I look up into his eyes, the water making lines like streams down my face and chin. My chest is rising and falling. The feel of his dick teasing my slit.

"I was with Reid a couple of hours ago."

I want to tell him so he can stop if he wants to. I don't want him to think any less of me. It's better to actually say it, even if he already knows it.

"Did he make you come, Jess? Did he make you feel good?"

I shake my head. "No. I didn't come."

He closes his eyes. "Bastard," he mumbles with a grin. "I guess I have to be the one to make you come."

He slides his hands over my ass, spreading his big hands over my skin. Valen is about an inch taller and leaner than Reid but is strong for his build.

He lifts me, and I wrap my legs around his waist as my back hits the tile behind me. He bends his knees slightly, his gaze not leaving mine, when he slides the tip of his cock inside my pussy inch by inch and we both groan.

"Fuck, you feel so good."

My pussy gushes, my arousal coating his cock as it makes noises while he thrusts inside of me.

"Yes," I say on a moan. "Don't stop."

I wrap my arms around his neck, giving him a better angle so he can plunge into me deeply. He places my lower back against the tiles, holding me at a certain height while angling his body.

"What are you doing?" I ask with a gasp.

He feels so good. He's hard but soft at the same time. He knows what he's doing and how to hit me in the right spot that has me falling off the edge. He may be younger than Reid, but he sure as hell knows how to make a woman come.

"Making sure I come inside this pussy. I want my cum dripping out of you in the morning while I eat my breakfast."

I grind my hips, hoping he reaches the right spot. Fuck. His words are hot. He grasps my thighs with his strong hands as if I were nothing.

"Do you like that, baby? Is that what you need? Me inside you."

"Valen," I mewl. "Right there."

He pumps into me while I gyrate on his shaft. I'm swollen and dripping. The water feels hotter, but I know it's my body and what Valen is doing to me. He has my body on the verge, and god, he's perfect. It's a shame he isn't the relationship type. This is just a good time, and I need a man to make me feel good, so he's perfect, and I don't want him to stop. I want him inside me, taking me away from my reality just for a little while. I'm on the pill, and I've only had sex with Valen without a condom. Except when Michael raped me. Valen has evolved into a guy I can trust with sex. A guy who doesn't judge and is comfortable in his own skin, and when I'm with him, I'm free. I feel like that girl in college exploring what she likes. He gets tested monthly like I do, which we only share with each other.

He places his lips on my neck, placing soft kisses. "I want you, Jess. I want you so much. Come on my cock, baby, it's all yours. I want to feel you milking me."

I meet him with every thrust over and over until my orgasm crests, and I feel him going at me deeper. His grunts and my moans echo in the shower against the sound of water hitting the tile. It's hot, and it feels forbidden. He takes what he wants, and I want to give it to him.

I glance down and watch his cock disappear inside my pussy, hitting my clit and causing me to clench my pussy.

"You're coming, baby. I can feel it. Let go, Jess. Give me what I want."

"What do you want?" I ask breathlessly.

He grins and slides his tongue up my neck and over the seam of my lips.

"To fuck you whenever I want," he responds, sliding his thumb over my clit in circles, and it throbs, pushing me over the edge. "Tell me I get to fuck you whenever I want. Tell me," he repeats.

My pussy floods in response, and I scream, "I'm coming! Fuck. Yes!"

He pumps into me and grunts with a smile, spilling inside me, jerking his body as his cock spasms, lighting me on fire from the inside.

"You're dirty and swollen now," he says, holding me steady while my heart rate slows down.

The door to the main shower opens, and I stiffen. "Fuck, someone's in here," I whisper.

He places his index finger over my lips, telling me to be quiet as he helps me slide down until my feet touch the tiles.

My forehead is touching his chest, and I wait, closing my eyes. My skin prickles in awareness at being caught naked in the shower with Valen.

I hear footsteps, but he remains still. Once they stop hearing the only shower running in the middle of the night, it is evident that we are the only ones in there.

I hear a snicker. "I knew he wouldn't keep her."

Veronica's voice booms inside the quiet bathroom. Shit. She saw us. How the fuck did she know we were here?

"I'll handle this," he whispers. "Don't be afraid."

"I'm not," I say, looking up at his beautiful face full of mischief.

"Play her at her own game. She wants you. Are you up to play, baby?"

It depends on what kind of game he wants to play, and I can't ask him with her right here. I wonder what she wants with me besides being a sex-crazed idiot.

She walks close to the curtain to the changing area right before you reach the shower curtain. The curtain is like a barrier. But you can still see who is inside the shower stall if you walk into the small changing area with a bench.

Valen turns around, not caring if she can see him completely naked, shielding me behind him. Valen is the type who doesn't mind who sees him. It's what I like most about him. He doesn't care what anyone thinks or says. He does what he wants and with whom he wants.

I can't see her, but I can hear her next words. "You're fucking her raw," she says, with a smile in her voice. "I like it. Did you come in her?" she purrs.

"What do you want, Veronica, and more importantly, why are you here?" Valen says with a firm tone.

"I was curious to see where you went. I had a hunch after you stormed in and punched the shit out of Garrett in her honor, and I guess I was right. You couldn't resist her. Could you?"

He punched Garrett? For me? My stomach clenches, and butterflies swarm, mixed with tears burning behind my eyes. No one has ever cared for me besides my mom. I feel bad for Garret in a way. He is fucked up, and his motives don't add up, but no one has ever defended me that way. Why would he risk himself for me?

"Your point?" he snaps.

"I was surprised, that's all. I would have thought it would be Reid, but then again, he doesn't care about a Prey. He had me confused earlier when he saw us and called me a bitch."

I snort. He called me a whore. I guess I got the short end of the stick. Being referred to as a bitch is preferable to being referred to as a whore.

"What was that, Jess? Did he say something to you, too?" she asks in a singsong voice.

Like she would give three fucks what Reid would call me. She's a manipulator. She sure as hell got me by screwing me over. But that was then, and this is now. I'm tired of people using me.

"I'm going to my room," I say, quietly moving from behind Valen and coming into view. She steps aside, but her eyes dip as she watches me walk with pure want in her eyes. Valen wasn't wrong. She does like to bat for the other team.

JESS

ONCE I'M in my room, I don't expect Valen to show up. I'm combing my hair in a fresh pair of pajama shorts and a cropped tank top. I hear a knock on my door, and looking at my phone, it's already three a.m.

I open the door and see Valen fully dressed, minus his jacket and gloves or the beanie he likes to wear. His light hair is a sexy mess, and his eyes roam over my body. Veronica is behind him, and they walk in and close the door, flicking the lock.

Veronica sits on the chair by my desk and watches Valen as he walks closer and tips my chin up with his finger. His eyes find mine, and the look he is giving me is different.

"Remember what I said?" he says.

Veronica raises her brows, but she is so fixated on me that she doesn't grasp the hidden meaning in his words. He pushes me down on the bed, and I break my fall by placing my hands behind me.

"What are you doing?" I ask softly, my eyes locked on his.

He smiles and looks over at Veronica and then back at me. "Showing her how much you like me. She wants to watch your cunt swallow my cock."

What is he doing? My elbows shake at the intentions behind his words. He wants to finish what he started, or rather, what almost happened at the party. The part with her in the room.

"I'm tired."

"It will be quick, I promise," he says, removing his shirt and pants.

Veronica bites her lip, but she isn't looking at the beautiful man standing in front of me, sliding his boxers down his muscular, solid thighs full of tattoos or his hard cock. She's watching my reaction to him.

"Yeah, Jess. It will be quick," Veronica parrots, her eyes transfixed on me like I'm a shiny dot in a dark room.

"Sit on my lap, baby," Valen says, sitting beside me and stroking his cock.

I should ask him to leave and get the fuck out or, better yet, kick them both the fuck out. But then I'll be left alone with my demon coming to remind me at night that I'm his.

How bad can it be? He's here to make me feel good. He won't hurt me, and he says all the right things—things that make me forget. I know he's saving me from her for whatever reason. The problem is, I don't know what that is exactly.

I sit up straight, and he reaches for me, pulling me so that the backs of my thighs rest on his muscular ones, the contrast of his tattooed hands against the bare skin of my thighs. My back to his front, I can feel the heat of his hard cock ready for me.

He slides my hair away from my neck and places a soft kiss near my ear, the little spot where my pulse beats wildly when his firm lips touch my skin.

"I want you to ride me this way. Reverse cowgirl," he says, nibbling my neck. "She wants to watch you take my cock. She wants to see how much you want me."

He kisses me again, and my body melts. My skin is on fire with goose-bumps from the heat. My nipples are hardening under my shirt like I'm cold.

His other hand slides the neckline of my top down, exposing my breasts and pulling it down so that it stays in place beneath my tits like an offering—a sample for someone to taste.

Veronica gets up from the chair and kneels between our legs. "You're so beautiful, Jess. Has anyone told you how beautiful you are? How hot and sexy your body is?"

I shake my head silently, telling her no, and watch as her forehead creases in a frown. She tilts her head to the side, licking her lips.

"Really. I guess we have to change that, don't we? Right, Valen? We have to show her how pretty she is and how good she tastes. What she does to us."

She glides her small white hands on my thighs. Her straight hair sliding forward like a curtain. I hold my breath, stiffening as she reaches for the hem of my shorts and slides them down my legs in one motion, exposing me.

Valen reaches around my waist to flick my clit and I explode from the sensation on a moan.

She looks up and bites her lip like she's in agony. "Does it feel good?"

I nod. "Yes."

She looks up at Valen like he's a disease but is only here for my benefit. "Make sure she's wet, Valen. Make sure it's good for her."

"It's always good for her. She's my favorite," he says, smearing my arousal all over my lower lips while playing with my clit.

"I know she is. I've never seen your cock work so hard or go... bare for a girl."

She looks at my pussy and then looks up at me, biting her lip so hard I think she is breaking the skin. "Did you know Valen has this special appetite? Not like mine, of course, but an appetite so bad it's crazy and borderline insane."

She angles her head, mesmerized by how wet Valen is making me, breathing fast and steady. "He loves to fuck, and I like..." She sticks her tongue out, wetting her upper lip. "To suck pussy."

"You don't like cock?" I ask.

I don't care, but I need to keep my cool. She's a lesbian, which is fine. No judgment. I don't like women, but this is just experimenting, I tell myself. I'll be clear: this is a one-time thing. I'm not going to touch her or let her stick anything inside me. It will just be a kiss, I tell myself.

Valen slides the tip of his finger inside my pussy, and I arch my back against his chest, and he widens my thighs.

"That pussy is so wet," she purrs. "Ready to be fucked. I like to call it a pootie." She smiles. "Do you know why?"

I don't give a fuck, but I can't tell her that. This sex-crazed bitch is insane. It's no wonder Warren dropped her like a bad habit. He's a creepy asshole, but this bitch is crazy. They're like a match made in heaven.

"No, why?"

"Because it's what my daddy called it. It's what I like to call it since I found out for the first time that I like them," she says.

"Fuck," I gasp as Valen slides a second finger inside me.

"Ready, baby?" he says in a rough voice.

His cock is hard like steel, and it's throbbing under the crack of my ass. He lifts me, and I impale myself on his cock, holding my breasts. "Yes," I moan.

"You feel so good, baby. You're always so tight and such a good girl," Valen says, pumping inside of me.

With my hips riding him, I meet his thrusts. He grunts and groans.

My nipples are hard and aching. Veronica kneels and leans forward, flicking her tongue on my nipple, causing me to jolt. Valen stiffens slightly but keeps going.

"I'm just going in for a taste."

Her eyes flick to my hooded ones. "Let me make you feel good, Jess. I need you to tell me I can suck your pussy and those pretty nipples aching for a touch."

I moan. Valen's cock is so hard and is swelling inside of me, stretching me. The sound of wet noises bounces off the walls, with only the lamp from my nightstand casting a glow on the wet nipples she just licked, causing my body to react biologically.

I want to feel good, and she licks it again, placing her lips over the tight bud. "Please," I whimper.

"More?" she asks.

"Yes," I moan.

God help me. I can't help myself. It feels so good. I'm hot and wet.

"Fuck, that's hot," Valen says behind me. "That is so hot, baby. You're in control, Jess. I got you."

I close my eyes, and she begins to suck my left breast and then the other.

While Valen's cock is fucking me, her fingers play with my clit. I moan and he grunts.

She moans against my skin, releasing my right nipple with a pop. "So good and so beautiful. She's gorgeous, Valen. Look how wet she is for you."

She leans closer to my lips. "Tell him. Tell him how much you like his dick inside your tight pink cunt."

"I like his dick inside me. It's so hard and big. I love it when he forces me to come," I whisper.

He grunts in response, going faster. "Yeah, baby. You're so beautiful, Jess. You're exactly what I want. I'll be inside you, pounding this pussy whenever you need me."

Veronica smiles and snakes her tongue down my torso to my clit and begins to suck my pussy like a woman starving to eat. "Oh my god. Yes!"

I grab her head, holding her in place. I lose myself, not believing what I'm letting her do to me. She makes circles over my clit, licking it and sucking my pussy at the same time Valen's shaft disappears inside my folds. Fuck.

"Mmm," she moans. "This pussy belongs to the Order. You choose, and we fuck," she says as she twirls her tongue against my clit.

This bitch is fucking nuts, but she can eat pussy. Fuck, I'm about to come. Valen increases his thrusts as I turn my head and he devours my lips.

His tongue fucks my mouth, and I can't take it. Her mouth on my pussy while Valen is fucking me is too much. I break.

"I'm coming!" I scream.

Valen places his hand over my mouth so no one can hear me scream while he grunts. "I'm coming. It's a lot of cum, baby. I'm going to fill you up so much," he says on a grunt, spilling inside me. He stills, letting his release, and I can feel his cock throbbing as it promises what his words just did.

I'm breathing hard after he's done, and he slides out of me, his cum leaking out. He places me on the bed with my legs open. My pussy used, swollen, and leaking.

Veronica kneels on the bed while Valen kneels beside my head. I turn and the tip of his cock is coating my lips. "Open. Clean me," he says.

I open my mouth and he slides his cock slowly inside my wet mouth. I can taste his salty cum on my tongue. It is not nasty but tastes a little sweet.

"Fuck, your mouth is perfect," he rasps.

He looks at Veronica. "Clean her," he instructs.

"Yes, sir," she says without protest.

Her mouth is on my pussy, and I lift my ass off the bed at the intense sensation. I'm sensitive and swollen, but her tongue is soft as she licks his cum from my pussy.

I moan when she places pressure on my clit. She dips her tongue inside, and I clench my thighs around her head. She places her hands on my outer thighs, caressing me. "Open, baby. I need to get all of it. He wants you clean."

I relax my thighs, and she finishes cleaning me off, sucking her lips when she is done feasting on me.

"All done."

He looks at her. "Good, now get the fuck out. You're done."

"Fine," she growls, getting up. "But I did what you wanted. Reid is going to be pissed when he finds out."

What? He called her? Did he lie to me?

I stiffen, but he is already between my thighs, sliding his cock inside me, thrusting. He leans over me with his hands on the side of my head.

"Shh."

His lips move closer to my ear while the door clicks after Veronica exits. "You heard her. Your pussy belongs to the Order." He looks down as his cock slides in and out, making me whimper. "When you want to fuck, you call me, and I'll fuck you so good."

"You'll fuck me whenever I want?"

JESS

I BOLT upright from the bed after being jolted awake. I look down, and my legs are open with a sense of relief. I was dreaming. Valen is between my thighs. My eyes are closed. I was talking in my sleep.

He nods, letting out a breath, sliding his hand behind my neck. "Whenever you want. Wherever you want. I'll come over, and we'll fuck." He lifts my head, allowing our lips to brush against each other's. "You were talking in your sleep. What you didn't hear me say to Veronica in front of you was that she wasn't allowed to touch you. Don't let me catch her touching what's mine. If anyone touches you without your consent, I'll kill them. Do you understand?"

I nod, my gaze fixed on his. He slides inside me in a hard thrust, causing my orgasm to crest again, and I tighten around him. His nostrils flare while he peppers kisses on my lips.

His words fill me with warmth, with the hope that someone cares. Veronica wasn't here. It was a dream. I must have fallen asleep, and he found his way inside my room. He cares right now, and that's the most anyone has ever done for a girl like me.

He's not my boyfriend, and I'm not stupid enough to believe he can offer more than what he's giving me.

The way he looks at me while he's inside me is the closest I have ever felt to feeling wanted. To feel free and be able to enjoy sex without being haunted by memories because of my bad decisions.

He runs his nose against my cheek, just the way I like when he does it. The smell of his skin mixed with my body wash.

"You're not a whore. You are not a bad person simply because you want someone to make you feel good sexually. You're sexy and beautiful, and if anyone can't see that, then fuck them."

"Valen," I mewl.

His words make me fall. I can't say it's love, but it's something I have never felt for someone.

"I know, baby, you're almost there. I can feel it. I want you to let go. I don't want you to hold back and not enjoy this. Enjoy us."

That's when I come. I come hard from his soft words. Tears pool in the corner of my eyes because it's all I want. I want to forget. I want someone to treat me right, even if it's just for a minute, to caress me like I belong to them, to love me for a second, to know what it would feel like when someone truly cared for me like I would care for them.

Some type of love. Even if it's a lie. My mind tries to make sense of why I dreamed of Veronica and Valen pleasuring me at the same time. Was it because Gia kissed me, which triggered what happened with Garrett, and I was at his house with Veronica before Reid saved me from doing something I would later regret?

I close my eyes, trying to make sense of it all. I'm losing myself, but I secretly crave two men and hate another. One is inside me, and the other treats me like the thing I hated the most, triggering a memory I'm trying to forget. Then, the other allows me to use him.

The sacrifice I had to make for the only person who truly loves me and sees me as a saint, despite the fact that all I have become is a sinner. I'm using their want for sex on a primal level to forget the monster that comes for me, but now I'm feeling things that I want. With them.

GIA

WALKING into Babylon after a late class on Monday, I scan the bar and spot Jess talking to the bartender. I smile as she animatedly waves her hands with a smile on her face.

Making my way through the crowd, it is surprisingly busy tonight, being a weekday, but it's Monday night football, and there isn't much to do so…

When I finally make it up to the bar, Jess smiles at me. She turns and sees me in my fuzzy jacket over wool leggings and UGGs on my feet. "You look so cozy, I miss you," she says, giving me a hug.

She turns her head, and the bartender she was deep in conversation with gives me a nod and asks, "What can I get you?"

Before I can answer, Jess blurts, "Cranberry and vodka, but not too strong."

I giggle. "I'm not a lightweight, Jess."

She waves her hand, taking a sip of a fruity cocktail she is drinking. "Yeah, but I'm not taking any chances with your man, or should I say…" She trails off.

She means the twins. I have been holed up in Dravin's house, being waited on hand and foot by two hot-ass men. My body is deliciously used, but I'm not taking anything seriously and just enjoying feeling safe. Wanted.

I didn't tell them my fear of being alone with Warren lurking around or his threats. I should have told them, but I was as caught up with both of them as they were with me. There were no discussions of the future, just being in the moment, and I was okay with that for now. No pressure. They held me at night when I cried about the miscarriage. They took turns holding me. When I was in the shower, the other was there supporting me and telling me everything would be all right.

Dravin repeatedly apologized for his actions, but what was done was done. Do I trust them? Not entirely. Do they want me? Maybe. Time will tell, but I'm not in a hurry to find out right now. I need to find myself, explore what I want, and discover what I truly need.

Jess twirls her glass between her fingers, the drops of water sliding down the glass. She looks happier—not entirely happy, but happy for now, if that makes sense. I heard she left with Reid, but then I heard Valen slept over, and I'm not sure what the deal is between them.

"You look happy," I say over the music playing from the jukebox.

She gives me a smirk. "Not as happy as you. So, how was your weekend?"

"You first," I counter.

She takes another sip of her drink, and I see her eyes are glassy from the alcohol. She's buzzed. I can tell with the way her mouth curls in a grin and her upbeat attitude. Usually, she's more reserved and borderline paranoid half the time.

She swallows and watches the bartender place the drink I ordered in front of me. When he walks away, she spills everything that happened with Reid, Valen, and Veronica, causing me to down my drink in one go.

"Hey, chill with that, or I'll have to call back up," she teases.

"I think it's too late for that," I say, nudging my head to where Drav, Draven, Valen, and Reid are making their way through the crowd. They are all dressed in black like they are part of a cult, except they look like cover models. All the females turn their heads to get a good look as they approach us. Some make it obvious, and some try to hide it by giving them a glance behind them as they pass.

Once they see us, I notice Reid standing a few feet away from Jess, unsure how she will take the fact that he's here. She doesn't look at him, though. Her eyes are locked on Valen, and they share a silent language that only the two of them can understand.

"Hey, gorgeous." Drav is the first to greet me, but Draven places a kiss on my neck. My lips rub together, nervous at their display of affection. People are staring at them because they look like two clones that were made in a lab somewhere. The good news is that I can tell them apart. The tattoos. A particular touch that is different. I have also been smart enough to share certain things with one and not with the other.

"Hey," I say softly.

Valen gives me a knowing smile, looking between the Bedford twins and me. My cheeks must be red because Draven leans close and says close enough to my ear but out of earshot. "Relax, or I could take you right now to the bathroom with Dravin and fuck you. No one would know the difference."

I bite my lip and Valen quirks an eyebrow. I swear nothing that has to do with sex escapes him.

"What are you guys doing here?" Reid asks.

Jess stays silent, but her eyes swing my way, telling me to answer him. She doesn't want to talk to him directly after how he treated her, and to be honest, I wouldn't either.

My eyes find his a few feet away. "We decided to meet up after classes were over. We wanted to catch up. We were both busy this weekend and didn't get to hang out," I answer.

He nods, though I can see he is trying not to look over at Jess. He tries to break the awkward silence by talking to Valen since he knows where the twins and I were all weekend.

"What did you get up to this past weekend after the party?" he asks Valen.

Jess stills and rests her forearms at the bar, facing the bartenders and giving them her back. She reaches for the glass and drains the rest of her cocktail.

She was screwing in our dorm room with Valen all weekend. It is obvious Valen didn't mention that part to Reid.

After a few seconds, Valen rubs the back of his neck and faces the opposite direction, leaning on the edge of the bar next to Jess. "I was with someone the rest of the weekend." He licks his lips and looks down and then back at Reid.

"No shit. Who was she? You're not the type to hang out with one chick all weekend," he says on a laugh.

My hand slides into Dravin's hand and squeezes it for support. His eyes land on mine, and it dawns on him to be quiet. Not to say shit. Draven, behind me, chuckles, but he gives Draven a look that tells him to keep his mouth shut.

Valen sucks his teeth, trying to keep his cool. "No one you care about," he responds.

Shit. He's keeping it from Reid. It must have bothered him the way Reid treated Jess. I look over at Valen and smile, seeing him in a friendly light. He's looking out for her. The things she told me she went through, and keeps enduring, and he's actually not being a dick about it and putting her out there.

Reid is quiet, not entirely convinced by his answer. It's like you can feel the uncertainty of Valen's response or the way he isn't talking like he smashed some random chick he usually does. He is typically vocal about the girls he sleeps with the few times he's been around. He's a total player.

Jess turns around and nudges Valen playfully. "So, who was the lucky chick? Was she good?" she asks.

Draven snorts and I widen my eyes. He takes the cue and looks over at the bartender, twirling his finger, silently motioning for another round of drinks.

Reid finally glances over at Jess while she isn't looking, totally checking her out. She's wearing tight skinny jeans and over-the-knee boots with an off-the-shoulder sweater. Her cute bra strap peeking out. Her hair is in loose, messy waves. She looks hot. It's no wonder even Veronica has a thing for her, but Jess clearly said it wasn't ever happening again after that time with Garret. College experimenting, she said on a laugh.

Valen pulls his bottom lip with his teeth, and he is totally going to talk about her in front of Reid without him knowing he is talking about her and what he thought of her in bed.

Fuck, she's playing with fire, making me smile at her. Well played. He deserves it.

Valen snakes his gaze over her briefly and tilts his head. "She was hot and tasted so good I didn't want to leave, so I stayed the whole weekend."

"You slept with her in bed?" I ask him, acting like I don't already know.

He gives me a mischievous expression, licks his lip where his teeth are, and then chuckles. "More like fucked nonstop. More fucking and less sleeping, and I stayed. The sex was so good I didn't want to leave. We even ordered food in between."

Drav scratches his head when he looks at Reid, but he notices he doesn't catch on.

"How about you?" Valen asks Reid. "What did you do after?"

Reid looks at Jess, but she's already turned away, disinterested in what he has to say. I can see the frustration in his brows as she continues to ignore him.

After the way he treated her, why should she feel the need to acknowledge him? He's lucky I don't punch him in the eye, but I'll let her handle it.

Reid swallows, trying to find the right words. "I had some family business to take care of after Jess left," he points out.

She snorts yet doesn't turn to look at him. When the bartender arrives with our round of drinks, he smiles at Jess and says, "I made this one just the way you like it."

Draven's eyebrows rise, and Reid slides his hand on the bar, his forearms taut with corded muscle and ink, tilting his head toward the bartender.

Oh, shit. Someone's a little pissed.

"How would you know what she likes?" Reid asks with a growl.

The bartender glances at Jess and answers without looking at him. "Because she told me. She told me what she likes."

Reid and Valen both chuckle, and my pulse begins to pound when Jess glances at me. The twins are flanking me on each side but make no move to intervene. They want to see how this all plays out. It's like watching two lions fighting for a lioness, waiting for someone to attack so they can pounce. This isn't about the bartender; this is about the way Jess smiles and is comfortable with Valen, and how Reid doesn't like the way she doesn't acknowledge him. She looks down her nose at him like he's no longer a factor. The way she is flirting and sharing what she likes with the bartender.

Reid's eyes travel down her body, making a point that he's undressing her with them. That he's seen her without her clothes on. It's obvious to anyone who is watching him next to her that they have been intimate.

The bartender watches him with annoyance and then flicks his eyes to Valen, who tilts his head, watching Reid make his next move with a devious smirk. It's like the rest of the place fades away, and we're the only ones trapped in our own makeshift bubble.

Jess raises her head and stares at the bartender with a worried expression. She must be nervous because Reid is unpredictable when pushed. He's mostly quiet and keeps to himself. Although the few times I have seen him, you wonder what is going through his head. Like right now, he may be looking at Jess with interest or maybe it's just part of their game. Games they like to play just to fuck with you.

He makes it seem like he's interested in her, but then, you never know with Reid. He could walk away and go to the back and get his dick sucked by some random chick in the bar. Jess is a memory all forgotten until... next time.

Two distinctive pings sound on either side of me. I look up to see Draven pull out his phone and then I look to my left to see his twin do the same. They both received texts at the same time.

I hear Draven mutter, "Fuck."

"I would love to see how this all plays out, but we have to leave."

Valen darts his eyes to Draven. "What's up, brother?"

"Family business," Draven answers for him.

"Let's go," Dravin whispers in my ear.

Jess turns around and our eyes meet. "Are you okay to stay, or do you..." I trail off.

"I'm good. I can have Valen take me back."

I nod, and Dravin places his hand on my lower back, signaling that we must go. I don't know how that involves me, but the twins have been very adamant about never leaving me alone. I wonder why?

REID

MY ARM IS CAGING Jess from her right side, and the sideways glance she gives Gia tells me all I need to know. She's nervous when I'm near, and I'm going to show her she should be. Especially when she's flirting with the bartender.

She thinks I haven't been watching her since I entered with Valen and the Bedford twins. Her sultry smile and the way her snug leggings are hugging her perfect ass. Her bra strap is visible from her shoulder. The asshole in front of her keeps looking at it, probably imagining sliding it off to see her creamy breasts and what color her nipples are.

My gaze moves over her shoulder, down her arm, and back up to her neck, where I'm sure I can feel her pulse beating if I place my lips there. Not the same way it beats when I'm inside her, but close.

I stare at the bartender and can see the look of annoyance aimed right at me. I smile when I rub my lip piercing and inhale her flowery-scented perfume. Intoxicating right to the head of my dick, straining in my jeans. Fuck, she is addicting. I hated the way she left my hotel that night. The way I let her go when I fucked up. It wasn't the way I wanted to end the night, not with her. I shouldn't give a fuck, but there is something that draws me to her, like a moth to a flame, something that needs to be awakened. There is something inside her that I see that is dormant, but once it is unleashed, I want to feed off it. I want her to want me. I'm just so fucked up when it comes to her. I was raised in a world where I was taught to not care.

To take.

To control.

"You don't want to look at me?" I whisper in her ear.

Nothing. No answer. She just stares at the bartender. The music fades in the background. My heart begins to pump inside my chest. My cock is rock hard, but I'm going to rectify my mistake. I didn't let her come. In my jealousy, I punished her. It's hard to admit that to myself, but that's what it felt like. The same way I'm feeling now with her attention on Valen. His attention on her doesn't bother me—or perhaps it does. I'm not sure yet. But the bartender? Now that I have a problem with. Him—or any other man she smiles that way for.

My hand finds the waistband of her pants, and she tenses. "You don't want to look at me, fine, keep looking at him."

Her face turns to gape at me. Her stormy expression is in those brown eyes.

"What are you doing?" she hisses.

My lips are just inches away from hers. "I'm finishing what you started. You didn't let me finish, but I will now."

My hand quickly slides inside her stretchy pants, and I find the elastic band of her panties and slide my finger over her clit.

She turns back to the bartender and parts her lips. At her entrance, I make languid circles with my thumb, teasing with my index finger, and softly say, "Tell him everything you like."

She doesn't say anything. Valen tilts his head forward to glance at me over the bar, with Jess between us. People are drinking, and the place is filling up quickly, which is perfect. No one will notice.

My name escapes from her lips, which are so soft, in almost a whimper. "Reid."

"Tell him."

The bartender pinches the skin between his brows in a slight frown. He doesn't realize I'm finger fucking her in front of him while he watches. She doesn't tell me to stop or scream. She wants this. She needs to come. She craves it. And I want her taste on my fingers.

"Hey, man. It's all good," the bartender says. "She's good. She doesn't have to repeat the types of drinks she likes."

"Oh, you thought that this was about drinks?" I ask, plunging my finger inside her tight cunt. She takes a deep swallow.

Fuck, she's wet and tight. I want to slide into her right here so bad, not giving a fuck who watches, or maybe I do. I don't want this asshole to see her perfect cunt or the way her perky tits bounce when I'm inside her or when her neck arches when she comes on a scream.

I slide my finger in her faster and swirl my thumb on her clit. She grips the bar with her hands, and I'm right behind her. My lips are inches from her neck, under her ear, while I look at the bartender with a grin. She's about to come, and I plunge into her one last time, and I feel her walls clench my fingers as she breaks.

"Yeah, baby. Come. Show him what you like. Tell him you love my fingers fucking you in a roomful of people."

Her mouth is parted, but I can't see her eyes. The bartender looks at me and shakes his head with his lips curled.

I raise my head, my eyes challenging him to say something so I have a reason to slit his throat. He sets her empty glass to the side so the busboy can retrieve it. A couple of girls across the bar are waving their money to get his attention. He hears them calling, but he's pissed. I'm not sure if he knows what I am doing to her or if she allowed it.

I remove my fingers full of her cum from between her leg and raise them to my mouth, tasting her. "One thing you will never have is her." I suck my fingers clean.

"I get it," the bartender says. Then he looks at her, but she turns her head away.

"Make sure that you do, or I'm going to have to pay you a visit," I tell him with a sigh, placing a small kiss on her hair. "And you wouldn't want that."

Valen laughs through his nose at the nervous look that crosses the bartender's face and he leaves to take the other orders.

Jess whirls with a glare. "Why? Why did you do that?"

"Because I can. Last time I checked." I wave the scent of her pussy under her nose with my fingers. "You didn't protest, and you sure as hell loved it. I owed you one, remember?"

"Fuck you."

"I plan on it."

"No."

"We'll see."

She sidesteps to the right to go around me. I'm about to stop her, but I let her go. I'm surprised Valen doesn't follow her. Instead, he stares at me with a glare.

"What?" I snap at him, annoyed.

He shakes his head. "You didn't have to do that."

I take my vape pen out, place the tip between my lips, press the button so it heats up, and inhale without giving a fuck. "I did," I say, releasing a cloud of smoke tinged with marijuana into the air. Some people can make out that it's marijuana in oil from a vape pen, and others don't notice. I couldn't care less. It's just convenient, and it relaxes me.

Valen walks away, pissed at me, but I don't care. I was making a point, which I'll keep making when it comes to Jess. She is mine, and I'm claiming her. She just doesn't know it yet.

GIA †

I'M in the back seat of the black Rolls Royce with Dravin and Draven sitting next to me while their driver is taking us to the Bedford estate. Apparently, their father wants to see the three of us. Dravin to my left and Draven to my right. I know this because I have picked up on some of their quirks. Dravin likes to place his hand on my knee, and the other twin likes to watch him do it.

I wonder if it bothers him to see Dravin touch me and for me to allow it. Draven isn't affectionate in public. He isn't soft or emotional like Dravin. He's more to the point, but he does have a soft side, which I saw when I was crying.

He's seconds younger, and by default, he doesn't get to marry. He has to share the woman who bears his children with his brother, but it doesn't appear to bother him. Maybe it's because of his freedom to choose who he wants to be with.

Feeling Draven tense beside me, I look down at his hand resting on the red leather seat. I glance at the rearview mirror and see that the driver is looking straight ahead and I look to my right and see that we are passing the cemetery. It's dark, and the glow from the pillar near the gate illuminates the front door of the old church. I see suited men leaving discreetly to the awaiting vehicles parked in a line by the path near the opposite entrance.

Trying to get a better look without being obvious is straining my eyes. I'm beginning to sweat under my jacket, and my feet feel suffocated inside my UGGs.

The Order. They had a meeting. It must have been between the main leaders and that didn't include the sons of Kenyan because they were with us. All of them, so that could mean that something is wrong.

I feel Draven next to me, and he seems restless, which causes me to feel nervous. Dravin must feel that I'm nervous and begins swirling his thumb over my thick winter pants. My right hand moves slowly down by my thigh and I reach for Draven's hand. I can hear the small intake of his breath when my fingers brush against the top of his left palm. His head angles slightly, and I can feel the burning gaze, watching our hands touch.

Slowly, I place my left hand on Dravin's, and my right hand grips his brother's. My skin prickles with awareness, and my body reacts to the warmth of their hands on mine. Identical hands from two different men. It's crazy but so erotic. Memories of their touch on me the whole weekend flashed back into my mind. When they were on me. Inside me.

When the car turns on the same street Draven took me on his motorcycle, I snap out of my thoughts. This time, it feels like I'm on my way to meet the devil. Mr. Bedford is a very powerful man. He serves a purpose: the Order and himself. Everything else is inconsequential.

The black iron gate opens slowly like it's taking its time, or maybe it's giving me time to flee. But I know deep down I won't. I'm not going to run. There are threats in the name of Warren. He threatened me. I haven't told the twins and fear what they might do. I'm sure they will kill him. It means they will risk their lives for me if they find out. Do I want the death of Warren on my conscience because of his threats? Do I want the twins to risk their lives for me? I know the answer in my heart is no. As much as they have hurt me, they have also made me feel like I'm a woman. They have made me love myself. Warren hasn't touched me or physically hurt me. Not yet, but I wouldn't put it past him. I'm stuck in a hard place. Tell them or don't tell them. Either way, there is a risk.

The driver pulls in around the fountain with the gargoyle. The reflection of the red light on the pillars gives him red eyes. The front door opens, and the staff, I assume, is present. Maybe they only appear when their father is home, or maybe that day Draven had them dismissed.

The driver places the car in park and opens the door on Dravin's side to let us out. Dravin slides out of the car first, but when I move to place my foot, Draven pulls me back. His hand grips my jaw, turning my face to his. His lips come crashing over mine. I gasp when his tongue plunges inside my mouth, and he groans. His soft tongue sucks my top lip and then my bottom.

"Are you done?" I hear Dravin's annoyed tone snapping me out of the kiss. For a moment, we weren't in the car. Dravin wasn't outside waiting for me to slide out. I was transported into another world—another moment—with Draven.

Draven releases me and tilts his head to look at his brother. "It was the kiss, or I was going to take her in the back seat."

"He's waiting, Draven. If he gets into one of his moods, you know how the night will end."

I frown and look at Draven to see if there is a hint. How will the night end? He sighs and gives me a peck on the nose. "Let's go. He's right."

I slide out, holding Dravin's hand, and he tugs me to his chest. "I'm not mad at you. I'm not mad that he kissed you. I just don't like being here."

I look up at him. The smell of the cold air and the way it's seeping into my clothes causes me to shiver from the change of temperature when exiting the warm car. His childhood home must bring him memories and thoughts of his mother.

"Okay," I say softly.

He smiles and slides his fingers down my cheek, and places a kiss on my forehead.

"Let's go," Draven says as he passes by us, walking ahead.

The front door is held open by a butler or doorman or whoever rich people hire to man the door—unnecessary if you ask me. The place looks like no one lives there, and it feels dark and haunted.

When Draven walks in, I follow him to the west side of the house. Just Draven's room on the east side of the home is the only part of the house I've seen. We make our way down the stairwell toward the middle. The gargoyles are just looking ahead, uninterested, as though they've seen it all before. The only sounds in the house are the sound of our feet on the red carpet runner and the thud of the front door closing. I wouldn't be so fearless if it weren't for the fact that I have the twins with me. It's almost as if they're stepping in front of me and behind me to protect me from... something.

Dravin's decision to go off on his own is understandable. His home looks sleek and sophisticated, yet it's rather dark. This house is dark, ancient, creepy, and holds secrets—secrets that could destroy you. These walls have seen things—terrible things—things that would have you question your existence. You can feel it in the bones of the house. It's solid, evil, faithless, and deceiving, like the people who own it.

GIA
†

WE MAKE it down to the end of the west wing, reminding me of Stephen King's *The Shining,* where the twin girls appear at the end of the hall. Dravin takes a right and turns the knobs of the double doors that appear to be an office.

His father is seated at a very old wood desk that looks antique and completely restored. It seems like it belonged to the house when it was being built. Not a piece you would find in an auction or a gallery.

"All three of you are here. Good," his father says, seated in his chair, which looks like a king's throne. In front of the desk, there is a young woman, probably a few years older than me. She looks at the twins with a smirk. A protective instinct flares inside my chest at her expression.

Three wood chairs mirror the one Mr. Bedford is seated at, but they're smaller versions. There is a floor lamp to the right and a painting of what appears to be old family members from their past. Men like their father. Their eyes witness everything that goes on inside the room. To the left is a bookcase filled with books. The carpet under the desk has the symbol of a family crest. When I take a seat in the chair, both men are at my sides. The young woman doesn't move except to lean close to Draven and whisper something in his ear. From the corner of my eye, I see him nod. A pang of jealousy snakes up my spine. *What the hell?* I look to Dravin, who is eyeing his father.

His father is watching me with his self-aggrandizing grin. He knows it bothers me that the woman is close to his son. The intimate way she touches his shoulder and the way she leans close so he can see the low cut of her black dress. The dress is formal in a way. A cross between office attire and a house-keeper's uniform. But not the way she bends at the waist. What throws it off is it's completely black and tight. It's deceiving. Fucking with a man's imag-ination.

Thinking about what Jess told me about showing no emotion, I'm trying to go with indifference, but my thoughts move into anger and rage. I want to claw her eyes out and hope an animal eats her face off when I'm finished with her.

Mr. Bedford clears his throat when he sees that I'm not amused by the woman or that she's touching him inappropriately for being an employee. If that is what she is. I'll soon find out. If Draven wants to mess around, then all he has to do is tell me. I'll accept it, but he isn't touching me ever again. It's his choice what he decides to do, and right now, it looks like he's making it.

"It has come to my attention that you were pregnant with my grandchild."

I raise my chin and cross my legs, one over the other. Mr. Bedford watches me, and his eyes slide over my thighs. I notice Dravin gripping the arms of the chair. Is his father checking me out? Gross. I get that he is a very handsome man. He doesn't have a protruding belly, it's flat. His dress shirt is open at the throat, and he looks like an older version of his sons, except he has a sprinkle of gray in his hair by the temples. He is muscular and toned, with a couple of tattoos peeking out from his chest and left arm by his wrist. He keeps them well covered by wearing tailored suits that must cost a fortune. The twin's father is a very attractive man for his age. He looks like he is in his late forties, maybe early fifties.

"Yes." I finally say. "I was, but I..." I trail off. It's still too painful to think about it. The sting of tears causes needles to prick my throat and I avert my gaze.

"You were poisoned. My son gave me the medical reports, and I had an investigation done on campus, as well as your whereabouts. I had a meeting with the leaders and it has been concluded that someone made an attempt on your life. Has anyone threatened you? I also need the last places you were before you ended up in the hospital. What you ate and where? Who was with you? And don't lie to me."

"Be careful how you talk to her, Father. I get you are upset about her losing the baby, but don't you dare threaten her," Draven warns him, to my surprise.

Dravin, to my left, is quiet, but he straightens in the chair. His glare, aimed at his father, is laced with fury and full of hate. It's obvious that Dravin hates his father. Resentment bleeds off of him in droves.

"Or what?"

"You will not like the outcome, I assure you," Draven replies.

Mr. Bedford trains his eyes on Dravin. "What? You're going to crawl over the desk and hit me."

"Maybe," Dravin challenges. "It all depends."

"On what?"

"If you look at her that way again. You know exactly what I'm talking about. Make no mistake. You touch a hair on her head or look at her like you are undressing her with your pathetic eyes, I will kill you."

Mr. Bedford laughs, and a wave of fear chills my spine. "You touch me, and you're dead, and your brother will have nothing. It is a stipulation within the Order. You might as well secure everyone in this room's death sentence if you go through with your threat against my life. I have treated you better than your mother ever could." He nods toward Draven. "Gianna knows too much to let them keep her alive."

He looks at the woman and nods. She kneels in front of Draven and my eyes fly to her as she slides her hands up his thighs. What the hell is she doing?

"What is she doing?" I ask.

The woman looks at me. "Taking what you didn't want," she says coyly.

"You said you didn't want to marry my son, so I'm going to show you what happens when you deny a Bedford. When you go against what you agreed to."

They already showed me the video they released to go viral on campus. It bothered me and hurt me to see it. How would they feel if I did the same thing?

"They have already shown me how easily they move on."

Draven tries to push her away, but his father's eyes darken, full of malice. This man is evil. He cares about himself and the control he has over everyone. He cares about me losing my unborn child because, in his eyes, someone took his legacy from him, even if it was inside my body. To a man like the twins' father, someone attempted to kill me because they knew I belonged to a Bedford and wanted to kill his legacy and get control.

This isn't about love or having a family. This is about power and manipulation. A pang of sadness consumes me for the twins and their mother. He didn't love her. He used her, like he expects the twins to use me. And if I don't fall in line, he will make me pay or, worse, kill me.

It's too late to turn back. I can read between the lines. He said I knew too much already. He isn't going to let me go. I either toe the line or pay. I look at the woman undoing Draven's pants, and my heart sinks. He wouldn't? He wouldn't let her. Not with me right here.

Dravin glances at me and then to his father. "I have done everything you have asked. I have sacrificed my entire life and future. "

"I'm helping you out," his father says with a smirk. "Trust me. I have never steered you wrong. You're not a momma's boy like your brother. You don't cry. You're just like me. You take what you want, which is why you are free and he isn't. You think you have sacrificed everything, but we all pay. She will look at him differently now, and maybe she'll think about the consequences the next time she decides to deny a Bedford." He looks at Draven. "Let her, or you'll be sorry. She needs to learn."

My chest tightens, and I close my eyes, not wanting to look at her grip Draven as she slides his cock out of his pants and slides her mouth over him like the greedy bitch she is, moaning while sucking him off, looking at me with a satisfied expression. Draven's cock goes rock hard while she is sucking him off and I turn my head away.

"Be a man and enjoy when a woman is sucking you off. What are you, a pussy? You like dick in your ass? Is that it? You're lucky I don't make her fuck you with her cunt."

"Fuck," Draven snaps. He grips her head and shoves his cock down her throat, and she almost dies of pleasure, and I want to claw her eyes out. The bitch.

He begins to fuck her mouth savagely. "This is what you want, you greedy cunt. You want my cock? Take it."

He grunts, and a wave of nausea climbs my throat. Bastard. He's enjoying this. The wet sounds echo in the room, and my eyes are trained on Dravin beside me, but he is silent. He doesn't look. He stays still, and I'm confused. He doesn't look at his brother or the woman. He is frozen, staring at the window behind his father, where there is nothing but the pitch-black night and a glow coming from what must be a garden or backyard. I have never been to the back of the house, so I don't know what the view is like. I'm trying to think about anything. Does the backyard have a pool or just manicured lawns like the front?

"Look at her while she takes his cock," Mr. Bedford says to me, snapping me out of my thoughts. "You want him? Now you will have him, but with the knowledge that you're not the only one that can make him come. Your cunt isn't anything special. Just a wet hole a Bedford sticks it in. You will dress appropriately and stay here for three days."

My eyes snap to his. "Why?"

Why do I have to stay here for three days? I don't want to stay in this creepy fucking house.

"Because I said so, and you will spread those legs and fuck my son until you cool off. You will learn what your duties are in this house. Your soon-to-be husband likes to live in his little playhouse. You will learn to play house in both. If you deny one of my sons again? I will make sure you pay. Trust me, it will be fun. There are other ways to make you pay. You will get pregnant, and you will have security. No contraceptives from here on out. Once you're pregnant, you will wed Dravin. You will accept that this is your life. You belong to the Order."

He thinks he can control me. That I don't have a say?

"What if the wrong son gets me pregnant?" I counter. I can feel the twins stiffen beside me.

One is getting his knob stroked, her moans and his grunts giving me the courage to challenge him. I'm not going to have sex with Draven, but I want to push. I want to annoy their father.

"It doesn't matter who gets you pregnant. Either way, you will give each of my sons a child from your cunt. My oldest son Dravin wanted you; he got you. There is no turning back. You belong to us, and you will learn to act, dress, and obey. You will not only honor your husband, but you will honor the Order."

Reid's evil smirk when I found out I was pregnant is coming full circle. The meaning behind his words comes at me in full force. *I belong to the Order.* Choosing to be with Dravin also means choosing to go along with everything that he is part of, including his brother.

"Tell her to stop," I say, turning to look at the woman as she is playing with herself while his hips lift and his hand is in her hair. "Better yet, tell them to leave and continue outside or in his room."

Their father raises his eyes in surprise and her mouth makes a pop when she releases his cock. "You don't care?" his father asks.

I lean forward, placing my long, dark hair to one side. "They don't leave anyone a choice once they accept and come here, do they? The ones you call Prey."

"I'm afraid not. It's the price that is paid when you accept. Tuition has nothing to do with it because when you graduate, you will make enough money to cover the tuition and more. The only problem is when they go against us. If you threaten us or our way of doing things, it messes with our purpose. Our control." He bends forward. "This is how we maintain the Order and control the world. We choose."

"You mean you choose people based on where they are from. People that have nothing else to lose. People you can manipulate and control."

"Let's not forget. Fuck and discard."

I snicker when I glance over at the woman with swollen lips and a smirk on her face. Her face falls when she sees that I'm not angry. I'm pissed off, but I'm not going to show anyone in this room that I'm devastated about my situation or, more importantly, that she is pleasuring Draven. I'm doomed to a life in a hell of my own choosing. Choosing Dravin or any son of Kenyan is accepting their life and rules that have you questioning what is right and what is wrong. If I have no choice but to accept Dravin and his twin, I'm not going to share them.

The memory of the painting in Dravin's room comes back to me: the woman depicting Lilith, the snake, and the man devouring what appears to be a woman's body, even if the history of the painting says otherwise. I know what I saw in the painting, and it was not about history. It is what they represent to them–the Order, lust, control, manipulation, but most of all... power.

I sneer at the woman with a look of hatred. "So, how did I taste?"

Her eyes widen but then she looks at Draven, but I can't see his expression.

"Answer her," Mr. Bedford demands.

She licks her lips and the rage burning inside me boils, causing my hands to grip the handles on the wooden chair.

"G-good. You tasted good."

I roll my eyes because I wanted her to say something slick so I would have a good enough reason to slap her across her face. I know she is a puppet for the puppet master, but it was the look she gave me when she had him in her mouth. It was supposed to be my mouth and now I can't look at him. It's one thing seeing it on video and another to be in the same room. He isn't mine, and he is allowed to do whatever he wants, but he was enjoying it. His grunts and her moans replay in my head.

My indifference is my armor. I shouldn't care, but I'm left with no choice but to care. I'm trapped in this, and it's obvious there is no way out. But I cannot lie to myself and say I don't want them. I crave them. My head lifts, and I see their father's smug face, watching the woman adjust her clothes and stand.

"I don't find this funny," I say, watching their father with his air of arrogance and devilish smile. "I'm not going to have his child. I'm not going to pollute my womb with her filth or any other's filth. That is sentencing me to hell."

He chuckles. "I know the only cock that has seen your cunt is from my two sons, but you actually expect my sons not to screw around? All men have mistresses. You need to accept that this is the present and your future."

His words are like sandpaper across my skin, burning with every word spilling from his mouth.

I'm about to tell him what I think, but Draven is quicker. "That's enough," Draven growls.

I'm relieved that he is defending me from his father, but I refuse to look at him. His father's eyes are like a pit of snakes, intimidating and always looking to strike. He chortles, and I have never hated someone the way I do their father right now. If evil had a face, it would be his.

He places his elbows on the wooden desk and leans forward. Dark eyes are fixated on Draven seated beside me. He made sure he gifted each of his sons a piece of the evil that lurked inside of him to ensure his agenda was carried out. They each have a dark eye that matches his as a reminder.

I can hear Draven adjust his pants in the chair next to me, and my head turns to look at Dravin to my left. He is silent, and I wonder why. I wonder why he hasn't said anything else to his father. He just sits silently, glancing at each person in the room as they speak. He doesn't reassure me or hold my hand. He is just... silent, like he isn't in this very room.

"You're playing a dangerous game, my son. Bringing a Prey to our circle has served no purpose. I applaud your efforts in trying to save her, forcing her to accept you both, but she denied you the first time and was against what was required."

"Save me from your incantations. Tricking her into believing a false pretense isn't fair. She didn't know that she had to accept both of us," Draven fires back.

He's trying to defend me, and my reasons for rejecting Dravin, but the truth is that I'm interested in both of them. I'd want to keep them all to myself and not share them with anyone else. I can't believe that their dad expects me to allow them to have mistresses whenever they want. There's no way I'll let it happen. I don't see why, but I just can't imagine choosing between the two. My dilemma is how to proceed without being destroyed by them or, worse, losing who I am. Now I know why their mother chose to end it. This is the reason she gave up. If you fall in love with a man, how do you bear to see him with someone else?

Their father chuckles. "The sins we remit on earth. I see it in your eyes. You want her for yourself. You were always the confrontational one, but you know the rules."

"Fuck the rules. They tried to kill her, and they almost succeeded. They killed our unborn heir," Dravin seethes.

"There will be others. It means she was weak. Unprotected. You failed her, but you will never admit that. Especially to her."

Recalling Dravin's hurtful words brings back painful memories. He assured me that he would provide for me and our child, that I would never have to worry about him or her, and that he would eventually marry someone else. Trying to recall what he said as he pushed me away, I stare down at my sweaty hands in my lap.

My eyes glance at their father, and it dawns on me that he is saving me from this—a life where heaven and hell make a pact among the scavengers of the damned. Children being born in the eyes of God corrupted by evil. He was trying to save me from this life. A life where they will try to kill me. They tried, but...

Everyone turns to gaze at me as I let out a startled sound. In my lap, my hands are shaking. Warren. It was definitely Warren. The café and the way he watched me sipping hot chocolate, the barista's knowing grin as I left the shop. How Warren found out I was pregnant is a mystery to me.

"Warren. It was Warren," I blurt.

His father's expression hardens as he stares the lady in the eye and motions for her to depart. She moves away from the desk, but her hand passes across Draven's shoulder, causing me to lash out. Getting out of my seat, I give her a backhand across her smug face.

She screams and covers her mouth, then looks down at the blood trickling down her chin from her split top lip and sees her hand-painted scarlet.

"Touch him again, and I'll split the other one," I sneer. "Now, do as you're told and get out."

She scrambles and exits the room, and Mr. Bedford gives me a diabolical grin. A deafening silence falls in the room when the door shuts with a click. Dravin gets up from his chair and moves over to the bar to pour himself a drink. The clinking of ice falling inside the glass and the decanter being uncorked. My hand begins to sting from the slap.

Dravin turns, his eyes resting on my face. "Tell me everything, and don't leave anything out," he says while he raises the glass to his lips.

His countenance darkens when he stares at me and at this very moment, watching his neck as he downs the full glass of amber-colored liquor in one go, I know there is a monster being unleashed. The man behind the black flowers and pretty words on paper is gone. A murderer is standing in front of me—a cold-blooded killer, to put it bluntly. Draven wasn't the crazier or more dangerous of the two, as I had assumed. Dravin is worse. In a more far worse way. I immediately think of Jack the Ripper.

He walks closer. Draven and his father quietly wait for me to tell them about the night I went to the café, and Warren showed up and how the barista acted. How afraid I was.

GIA

I'M SITTING on Draven's bed while he talks to his brother outside the door. I can hear their loud whispers but can't make anything out. I'm upset about having to stay here in this house. I have to get my clothes from my dorm, and the only reason I don't stomp out of here is because of Warren and his threats. If he attempted to kill me by having me poisoned so I could lose my baby and die, who knows what else he is capable of? I'm about to hop out of bed when Draven enters the room and shuts the door.

"Where's Dray?" I ask when I see that he doesn't come inside with his brother. I have begun to shorten his name and use the nickname his mother gave him to identify them in conversation.

Draven lowers his head and wipes his hand over his face. He looks up and takes a deep breath. "He'll be back in three days to pick you up. He has to take care of business while you're here. He left you a note."

I frown when he hands me the note. "What do you mean, he left? Why didn't he tell me? Why did he just leave me here? I don't want to be here."

I scan the note similar to the ones he always leaves for me in his handwriting.

Gia,

I would search the world if you were lost. I would ask the stars for guidance. The moon to be the light in the dark and the sun to shine bright, knowing it would all lead me to find you.

Love,

Dravin

I look up and meet Draven's gaze, feeling my heart squeeze. "You don't have a choice. He asked that I take care of you while you're gone. He doesn't need to ask, but he needs to hear it from me."

I shake my head. "I don't want to be here with you. I want to leave."

"I'm afraid that isn't an option. You will have everything you need," he says while he walks toward his en suite bathroom.

I slide off the bed and follow him inside, not caring if he has to take a shit. I'm pissed off at what he allowed that bitch to do to him.

He whirls around and begins to undress. When his clothes are off and he is standing naked in all his delicious glory, he raises a brow. "Are you joining me?"

I snort. "I'm good. I'll be on my way."

When I turn to leave, he grips me firmly on my arm and pulls me toward the shower, pressing the button that causes the warm water to spray like rain against the tiles.

"What are you doing? Let go of me!" I seethe in fury.

"What is your problem?" he asks, pulling me under the spray.

"Are you insane?" My clothes and hair are drenched, and my shoes and socks are soaked. I'm relieved I left my phone on his bed.

"Just a little."

I back up to leave through the shower door, but he pins me against the tiled wall. "No. You're not going anywhere."

"I don't care. I'm wet."

Draven begins to tug at my clothes, and I stiffen and pull away. He rips off my shirt and bra.

"What the hell?"

His lips slide over my jaw near my ear. "You are in hell. You're just my heaven."

"I'm nothing of yours. Now let me go. Go ask that bitch to be your heaven. You were certainly enjoying it. Now, fuck off."

His lips form a smirk. "You're jealous."

I turn my head away. "I'm not."

I am, but I won't admit that to him. I won't tell him that he hurt me. I don't know why he did it, but he did, and I can't look at him the same way. It's stupid, and I should only have these types of feelings for his twin, but I feel them for him, too. Dravin's words in his letters hit that part of me. The part that I felt when I fell in love with him. It's crazy and weird, but the feelings are there. The desire for him is there.

He turns my head by placing his fingers under my chin. "Look at me," he demands.

The sound of water surrounds us, and the steam from the warm water fogs up the glass.

My eyes finally look up at his and begin to sting from the tears that are building up.

"I did it for you, Gia." My brows pinch in confusion. "My father thought I was Drav."

I shake my head in denial. "There is no way. How?"

"We have perfected it through the years; we did it for our mother when he wanted to hurt her, and now we are doing it for you. We've had a lot of practice since we were kids. Drav kept quiet so he wouldn't notice. He wanted to use him to hurt you. If you notice, he addressed Drav like he was me. He said that he loved me more than my mother. My mother favored Drav, and he favored me because I always protected my older brother. I—we did it for you. We knew that it would hurt you if your husband took pleasure from another woman. I put myself out there for you. When she asked me if I was the older twin, I nodded yes. She mistook me for Drav.”

“But you liked it.”

While his other hand continued to hold on to my chin, his fingers pushed my hair away from my face. I avert my eyes so he can’t see the hurt I’m feeling. “I didn’t come, did I?”

No, I shake my head. He didn’t, but it hurt to watch. It hurt to see and to hear.

“We did that to hurt you the first time, and we both regret it. We tried to get over you. I tried it, and it didn’t work. I haven’t fucked anyone since you.”

My eyes meet his as I listen. I’m trying to understand him. His reasons.

“It hurt me,” I whisper.

He leans in close and places a soft kiss on my forehead. His words and breath welcome on my skin. The drops of water slide over my face and neck.

”If you only knew how much it hurts me that I can’t marry you. I want you so badly that I’d gladly live in my brother’s shadow if it meant I could have you in any way. I’ll sacrifice myself so that you never have to look at the man you marry and know that he slept with another person while being with you as your husband. He won’t allow it, and neither will I. I’ll be the sacrifice for your happiness.”

Tears escape down my cheeks like carved words on wood—his words, words that etch themselves into the depths of my soul.

I sniff and close my eyes. How do you give yourself to two men who are identical twin brothers without cheating on them?

“Don’t cry, our little Raven. If he gets your heart, I want your soul, and your body is our playground. You’re perfect.” He steps back and looks down with a side grin. “Let’s get you out of these wet clothes so we can clean that bitch off me.”

I open my eyes and feel his hands lift my torn shirt over my head, then my bra, letting it drop in a wet heap on the tile floor. He helps me with my shoes, socks, pants, and finally, my panties.

His eyes smolder when I’m completely naked. My nipples harden under his gaze when the water sluices down my body. The backs of his hands slide down my chest over my nipples, causing them to strain into two stiff peaks.

“I can’t wait to see your beautiful breasts full of milk nursing our children and feeding them the way we feed you.” His fingers slide down my torso to the apex between my thighs, igniting me from within. “I’m not going to be the one to give you the vanilla sex you read about in a love story. I’m going to be the lover that fucks you hard and fast.” I’m about to mewl when his finger grazes my clit. "I'm going to rip your clothes, make you sore, and fuck you so hard and so good in every hole my cock can fit in." He leans back and whispers against my lips. "And you're going to like it."

Fuck. I shamelessly want him. My body needs him. It needs them both. His lips brush against mine, and he pushes me up against the tiles. He pushes the soap dispenser and takes my hand, sliding the soap between our hands and making suds. I look down between us, and his hard cock is aimed at my belly. His fingers are entwined with mine, and the smell of body wash is the same one his twin uses.

He places our hands over his cock and strokes his shaft from base to tip, washing himself. He steps back so the water can rinse him off. He raises our hands under the spray, and the soap slides down my arms, raising goose bumps over my skin. He places more soap on his hands and bathes me thoroughly, and I return the favor.

My hands slide over taught skin just like his twin brother, yet inside, he's so different. Different in a way that is forbidden. He is like a dark secret—something no one knows about. My own personal release. My hands slide over his chest, feeling it rise and fall like he is about to snap. His cock sticking out painfully hard against my stomach. My head angles up toward his gaze, his nostrils flare slightly, and he snaps on a growl.

He pushes me up against the tiled wall and lifts my thighs over his hips, grazing his teeth over my neck, knowing that he will leave marks.

"I'm going to take you hard," he growls.

"Yes," I moan. "Please."

I can't think of anything else at this moment except for him being inside me, filling me, and reminding me why I want him. I want him to take the pain away from me, of seeing someone else's mouth on him. I know it's selfish, but my grasp on what is right and wrong is blurring. These are my boys, and I'll give them all of me.

He slides his cock inside to the hilt, and I gape at how big he is. "Fuck. Yes!"

He pumps into me hard and fast without stopping. "You're mine. You're his, but you're mine."

He continues his assault on my pussy, which is deliciously unforgiving. I slide up against the tiles with each thrust he gives me. A demon who is nothing but pure evil and desire. My arms are wrapped around his neck while he presses his face into mine, placing his kiss on mine and biting my bottom lip until it bleeds.

"Bleed for me. Come for me. Milk me. You're perfect, my little Raven."

"I'll bleed for you. I'll come for you as long as you're inside of me. Filling me," I say, as my pussy spasms on his cock, coming for him. My breasts bounce with each thrust until he arches his neck and stills, spilling inside me as he comes on a roar.

The sound of water hitting tile is mixed with my rapid heartbeat as we both come down from that place. A forbidden place where there is only room for feeling what the body can take, and the memories of that place are the notes left on your skin.

DRAVIN
†

"PLEASE!" he pleads like the piece of shit he is.

It didn't take long to track down the jerk from the café. I didn't want to involve the others so they could tip Warren off.

"Tell me. Why?" I say it through clenched teeth.

"He threatened me. H-he said he would kill me and my family. He knows where they live. He knows everything. Please, it hurts. Take me down," he begs through each measured breath of agony.

"Are you sure this is a good idea?" Father Jacobs asks, taking a deep breath as his forehead drips with sweat. He's been sweating profusely since I barged in, barking orders to set up the church.

"Shut the fuck up and do as you're told," I snarl.

I glance up and see the barista from the coffee shop loll his head to the side. I nailed him to a wooden cross like a sacrifice, rope around his neck, waist, and thighs. I had the fake priest cover the statues behind him with a black backdrop with a giant wooden cross in front and the pussy I nailed against it. Candles are lit to give the massive area light, closing the church for three days. The glow reflecting off the stained-glass windows illuminates the messengers of God like judges, watching me torture the sinner for his sins—an eye for an eye and all of that.

I glance up with the hammer in one hand and the concrete nails in the other.

"Who is he?"

"Christ." He closes his eyes. "Warren. His name is Warren. He wanted me to poison her. That is all I know. He told me her name and came into the coffee shop as soon as she arrived."

"How did he know she was there, and how do you know her?"

"He texted me. He told me her name; that is all I know. He made me do it. He said no one would find out because she was considered Prey, and he assured me it was all part of the Order. I did what I was told."

That motherfucker is dead. There was no such meeting about Gianna. Something isn't adding up. There is something bigger at play here. They are trying to eliminate our power and control by making us weak.

"You were told to kill an innocent woman. She almost died," I roar.

I grip the hammer and drop the nails on the floor, leaving just one in my hand. I move to where his feet are and place one foot over the other.

"Please! No!"

I place the sharp tip of the big nail and hit the nail in the head, causing him to scream like a person being mutilated. Blood begins to ooze like the blood on the airport bathroom floor from my baby dying in his mother's womb.

"She was pregnant!" I scream. "Pregnant!"

I spit at him while watching him suffer. This is nothing compared to what I'm going to do to that piece-of-shit Warren. There is nothing no one can do that will save him from my wrath and from his fate.

Jacobs comes up behind me. "I'm sorry, Dravin."

But there are no words that can describe the carnage I want to inflict on him. Our pain. My pain. The pain of losing our baby. The agony of almost losing her in the hospital. I lost my mother. I failed her, but I will not lose Gianna. They will have to get through me and my brother to get to her. Warren understands that killing her is a way to destroy the Bedford legacy. He wanted her for himself, but all he did was fuck himself. He knew. He knew she was pregnant.

I hang my head and close my eyes because all I see is red. Death and destruction are all I can think about. Leaving Gia in that house is a risk, but my twin brother would never allow anything to happen to her. What he did saved me from my father and his manipulation to hurt Gia for changing her mind about marrying me when she found out about Draven and that we were twins.

Once he had sex with her, I couldn't tell her. I wanted to, but I couldn't tell her. My father advised against it until she fell pregnant. She was untouched and perfect. I desired her as if she were my next breath. I'll always want her.

Draven sacrificed himself like he has always done for me, but I know he didn't do it for me. He did it for Gianna, so my father couldn't hurt her because I knew my brother was in love with my future wife.

He might not know it, but I do. He only sacrifices for the things and people he loves. He will gladly be the villain in her eyes as long as she sees me as the god in hers. It's the only way he can ensure she doesn't suffer the fate of death by her own hand, like our mother. It was the only way she knew to end her suffering.

I look up and meet the eyes of a dead man hanging from the cross.

"Please," he whispers. "Take me down. Please, God. It hurts."

I chuckle and laugh maniacally. "Pretty, pretty, pretty, pleeeassse," I mock him, tilting my head to the side. "If you play in hell, you get fucked over by the devil. God has no room here. He checked out a long time ago." I look up at the old cathedral-style ceiling and then down at the pathetic piece of shit nailed to the cross.

"Oh my god! It hurts." He continues to scream.

I look over at Jacobs. "Gag him. Shut him up."

He nods with a look of fear. He hasn't seen the dark games we play. My brother is a little more sinister when he commits his sins. He lets them pray before he kills them. I... don't.

Jacobs is getting the ladder, making clinking sounds as he places it to safely climb up to reach Timothy's face. I look up while I watch Timothy cry, not feeling an ounce of sympathy or empathy. He didn't feel that way when he tried to kill the mother of my child, causing her to miscarry.

I slide my phone out and call Draven, listening to the phone ring and waiting for him to answer.

"Hello."

"We have a problem."

"Tell me, and whatever you do, make it quick. She's wondering where you are and why you didn't say anything to her when you left."

"I'll be right over, but I can't stay long. Call the others. There are people within the Order who want to destroy us. Only the ones we have on the Consortium are to be trusted. She was right; it was Warren, but he isn't working alone."

"I'll make the call."

"Do it. I'll be there in fifteen minutes."

I hang up and look at Jacob's stricken face when he sees that I'm leaving him.

"Don't look at me like that. I need you to babysit for a while."

"W-what do you mean? You can't possibly expect me to stay with him like this. Do what you and your brother normally do: chop him up and bury him somewhere."

"No. You stay and watch him." I look up before I turn to leave. "I have a purpose for him, and it's not that," I tell him, heading to the side door and hearing Timothy's muffled screams as I take out my vape pen for a smoke.

"You're crazier than he is. You know that, right?" Jacobs says.

I turn around before leaving through the door. "No, I'm insane."

GIA †

"THIS IS THE KITCHEN," Draven says, showing me the massive kitchen with dark wood cabinets and black-and-white marble counters. A window leads to the backyard, and I wonder what it looks like.

"It's beautiful."

"I'm glad you like it. We always have five members on staff. The butler and doorman are Norman, Sasha is the cook, Nikolai is the head groundskeeper, our driver, whom you have seen many times, is Germain, and there are two housekeepers, Miss Jean and her daughter Pricilla."

"Who was the woman in the office yesterday?"

He walks to the island and leans his forearms on the marble, with the massive centerpiece, which has black feathers glued to it like those on a masquerade mask. I want to know because I refuse to have her around me.

"Just a woman my father entertains. He prefers Pricilla."

"And you?"

His eyes smolder when he raises them to me while I lean my back near the kitchen sink. "I prefer you."

"You hardly know me."

"I know enough. I know a lot of things about you."

"Like?" I ask, intrigued.

How would he know me? I've never gone out with him knowing who he is. I know Dravin on a deeper level. Our long talks before and after sex, his letters. He's met my parents, but Draven hasn't.

"I know you prefer red roses to black. I know you like to talk to my mother, whom you think is actually buried in the empty grave."

My eyes flick to his. "What?"

"I'm afraid so. You have been talking to an empty grave. It is why he told you not to visit the grave. It is why you see that there are no flowers left there."

"Then where is she?" I gulp. "Buried, I mean."

I have been talking to an empty grave like a lunatic. I want to kill Dravin. He could have said something. I know it was my fault for assuming, but it's a grave with her name on it, like a normal person. I asked him before, and he said yes.

"We had her cremated. The necklace he gave you when you thought it was me—her ashes are inside the crow. She is with you and will help you see the light in your moment of darkness. You carried a part of her inside you. It is only right you carry a part of her with you, always and forever."

A tear slides down my cheek when I look down at the necklace, sliding my fingers over the crow. He walks over, wipes my tear away with his thumb, and slides it between his lips.

"Don't cry. We hate to see you cry. To see you cry is like watching our hearts bleed out. We need to stop it, or we end up dying. It's like hearing my soul cry out in pain, and your tears are the fire burning it to ashes." He places his finger over my chest where my heart beats and his eyes follow the movement of his finger as he talks. "They say there are only two halves to a heart, but ours isn't like that. Ours has three parts, like the pieces of a magnet coming together. See, we are your two halves, one on the left and one on the right. When you first draw it on paper, it starts in the middle. The beginning of the left and right always unite us in the center. Without you, we are never whole. With you, we are complete. The center is you and will always be you.
"

He speaks like his brother is always with him and part of his thought process. Two souls linked to each other are trying to find their heaven. I'm their heaven and their salvation from the hell they live in.

I look up to find him watching me. "Where's your necklace?"

He raises his hands and removes a chain I've never seen before, one with a wolf and the raven from the necklace I gave Dravin that night at the cemetery. It's longer and hangs like a *T* at my navel. The crow and the raven meet in the center, near my heart, when he places it gently around my neck.

"I have been meaning to give it to you, but I never found the right moment."

"Thank you," I whisper. "It's beautiful."

"There is nothing more beautiful in my life than you. You're everything to me, Gianna. Did you think it was only Drav with you? I've watched you. We watch you. We talk about you and how much we want you in our lives. You don't have to love me, Gianna, or feel guilty for loving me less. I'll accept anything as long as it's from you."

I fan myself because I'm about to cry—not from sadness but from happiness at hearing his words.

"I want to get to know you. Both of you. I want you to meet my parents. I want you to meet my mother." I sniff. "Drav met them, and it's only right for you to meet them."

He smiles, and my heart melts. "We will meet them tomorrow. Call them, and we will have dinner. It can be their house or a restaurant. Whatever you want. Tell them whatever you want."

Shit. I have to think of something. I'll tell them the truth: he is a twin. What could go wrong?

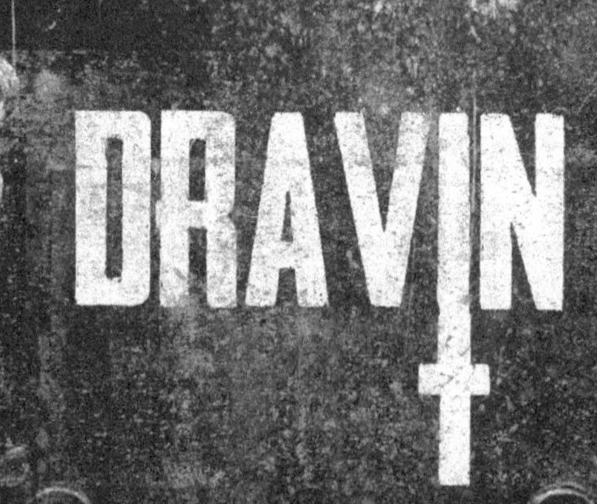

DRAVIN

THE DOOR OPENS, and Norman, the doorman, nods his head in a silent greeting. "Dravin."

He knows I'm Dravin because my brother is inside with Gianna, and they usually call my brother, Mr. Bedford, to address us. Sasha, our cook, has been here since we were born and knew my mother very well. She is like a secret confidant. She can tell us apart, though she was sworn to secrecy by my mother so as not to let anyone know that she knows how. Especially my father.

I'm walking toward the staircase, but I can hear voices traveling from the kitchen, and one of them I know all too well. Her voice is like a sweet whisper in my dreams, singing to me like a lullaby full of promise in the darkness of sleep.

I walk through the dining room into the archway leading to the kitchen and see them together. I smile when he adjusts his necklace over her chest.

When she hears me enter, she gives me a sidelong glance. "Dravin."

My brother watches me and gives me a curt nod. He knows what I came for—my time with her. When I reach her, I slide my fingers over her throat, watching goose bumps rise on her skin in the soft light.

"Raven," I say softly.

Her eyes shift to Draven and back to me. Unsure. Torn.

I see it in her eyes. She is falling for my brother. It doesn't bother me because he deserves her. He deserves her love, and she deserves ours.

I slide the fluffy red robe down her shoulder so I can see her creamy breasts and puckered nipples harden against the cold air. My tongue meets her flesh and flicks, twirls, and trails down until her nipple is in my mouth. Her gasp causes me to increase the suction and her robe to widen.

I grip her waist with both my hands, carrying her to the island, pushing her thighs wider so I can see her wet pussy drip for me. I look down at her swollen lips. My brother fucked her hard.

Her pussy is pink, wet, and swollen. My head turns to the right. "Damn, brother, you took her hard."

His eyes flick toward her. "She can handle it. Right, baby?"

She leans back, placing her palms behind her to arch her back. "Are you ready for me, baby?"

Her long hair slides over the marble counter like silk. She opens her legs wider, and I nudge my head toward my brother. "Get me some ice."

Gia quirks her brow, but I don't tell her what it's for. She knows I'll never do anything to hurt her. My brother opens the built-in fridge, grabs the ice cubes, and puts them in a glass. He walks over and clinks the glass on the counter.

"Do you trust me?" I ask her.

She slants her head, licking her lips with her tongue. "What do you think?"

I smile at her sassy mouth and look at her pussy dripping on the counter. "I think you want me inside you." I grab an ice cube with my fingers. The cold is freezing my skin as I place the tip on her nipple.

She gasps. "Dravin."

I slide it in a circular motion over each nipple. Her breaths come out slowly and evenly. She's trying not to shrink away. I lean in close and take one breast in my mouth while my brother takes the other wet nipple, warming her back up. I slide the cube down to her pussy lips and circle it at her entrance.

She moans. "Yes! Fuck, that feels so good."

I don't want anyone getting off on her moans, especially Norman. Releasing her nipple, I take out my phone and link it to the speaker in the kitchen, connecting with two distinct beeps. Marilyn Manson's "Sweet Dreams" begins to play softly.

"I told you, baby. Your body is our playground," Draven says.

We lick every inch of her, feasting on her tits, her pretty stomach, and her swollen pussy. I suck the inside of her left thigh while my brother takes the other. We take turns in rhythm, sucking after every melted cube of ice to ensure she doesn't feel a sting.

I slide my cock out of my jeans, fisting it in my hand. My brother removes the centerpiece and climbs over the counter, turning his head to watch her from above.

Her eyes flick to me, and I climb on top of the counter, taking the glass with me while my brother slides her down the smooth marble. Her robe is entirely open, exposing her flushed, naked skin.

Taking a cube, I slide it inside her hot cunt as "Beautiful People" by Marilyn Manson plays. I slide my cock inside her with a groan after the ice cube melts from the heat of her pussy.

My brother kneels and slides his cock out of his sweats. Her pretty lips open, and he slides his cock inside her wet mouth. I grip her thighs over my waist and take her soft and deep, being careful not to hurt her.

She pops my brother's cock out. "Faster, please," she purrs.

I bite my bottom lip and take her hard and fast, pumping into her.

She moans on my brother's cock as he fucks her mouth, placing his thumb on a cut on her lip. Fuck, he took her hard. I think we've corrupted our little Raven.

My brother holds her neck gently while he grunts. I pump into her, watching her pretty tits bounce.

"She's beautiful," I say quietly.

"Yes, she is," Draven says, watching her like she is a fragile piece of glass.

Her eyes are filled with tears as she takes him deep, relaxing her throat. My balls tingle when I'm close, and her pussy clenches my dick. "Fuck, she's tight," I say with a grunt.

"Everything about her is tight," Draven says.

She responds with her fingers playing with her nipples, her legs open wider for me so I can come inside her. I place my thumb on her clit and her fingers meet mine while we both play with her clit.

She moans when she comes with her mouth full of cock. My brother's cum spills down her chin like overflowing milk in a cup as she tries to swallow it all. Her pussy squeezes my cock as she comes, arching her back, and I groan, coming inside her, holding her thighs in place as my body slams into her until I'm spent.

I slide my cock out of her swollen pussy. Her tongue licks her lips and slides down her chin, licking my brother's cum. Her legs are wide open. Her pussy is a mess.

"You're a beautiful mess, Gia." I circle her clit softly, and she mewls. "Our beautiful mess."

JESS

AFTER GETTING to the dorm last night from the bar, I was ashamed of myself. Of how easily I lose my head when Reid is around. I can't help the way he makes me feel. It's like he tests my limits every time without taking it too far, but I think I'm past a point of no return. I've reached the point where I don't care and will take pleasure in being offered my two hot as fuck guys who are fucking insane. The things they have me do, no fantasy will be left unexplored. There will be no secret bucket list when it comes to sex with those two. The only problem is that I get the feeling Reid is more possessive than he lets on.

My phone lights up from a text notification. Gia is with her twin duo, probably holed up at the Gothic mansion. When I get out of bed to finish my class assignment, I notice a text from Michael. I have him saved under Fucking Loser.

> Fucking Loser: I'm parked on the curb by the main entrance. Meet me there. You have five minutes. Don't be late. Ticktock.

I close my eyes. He's here. He knew where to find me, but he did warn me he would find me when he wanted his dick sucked. My fingers shake when I close my notebook.

"Fuck," I mutter. Every time I do this, I fall deeper into the rabbit hole.

It's a good thing Gia is not here, so I don't have to explain. I look at the corkboard on the wall near my old desk and see the hundred-dollar bill from last time. How many will I have to collect to remind me what he thinks I'm worth?

I make my way to the main entrance, making sure no one is following me. The sun has set, setting off a twilight in the sky of different hues. The trees sway and groan as the lights on campus become brighter as the sun disappears beyond the horizon. It's like darkness is falling, and the demons of the night have come out to play. The light disappears so the demons can collect and feed off the less fortunate.

I see his Mustang idling at the curb like it's a death sentence. I shiver under my winter coat. My boots are hitting the concrete pathway as I reach the passenger door, pulling the handle like a finger on the trigger.

The scent of leather mixed with Michael's cologne makes me want to puke. The bile that rises in my throat almost has me turning my head and emptying my stomach, but I take a deep breath and slide into the seat.

I close the door, and the car lurches forward at a fast speed, pinning me to the seat. My hand grips the door. "Did you have to do that?"

He grips the steering wheel and changes the gear down to third. "Put your seat belt on," he says.

I grip the seat belt and pull it across my body, hear it click, and glare at him. "What is your problem? Why are you here?"

His features are tight. His teeth are clenched, and I don't know why he is angry, but he's scaring me. It is a stupid question to ask him. I know why he is here, and it's not to talk about my mother's job performance.

He glances at me briefly as he winds down the road, finally slowing down to the forty-five miles per hour speed limit. "You know why I'm here. I'm here for you."

"I get that, but you can't just show up whenever you want. I don't live by myself, and for someone that doesn't like to be seen with trailer trash—"

"Who do you live with?"

"None of your business."

He grips the steering wheel, and I'm cursing myself for telling him that I live with someone else. I look out the window, watching the sun finally set.

"Tell me, or I'll find out my way."

"Why do you care?"

"I asked you a question. Who is he?"

He? He thinks I live with a guy.

I turn my head and snort. "I live in the female dorm. Why would you think I live with a guy, and more importantly, why are we having this conversation? You want to use my mother to blackmail me so you can fuck me? Fine. I will lie there so you can fulfill your sick little fantasy and slide me a hundred-dollar bill for my trouble, like that is going to make me feel any better for being a whore. Now, take me wherever it is you're taking me, and let's get it over with."

I hate him, and I hate myself for agreeing to do this, but every time I call my mom to check in with her, she sounds so happy, and he is keeping his end of what was promised. He made sure she got her bonus and the best shifts while giving her a raise.

After driving for nearly twenty minutes out of town, he stops at a hotel.

I raise a brow. "A hotel?"

"What's wrong with a hotel?"

I take a deep breath. "You know, for someone who has a problem with a girl who lives in a trailer, you've got no problem being seen with me."

"Don't get your hopes up. It's too fucking cold to take you into a parking lot, and my car isn't exactly comfortable. I can't take that cunt on top of my hood like last time, can I?" He pulls the parking brake when he pulls into the couples-only type of hotel. "I'm doing this for me and for the sake of not freezing my balls off."

"Gee, lucky me."

"Trust me. You are lucky. It could be worse. A whole lot worse, Jesse."

I hate that he calls me by my full name. It's like a pain in my ears to hear it coming from him. He loves to annoy me, and all I can think about is the hot shower and the scrubbing I'll have to endure after he is finished with me.

He gets up, and I make no move to open my door. I'm dreading his touch and the things he wants to do to me. I close my eyes for a few seconds, hating myself a little more, but I won't cry. I have to be strong for my mother.

Apart from Gia, she is the only person who cares about me. I can't tell anyone what I need to do to help my mother. She looked exhausted when I saw her on winter break.

If I dropped out, I'd be working a low-paying job back home or, worse, be preyed upon by Michael. This is only temporary. I have six months until I graduate, and I can start looking. I wish I could find a job between classes and send the money home, but knowing my mother, she wouldn't take the money. Her pride as a single mother won't allow it. She loves to tell people I was accepted to a fancy, elite college.

If she only knew that the fancy elite college is dark and evil. The church is just a front for what truly goes on in Kenyan—the parties and the mind games. Kenyan college students are the children of the people who control the major corporations—the corporations that control the economy. Those are the real players. They use people for their own gain and cover up the mess they create in their wake.

My problems back home and living in a trailer are nothing compared to the havoc the Order can create. I just have to find my way out of this maze unscathed. I'll have battle scars from what I have to endure, but I have a goal, and that is to use my affiliations from attending Kenyan, shut the fuck up, and turn my head the other way to provide a better life for me and my mother.

The door opens, and I look at my tormentor. If he sees the hate aimed at him through my eyes, he doesn't say anything about it. His eyes skim my pants slowly until they reach my eyes.

I step out of the car, and he pulls me up until my face is level with his chest. He looks down at me, and for one second, I remember when I thought he was the most attractive person I had ever laid eyes on. That crush in high school I had dreamed of doing everything with.

My first date, a kiss, lunch at school at the popular kids' table, and the guy I wanted to spend my first time with. Then, that memory goes up in smoke, and it's replaced with the night he spiked my drink and raped me with his friends.

My eyes sting from the memory, like a window looking into a past nightmare. That memory creeps into my mind when I least expect it to, and then I ask myself, *Why did I have to go to the party? Why didn't I just say no? Why did I ever think I stood a chance, knowing what everyone thought of me?* A poor girl living in a trailer with a single mother and a pipe dream.

"I think tonight is the night I make you come. You have never come for me, Jesse."

I harden my jaw and lift my eyes to his face, a face that belongs to the demon in my nightmare, the face I try to forget, and the scent of him I try to scrub off my skin. If you ever asked me if I hated anyone, I would say Michael.

"This isn't about me, it's only about what your twisted mind wants."

He pushes me hard against the car, and I remind myself that I have to play along. How will I get off when he is on top of me?

"Let's get inside before we freeze out here. We'll talk about it when I warm you up."

I wait for him to move toward the hotel's entrance, not wanting to be near him more than I have to, dreading the things he wants to do to me. He doesn't hurt me, but it is worse when he thinks I like the things that he does to me. In his mind, he thinks I like it. He thinks I want him. If he only knew the truth.

He pays the clerk for the room, and I stay silent, looking at the cream-colored walls and fake plants. This definitely is not like the hotel that Reid owns with its luxury carpets, bellman, impressive entrance with valet, and even the elevator he fucked me into was better than this place, but at least it's not a roach motel.

We make our way to room 504, and he unlocks the door. It doesn't have electronic key cards, but for a girl like me and where I was raised, this is better than my own room in the trailer. The difference is that I had happy times there with my mother growing up. It didn't matter if we were in a one-room shack; it was home as long as we were together.

When he opens the door to the room, at least it isn't cold, but he turns on the heater. When he flicks the lights on, my heart drops. There are mirrors everywhere around the bed. On the ceiling, the back wall, and the sides, there is even a heart-shaped Jacuzzi to the right.

"Really?" I ask.

He turns his head, removes his corduroy jacket, and begins to remove his sweater. I want to keep my jacket on for longer if I can before I strip my clothes off for this asshole.

A smirk plays on his lips, and all I can think about is punching him, but I can't; he will make me pay somehow.

"Come here, Jesse."

"Don't say my name."

"I'll keep saying it while I'm pumping my cock inside you until you come. Stop being a bitch and get over here."

I ball my hands into fists and walk closer. He removes my jacket over my shoulder roughly, and I flinch. "Don't make this harder than what it really is. I promise to make it good for you."

I raise my chin, but the expression across his face doesn't sit well with me. "Why are you doing this to me, Michael? Don't you have a girlfriend? You're a good-looking guy. You have money and could get any girl you want."

He laughs and pulls me to the bed, so I plop on top of it. I turn my head and lie there motionless as he takes my clothes off. Once my shoes and thick socks are off, he slides my bra off and leaves me in just my panties.

I raise my hands to cover my breasts. "No, no, no. Don't cover up, Jesse. I want to see you, all of you."

I close my eyes, thinking of anything but being here. On this mattress, in this pink room, with its unforgiving mirror and matching dreadful carpet. He wants me to see it. He wants me to remember him while he fucks me. I hate him even more.

"I had a girlfriend," he says, kissing my skin, and it's like a burn with every kiss of his dry lips. "But I couldn't keep fucking her while thinking of you."

What the hell? He's sick. There is no other way to describe him. Michael is sick. Infatuated with... me.

"I had to let her go. A girl can only take so much when her boyfriend keeps calling her another girl's name. Do you know how hard it is to not want you, Jesse?" He slides his hand down and cups my mound, and I cringe. "To want the girl who lives in a trailer so bad but can't risk being seen with her in town because his parents will never approve. The town would never approve of me choosing you, Jesse. Do you know how they made fun of me back in high school because I said you were pretty? I had to show them that I didn't. I had to lie. I had to do what I had to in a way that I could have you."

Bastard. He could have left me alone. He didn't have to treat me like that. He didn't have to drug me and rape me. His fingers grip my face hard, and pain radiates from my jaw.

"You're hurting me, Michael. Please."

"Then look at me when I talk to you," he snaps. My eyes open, and I look into his smoldering eyes full of hunger. "Good girl. Now open your legs and let me see. I want to taste you, Jesse. I want you to come on my tongue."

He slides down the bed, releasing his hold on my jaw, and places his face between my thighs. He slides his finger over my panties near my slit and makes me squirm.

"Don't resist me, Jesse."

I'm trying, but everywhere I turn my head, there is a mirror, and I can see myself practically naked in a cheesy lover's hotel suite with a blond head belonging to the man I hate. He raises his head, and his light eyes watch me.

"I want you to look up at the mirror on the ceiling so you can watch how I make you come."

I try to blink back the tears when he slides my panties off and begins to eat me out.

"Mmm. You taste so good, Jesse," he rasps.

My body biologically responds to the stimulation. I could kick him and scream, but it would make things worse for me and my mom. I have no control. He knows me. He knows my weakness is my mother. He knows what to do to get me in this position.

He slides his tongue inside me, and I close my eyes, refusing to look at what he is doing to me. I'm losing myself while he groans against my pussy. He slides two fingers inside me as deep as he can go while sucking my clit. My body shamelessly betrays what my mind wants and responds to the stimulation.

Needles prick my throat, and I tell myself it doesn't mean anything, but that is a lie. When you tell yourself something doesn't mean anything, it just means it does.

He grips my hips hard as my pussy gets wet, and I tell myself it's just me in the room and this is all a dream. I don't imagine it's Michael but someone else so that I can get through it. After a minute, my pussy comes, and I hate myself. I hate the way it responds to him. I turn my head and shut my eyes so the tears don't leak out and make it worse if he sees me cry.

When he licks me clean, I hear the rip of the condom wrapper, and I know it's just going to get worse, but this I can fake. This is the part where I have to act. I have to be the actress. When I look down, his condom-clad cock is near my entrance, and his lips, which I once found so appealing, are glistening.

He hovers over me, his palm flat on the flimsy pink comforter with ugly graphics, and slowly guides his cock inside me. He doesn't take me hard like he usually does but patiently waits.

His lips are inches from my ear, and I can smell myself on his chin. "Look up, Jesse."

I open my eyes and hate the sight of him between my thighs. My chest wants to cave in when he goes slow, like he is making love to me. His breath is on my skin, and that is when I give up. This is when I stop caring, and maybe it's a good thing to not care. That way, I don't need anyone else to erase the memory. One person treating me this way and not caring is better than hoping one will care for me. Maybe. Someday.

"I'm in love with you, Jesse."

"This isn't love, Michael. You know that, right?"

He pumps into me faster and rasps against the skin of my neck. "It is to me. I love you, Jesse. This is me loving you. I'm sorry, but it's all I can give you."

It's all I'm worth, a secret dirty fuck, but I don't tell him that. The irony of it all is that my high school crush raped me, blackmailed me, and now says he loves me. I let him fuck me and place the memory among all the other ones I have that I hate, becoming what I hate the most.

JESS

I shake my head. "No, that's okay. It's a short walk from here, and you won't be able to get into the building," I lie as I open the door.

Before I step out of his car, he grips my wrist firmly, causing me to whip my head around. "I love you, Jesse. I'll see you when I can, okay?"

My eyes watch him like a psychopath. He reminds me of the face Jeffrey Dahmer puts on when he talks about his victims. His gaze is maniacal, as if he knows exactly how everything will turn out. I'm the victim on the outside, even if, on the inside, I refuse to be.

I just don't have control over what happens to my body anymore, and that's the saddest thing, to lose control of yourself. He claims to love me, but when he takes me or fucks me, it's like walking on a bed of nails. That's not love. My body can't fight him anymore. My soul is falling, afraid to let go.

I hate you, I tell him inside my head. *I'd rather die than ever have a man like you love me.* I can't say the words because it's too late; I've found my fate. The pain all over my body reminding me. I nod, slide out of the car, and close the door, watching his hand grip the shifter, hoping he leaves. I'm hoping I never see him again.

When I turn to walk toward the female dorm building, limping, he slides the window down and calls out, "I forgot to give you something, Jess."

I turn around, and he reaches the edge of the window; I hope it will close on his fingers with that hundred-dollar bill. His signature of what I'm worth every time he comes for me. My pride won't let my feet move, but he releases his hold, and it floats away to the concrete, and he takes off, peeling out onto the street into the dead of the night, hoping he disappears. For the first time in my life, I wish death on someone.

The smell of a strawberry mixed with marijuana hits my senses. "Who the fuck was that asshole?"

In the dark, by the wall of the side building leading to the quad, Reid is leaning against the wall with one leg bent, taking a hit from his vape pen. He pushes himself forward and walks toward me with a look of fury in his expression.

"Huh?"

My body feels dirty and unclean. I feel numb, and I don't care what he thinks. I won't try to erase the memories of the way he used my body. Reid bends down, picks up the hundred-dollar bill, and holds it up like a dirty rat.

"One hundred dollars."

I turn around, not caring about anything more, especially what he thinks of me. He has already expressed his feelings or thoughts about me. I'm a whore. Tears that I have held back silently slide down my cheeks as I pick up my pace, limping as fast as I can to go to my room, where I can take a shower and scrub.

"Where do you think you're going?" He catches up right beside me.

"I don't want to talk, Reid. Go home."

JESS

HE GRIPS MY WRIST, and I inhale from the pain. It hurts because it's red and sore. Michael held my wrists so tight because I couldn't come for him with the chains.

I thought he was taking me slowly, but I was wrong. It got longer and harder as the night progressed. He got frustrated when my body could no longer respond biologically. His words lure you in, and then the mask falls, and you see the true monster that's inside. The leather straps and the bindings I have never endured before on my skin were too much. It was all too much, too fast.

"Please let go of me. You're hurting me."

He looks down, slides his phone out, and presses the flashlight. The light reveals the red marks on my wrists.

"That motherfucker! You let that piece of shit do this to you?!" he roars.

I flinch and turn away. "It's not your problem. Please, just leave me alone."

I try to back away, but his lips turn into a frown. "No. I'm taking you with me, and you tell me where to go. You tell me who and what, Jess. He's dead. Do you hear me?"

My body begins to shake. "I-I need a shower. P-please."

It's all I can think about. My body feels sore, and my core aches. Reid's arms wrap around me, and my knees buckle. "Shit, Jess. I got it. I'll take care of you. I promise, Jess. Please, don't. No," he pleads. "Jess!"

My brain goes into a fog. There is a terrible ringing in my ears, and everything goes dark.

GIA
†

I HEAR a noise coming from inside the room, and when my eyes flutter open, I wince at the light filtering through the vast window to the right of the room from the curtains being drawn by an older lady. She must be the housekeeper. I must have fallen into a deep sleep after Dravin showered with me and placed me on Draven's bed.

I'm wondering why I'm in this massive room, which has black antique furnishings and blood-red curtains. When the older woman turns around, I grip the black satin sheet and raise it to my neck for modesty.

"Good morning, Gia. I'm the head housekeeper, Miss Jean."

"Good morning."

"Mr. Bedford is waiting for you downstairs for breakfast at the dining table. All your clothes and everything you need will be in the walk-in closet through those wood doors." She points to two massive double doors with brass gargoyles in the center. "I hope you don't mind. I have taken the liberty of picking something so you could have an idea of what he expects you to wear."

Great, I don't get to dress myself either. I have new clothes and a new room.

"How medieval," I blurt, my cheeks going red.

I hope I didn't sound like a bitch.

"It's all right. The late Mrs. Bedford felt the same way, but you'll get used to it. All your clothes and whatever else you need will be provided for you. Of course, you can pick and choose, but I must warn you. It's either black, red, white, or lace." She gives me a wink. "One thing the Bedford men have is, good taste in everything. You will not have a problem showing off your assets. They enjoy seeing how beautiful the lady of the house is and have no issues with showing her off."

It's fine for me to walk around half-naked. Not that I'm planning to, but that's what she's getting at. I'm about to ask her about the room and who it belongs to, but she beats me to it.

"This was Anastasia's room." She clears her throat, and her brown eyes turn glassy. "Excuse me. Mrs. Bedford's bedroom. Dravin has asked that all his things be moved to the closet from his old room for when you come to stay with us. His father sleeps in another room by his office in the east wing. He prefers his privacy."

She moves to open the doors and freshen the room. As it shines on the dark wood furnishings, the sunlight creates a sense of clarity. The bed is massive and looks custom-made for a king. There is an oversized nightstand on each side with white-and-gray marble tops. The walls have dark wood paneling that matches the dark wood floor. I look up, and a massive crystal chandelier is above the bed. The crystals glitter in the light like tiny mirrors.

"Thank you."

"My pleasure. If you need anything, all our direct numbers are programmed on your phone."

I give her a grin when she turns and heads to the door. "Thank you, Miss Jean."

"Of course, Gia."

She closes the door, and I hear the slight creak and a thud from the antique knob turning.

My gaze darts around the vast space, taking in the aromas of rich wood and bergamot. The scent of the twins. It's amazing how two men are so alike in many ways, but as I'm sucked into their world, they allow me to see, touch, and feel them. They are different and feel things differently. Drav is more emotional, feeling things on a deeper level than his twin brother. Draven is not colder, but harder. He sees things in a practical way. Maybe it is why he is more accepting of his future. He risks himself for the people that he values the most. I notice a piece of paper and my heart skips a beat. It's a letter but from Draven.

> *Gia,*
> *There are so many stories of happily ever afters—plenty of books written about them. You probably have a favorite. Mine would be the one I want to create with you, the love story you can't find on paper, in a poem, or in a book. It's the one no one could ever find because this one is ours.*
> *Love,*
> *Draven*

Tears flow down my cheeks at his beautiful words. The books he must have read in his room.

I don't want to keep him waiting, so I freshen up in the shower while keeping a wary eye on the marble bathtub. I can't help but wonder whether she committed suicide there. At the point at which she made the decision to give up, due to the fact that I now know it was how she ended her life, I won't ever use the bathtub when the twins are around. I would never, ever bring up the painful memories of how their mother died in front of them.

Thinking how horrible that must have been, I'm happy that I will get to see my parents today. Even if they are divorced and my father lives with another woman, I want to look past the hurt and pain my father has caused and my mother's decision to not fight and accept another woman coming between them. She knew that she was breaking up a marriage and that I would be affected in some way, but that didn't stop her. She did what she felt was right for her, and so did my father.

I press the electronic button that turns off the water from the shower and open the glass door, stepping out onto the plush white bath rug, my toes sinking into the luxury carpet. When I step on the tiles to make sure my feet don't slip, I notice the tiles in the bathroom are warm and not cold like I'm used to back home. The luxuries that money can buy are paid for by the souls of the departed. Nothing in life is free, even if you think you got away with it.

I make my way out of the massive bathroom with matching vanities fit for a queen to the right, where the double doors have the gargoyles in the center, watching everything that goes on in this house. I grip the antique brass handle, turn the handle, and pull.

I gasp when the door opens and enter the massive walk-in closet. Just like Miss Jean indicated, there is a hanger with a tiny black lace minidress and a matching silk robe. Not what I expected, but the housekeeper did warn me, and I guess their mother did the same. I touch the necklace hanging from my throat and close my eyes, saying a little prayer for the woman who was gone too soon.

I tie the red sash at my waist and slip into the soft house slippers, with a red mink tickling my toes. I make my way down the hallway toward the stairs. My hand slides down the railing, and my eyes fall on Norman. He looks up at me and nods in silent greeting, and I'm thankful for the robe concealing my body from prying eyes like the staff in the house.

I walk past the living room and pause when I see Draven seated at the head of the table with a red rose in his hand. Flutters form in my stomach when I watch him look at the soft petals like they hold the secrets to his desires. When he notices me, his face brightens. His gaze slowly travels from my feet to my face. He smiles, and I swear my heart skips a beat for a second. Gorgeous. He is utterly gorgeous. He isn't wearing a shirt, and all his muscles are on display like a god seated on a throne.

"Sleep well, gorgeous?"

"Yes, but why did you move me to the room?"

He slides the chair back, and I pinch my brows when I notice there aren't any plates or breakfast served. I point toward the massive table for fifteen. "Where's breakfast? Do you want me to make you something?"

He chuckles and shakes his head. "No, you don't have to cook unless you want to, and to answer your question, I didn't move you to the main bedroom, Drav did."

"Oh," I say, pursing my lips.

Well, that explains why I ended up in bed.

"He's away, taking care of some things. He left early this morning. He will meet us there. After I eat, I'll feed you, and we can get ready to head out. The plane will be ready within the hour for Wisconsin."

I step closer, and he holds his hand out for me, and I take it. He places a kiss on my hand, his lips feeling like soft petals over my skin. His dark hair is falling forward over his brow. The wolf and the raven tattoo are calling out to me from his skin like a three-dimensional mural. I love that they placed the tattoos in such a way that I can tell them apart. They are identical, but I can see through the placement of the tattoos that, if you look really closely, there is a glimpse of a difference in their features. Tattoos can hide things in their bodies, such as birthmarks and minor differences. I researched how it is possible that they look so alike and are identical, and any differences they have, they have mastered the art of looking like each other while hiding it. The Crow is Dravin, and the Wolf is Draven.

He placed the petals from the rose on my skin like the satin already on my skin.

"So, what are you going to eat?"

He gives me a grin and watches a rose petal fall. "You."

DRAVEN

"WELCOME," Mr. Taylor says when he opens the door to me and Gia.

"Thank you for having us, sir. It is a pleasure meeting you."

He looks at me like I'm fucked in the head, but he doesn't know that I'm a twin. None of them do. I'm dressed to impress. Gia filled me in on the details of what happened when she was here for Thanksgiving with Dravin. I almost showed up to switch with my brother before she knew there were two different men who were interested in her but didn't want to risk it, and Dravin was serious about her.

Their house is a typical modest home. White railings and the white door that most homes have made it seem like a heartwarming family lives there with their two kids and Labrador retriever they call Ben. But I know the truth. This is her father's house, which he shares with his former mistress, Carolyn. No small children and no dog. A house full of hypocrisy.

"I was afraid you all weren't going to make it. Gianna's mother is waiting in the living room."

"My apologies. We had a long breakfast."

Gia's eyes widen, and a cute blush creeps up her cheeks. "Right, baby? It was good, wasn't it?"

Her father swallows, but I think he caught on that I wasn't talking about the eggs or the coffee. He has the same dark features as her hair and eyes, but her other features must belong to her mother.

Her mother is looking at me with a reserved expression, and I remember the hospital. She must feel like we abandoned Gia. We weren't there like we should have been, but that all changed when we almost lost her. My brother and I weren't thinking. We didn't anticipate a threat so severe that it would endanger Gianna in that way.

"Hello, Laurie," I greet her.

Another knock sounds at the door, and Carolyn, her father's girlfriend, watches me with appreciation. I expected it. Laurie glares at her, but Carolyn smiles like she isn't caught. Gia stiffens, and I murmur into her hair while inhaling her flowery scent.

"We'll handle it," I tell her.

The sound of clearing throats and holy shit from her father at the front door has me smiling like the Grinch who stole Christmas.

When Laurie glances behind me, her mouth slacks open. She points behind me at my brother. I turn around and watch as my brother kisses Gia in a sweltering kiss. The silence that falls in the room is almost comical.

My father stands while her father closes the door. "Father." I nod, and he smiles like the devil was just granted permission to enter.

"So, you're twins," Carolyn says, stating the obvious.

The clanking of glasses and utensils scrape the plates at the dinner table. Carolyn insisted on catering a meal because, you know, she is a coldhearted bitch that hates to cook and is fucking her boss behind her father's back. Colin. The same one she tried to put on Gia to hide it. She's a real piece of work, but she's just fucked with what's mine. Now we need order.

"That's right," I answer, eyeing my brother across from me. Gia is seated between me and my father, with Dravin directly across from her. My father hasn't returned to the table, so I can look directly at the home-wrecker. She wreaks havoc on Gia's, and I'll annihilate hers.

"The same name spelled differently. That's..." Carolyn trails off.

"Perfect for Gia. She can't ever forget our names."

"Excuse me?" her father asks, perplexed, his fork in midair crossing his features. The room fell silent.

"Are you trying to say both of you are fucking my daughter?"

My father returns with a flustered Laurie following behind him.

"Excuse me," Laurie says, taking the glass of water off the table and downing it in one go.

"Yeah," Dravin answers.

"Gianna!" her father bellows. "Are you insane?"

"Wow," Carolyn says, staring at her plate with a nervous laugh.

"Laurie, did you know?" her father asks, but she is silent.

"You are all sick, twisted individuals, and I'll not allow you to corrupt my daughter with your filth."

"Dad, I'm a grown woman, and you are the last person to tell me anything," she quips.

"Are we, Mr. Taylor?" I ask, quirking a brow at him.

My father laughs like a puppet master ready to make the puppets dance on their strings. He throws the napkin over his plate. "Touching, Mr. Taylor, but you should be more concerned about what happens in your home than what happens between your daughter's legs; her legs are the ones you shouldn't be concerned about. See, as a rich and powerful man who has raised very rich and powerful sons, I have a few things at my disposal, such as power, connection, wisdom, and a big cock with a big set of balls."

He gets up and buttons the top button on his immaculate black suit jacket. "Your daughter has made a very good decision; she is set for life, and she will produce heirs for the Bedford name, and yes, I meant plural, from whichever son can get my grandson into her belly first. She will marry one, and her lover will be his twin brother. On the other hand, you are no different, fucking a woman while married, then divorcing your wife, breaking your home, and driving your daughter away so that you can act like this." He leans forward and places his hand on the table so his eyes are level with her father's hard glare. "This is for the soap dish I broke while I was fucking your ex-wife Laurie in the bathroom while she milked my cock."

Carolyn gasps, and Gia's head snaps to her mother's flaming red cheeks. I stand up, sliding my hand and tugging on Gia to get her to stand. "We're leaving," I say.

"Good idea," her father snaps. "And take that whore with you."

"How dare you," Laurie seethes, getting up from the table and throwing her napkin.

"Don't call my mother a whore," Gia snarls.

Her father raises his hands. "I'm sorry, Gianna."

Dravin lowers his voice. "Your girlfriend Carolyn is fucking her boss Colin behind your back." He opens his jacket and slides an envelope with pictures of them fucking on the table. "Have a great rest of your day."

"You bitch!" Gianna's father bellows at Carolyn. He lifts the table, flipping it over in a fit of rage.

Fuck with what's mine, and I'll destroy it. I'll lift the world and drop it on their fucking heads.

GIA †

"WHY ARE we going to the church?" I ask.

We're driving toward the school, and it's already nightfall. I'm seated across from the twins, but they are silent since the showdown with my parents at dinner involving my mother and their father. I wonder if Dravin planned it that way, instead of him wanting to meet my parents.

"You'll see," Dravin says. "Just remember, I love you, Gia. Everything we do has a purpose. What happened at your father's house was for you and your mother's benefit."

"My mother?"

"Since the hospital, your mother and my father have been in contact with each other, but that is the first time my father and your mother had sex. I think he planned it that way."

"Why?"

"Because it's what my father wanted. Don't worry, we won't hurt your parents, but Carolyn is a two-faced bitch that needed to be outed that way."

I agree with him on that. The look on my mother's face when Mr. Bedford threw the money for the soap dish on the table was priceless. I bet she couldn't get that satisfaction anywhere. I never thought my mother would be that promiscuous. Good for her.

The driver pulls up to the gated cemetery and opens the rear passenger door. We arrived from Wisconsin three hours ago, and they brought me here. They didn't tell me why we were coming to the church, but I'm curious. Is it a meeting with the Order that I've been mandated to attend?

"Is this a meeting with the Order?" I ask when the door closes behind Dravin.

"No," Dravin says. "We've created a society besides the Order in case there's an attempt to disrupt or annihilate the legacy built by our founding fathers. It is known as the Consortium."

Draven knocks on the door, and it opens; once inside, people wearing black leather plague bird masks with black robes simultaneously turn their heads in our direction. I notice they have white crosses marked on their foreheads with what seems to be ashes, and under the cross, it reads *Sinner*.

When I walk inside behind the twins, my first reaction is to turn my nose up at the putrid smell of a rotting corpse. "Oh, dear God," I say, placing a hand over my mouth.

"Welcome to the Consortium, my love," Dravin says.

THE PREY SERIES

APPETITE

GIA
†

MY HAND TREMBLES as I cover my mouth, struggling to bring oxygen into my lungs from the images in front of me. The masks cover the faces of everyone sitting in the pews of the church, and where the altar is supposed to be, there's a man nailed to a cross, someone who seems to have been sacrificed for sacred worship. I pinch my nose and try to get air into my lungs through my mouth, watching everyone slowly face forward, acting as if this is a normal occurrence and there isn't a man in front of us with his eyes fixed in a wide, unblinking stare. A man I recognize as the barista from the coffee shop.

His head hangs, his eyes wide open, bulged out from their sockets, the whites tinged with a sickly yellow hue. His pupils are dilated, and the irises have lost their color, giving them a lifeless, glassy sheen. It's as if the very essence of his being has been sucked out through those gaping, staring orbs, leaving behind nothing but a shell of a man, forever trapped in his last, fearful expression.

Unflinching.

Dead.

On the cross, the man is completely naked and his arms are spread wide and large nails are hammered into the flesh at the wrists on two wooden beams. As my eyes trail down his chest, a path of blood flows from the wounds down his body. His feet are placed one over the other and nailed by the ankle and heel bone to keep him pinned on the beams.

Dravin leans close, his lips ghosting my ear, and whispers, "Scientists are indeed correct. If Jesus was nailed to the cross, it had to be by the wrists and not the palms of his hands because there is no way to keep him from falling if he's not nailed at the wrists."

My eyes fill with tears. I have never witnessed a dead body before, and even if I had, I would have never imagined this would be the way I would encounter one. What I am witnessing is another level of depravity and sacrifice. Shock and disbelief course through my body, amping up my nerves and making my stomach clench as a wave of nausea hits me. I try to keep my balance, but my body bends.

"None of that, my love," Dravin says, holding my arm then handing me a mask. I take it from his hands. It is a full-face silver mask and I notice it has a built-in filter that completely blocks the putrid smell that's causing my stomach to revolt.

Once I get my breathing under control, I close my eyes, hoping I will wake up from this bad dream, but when I open them, I know that this is real. I try to look away but can't help myself. My mind wants to know who and why they have decided to do this this way but, deep down, I know the reason. This is revenge for what happened to me. What he did was irredeemable. It was inhumane to purposely drug someone. Especially, a pregnant woman that could have died along with her baby.

That motherfucker killed my unborn baby. He almost killed me and what scares me the most is that I feel no remorse. How could I? I wonder if that makes me the same as his killers. A chill slides up my spine because that means all of the people sitting in the pews of the church are sinners and killers. The only two I recognize are the two men that have my heart and soul in their hands because they were the ones walking to the altar as soon as we entered after donning their masks. The rest, I have no idea who they are, but they know who I am.

I watch as Dravin heads toward the center of the church, directly behind the pulpit, and places his hands on the wood like he's the church's priest. "I apologize to all of you for taking so long, but we can all agree that Gianna must know that she will soon be part of the Consortium. She must know what we do when someone disrupts the Order or tries to take a life without a vote. In his case...our child from our chosen's womb. An innocent life that wasn't his to take."

Dravin's voice echoes with conviction, and I can feel his eyes on me, the feel of anguish and hurt rip right through me. Raw pain from the loss of my baby grips my heart, and I don't feel an ounce of sorrow for the man nailed to the cross because he didn't feel sorry about me or my baby.

Dravin clears his throat, his voice sounding muffled behind the plague mask he donned, making him look creepy and signifying that death is coming or that it has already came and taken the soul in which it needed to claim.

The tiny hairs on my skin rise because I know more death is coming and it will include Warren.

I watch as everyone nods in agreement. Draven puts his hand on my lower back, urging me to walk toward the center. Once I'm there and in front of the ambo, he turns me around, stands behind me and continues, "She is ours as much as we are hers. Anyone harms her, they die. Anyone causes her to be distressed, they die. We can all agree that Warren is not one of us. He is not part of the Order, but of his own order and anyone who follows him, must die. All agreed?"

The beaks of the plague masks all nod in agreement. No one says anything; there's not a single sound made or heard. I swallow hard and my eyes try to match a face to each of the masks staring straight ahead, but I can't. I don't recognize anyone; it's as if who they are is one big secret. A secret that must be kept. But I still want to know who or what they are.

The only thing that makes sense in my mind is that the people before me are the true rulers of society. The Consortium's way to balance the Order, which in turn, balances the world.

Right now, this is not a mass taking place inside a church but a house full of judges passing judgment. The setting where the gauntlet is thrown down to determine who lives and who dies. Sacrifices must be made in order to account for the deaths that have occurred and the reasons why.

Fear snakes through my body and overtakes me as I realize that no one is safe from their persecution. They are the persecutors. Both the devil and God have taken a back seat to the Consortium because they are not human, but these men are. They all have blood on their hands, which is normal to them.

And now I'm part of them.

I hear a phone vibrate followed by a ding. Dravin looks down and slides his phone out of the black robe and opens the message, the light casting a glow on the black leather of the mask. I hear a string of curses and my stomach drops; hurt grips my chest, signifying that something is wrong. Terribly wrong.

JESS

MY EYES FEEL heavy and I roll my head from side to side, trying to remember what happened. All I remember is Reid catching me when I fell, after getting out of Michael's car.

Michael gave me something in the hotel room. All I can remember are flashes, like a picture book of the things he did. The things I allowed him to do because a girl like me against a man like him doesn't have much of a choice. My legs were spread wide, and I closed my eyes, wanting to think of anything that would get me through what I had to do. He told me to drink, and I was so thirsty, so I did. I tilted my head forward and he caressed me in that insane way of his that makes me shudder every time his hands, or any part of his body, meets my skin.

My eyes slowly open and I notice I'm in a room illuminated with soft light, casting shadows against the wall to my right, like they're watching over me. Looking down, I notice that I'm on a bed and I want to scream. Lately, this is where I have had the worst happen to me. Sleep being the last thing that comes to mind.

Turning my head to my left, my eyes regain focus, and I sigh in relief. I'm in Reid's room. His computer desk is hard to forget the one time I was here. He has these high-end computer monitors with neon lights that fade in and out, changing colors. It was the first thing that stood out when he brought me up here that night after the party. I remember sleeping over. Well, he was screwing my brains out more than anything. No kissing, no caresses, just straight fucking with no fucks given. I think I slept an hour or two the most until he went downstairs and told Gia to come up.

When I take a deep breath, I can smell the hint of his cologne mixed with his manly scent. I can hear movement below and all I want is a shower to scrub away the memory of Michael and what he did to me.

My tongue is stuck to the roof of my mouth and my throat feels raw, I'm thirsty and I feel groggy. My limbs feel heavy and my wrists are sore from the restraints. I'm such a stupid woman, allowing him to tie my wrists, but with Michael, there is no winning. He will make me pay through my mother. When I told him it was the last time in the hotel room, he threatened my mother's life, making the stakes go even higher and giving me no choice but to pay with the only currency he's interested in, my body.

The sounds of footsteps outside the door cause my heart to pound and my head to look down. I lift the comforter and notice I'm only wearing a thong.

"He couldn't help himself could he. Bastard," I mutter.

The night in the elevator at his hotel replays in my mind. The way he treated me has my lip curling. If he walks in at this moment, I'm not sure I should tell him what I really think about him.

The door swings open and Reid walks in with concern etched across his gorgeous face. He's an asshole but a gorgeous one. His long-sleeve black shirt is stretched across his chest and biceps. His dark, straight hair flipped to one side. His eyes are the color of midnight as they sweep across me in his bed.

He places his finger over his mouth cocking his head. "I'm not going to ask questions you probably won't give me answers to, but you need to pick your boyfriends a little better." He walks inside, closing the door with a thud and flicking the lock, and then reaches out with his hand to tug the comforter down my chest, exposing my breasts.

My heart begins to beat faster and my instinct is to cover my chest with the palms of my hands, flinching when my wrists sting, causing me to remember that the skin is raw. I notice a Band-Aid with a piece of cotton on my inner right elbow and my eyebrows pull into a frown.

"I had a doctor draw blood from you to see what that piece of shit gave you. All I want to know is if you went willingly, or did he rape you?" he asks in a harsh tone.

I avert me gaze because his question is complicated to answer. Has Michael raped me? Yes. Did he rape me tonight? Maybe. Did he drug me without consent? Yes. Did I go willingly? Yes. Did I want to? Absolutely not.

There are a million ways to answer him right now and all my answers would be to scream rape, but what would that solve? I believe Michael when he says he will hurt my mother. He's unhinged and last night proved that he is willing to take this as far as it will go. In the end, I lose. And people like Reid and his secret society give two shits about someone like me.

The best answer I could give him is my silence because why would a guy like Reid care? Him bringing me here is what any moral, sane person would do. I stare at the wall and reply the best way I know how because the concern that was written in his expression has turned to annoyance.

"I went willingly, but I didn't think he would–"

"Drug you," he interrupts. "Well, he obviously did." He points to my wrists. "I didn't think you were into...other shit." He walks over to the side of the bed and leans close; my eyes flash in challenge. His upper lip curls in disgust when his finger lightly lifts my chin. "You're dirty and for the record," he pauses, and his eyes slide over my skin to where my breasts are exposed to his gaze, "drugging a woman to have sex with her is for pussies."

His eyes flick up and darken like a man possessed of something sinister. "Men that do that to women deserve other things."

I swallow thickly and I grimace because my throat feels like sandpaper. His eyes narrow at the marks on my skin on each of my wrists and I squirm when my mind starts flashing back to glimpses of what Michael did to me.

It is too late to protest when I feel Reid's hands slide under me and lift me into his arms like I'm a bride. He walks over to the door right next to the closet, pushing it open with his boot. The light senses his movement and flicks on. Instead of telling him off, I look around at the luxurious bathroom with black slate tile and cool lighting behind the vanity mirror, highlighting the modern luxury. He stops in front of a white free-standing tub and slowly places me down on my feet, keeping one arm around my waist. I forget that I'm standing against him, and my mind brings me back to the present. To the presence of him and the scent of his cologne.

"Hold on to me. Okay? Whatever that piece of shit gave you can make you feel off-balanced for a while."

I bow my head and nod. Ashamed that I let someone like Michael do the things he did to me. That I am risking my life, but in Michael's obsessive craziness, he wouldn't kill me. It wouldn't make his game seem worthwhile. If he killed me, he wouldn't have anyone else he could manipulate and black-mail. He has me cornered. I just hope I can survive it all. Graduation is not too far away and then like all Prey, I can be free.

Reid leans and turns on the water, checking the temperature with his fingers. My hand grips his bicep when I feel a wave dizziness. His head turns and his eyebrows draw in when he notices. This is the part of Reid that draws you in. The part that drew me in. The few glimpses of kindness he can bestow on you, making you feel like you are all that he cares about. The few moments.

The ones I wait for.

The ones that I have fallen for.

"Thank you," I croak.

It's all I can think to say to him because he doesn't have to bother with me. He could have called campus security and they would have called the police and handed me over, but he didn't.

"You could thank me by telling me who he is, but we both know you won't for whatever reason, and I have the suspicion this isn't the first time he's done it." He leans close, sliding his hand on my cheek and wrapping his fingers behind the nape of my neck. My head tilts to look at his handsome face, but he's looking above my head, like he's picturing something in his mind. "Did you know that an animal when preyed upon screams when it's caught by a predator as it begins to eat them alive." Chills crawl over my skin when his eyes drop to meet mine and are pitch black. My heart pounds inside my chest and my ears begin to throb, the sound of the water filling the tub is like the blood rushing to my ears. He continues, "It goes silent and watches as the predator feeds on its flesh." His thumb caresses my cheek, while he studies me and his lips break out in a grin. "Until the predator becomes the prey, when something bigger comes because he found the source of the screams."

Only three animals pop into my mind. I read an article of things you hear in the woods that scream like humans and I remember the article mentioned foxes and rabbits. The fox eats the rabbit, and the lion eats the fox, but it's the screams of the rabbit that called the lion.

"The fox and the rabbit. A-and the lion," I say breathlessly.

"Smart girl."

JESS

Gia is pacing back and forth in the dorm room. When I was able to walk on my own, Reid dropped me off at my dorm. Back at the house where he lives with Dravin, he placed me in the tub of his bathroom and left me to bathe myself. I was relieved he gave me privacy, so I could lick my wounds and deal with my shame. I'm also glad they called Gia and she showed up here to check on me.

My refusal to say anything is obvious. Michael will harm my mother if I open my mouth and the fact that he knows I'm here doesn't sit well with me. He knows where to find me, so running from him isn't an option. I'm not sure how much influence he has or how much money is at his disposal. I know he's rich, but I don't know how rich. I have never been to his house so what do I know. All I know is that he owns a town and everything in it. Including the people.

"I can't," I say quietly.

She whirls around, her black hair fanning out toward me and her eyes almost bulging. "Are you fucking kidding me right now!" She places her hands on her head and walks closer so that she is facing me while I sit on the bed with my feet together, as if I'm being scolded like a child. She lets out a puff of air and stretches her arms out wide. "Why?" she asks, lowering her voice and breaking on the last part, before dropping her hands to the side and plopping beside me on the bed.

I close my eyes briefly and hate that I'm disappointing her. I hate that I sound so weak, but I really don't have a choice. Michael has me by the balls, and he knows it. There has got to be a way to get off his radar, but I need to finish school first to be able to support me and my mom. Once I have a job, I can figure out the rest. Like how to get rid of Michael.

"I just can't right now. I'm in no position to report him. Not yet. Not right now. You have to trust me on this."

I swallow thickly. I know she is struggling to understand why I won't do it but telling her this is futile. I know she will tell the twins, but by the time they look into it, my mother is fucked.

Michael is beyond fucked up, and obsessive people like Michael will stop at nothing if they don't get their way. I have to find a way, but I know the twins are not the answer. Killing him is probably the only way to get him to leave me alone. But how would I ask someone to do that or ask that of myself? It would make me a killer. Like hiring a hitman to whack somebody. This isn't a movie. This is my life. My future. I would go to jail and my mother would suffer either way. There has to be another way; Dravin and his brother are not the answer.

I can't ask Gia to get involved. It would be too risky, and she has enough on her plate with Warren. This is my problem.

I shake my head when we both fall silent. Her mind must be turning, trying to figure out why I won't tell her more.

"I can't," I repeat. My head turns and my eyes find hers. "You have enough on your plate with the twins and Warren. Anyway, what happened at the church?"

She looks away and I know that there is something she isn't telling me. I'm deviating from the topic of what happened with Michael. How Reid found me, and I passed out from whatever Michael had given me. When she showed up after Reid called Dravin, she came over telling me that they took her to the church. I wonder if they introduced her to the Order. I feel her tense beside me, and the same way I'm not telling her everything in detail, she is doing the same. Maybe she can't or the twins could have sworn her to secrecy from what was said.

"They killed the barista from the coffee shop," she deadpans.

My body begins to feel hot and cold. The room goes silent and all you can hear is the humming of the air conditioner from the old building. I can feel the pressure from my heart beating in my ears. They killed him?

I knew the twins were ruthless and what he and that asshole Warren did to her, I wouldn't blame them, but she's saying it like it was a normal situation.

I take a deep swallow and lick my lips that have suddenly gone dry then ask her the only thing that comes to mind. "H-how?"

She rings her hands together and clears her throat. "T-they nailed him to a cross in the church. When I got there, he was already dead." She gets up from the bed and her hands are shaking a bit. I watch her and it's clear that she is scared, sad, and relieved all at the same time because he wasn't a good person. He deserved it in my opinion. I mean, yes, a man lost his life, and they must have tortured the asshole, but Gia's baby died. She lost the baby, and that piece of shit was smiling and was a fucking creep that night. She was scared when I got there. I remember it like it was yesterday.

Not wanting to force her to tell me something that would probably get her in trouble or worse, killed, I slap my hands on my thighs and get up, leaning on the bed as a wave of dizziness hits me.

Gia moves over to me quickly, but I steady myself. "Woah."

I let out a laugh, holding myself steady. "I'm good. It's probably from whatever that asshole gave me."

"Are you sure?"

I wave her off and nod. "Yeah, Reid had a doctor check me out. It was some medication they give people for depression and anxiety. The asshole gave me more than I should have taken and it kinda made me go in and out of consciousness. I hardly remember some of the things he did."

"Fucking asshole. I hope they find him even if you can't tell anyone."

"Yeah, I doubt that. I'm sure they couldn't care less and Reid was just being...Reid."

Gia pinches her brows. "What do you mean? He was just being Reid?"

"He blows hot and cold. You never know what mood he is in or what spills out of his mouth that turns you on or gives you the creeps or worse... insults you." I roll my eyes dramatically. "Like I said, Reid."

"I guess. I never know what is up with you two, but please be careful. What I saw, Jess," she says, lowering her voice. She slides her fingers through her dark, straight hair. I notice her bottom lip quivering and fear grips my spine. Shit. Her eyes are glassy, and I know she's scared. Whatever she saw was fucked up and I get it. Maybe the crap that is in my system is not allowing it all to sink in. This whole place is fucked up with mentally fucked-up people. The only thing I can figure out that is holding her together is the fact that it was an eye for eye. A way to show Gia that she is protected. Loved in their crazy-ass way and that the twins will not let anyone hurt her. Even the people sworn into their fucked-up society with their archaic rules. "I get it. I know why you don't want to tell me. You must be scared."I purse my lips and let out a slow breath. "Are you scared of them, Gia?"

"I'm not scared of them, just the people they have in their circle. I don't think you have anything to worry about with Reid or Valen, but the rest of them..." She pauses and shakes her head slowly from side to side and then whispers, "Don't trust them."

I know she is trying to warn me or whatever, but if I was worried about telling anyone what the deal is with Michael before, I'm better off dealing with my own shit and my own crazy monster. We have that in common at least. A crazy asshole on the loose that is obsessed. Except, for one thing: I don't have a pair of guys willing to do anything for me, except have sex with me because I allow it. Because I need to forget. But they don't know that. I took that saying of a girl forgets a man by getting under another one to a whole new level. It's like a ritual for me. A way to get through the aftermath. A Band-Aid for the wound.

"I won't," I say softly.

Here, they say the Prey chooses, but I choose to survive.

JESS

THE STUDENTS ARE FILING into class. One after the other they walk in. Some glance at me and others have a knowing fucking grin on their face when they spot the less fortunate. The dorm bunnies I call us. Prey. I used to think that they were curious when I first started here at Kenyan, but I learned quickly.

After everyone is seated, the door swings open and the professor walks in and my chest tightens. My chest begins to rise and fall like I just ran a marathon because he doesn't walk in alone. Professor Krupp is with the last person I would ever expect. I blink rapidly, hoping it is a trick of the light or that I'm having a fucked-up dream and I'm the joke.

Professor Krupp turns to face the class with a smile, reminding me of the old man with creepy teeth in the movie the *Poltergeist* that wears the black hat. Professor Krupp breaks an even wider smile with his coffee-stained teeth when he speaks. "Good morning, everyone, I would like to introduce you to a new student that has decided to transfer from our online school to on-campus for the rest of the year to our economic class. You will most likely see him around. I would like you all to welcome, Mich."

Fuck! He's here. Out of all the places and schools, why here, but I know the answer. Me.

Michael or Mich gives a slight nod, but when his eyes find mine, his lips curve into a knowing grin. I shrink in my seat under his sharp gaze. The tiny hairs on my forearms stand, due to a mixture of fear and awareness. I feel like a helpless animal trapped in a cage. A cage he created just for me, like a dog chained up against its will, only able to go out so far before it is yanked back inside.

"Thank you for the introduction, Professor Krupp," he says, but his eyes never leave mine. "I look forward to finishing out my senior year on campus."

Mich, huh. Why not be addressed as Michael, but then I remember some of his friends called him, Mich. His close friends, from his circle, and the assholes that were with him that night I went to the party my senior year of high school and he drugged me. I always called him Michael because that was what he wrote on his assignments in class and how the teacher addressed him when they called on him.

The professor continues to talk about current events on global currency, while Michael takes a seat behind me to the right, where he has a clear view of the class, including me, but I would have to angle my body to see him. Asshole.

My eyes scan the room and everyone is facing forward, while my head is screaming, not paying one ounce of attention to what the professor is dictating.

Deep down, I know there is something bigger at play here. In Kenyan, you are either Prey or part of the Order. I have the sinking feeling that I know the truth of which one Michael is a part of. And Prey is the last thing that comes to mind because that is what I am and have been since I set foot on campus. A pawn. A challenge.

REID

STARING at the wide monitor in my room, my eyes scroll over the information I was able to pull up on Jess, wondering why I even bother. I shouldn't care. But I do. The look in her eyes when I'm with her––inside her--is haunting. It calls to me on a deeper level, like she is there in the moment, but for an entirely different reason other than to have sex. Other girls want to sleep with the sons of Kenyan for popularity and to get ahead. For social status. But with Jess, she is doing it for something else. A reason I want to find the answer to.

When I saw her get out of that piece of shitty car and proceeded to pass out in my arms, it broke me. It called to something inside me I've had buried for a couple years now. She brought it out and I want to embrace it. It is one of the reasons I moved in with Dawin and left my parents' house. The constant bickering between my mother and father over my behavior was too much and I couldn't take it without snapping.

The constant questions.

Where was I?

Who was I fucking?

Every conversation centered around my need to marry because of the Order and the importance of making alliances with the right families in order to gain more power and more control. Every time they would look down the long dining room table and see the look in my eyes and the expression on my face as silence stretched throughout the room, I would see it. The reason. The fear. I knew in those few encounters, I could no longer sit there and watch them.

They are probably afraid of what I might do or what I'm capable of, but the thing is, I don't remember the things they said I did. They said I killed a certain way or slaughtered the ones responsible for my sister's death, but to me, they're merely lapses in memory that started right after my sister died when I was twelve.

Deep down, I blame my parents. I blame the Order. The fucked-up rules made in archaic times that are followed by leaders with their own agendas and the reason my older sister died. At the young age of twelve, I understood what men in power do to women that threaten their control. They destroy them by bringing them down mentally, emotionally, and physically.

I study the screen; there are several windows open on the ultra-wide display, detailing Jesse Sharpe's background. Cedar Lake, Ohio, is listed as her place of birth and residence. I use the track pad to zoom in as I put her address into the map's search bar, and a red pin appears above a trailer park.

Lot 606 at the Cedar Lake mobile home trailer park. She did say she didn't have much growing up. Clearly, she wasn't kidding. The trailer park is a shithole. The type of cesspool meth heads and druggies come from, but I don't get that vibe from Jess or Jesse, as her birth certificate reads as her full first name. I have never witnessed her on anything, except alcohol at the bar. Draven had me keep an eye on her during the party, while he dealt with Gia, and I noticed she didn't touch anything that was offered to eat or drink. Smart girl. You never know what kind of creeps are lurking at a college party.

As I expand the window, I can make out the dilapidated trailer, the over-grown grass mixed with filth, and the yellow stains trickling down from each window like a dog has been pissing out of them.

I need to know more about her, so I keep reading. She was top of her class her senior year at Cedar Lake High on the outskirts of Ohio. She has no social media accounts, which means she wasn't popular or was trying to hide where she was. She would definitely be memorable with a face and body like hers. She's curvy in all the right places with a straight nose, honey-colored eyes and a sun-kissed complexion. I shift in my chair, my cock remembering all too vividly the way she felt the first time. She took everything I had to give her, and I loved watching how her eyes would turn the color of fire when she came. Mesmerizing.

If she only knew she was the first woman I could watch for hours on end and yet find something new and interesting in her every time. But what draws me in is the darkness that lives inside her, consuming her from within. Her lack of emotion when she gets what she needs every time she fucks is like she is feeding a demon. Everyone sees her as Prey. An unprivileged female given the opportunity of a lifetime by fucking around at an elite university with the rich and powerful. But I don't. What do you do when you are trying to feed one monster? You get in a pool of monsters, hoping they will turn on each other, so you can escape.

The mystery is what or who she's trying to get away from.

The town sounds familiar. Cedar Lake was discussed in an Order meeting, but I cannot remember who brought it up or why. It's a pain, but I have to attend these meetings, or I won't know what's happening. Then we have the Consortium, which is like the internal affairs department of the Order, run by selected members only. The sons of Kenyan are at the head, but we recruit and set our own rules.

It was necessary and what we agreed to do after the deaths of my sister and Dravin's mother. We still meet in the same fashion in the church, but the high-ranking members of the Order have no idea when these gatherings are held or who we could decide to execute if they disobey our rules. It's what separates us from them. That's why the other members, and even our parents, cower in dread of us and the power we wield.

I continue to scroll through the page with all her information and notice there isn't much on her. She has a mother but no father in the picture. No surprise there. No siblings. No family. Something doesn't add up. I can't ask Gia about her because I'm positive I'm not a fan favorite.

I sigh, closing all the windows on the screen, and let out a puff of air from my mouth. Fuck. I place my thumb and close my eyes, relieving the sting from staring at the screen for so long.

Knock. Knock.

"What?"

"It's me, Dravin."

The door makes a small sound when it opens. I rotate my seat so that I'm facing my bedroom door, pushing to recline the chair. As I relax in it, the screensaver starts up on my computer and I watch Dravin cross his arms over his chest, leaning on the door jam.

"What are you up to? You have been up here for the past three hours." I look at his hand not saying a word. My eyes narrow because he is gripping something.

"Is there something you want to give me?" I ask, raising an eyebrow.

He uncrosses his arms and tosses a pill bottle at me. I catch it due to my quick reflexes and hold it up. "Your delivery came."

I look at the prescription bottle with my name on it and a low chuckle climbs up my throat. "Are you worried, Dravin?"

My eyes flick up to meet his, and he scoffs. "I'm not, but everyone else is another matter entirely."

I toss the bottle in the trash bin near my desk, not giving a fuck. I hate taking them because they mess with my concentration. I prefer Adderall because I can get shit done instead of the crap they want me to take. After my sister died, my parents started to take me to psychotherapy. It didn't help because I took care of it my way. They thought they were right to take me, but there is no line between revenge and crazy. It goes hand in hand. I don't want my parents to freak out, even though Dravin is cool about the whole me not needing psychotherapy after my sister died, but the thing is, I haven't gone in a month. I don't want to talk about it to some asshole with a degree who thinks that getting inside my head will solve all my problems. Where were the doctors when they killed her? I've accepted that she's dead and nothing is going to bring her back.

"Do you want to talk about it?"

"Are you my therapist?" I counter.

He lets out a soft chuckle. "You know how I feel about therapy. Ask Draven?"

"Must be cool to have a twin and one of you go for the other. Help keeps shit balanced."

Strangely, Dravin has been seeing the therapist who also treats his brother for years. The Bedford siblings just muck things up, that's what they do. I remember the time Dravin fucked the therapist's daughter right under her mother's nose and then let her think he was the one in need of therapy so that she could report his "progress" to their father. The stupid bitch never figured out she had been giving therapy to the wrong twin. But I think Gia is the reason he stopped fucking the daughter. Gia is his chosen. Their chosen.

"I wouldn't know any more because I stopped going and so has Draven. Obviously."

There it is. I was right. And they say I need therapy.

"No shit. That makes three of us."

His expression morphs from playful to concerned. "Dude, are you sure that is a good idea?"

"Why, you have a better one?"

"Yeah, take the pills and go to therapy. Your parents are going to freak out."

I wave him off. "I am on medication."

"Weed and Adderall are not what they had in mind."

I shrug. "It's what has me working and concentrating on shit." I point to the offending pills in the basket. "That doesn't allow me to be who I am. That shit gives me weird dreams and makes me feel slow when I'm trying to get shit done. I hate it. It will probably keep me from having a kid when it's time. If they ask, tell them I'm taking them."

"Brother, I didn't think you would ever want kids, but then again, Tara might."

The thought of marrying Tara causes a little twitch in my left eye. Nobody knows this, but I'm not going to marry her. I don't give a fuck about her filthy family or the alliance they provide; she's obnoxious. She should marry my cousin, Alaric. He will keep her busy or fuck her to death, literally. The rule is that I have to find a wife at the end of the year. All I know it's not going to be her.

"I think you need to worry about Gia and decide which one of you is marrying her." He sighs and I know he is battling a decision. Which twin should Gia marry, him or his brother. It is crazy to think they both have fallen in love with the same woman and plan on letting her keep them both. "Have you three decided?"

"I think it should be my brother. He deserves to have a wife."

"And you don't?" I roll my head on the smooth leather of my chair and give him an idea. Unorthodox, but they both can have what they want. It's brilliant, and it steers him away from the current topic of our conversation.

"I have an idea."

JESS

"EXCUSE ME," I say to a couple blocking the exit to the door, as I make my way down the hallway from the classroom. I'm about to turn into a darker hallway when strong hands grip my arm, and I pull hard to my left to try and escape. Before I can scream, a hand covers my mouth, and I know by the smell of his skin and the cologne that I detest, it's Michael, or what everyone calls him, Mich.

His hot breath is near my ear, and it makes me cringe. "You think you can run away from me, don't you?" I shake my head nervously, averting my eyes to stare at the dark wall behind him. "You know the rules. Tell anyone about our little arrangement, and your mother will disappear. Got it." I sag in utter defeat.

Tears pierce the corners of my eyes and I want to scream, kick, and tear him apart.

I hate him.

Six months, I tell myself. That is all I have left of my senior year, and then I can leave here to start the next chapter of my life. I just have to play it smart. I have to act like Prey. And Prey get to choose. I may have to meet the devil in his bed, but he isn't the only one, and he can't do shit about it. Rules are rules. If you break the Order's rules, you die.

My mind plays back the conversation I had with Gia and the man on the cross comes to my mind. *What happens when you break the rules?* Right now, I wish nothing more than to be a rule that is broken when it comes to Michael.

"Nod, princess." When I nod my head slowly, he smiles, but it's evil. "I'm going to slide my hand away and if you scream, I know where to hurt you the most, besides that wet cunt you have between your legs that I like so much. Understood?"

Cold air stings my lips when I nod again, and I hate myself for nodding. He takes a step back, like he is admiring my face, but I know better. He is calculating how he wants to use me next time. "So pretty." The backs of his knuckles slide down my cheek and I stiffen.

He leans close. "Shh, it's okay. But I'm glad we understand each other." I'm about to sigh in relief when he moves away, but it's short-lived. "Oh, before I forget. Don't call me Michael." He lowers his voice. "My friends and family call me Mich. You can call me Michael when I make that pussy cry for me when I'm in and out of it. He gives me a wink and bile rises from my stomach, and I hope it makes an appearance up my throat, so I can spit it in his face.

"Of course, Mich. Whatever you say," I respond with a hint of sarcasm.

He grins slightly. "Be careful, Jesse. I might take you somewhere to show you how happy I am that we go to the same school. It can be like old times," he says calmly as he walks away, referring to the party from our senior year in high school.

My skin crawls with terror remembering that night, and he senses it. He's picking up on the scent of fear. Vulnerable people are easy prey for predators, yet sometimes, there is little you can do to avoid being vulnerable.

If I report him, the Order will make it go away, starting with me and then my mom. No one will miss the poor mother with the trailer-trash daughter from Ohio. They will probably make it look like an accident. Who will question people like Michael and the Levines. If he's here, it means he has money, power and influence. Three things I don't. Like all the assholes here, he wants to play me like the strings on a guitar. He doesn't know that he isn't the only one playing with my strings. But he will soon find out.

I walk out of the dark space and almost run into a hard body. "Woah, there."

I look up about to tell the asshole to watch where he is going, but then I meet light eyes to my brown ones. Valen.

"Oh, shit. I'm sorry," I say, letting out a breath and pressing my fingers over my brow.

"Don't be sorry." He looks over my shoulder to where I jetted out from, probably noting that there is no one in class and the window light by the door is out. He leans his neck back and tilts his head to meet my gaze. "Are you okay?"

I give him a fake smile. "I'm fine."

I'm not fine. I'm a victim of a rapist stalker that has blackmailed me into fucking him for his pleasure at the expense of me and my mother's life. Valen's tongue flicks the corner of his lip piercing, and my eyes follow the movement of his tongue, watching the tip caressing the metal. The scent of him hits me in full force, replacing Michael's unwelcome one. Valen is fun and familiar. Young and carefree.

Valen rolls his bottom lip inside his mouth with his tongue and it's sexy. He's sexy. People walk by us and around us, but we are still standing in the middle of the hallway studying each other. Him trying to figure out what I'm really thinking and me trying to keep it together by using him as eye candy.

"Want to get out of here?"

My heart begins to pound in my chest, humming a tune. I think about my next class and if it would be a huge deal if I miss it. Then I think about what just happened, causing the pounding in my chest to travel to my head and telling me that I need a release. The need to feel wanted and safe beating out the guilt and shame of using him for my own selfish needs. Maybe he is doing the same and we need each other for whatever reason. Right now. In this moment.

"Yeah. What do you have in mind?"

His eyes travel down my knitted sweater and wool leggings to my cheap knock-off Uggs I bought in the kiosk at the mall. He slowly lifts his eyes like he is picturing me without any clothes on. "Everything."

JESS

THE BLAST of cold air hits my cheeks like a slap in the face when the front door of the building swings open. I welcome the sting and cold air filling my lungs as I follow Valen outside the campus building. The trees are bare, with a unique texture and color. Some have smooth, grey bark, while others have rough, dark brown bark, full of knots. It hasn't snowed, but the harsh cold hasn't let up for two weeks, which is no surprise since it's the middle of winter.

"Your car or mine?" I ask.

"I think you know the answer to that, princess."

Of course, it would be his car. He had to drive my car back when I left the pool party with him that one time and it showed him what a piece of shit my car really is, which means he isn't interested in another test drive.

As I walk behind him into the parking lot, I reflect on the fact that the closest I've been to Valen always has to do with his cock. I've ridden it a few times, and it's always a pleasant experience.

I'm also sure his car is much better than mine. I didn't have much growing up, and most people, compared to me, are well-off. I think even poor people are more well-off than me at this point. I'm a generation away from being homeless after I graduate. When you are used to people having more than you for so long, you get used to the fact that you never will have more than you already do. You can't cry for something you've never had. You just have to work harder and make sacrifices for what you do have.

He turns left in the parking lot and stops in front of a sleek black sports car that reads Mercedes with the letters GT on the back.

"Do you like it?"

All the rich boys around here drive nice cars and live in even nicer houses that look like hotel resorts. It looks new. If it's new, what is not to like.

"It's better than mine," I say, shrugging my shoulders.

He smiles. "I think anything is better than your car. No offense. I just got it for Christmas. Listen, I need to head to practice and want you to come along. If that's okay. Dravin and Reid are in their last year at Kenyan, and I'm taking over as swim team captain, and I would love for you to be there."

I thought he was taking me to have sex somewhere. I guess my encounter with Michael affected my brain cells more than I thought because the only thing I can think about is wiping the memory of his touch off my skin.

I don't want to disappoint Valen, but I really need a shower. The need to scrub my skin raw overpowers my guilt in turning him down as I stare at the handle of his nice car, knowing I'm not the type of girl that should be seen with him. I step back when I see him slide into the luxury sports car and hear his door shut.

He probably thinks I'm agreeing to come along. As much as I want to, I can't because we would never work. He is young and he deserves better. Better than someone like me and I feel like I'm using him for all the wrong reasons. He has to know what happened to me. That I was drugged and dropped off on the curb like a prostitute, but he doesn't mention it or bring it up. Him asking me if I'm okay in the hallway was a sign that he knows, but knowing how Valen is, he won't bring it up because he's a nice guy.

When I hear the deep rumbling of the engine, he lets down the passenger window. I can almost taste the smell of new leather, and its combination with the chilly air makes me think of a pair of fancy shoes I'd seen in a shop but could never afford.

"Come on," he says.

I bend down and place my hands on my thighs, not wanting to put finger prints on his nice car. "You go ahead. I'm sorry, but I just remembered I have an assignment to turn in for my next class," I lie.

I watch his expression turn to disappointment when I back away, but I know turning him down is the right thing to do.

"Jess–"

I hear him call out, but I don't turn around, so he can't see the tears welling up in my eyes. I'm no good for him. He doesn't need a woman in his life with my kind of baggage, and besides, I would never be accepted. Maybe, deep down, I don't want to go because Reid will be there. I don't know how I would act around him after what happened. He hasn't reached out. He is probably disgusted with me.

On Sunday, the effects of the drugs wore off and I was practically back to my old self, except for the red marks on my wrists, currently hidden under my sweater, and my ankles. Mentally, is another matter. As for Reid, I'm still trying to figure him and his mood swings out.

There are times that I think he cares and then there are times when I think he hates that he shows me any type of attention. When I sat at the bar with his cousin Alaric, he was jealous for whatever reason. I wasn't going to jump and have sex with the guy. Reid was talking to his ex-flame, or whatever, and I was just standing there. He didn't introduce me, which made me feel unimportant.

I mean, I let him fuck me in the elevator because that is what my subconscious needed and after he was finished, the guilt set in. Calling me a whore cut me deep, filling me with guilt mixed with my jealousy when seeing him with that woman. I blamed it on clouded judgment, but I knew that was all a lie. I wanted him more than I thought I did.

It hurt when the words spilled out of his mouth, but I can't help if that is what he thinks of me. I'm sure that's what they all think.

And letting someone like Valen, one of Kenyan's sons, treat me differently would make the fall hurt even worse.

When he realizes his time is up playing the college student and has to fulfill the Order's rule when he graduates, then what? Where would that leave me? Alone.

VALEN

I SLAM my hand on the leather steering wheel. "Fuck."

I have never been turned down before, but the sadness in her eyes gets to me every time I look at her. A protective instinct overwhelms me, mixed with the nagging feeling of needing to save her, but what gets to me is what I am protecting her from. She doesn't let me in. Sex is transactional for her, and most girls would be expecting more. An invitation. A phone call. A date. But not Jess.

She has my number, and she doesn't use it. No phone call begging for me to come over. If we cross paths, then it's on, wherever we are at. Something happened when she was drugged, and it wasn't a sex fetish she was into, and none of us know with who, but she told Reid it wasn't forced. But I'm positive she didn't agree to be drugged. It can only mean she knows whoever did it and doesn't want to say. I wonder why she would protect a piece of shit like that. Whoever it is knows the rules and is pulling the strings like a puppet master, but he's playing a dangerous game.

It shouldn't matter. I know the rules with girls that are Prey on campus. Use them and move on. A good time and nothing more, but with Jess, it's different, I care. I should have gone after her and pushed her to accompany me to practice. I wanted her to be there so I could keep an eye on her. I found it weird that she came out of a hallway where there was a vacant class-room. What was she doing there? Her eyes were full of dread, but when I looked over her shoulder, no one was there, except a closed door leading to a dark classroom.

I pull into the sports complex where practices are held in the indoor pool, finding a spot next to Reid's Aston Martin. Reid and I have shared girls in the past, but the fact that he goes all ape-shit over Jess says a lot. He's interested. More than I thought from how he stormed in and took her from the pool party that night. Makes me wonder what his motive is. The way he looks at her can start a fire in a room, but he claims she is just another girl. Another Prey.

"What's up, Vikiar? Are you ready to receive the torch from Dravin?" Geo says, when I walk into the locker room to change. He loves to call me by my last name because he is a prick that loves to get under my skin.

"Yup, it has to go to the best. And I'm what is left."

I sound like a cocky asshole, but, after Dravin and Reid graduate, I am the best. I love to swim. Garret is always a second behind my lap time, and I'm third behind Reid. I would have been fourth, but that particular twin prefers other types of business and thinks school's a waste of time, but it's his loss.

"Cocky, asshole," he mutters.

I pull my shirt over my head, playing it off like I'm not looking for a particular asshole named Warren. I'm sure Dravin is somewhere in the back thinking the same thing. Maybe they are playing dumb and really have him holed up somewhere. Warren must be stupid to think we wouldn't retaliate for what he did to Gia. Motherfucker thinks he could outsmart us using the barista to cover it up and to throw us off.

He thought that Gia was just Prey and she didn't matter or that the Order would not allow us to kill him, but he didn't know the Consortium existed. Members like Warren are kept in the dark.

My phone vibrates, and I check the unknown text.

> Unknown: Order meeting. 8pm.

I look around and see all the members looking down at their phones, reading the same message. I pull up the Consortium's thread to ensure no one can see me type on my phone.

> V: What is this about?

> C: Member attending last semester before graduating on campus.

> V: Who?

> C: Some asshole who is owed a favor for taking care of our mess. He bought his way in.

Fuck, that means there is someone we don't know walking around campus. It means we all must attend to be properly introduced. Members of the Order and their sons are spread out across the U.S. Sons of important politicians and leaders with special issues are sent to Kenyan. I wonder what this guy's poison is? Mine is sex. I'm a sex addict, amongst other things. I like drugs, fast cars, and pussy. Every rockstar's dream, but I'm no rockstar. My fix is the next orgasm, but luckily, I don't have any problems getting my fix. I have more than I need when I want, where I want, and how I like it.

Except for a brunette that turned me down. I'll have to rectify that a little later. I'll fuck the guilt or fear right out of her, and she will be smiling by morning. All better. But only when I find the bastard responsible for fucking with her.

V: Who is it? We have other shit to worry about.

They know I mean Warren and how we will dispose of our little problem with a small dick. It slipped out of a girl's mouth at a party I attended. I think her name was Melly. She said it felt like a tampon going in. Her words, not mine. It is a wonder why Warren is obsessed with Gia, but Veronica's obsession with Warren has my mind on the fritz. It makes no sense to me, but that bitch is Satan's spawn so there must be a reason. The only thing that comes to mind about Warren that the twins, Reid and me can agree on, is that Warren is a predator.

"Did you get the text?" Geo asks behind me, and I slip my phone inside my locker after locking the screen.

"You know I did. What do you want to ask?"

Of course, I got the text, but this asshole has been making small talk since I showed up, and I can't slip on my swim shorts while he is standing behind me. He isn't stupid. I'm one of the founding sons of Kenyan.

"Dude, are you Greek?"

Geo looks at me, confused, ready to head out. "Nah, man. Why would you think that?"

"Because I can't get dressed with you standing behind me, looking at me from behind. I mean, it's all good if you are, but fuck. Not all of us are down like that."

I hear laughing from the left. "He has a point."

I turn my head, and Reid has a sinister look in his eye. "Get lost, Geo. If not, I might have to see how long you can hold your breath underwater."

Geo holds his hands up nervously. His eyes projecting fear at Reid's threat. He knows Reid doesn't fuck around when he is in a mood to play. "I just wanted to ask if he is serious about a girl I've seen him with."

I slide my pants down along with my boxers, not giving a fuck that my dick has sprung out. Reid leans on the metal lockers with one of his shoulders, loving how uncomfortable Geo is. He didn't leave when I warned him. I want to laugh in his face while he is trying to keep a straight one.

"I'm around a lot of girls, so it doesn't matter. Go for it."

"Go for the blondes," Reid tells Geo. "The blonde ones," he repeats.

"I kinda like the brunettes."

Reid laughs, but it's different. I slide my shorts on, adjusting myself. Geo said nothing funny, but Reid can act like that sometimes.

I turn around, securing my locker, and notice Reid smiling at Geo as he shoves at his shoulder. "The blondes, dude. They're more fun when finding out if they are true blondes. It's like a scavenger hunt."

The strange thing about what Reid just said to Geo is that Reid doesn't like blondes. I don't think I have ever seen him with one.

REID

I'M SITTING in a pew inside the church, waiting for our fathers to take the front and address the members. The Bedford twins are standing next to their father as I should be standing next to mine like Valen, but I'm not like them. Never have been and never will be. I have my own set of rules that I adhere to and that includes not following certain rules. Maybe all of them, but who's counting.

Everyone knows who I am. I don't need to remind everyone by standing up next to my father. Only when it's necessary. My sister isn't here anymore, so why should I stand. She's in the cemetery behind me, feeding the earth as we speak.

"I would like to introduce you to Mich Levine. His father, Mr. Levine, has been a member of the Order for fifty years since he bought and took over Cedar Lake in Ohio. He was attending classes online to help with our business matters."

My head snaps to attention at the mention of the town where Jess is from. It isn't uncommon and it may be just a coincidence and he doesn't know who she is. All eyes are trained on a particular man to the right with a strong build. You can tell he was handsome when he was younger, and still is for his age. If his son was taking care of matters, it means disposing of the mess we made in Ohio. Cops, burying bodies that can never be found and that sort of thing. I call it bottom-feeding, but someone has to do it and they do it gladly in exchange for the wealth and power it yields.

So, the prick's son didn't buy in, he was already a member by proxy.

My eyes follow the man's son named Mich. Mich looks like an uppity asshole that has gotten everything he has ever wanted. Now, he has to find a wife. Rules of the Order and why he is here. I wonder what idiot would like to be on his arm with his collegiate looking sweater and slacks.

He isn't unattractive, but you can tell he has to hit the gym to get his build, but he will have no trouble getting females on campus. Especially, Prey. He looks like he could be the head of a frat house. A boring jerk that looks forward to getting drunk on the weekends and spending his father's money. But he doesn't have time to do that, does he. Time is ticking.

Mich looks around like he struck gold and won the lottery. He doesn't know he is in the church of hell. *Keep smiling, asshole. You have no idea what you signed yourself up for.* I roll my head, hearing the crack in my neck, and try not to lose my patience. Lack of sleep will do that to you when you keep trying to find more information and keep hitting dead ends on a particular girl. There is also the added pressure of having to help Dravin kill Warren under the radar and make sure him or his brother marries Gia. We can't keep Warren holed up in a cage forever.

When the introductions are done. The twins step forward and the look on Warren's face is priceless when they mention Gia as their chosen and the one that they will marry. Warren's eyes are sunken in with dark circles, reminding me of a raccoon. The guy looks like he came off the set of Resident Evil. Warren looks around like he is lost in space, totally out of it, but no one notices what we do. *Time to go back to your playpen, asshole.*

My eyes dart over to Veronica, seated two pews down, and the smile on her face is priceless, but I also find her staring too hard at Mich. Probably her next victim. Poor guy. She will fuck him dry by the time the week is out. Hopefully, she will forget about Warren and we can get rid of him as planned, without her getting hung up on the idea of him when he is gone. Like the saying goes, loose lips sink ships.

There is a meeting taking place after the Order with the sixty-six members of the Consortium. Draven disposed of the barista, sending a message to Warren, but the bastard thinks he is going to be absolved of his sins by going away for a while. He wants to fuck with the sons of Kenyan, but he forgets that no one fucks with us. No one.

Garret turns slightly, the wood creaking from his weight on the pew and our gazes meet. He knows there is tension in the church. You can sense death knocking at the church's door waiting to collect. Beginning with Warren.

For the next thirty minutes, the Bedford twins remind everyone of the rules when it comes to Prey. *They choose. Whoever breaks the rules dies.* It is all simple really. The same bullshit narrative. Just follow the rules and you will have the power that is meant for you and the wealth that you are entitled to. I get it, if rules aren't followed, where will that leave everyone, with the crazies.

JESS

"I'M FINE," I say to Gia through the phone, counting the minutes in my head on my prepaid phone plan. I have to pay as I go. It's not like I have an income to pay a cellphone bill.

"Are you sure you don't want me to stay the night? Or you could come to Dravin's house."

I think of Reid being there and I know that is not going to happen. I can't forgive him for what he said and the fact that I'm attracted to him doesn't help the need inside me to purge my own demons of looking like a desperate woman vying for his attention. Not happening. That would be like walking into the devil's lair and expecting to come out baptized by God. The reminder of my need to shower and scrub causes my heart to beat in anticipation. Seeking relief.

"I'm sure. I'll be fine. I swear."

Gia whines. "Are you sure, Jess?"

I nod, even though she can't see me. "I'm sure. We'll catch up tomorrow at Babylon. We can have a couple of drinks since it's Tuesday. Ladies' night."

It's fun to hang out with her, and because it's ladies' night tomorrow, I can get free drinks, despite being a broke college student. We can shoot the shit and I can assure her that I'm fine.

"Fine, but make sure you show up after class. Happy hour."

"Happy hour," I repeat. "I'll see you tomorrow. Bye, Gia."

I hang up, closing my eyes and taking a deep breath as I grip the handle of my shower caddy, tossing my cheap basic track phone on the bed, and head to the shower with my towel under my arm.

It is already ten, which is lights out on school nights. The perfect time for me to head to the shower when no one is there.

The hallway is dark, with only three lights separated by the fire alarm. I make my way down the dark corridor, but a nagging feeling has my nerves on edge. Taking a few more steps, the hairs stand up with the feeling that someone is watching me. I stop in the middle of the hallway, awareness creeping through me. The light shines down on me, between the dark sections of the hallway, and I turn around, gripping the handle of the caddy with my fingers. My knuckles are white from the effort, and a sheen of cold sweat slides down the base of my spine.

My eyes try to focus, but it's dark, and no one is there. The hallway is empty.

I'm probably just feeling paranoid because of Michael and the fact that he is close by and knows exactly where to find me. He is always near when I think he isn't, but with Michael, he always calls. I hold the change of clothes wrapped in the towel under my arm and let out a slow breath. I blink hard to ensure my eyes are not playing tricks on me and head to the women's shower.

I'm under the hot spray and I'm scrubbing my skin like I'm filthy, but all that stares back at me is reddened skin. I scrub every part I remember he touched. My mouth, my thighs, and I close my eyes, letting tears slide down my cheeks mixing with the spray of the water.

"You know. There are other ways to deal with flashbacks of things you'd rather forget."

When I hear a man's low baritone voice, I drop the loofah from my fingers, closing my eyes. When I open them again, it's as if someone has sucked the oxygen out of my lungs. Across from me, a man in a plague mask leans against the wall, his leather beak pointing directly at me. The eyes and head on the mask cover his entire face.

My back hits the tile behind me, and I'm about to scream, but his voice keeps the scream locked in my throat. "I wouldn't do that if I were you. I'll just leave, and then they will think you're crazy and unstable. Seeing things. Hearing things that aren't there. Then you will tell them you think someone is watching you. What do you think they would do to you then?"

"Wh-o the fuck are you and why are you following me?"

When he tilts his head, dread spreads over me. The thought of being naked in the shower in front of a psycho stalker has left my mind, replaced by the pure instinct of survival. Or, I'm losing my mind. No, I'm not losing my mind. In the corridor, he had been watching me. Waiting. Gia said that she couldn't identify the individuals at the church where the lifeless barista was crucified and were all wearing masks like they were protecting themselves against the plague. The plague meaning the death of evil. And, recognition.

The silence stretches and the shower runs like rain between me and the man in front of me. I look down and cover myself with one hand on my sex and my left arm across my breasts.

"Don't be afraid, Jess. I'm here to save you from yourself."

I shake my head, frustrated by him deviating from my question. "That is not what I asked. I asked who the fuck you are and why you're here," I snap. The water tickles the skin on my face, but I refuse to remove my hand to relieve it. Is this some kind of joke?

My eyes focus on what he is wearing, trying to figure out if there is a clue to who he is and if he is here to kill me, but I don't see a gun or a knife. Maybe they sent him to get rid of me, the Order simply waiting for an opportunity. He could use his hands and snap by neck.

My body shivers as he stands still, the creepy mask with the pitch-black eyes aimed right at me. I look to see if I can run out and scream for help, but he isn't a small man. He has broad shoulders and fills the space. He's wearing a black long-sleeve shirt with black slacks and black leather gloves. I can't see an inch of skin, which makes trying to identify him futile and that is what scares me the most, besides the fact that I'm naked in the shower and he could do whatever he wanted to me.

"I was getting to that part, but you won't let me finish. It is impolite to not allow someone to finish answering a question when asked."

"Fuck you."

He points his leather gloved finger toward me in a sweeping motion gesturing no. "Not tonight. In time. I would like to get to know you first. It makes the experience that much better."

"Please leave me alone. Get out of here and I'll act like this never happened."

"I'm sorry but I can't do that."

"Then I'm going to scream and they will come running in here."

"Try it and you will suffer the consequences."

I move to the side and that is when I bolt. I try not to slip on the tile as I make my escape, but he is faster, and when he pushes me against the stall, I understand the mistake I just made. He is strong. Stronger than I thought he would be. His hand is over my mouth and the protruding beak of his mask is to the side of my neck. The hint of leather and smoke mixed with a cologne I have never smelled before fills my senses. It smells of spices and man. I close my eyes because I know he is not going to let go. I'm trapped. I'm fucked.

"Please," I plead, sounding muffled. "Let me go. I won't say anything. I know the rules."

He chuckles and it causes me to stop pleading as he mocks my attempt. "I don't believe in rules. I don't follow them because I'm not a puppet."

His voice is muffled behind the mask and my ears are trying to capture a hint of his voice, a sound to give me a clue. My legs are shaking, and it is not because I'm chilled. I'm scared. I'm terrified. The shaking has reached my hands and tears run down my cheeks.

"Don't cry for me. I prefer to hear your screams. It does things to me. It calms me. The same way it calms you when you get fucked." His fingers covered in smooth leather slide down the sides of my bare stomach, and I wonder how much he knows about me. Who is he and what does he want. "Let's take care of the little problem you're having, Jess. Scrubbing is obviously not working. It stings. It infects. It opens wounds."

"H-how do you know my name?" He is sliding his fingers over my skin down to the apex of my thighs, and at this point, I'm as good as dead. "What are you doing?" I ask.

"Keeping you from crying. I don't like the weak but I have found that you are not weak. You are just outnumbered. To answer your question. My name is Zero. Zero, because I don't exist. They see me, but I'm not really there. I hear and see things. I know things and when I want something, I get it."

"What do you want?" The tip of his finger grazes my clit, and I tense. Please, God. "I want you, Jess. The real you. The fucked-up version you hide from everyone. Even the three cocks you get off on on-campus and the other one that shall not be named. Am I right, Jess? The one that has you scrubbing your pretty skin until it turns the shade of red, hoping he bleeds out of your skin like an infection. The one that has you skittish, crying pathetically when the real you wants to kill. To destroy." He brushes the side of the smooth black mask over my cheek. "Have you ever liked someone, Jess? Truly wanted them dead and not to aid your sickness like a pill."

"Get fucked." I seethe under his hand.

He inhales and I shouldn't be pissing him off, but he knows too much. He slides his finger inside me, hitting a spot that has my mouth parting on a gasp.

"The thing about being sick like you, Jess, is that it's like a drug, and this––he rubs my clit with his thumb, causing my body to respond––"is what you need. Isn't it? The release to remove what you want to forget. A drug to take you to that place. The place you secretly wish to be. A nirvana of sorts."

I don't know how or why, but he gets me. He must be a psychologist or someone older with the way he speaks to me. He is someone that knows what suffering and wanting to escape feels like. My body betrays me and I moan when he increases the pressure, taking me off the edge, it is all I can think about, and nothing else. I hear him growl, lifting my leg and spreading my pussy wide, and God forgive me, I let him. I let a stranger finger-fuck me in the women's shower. I'm so messed up.

"Yes," I manage to say after he breaks me, and I feel it. The drug I crave. The one he knows I would do anything for. Release.

JESS

I WAKE UP WITH A START, bolting up from the bed. Naked. The chill freezing my body into stone. I look down at the skin on my thighs, watching the bumps rise all over my skin like an electric current. The twin comforter is on the floor. My hair is a mass of curls from not drying it like I usually do. Last night must have been a dream. An episode of my past trauma or something. There is no way it was real. He couldn't have been real. Swinging my legs over the bed to get up and get ready for class, I notice there is a piece of paper on my nightstand.

I place the comforter over my shoulders to ward off the chill and my stomach clenches when I see there is a note scrawled on a piece of paper I recognize from my notebook. My eyes dart over to where I left my bag and see that it was left open. Clearly, someone was in here last night.

Do you remember your heart pounding, screaming for its release? This is the moment where everything you thought was a dream, isn't.

We are real.

We are right.

Every tremor your skin made when I held you called to me. Do you remember, Jess? Do you remember coming apart for me? You are not strong enough to carry what you feel alone, Jess. But you have me. You can search for me in every stranger's eyes, trying to get that fix you so desire, only to find out that in the end, all you ever needed...was me. I'm immortal between the lines. You can see me, but I'm not really there. Only for you do I exist.

Zero

I drop the letter on the bed and slide my finger to the spot he touched. To the spot that gave me the release I needed, feeling the slight ache. I slide my fingers and rub myself and close my eyes, remembering the man in the plague mask and what he gave me without judgment. No face. Not even a name that seemed real, but he was *real*. He didn't hurt me like I thought he would. He just showed up like a shadow in the dark, peeling itself from the wall.

I pleasure myself to the thought of someone I can't see but only feel. I should be ashamed or feel crazy for what I allowed to happen, but I don't.

This is my secret. Apparently, a secret that can't leave the recess of my mind because my mystery man doesn't exist. There is nothing to report. Nothing to tell. No evidence except for me coming all over his leather-gloved fingers and me falling asleep in his arms, exhausted only to wake up alone.

No trace.

No fingerprints.

He could have done what he wanted and there was nothing I could have done about it. But he didn't and I wish I knew why.

JESS

AFTER CLASS, I enter the bar with the Babylon sign flashing as I make my way inside, looking for Gia at our usual spot in the same booth. She smiles as I slide in, but I notice her fidgeting.

"Is everything alright?" I ask.

Her dark hair looks shiny, even in the dim light as she nods. "Yeah, I'm just nervous with class and the other situation. Meaning, Warren. I haven't seen him, but I bet they are gunning for him. Waiting for when the time is right."

"What can I get you two girls?" The waiter asks, coming up to our booth with a smile.

"I'll have a Black Plague," I say with a smile. The fact that the mask is on the beer has me almost laughing at the irony.

Gia raises her brow. "Really?" I nod. She turns to the waiter. "Cranberry and vodka please."

Once the waiter leaves, she asks, "What's up with the beer?"

"I'm trying to blend in with the underground." At least we know why they chose to stock it here. We also know that this place isn't owned by some bar owner who got lucky years ago when he invested across the street from Kenyan."

She snorts. "I agree with that."

"Have you seen him?"

She knows I'm referring to Warren when she shakes her head slowly, looking at the bar's entrance every few seconds. If she only knew I'm just as paranoid because we both have a stalker.

I hear the squeak of the door to the bathroom open from the hallway in the back, and Veronica saunters over with that predatory smile of hers. Great. The beauty of evil. Just what we needed.

She walks over and slides in next to me. Gia's eyes narrow in her direction, and I can feel Veronica's eyes on me.

"How are the famous ladies of Kenyan doing this evening? I would have thought you would be out polishing."

She means fucking. Of course, that is all she thinks about. It is the first thing she talks about when she opens her mouth. It makes you wonder if she was groomed to be this way. Created by someone. It makes you feel sorry for her. Almost. If she wasn't so fucking evil.

"I wouldn't say famous," Gia replies.

Veronica whips her hair to the side and smiles with her freshly applied red lipstick, flashing a smile toward Gia. "You are fucking the Bedford twins, sweetheart. You live with them and practically breathe the same air. You are watched by people they employ when you think they are not watching. Everyone that values their life knows not to touch a hair on your head or the muff on your cunt."

"Who is everyone?" I interject.

Her head turns and her eyes slide down my face. "Everyone that needs to know. As for you––" She lowers her voice. "Six months of fucking left. You are on everyone's radar. Not a fan favorite amongst the ladies. Well...except me, of course. You know what I like. Don't you," she says, giving me a wink.

"Fuck off, Veronica." Reid's voice booms from behind the booth. Gia looks up and smiles, relieved by the interruption. Dravin and his brother slide in next to Gia and her cheeks blush.

It is crazy how you can't tell them apart. Even their names sound the same, even if they're spelled differently, but to Gia, it is like they are one and the same.

"I was being friendly. I don't bite. Right, Jess?"

I swallow the anger that begins to rise to the surface. Bitch. She loves to mention that day with Garret and Melissa. It was her games and my stupidity that ruined my freshman year, but she doesn't let that shit go. Everything is a game to her for whatever reason.

"Aww, Veronica. I thought you would have been over it by now. Are you not tired of trying to get the juice between my legs? It has been what...three years?"

She licks her lips like she just saw a juicy steak." She is insufferable but turns her face to address Reid instead.

"Don't worry, Reid. I won't ruffle her feathers, but I think it looks like she'd rather have a big dick pluck them out of her." She slides out of the booth. "Someone more likable, more prestigious," she continues leaning close, and Reid's eyes harden. Because she is mentioning Garret from that night and everyone knows that I have slept with him and Valen. "Not an uptight asshole with an arranged marriage hanging over his head."

Reid's jaw tics, and he clenches his teeth. "Leave. You got what you wanted." She snickers, walking away.

"Dude, it is a shame she is like that. I wonder what happened to her?" One of the twins says, and I'm assuming it's Dravin. The other twin has his hands laced through Gia's fingers studying me.

Reid has an arranged marriage to someone? I have a gut feeling it is to the woman I saw in his hotel that night. It is the only one he has ever paid attention to in that way. The only one that has the balls to come up to him the way she did. An ex-flame my ass.

I feel hurt by his failure to mention that piece of information before sinking his cock inside me. I look away, trying to convince myself that she can have him and she will, apparently.

I'm sure Valen has a similar agreement. I was right in turning him down the other day. I purse my lips and look at the entrance to the bar. My beer appearing in front of me when it slides over the glossy wood table from the waiter. I turn it in a circle, looking at the mask printed on the bottle like it's speaking to me. My secret.

"What are you thinking about?" Reid asks as he takes Veronica's spot next to me.

From the corner of my eye, I take my fill at how attractive Reid is. I like the tattoos on his skin and the smell of his cologne. The way his lashes always look like they are darkened with mascara, but I know they are natural.

I'm unsure why I'm drawn to him the way I am and can't shake it off. I'm still trying to figure it out. I'm trying to make sense of the emotions I buried after the first time I slept with him.

"Nothing. Me and Gia were catching up before Veronica announced your upcoming nuptials."

I feel him tense and I sense that wasn't supposed to be said and not many people know about it, or at least I wasn't supposed to know about it. A wave of hurt filters inside me because I loved how he made me feel in his arms, even if he was promised to another the whole time. I'm such a tramp. I let him fuck me in the elevator while his soon-to-be wife was downstairs on the first floor. I'm disgusted with myself. It's one thing to have sex with him or even with Valen, but not when they are promised to be married to someone else. I can also overlook the fact that he hasn't contacted since he dropped me off at the dorm.

"I think I better get going. I have class in the morning and I need to study if I plan to pass any of my classes and graduate, so I can get out of here." I give Gia a fake smile.

Gia's lips form a thin line and when she looks up, her eyes soften. "Are you sure?"

I sigh. "Yeah, I better get going. Thanks for meeting me. You two take care of my friend, okay?"

"Always," the twins answer at the same time. I push the untouched beer away from me and collect my things.

"You need a ride," Reid says, getting out to let me slide out as well.

"That's okay, I know my way back."

"I wasn't asking. I was telling."

I FOLLOW Reid out back because it is better than going against him, refusing his offer and running into Michael. No one needs to know about him because it doesn't matter. My plan with the sons of Kenyan looking out for me is unraveling fast. Michael has me exactly where he wants me. Trapped.

Reid unlocks his fancy sports car. The cold air whipping my unruly hair while he opens the door for me. "Curly today," he says, before closing the door and walking around to the driver's side and sliding in the driver's seat. "I like it."

He is probably trying to flatter me because he fucked up. Typical guy move. He pulls out of the parking lot and turns in the opposite direction. I furrow my brows and ask, "Where are you taking me? The dorms are in the opposite direction."

"I'm taking you to eat. You haven't had dinner, have you?"

He is right, but it's nothing a good vending machine on the first floor of the dorms can't fix. I'm used to it by now, being on a strict budget.

I nervously slide my hands between my thighs. "I'm good."

"Liar," he teases.

I snort. "Look who is talking about lying. You're engaged to be married. It would have helped to know that part about you before I became your fuck buddy."

I see his hands tense on the steering wheel, and I know I have no right or claim over him, but he could have said something. He could have shared that little detail about him and where I stood, besides being his Prey and him taking advantage of me. But he doesn't have to, does he? None of them do. They can do who they want, what they want, and how they want it.

"I don't want to talk about it and I'm sorry I made you think you were a whore by calling you one. It is not my style, but you love to push me... more than anyone."

"Good to know."

"What do you mean?"

"That I push you."

"Do you like pushing me, Jess? Do you like when I punish you?"

As he maneuvers the car down the street, I watch his forearms flex under his fitted long-sleeve shirt. My eyes slide over the side of his face. Was that what he was doing in the elevator? Punishing me.

"Where are you taking me?"

"To eat. I'm taking you out to eat," he repeats.

"Why?"

"Because I like watching your ass fill out those leggings you wear. I wouldn't want you to lose it. I'm looking out for your best interests. Some men like something to hold on to when they take a woman from behind or when she is on top slamming her ass on his thighs."

"Of course, what a great reason," I say with a drip of sarcasm.

He turns his head slightly and grins. "Your ass will thank me."

His phone rings through the speakers, interrupting our conversation. He presses the button and Valen's voice comes through. "Where are you taking her? Dravin said that she left with you the bar when I arrived."

"I'm taking her out to eat. Why? Jealous."

"When it comes to her, of course, I am. Right, Jess? You know how I feel about you, sweetheart."

All games. He knows I'm in the car and listening to their conversation. He is probably upset that I turned him down, or maybe not, maybe he got over it. Maybe he doesn't care, and I'm making things up.

"I'll see you there," Reid says, hanging up.

"H-he's coming?"

"Shh. It's a surprise."

JESS

FOR THE NEXT TWENTY MINUTES, I relax in the car, watching the streetlights speed by, as the car glides down the road, wondering how the shadow of my past can find me so quickly to the point I can't escape. It feels like hope is a lie in disguise, like a trick of the light.

"Control" by Puddle of Mudd plays in the car and the back of Reid's hand brushes against mine. I should pull away, tell him to stop, but the need to be caressed overpowers what I should do.

There is something about the way that he touches me that is soothing. Possessive. The song lyrics that surround us cause my mouth to lift in a grin. My eyes find his dark black ones for a second, and he winks. I feel the pressure between my legs, begging him for more.

My eyes follow each stroke of his fingers as they slide over my skin until the spell is broken when he pulls into the valet of a hotel similar to the one he took me to the first time. The one that he owns.

He opens his door, and I look out the window and notice a fire pit in front with tables around it. People are deep in conversation, eating their meals from the restaurant attached to the hotel. It's something you see in a movie and nothing I have ever been to personally. I look down at my simple winter coat, feeling out of place compared to the nice ones seen on the women seated at the tables.

"Um, I don't think I'm dressed——" I trail off as he finishes getting out of the car and barks at the valet, trying to open my door.

He has this thing where he doesn't let the valet open the door for me. I thought it was just at his hotel, but it's a Reid thing.

Instead of heading toward the restaurant like I expected, we head into the warmth of the impressive, modern opulence of the hotel. He walks up to the front desk, and I admire how he commands a room, not paying attention to anyone except those who give him what he wants.

He heads to the elevator with a key card in hand, and I silently follow him. He doesn't say a word while we wait inside the elevator. I find my voice once I see the elevator climb to the top floor.

"Why are we here?"

When we reach the designated floor, the doors automatically glide open and make a beeping sound, and he steps out. "Like I said, dinner is on me. No elevators this time."

Letting the mention of the elevator slide, I bite my lip. I know he is trying to lighten the mood. Regretfully, I run my fingers through my curly hair, upset at myself for not straightening it. I hate when it frizzes up.

A smile forms on his lips as we step out into the hallway. "Leave it. I told you I liked it."

I stop fiddling with my hair, adjust my medium-sized handbag on my shoulders, and let my hands fall to my sides.

After walking through a modern hallway with patterned carpet and contemporary lighting, we reach the door of a suite. The key card scans, and the entrance to the penthouse opens to an expansive room--more like an apartment that greets me with plush carpet and marble floors. To my right is a big dining area and kitchen. The doors leading to the balcony beside the living room look like they don't exist. They are so clear, it seems like they forgot to install them. In the middle of the living room are two L-shaped sofas and a huge coffee table supported by chrome legs.

"Wow," I breathe.

Knock. Knock.

I turn around as Reid pulls the door open, allowing Valen to walk through. His blond hair sticks out everywhere, like he has been running his hands through it. He is wearing a thick black jacket over dark jeans and boots. He has that sexy grunge look, like he just left the stage from a concert.

"Hey, gorgeous. Has he behaved?"

My eyes follow Reid as he makes his way toward the dining table, where there are silver covers over plates I didn't notice before, and a place setting for three.

I gesture to the dining table. "Hi...did you guys plan all of this?" I ask. Valen walks toward me, greeting me on the cheek with a simple kiss, sliding my jacket over my wrist like he is inspecting a child after a fall, looking at my wrists. They obviously talked about me, and Reid told him what happened to me, in detail. My thoughts go to the mystery man that visited me in the bathroom. *Zero.* Does he know? Did he notice them?

"Yes and no. It depends on how you look at it. We plan on the fly." He slides one of my curls behind my ear. "There is nothing we can't do, and we practically own everything or know who does."

The sons of Kenyan are also business entrepreneurs, schooled since birth. I wonder if college is mandatory or if they could actually choose. It isn't my business, but I'm curious.

"You didn't have to go through the trouble."

"We did," Reid says, standing by the dining table and pouring sparkling water into glasses as I notice an unopened bottle of wine for one.

My eyes meet Valen's light ones. They remind me of the fall foliage of colors. Moss greens with a touch of blue in certain places and the lightest part of honey in the center. It reminds me he has that boyish charm under-neath the bad boy demeanor.

Reid walks up behind me and leans close. His fingers slide on my shoul-ders under my jacket, pushing it over my shoulders. I can feel the heat coming from behind me and his fingers ghosting the skin behind my neck.

"We want to see you while we eat," Valen says, sliding the sleeves off my arms and removing the rest, leaving me in my sweater and leggings.

We are seated at the dining table with Reid at the head, myself on his right, and Valen on his left, facing me. The smell of perfectly-cooked meat takes over, making my belly groan. Reid lifts the silver cover, and the most glorious steak I have ever seen sits in its juices, promising flavor on my tongue.

AFTER DINNER, the plates are cleared from the table by room service. Valen takes me by the hand to the bedroom and my mind begins to spin because I have never been with them at the same time, and to be honest, it isn't some-thing I have thought about. It is always one or the other. An intimate trans-action to which I always agree and nothing more.

He pauses, turns to face me at the foot of the bed, leans close to my ear, and whispers, "Is this what you wanted yesterday?"

My eyes meet his, and I know I can't lie. I'm ashamed to admit it, but I will because it's true, it's what I wanted. What I needed. This is what my life consists of.

"Yes."

"Reid wants to watch. Is that okay, gorgeous? Is it okay for him to watch me fuck you?"

There is a chair in the corner of the room, and Reid takes a seat, removing his jacket. His face is stoic, but his eyes are dark like the sea. He doesn't say a word. He just watches us, and it feels like we are the only ones in the room, and it's not Valen and me. It is Reid and me.

Reid nods, giving me the signal that it is okay. That he agrees to watch me with Valen.

It's okay, beautiful. Act like he isn't even here."

I pinch my brows, a little confused, but he is trying to make me feel comfortable. He is giving me what I wanted yesterday, not denying me.

"You don't need a man to leave marks that hurt, gorgeous. Unless you like it, Jess. Do you?" he asks, slowly lifting my sweater over my head.

"Do I what?" I ask, dropping my hands. He removes my bra with expert fingers, sliding the straps down my arms and flinging it across the room. My nipples are like twin peaks under his gaze, a chill awakening my skin for what is to come. What I need.

What I crave.

To be set on fire burning the poison.

Valen is so sweet and kind to me. His touch is soft, but there is something that only the man sitting in the chair in the corner of the room can give me. The spark I need to light my fire that leaves me in a mess of ashes.

But he isn't available. He belongs to another; as much as it hurts and pains me, I must accept it. I refuse to be the very thing I never wanted to be, a man's secret. A secret he hides because he is ashamed of being seen as something to be used, and I'm afraid that is the very thing I have become to him, to them.

"Do you like feeling pain on your skin? The marks it creates? Is that what you like?"

I shake my head slightly and answer, "No."

Valen lowers his head, and his lips brush over mine, whispering, "I wanted to make sure."

He presses his lips to mine, kissing me gently. My tongue peeks out and plays with the black metal piercing on his bottom lip. He groans and devours my lips in his, sucking on my tongue.

He lifts me, laying me on the soft bed with white sheets like a soft cloud. My head turns slightly, and my eyes meet pitch-black ones. Reid's chest rises and falls, and I sense he is battling something within him, but I brush it off and give my attention to the man showing me attention. The one that always asks if I'm okay and gifts me with his playful, gentle touches, making sure to wash away what I don't want.

"Valen," I breathe when the cold hair hits my thighs, and his hands spread my legs after removing my leggings and panties.

Valen hovers over me and I break eye contact with Reid for a split second. But then my eyes find Reid's again and he stills like a statue. He blinks hard, and he is not watching Valen between my legs. He is studying me.

"Condom," I blurt.

Valen nods and produces one from his back pocket. He tears the wrapper with his teeth, and he smiles. "If that is what you want."

Trust me. When you find out the reason, you will thank me. I'm thankful Michael always wears one, but Valen loves to go bare with me, and I don't know who he has been with. He is younger and has a beautiful heart underneath his craziness, but he is very sexually active. I'm sure he gets tested but still. It is better to be safe.

But if there is a guy a girl should choose to be with, it would be Valen, but I'm not a girl that comes from his circle. I'm the trash they allow to play with, like scrapbook paper. Something that they use to have fun and then discard, like the condom he has donned. Disposed of when done to avoid leaving a trace.

The tip of his cock is at my entrance, and my eyes find Reid's again. His eyes are still fixed on mine and not on what Valen is doing. I feel the tip brush against my slit, I arch my back, and my lips part, anticipating the feeling of being peeled apart. The sensation overpowers the last. The feel of something I want versus something I didn't ask for but had to accept.

Reid's nostrils flare, but his eyes harden as he watches my face, and I wonder what he sees through his eyes. Does he like to watch? Is he mad? Jealous?

But I know better because I'm just a good time to someone like Reid.

Valen groans, and I moan when he slides into me, but my eyes never leave Reid. Not when Valen kisses me while he fucks me. Not when I moan his name to never stop, or when I come on a scream or when my cheeks flush because I want it to be Reid.

When Valen pulls out of me and gives my pussy a soft kiss, I watch Reid quietly get up from the chair like a ghost in the room. He leans over the bed, grips me by the back of my neck, firmly locking me into place, and gets close. He licks my parted lips. He straightens, releasing me from his hold and walking out of the room. I'm stunned, aroused, and confused, staring at his back when he leaves without a backward glance. A tear escapes the corner of my eye.

For the first time, I feel it. The sting of a piece of my heart breaking for a man.

JESS

VALEN DROPPED me off at the dorm and walked me to my room. He didn't say anything on the way. It was like nothing happened, and we didn't have sex with Reid in the room; what was weird was that Valen was okay with it. It didn't bother him that I was looking at another man while he fucked me. It seemed normal. He got me off, and he got what he wanted. But I still feel empty.

Valen gives me a peck on the lips and ensures I'm safely inside. For some reason, I feel like a cheap date.

If Zero is watching me right now, he hasn't made it known. I still walk back to my dorm room paranoid, but I've given up expecting to see him. I have accepted I'm damaged, and my bandage is the men I use for sex to cover the wound that I know will leave a scar or, worse, a gaping wound that never closes.

When I look at myself in the mirror in the silence of the night, I see the parts of me missing. I'm falling apart, leaving pieces of me everywhere. I wonder when I leave how much of me will be left. I wish I could move time faster so I don't have to watch myself fall into an empty hole, hoping there will be something left when I reach the bottom.

When I'm done feeling sorry for myself in the mirror, I turn to find a piece of paper on my bed. It is old, like it came from a leather diary found in an ancient library. The red script is elegantly scrawled over crème fine paper as I take it between my fingers, feeling the thickness.

Mistakes you have made are filled with regret you cannot shed. Your hands slide over your skin, washing away filthy secrets you dare not tell. Eventually, they will burn your skin. That is the part of you that I will take away because every time you try to say the name across your lips, it never reaches that point, only digging yourself deeper into the soil until you make a grave for your soul.

When you think it is over and the pain is dormant, I will always be there when you think I'm not. Watching you.

I will always be where the darkness and the light meet, waiting until you realize I'm already there when you cannot see.

Z

I re-read the letter three times because he writes in riddles. I don't understand what he means, but if he is always watching me, this means that he isn't going to stop. My mind is spinning a million miles a minute, wondering where my fate is headed. Death or destruction.

I stare up at the ceiling, hoping for a different life. A life where love and trust meet and mix into something beautiful like the colors the world has created.

A kaleidoscope of colors morphing into each other, creating a peaceful paradise.

A place where there is no regret and nothing but good things to come, but where I come from and where I am now, it all seems like a pipe dream. A well you are trying to crawl out of, and when you think you reach the top and are about to climb out, you slip and fall right back to the bottom.

My eyes drift closed, trying to stay awake in case Zero makes an appearance. I have so many questions to ask, but my eyes feel heavy with sleep, and I fall into the dark abyss, waiting for the memories I try to forget to appear. The ones that play on repeat.

It is always the same.

I wake up trying to breathe, looking around and seeing double. Re-living the moment of the first night Michael took advantage of me. My vision is blurred, and the sting of the burn between my legs leaks out, mixed with fluid and my innocence. Tears fall down my cheeks like blood from the shame.

I wake up, bolting upright from the small bed, like I'm being pushed to the water's surface and gasp for air. My body sags in relief when I realize it is just a dream. The sunlight streams through the small window, but the empty bed where Gia used to sleep is now occupied by a masked figure. *Zero.*

My body trembles in fear because it's one thing in thinking you can handle someone's presence when you feel ready to confront them. It is another when they finally show up. The black mask with the long beak of a bird stares back at me like a crow watching its prey.

I let out a breath of air, making tiny half-moons on the palms of my hands with my blunt nails, seeing if this is real and I'm not going fucking crazy.

I lick my dry lips. "What are you doing here?"

He cocks his head. "Bad dreams. Suffocating, aren't they?"

My eyes sting because he isn't wrong. I comb the knots of my curly hair with my fingers and respond. "The bad ones always are." My eyes scan his black pants and fitted dress shirt, trying to look for a clue of who he his. "Do you always wear a mask?"

"Don't we all."

I gesture my hand over my face. "I meant literally. Isn't it hot under there?"

"No, but I like that you can't see me."

" Why, are you ugly? Do you have imperfections you don't want others to see?"

"We all have imperfections. We hide what we don't want others to see, but this is me. This is my face and what I choose to wear. What...I choose to let you see. The same way you don't want me to see the real you. The part of you that you hide behind that fake smile you plant on your face for your friends to see. So, you see, we all wear masks." He stretches his legs over the bed and leans against the wall. "You intrigue me. I like the fact that you are all alone. What intrigues me the most is how you deal with your emotions and the sickness you carry inside."

"Is it because I'm considered Prey? Because you see me as vulnerable and want to take advantage of me?"

I'm getting annoyed. He may have power because he is one of them, but I won't sit here and let him taunt me and toy with me like I'm a pet he wants to keep in a cage.

He chuckles, a deep vibration coming from his throat. His voice is deep when he speaks. Demanding, dark, and twisted. "I don't think you are weak. I think you are underestimated."

"What are you doing?" He moves to get up from the bed, and I shrink back when he stops at the edge. His gloved fingers pull the comforter back, exposing my legs.

The tip of his mask is aimed at me, and I can feel the heat from his eyes watching me. I don't know how, but I do. It is electrifying, not being able to see what he looks like.

"I'm showing you the nature of us. The line where friendship and lovers exist. A place few people ever find."

I close my thighs, swallow deeply, and let out a shaky breath. "You're crazy."

He shakes his head slowly. "No, Jess. The ones that hurt you are crazy because I'm your savior. Your lord. The one you crave and beg for on your knees when you need saving because God won't listen. Your secret weapon to survive the depths of hell you are in–– the gasoline to your fire. The one that no one will see coming. Isn't that what you need, Jess? Your very own dark demon. A demon you can unleash upon those who have wronged you."

"What the fuck are you?" I ask through clenched teeth, but inside, I'm quaking in fear.

"I'm the anarchy of the Order." He cocks his head. "The secret...no one talks about." He holds his leather-gloved hand like I'm drowning and I need a savior, "Take it. Let me show you."

I hesitate for a second, and I remind myself if he was here to kill me, he would have done it by now. I place my hand in his, and he pulls me to stand. When I put my feet on the floor, I'm reminded of how much taller he is than me. He steps to the side and pulls me toward the mirror over my desk. I can see myself in the reflection. My messy bed-hair frames my face. My lips are swollen from sleep.

I tilt my head to look at him. "What?" I mock.

He stands behind me. "Look at yourself in the mirror, Jess," he demands. He tugs on my hair so I don't look away and holds me firmly with his hands, watching the reflection of the bird mask next to my ear. "That is what love looks like." He places the palm of his gloved hand over mine, and I can feel the fine leather like a second skin. He guides my hand to the apex of my thighs over the fabric of my boy shorts. "Come for me. I want you to see what I see when you come. The need you crave that chases the sickness away. Show me, Jess."

"Why?" I croak. My eyes brimming with tears. His words bring out emotions I thought I had buried inside me about the way I view myself.

"Your pain is relieved by my pleasure, and my pleasure is the drug you would secretly die for. The high running through your veins. The feeling that will take you to the place we both meet. The blur. You'll cry when I'm not inside you, giving you what you want. I'm everywhere, Jess. In your head. In your cunt. In that forbidden hole, I have yet to explore. Even when you are with them, I'm inside you. Always. Nothing or no one will ever be able to tear me away from you now that I have claimed you as mine. A soul mate of sorts. Now...show me," he says, his breathing audible from the mask. "Come for me. Break for me, my little Sparrow."

My head falls against his chest as I watch him in the mask. He looks at me through the mirror with the tiny black saucers from his mask like a window peeking into my soul. He lifts my shirt over my head, releasing my breasts and leaving me in only my boy shorts. My hand slips inside the band, and his hand hovers over mine like I'm teaching him how to pleasure me.

I can hear his breathing through the mask pick up and the stiffness of his cock through the fabric of his pants. I rub the pad of my finger over my clit, and his leather-clad finger is moving with mine, wrapped like a vine rubbing in circles, making me wet. Preparing me for my pleasure.

I rest my head, rolling against his hard chest, breathing slowly. My chest rises and falls in a rhythm. His other gloved hand slowly glides over the skin of my ribs, causing electric currents to pass through me like a storm that is brewing, lighting a fire inside me. The spark I need to fuel the flames. He dips his finger inside me, and I moan. My breasts are high, and my nipples are hard like pearls.

"More?"

I nod, and he does it again, deeper this time. I moan, grinding my hips, seeking more of his thick finger. My finger joins his inside me, and I'm wet, feeling the double penetration. I'm so wet, tiny drops drip down my thighs. I bite my lip, and his other hand rubs lazy circles over the nipples of my breasts.

"You're beautiful. I love watching you. Even in the dark, you shine for me. In your sleep, when your demons try to take you to that place, I will find them and burn them all into ashes for you. I promise, my little Sparrow. When you fall, I'll catch you."

He rubs his hard cock against my lower back, and I think I'm going crazy. I'm letting a stranger do things to me that feel so right. He feels so right. I never knew that fear and pleasure could be so good.

When he pushes deeper, my eyes widen, and I gasp. "More. Please."

He continues to meet me stroke for stroke until I'm on the brink of a climax, but he pulls out, not giving me my release.

"Please," I beg.

He raises his gloved fingers, glistening with my arousal, to my lips, and slides them inside my mouth so I can taste myself. I lick and slide my tongue over and over, licking them clean.

He growls, and I bite my lip. "Remember to do that when you suck my cock, and I paint your pretty face with my cum. In time," he says in a raspy voice. "Do you want to come, Jess?"

"Yes."

"Lie on the bed and show me my cunt."

My cheeks flame, and I look away. "Too harsh, my little Sparrow? You'll get used to it." He taps my ass gently. "Now spread your legs for me. I want to see what's mine. Don't worry, I won't stick my dick in your pussy. When you're ready, I'll fuck you. I'll fuck them all out of you, and the only cock you will be begging for will be mine, like it's your salvation."

I sit in bed, and he waves his hand so I scoot back and part my thighs. He kneels on the mattress between my legs. His hands slide up my thighs. "Open." I let my thighs fall. "Wider," he demands.

My thighs are spread open as far as they can go, wondering what he will do next, hoping he takes his mask off. He slaps my pussy, and the sting mixes with pleasure, causing my throat to release a whimper.

"Play with your tits." My hands slide over my chest to tease my nipples, and he slides two gloved fingers inside my mouth. "Good girl," he says when my lips wrap around the leather, wetting his fingers with my tongue. "I can't wait to taste you, my little Sparrow."

I arch my back and look at the mask. I want to rip it off so I can see his face to match the man's voice. "Taste me," I taunt.

He laughs through his nose. "Clever girl. Soon. Patience. Besides, we have to get to know each other first. Showing you my face will ruin things. It's more exciting this way. I promise you when I let you see me, you won't be disappointed, but I need you to trust me first."

"It is not fair that you can see me, and I can't see you."

I know what I'm saying sounds crazy––childish even, and maybe it is, but I want to see what he looks like.

"Would it matter if you were blind? You wouldn't be able to see me then. How do blind people fuck? They can't see, but they can feel." He slides his finger inside me on the last part, and my hand flies to his wrist, holding him to the spot I crave.

"Mm, right there." The man is a magician with his fingers full of deception. It feels so good.

"Play with your tits, or I'll pull them out," he warns.

I release my grip on his wrist and do as he asks: rubbing my nipples while he rubs his thumb over my clit. He hovers over my body. The crotch of his pants right where his hand is between us. The mask above me casts a shadow with its long beak. I want to touch his chest, but then I remember his warning. If I remove my hands, he will release his gloved fingers inside me, not giving me the orgasm that my body's begging for.

He holds himself, placing his palm near my head on the mattress, and I watch as he fingers me in a rhythm. My walls clench around his fingers, and a deep rumble escapes his throat.

"Fuck, you're tight."

I grind my pussy against his fingers, finally seeking my release when I come. He removes his fingers and presses his hard dick against my pussy, ruining the fabric of his pants. He pushes into me, dry-fucking me, and I can feel his hard length. He's big and thick, promising me more.

He smears my arousal all over his pants, and I wonder why, but nothing with him surprises me, and it shouldn't. His hands are spread around my hips, his fingers gripping the sides of my ass while he angles his head, careful he doesn't poke me with the mask.

"You made a mess. A beautiful mess. When I make you come, the light in your eyes burns like a thousand suns defying darkness. When I leave out that door, I truly didn't leave. I'm around you, even if you can't see me. And I'll always come back. Only for you."

He releases me. He slides off the bed, moves to my desk, and writes something on paper. Something he won't say in case I forget. I think that is why he does it. So that I don't ever question myself or doubt that this isn't real. That what transpired in this very room is not just a figment of my imagination.

I cover my body with the bed sheet, and he opens the door and walks out. I look at the time, six a.m. No one is up this early. Classes don't start until much later. I look at the paper from my notepad to see what he wrote after he leaves.

 Music is like planting a seed in the soul-filling the emptiness inside you.
  I Hold You by CLANN
  Haunting you forever,
  Z

ZERO

I HAVE BEEN WATCHING her for some time now. Watching her break herself into pieces, trying to find the glue that would hold her together. I didn't mean to frighten her by showing up the way I did, but she could not know who I was.

I'm the Order's secret.

The Consortium's ally, so to speak. The one that walks in the shadows when judgment must be made.

Jess has become my obsession. My need to exist, and I will not let anyone harm her. I will save her, even from myself, because I'll do anything for her.

I would burn the world into ashes, some would say, for the one they love, but for her, I would build a world where she felt loved. Her nirvana. A place where no one could touch her unless she wanted them to do so.

For now, I will visit her in the dark, in secret. I will show her pleasure and how to deal with her pain, peeling her apart before I break her. It's sad to think I have to, but there isn't any other way. She was never meant to exist for me in the first place.

An innocent, underneath all her sin. I taste it as I slide my fingers in my mouth with the wetness of her arousal on my fingers. Women like her don't exist to monsters like me.

I close my eyes and savor the sweet honey that is Jesse Sharpe. An angel living amongst demons. My angel. My little Sparrow with broken wings.

I wonder who keeps my little bird from flying. A cage was created just for her to keep her from being free. A predator grooming her for their selfish games.

A manipulator.

He walks among us, projecting the evil spirit of fear into Jess. Tormenting her. When I find him or what crevice he crawled out of, God can't help him. Not even the devil. Because...I'm here.

JESS

I AM AT THE LIBRARY, with its old bookcases and shiny Mac workstations. A stunning contrast to the historic buildings within Kenyan. The more time that passes, the older this place seems. I examine my earbuds from the dollar store and discover that I need an adaptor to use them with the computer. *Damn it!*

I really needed to hear the song he dedicated. I can't use a prepaid phone since I can't afford applications or internet service. I could ask Gia for her phone, but I'd feel awkward asking her for it and explaining why. I know she wouldn't judge me because Gia is perfect in that way.

I haven't contacted her because she is going through her personal shit with the Bedford twins, recovering from Warren's attempt and planning her wedding. I'm looking around when someone taps my shoulder. I jolt and turn to see who it is.

"Woah, I'm sorry." Marc says with raised hands.

I place a hand over my chest to calm my racing heart. "You scared me."

"It's okay. I was just wondering if you needed help." He grins.

I hold the cheap earbuds in my hands by the string. "I was trying to connect these, but I don't have the fancy Bluetooth kind."

His expression softens. "Oh, I can fix that."

He moves to the help center, where his desk is located, and holds out a fancy pair with the Bluetooth function. "Here, you can borrow mine. Anytime."

I take them and smile at his kindness. Marc has that boy-next-door look. Fitted Henley and khakis with a pair of Sperry shoes. When I stopped by the library several times, I noticed his brown hair falling over his brow. I also noticed he needed to wear his glasses. It was the only time I had come to the library to study when people wouldn't stare at me because of what happened freshman year when I noticed him. Now, I try to remain unseen.

"Thank you, Marc," I say softly, turning around and heading back to the computer.

I connect the headset and listen to the song Zero wrote down. I hear the words. The music is ethereal and haunting. The sound of rain in the background mixed with the soft vocals underneath a storm of thunder. It reminds me of him, of me, of us. The words call to me like he is holding me in the echoes of chaos when no one has understood or bothered to pay attention to the pain in my heart. A single tear rolls down my cheek when the song ends. Not because I'm sad. But because I didn't want it to end.

When the song's finished playing, I walk toward Marc with the headphones in hand to express my gratitude as he looks up." Thank you," I tell him.

He twirls a pen between his fingers but doesn't take them. "You can hold on to them. We can meet at the café around two, and you can return them to me then. It would give you time to use them for a bit longer."

I'm about to turn him down, but then the sound of something large falling has me whipping my head around to see a large bookshelf collapse, causing books to rain down and the wood to break into splinters.

Marc jumps out of his seat toward the catastrophic mess.

"Shit," he mutters when I catch up to him.

The whole shelf has tumbled down, and books are scattered everywhere. The librarian makes an appearance, looking like an old caretaker of an estate. "Oh, dear. What a mess. I wonder how that happened?" she asks, dumbfounded, with her hand on her hips. "Marc, would you stay and help me clear all these books?"

Marc's face falls and I feel bad, but I have to get to class. I'm relieved I didn't have to turn him down on the offer to meet at the café. There was no need to hold on to the headphones when I don't have anything to connect them to, but I'm saved from having to explain.

"I would love to help but I have class."

Marc looks like he wants the ground to swallow him up. With a look of disappointment and disbelief, he stares at the mountain of books and the ruined bookshelf like they will magically right themselves. I hate to leave him with the librarian on his own, but I can't miss class. It's economics and I haven't begun the assignment that is due in two days.

I walk into class and my eyes are scanning, searching for Michael. Fear claws my insides for what he has in store for me. I have been so consumed with my masked stalker that there is nothing I can think about other than his words, his letters, and his touch.

I take a seat and watch as people filter in the classroom. I didn't realize I was holding my breath when I finally see Michael come through the door. His eyes immediately scan the room and land on mine. His dirty blond hair is styled with gel, making it stiff. I bet it would catch fire if I threw a match at his head. It would be a good way to get revenge for what he has done to me.

"Hey, I plan to take you to a party on Friday. Be ready at seven," he says softly when he passes by my desk.

"I can't," I reply, watching his eyes harden in satisfaction. "You're not the only one I go out with."

I need to throw the sons of Kenyan out there. Maybe he will back off. It isn't a lie. He raises a brow in challenge and catches his bottom lip between his teeth.

"Is that right?"

"It is," I deadpan.

"I guess I'll see you at the party. Make time for me after."

Asshole. I'd rather walk on glass.

JESS

I WALK INTO MY DORM, shut the door behind me, and close my eyes. I'm trying to hold on. I prefer to be Valen and Reid's plaything any day of the week than be Michael's. My phone rings, and I pull it out of my jacket pocket, hearing the sound of a basic telephone. I hate the generic ringtone. I feel like an old lady who doesn't know how to use a smartphone and needs a phone with large numbers because she can't see very well.

I answer and smile as my mother's sweet voice comes through. "Jesse, is that you?"

"Yes, Mom. It's me. How are you?"

"I'm fine. The bar is doing well, and I still have my hours," she says, and I sag in relief. The bastard has kept his word.

"That's great."

"Yeah, I was wondering if you could come home to visit. I miss you, and your birthday is coming up. You didn't let me get you anything for Christmas like always. When was the last time you had a Christmas gift, Jesse? How about a birthday gift?" she asks.

Tears sting like needles in my eyes because I didn't think it would make her feel bad for me not allowing her to get me anything. "You always try to get me something. I don't want you to work more hours because of me. I was nine, and I didn't want to worry you. I'm fine. I'm almost done and then I can get a real good job, Momma, and come and get you. We could move somewhere really nice. And get that kitchen you always wanted in a nice house. No more trailers and cold winters."

"Oh, Jesse. They don't make them like you anymore. Girls around here are on drugs and drinking. Sleeping around and getting pregnant. God was listening to me when I had you. You deserve a nice man that loves you. How about that young man Michael?"

Silent tears run down my cheeks. I would do anything for her. Anything. If she only knew he was a wolf wrapped in sheep's clothing. She thinks he is a great guy looking out for her because he is my friend. If I told her the truth, she would quit on the spot, and then what? My mother would be homeless, which means I would be homeless because I would have to drop out.

"I think he mentioned he had a girlfriend. Guys like him don't date girls like me, Momma. It's different for me. He is just an old friend from school who needs good help at the bar. You're a good worker. You never miss or call out."

"Did he say that? Is it because you live in a trailer? He's ashamed, Jesse. I'm sorry, baby. I tried. I really did, but your father left me; this was the best I could do for us. If that boy doesn't think you are good enough, he isn't worth your time. You're really smart, and you were top of your class. You worked hard and never skipped school to hang out with a boy. You didn't even go to prom."

She keeps bringing that up. She wanted me to have a prom and for a boy to pick me up, so she could take a picture of me in a nice dress. I couldn't go. I could never tell her what Michael did. I close my eyes, ashamed of hurting her feelings.

"I'm sorry about the prom thing. It was stupid, and they didn't have a dress in my size. They were all sold out. Besides, I didn't have a date."

I didn't know what else to tell her. We were broke with no money, barely making it, and no one wanted to take the trailer trash whore to prom.

"Alright, I get it. But could you come to visit your momma? I miss you, Jesse. You're all I've got. I can send you money for a plane ticket and pick you up from the airport?"

"No, please don't do that. I gotta go. I can't go over my minutes. I love you. I promise I will come home to see you soon." I hang up, acting like my minutes ran out, feeling like a horrible daughter. I know why she is insisting I go see her. She wants to do something for my birthday.

I hear the door open and sag in relief when it's Gia. "Hey. I didn't want to call you because of the minute thing. Are you sure you don't want me to get you a phone?" She pauses and frowns when she sees me crying. "Woah. Who did it? I'll call the twins right now, and they will kick his ass."

I laugh. "You would do that. I just got off the phone with my mom and feel bad. I don't want her to spend a dime trying to get me home, and I feel bad for hurting her feelings because I didn't go to prom or have a social life."

"Oh, that sucks. Do you need money? I could ask?"

I shake my head. "No, please. Don't do that. I'll be fine."

"Is that why you eat from the vending machine and drink coke at the bar when it's ladies' night and the drinks are free instead of finishing your beer?"

She figured out my hustle.

I scrunch up my nose. "Is it that obvious?"

"Kinda. I figured it out since it is the only time you are out. Since I have been here, you don't date. You hate parties, but I know the reason for that one. And you hardly use your car."

"Gas prices are high. Walking is good exercise."

She snorts. "Not in this cold. That is why I came to get you."

"What? Why? Where are we going?" I ask, wiping my face with a tissue.

"Dravin's."

"I don't think that is a good idea."

"Why not? Is it because of Reid? I saw the look on your face when Veronica mentioned his arranged marriage. You like him, don't you?"

"He's off-limits." I manage to say, not admitting to her that I do or how I truly feel.

Not just physically or because of the hot sex. I know he isn't the type to sweep you off your feet. He isn't soft or romantic. He's hard and hot. At least with me, he doesn't see me in the romantic way you read about in romance novels. He has never treated me like he is interested in anything more, and I have accepted that you can't change someone.

Gia sits on her old bed, facing me. "You didn't say you didn't, though. Would you still be interested if he wasn't off-limits because he is marrying some chick?"

I toss a pencil from my desk at her, and she moves to the side, dodging it and giggling. "You do like him. More than Valen?"

I roll my eyes playfully. "It doesn't matter. Valen is a sophomore. He has two years of sex, fun, and parties. I graduate in six months; it would never work out. You sometimes forget that I'm considered Prey and still the common folk. Reid is marrying someone the Order agrees to, and I'm...nothing." I shrug my shoulders. "It's pointless to dwell on it."

"Don't say that. You're smart. You don't even study, and you pass your exams. You're beautiful and the strongest person I know."

"Aww, Gia. You're going to make me cry."

"No, don't cry, but I do want you to come with me. Get dressed. The driver is waiting outside. A tight dress, long coat. Boots. Let's go."

* * *

We make it to Dravin's off-campus house. I still wonder why Reid lives there with him. Valen still lives with his parents. I wonder what his story is. Maybe it's the *I hate my parents and want to fuck and party without them breathing down my neck* story. I doubt they care as long as he does what is required, like all rich families. The sons take over, marry who they deem worthy, have babies, and rule the world. Rinse and repeat. The next generation of assholes is born.

The trees groan on their branches, blowing in the cold wind. The lights from the modern sconces shine bright against the house's walls. Leaves are on the ground from the wind dragging them to the walkway, causing them to crunch under my boots with each step I take behind Gia.

Gia walks up to the main door and punches in the code to unlock the door. The smell of luxury greets me from the moment I step inside. The fireplace glows on the white walls, casting a shadow from us walking inside, making us look like we are in a Tim Burton movie with a nice house. Our silhouettes grow as we step inside.

Gia closes the door, causing it to beep, signaling that it is locked behind us, and I can hear voices coming from the patio.

I can hear Valen and one of the twins laughing. I have to see if I can figure out which one is Dravin and Draven. I guess it doesn't matter. They both look the same, sound the same, they even walk the same. I need to give up trying every time I see them.

My eyes scan the area, the cold hitting my face, mixed with the heat from the heaters placed around the pool.

"Hey, baby," one of the twins says, greeting Gia.

The other twin grins when he spots me. One eye is dark, and the other the color of the bluest ocean. "Hello, Jess. I'm glad you could make it."

"Thank you for having me."

"Hey, gorgeous. Of course, you are their fiancée's best friend. You're always welcome," Valen says, realizing with a grimace how that sounded when he moved forward.

Thanks for giving it to me straight, Valen. I get it. I smile and look away to the dark sky glittered with stars. The sting of his words was like a slap to my face. "Lucky me." I guess that is the only reason I'm here. *It is better than just having sex with Reid as the reason*, I tell myself.

"I-I didn't mean it like that, Jess. I'm sorry. I–"

"Hey, Valen. Why don't you get us those beers you brought." One of the twins interrupts. I wish I knew which one said it because I want to thank him.

Sometimes you hate to be right about someone. You think you're smart for figuring them out, but when they prove you were right, removing any lingering doubt that you were wrong, you're left with the sting of the truth.

VALEN

WHAT THE FUCK *is wrong with me? Why did I say that? Why?* The look on her face gutted me. She must think I don't care about her or that I think she is beneath us, and the only reason we have her around is because of Gia and for sex. Everything I did to show her otherwise, I fucked it up with a few words.

I grab the beers and kick the refrigerator closed with more force than necessary, hearing the rattling of the things inside.

"What the fuck crawled up your ass and died?"

I look up, and Reid is staring straight at me. I wonder how long he has been standing there. He must have checked the cameras and seen that Gia and Jess had arrived.

"Nothing."

He walks closer and leans on the marble island, placing his elbows on the surface. "What did you tell her? What did you do?"

He isn't stupid; he's actually quite astute. Genius even. He goes to school and runs his businesses and hotel from his computer in his room.

"Nothing. I said something stupid. I'm probably in the doghouse like you."

Reid chuckles. "You know that is impossible. You know that, right?"

I grab the bottle opener and slam the drawer shut. Lifting the bottle caps off each brown bottle, and when I'm done, I look up and watch him give me a smirk. "Did you tell her who you must marry when the time comes?

"Why, so she can avoid me like she does you?"

"You think she is avoiding me?" he challenges.

"I know for a fact that she is, and I also know that you are too chicken shit to tell her the truth. You don't want to admit you like her, and it's not just to fuck."

He chuckles and places his hand under his chin with a predatory smile. "What did you say, asshole?"

I know a threat from him when I see one. If I hurt her, he will kill me. Not literally, but he will make me pay in the worst way. I sigh because Reid isn't my enemy. We're like brothers—more than that. We trust each other with everything.

"I told her that we invited her here because she is Gia's friend, that also happens to be Dravin's fiancée. I made it seem like that was the only reason."

He scratches his ear, twirling his piercing between his fingers, lost in thought. His gaze finds mine after I toss the bottle caps in the trash with a resounding clink.

"What did she say?"

"She wouldn't look at me after that and just said, "Lucky me.""

"Hmm. Yep. You're fucked."

"Fuck you," I snap, glaring at him.

He raises his hand in surrender. "I'm not your guy, but I'm just pointing out the fact that you fucked up with her and when she finds out you are also to marry and who the bitch is...good luck with that."

"What do you suggest I do?"

He grabs two beers and says, "I think you should tell her. You know Gia is going to invite her. She's going to find out at the ball anyway. It should come from you rather than how she found out about me."

"Who is taking her?" I ask.

I can't. He can't. Not in front of the members of the Order. She will become their newest target of interest. We have had enough with Warren, and he will obviously be there like the snake he is.

"No one."

I grab the rest of the bottles and grit my teeth, thinking about her dancing with another man that isn't Reid or me. "Dude, I can't sit and watch her dance with someone else."

"Then...we will. We can't show up with her, but we can dance with her. There is no rule against dancing with Prey."

Yeah, I don't think she will want to dance with me after I tell her my fate when I graduate. I don't think she will ever look at me the same way. The big secret I have kept from her. The secret that will unravel every moment I have had with her, evaporating it into thin air.

JESS

I WATCH Reid and Valen come back outside with the beers in hand. I'm still hurt by what Valen said. He is sorry, but it's better to rip the Band-Aid off the wound. He doesn't have to pretend I'm here because I'm his favorite because I know, deep down, I'm only his favorite when I spread my legs. There hasn't been a guy that has taken the time to care what I like or know what my favorite color is. It goes for every man in my life. It looks like I never will, or maybe it will when I start my life and become the first generation to move out of the trailer park.

My eyes take in Reid with his inky dark hair. The same straight hair I remember gripping with my fingers while he was thrusting inside me, the first time we had sex. I never knew piercings were sexy until I saw them on him, but then again, I don't have much experience to go by when it comes to guys or sex. It was kind of forced on me, like a kid being thrown into the deep end to learn how to swim, but instead flailed her arms and began to sink to the bottom.

His dark lashes make his eyes look like he is older than he is. The piercings on his nose and lip are my favorite compared to the extra ones he had in his ears that I love to swipe my tongue over. His tight muscles and abs that ripple when he's on top of me make my clit throb inside my panties, wanting a repeat.

I can't forget how he treated me the night I collapsed in his arms from being drugged again by Michael. I hate to say that it is weird to feel thankful that he did that when I had agreed to his proposition for sex in exchange for giving my mother a job and now for sparing her life, according to Michael. His words, but then again, I get confused as to why he goes to all the trouble, knowing I'm sure when it comes to the random encounters I must endure when he shows up.

Reid walks up to me, and I must have been staring at him longer than usual because he hands me a bottle of cold beer. I'm hesitant to take it. I don't think they would purposely drug me. Reid and Valen aren't the type of guys that need to take advantage of women. Not them. I don't think they are sick and would do that to me, but a girl is paranoid, thanks to the asshole that is Michael. I swear he has ruined me for anyone else, not in a good way.

"It's okay. I wouldn't. Ever," he assures me, knowing why I'm hesitant. I lower my eyes and stare at the bottle he is holding out to me. He pushes it in my hand to convince me. "Take it, Jess."

I take it and bring it to my nose. Paranoid. My eyes find Gia's, and her expression softens. She gets up from the chair and walks over. "Here. Take mine," she says with a smile. "I drank from it, Jess."

"Go get the girls two beers, sealed, and bring the opener,"Reid tells Valen when I take it with a nervous laugh, embarrassed, and hand her mine, but Reid cuts in and brings it to his lips and drinks. When he pulls the tip of the bottle from his lips, his pitch-black eyes find mine like he is possessed, staring at me, and I watch his lips move.

Valen disappears back in the house, and Reid lowers his head to my ear and hums softly before he whispers, causing chills to run like a river over my skin. "I'm not stupid. When I find him, I'm going to kill him extra slowly. The barista Gia told you about was child's play. And I will find him, Jess. It is only a matter of time. The maggots come crawling out sooner or later."

Valen returns and Reid pulls away from my ear to kiss me. He changes his demeanor like whatever possessed him for a few seconds left his body. "You're staying the night. Drink up."

Valen hands me the bottle opener and the beer. Gia has a blank expression because she is probably wondering what he said. My eyes dart to hers, and she grins, trying to play it off, to make me feel more comfortable holding the unopened beer.

"You boys sure know how to make a girl feel comfortable," Gia says, trying to lighten the mood.

"Of course," Draven says, pulling from his beer. "Anything for you girls. It's good to ask and question when someone gives you an opened drink. Good practice, so to speak. Don't take anything offered when you're not sure."

I can tell it's Draven because he is quieter and more observant than his brother. He is astute like him too, and one could tell nothing gets passed him.

"There is a ball this weekend. It's on Saturday. We are not going to that party on Friday. None of the members' offspring are going because they have to prepare. It's mostly Ohio State that is going to the frat party anyway. Gia would love for you to be there since she doesn't know anyone too well. Moral support."

I nod. "Of course, but I don--"

"Have anything to wear?" Dravin interjects.

"We wouldn't dream of inviting you knowing you would need a dress. That will be taken care of. It will let you go have a shopping day."

Gia smiles and bites her lip, bouncing on her toes. "Will you go?"

I smile because I could never disappoint her. She probably feels like

Cinderella, and I want her to be happy. We both don't belong in a room full of members of the Order. I can even send pictures to my mother, and she will be excited. She will probably blow it up and frame it. I don't mind being a fourth wheel for her or Gia.

I glance at Valen. His expression looks torn. I wonder why? Reid's face is stoic.

Gia is looking at Reid and Valen with a giddy expression. She's excited that we are all going out to a fancy ball. "So, which of you is taking my best friend to the ball or both of you?"

My eyes widen at her. I didn't expect to go with either. They didn't ask me to go. The twins asked me for moral support to Gia. I know she's just trying to make me happy, but she shouldn't have asked them.

"We're not. She is going as your guest," Reid answers dryly.

My ribs feel like they are cracking, breaking me in half. My thoughts run to Zero. My masked stranger. Where is he when I need him? Where is he when my insides are breaking me in half? I shouldn't feel this way, but I do. I'm alone. I feel abandoned. Not wanted. Unworthy. It reminded me of when I was back in high school, and the guys wouldn't ask me out because of the rumors of what Michael did to me at the party. The whispers in the hall-ways. No one wanted to be seen with the trailer trash whore at prom.

Gia pinches her brows in confusion, looking between them. "Why? Who are two going with?"

"Let it go, princess," Draven says, pushing Gia's hair behind her ear.

Valen takes a hard pull of his beer, sucking his lip when finished. "Members of the Order go with their wives or their betrothed to the annual ball. Unless one hasn't been chosen," he says grimly. The silence stretched between us.

"I understand."

What can I say? He has a betrothed, and so does Reid. One he never mentioned either. Needles prick my throat like razors scraping down the words I can't say. I hate you. I hate both of you.

The men I thought of as my saviors are deceitful liars. Pulling me away from everyone so I can be their own personal toy is no different than Veronica and Garret. So what was the point of putting on a show and punching Garret or walking into a bar, intimidating a guy that shows me an ounce of interest, so I don't sleep with them? Selfish bastards.

"I'm sorry, Jess. I should have told you. I haven't touched her since I've been with you."

"Who is it?" I asked, clenching my teeth.

"Melissa."

I hear Gia gasp through the ringing in my ears.

Valen moves toward me, but I step back defensively. "I'm sorry. I asked them not to tell you because I knew you wouldn't talk to me. The guys know I would never do that. I knew you would think I was part of what they did to you, but I wasn't. I didn't choose her. It was done a long time ago. I-I'm sorry, Jess."

I can't think past the pain of a lie laced with a betrayal. She must have loved to watch them make a fool out of me. Veronica showed up when he was with me. Reid was probably there to take me out of there and cover for Valen. Veronica would probably tell me the same way she told me about Reid.

I walk up to him and swing. Smack! The palm of his hand lies flat against the sting on his cheek. "Fuck you. And stay away from me," I seethe.

Reid comes up behind me, and I whirl around to face him. "I'm not staying here with you. The last thing I need is for you to touch me," I warn, walking back to the house. He pauses, but his eyes harden into two black slits. My gaze meets Gia's sad expression. Her eyes are glassy. "Gia, I want to go back to campus, please. I don't want to be here."

"Of course."

"I'll go with you," Draven tells her.

Gia shakes her head, placing her hand on his shoulder. "Please, let me take her back."

JESS

WE MAKE it outside to the driver waiting in the driveway in the black Rolls.

"I'm so sorry, Jess."

Gia places her hand in between mine. I wring my hands, feeling the sting of the slap I gave Valen. I have never slapped anyone before. My breaths are heavy from trying to breathe, but I know it is all in my head, and I can breathe just fine.

It's the false hope I was fed by them. I got used to running to them while trying to forget and got caught up in their game. I promised myself after Garret I wouldn't. It wasn't like they were my boyfriends, but out of all people, Valen knew what Melissa and Veronica did to me and how they used me. He lied to my face. Smiled even.

God forbid they are seen with the Prey from the trailer park. I'm so vulnerable and fucked-up I take what scraps are given. I settle for anything because I'm trying to forget. I'm trying to survive. I feel like a living ghost.

No one loves me. No one wants me. No one wants to be seen with me.

As a little girl, I used to think we were brought to this earth and that someone was destined for us, and we just had to find them. When I was raped, I knew that wasn't true. That he didn't exist. I still hoped I would be proven wrong, but all I found were lies in the eyes of deceit.

"It's not your fault. It is my own for being so stupid. For wanting something that didn't exist. I should have taken my own advice, huh?"

"Don't say that. They weren't thinking because they don't know you. I'll stay with you if you want. You don't have to go to the ball."

"I'm going. I said I would, and this doesn't change anything. It is better this way, you know." I look at her before I step out of the luxury SUV. "The need to be wanted gets us all."

I close the door, and the car moves forward. I stare at the imposing building that is Drury Hall. My home for the last four years at Kenyan. I hear the snap of a twig in the dead of night.

Evil can be felt. It is instilled in all of us like a mechanism. The sixth sense is in all of us. I feel him before he appears. I don't turn around because I don't want to see his face.

"You weren't kidding. Were you? You are their little toy. A broken little toy."

"What do you want?" My breath blows like a white cloud in the cold air under the yellow lamppost.

"You know exactly what I want."

Dread fills my veins with ice, but this is what I'm good for. I have to do this, and nothing matters at this point but survival. The power of deceit is a fixed illusion that can be used as a weapon. In this case, creeps like Michael.

"Let's go."

I follow him, watching his broad back under his jacket. He walks to the parking lot, and I know he is taking me off-campus. When we round the corner, he lets out a string of curses. My eyes widen. His car.

I want to laugh, but the look in his eye has me holding it in. All of his windows have been smashed. The only glass that hasn't been broken into pieces is his windshield. His tires are flattened with his headlights busted, and the condensation from the cold has allowed words to be written on the windshield. Two words.

WE FUCKED.

"Is this some kind of joke?"

"Looks like you pissed someone off. I don't think she likes you fucking someone else." He glares at me. His lip curled in disgust. I point at his beloved Mustang. "You should get that fixed."

"Leave," he barks.

"Gladly."

I turn and walk like I have to pee toward the dorms. I wonder who did it because I wish I could thank whoever did. If it was his little girlfriend, he would have been fucking somewhere. I could kiss the ground she walks on.

Once I'm inside my dorm room, I shut the door and lock it, checking it twice, and place my bag in my desk chair. I pull my coat off, and I see it. A note and a black gift box.

I bring the note under the small lamp and notice the familiar red script and crème paper.

The sound of music becomes a part of you when my words dedicated to you are composed in a song, taking the pain embedded in your soul away and making you mine. My words scrawled on simple paper are nothing without you reading them.

Ps. Your smile is a priceless treasure that, particularly if I placed it there, no other man has a right to see. Hold on, my love. I am never near or far. I'm right where I need to be...inside you.

Eternally yours,

Z

I look at the black box with a red ribbon. I pull the string, and it unravels. The latest smartphone sits on top of another white box of Bluetooth headphones. I pick up the smartphone, and a sticky note is stuck to it that reads.

Turn me on and play with me.

I lift the box and close my eyes and grin. I remember the bookshelf and all the books toppling over. It was him. It was Zero. I turn on the phone and see it is programmed with one number. The contact reads Z. A simple letter with a phone number.

I decide to punch in the service number. I'm trying to find out who Z really is. All smartphones have an account with a name. I might sound stupid for asking if the account belongs to Zero, but it's worth a shot.

"Hello, I wanted to know if I can find the amount of my bill?"

"Can I have your name, please?"

"Zero."

"I'm sorry. Did you say Zero like the number?"

Damn it. "My name is Jesse Sharpe," I correct her. Even though I did say Zero like an idiot.

"Yes, Miss Sharpe. You have a zero balance, and your account is on auto-pay."

"Okay, Thank you.

"Will there be anything else that I may assist you with?"

"That will be all, thank you."

Shit. It is under my name, meaning he has all my information.

The phone vibrates, and I look at the screen.

Z: Do you question every gift you receive?"

Jess: When it comes from a man with no face that
wears a bird mask, yes.

Z: No faith. Do you like it?

I smile.

Jess: Who wouldn't. Where are you?

Z: Close.

Jess: How did you know I called customer
service.

Z: I know many things, and I'm always watching
you.

He thinks he is funny.

Jess: Oh, yeah. Where was I?

Z: The Bedford residence off-campus with his companion Reid. I know your friend Gia and Valen were also in attendance, but you didn't stay long. Why did you leave so suddenly? Were the sons of Kenyan misbehaving, my little Sparrow. Do they need a little persuasion?

The reminder of what they did and how they lied to me still stings. I thought Valen and Reid were my friends. I thought I meant more to them. When Gia dropped me off, I thought about Michael and how he waited for me. Was he watching? Does Zero know?

Jess: How about after?

Z: I'm not sure what you mean.

I guess he doesn't know about Michael. It means he isn't always watching. My phone buzzing vibrates on my lap as I slide my boots off my feet. I sit cross-legged on the bed and swipe up to read the message.

Z: Didn't your mom ever tell you not to get in a car with a stranger.

Jess: It was you.

I smile to myself. He busted all the windows and flattened the tires on Michael's Mustang. Michael deserves it, but it could also be a game. Members of the Order like to play games, and Michael is one of them, and so is Z. They probably know each other, and I shouldn't trust him. I shouldn't trust anyone except Gia.

Z: You do have your own car.

I have been here almost four years and have never seen him before. I want to know why he watches me. Why me all of a sudden?

Jess: How do you know so much about me? Why me?

> Z: It is my job to know things. Things others overlook. Like I said, you intrigue me. Don't you want a guy to pay attention to you? I thought girls love male attention unless they like the same sex, and from what I have seen, felt, and heard, you love cock. You want to wipe away the shame that haunts you. You use your body to calm the need and hunger to forget. When your cunt gets fed, you don't have the need to scrub your shame. Isn't that right?

He is psychoanalyzing me. These are the type of questions a therapist asks a patient. He must be a doctor. They have a psychology department in Kenyan. He must be one of those psychotherapists with a fetish for students. A fetish for female Prey.

> Jess: Are you a doctor?

> Z: Maybe? Maybe not? Do you need a doctor, Jesse Sharpe? Would that help with the nightmares? The need to scrub the filth that has touched your skin like a disease? Did a father or stepfather fuck you? Did he…sodomize you? Touch you? Watch you?

Bastard. Tears slide down my cheeks from the memories of what Michael has done. What he allowed his friends to do to me my senior year. How I lost my virginity in the worst way. I live in fear and disgust with what I have to do every time.

> Jess: Fuck you.

> Z: I promise you, my love. It will be special when I take you. I'm not the enemy here, Jesse. I'm your savior. Your little secret. Sweet dreams.

> Jess: Z

I stare at the phone screen, waiting for him to respond. I try again.

> Jess: Z

Nothing.

When I close my eyes, nothing sweet greets me, just the darkness of my dreams. My reality and my dreams are blurring together. It doesn't matter if I'm asleep or awake. It is all the same. It's not ghosts I'm scared of; it's people.

JESS

"ARE YOU READY?" Gia asks with a hopeful smile.

I check my new phone, my fingers flying over the keyboard, sending a text to my mother with my new number and that I have been invited to a ball. Gia fears I'll change my mind because of Reid and Valen, but I won't. It was Friday, and she showed up so we could shop for the ball.

"Yeah."

She opens the door, and I follow her out, as my phone vibrates with a text from my mother.

Mom: Oh my God. I'm so happy you have a new phone. Please send me pictures, Jesse. Who is the lucky young man that is going with my Jesse?

Jess: Just a friend. I'm shopping for a dress. I promise to send pictures. Gotta go. Talk to you soon.

"Nice phone. A secret admirer?"

Gia slides inside the black SUV, and I contemplate how to answer when I follow her inside. I slide the phone away into my pocket and look up. I don't want to lie, but I don't know who the man in the plague mask is. So, I do just that.

"I saved up and got one. I make payments, but at least it is in my name. Almost four years of saving on meals." I smile.

Not a total lie. The account is in my name, and I have saved money that way. The only problem is that I didn't make the payment and didn't actually go to the store to purchase it.

She smiles and holds out her hand. A big rock glitters on her ring finger, and I gasp, taking her hand and admiring the beautiful engagement ring. An emerald-cut diamond with red stones on each side. "Gia, it's beautiful." Her eyes get glassy, and I know it's from happiness.

She deserves happiness and, in the best way, with her boys. She lost a child and almost died because of that monster or monsters.

"I still can't believe it, Jess. Sometimes I want to pinch myself to see if I'm dreaming."

"You're not dreaming, Gia. You're happy because they make you happy. So which one gets the ceremony?"

I always wondered how that worked. How do you marry twins? The three of them.

She clears her throat. "Dravin had an idea that Reid mentioned."

I arch a brow. "Reid?"

She lets out a small laugh. "Yeah, who would have thought he was a genius when giving a romantic solution we could all agree with." She licks her lips and continues, "I'll marry Dravin in church and Draven legally. I'll give them children as required, but Draven wants me to have Dravin's child first. He wants to give him or her the entitlement of firstborn," she says, emphasizing the i and the e in their names to tell them apart.

I smile. It is a clever solution. The three of them get what they want, but she would be legally married to the hidden twin.

"Oh."

"It is unorthodox, but the Order, in general, is unorthodox, and let's not get started on the Consortium."

My head snaps up, and I let go of her hand and wonder if she knows more about the Consortium. She said they wore plague masks in the church when they killed the asshole from the coffee shop. Z wears a plague mask, and I know he is part of the Consortium, but maybe I can narrow it down to find out who he is.

"Do you know how many are in the Consortium? They have more power than the Order, I'm assuming."

Gia looks nervously at the driver through the open partition. He is looking straight ahead, but you never know if he is listening, and I bet my ass he is. She reaches over, presses the button, and the soundproof divider slides up.

Her gaze meets mine when it rises all the way. She lowers her voice and says, "They are, and the sons of Kenyan started it. Dravin told me sixty-six members are to be trusted. It started after they lost their mother. Dravin thinks that they could have saved his mother in time. She was sick with depression, so why didn't their father always have someone with her. He also mentioned that Reid wanted an alliance after his loss."

I pinch my brows in confusion. "His loss?" Who did Reid lose?

She nods her head. "Yes, he had an older sister. She was murdered, and the Order covered it up, but he took care of it. Then Dravin's mother committed suicide. After Dravin's mother, that was the nail in the coffin. The Consortium was born to weed out the rule breakers. The murderers. The depraved." She swallows thickly, and her eyes lift. "There is one more thing I learned after last night. Valen is on a warpath after you left. The twins and Reid had to calm him down. They mentioned he needed to see his doctor, and I was confused. I had never heard of them mentioning a doctor, and that is when Draven sat me down and told me the truth about what Kenyan really is and not what people think the university is. To society, it is an elite Catholic college for the rich, but they don't know there is a fourth floor."

The tiny hairs on my forearms stand up under my coat. My skin turns hot and cold, and I know what comes next will put the E in evil and where we are in the middle.

"Let me guess. There isn't a second pool in the building on the fourth floor for the rest of the students to use."

She shakes her head slowly, and her expression goes blank, staring into space. "It is a psychiatric ward for the mentally insane and it's where people go to get therapy. The sons of Kenyan and all the children from the richest families in the world send all their unstable offspring to one place to get an education off the grid to shape them for society. To be able to take over and lead. The ones that can't cope. The ones with mental issues, addictions, traumas of all kinds. They send them here."

"Holy fuck," I whisper.

Her eyes flick to mine. "I'm sorry, Jess. But we are here for their game. We are their Prey. Valen has a sexual addiction, and that addiction is...you. I think Reid has PTSD, I'm assuming. Dravin and his brother have PTSD and another disorder he didn't want to say, but he says he doesn't have it. I'm not a psychiatrist, so I can't say for sure. I didn't want to hear more because...I love them."

"We are in a school with insane, rich people."

She nods slowly and looks at her hands in her lap. "I'm sorry I told you."

It means Michael is mentally unstable, which makes sense. Who knows what else he has done. I don't know much about it. It makes sense as to why they are waiting to get to Warren. The first year I was here and fell Prey to Veronica and her games. It. All. Makes. Sense. Zero is one of them, so that means he is mentally unstable in some way. I knew that, but maybe I wanted to overlook it. Maybe I wanted something real.

"The Consortium are––"

Gia interrupts me. "Considered criminally insane. Allegedly. But so are people in the world. Look at the monsters at your high school. Michael wasn't the only monster in that room that night. There were more. His so-called friends."

I know she doesn't want to bring up my past. My past trauma. The Order gifts the underprivileged an opportunity in exchange for being a test subject. The separate dorm. All Prey are identified somehow and kept in the dark by dangling a better future at the end of the tunnel, like a carrot to a rabbit with a room full of foxes.

After the drivers drops us off, we walk into a designer boutique and a woman immediately greets us wearing a black pants suit. Her blonde hair is pulled tight into a low bun.

"How may I help you?"

Gia makes the introductions and upon hearing our names, the woman's face lights up. She immediately shows Gia the latest collections of gowns from different designers.

Feeling overwhelmed looking at all the colors, patterns and lengths of different ball gowns, I step to the side and wait. I came because Gia invited me and I don't think I have enough to even purchase underwear from a place like this.

Gia's head turns and she smiles at me. "Come, on Jess. Pick one. Whichever one you like."

The stylist from the boutique turns to me once again and I think she said her name was Carol. "Jesse Sharpe. Right this way."

I furrow my eyebrows, trying figure out why she is leading me down the hallway toward the back of the store when there are perfectly good dresses on the rack in front of Gia.

She stops where there are dresses in glass cases like they are memorabilia. There is one in the center of the room made of lace that looks expensive. It's black with cream silk underneath with a deep v down the front stopping right before the mannequin's fake belly button. The crystals are woven into the lace, glittering when it catches the light. I wonder if there are real crystals.

I must have been staring for a while because I hear Carol clear her throat. "It's beautiful, isn't it? A masterpiece."

"Yeah," I mutter.

Carol walks forward and opens the glass case just as Gia walks up behind me. "Wow," Gia says.

"I know. I couldn't help myself. I had to stop and look. It's...gorgeous."

Carol faces me and grins. "The dress was imported from France. It is made of the most expensive lace in the world, which is known as the "Reticella" lace, which originated in Italy in the 15th Century. Reticella lace is a type of needle lace that is made by hand, using very fine thread and intricate stitching techniques. It is known for its delicate and intricate design, which often features geometric shapes, floral motifs, and other ornate patterns. One of the reasons why Reticella lace is so expensive is because it is incredibly time-consuming to make. Skilled artisans must work for hundreds of hours to create a single piece of lace, using specialized tools and techniques that have been passed down through generations––" she nods to her assistant wearing gloves so she can take it out then continues––"Another reason for the high cost of Reticella lace is its rarity. The purchaser wants to remain anonymous but this dress was made for you, Miss Sharpe. I was given specific instructions to make sure you receive it and leave here with no other dress and shoes."

Gia steps close to me and whispers near my ear, "Someone wants you bad, Jess."

JESS

AFTER A NICE HOT SHOWER, I return to my dorm and shut the door. I have made it a habit to shower when the rest of the girls occupy the showers, so I don't run into any visitors.

I pull on the door to ensure it is locked, and when I turn around, I drop the caddy containing my soap with a thud. "What are you doing here?" I ask him.

"Whatever I want," is Zero's response.

He is sitting on my bed, but his mask is black with his eyes covered. It isn't the same one he wears with the beak. Walking around campus in the evening with a plague mask that resembles a creepy bird would probably look weird.

I inhale sharply, getting annoyed that he keeps hiding his identity. I want to know who he is and why he keeps stalking me. Buying me overly priced gifts I can't afford for no other apparent reason except to confuse and torment me. Except, when he makes me come. For the first time, a man has pleasured me, and it is not right after I have done something I regretted doing. A sin washing away another sin.

"And what do you want?"

"Is that your way of thanking me for the dress?"

It was him. I thought maybe it was Reid or even Valen trying to apologize, but I guess not.

"How do you want me to thank you? Have you come for your pound of flesh?"

He chuckles maniacally and places his hands over the stomach of his fitted black dress shirt, which I notice is pressed against his flat stomach. Z is a fit man with broad shoulders and muscles.

"I would rather prefer for you to want me."

I run my fingers through my hair in frustration. My plan of blow-drying my wet hair going to shit. I bend and pick up the bottles that fell to the floor.

"You're upset with me." I place the bottles with more force than necessary and glare at him. "I like the fire you have inside. I like that you hate me at the same time." I pause, and my eyes narrow at his haughty tone. "It will make it pleasurable."

I place the bottle of lotion in the caddy and straighten, blowing out a puff of air to get the wet strand of hair out of my face. "Make what pleasurable?"

He cocks his head like a life-sized puppet. "When I fuck you. When…I pluck the hate for me out of you, replacing it with my cum."

'You're sick," I spit.

"Tsk tsk. Not all that attend here are sick. Just misunderstood. Like you. So tell me, who was it? The one you're trying to forget? The one you try to exorcise like a demon that has possessed your body, causing you to do the devil's tango."

I shake my head and clench my teeth. "Stop psychoanalyzing me. Are you a doctor? Is that it?"

He straightens and shakes his head slowly, reminding me of a serial killer with his victim. "Nice try." He makes a buzzard sound that's muffled underneath the full head mask. "Try again. I know what you are doing. You are trying to figure out who is behind the mask. I give you an A for effort but an F for the wrong answer. Tell you what. Tell me who or what hurt you, my little Sparrow, and I'll tell you who I am."

I place the caddy on my desk and charge over to him angrily. "Get fucked. You crazy son of a bitch, how dare you!"

He grips my wrist hard. My hands fisting his shirt, wrinkling the soft fabric over hard muscle. I can hear him breathing under the mask.

"I don't want to hurt you, but I will." I try to pull away but he spins me around and pins me to the mattress with my hands over my head. He's between my legs. My chest is rising and falling. My t-shirt rises up, exposing my stomach, making me curse myself for wearing really short shorts.

My jaw hardens, and stupid angry tears threaten to fall. "Then do it. Do your worst. Rape me. Kill me," I taunt him.

Silence.

I'm ready. I don't stand a chance in this place, and he knows it. I know it. In here. Out there. I'm doomed. A helpless animal with no escape.

More silence.

It stretches in the room over his breathing, my chest rising and falling under him. His mask staring back at me like a bad joke.

"Shh…" His head dips to the flash of skin exposed above the band of my shorts, and I can't even see the color of his hair. I can only smell his cologne mixed with leather, like a poisoned chalice. "Don't get upset, my love. I'm just thirsty. I'm starved."

"For what?"

"To kill," he says softly. "I need to kill."

My legs begin to shake, hanging over the side of the bed. I swallow thickly and know danger when it is in front of me. I know it's scent. This man is dangerous. He's evil in the worst way. Insane. The tears threatening to fall slide down my cheeks, and I turn my head so he doesn't see them.

His head snaps up, and as much as I try to hide the wetness trailing down the apple of my cheeks, he catches them with a gloved finger, holding them up like they are evidence of a crime.

"Please," I plead.

"Don't be scared, my love," he says, pushing himself off the bed.

I freeze, afraid of what he will do next. He picks up my phone, and I watch him go through it and set it down. He turns to face me and holds his hand out for me to take it.

I wipe my face and slowly place my hand in his. A haunting melody begins to play from the playlist saved on my phone. A playlist he left for me to listen to. He pulls me close, gripping my waist, and his head is bent, looking down at me from behind the mask.

I sway with him to the music. The words feel like they are floating around us; we are in a place only he and I can go. A place that only exists as long as he's in it.

The backs of his gloved fingers slide over my damp cheek down to my neck in a soft caress, and I shiver from the electricity running over my skin from his touch. I place my hands on his chest and feel his heart beating fast, thumping under my fingers.

He's nervous.

He's afraid.

But of what?

"Don't fear me. I couldn't bear the thought of you fearing me. I prefer your hate," he says softly.

I lay my head on his chest. The feel of his fingers caressing my head. "Don't give me a reason to fear you."

"I can't make you that promise, my love. But I won't hurt you."

"You're one of them. The Consortium."

"Yes."

"A-are you crazy?"

"Some think so."

I look up. "And you?"

"Asking a person with a mental illness is like asking a drunk if he's an alcoholic."

I snort. "You're crazy, aren't you?"

A deep rumble comes from his chest when he says, "When it comes to you, I'm insane."

"You don't know me."

"I know that you have never had what you truly want. I know that something inside you is trying to get rid of something dark. Something, someone put there. It is not Reid or Valen. Or that idiot Garret with a small appendage.

I giggle. "How do you know that?

"A little bird told me, but I want to know your secrets, your darkness, and your hell. Secrets so deep, not even the devil knows."

"Why don't you tell me yours, Z."

He stops moving and looks above my head. "I can share one of them. A truce."

I step away, and he slides his belt off, and I frown. "Lie on the bed and hold your hands above your head."

My eyes dart to the bed behind me, and my curiosity outweighs my logic and I let him tie me to the old headboard. He makes sure I cannot get free. He moves to turn off the lights, and before I can protest, the room is dark.

"Z," I call out.

"Don't fear me. You need to let me show you."

I feel his gloved fingers pull my shorts down and freeze. "Zero," I whisper.

Silence.

I'm not wearing underwear and begin to panic, pulling on the belt, preventing me from getting free.

I feel his hands on my thighs, they are bare, free from the gloves and I'm dying to know what they feel like. I need to understand like a person that is staring at a tornado, knowing it can destroy them as it gets closer, but they stand there like a statue. Waiting for its destruction.

He parts my thighs, his wet tongue licks my slit, and I whimper.

"Z," I protest with a moan, trying to grip the side of his head with my thighs, hoping I can feel his face to make out his features.

"Relax, and I'll give you what you want."

"You don't know what I want."

He flicks his tongue over my clit, and my ass lifts off the bed. My clit is throbbing. My pussy is wet and dripping. I can feel the drops sliding between my thighs. I search in the dark for a glimpse of his face, anything to identify him.

"Fuck. You taste amazing, my little Sparrow, like a jar of honey. Tell me you want me to make you come," he says, sliding his tongue inside me. "Tell me you want me to fuck you with my tongue so you can give me my secret. The secret of your pleasure. A pleasure you give no other."

My nipples are hard, my legs open wider, and I shamelessly tell him what he wants to hear. What I want. For him to show me what it is like to be desired. To be truly wanted. "Yes," I croak. "Make me come, Z."

The man is wicked. He plunges his tongue like an animal feasting on his prey. He eats. And eats me. Fucking me like he promised with his tongue.

I bite the inside of my cheek to keep myself from screaming. "Oh, fuck."

I whimper. I moan. I grind my hips, seeking my release. He grips my hips in his hands and flicks his tongue until I shatter in my release. I see sparks behind my eyes like fireworks in the dark sky. My words echo for him in the dark room. "I'm coming, Z. I'm coming."

I can feel what appears to be his nose rubbing over my pussy, smearing my cum all over his face. It's dirty and hot. He licks me and sucks hard in different spots on my skin near my entrance, and I think he is trying to leave hickeys as evidence.

I can feel his breath on my swollen clit begging for more. "You are so fucking beautiful. Now the memory of me will haunt you in the dark and your thoughts when you wake up to the light of day."

When he gets up from the bed, the cool air blows directly on my warm body. There isn't so much as a glimmer of light coming in through the window. It's as if the moon agrees with him and has chosen to stay dark in the sky.

I can hear the rustling of him re-placing his mask, and all the nerve endings on my skin awaken when I feel the heat over me, undoing the straps of his belt on my wrists–– a different experience than the one I endured with Michael.

I arch my neck, wishing he would let me kiss him. Because for the first time, I'm falling for a man with no face. A man replacing bad memories with each encounter I have with him with ones I want to repeat. And I don't even know what he looks like. When he is done, he unties me, he leaves me in the darkness of my room, wishing he would stay.

JESS

"BOTH OF YOU LOOK STUNNING," Dravin says from inside the dark SUV.

He preferred to drive us himself, which means Gia is seated in the back with me, while Draven is in the front passenger seat.

"Thank you," Gia and I say at the same time.

"It's true. Both of you will be the talk of the evening. There is no doubt about that," Draven says, looking out the window at the black SUV following us. They have hired security to make sure the evening goes smoothly. Especially with Warren being there. I'm also nervous. Knowing they will be married soon, I'm unsure how I will feel about watching Reid and Valen with someone else. Especially Reid.

I never thought I would get attached, even if my reason for sleeping with them was a way to get over the feeling of self-destruction. The guilt would come after knowing I was using them for the wrong reasons and never thinking about the future. But I got used to them always being there for me and only me. I never once thought I would feel lost when they finally got tired of me or went away.

My mind also wonders about the mystery man that has been taking residence in my mind every waking moment. His touch. His words. Even in his absence, he is everywhere. The fact that the dress I'm wearing was created for me by him is something no one has ever done. Everything Z has done to me has never been done. The need for him is not based on me trying to forget Michael.

"Isn't her dress gorgeous?" Gia says with a smile. "Reid or Valen certainly have good taste."

Gia thinks they were the ones who had it made. If she only knew. If they all only knew.

"The woman at the store wouldn't say who purchased it, but I would love to thank them personally tonight," I add, but then contradict my statement. I know that I will be doing no such thing. "Maybe not. I don't want to cause trouble. I'm sorry for even mentioning it."

They wouldn't even notice the dress, assuming Gia and the twins did me a solid since they were the ones that extended the invitation.

"Don't be nervous. We have each other," Gia assures me warmly.

"If they ask you to dance, Jess. It is normal. You are considered single and

Prey. I hate to say this, but you are available in their eyes, and some might view you as one of two things, a potential fuck or a potential wife," Draven says.

I let out a deep breath I didn't think I was holding. "Good to know, "I reply dryly.

It isn't his fault. He is just being nice and preparing me for the vultures of the room. There are only two I'm worried about that are dangerous to me: Warren and Michael.

The car pulls up to a large estate, resembling a hidden palace in the woods. I would have never thought a place like this existed. Expensive cars with drivers line the driveway of the expansive estate. The walls are ancient with history, like the Colosseum. Men in suits open the doors of the cars as they crawl forward. Vines covering the walls of the estate give it an enchanted feel. The stairs look like they are made of stone that has stood the test of time.

Two wooden doors open and close as guests in tuxedos and ball gowns are screened to enter. My eyes are transfixed, so taken by it all that I don't hear the door opening or the man waiting for me to exit.

"Let's go, Jess," Gia whispers.

I'm embarrassed that I was caught staring into space. I didn't realize the twins were waiting outside or that we were the only two who needed to still exit.

"I-I'm sorry," I stammer, trying to plant my heels on the stones that lead to the stairs and not face plant on the concrete.

I'm not used to wearing heels and didn't own a pair until yesterday. When we reach the interior, everything is black and red. There is a photo booth, where everyone stops to take a picture. Embarrassment sings in my veins, and my heart begins to pound. Gia is in front of me with the boys, and it is customary to take a picture. I haven't seen one person avoid it. Taking a deep breath, I look around at all the faces I don't recognize, with their expensive suits and beautiful dresses. When I look to the side and watch as the photographer snaps pictures, the flash rapidly going off, my stomach clenches when I see it is Valen with Melissa. His smile is tight, but he looks handsome. My hand immediately flies to my neck, and I tug at the necklace he gifted me like it's burning my skin. I received a box earlier with a necklace from him. I wasn't going to wear it but I didn't want him to think I would never forgive him.

Forgiveness is given but not in the currency of a gift. Growing up, I was never given anything unless it came from my mother's hard work. Accepting a gift from Valen was a mistake that I now regret. I tug harder, and the necklace gives, and it falls in the palm of my hand. I stare at the offending necklace, wondering where I will put it. I didn't bring a clutch because I don't even own one. My phone was left in the car in the seat pocket.

The line moves forward, and Gia turns to give me a reassuring smile. *I'm doing this for her and the experience.* I repeat in my head when our eyes meet. When Valen steps forward, his eyes find mine, but I look away, staring at a painting with a naked woman. Her nipples are visible underneath the fabric of her dress and her eyes are staring at her lover.

When I turn my head, it is my turn to have my picture taken. "Right this way, Miss. You will have two sets of pictures at the end of the evening," the photographer says.

"Thank you," I say softly, moving forward on steady feet. I rub my lips together and paste a fake smile on my face.

"Is there anyone with you, Miss?"

I shake my head, telling him no. Embarrassment covers my skin. I'm the only one alone, standing before the red backdrop. The photographer gestures so I can stand in the middle.

All eyes are on me, and I want the ground to swallow me whole. My dress swooshes over the lush black carpet as I hold my head high and pull the fabric delicately to the side. I don't care that I look like someone's mistress. I don't care what they think of me. For me, there was no prom or fancy date. Fuck them. I'm taking a picture to send back to my mother. The only person that stuck by me through it all.

I can see the women craning their necks, covering their mouths and whispering amongst themselves, but then the photographer places the camera down, and I stand confused.

"Excuse me." I hear someone say in a stern tone. "Excuse me." I hear the voice say again.

The crowd parts, and the last person I expect stands before me. His dark eyes find mine, holding them for a second longer than necessary. *Reid.*

His mouth breaks into a small smile. "Now, smile," he says.

My palms are sweating, my pulse is racing, and I take the time to admire his clean-shaven face. His piercings are gone, and he looks like a dark prince. His hair is jet black and worn to the side part, and I know from experience that it will fall over his brow before the night ends. His black lashes seem even darker than normal because they are so thick, and his strong lips are nicely sculpted. Sinfully beautiful. His tattoos peek out of the collar of his black tux and over his hands.

His expression softens when he takes my hand and places it over his chest. I can feel his heart beating a million miles per minute, and then a flash of the camera goes off. My other hand grips the necklace in a fist. He turns, and I follow his lead. His fingers slide softly over the lace on my waist, and I feel the electricity over my skin. It has me confused, thinking that being away from him for a while would cause me not to feel anything, but I do. I always have. With Reid, it's different. Deep down between the need to remove Michael's touch from my skin, my heart fell through the cracks for Reid. The harshness of his words buried my feelings for him in a place deep inside, lost in the chaos of my suffering. But every time he softens his touch and looks at me with his midnight eyes, the color of the deepest ocean full of secrets, I remember that the feelings I have developed for him are still there. Whatever I'm missing from Zero, I find it in Reid.

Flash, the camera goes off, but when I think the photographer is done, he stops us with his words.

"One more," he says, holding up his index finger with a camera lens aimed at us. "You two look amazing. One of the best I have seen all night. Truly, it is a pleasure to photograph you both." I smile, showing my teeth, and the camera goes off again.

VALEN

I STAND to the side watching her and I see it. The way she looks at him. The way she has always looked at him and I hate to say that I'm jealous and ashamed at the same time for keeping the fact that I have to marry Melissa from her.

When I think of sex, the itch that overtakes me is like a drug that I need to take a hit of over and over. There is one woman that is like my favorite drug of choice that comes to mind and it's Jess. There were times I felt guilty to use her like that and not tell her my problem. Letting her think that sex with her meant more but in fact it was like taking a hit from a pipe of heroin. There is no emotion and it's just a high reaching a climax, only to fall right back down hitting rock bottom. But with her, it was more in a way because we would take from each other what we needed. I wasn't stupid enough to think that she was into me and had stars in her eyes every time I showed up. We were both willing to fuck to get what we needed out of each other.

There are times I want to feel normal, but I can't. A body is a body to me and my need is the euphoria of coming to get my next fix. Like a coke head chasing the white horse. The urge of satisfaction is what I crave and nothing else. If the woman is willing, it is all the same to me but that is what is killing me the most. I want it to be her and no one else, but I could never be that selfish. If I care about her, the way I know deep down I do, it is best I let her find happiness, allowing another man to replace those haunted eyes with joy. Even if that man isn't me. Because she deserves that. Jesse Sharpe deserves everything.

"Stop embarrassing me. You have been staring at her long enough," Melissa says next to me in an annoying voice. It sounds like nails on a chalkboard, grating on my nerves.

"It isn't her fault. She's gorgeous and eyes are made to stare and admire things that are rare and beautiful."

"She knows about us. It looks to me like she hasn't even noticed you're in the room. Why bother, Valen?"

My jaws hardens and I grind my teeth. "All thanks to you and Garret. Veronica is a ferocious being all on her own. Everyone knows that."

"Oh, come on. You remind me of the Bedford twins and Gia. You can't possibly think that underprivileged pussy is a better option than what you have right in front of you. We know the rules. We know what we are marrying into. We have doctor's notes to prove it, but we also have enough money to start our own country. Prey are weak and vulnerable. They were given an opportunity in exchange for being our little dog toys."

I scoff. "Let me guess, you're the dog. The bitch in heat."

Her eyes harden. "How dare you."

My lip curls in disgust. "Fuck like a bitch, get treated like one."

The thought of what she did to Jess makes me sick. Manipulating her into having sex by using Garret and knowing Veronica loves to play games. All because she felt Jess was a threat the minute she showed up at Kenyan when I mentioned that I would love to fuck her.

"You are just upset that I ate her cunt before you and she liked it. She sure as hell wasn't thinking of you."

"I guess you got what you wanted. It's going to be fun keeping you on a leash so you can watch me fuck. You wanted me so bad, you got me. Just not the version you thought."

"Fuck you," she spits.

"Nah, I don't fuck bitches," I retort, walking away from her and leaving her alone like she deserves.

My eyes scan the room and I find Jess with Reid standing near the champagne table. I make my way over and I notice Jess's gown. It has a deep neckline but what has me stunned is the fact that it gives the illusion that she is practically naked underneath. Her dress looks transparent, the lace covering only her nipples down to almost her belly button.

I catch men trying not to stare at her beautiful body. There is no way she is wearing underwear underneath that dress and that thought alone has my cock stiffening with the urge to fuck. But I have to calm down. This is not the place or time. I can't go to a room on the second floor after picking a random chick. I'm not here for that.

"You look gorgeous, Jess," I say, praising her and wanting her attention on me.

Her eyes find mine and she automatically holds her hand toward me in a fist. I look down at the diamond necklace hanging from her fingers and I feel the pain of rejection stabbing me like tiny needles. The urge to fuck dying a slow death.

"I forgive you, but I can't take it. I wore it, but I don't think it's right. My forgiveness doesn't have to involve a gift. There are things we don't have control over and some things we do." Her expression softens when I take it from her. I have no intention of not letting her have it, but for now, I slip in my pocket.

"I understand."

"You are young. When I'm gone you will have two years to have fun and explore college life before you have to take over your family's obligations."

She means fuck around with other people and go to parties. In her eyes, I'm a player that doesn't have feelings and is incapable of them. I can't blame her for thinking that of me. It's always been true, until her. She taught me that emotion does exist because she was the only woman that didn't give it to me in return when I wanted to feel it. Jesse is the first woman that didn't ask for more than I could give. One thing I promised myself when it came to her, I would make sure she was taken care of.

"I'll always be by your side, Jess. I'll always be here for you."

"That's enough," Reid interjects and then lowers his voice. "We have company."

I arch a brow because I can't believe what I am seeing. I can see right through his bullshit; he's jealous. Reid likes her more than he lets on. Which means the show he was putting on earlier, showing up like a dark knight to save her from taking pictures alone, was genuine. God help the other souls who try to fuck with her. What's amusing is that she is oblivious to the whole thing.

He wasn't lying when he said we have company. Reid's parents appear with Tara in tow. My lips lift into a fake smile, mimicking the one Tara is aiming right at us, reminding me of a possessed demon waiting to lure you in for the kill.

The woman Reid is supposed to marry, and his ex-fuck buddy, pausing in front of Reid and narrowing her eyes at Jess like she is an unwanted pest. *Good luck sweetheart.*

"You must be Jess," Mrs. Riordan says warmly.

Mrs. Riordan watches Jess with intrigue. Reid never takes an interest in a woman for long. Reid's parents try to keep up with Reid. Where he goes and what he is doing. They want to make sure he stays in line, following the Order's rules. They know first-hand what happens when you don't. Reid's sister was killed for eloping with a Prey against the Order's rules – one that states, *by being the first born and a female, she has to marry a member of the Order and is not allowed to marry a Prey.* The poor guy she eloped with suffered the same fate.

You can run from the Order, but you can't hide. They will find you when you least expect it. When you fuck up, there is no God inside the church who can save you. There is only the Consortium. The judges from the entrance to hell that serve as the gateway between both worlds.

JESS

SO MUCH HAS HAPPENED since my last run-in with Michael that I cannot drag Valen into my mess. Guilt claws at my insides when I watch the look of hurt and disappointment crossing Valen's face, but I can't lead him on, thinking I will forget and everything will go back to the way things were. Then there is Z.

Valen has a sex addiction. In health class, I always paid attention on the subject. Sleeping with each other for the wrong reasons is not me caring for him. If you care enough about someone, you can't make it worse for them. In Valen's case, I can't be the pipe to smoke his drug.

I could feel Reid tense when Valen promised he would be there for me, but then his parents showed up with Tara. The woman I recognized in his hotel that night we had sex in the elevator. The woman he is engaged to be married to that he has a history with. She is obviously accepted by his parents and the Order. But what confuses me is how his mother smiles warmly at me as she introduces herself. I find it weird she wouldn't turn her nose up at me, making it known that I'm gum on her shoe.

"So you're the Jess I have heard so much about," Mrs. Riordan says.

"Yes, ma'am. I am," I reply.

I'm nervous, but I feel Reid's hand on my waist. His father's eyes dart to where his son is currently caressing me with his thumb, causing awareness to skirt up my sides, and I bite my inner cheek, tasting blood, trying to stop my nipples from hardening under the fine lace.

What is Reid doing?

Mr. Riordan smiles, meeting my gaze, his lips moving, speaking to Reid, but his eyes never leave mine. Calculating. "It's okay, son. I think they all get it. But some might disagree."

"Honey, let it go. Let him be. He knows what he is doing," Mrs. Riordan says.

I have never wanted to disappear or wish to be invisible like I do now.

"He's embarrassing himself. He knows what must be done. And she isn't part of it. She is just his current plaything. I've heard they pass her around like a Frisbee," Tara says, her voice with malice dripping, talking to his parents like I'm not standing here.

The possessive streak inside me regarding Reid rattles awake, wanting to be unleashed. I don't care if his parents are present. They know I'm a means to an end, but still, fuck her. I can tell when a woman is into a man, and Tara doesn't like the idea of being married to Reid any more than he does. It seems this is a power move. And it helps the cause that Reid is hot as sin.

A nun would break all ten commandments if Reid walked into a room and she was offered a chance to be with him.

I smile politely, placing my finger on my bottom lip. "Tara, is it? I can tell he is dying to take you down the aisle. It looks like he can't wait, and be careful with Frisbees. They can come out of nowhere and hit you in the face. I know you're a little slow, and it will take some time to understand, but in the meantime. Be careful how you say my name. You might choke." I pause and smile at his parents' surprised faces at my behavior. I don't miss the deep chuckle coming from Reid next to me. Valen has his hand over his mouth stifling a laugh, and the wide-eyed look on Tara's badly caked-up face makes her look like a dollar-store Barbie.

"If you would all excuse me, I need to use the ladies' room," I say, excusing myself before my mouth gets the best of me, or worse, the urge to smack Tara in the face overtakes me. I have never wanted to put my hands on someone so much.

"Good, that way I can dance with my fiancé. It would give you time to clean and spread your legs for the next one."

"That's enough!" Reid snarls, moving his arm away when she places her left hand on his jacket, but I don't miss the big engagement ring on her finger that could probably feed a third-world country.

"I'm your future wife," she retorts and points. "She is just a whore. I think she forgot that the only reason she is here is that the Bedford twins chose a Prey as their chosen, and she is the best friend, and was invited. No one escorted her here. She tagged along like a pet. We came here together as the future Mr. and Mrs. Riordan."

People stop and turn to stare me. My feet move like skates across the floor until I reach the end of the ballroom. The music begins to play in the background. I recognize the song-- "Something I Can Never Have" by Vitamin String Quartet.

I'm trying to hold back the tears that threaten to fall, running inside the women's bathroom and finding the bigger stall open, holding the skirt of my dress as I lock the door frantically, finding a small couch. Probably so you could get out of the gowns to use the toilet. I let out a strangled laugh at the fact that the bathroom stall is bigger than my room in the trailer. Anything to stop thinking about my heart breaking inside my chest.

I stare at my hands, that are shaking from shame and anger. I'm angry at myself and what I have become. Seeking scraps of affection to cover up the shame and guilt of allowing myself to be used. Over and over, I'm swallowed into a web of lies try to be free. The voices in my head scream in agony for it to stop, but when I think the worst is over, they come knocking, laughing at my stupidity.

I clamp my mouth shut to keep it from trembling when I hear heavy footsteps approaching. I listen to the turning of the doorknob. I think my heart skips a beat in my chest hoping it's Reid, Valen or even Z. My palms sweat when the door swings open slowly.

A sob escapes my throat. My heart begins to pound like a machine.

"Did you think I wasn't going to come for you? Look at you. It's a shame you are all alone, but I have to say, you look so beautiful in that dress. I couldn't resist," Michael says, undoing the belt of his pants and sliding his hard cock out of his boxers.

I turn my head away in disgust, not wanting to look at him. I can hear him fisting himself, and I cringe. My stomach revolting.

"Hurry up and make it quick. Give me that dirty mouth, and I promise to dance with you."

I'd rather die than be in his arms.

"I wouldn't want to sully your reputation. I was surprised you didn't bring your girlfriend."

He gives me a smirk. "Now that I know there is a way to marry Prey, I might consider you to be my wife. I saw how they treated you. Tsk, tsk. They don't know what they will be missing. Kneel and open up, my love. I've been dying to watch you on your knees praying for your sins."

No, I tell myself.

You're just a monster who thinks he is a God.

JESS

THE SOUND of the water running in the oversized stall with a private sink assaulting my ears as I try to clean off the cum stains Michael gifted me is a cruel joke. The one-hundred-dollar bill is wet and plastered on the mirror, mocking me. *My bonus,* he said.

Hot angry tears slide down my cheeks as I scrub frantically. I threw up as soon as he left. His words about him marrying Prey came out of his rotten mouth. I was tempted to bite his dick, but all that would earn me was a one-way trip to ruin.

I have to think of something, and only one thing comes to mind, getting him to break the rule of the Order. Him telling me that he just found out about the possibility of marrying Prey means one thing, he doesn't know all the rules.

I wash my mouth with soap, not caring about the weird taste in my mouth. I keep scrubbing as gently as possible, without ruining the beautiful dress, hating that piece of shit, Michael. My body shivers at the memory of him cupping my breasts and licking them.

I turn around and push my butt as far as it can go to throw up in the sink for the fourth time. My stomach is sore, and my eyes are watery from the effort. I breathe through my mouth when I'm done.

The door is pushed open, and I see Veronica standing at the entrance of the private stall.

"Well, well. Aren't we full of regrets this evening? Your little boy toy looks like a lost puppy out there scanning the crowd like a little boy who lost his favorite toy, "she coos.

The woman is so beautiful, she looks like an enchantress. Her dress is red, like the evil person that she is. Her blonde locks are in loose waves.

She steps closer, and I back up. She is taller than me by about an inch or so. "I'm not here to hurt you, Jess. But I am tired of seeing you suffer, No one appreciates you. They...fuck you like you're an object. No feelings. No remorse. They take and take," she says, shaking her head and sighing. "I take it you didn't enjoy it, did you?" My eyes widen because that means she saw Michael come in and out of the restroom. She isn't stupid. She slides her perfect red-manicured fingernails into her blonde tresses. "I need to show you something, but you must leave with me."

"Pfft. Why? So you can perform a ritual and drink my blood."

She laughs. "No, I need to show you what they don't want your kind to see."

I arch a brow. "My kind?"

She rolls her eyes. "Prey," she deadpans.

"I want you to see what they do to little boys that don't know how to keep their little pricks inside their pants."

That has me all ears, listening to this crazy bitch. But I don't trust her. Why would she help me?

"What's in it for you?" I ask.

"Let me ask you a question. The night with Garret, who was sucking your cunt while Garret watched like a horny teenager with a baby dick?"

I try not to grin. "Melissa."

"Melissa," she repeats, looking at her flawless complexion in the mirror. "Do you think if I liked to suck cunt, I wouldn't have that night? I would have let that dumb bitch who is too chicken shit to tell her daddy she enjoys pussy to let her have you if I was interested?" She wipes the corner of her mouth to ensure her lipstick is perfect. "I'm gonna let you in on a little secret, Jess. I don't like pussy. I act like I do for other reasons that are not your problem but my own. I like cock. The bigger, the better. You can ask your besties' men. Well...one of them."

My jaw clenches, and I want to slam her head against the mirror for mentioning that she fucked one of the Bedford twins out of respect for Gia.

"And is that supposed to make me feel any better?" I snap

Her lips form a smile. "I thought you should know if you thought I was hung up on your juice. I fucked Draven before he met Gia. One time. I haven't fucked Reid. He thinks his dick will fall off if I sit on it, and I'm sure you have heard that Valen doesn't count. He fucks anything but is safe. He gets tested as required." Her eyes look up at me through the mirror. "On the fourth floor."

That has my eyes trained on her. The fourth floor. I want to know what and who the fuck is on the fourth floor. I can find out if Zero is up there.

"The fourth floor?" I ask, playing stupid.

"Oh, come on. I'm sure the Bedford twins have mentioned it to Gia, and that Gia has spilled the beans," she says, pronouncing the S like a Z.

"I have never been to the fourth floor. I don't think the faculty allows students to go up there. I have noticed the building's architecture is high so that it appears to have room for multiple levels, but I never imagined what is on the fourth floor."

"There is...do you want to go?"

"Like, right now?"

"Yes, before your best friend sends the search party with her men and your little boy toy. It must be fun to watch you two fuck. The way you two set fire to a room. You would think you two just came from fucking every time you look at each other."

"I wouldn't know. He is getting married to Tara."

Veronica tilts her head back and laughs. "I would love to see that. No...I would *pay* to see that. She wants money, power, and a good dick to ride at night when she isn't fucking his cousin. She loooves breath play, and that animal loves to push the limit. Reid is a better catch, though. More money, more power, and more danger."

So that is why he went apeshit when I was talking to Alaric that night. His references in the car of him punishing me.

"Does he know?"

"Of course, he does. You don't think Reid is a pushover and will allow his wife to fuck his cousin behind his back, do you?"

"Why are you telling me all this?"

I see her eyes go glassy for the first time, and she looks away. "Reid had an older sister, and she died. Alicia Riordan was my best friend. She was older, and she knew secrets. Secrets that I told her about me. About the Order. Things I heard my father say and the things my father made me do. Things I can't tell you."

"Why?"

A single tear slides down her cheek, and I realize she hides who she really is.

"I can't watch my best friend's little brother spiral out of control if he loses another person he cares about. If I tell you certain things, they will kill you. I'm taking a risk by taking you where I need to take you, but I know if I don't, they will take you from him."

"Who will take me from whom?"

"Do you think everyone didn't see? The pictures. The way he looks at you. The way you look at him. No one exists in a room when he looks at you."

I shake my head. "You have it all wrong. Reid doesn't feel that way about me."

"I'm not going to argue with you, but whatever the fuck happened with that pig that left here. There is something bigger at play, and you're the prize."

JESS

VERONICA SNUCK us out the back door to the right of the east wing. There was a dark corridor that led to the exit opposite from the ball. I hated not telling Gia that I had left with Veronica, but I knew they wouldn't let me go with her, and I had a feeling that what Veronica wanted to show me, I would never get another opportunity to see. She could easily spread rumors about Michael leaving the restroom and me being the only one inside.

She could tell by what she saw that he wasn't my secret lover. I shiver as the warmth of the luxury car hits my skin from the brief exposure to the cold air. It wasn't smart leaving my phone and not telling anyone, but I'm at my breaking point. I'm past the point of no return. I'm way past caring.

I need a way out of this mess.

"I want to graduate and leave here."

She looks at me but presses the button raising the divider so the driver doesn't eavesdrop on our conversation.

"I like Thomas but don't trust him enough for his tongue to slip and tell my father what he shouldn't. I'm afraid that you hold too much interest. Especially if I'm talking to you and you are mentioning leaving Kenyan. You have caught the attention of the most important members of the Order and are the best friend of a girl who did the unthinkable and is now chosen by the Bedford twins.

"But I didn't. They are marrying other women. I'm not a threat."

"Keep lying to yourself and think you are not part of their games. I used to think that way, and my best friend and her boyfriend were murdered. They left. They ran away thinking that laying low and out of sight, the Order would just let them go and not make them pay for defying them."

"Who are they. To my understanding, they have to vote."

"Not if you have a father like mine, like Garret's or like Mr. Bedford. There are more. Men like that prick that showed up in the bathroom. Some follow old rules from ancient times. Some don't. The desire for wealth is from a lack of separation, which fuels men like them to fulfill all their desires. Sexual and material. They will do whatever they must to get it, but in the course of generations before these types of men, some of the women and children have suffered from depression. The wealthy get depressed, too, you know. It can get boring really fast when you can buy whatever you want. Have whoever you want."

"Is that why some of you have...issues?"

"You mean that some of us have to see the wizard?"

"You mean shrink?

She rolls her head on the seat and looks at me as the sedan cruises toward Kenyan. "Psychiatrist, the wizard, the magician. Whatever you want to call him. A God. That is how some of us deal with shit when we become unstable. The. Fourth. Floor."

"It's a clinic?"

"No, it is both. Kind of like the movie *The Girl Interrupted* and an asylum."

"Oh."

"Relax, it sounds worse than what it really is, but I want to show you."

"Why?"

"Because the only way to deal with a psychological cacophony is to relieve it. I have the feeling you don't like sleeping with random men from what I saw when the one you truly want is outside dancing in the arms of another woman."

I look out the dark-tinted window watching the gold lights pass by. The shame of what I had to do if he found out. If they all found out and what Michael's plan for me is.

"How do you relieve it?" I ask, meeting her gaze.

"You defeat the evil that put it there. You outsmart the devil who wants to play God."

REID

FORTY-FIVE MINUTES HAVE PASSED since Jess bolted from my side, and I haven't been able to tear myself away from the members of the Order coming up to greet me and wish Tara and me well.

"...is there a date set, Riordan?"

Hearing my last name being addressed and failing to catch the first part of the conversation has me turning my head to Veronica's father.

"No date."

"Well, you can't keep the lady waiting." He steps forward, lowering his voice so no one overhears. "You could still have the girl on the side until someone scoops her up. A woman who looks like she does won't be single for long. She is the talk on campus ever since the Bedfords picked Gianna as their chosen."

My jaw hardens at him playing matchmaker, and I throw a shot at him where it hurts, Veronica. She has become an evil bitch since my sister's death. It is the only reason why I don't slit her fucking throat. She was her friend, and some say she was in love with her since everyone thinks she prefers women, but no one wants to address the elephant in the room, including Melissa.

"I should say the same for your daughter, Veronica. When is her upcoming wedding taking place?"

His brown eyes harden and I give him my best smile. I struck a nerve. *Asshole*. Warren has already left, needing to go back to his cage. Keep coming at me about Jess, and I'll make you disappear, you old bastard.

I never liked him, and how he raised his daughter has me questioning everything he says. Everything he does. When it comes to him, something doesn't add up.

Gia and the Bedford twins walk up behind him, and I can tell that something is up with how Gia fidgets. A smile that tells me she is faking the funk because I have an unwanted guest in front of me.

"Have you seen Jess?" Gia asks with a smile. "I have her phone and wanted to ensure she gets it."

A sinister feeling explodes in my gut. I know it before I have to question it. Jess isn't here. But in front of Veronica's father, I can't show how much the knowledge that I don't know where she is affects me. I can't show him how much I care. I have already shown everyone here more than I was supposed to.

I give the twins a knowing look, dryly answering, "No."

Dismissing Gia, my eyes land on Veronica's father like I couldn't care less, but in reality, I'm raging inside.

He arches a brow, probably shocked by how I answered and chuckles. "There is no emotion in you, is there, Riordan?"

Not since I killed his friends for killing my sister, simply because she didn't want to follow the rules. My sister fell in love with a guy that was Prey and he outed her for it, so I made him pay. She did break the rule being a first born, but she was my sister. I wanted to destroy his family the way he destroyed mine. That is why I talked Mr. Bedford into screwing his wife. In his bed. Then had his evil son defile your pretty daughter, making sure everyone knows who and how she fucks.

It makes us dicks, but Veronica isn't a saint. She may be collateral damage, but my sister was innocent. She was in love, and they killed her for it.

My phone vibrates in my pocket, and I hold up my finger. "If you'll excuse me," I say, fishing out my phone, "Business."

Veronica's father smiles, but it doesn't reach his eyes. *Yeah, asshole. I haven't graduated college yet and have more money than five generations of your pathetic DNA combined.*

I look at the text.

> Valen: Jess isn't here, and Veronica is nowhere to be found.

Fuck.

JESS

"THE DORM ROOMS ARE SHITTY," Veronica says, leaving Drury Hall after I changed out of my dress. She brought a change of clothes that her driver Thomas gave her.

"It is better than my room back home. It's actually nice."

"What kind of house did you have back home?" she asks, walking toward the church.

I clear my throat and squint my eyes a bit. "I didn't have a home. I lived in a trailer with my mom. It was just me and her growing up."

"Oh. I'm sorry. I didn't mean——"

I shrug my shoulders and interrupt her. "I'm not ashamed of it. I just hate when people judge me for it."

We make it to the church's doors, and she pulls it open. I'm surprised it's ten at night and still unlocked. When I walked inside the first time to pay my respects, I always thought the priest was sketchy. The younger one. The older one felt more genuine and a man that serves the church.

The smell of old wood and candles hits me all at once, and I try to picture the barista crucified on the cross, but I can't. I look at the pews and try to imagine Zero sitting at one of them, watching them commit their sins, but right now, it feels like a normal church.

"Come on," Veronica says, walking toward the back, where the priest's office is supposed to be.

When we reach the back room, I hear voices inside. I expect Veronica to knock like a normal person, but then I remember there is nothing normal about this woman.

The door swings open, banging against the wall. I can hear a female shriek and then blink a few times, trying to process what I'm witnessing. My mouth is hanging open like a nutcracker.

The priest is fucking the nun on the desk. Her habit is lifted, his cock is shoved inside her, and he is glaring at Veronica.

"Do you knock?" he asks with a hard edge to his voice.

"Do you pray? I thought that is what they hired you for when the real one wasn't there. Not to be fucking the nun that is supposed to be a virgin."

"You could have knocked," the nun purrs, shaking her ass with the priest's cock inside. She stretches her arms across the table. "Or, you could watch. The choice is yours."

"No, you perverted bitch. Have some respect for yourself and go to a hotel or fuck in a car like the college students that go here," Veronica says, snapping her fingers toward the priest. "Keys to the fourth floor. Where are they?"

"Behind the door, and what the fuck do you need to go to the fourth floor for?"

"I'm giving a fucking tour? What does it look like? I have company?"

He shakes his head, and apprehension begins to set in when his expression tightens. Both are sinners and liars, but what should I have expected? The guy's full of shit and doesn't know how to lock the door, let alone say a prayer. I can even overlook the fact he is balls deep in the nun.

I back out slowly from the room, when Veronica unhooks the keys from the hook and turns around to close the door.

"What the fuck was that?"

She giggles. "Campus security for the church," she teases.

I shake my head in disbelief. "That is so fucked up. How many people go to him and confess?"

"I'm sure he has heard plenty, but they are hired by the Order. The real one is old and comes during the day. If you want to confess your sins, I would start there."

We are back outside, and the cold air greets us. The hot and cold are getting to me, causing me to sneeze.

"Get it all out. You wouldn't want them to hear you."

"Who's them?" I ask, trying to keep up with her.

She smiles. "You'll see."

* * *

After the last step up to the fourth floor, I catch my breath, and there it is, blocked off by a door. Veronica looks up at the camera and, with the key in the lock, waits for the green light to the camera pointing down to turn red, then she turns the key, releasing a lock that makes a buzzing sound.

She pulls the door, and it sounds like an air pocket being released from an air lock. She pulls open the door, and when she moves forward, the smell of a sterile hospital burns my nose.

She wasn't kidding. The entire floor looks like a hospital. White walls and shiny floors in a dimly lit hallway with sealed rooms on either side. Another hallway with carpet leads to what looks like doctors' offices.

"That is where you get therapy and prescribed medications. There is a receptionist during the week."

My eyes scan the hallway and the doors, filing it away to memory. What Gia told me is true, Kenyan is full of surprises and fucked-up students with money.

"This is where the wealthy, not rich, send their kids. I'm not talking about Beyoncé rich. I'm talking about middle eastern rich. The kids that are sent to Kenyan are from U.S. leaders. Not the people you see on TV. The ones behind the scenes telling them what to do. All those people are bottom feeders compared to the Order."

"That is why everyone is losing their shit over Gia."

"For you too, I'm afraid. It is either they will kill you, or they keep you. So, you can kiss leaving here goodbye. You know too much. You will not graduate here without being married to a monster or ending up in a box buried in the cemetery. The fucked-up part is that whoever you choose, you will lose your right to do whatever you want and will be at their mercy. All the safe ones are taken. Unless you marry Garret, his family will not allow it, and Reid and Valen would probably drown him in the pool and call it an accident."

"You're giving me too much credit."

Her telling me this sets a smoke alarm in my brain, suffocating me. That is Michael's sick plan. Blackmail me to agree, but he isn't sure how to approach the Order. I have to figure out how to outsmart him and end his sick twisted mind games.

We pause in front of a room with a glass window, and she stops like a tour guide and shows me an exhibit at the zoo.

"This is where they are keeping him," she says, pushing a button, and a light turns on.

I let out a gasp, my hands flying to cover my mouth. "What the fuck?"

Warren is in a straitjacket talking to himself. The weird look in his eyes I have seen lately makes sense. He keeps shaking his head and talking to himself with his eyes and lips moving.

"The Bedford twins don't fuck around. They don't want to worry Gia, but according to the medications they are feeding him, it is melting his brain. He will be dead in three days. They allow him out for a bit. He was at the ball, but I came to get you when they brought him back. This is one of the reasons the twins have security around Gia all the time: to ensure Warren doesn't go nuts and do something when he is out. People will wonder too much if he doesn't show up. Ask questions."

I purse my lips and gaze at the ground, looking at my worn-out bootleg Uggs. Observing a person suffering that deserves it messes with your head. You think it's inhumane, but what he did to Gia was irredeemable. What doesn't add up is Veronica's interest in Warren and the fact that his parents don't do anything.

"I thought you were into him? And why don't his parents do something? Retaliate."

Her lips twitch. "He broke the rules like my best friend did, and she paid the price. There is nothing anyone can do. As for me being into that pervert, he forced himself on me before freshman year began. He cornered me, and when I told him I wasn't interested, he shoved me against the wall, and I did what I had to do."

I raise my brows to my hairline. "Which is?"

"I played possum and let him think I changed my mind by luring him to my bedroom, and then I fucked him in the ass with my dildo. He screamed. I laughed. He came. He left me alone after that, and I made it seem like I was obsessed with him."

"Holy shit."

She was trying to save us from it happening to Gia and me.

She giggles, and then her lips twist into a pathetic attempt at a smile. "I knew something he didn't want everyone else to know. Of course, he wouldn't want to be married to be around me, fearing what I knew and how I would stuff his ass with my six inches of silicone."

My head lifts, and the tiny ounce of remorse fades into oblivion.

"He can rot for all I care. He deserves it."

"So does that animal that left you in the restroom at the ball. Messy. But I know you won't tell me or anyone the truth."

She knows I won't because I can't trust anyone here. They all have an agenda; I'm at the bottom of the list. Gia can't help me. It is a risk telling them Mich is actually Michael, without it getting back to him. He has direct access to my mother, and he will kill her. Too risky.

Veronica turns off the light, and we walk the same way we came.

"Other unhinged creatures are lurking around Kenyan. PTSD, mental health issues, and addictions of all kinds. They all hide it well and supposedly get treatment but continue to rule the world in their fucked-up states. Then, there are some like you, me, and Gia who suffer at the hands of monsters trying to escape the fate of becoming fucked up."

"What happened to the people that had to kill Reid's sister?"

I wonder how Reid and Veronica could deal with knowing the person responsible for actually killing her and her boyfriend.

"They are dead. Some say it was Reid in a rage but couldn't prove it was him. Then the Consortium was formed after Dravin's mother committed suicide. They think something drove her to do it and that she could have been saved."

My stomach somersaults at the mention of the Consortium, my mouth salivating for more information as the door makes a whooshing sound when it opens.

When the door closes behind us and we make our way down the stairs, I ask, "Who are the members that make up the Consortium?"

From the corner of my eye, a slow smile spreads across her face. "That is a question no one has the answer to. Obviously, the sons of Kenyan are part of it, but the rest, no one knows. There is a rumor that there is one. This vigilante that no one knows who he is or where he came from. A killer. He doesn't exist and doesn't have a name. It's because they all fear the Consortium's wrath and judgment from him. The grim reaper, so to speak."

Zero. He's the answer.

JESS

KNOCK KNOCK.

I hear banging on my door, and I place my textbook on the bed to get up. It was too late to find a way to call Gia, and I couldn't ask Veronica for her phone because I wasn't supposed to be out with her, so I decided after she walked me to my room to catch up on my economics assignment hoping Zero would show up. I needed to talk to him, but he never showed.

I twist and pull the knob pulling the door open. The twins, Valen and Reid, are in the hallway, all giving me haughty looks when they see I'm safe and sound.

They should be smiling.

"Are you fucking kidding me right now! You're studying?" Gia roars. "I've been worried sick, and you're studying?"

"How did you get back, and more importantly, you left your phone," Dravin adds.

"Please tell me you didn't leave with Satan's female spawn." I back up, and Reid is the first to enter, with Gia trailing close behind. Reid's fingers pinch the bridge of his straight nose, trying to keep himself from losing it.

"I did, and she isn't that...bad," I shrug.

What can I say? I was too busy cleaning up Michael's mess when I was on my knees, sucking him off to keep him from hurting my mom and me. Veronica gave me a way out.

"What have you done with my friend. She wouldn't leave with someone like Veronica. What happened?"

Valen finally speaks up. "You're playing a dangerous game, Jess."

"I'm not the only one playing games," I retort.

"We were all worried," Gia says, her expression softening.

"I'm fine. I didn't want to ruin the evening for you all, and I thought it best for me to leave. The ball wasn't my thing, and I shouldn't have gone, I felt out of place and alone. But thank you for the invite and the opportunity. I don't want to seem ungrateful."

Reid's head lifts his eyes, finding mine holding them for a second, but I can't read him. He's gone quiet and walked over to my nightstand. I dart around, snatching the black string bracelet in my hand. He broke the other one, and I was planning on making a second one to match so I could replace it and give it to Gia, but I haven't gotten around to it. I never thought he would be in my room again, so I left it there.

"I wasn't going to break it. I'm sorry for breaking the other one."

"Yeah, well, I'm not taking any chances. I made them as a kid and wanted to give one to Gia, but didn't get the chance when you broke one. I have to make another one. It doesn't mean much to you but does to me."

"Dude, you're such a dick. Why did you do that?" Valen asks with a stern expression.

Reid blinks, but he keeps watching me with a blank expression. His eyes traveled down my legs and then back to my face, his eyes shifting like a raging storm. Since he lost his older sister, he doesn't feel sorry much. A normal person would apologize for what they did but not Reid.

"Let's get going. It's late. You two can catch up later." Dravin says to Gia but then looks at me. "Meet her at Babylon. Tuesday is your day isn't it," he smirks.

My eyes narrow. I guess Gia wasn't the only one who noticed my hustle.

"Tuesday. Don't be late." Gia gives me a kiss on the cheek and a hug.

"I won't."

Valen approaches me and hugs me tight, lifting me from the ground. "Be careful, princess. You don't want to wake up my crazy side."

After setting me down, he gives me a wink and leaves behind the twins and Gia, but Reid stays rooted to the spot.

His blank expression firmly back in place, he says, "Let's go. Get dressed."

I sit back on my bed and grab my textbook. "I can't. I have work to do."

He takes two steps and takes the textbook out of my hands, watching his eyes read the assignment I'm working on. He shuts the book with a thud and tosses it on my desk. "You already have the answer, and it's completed. He'll give you an A, or he will answer me. Let's go."

"Where are we going?"

He removes his jacket, tosses it on Gia's old bed, untucks his dress shirt, and my mouth waters getting a glimpse of his rock-hard abs. Fuck he's beautiful. Too bad he has to marry that stuck-up bitch, Tara.

I watch him roll his sleeves up his forearms revealing the tattoos on his arms like a second skin down to his knuckles. He looks like a devil in an expensive tux, ready to sin. He finishes by running his fingers through his hair, falling over his brow.

I walk to my extremely small closet, pull out a sweater, and then walk to the drawer and pull a pair of leggings out. His eyes follow mine, and I remember he isn't mine when I pull down my shorts.

"You could wait outside," I tell him, watching him lift his brow to his hairline and continue, "I don't think friends should watch other friends get dressed when one is practically married." His eyebrows drop in place, and then he scowls.

"Who said I was getting married?" He asks, pulling the band of my shorts slightly.

My eyes are transfixed on his lips, moving when he speaks. He walks closer, and I suck in a breath when I feel his index finger caress the skin above the band of my shorts, causing my panties to get wet.

"But–"

I don't get to finish because I gasp when his finger grazes my clit over my panties. My cheeks heat because he must feel how wet I am for him.

His nose grazes with mine, his soft lips ghosting mine. "Hmm... I think you like that idea."

"You have to or––

He plunges his tongue inside my mouth, and I can taste a hint of spearmint. I whimper, moan, and slide my fingers in his hair, pulling tight on my tippy toes.

He devours my mouth out of tongues dueling with each other in a battle of submission. His hands slide under my ass, and he lifts me. My legs wrap around his waist, and he deepens the kiss.

I'm lost.

There is nothing I want more than this moment. For Reid to be mine for a minute. I imagine him meeting me somewhere. I run and jump into his arms and end up just like this. Lost in his embrace.

My heart is pounding. My legs wrapped around him, not wanting to let go. His strong arms holding me, but I know it has to end. Moments with Reid are few and between. It is like winning a scratch-off. You have to savor that moment when you win just a little, hoping it is more.

This is the moment I dreamed about having with a boy in high school. These are the moments with Reid that has butterflies swarming my stomach. The rest is noise.

When he breaks the kiss and my feet find the floor. Our eyes are locked. His lips were swollen from the kiss.

"Come on," he says softly and steps back, watching me dress.

REID

I HOLD the door open for her because she deserves to be treated like a princess, but I'm selfish when it comes to her, and I want to be the only one to do it. I pull the seat belt tight when we are both seated inside my Aston Martin to ensure she is secure.

She lifts her arms and lets me. I graze her breast with the back of my knuckles to ensure it is not too tight and lean back in my seat to grip the steering wheel. I won't leave the parking lot with her if I keep it up.

I was scared something had happened to her when she left with Veronica but relieved when we found her safe inside her dorm. My heart constricted, and I hadn't felt pure fear like that since Alicia's death. I didn't know what I would do if something happened to her. A possessive instinct for her overrode my normal thought process.

I pull out onto the main road and head to the twenty-four-hour diner on the outskirts of town. It takes thirty minutes to get there, so I pull up my playlist and relax, enjoying her company. Lately, she has been on my mind, and what I can't find out online about her, I'll have to find out in person. Jesse Sharpe is a puzzle I want to find all the pieces to. I want to know things that no one else knows, like the fact she made string bracelets when she was twelve, even though I was the dick that broke one of them in a fit of jealousy.

A foreign emotion I have never felt before for another woman. I didn't know how to deal with it, and I didn't know how to say I was sorry.

I never had to apologize for anything, except not being older than my sister so I could protect her. The pad of my thumb touches the hard ridges of the little wheel scrolling through my playlist, selecting "Feel" by TWO LANES.

The low beat of the music creates a chill vibe in my car's cabin. I slide over the center console to reach for her hand sliding my fingers through hers. My thumb stroking her soft skin.

"So you're not going to marry her then?"

I lean back in my seat, and I tell her the truth. "No. I was never going to marry her. She just thinks I am."

"And Valen?"

My left-hand tenses on the steering wheel because, for the first time, I feel like I have competition. I know I'm far from the image of the perfect guy she has in her head.

"I don't know. He still has time to decide, but I'm not marrying Tara. Where are you from?"

I know where she's from, but if I act like I already know, she will know I have been stalking her like a creep.

She tilts her head looking down. "Cedar Lake, Ohio."

She doesn't like where she is from, which means she is running from something or someone. Maybe her parents were real assholes. But I go for another angle.

"Brothers, sisters, or family."

"No, it was just my mom and me. My dad skipped out on her when I was born. She raised me all by herself. We didn't have much. Typical story. Single mom raising a kid on her own. No other family."

I can empathize with her feeling alone and not having siblings. It was how I felt when Alicia died. I was alone, and nothing mattered. Everything around me faded in the background.

"How's your mom?"

I see her shoulders stiffen from the corner of my eye, and I'm curious, maybe her mom's a piece of shit.

"She works at a diner in town but had to take hours at a biker bar across the street to get make sure she could ends meet. She's a hard worker and has done the best she can with what she has been given. She didn't mean for us to struggle, but in a small town, there aren't many options for people in our situation. Not when you're a hundred dollars over the threshold to receive food stamps." Regret begins to sink in at how I've treated her when she sighs and continues, "I wouldn't ask for much. You know, so she would stay home longer and not have to leave me alone."

"Did you have friends?"

So, it isn't a drunk father or a drug-addicted mother. There is no stepfather, so who the fuck messed with her? It's a simple lame-ass question, but I'm trying to find out more.

She exhales. "No time for friends, and they kinda didn't like the idea that I lived in a trailer. That didn't help my cause."

"How about a boyfriend? Do you have one of those back home waiting for you so you can experience college life? You made the grades, or you wouldn't have been accepted at Kenyan. You don't play sports."

She mumbles something under her breath that I can't catch over the music. She must have had a boyfriend because she isn't a prude virgin kneeling inside the church praying to God.

She hesitates, and I think she is choosing how to carefully answer the boyfriend situation based on our conversation in the past and the way she has chosen guys on campus. My nostrils flare thinking about her fucking someone else that isn't me. I would punish her with my silence and indifference when she chose to have sex with Valen. I can't get mad about anyone before me, but there hasn't been anyone for me since her.

I wish I could say the same about her, but there is a reason deep down. Something she is hiding that I want to find.

"No sports. I was top of my class and didn't have a boyfriend. No one wants to be seen with trailer trash. It doesn't matter who I really liked," she says, looking out the window.

Anger at how they judged her back at her school has me wanting to go over there and burn their fucking building down until it's a big pile of shit. All those idiots at Cedar Lake are pricks. Jesse is gorgeous. It doesn't matter where a girl lives. It is where you live in her heart that does.

I wonder if she liked someone back home, and she is hoping that attending here for four years will make them see her differently. The selfish part of me hopes not. The selfish part of me wants me to be the one she likes more than any other.

"Did you like anyone? Maybe you were hoping they would ask you to prom?"

I feel her tense beside me, knowing I struck a nerve. I sound like a chatterbox, but fuck it. Fuck.

"I thought I did, but it doesn't matter. I wasn't asked to go, and I didn't have the money for a dress. I didn't go to graduation. I was happy I was able to get a better education. I will be the first Sharpe with a college degree where I come from. Did you go to prom?"

My jaw locks, not so much by her question, but by the fact she has never been to prom. She's probably never had a boyfriend, but then I grin. She's out with me.

"Yeah, I graduated from Kenyan Preparatory. My parents made me go with Tara," I say, the words bitter on my tongue.

"Oh."

She doesn't say a word or push. I should be grateful the music is playing, but the silence stretches uncomfortably.

"It feels the same. Going with someone you don't want to go with and not going at all."

She shrugs. "Yeah, I guess. It would have been nice, though. My mom wanted me to go. It was one of those things parents want their kids to experience, but at the same time, it is an experience for them too. To watch their kids grow up and take pictures. Memories they can look back on."

"I would have asked you."

I may sound like a dork, but it's the only thing I could think of to make her feel better. Besides, it's the truth. I want to know what she wanted and didn't get.

I pull into the parking lot and find a spot to park. She turns to me. "Asked me what exactly?"

My hand is on the handle to open the door, but before I exit the car, I give her a genuine smile. "To go to prom with me."

JESS

MY CHEEKS HURT from the smile plastered on my face as I sit across from Reid. He said he would have taken me. And I believe him.

After we place our orders, his eyes never leave my face. It is like he caresses me with his eyes instead of his fingers. My eyes take in his clean-shaven face without his piercings and file it away to memory. The way his dress shirt stretches across his wide chest and tight muscles as I shift in the plastic seat of the booth.

"Why are you always taking me out to eat?" I wave my hand at him. "You could have asked anyone else. Why me?" I push.

"Because I never see you eat. I'm looking out for you. You're always holed up in your room. Your car doesn't move from the same spot in the parking lot," he says.

"You have someone watching me or something?"

He gives me a playful smirk. "You're hard to miss when you're around, and when you're not around, it's not hard to find you."

Is he flirting with me? I bite my bottom lip because I have never had anyone flirt with me this way before.

After we're done eating and he pays the bill, we drive back. I purposely leave my hand near the center console to see if he takes it. I've become desperate for his touch. This is a side of Reid that I have never witnessed. He leaves clues. Little tidbits that make you fall for him, and I'm falling. Hard.

When we turn on a familiar road back to campus, I pull my hand back, disappointed he didn't hold it. I guess this is all I'm getting for the night.

"Thank you for the food. It was nice."

"You're welcome." I see his fingers tapping the steering wheel nervously. He slows the car down at the stop sign. If he goes straight, it takes us toward Kenyan. If he makes a right, we end up at Dravin's house off-campus. It feels like we are at a crossroad. "Do you want to stay the night with me? It's late, and it's just to sleep. I don't expect—"

I turn my head, giving him a smile and flashing my teeth when I blurt, "I would love to." He smiles, turning the wheel and heading to where he stays with Dravin.

WE ENTER THE HOUSE, and it is quiet. It is the beginning of February, so it is still cold outside. The fire is lit, casting a romantic glow in the living room. Is Gia here with one twin or both? Maybe she is at the main house with her men.

Reid closes the front door, brushes past my shoulder, and whispers, "They're not here. It is just us."

Despite my nervousness, I'm excited to be here alone with Reid. I can't think of anything except how he is and acts around me. There is something about the way he consumes me. If he stares at me, I get lost in his black eyes, the color of a dark galaxy. There is nothing and no one at that moment except him. Except us. Everything else just fades away.

I follow him up the stairs to his room, remembering the last time I was here and practically out of it. He took care of me, and he didn't take advantage. He discreetly called a doctor to check me out and ensured I was alright. Even though he didn't follow up with me afterward, it doesn't change the fact that he saved me in a way. He didn't judge me, even if he was upset that I didn't tell him what happened and with whom.

He turns the knob of his bedroom, pushes the door open, and steps aside to let me in. Both times I have been here, it was under different circumstances but now I can take my time and let it sink in. My eyes find the king-size bed, promising comfort. A big contrast to the bed back home with the hard springs that dug into my sides as I got older.

I honestly prefer the reason I am here now. I couldn't appreciate Reid when we had sex the first time in this room because I was too busy chasing away a demon, but not tonight. Tonight, I'm with him because I want to be here. I want to feel him next to me.

Deep down I have fallen for Reid without meaning to. My thoughts fly to Z, and a wave of guilt filters over me, but then it fades because a few encounters and a couple of letters don't count as a relationship. What I truly want is behind me, and he doesn't know it because I'm too much of a coward to express my feelings for him. It just happened, and it doesn't matter how often Michael blackmails me, and I try to erase what he has done to me. My feelings for Reid stay the same. I think they always will.

Reid pulls the covers back, and his head lifts when he notices I don't move. His midnight eyes lock with mine. "I won't touch you if you don't want me to, Jess. You have a choice. If that makes you more comfortable, I can sleep in the spare room."

My lips part because that is the last thing I want. I want him to hold me. I want him to make love to me. Even if it is just for one night, I like sex to feel different...with him.

"What if I want you to touch me," I say softly.

He looks so grown up in his dress pants and shirt, and I imagine we just came from a dinner with our friends, and I'm his wife. He's turning the bed down, waiting for me to undress, so we can make love for the millionth time, and it feels like the first time every time.

"Then, I'll touch you how you want me to, and if you tell me to stop, I will."

A silent tear slides down my cheek, and I approach him. He stands at his full height when my chest ghosts his torso. "Don't stop," I say.

He lifts my sweater over my head and undoes my bra, throwing it across the room. He pushes me onto the bed, my feet hanging over the hedge. He bends to remove my boots and pulls my leggings off one leg and then the other.

I'm left in my panties, leaning on my elbows on the mattress, watching him undo the buttons on his dress shirt. His skin is perfect, with no blemishes. His tattoos of death and angels are drawn over his skin like beautiful works of art.

His eyes skate down from my nipples to my thighs and then back to my face. "You're beautiful, Jess. Has anyone told you that?"

"Not the right people."

He undoes his belt, and his pants drop along with his boxers. His cock juts out with a piercing at the tip. "Am I the right person, Jess?"

I lick my lips nervously because I want to wrap my mouth around the head of his cock and taste him. I close my eyes because, with sex, I always erase what I didn't want to happen, but I can't use him for that. The first time I have given oral sex was when Michael forced me to that night in his Mustang. If I allow it, my heart wants it, and my soul begs for it. Right now, it's begging for him.

"Yes."

He grips the base of his cock, and I look up at the beautiful head with a Prince Albert piercing, wondering how it would feel raw against my tongue.

"Do you want me, baby?"

I nod slowly, my chest rising and falling. My nipples pearl under the heat of his gaze, and I push myself off the bed to swipe my tongue over the head and hear him growl. I moan, taking him inside my mouth.

"Fuck, Jess."

I take him as deep as I can; there is still room left, but he doesn't push. He slides his fingers into my wavy locks in the back of my head, holding me so I can bob my head in and out, deep and slow. He hits the back of my throat, and I relax. Gripping him by his narrow hips, I fuck him with my mouth. The salty taste of his precum sliding down my throat.

I could suck his cock forever if he let me. He pulls out, and I lick my swollen lips, hoping it was as good for him as it was for me.

"I'm not going to last, baby. You have a mouth that I would kill for."

He leans and takes my lips with his, tasting himself. I smile at his praise, and he cups my breasts, teasing my nipples. His head lowers, his tongue flicks one nipple and then the other, sucking each one with just the right pressure.

He pushes me back on the bed and reaches between us, ripping the panties off my pussy. The head of his cock teases my slit. His nostrils flare like he is struggling, but he takes it slow.

He rubs his cock on my clit, spreading my arousal between the lips of my pussy, dipping the tip of his finger inside and then out. Repeatedly.

His head dips again as he takes one nipple in his mouth and then the other.

My hands respond to the delicious torture by pulling his hair tighter. "Mm, more, Reid. I need more," I plead, my voice soft and needy.

"I'll give you whatever you want if you ask."

His neck arches, and he is holding himself above me. "I want you, Jess."

His head dips, and he furrows his brow as the tip of his cock slides inside me, stretching me.

"Yes. Fuck, yes."

My legs are wide open, and I watch as he slowly enters me, and his eyes lock on mine like our souls are connecting. "Perfect. You feel perfect."

I bite my lip when he is all the way in. I close my eyes and wait until I can adjust. He is so big. Bigger than anyone else I have had.

I grind my hips when my pussy throbs seeking more. He grins and lowers himself over me, holding his weight by framing my face with his hands. He captures my lips, while moving inside me, making love to me.

My hands slide down to the hard muscles rippling on his back, and my soul wants to stay locked with him forever. There are no words that can explain the emotion I'm feeling. With each tender kiss he gives me, he takes the hurt and shame away. And I desperately fall into him.

I arch my back when his lips fall to my neck, licking my skin with his tongue. My hands stretch above my head, and he pins both my wrists, grinding into me. Beads of sweat have pooled on my lower back, and our skin is slippery like we just took a shower. The sounds of wet skin smacking echo in the room. Our hips move in sync with each thrust faster and faster, causing my climax to build.

I moan his name on my lips, and he whispers, "This is the part where you fall, and I catch you." He thrusts into me and stills. My walls clench, and I hear him groan.

I'm holding my breath when I come hard and then gasp, taking in large amounts of air and trying to feed my lungs. His cock twitches, and I feel the heat of his cum dripping inside me, marking me as his.

REID

THE TIP of the pool stick hits the ball, making it into the left corner pocket, and my eyes straighten and dart to Valen.

It's Tuesday, and the Bedford twins are playing pool on the next table over, while I play a game of pool with Valen as we wait for Jess and Gia to show up at Babylon like we planned after school.

"I heard you were with Jess Saturday night," Valen says.

I nod, without looking him in the eye because I would rather not discuss Jess with a guy she has slept with, even though we are like brothers and there is no bad blood. I don't think I could handle him talking about her sexually.

"We hung out on Saturday and Sunday. I helped her with an assignment she had due."

He snorts, and my head lifts, giving him a glare. "Damn, it's serious," he says with a grin.

"I'm not going to answer that," I reply.

He wants me to admit that I have fallen for Jess, and honestly, I don't know because it has never happened to me before, but all I know is that I don't want her to go. I want her to stay with me. I want to breathe in the smell of her hair, taste the sweetness of her skin, and suck the juices from her pussy. It is all I can think about.

"I will," Dravin says with a knowing smirk. "It is very serious." He points at me, and I roll my eyes. "This motherfucker will cut your dick off and bury it in a pile of shit if you touch that woman. Jess is off-limits. Playtime with her is over, my friend. He was helping her with an assignment, alright. More like fucking like bunnies all day and all night Sunday. He was giving Gia and me a run for our money."

"You are aware that I'm standing right here, right? I can hear the shit you two are talking about Jess and me. Make sure that this conversation is not overheard by the assholes that just walked in," I say sarcastically, the last part causing Valen and the twins to look up.

Garret, Geo, and Mich show up with some guys from the swim team. My eyes immediately follow the newbie Mich, and there is something that doesn't add up, and then I remember that his father owns Cedar Lake. I know a rich asshole like Mich goes to private schools and probably doesn't know Jess, but it doesn't hurt to fish out information.

What's up, guys? I got next game to whoever loses first," Garret says, walking up the steps where the two pool tables are to the left of the bar.

Geo nods and Mich smiles at us, like he is in a room with a group of celebrities and hopes one of us acknowledges him. *Not in the way you think, asshole.*

For some reason, I feel like beating his ass and cutting him from the bottom up.

Draven looks at his phone, and his lips break in a smile. The glow from the screen makes him look like a creature of the sea with two different colored eyes. "Gia and Jess are on their way," he says more to Dravin and me.

Valen walks up to Garret with an evil gleam in his eyes. "Don't fuck up, Garret. You know the rules. Keep your hands inside and your dick tucked in your ass when Jess shows up, or I'll shove this pool stick up there."

"Y-yeah man, whatever," Garret stammers.

We threatened Garret to stay away from Jess. He makes her uncomfortable because of what happened, and we couldn't care less if he's infatuated with her. He has obsessive tendencies, but his medication is through us, not the kind you get at the pharmacy.

"Wait, he was with Jess," Mich asks, looking at Garret like he is planning his murder.

While I align the pool stick to prepare the next shot, I ask Mich, "you're from Cedar Lake, right?"

"That's right. My father owns the town," Mich replies.

I didn't ask for your resume, asshole, but now this just got more interesting.

"Did you know Jess when she lived there?"

He arches a brow and grins like I said something funny. He shrugs and says, "Maybe. Apparently, a lot of people know Jess."

I give him an attempt at a smile. Valen watches him from the corner of his eyes, calculating. "I didn't ask you that. I asked if you knew Jess when she lived there. It's a simple yes or no question."

He chuckles low in his throat. "Hey, man. I get it. You all have this thing for the chick. Prey choose and all that. I knew her from school. Obviously, she was top of her class, and I had heard around here that she sucks dick like a champ, just like I heard when they talked about her back home. I saw her at a party once, and that's it. She was quiet and studied all the time."

My fingers tighten on the pool stick, ready to snap it in half. My knuckles turn white because he's calling her a whore.

Dravin's face is ashen when he looks at me and then back at Mich, like the son of a bitch grew three heads suddenly.

I recover quickly, masking my feelings inside, wanting to shove the pool stick down his throat, but I don't miss how Dravin keeps looking at him.

"Is that right," I say, trying to sound indifferent. My ears are ringing, like I'm about to blow a gasket.

The door to the bar opens and Gia and Jess walk in, wearing their hair straight, catching several appreciative male glances. They both look beautiful, but my eyes are only for her. They scan the room, and Gia's face beams when she spots us, but Jess's smile dies slowly. My eyes flick back to Mich, and the sound of wood splintering causes me to look down.

Fuck. I broke the pool stick. My head lifts, and Jess and Gia sit at the booth with Jess's back to us.

"Dude, you broke it," Geo says, but his eyes keep darting to where Jess and Gia are.

I'll drown the bastard if he gets close to her. I toss the broken stick in the trash and walk over to them.

"What about the game?" Valen asks.

"I broke the stick, dick."

Valen sucks his teeth, shaking his head. "I was right," he calls out behind me.

REID

I SLIDE in beside Jess and feel all the tension leave her body in waves. Something is wrong, but this isn't the time or place.

"Hey, beautiful?"

Gia waves her hand in my face, and I pull mine back. "I'm right here too."

"I see that, but I didn't come here to see you. I came for her." I slide Jess's hair behind her ear. My stomach clenches into knots, and I need to feel her. "Are you hungry? Would you like anything?"

Jess turns her head, and I kiss her cheek, slowly moving toward her ear and whispering, "Go to the bathroom."

I look at Gia. Her eyes widen, and she gives me a little nod. I slide out and watch Jess walk to the restroom as I asked. "I'll be back."

Gia arches her brow. "Are you seriously going to fuck my best friend in the bathroom?"

"Don't act like you haven't done it and you take two cocks." Her cheeks heat, and I chuckle, walking away.

I open the door to the restroom and turn the lock. I push open the larger stall, and she is there waiting.

"Miss me?"

She nods like I'm her savior and I'm here to rescue her or some shit. She jumps in my arms, but I turn her around and bend her over. "Hold on to the wall."

I tug her pants over her ass, while my other hand pulls out my dick. I slide it toward her slit, testing to see if she is wet enough to penetrate her cunt. When I'm satisfied, I ram my cock inside her, causing her to push back, holding her hand on the wall for leverage.

I fuck her.

I fuck her hard, loving the way we fit. Her ass hits my thighs with each thrust, causing little whimpers to escape her throat.

"You like that, baby, huh? Is this what you need?" I ask while her pussy is milking my cock.

"Yes, I need it. I want it deep and hard, Reid. Please."

We have been fucking like animals since Saturday night, and I have no intention of stopping. Jesse Sharpe is mine. Her pussy is mine.

"Tell me you're mine, Jess. That this is the only cock that belongs inside your pussy. Say it," I demand.

"I'm yours. I'm coming," she says and then lets out a moan.

"I'm coming–– fuck, this pussy is so tight," I say, feeling her pussy clench around my dick, and I want to live forever inside her cunt.

I pull out and she turns around, adjusting her pants. She drops to her knees. She takes my semi-hard dick and cleans me off with her mouth, and my eyebrows rise, loving this side of her. Her eyes flick up to mine with my dick inside her hot mouth swirling her tongue and tasting our cum mixed together.

I pet her head, pull her beautiful hair, and snag my bottom lip with my teeth. "My...my...Jesse Sharpe. You have such a pretty mouth. Let's fill it up."

REID

DRAVIN and his brother called me over to the house after I dropped Jess off at her dorm and made my way here. I didn't want to leave her, but they said to come alone. That it was important.

I jump out of the car, and unlock the front door. I walk inside. Gia, the twins, Valen, and the last person I expected is leaning on the counter with a predatory smile.

"What the fuck is she doing here?"

"I'm here to discuss matters about your girlfriend."

"There is nothing I have to say to you."

Veronica exhales, and her eyes harden. "I promised Alicia I would look out for you."

"Yeah, by playing little cat and mouse games with the Prey and fucking everyone in sight."

"I agree with him," Gia says.

"Your bestie might disagree."

"If you have done anything to harm a hair on her head, I'll slit your fucking throat, you evil bitch," I grit out, watching the hurt reflect off Veronica's face.

"I think you should hear her out. You need to know, tell him, Gia," Draven says.

My eyes land on Gia, and for the first time since I walked in, I notice that her eyes are red-rimmed. She is wringing her hands together. "I'm not saying this because I'm outing a secret Jess trusted me with, but it is for her safety that I'm telling you this, and something must be done because I'm afraid of what will happen to her if I don't."

Dread creeps in like a disease in my gut, trying to cut off my air supply. The need to protect someone so much since my sister's death is front and center. I want names and details because nothing else matters to me but her.

Gia closes her eyes, and a tear escapes down her cheek, and I know what she will say next is bad. It is going to change everything. "Jess told me that in her senior year of high school, she was invited to a party by a guy she had a little crush on. She just wanted to experience going on a date. She told me she was excited because she had never been asked before. His name was Michael. She didn't think that he would...." Gia trails off, her hand covering her mouth as a sob escapes her throat. Draven is holding her to his chest.

My insides burn, like they have been lit up on fire. Cold chills snake up my skin from the rage, causing me to clench my fists. The backs of my eyes go black like a dark abyss; all I can do is hear the next words that will break me in two.

Gia pulls away from Draven and wipes her face, trying to steady the sobs wracking her body. Her eyes find mine, and I give her time to compose herself so she can tell me what I need to hear.

"I think you need to sit down, Reid. What I'm going to tell you, and everyone else, cannot leave this room. It stays here, and how you deal with it is up to you but don't judge her. Don't treat her differently. Just...heal her."

Veronica clears her throat and my eyes dart over to her. "When Gia is finished, I have to tell you what I saw that night at the ball."

I'M SITTING in the church, staring into space, listening to a meeting take place. Dravin's father is talking about some asshole they have to take out in corporate America, but like always, it's all white noise to me. There is nothing I care about more than going and visiting my girl, but duty calls. The gauntlet is thrown, and I stand to address the Order.

I clear my throat and begin. "I have an announcement to make. I will not be marrying my betrothed. Unfortunately, she has decided that my first cousin is more appealing to her appetite." I pause and watch as pictures provided by my cousin of Tara with her legs spread eagle, waiting for my cousin to fuck her, are being passed around.

She wasn't called to this meeting for obvious reasons, but my plan has been set in motion. I would never consider marrying her, not while she fucks around with a family member. It is against the rules of the Order, unless there is an agreement with all parties involved, and I have no intention of sharing the woman I would call my wife.

Alaric is a man who doesn't turn down a willing woman. Of course, he asked if I was okay with it, and I told him he was doing me a favor. He smiled that evil smile of his and proceeded to do whatever the fuck he wanted. He knew I wouldn't agree if I wanted her.

"What you are seeing is something I don't agree with."

"What are you proposing?" Mr. Bedford asks with a gleam in his eyes.

"Not marrying her and marrying who I want to marry."

"Do you have a person in mind?"

"I will before graduation. I'll fulfill my obligation. You will be notified once it's done legally. I just ask that I have the option to choose my wife. I will have a wedding at the church as required."

Mr. Bedford turns and addresses my father and Valen's father. Then the rest of the top leaders. "All in agreement with his proposal and his decision?"

They all nod, and the gauntlet is thrown, echoing inside the church's walls. I'm a free man.

JESS

AFTER CLASS, I look over my assignment. The sun is setting. The yellow and orange hues filtering inside my room from the tiny window. My hand itches to call Reid, but simultaneously, I want to speak to Z. I need to tell him about Reid, hoping he will stop appearing like a deranged creep.

I pick up the phone and jolt when I hear my phone ring. I laugh at myself for being so jumpy and look at my mother's name flashing on the screen.

"Jesse?"

"Hi, Mom. How are you?"

"I'm good. I was wondering if you would make it here for your birthday."

I bite my lip and stare at the dress hanging outside my closet, remembering the night at the ball, the good parts and the bad. I left before getting the pictures that were taken, so I could give them to her to make her happy.

"Yeah, I'm coming."

"Really?"

"Yeah, I will be there this Saturday."

After hanging up, I check my bank account balance and let out a breath, a strand of hair flying forward. I'm trying to find the most affordable way to make it there and back. I've never looked forward to celebrating my birthday. It was always a hard day for me personally, especially when you know the person that wants to make the day special is struggling to do it.

A flight isn't an option, so driving is the only way I can afford to go back home and make it back here. I grab my keys to make sure my car starts. I try not to use my car as much as possible, so I can save money, but right now, I don't have a choice.

Making my way to the Drury Hall parking lot, I'm relieved to see some students milling about. The sun has already set, and the temperature is slowly dropping. The trees are starting to sprout leaves as spring is looming. The flowers around campus are the only things that give the campus life. Other than that, it looks like an academy for Vampires with the gothic style architecture and the cemetery right in front of the church.

I place the key in the lock and sit in the dingy car with leaves strewn all over the windshield.

"God, this thing is a piece of junk," I mumble.

I start the ignition, and the engine turns over, but it doesn't start. I place my forehead on the steering wheel. "Fuck."

"You need a ride?"

The hairs on the back of my neck stand. I turn my head, and Michael stands outside my open driver's side door.

I stare straight ahead. "No," I reply.

He steps closer, and before I can close the door, he places his hand inside and pulls it toward him. "I'm surprised you still drive this piece of junk. You would think with all the bonuses I pay you, you would get a better piece of shit, if that is even a thing."

"I can give you a ride this time if you need to go somewhere, but of course, like everything in this life, nothing is free."

I take a deep swallow and close my eyes. "No, thank you."

"Now, I'm not asking. I'm telling."

"I said no."

A couple of students walk down the sidewalk, and I take my cue and step out of the car. I know he won't try to do something if there are witnesses. Weasels like Michael are calculating but also cowardly. They wait like predators but hate confrontation.

I slam the car door shut and lock it. I smile at the girls looking at Michael, giving him appreciative glances. If they only knew he's a rapist and a blackmailing piece of shit. I swear, if my car started, I would run him over repeatedly.

"Do you go to church?" I ask.

"Not for what you think," he replies.

I turn around and face him, my lip curling in disgust. "You should. You need to start praying."

I throw the insult in his face like he did in the bathroom at the ball but for an entirely different reason.

He chuckles. "Now, why would I need to do that if I have you to do it, silly."

I tilt my head back and laugh, a confused expression crossing his features.

"What's wrong, Mich. Am I supposed to quake in fear? Beg?"

"If you know what is good for you, yeah."

Whatever he has planned, let it happen. I can't keep hiding, trying to cope with the agony when he toys with me every time he comes close. I stopped trying to suppress the pain I constantly feel.

"I'm not going to fuck you. I'm not going to go with you, Michael."

He laughs maniacally. "Oh, yeah?"

"Yeah," I snarl.

"We'll see. Don't worry, I'll make you pay for your little outburst later."

"Do your worst, you piece of shit," I spit and walk away, catching a group of girls walking into Drury Hall.

When I make it back, I stop to catch my breath for a moment in my room, making sure I lock the door. I walk to flick the light switch on and suck in a breath.

"I've been waiting for you."

Z is sprawled on my bed wearing his mask, dressed in all black. His gloves are tight on his fingers resting on his stomach.

"You think you can just show up when you want. I haven't seen or heard from you for a while."

"Aww, miss me? I thought you were entertained these past few days with a certain someone. Tell me. Do you like the way he fucks you? Do you like the way he takes you to that place you crave to go, or do you like it better when my tongue fucks your cunt."

"Fuck you."

"I plan on it. It is convenient. Lucky for you, I'm not jealous of him.

"What the fuck are talking about?"

I hate the way he mocks me and evades the question. I'm on edge. Two assholes in one day is my fucking limit. I'm pissed.

"Did you tell him about us, little Sparrow? Did you tell him how much we enjoy each other's company?"

"I thought you didn't exist? It doesn't matter because whatever this is, it will stop?"

He sighs under the mask. "I'm afraid that isn't possible. He gets you when I'm gone, and I get you when he's busy and can't handle matters the way I can. If that makes sense."

"It doesn't. You're crazy. Your whole existence doesn't make sense."

I stride up to him, not afraid anymore. I don't care because I know who I want in my heart, and I choose myself after everything I have gone through, I have learned I need to love myself.

"I would be careful if I were you. You might regret the words on your tongue."

"Oh yeah, why. You going to kidnap me?"

He gets up, and I take a step back, flinching when he lifts my chin. "Who pissed you off? Was it that little bastard standing by your car?" I avert my gaze because he saw, and it doesn't take a genius to guess he is the reason. "Look at me!" he demands.

I jump at his deep tone. "Now you know why I'm here. I needed to make sure dirty dogs don't sneak in the wrong house."

He was protecting me. That is why he is here. He cocks his head. The eerie way he does it with the mask on has bumps rising on my skin.

"I need you to leave. I have to go somewhere."

I need to be alone. I don't dare call Reid because I don't know where we stand. We have yet to talk about it. About us. Is he my friend? Boyfriend? All I know is that I'm done being a pig's toy.

"There's an idea? Where do you wish to go?"

"Nowhere with you," I reply.

"With him then? Your cock of choice. Okay, I'll wait."

I furrow my brows. "For what?"

"I'll wait to inflict my carnage and...to fuck you until your eyes roll back in that pretty skull of yours, like you're a demon possessed. Possessed by me and my cock."

"Good luck."

He rolls his neck, and I hear his bones crack, easing the ache of his muscles. Whoever he is, he must be strong on top of the fact the man gives off the air of danger. I'm so used to being around it that I've given up, letting it consume me if that is what it wants. I remember what Veronica said about the one that doesn't exist. He comes and goes as he pleases, and no one can stop him.

"Until next time, it's a date. One that you will enjoy or...not. It all depends."

"On what exactly?"

"How much you are willing to take. How much you can handle because, like it or not, I'm not going anywhere, Jesse. I'll haunt you because I choose you."

"What if I don't want to be chosen," I say to his back.

He heads to the door and turns his neck, the beak of the mask hiding his eyes.

"It doesn't matter, Jesse. You will understand when the time comes. You will understand there isn't a choice." Then he walks out, leaving me more confused and out of control.

REID

IT'S DONE. Warren is dead. The Order sent the alert, and his parents have been notified. He killed himself. He was sent home with enough drugs to make any sane person go crazy with suicidal thoughts, and the bastard hung himself. His eyes were sunken, bulging out of his head.

"The trash has been taken out," Dravin says.

"Does Gia know?"

He nods. "She is relieved and has accepted it."

"Does she know the truth?"

I'm asking whether she knows he killed himself slowly, painfully, and tragically.

"She suspects but not the details. I wanted to spare her from knowing more. The barista was enough to know what I would do for her. She doesn't have to look over her shoulder and wonder. His parents will announce it to the school once all the preparations are made to bury him. How about you? How are you holding up?"

Like I want to commit murder. I'm still working on the details for Jess. She needs to heal. Valen understands where they both stand, knowing why Jess has done what she has done. The scrubbing in the shower. The way I found her when she collapsed in my arms. The puzzle pieces are all coming together. I just hope she can handle what I have planned for her. I have never tried to win a girl's heart before, but she's worth it. I just wish I had known that sooner.

I turn off the faucet and shake my hands in the sink, hearing Dravin flush the toilet. I'm drying my hands when I hear voices in the hallway, but the class just outside isn't over yet.

I furrow my brows and turn to see Dravin wash and dry his hands, and then I hear it again, the voice louder this time.

What the fuck?

I open the door, and people are taking pictures and recording with their cell phones, aiming toward the wall. I walk up to it and see it dripping with red paint and then read: ARE YOU INSANE LIKE ME?

I see the classroom door open, and Jess walks out, followed by the bastard I want to rip into pieces as he stares at the wall.

"Did you?" Dravin asks.

I shake my head. "No, I—"

"Yo!" Valen shouts, interrupting me as he strides up to us with a smirk on his face, but my attention is held by the woman walking in front of me.

Jess lifts her head, and our eyes lock. She looks edible in her comfy sweater and signature leggings. I grin, and she smiles.

I waited for her so I could make sure the bastard didn't corner her, but I didn't want him to catch on.

When she walks up to me, I smile wide, showing all my straight teeth, and slide my hands around her waist, giving her a peck on her delectable lips. I close my eyes and breathe in her sweet scent.

"How's class. Did you get an A?" I ask. "Do you need me to go in there?"

She giggles. "I did and no, I'm okay."

No, you're not, baby. You haven't been okay, but I don't tell her that.

"Good."

"Where's my kiss?" Valen asks with a grin on his face when he comes up next to us.

Jess gives him a pointed look, not knowing how to answer. I tighten my hold on her waist and drag her toward me.

"I'm afraid you'll need to find another girl to ask because this one is taken."

I make it a point to say it loud enough for the asshole in her class to hear. His eyes narrow, and I could have sworn he curled his lip in a snarl, but I don't break my stare. I hold it, aimed directly at my intended target. *Touch her again and die, asshole. Your days are numbered.*

"Taking charge, Riordan. I like it."

People in the hallway begin to do their business, but Mich keeps looking at the words sprawled across the wall. He stills and stares at it for another minute.

When Jess heads back inside the class, I walk up behind him, wishing I could snap his neck. Not yet. But in time.

"Are you?"

He turns. "What? Was this you?

His blond hair is glued to his head like a helmet with so much gel I'm surprised he even has hair to begin with.

"Does it look like it was me?"

"The way you asked. It seemed like..."

"It couldn't have been. I was in the bathroom, and I don't remember seeing it there when I walked past. I was just wondering if you were insane?"

"No, why would you think that?"

I smile at him like a Cheshire cat. "There are three types of people. Mad, crazy, and insane. Which one are you?"

"None, but if I had to choose, I would choose crazy."

"For some, that isn't enough, and for others, they didn't choose wisely," I reply, nudging my head to the door. "Get back to class; you never know if there is an insane person on the loose fucking around."

I turn around and wait out of sight until he enters the classroom, while I patiently wait for my girl.

JESS

"JESSE?" My mother comes outside the bar. I was waiting until her shift was over so I could surprise her this weekend.

Reid convinced me to allow him to drive me over. I couldn't pass up the hours I would be able to spend with him so I agreed. He offered to fly us but I refused. He had already offered to have a driver take me anywhere I wished to go since my car wouldn't start. To be honest, though, I preferred to spend the six hours it took us to get here just the two of us.

We stopped to fill up and get snacks: potato chips. I told him which ones I was sick of and couldn't stop eating if I tried. For me, it was regular Doritos, and he likes anything barbecue.

Gia told me what happened to Warren and how he died, but we all know the truth. I have to give it to Dravin and his brother. The way they made it look was brilliant. No questions. No deep investigations. And no one questions anything, not even his parents.

"It's me, Momma. I'm here."

I'm embarrassed that I don't have money to stay at a hotel in town, but my mom always keeps the trailer clean as best she can inside. On the outside, it looks like a bunch of alley cats raided it, but it's home, and she makes me feel loved no matter what. Amanda Sharpe is a saint.

"Oh my God, I can't believe you're here." She breathes me in when she hugs me tight. I don't care if she smells like alcohol and fried food. She's Mom.

"Are you ready for the best birthday ever?"

"As long as it's with you, Mom."

"It looks like you picked a good one over there," she whispers. "He's eye candy that has stolen my baby's heart, hasn't he?"

I nod, not wanting Reid to overhear that my mother has noticed since I arrived that I have fallen hopelessly in love with him. I knew she would see it when we showed up. Why hide it. I'm tired of hiding. I'm tired of hurting.

REID

A WOMAN in a waitress uniform and an apron walks down the steps and stops in front of Jess, giving her a tight hug that causes me to smile. You could feel their love and respect for each other, just by watching them together. The bond between mother and daughter.

I look up at the bar sign her mother works at, and I know it is owned by the Levines. The whole town is. A thought formulates in my head, and I smile to myself.

"Momma, I have someone I would like you to meet," Jess tells her mother.

I step forward, giving her my best smile. "Miss Sharpe. My name is Reid Riordan."

Her mother pulls away from Jess, and her eyes take me in. "Jesus, Jesse. He's gorgeous." She walks up to me and tries to wipe her hands on her apron. "I apologize for my rude manners. I'm not used to Jess bringing someone home."

I'm the only one she will ever bring home.

"It is a pleasure to finally meet the woman responsible for raising the perfect woman."

She blushes, and I have never wanted the approval of someone like I do right now because it would mean so much to Jess.

"Aren't you a charmer," Miss Sharpe says with a smile. "Please call me Amanda."

Jess is the exact replica of her mom. She reminds me of an older Jess. She looks like a hard-working lady that took care of her responsibility the best way she could. I look across the street at a diner and then back at the bar.

"If you don't mind me asking, how long have you been working at the bar?"

"Oh, not too long. My hours were cut , but Jess's friend Michael from high school was kind enough to give me a job here. Business at the bar slowed down, and they cut my hours at the diner across the street."

I see Jesse stiffen and recognize her body language when the underlying cause——when the piece of shit--is mentioned.

I open the driver's side door to my black Mercedes. "You're driving, babe. You and your mom can sit in the front; I'll take the back."

"Oh." Her eyes soften when she hears me call her, babe. The endearment is new, but it fits when it comes to Jess.

I sit in the back seat and fire a few texts to my father. I have a business proposition for him. One he would take an interest in.

WE REACH the dirt road leading to Jesse and her mother's trailer, recognizing it immediately from my research on Google Maps. I hate to say it but Google accurately depicts what it looks like.

She must feel embarrassed about her living situation, but she shouldn't. I have seen countless pricks at school that have everything and become the worst human beings on the planet. Jesse and her mother are just victims of people like that. But all of that is going to change.

Jesse stops in front of the shitty trailer and parks in the only parking spot by the pissed-stained door.

I look around and see a crackhead twitching across the street. The burnt grass that hasn't been mowed mixed with dirt and weeds. The car doors open, and I watch her mother walk up to the door with a small smile.

"I know it looks bad, but I try to keep it tidy inside, especially for Jesse. She always did the cleaning for me while I was working after school. She would take odd jobs to help me out. It was how she bought her car. Did she tell you that?"

Her mother rambles on, trying to make a good impression like any good mother would.

"No, but she doesn't have to, Miss Sharpe, because I know she is a hard worker. She doesn't party like most college kids. You raised her right."

Jess walks by and gets on her tiptoes to kiss me on the cheek. "Thank you," she rasps against my skin.

I'm fighting the urge to take her in the car and fuck her in the back seat but I need to behave with her mother around.

I walk in behind Jess, taking in the small trailer. It smells like an old storage closet mixed with those little smelly things in the outlets. The carpet is old but clean. The counters are spotless, if you overlook the peeling cheap Formica on the surface. In what is considered the living room, the couch looks like they picked it off the curb for bulk trash.

"This is home," Miss Sharpe says, closing the yellow refrigerator.

I didn't think they made those, but I guess they exist. There is no fucking way I'm letting them stay in here. Not with that crackhead outside. I'm surprised he hasn't come in here and hurt them.

I don't know what to say. Thousands of dollars in education doesn't prepare you to answer a question like that when you see someone living in a shitty trailer. What do you say? How do you respond? You have a lovely home and sound like a lying douchebag. A fake rich prick from wealth, lying to her face after she rode in a car that costs just as much as she makes in five years, including tips.

I feel the draft of the chill from outside seeping in and notice no heating or central air. There is only one air conditioner on the wall, and I can't take it. I can't.

"I was going to wait to tell you both my surprise, but since we are here, I would like for you to pack a bag, Miss Sharpe. We are going somewhere special."

Not a total lie. I have to check to see if I have any of my five-star hotels in the area because there is no way I will have them stay in anything less.

"Oh, but I have to be back by Sunday so I can get ready for work."

"You'll be back, I promise." I smile.

Honestly, she'll be back, but not in the way she thinks.

JESS

I WASN'T aware Reid had anything planned, but I think it was Jimmy the crackhead walking out after his last crack hit that changed his plan. Not the best thing to come home to, but he's harmless, considering. He keeps to himself, doesn't bother anyone, and just stands with a cardboard sign that reads:

YES, I'M ADDICTED TO CRACK. ANYTHING HELPS TO KEEP ME FROM DYING.

I used to think it was funny until I realized it wasn't, but at least he was honest. Being honest got me bullied at school when people would see where I lived.

Maybe Reid was so disgusted he refused to be in the trailer another second, and I can't say I blame him.

"Where are we going? What is the surprise?" I ask.

He clears his throat. "I'm taking you to my hotel. You ladies are going to be pampered for the weekend. And I can't tell you about your birthday present because it wouldn't be a surprise, would it?"

I smile, falling more in love with him with each passing second.

"I guess so."

"Jesse, let the poor man surprise his girlfriend," she scolds.

My mother likes him. She likes him a lot. I was afraid she would be intimidated by the tattoos and the piercings, but Reid is perfect, and he said all the right things. It felt genuine.

He parks in the valet at the same hotel he first took me to the night we had sex in the elevator, and it is déjà vu all over again with the valet. It is late, but the hotel operates at full capacity twenty-four seven.

I wait for Reid to open the door, but he surprises me by opening both for my mom and me.

"Oh, boy. You have outdone yourself, young man," Mom says, looking around with wide eyes, taking it all in.

"Mom," I rasp out, smiling but also trying not to feel embarrassed.

It really is a beautiful hotel. My mother has never experienced something so lush and her reaction is understandable. Reid has his staff taking our few bags up to the room.

I inwardly smile and can't stop looking at Reid and how he carries himself. We walk into the lobby, a very different experience since the last time I was here.

"Right this way, sir. Will you be requiring anything further?" I hear one of his staff ask in a professional voice.

"Yes, I would like dinner to be served at the restaurant below for three." I hear him say it is his girlfriend's birthday, and my stomach swarms full of butterflies. "Please have the kitchen staff available."

"Is this all really yours?" I ask.

"Yes, it is. I run everything remotely. My major is computers and hospitality. Even though we both know it isn't necessary, I didn't want anyone to think that I didn't have an education and was just a byproduct of my inheritance."

Reid is proud of who he is and doesn't take his businesses lightly. He has earned his place within his family. The way he treats his staff tells everyone who he is underneath. Not some spoiled man who thinks people should bow to him because he comes from wealth and has power.

"I can tell you are very good at what you do, and you know how to run things efficiently, but most of all, they all respect you. It says a lot. I love that about you."

He smiles, and I can tell by his expression not many people compliment him for his effort and hard work.

"Do you or your mom need anything? Anything at all, you just ask, and it will be provided."

"Being here and allowing us to be your guests is more than anyone has done for us. We have never stayed in a hotel this nice. My mother can't stop looking around at it all."

Lust-filled eyes look back at me, darkening into black orbs. He leans close and grazes his lips by my ear. Chills rise over my neck, causing me to quiver. His manly scent fills my senses, and I almost feel dizzy. "I have a nice treat for her while I'll have my dessert."

MY MOTHER LOOKS AROUND, worried about what she is wearing compared to the other guests in the restaurant by the bar, but I assured her it was fine. She keeps touching her hair, trying to tame the massive curls.

"It's ok, Mom. You look fine. I didn't have time to straighten my hair," I soothe. I touch the tips of my curls to assure her, but she still looks unsure.

Reid places the menu down and smiles. "I'm always telling Jess how much I love her hair. I love it the most when it's in a natural, wild state when she wakes up in the morning. Trust me, no one will say anything."

My heart catapults in my chest as he smiles broadly at the innuendo. I watch the tip of his tongue lick his piercing, and all I can think of is dessert.

Him being the dessert.

JESS

AFTER DINNER, Reid had my mother retire to her own private room with a masseuse and all the luxury toiletries to prepare for her bath before bed.

We are in Reid's penthouse suite, and my ass is perched on the edge of a black Grande piano. After a hot shower, my robe is unbelted, and I'm naked underneath. My legs are wide open, and Reid is staring at my pussy with his head cocked.

"I'm going to cum inside your pussy all night. Would you like that?"

"Yes," I plead.

My eyes take in the gothic-styled penthouse. It reminds me of an ancient hotel mixed with modern touches like the stainless-steel appliances in the black wood kitchen with white granite counters. Everything is black and shiny like the piano I'm currently sitting on. He slides on the thigh high panty-hose up on each of my legs. The silkiness of the fabric feels soft. The black lace at the end of each thigh.

He places his hands around my waist and grips my hips. His face dips to capture my lips. "Fuck me," I beg.

"Hard?" I nod.

"Fuck me. The way you really want to."

He bites his bottom lip, the tip of his cock at my entrance. His eyes flick to my face, and I hold my breath when they smolder. The moonlight filtering in from the large windows behind us glow on his face.

I arch my back and widen my thighs, giving him open access to my pussy sliding my smooth legs over his hips. I tilt my head to watch the piercing on the head of his cock rub against my swollen clit.

"Are you ready to take me, Jess?"

"God, yes," I beg.

I want him to claim me. I want to feel him the way he wants to touch me. Nothing held back.

He plunges inside me, and I gasp. He doesn't stop. He fucks me hard. The back of my heels hit the piano's keys, making a loud sound, but he doesn't let up. My tits bounce with each thrust with only the thigh high panty-hose on my legs. Reid is like an animal fucking me into oblivion. My pussy clenches on his cock, and he lets out a grunt.

"Are you mine? Is this...mine?"

He releases one hand from my hip and pinches my nipple, causing me to moan loudly.

"Tell me, Jesse. Is this pussy mine?"

"Yes," I say on a whimper.

He pumps into me, and I arch my neck. He slaps my nipples, and it causes me to come. "Oh. Fuck."

My head tilts back when I come and come. I struggle to form words, but he doesn't stop fucking me. The noise of our skin slapping is all that I hear. A train can be heard in the distance, but my ears are only privy to the sound of our bodies.

He pulls out and flips me around, letting the tips of my toes hit the black marble. He pulls the robe from under me and drops it to the floor.

"Now the fun begins," he says with a growl, bending me to take me from behind. His fingers wrap around my hair, and he plunges his cock inside my swollen pussy. He thrusts and grunts, his movement turning erratic.

"More," I scream.

I want more. One time is not enough. I feel the need pull low in my belly; all I can think about is the next time.

He chuckles and pulls my hair, whispering, "That's my girl. Don't worry, baby. We haven't even started."

JESS

AFTER BREAKFAST IN BED, Reid had scheduled appointments for my mom and me at the spa. My mom was so tired after all the pampering she received and fell asleep. I had to wake her after too many hours went by. I'm worried she works too hard, and one day she will faint from exhaustion.

Reid fucked me hard all night. The man has stamina and a beautiful body. He's like a well-oiled machine. There isn't an ounce of fat on him. He is pure muscle wrapped in sin with a face like a model. I couldn't tear my eyes away from him when he pranced around naked in the room.

I hear the sound of a doorbell, pinch my brows, look around, and then smile. I'm not used to a doorbell. I wince when I get up to answer the door because I'm sore from the delicious rough sex.

"Can I help you?"

A woman is holding a very large garment bag and smiles. "Yes, Mr. Riordan requested I bring you this dress."

"Oh."

I step back and let her pass. He bought me a dress?

I watch her placing it inside the master bedroom, and a shoe bag hangs from the hanger.

I wait until she leaves, desperate to take a look. My heart is slamming inside my rib cage in anticipation. He said he needed to take care of some things when he woke up this morning, but I never thought it included a dress.

I lay the black garment bag on the huge bed with black sheets. I pull the zipper slowly and gasp at the black silk dress with a thigh-high split. I peek inside the shoe bag and smile at the red open-toe sandals.

My phone vibrates on the table, and I see it's a text from Reid.

> Reid: Be ready at six sharp.

> Jess: Okay, Thank you for the dress.

> Reid: Thank me later. ;)

I smile and look at the dress once more. I feel like a fairy-tale princess, and my biggest fear is for it to be taken away, or worse, to be back in the nightmare that was my life.

As promised, Reid knocks on the bedroom door at six in the evening. I open it, ready to go. My mom said she was staying in her room to relax and would see me later.

All the pampering got to her, and I have to thank the man staring at me right now. I'm speechless while I take in how good he looks wearing another tux with a red rose in his pocket jacket and a red silk bow tie.

"Hi," I say.

He visibly swallows, while his eyes slowly travel from my toes up to my face.

"You look stunning."

A blush creeps up my cheeks. "You look very handsome, and I love the red."

He pulls a little black box from behind his back, and my eyes widen when I see a red corsage. He takes it out and holds it in his hand.

"Red is the color of presence and absence. Life and death. And most importantly, love and passion."

My heart somersaults inside my chest when he slips it on, and I smile. He holds out his arm, and I slide mine through, my cheeks hurting from constantly smiling.

"Thank you."

"Happy Birthday, Jesse."

The elevator dings once it reaches the penthouse floor. We enter and I can't stop smiling on the way down. We reach the hotel's ballroom when the elevator doors open, and I gasp.

There is a sign above the entrance that reads **Welcome to Prom**. My mother is standing in a beautiful high-necked dress, waving at me. I blink back the tears that well up in my eyes.

"Jesse Sharpe, will you do me the honor of accompanying me to prom?"

I nod. "Yes," I say with tears in my eyes.

"Please don't cry."

I fan my face, trying not to ruin my makeup. "I'm so sorry. I just never thought I would..." I trail off.

There are black and red balloons replicating the arch you see in a typical high school prom. A photo booth is next to the entrance, and a photographer is waiting for us to approach.

"Oh my God, Jess. You look beautiful," my mother beams.

"So do you, Mom."

Reid poses with me in the picture, and I smile like a schoolgirl. My mother dabs her eyes because she got her picture, and I got mine.

"Thank you," I whisper when we face each other.

He slides loose hair away from my face. "No, thank you. We both get what we want. A prom with the person you imagined you would go with."

The doors are opened by his hotel staff, who are all wearing tuxedos, and I feel like I'm dreaming. Chandeliers are in the center of the ballroom, and tables are to the left, with everything decorated in black and red. The theme is beloved. Red punch that looks like blood is inside a bowl in the center at a buffet table with hors d'oeuvres. Couples are dancing, and they look like high school students.

I lean close and whisper, "Who are these people?"

"Not all of us were able to go to prom," he says, while looking around the ballroom full of different people, all wearing formal clothing. "These are some of the staffs' teenagers and their boyfriends and girlfriends.

"It's perfect."

"You're perfect," he says.

Music begins to play in the room. A slow ballad with a key from a piano, and I recognize Amy Lee's voice.

"Even in Death" by Evanescence plays, and Reid, guiding my hands, leads me to dance in the center of the room. His hand is on my waist in a formal stance, his eyes never leaving mine. He begins leading the steps perfectly in sync with the music, like he has been dancing for years.

When the song ends, the crowd erupts in applause. He dips his head and says softly, "I love you, Jesse Sharpe. This is the beginning of us and of the things I will try to make right in your life.."

ZERO

I WATCH her toss and turn in her sleep from the other side of her dorm room. After the weekend celebrating her birthday, I hold up my little gift that means so much to my little Sparrow.

It is a shame I must give it to her under different circumstances. She needs to learn to accept me if she wants me to allow her to be with him. She can't have just one because that will not work.

She's ready. I just hope she realizes it and accepts me for the monster that I am. The one that walks in the dark and no one sees. The one they all fear when I come out at night to play.

I walk over to her and watch her chest rise with each breath she takes. The love seeping out of her for him is the same love that can destroy her. An internal battle between good and evil burns inside me, and all I can think about is how to keep her. Keeping what I am from her is shortly coming to a close.

It is hard not to fall for her beauty; I can't blame Reid. He has the gift of her heart. But...we fell in love with her darkness. She fell in love with our demons. We were the perfect hell. But, she's mine. I'm the fire she feeds that will allow her soul to break free.

I leave her and walk down the dark corridor and meet Valen.

"You promise not to hurt her?" he asks under the mask once we are outside.

"Have I?"

"No, but you have to tell her what you are, Zero."

I back him up against the building pissed that he said my name out loud. "Shut the fuck up."

He raises his hands in surrender. He knows there is something more important I have to deal with right now. It cannot wait.

"He's in the room like you wanted."

"Good. Now let's go."

We walk through the secret door on the side of the building. It is how I get in and out of here without anyone seeing me. We make it to the fourth floor and use the master key in my pocket.

The area is dark, except for a white light flickering from the TV inside the room. The rooms are soundproof, and you cannot hear anyone inside. Perfect for the screams.

I take the lead, with Valen following behind me. When we reach the room with the biggest window, I cock my head and watch the look of fear expressed on his features. I'm sure he's going crazy with the sound of the TV as high as it can go. The sound must be bouncing off the walls.

"I can taste his fear," I say with a growl.

"W-what do you have in mind?" Valen stammers.

I watch him like a curious bird. I flip the switch, and the white strobe light flickers and I see him try to squint and his mouth opens. He's screaming in agony because he can't close his eyes. I'm sure I look scary as fuck through the glass.

"Have you ever seen the film called *A Clockwork Orange*? It's quite spectacular. The more I interact with him, the longer I can stay and feed off his screams."

"Dude. You can't show her this shit. You can't tell her..." Valen trails off.

I increase the speed of the strobe light, and his mouth hangs open, and I can see his tongue. Definitely, screaming.

"What I do with my future wife is my problem, not yours. I suggest you deal with your own. She has more carnal tastes than you do."

"You can thank Veronica."

"I didn't hear Veronica putting a gun to her head while she feasting on Jess's cunt. She swallowed more than she could chew."

"How do you know that?"

I chuckle. "Apparently, I know more than you."

Mich or Michael jerks in the medical chair I rolled in here from the Ophthalmologist's office to tie him up when Valen brought him in.

Valen knocked the fucker unconscious and gave him a hallucinogen. He likes to drug my girl to fuck her, which is what I'll start with.

I smile, open the door, and walk in, dragging the metal seat, making sure it squeaks really loud so I can sit and chat.

I turn the TV down but leave the light flashing. "Ah, ah, ahh!" I scream, laughing, loving the fear dancing in his eyes.

"P-please turn the light off. Make it stop. I'll do whatever you want," he pleads while the drool drips down his chin. Disgusting.

"Michael, Michael, Michael. Tsk. I see that you got yourself in a pickle.

"What the fuck are you? Who are you? How do you know my name?"

I cross my legs and angle my head, watching both of his eyeballs protruding from his pathetic skull.

"I know a lot of things. But I have recently found out that you're the disease, Michael. And I'm the cure."

His eyes widen when I stand, and he sees the long knife I pulled from its sheath from my coat. The perfect knife.

"What are you doing with that?"

"What normal people do is cut meat, but, in my case, insane people cut flesh."

"Please let me go."

"Why? Why should I let you go? I can't let you infect other people. I need to cure you of your sins."

I twirl the knife and know Valen can see me, probably wondering what lengths I will go to for my little Sparrow.

Michael can see out the window with the strobe light on, he doesn't know who the fuck is behind the mask, but I think before I'm done, he should see. So it can sink in when I revel in his screams and the reason that brought me here to hand him his fate.

I get up and walk around him and bend so he can feel the leather beak of the mask. "Do you want to know why you're here?"

"No, please. I'll give you whatever you to want."

"Can you go back in time? Can you undo what you have done?"

"I haven't done anything."

"Then I'm afraid there is nothing you can do."

"I'm telling you the truth."

"I'm sure you are, but if there is one thing the Order hates, is liars. They take what has been given when you break the rules."

He tries to close his eyes, but the device keeps his eyelids open. "What have I done?"

"The worst thing anyone could have done. You touched something that is mine, and I will take everything away from you and the piece of shit ball sack you came out of. You're a waste of sperm, honestly, and I'm doing the world a favor right now."

"I'm sorry. Please, I won't do it again."

"I'm afraid you're at the point of no return."

I walk behind him, bend to see his Achilles heel, and swipe the knife. I close my eyes and hear the guttural screams as his flesh slices open, the blood pouring out to pool on the sterile white floor.

Tears begin to trickle down his pathetic face, and I cut the binds of his hands, and he tries to stand, only to fall flat on his face.

"I wouldn't try to run if I were you. I ruptured your tendon, and it hurts like hell, but that is nothing compared to what I have in store for you," I say sharply.

I lean down and begin to swipe the knife, hearing it touch flesh. He screams in agony as I slash his skin.

"Please," he says with a sob, crawling on the floor like a snail.

I can't stand weak, pathetic humans. "Did she say please when you raped her? When you made her suck your pathetic cock?

"W-what?"

"Jesse Sharpe. You know her?"

"She's just a girl, man. She's a trailer-trash nobody. She liked me in high school. She had a crush on me, and I asked her to the party. It was just a little fun."

"Wrong answer."

I pull off the mask and smile at his bewildered face when he sees me. "No!"

"I'm afraid so. I'm afraid you have fucked with what is mine, and it is only fair I take what's yours, along with your worth as a man, which is small and insignificant."

I pull at his pants and cut off his pathetic flaccid cock and toss it across the room, letting it hit the window with a thud."

The strobe light flashes make the blood look trippy as hell while it oozes out. His screams are like a symphony to my ears. "Ahhhh! Ahhhhh!" I mimic his cries.

Such a waste of space.

I sit on the chair and watch him look at his missing dick as he swipes to see if it will magically grow back. His eyes widen, watching himself bleed out.

His chest is rising and falling, getting labored.

"You cut off my dick! You cut off my dick," he repeats with a sob.

"You stuck it in the wrong hole. They didn't like what you did. You can't blackmail Prey to fuck you, I'm afraid. It goes against the rules. They choose. You had balls walking in here and thinking we were stupid enough, and they wouldn't find out."

"You're insane."

"I've been called worse, and now you have pissed me off."

I aim the tip of my knife at his eye and feel a slight resistance as it enters his eyeball. He begins to convulse, and I pull it out, the blood splatting across the room. I stand and watch as the life leaves his other eye.

After donning my mask, I leave the room and hand Valen the large knife.

"Clean it up and send his cock in a jar to his parents."

"Jesus," he whispers.

AFTER A LONG HOT shower in the men's dorm, removing the evidence of what I have done, I go to the back side of the building to see my little Sparrow. Taking my time to look presentable. I scrub all the blood from my hands and hair.

It is time I take her out of that lonely room. She sleeps alone night after night when she is not with him. I want to sink into her body and feel her come apart for me.

I let myself inside her dark room with the skeleton key, softly closing the door. Her back is facing me, and I can't help but admire the curve of her waist. Her curly hair is full of waves, ending in a mass of curls.

I stride softly and slide my gloved finger over her exposed skin, watching bumps rise on her flesh from the light coming in from the window. I pull my hand back when I see her flip over on her side.

Her eyelashes kiss her cheeks, and the leaves from the tree branches cause shadows to dance on parts of her face. She looks like an angel, and I am about to free her soul from the demon that haunts her, keeping her mind in a cage on the edge of hopelessness. I can't erase the past, but I want to create memories with her to erase the ones that plague her in the dark. I want to be the one she turns to when she is afraid. The one she trusts.

I slide the backs of my fingers over her cheek, and her eyes flutter open. It takes her a second for her eyes to adjust to the dark and the dim light.

She gets up, sliding herself on the mattress until her back hits the wall. Her knees are almost to her chin in a defensive pose. "What are you doing here?" she asks.

"I have come for you."

She shakes her head, wiping her eyes. She pulls the sheet like that will stop me from taking her.

"I told you no."

"I'm afraid you don't have a choice. I have handled the problem, and it is the least you can do."

"Took care of what problem?"

I sigh. "Michael."

"M-Michael? How do you know that name?" she asks nervously.

"Like I said before, I know a lot of things. He touched what is mine, and so I took away what is his. Eye for an eye and all that. You can go to church and confess if it makes you feel better. I suggest mornings are the best time to go."

"What the hell are you talking about?" she asks with anger in her tone.

I know it is hard for her to talk about it. To admit it. It makes it more real when you do. Everything comes full circle.

"No more scrubbing your sins off that pretty skin."

She lunges off the bed and fists my shirt sobbing. "Don't lie to me. Don't play games. Please." She sobs on the last part.

"He's gone. You don't have to worry about him anymore. You have me, and you have him."

"I can't see your face."

"I promise. I will show you if you promise to hold me. It is all I ask, but I need you to go with me."

"A-are you going to hurt me?

"No. I'm going to save you."

JESS

I GET DRESSED while Z watches me seated on the bed. I can't see his eyes behind the black mask and hoodie over his head. I thought of running and calling Reid but feared he would hurt me if I tried.

He said he took care of Michael. I'm not stupid, if he is telling the truth, he killed him. I saw the message in the hallway and knew it was Zero, but I couldn't say anything to anyone.

"Hurry up, my little Sparrow. I don't like to be kept waiting."

I have been taking my time, but I know there is no way out. I don't have much of a choice.

"Will I be back?"

"I'm not going to kill you, but you will not be back to this room, except to get your things. Now, I want you to hold your hand out."

I sigh. "Why?"

"Because I asked nicely and want to give you something."

I hold out my hand, and he wraps his fingers around my wrist and tugs me closer, so I'm between his legs. I hesitate, and then he pulls hard, flipping me so I'm on my back, and he is pinning me to the bed.

I struggle for a minute at the shock of being tossed on the bed. "Get off of me," I say through clenched teeth.

He lowers his masked face. "You won't be saying that much longer, I assure you. Not when I'm pounding that sweet cunt."

He pulls my shorts down my thighs and I try to push him off, but he is too strong. He slides his pants off and releases his cock, pining me with one hand holding me in place. I can't move my head and can only look at the top of his mask.

He presses his cock, rubbing his hard length over my slit, and I close my eyes. "Please," I plead.

He rubs his dick over my pussy and grinds into me in a hard rhythm. Rage begins to course through my veins, and I manage to slap him across his face, and his head rears back, but the mask doesn't fall off.

He laughs. "You hit me. Now, you're being a bad girl."

"Fuck you."

He pushes my hands over my head and holds them with one hand. It is no use struggling. He is too strong and can do whatever he wants.

He pulls at my shorts, and I try to kick, but it gives him more of an advantage. He frees me of my shorts, flings them to the side of the bed, sinks his fingers inside me, and I gasp. I'm truly fucked.

"Shh. I promise you're going to love it, Jess. You're going to love it when you see."

He plays with my clit, circling it with his fingers, it's different and frantic.

He takes out his cock, and I am still. My body biologically gets wet, and I turn my head. I wait until I have a chance to escape and relax my thighs.

He plunges it inside me, and I whack him with everything I got. His mask flies off his head.

Dark inky hair is matted to his head, and I feel something on the tip of his cock. I freeze when my eyes focus, and he sinks inside me all the way to the hilt, my mouth flying open.

"No, it can't be. Your voice."

Black familiar eyes stare back at me, but they are different. Dark and unfamiliar at the same time.

"He's still here, Jess, inside me. We're two people in one, but you are mine. You're ours. I promised. This is the part where you fall, and I catch you."

Tears slide down my cheeks. Not believing what I'm seeing.

I reach and touch his face, but his movements are different. His body language.

"Hold me, Jess. I need you to hold me. I love you."

I nod and wrap my arms around him, holding him tight, wondering how I could have missed it. He's been here the whole time. Watching me. Protecting me.

He must have a multiple personality disorder. That's why Zero wouldn't show me his face and why he hides it.

Why Zero doesn't exist, but he does, inside Reid.

REID

SHE KNOWS MY SECRET. A secret I have kept from almost everyone except Valen, the twins, and, of course, my parents. I never meant to let it get this far, but there are things I do as Zero that I need to remember and some parts I do.

I stopped taking my medication because I needed to help Jess. Watching her that night when she was drugged triggered it. I had to save her because, deep down, I was already in love with her and couldn't lose her like I did when my sister Alicia was killed.

"So she knows?" Draven says.

"Yep."

"What about her mom? Where's she?"

"I had someone call her from the bar and tell her they would be closed for a few days and she would be notified, so I convinced her to stay at my hotel, all expenses paid, until they transfer the new ownership into her and Jess's name of the bar and everything those pricks owned."

"The town."

"Yeah, she's been working in that shithole for years. If anyone deserves to own it, it's Amanda Sharpe and her daughter." I nod my head.

"You bought a town for the girl that you love."

I nod. "And I took her to prom."

"And she met your other half. You can't forget about him."

"She gets two rides for the price of one. You're a genius."

I grab an orange and toss it at his head. "Apparently, not quite. I still have to ask her to marry me as my chosen and I'm not sure she loves me."

He catches it and tosses it on the counter and smirks. "So, get a marriage license and schedule the ceremony like the Order dictates at the end of the year. Get married on paper and wait" ––he makes silent quotation marks–– "on the church. Then ask her. Tell her to sign on the dotted line, and it's done."

"Do you have an idea of how I can ask?"

He grins. "Who's asking?"

He is trying to give me shit because of his brother and how he asked Gia to marry them both, but I don't have a choice, and they did.

"Yeah. Let me call him, and I'll get back to you," I say sarcastically, glaring at him.

He places the cup down that he's drinking, laughing at me. Fucker. He thinks this is funny, and all I can think about is the girl currently upstairs in my bed that means the world to me.

I MAKE my way up the stairs with the ring in my pocket. I found it in the clothes I was wearing last night. All I remember is that I was in Dravin's house with Jess in bed with one of the masks I wear on the desk. When it happens, I black out. I never leave it on the dresser, and I never leave it out in the open when I go to the Consortium's meetings.

I knew what happened before having to ask; it has been happening more when she is around, and of course, I haven't been taking the meds for obvious reasons, and I don't plan to.

I open the box, the flawless white diamond with two black diamonds on each side and I smile. I know what to do. It is the only way I can express how I feel. Jess isn't the type that needs an announcement. It needs to mean something. I just hope she can accept me for who and what I am.

JESS

MY EYES SQUINT, and I feel safe, floating on a cloud. One of my legs feels the cold air, and the other feels warm under the thick comforter, and I know by the feeling that I'm in Reid's room.

I peel my eyes open and feel something heavy on my hand. It's a ring. I rub it between my fingers and feel something smooth on top near my knuckle.

My eyes focus, and I stare. I just stare at the massive three diamonds on my finger.

"Good morning, my love."

My eyes find Reid sitting in the chair, and I know it's him because of his voice. It isn't as deep, and he enunciates his words differently. I fell asleep looking through my phone at his condition. Multiple dissociative personality disorder. It manifests when something traumatic can affect you mentally. In his case, his sister, Alicia's death and how he just had to accept it but couldn't deal with the blow of the pain.

Things can trigger it and manifest the disorder. I believe I was the trigger. He confessed he wasn't taking the meds they gave him, which made him so moody.

"Good morning." I smile and point to my crazy bed hair. "I'm sorry, I look like a wild animal this morning.

He was tugging on it last night and in the shower, or Zero was. He worshipped my body, telling me how sorry he was and to repeatedly hold him. I held him until Reid came back to me. I cried when he didn't remember everything. I showed him the letters and he read them to me. He also told me his plans for my mother and me.

I sit up, and there is a folder on the bed.

My gaze finds his, and he points. "Open it."

I nod, open the folder, and see his name scrawled on a signature line. I try to blink back the tears of happiness, but I can't. My tears slide down my cheeks. All the paperwork from his lawyers that has been drawn up. There is a pen and a sticky note where I need to sign.

To my wife Jess,

Meet me where the light meets the dark, and I will always find you.
Without you, I'm nothing. I want you to be part of me...all of me. Forever.
Will you marry me...right now? I can't wait, and you shouldn't either. I
love you, Jess. I hope you love me too.
Reid

I nod and pick up the pen and sign with my answer leaving my lips. "Yes! I love you, Reid Riordan. All of you. The fucked up parts, the crazy and insane parts."

He bolts out of the chair and picks me up in his arms, burying his face into my neck. "Fuck, I was so scared you would say no."

The door to his room opens, and Gia is standing with Dravin. I look up, and she frowns when she sees me crying.

"I could never say no to you. I love you, Reid. I love you."

"I take it she said yes, and from the looks of it," Dravin says, pointing at the paper, "she is Mrs. Riordan now."

Gia runs to the bed and screams with excitement. "You signed it! You're married, and we can have babies, and they can be the best of friends and we can raise them as brothers and sisters," she says, rambling with tears in her eyes.

I get up, donning my robe for modesty. I smile when Gia watches me from the mirror.

"I'm so happy for you, Jess."

I turn and give her another tight hug. "Thank you, I love you."

I look at the door when I hear footsteps down the hallway. I look up, and then I hear a familiar voice. My head turns, and I walk out with Gia to the bedroom and find Reid smiling, giving me that sexy wink.

"Jesse? Jesus, this place is gorgeous." I hear my mother's voice.

She comes into view. She looks like a boss lady. Her hair is done, and her makeup is delicately applied. Her clothes are all tailored, gone is the waitress uniform. Her black pencil skirt and cream-colored blouse look beautiful on her.

"Oh, Momma. You look beautiful," I tell her with a smile.

"Hello, Mom," Reid says, kissing her on the cheek.

"Oh, there is my boy. I can't thank you and Jesse enough for giving me a makeover and a wonderful vacation at your beautiful resort. I just found out that ballroom dancing is even offered in a hotel.

My mother is considered a millionaire overnight with all the newly-acquired businesses Reid signed over to her with his business plan. She goes on and on about all the activities she did at Reid's hotel for the four days there. He had a personal shopper pick out her clothes and take her to get a makeover as the new owner of all the businesses back in town.

"We have to get going, I'm afraid," Reid says.

"Where are we going?" I ask.

"House shopping, and you girls have a wedding to plan right before graduation."

AFTER THE WEEKEND full of house shopping for my mother back home, courtesy of Reid, I look one last time at my now empty room and furrow my brows when I see something on the floor by Gia's bed that I must have forgotten.

Holding the box in my right hand, I pick up the two string bracelets. I rub the pad of my finger over the red lettering, HER BELOVED, and the other bracelet reads, HIS BELOVED. Inside the box there is one of his notes.

> *My Dearest Sparrow,*
>
> *Some may perceive the villain as beyond redemption, but deep down, we all yearn for the same thing—to experience love or avenge it. And my love, that is precisely why I affectionately call you my little Sparrow, for you embody the essence of true love. No love surpasses the magnitude of what you mean to me, my beloved. There are no limits to what I would do for you. While you may have believed it was him at times, know that I was there too, by your side during your darkest moments. Even in the quietest moments, where silence prevails, I am there, unconditionally. The gentle touch of our intertwined fingers draws me closer to you, igniting a profound connection. He may represent light, and I, his shadow, yet it matters not, for we are inseparable and intertwined. You are an integral part of us, just as we are an intrinsic part of you. Across this lifetime and beyond, through the brightest days and the darkest nights, we shall forever be part of you. You are eternally cherished, our beloved.*
>
> *Eternally yours,*
> *Zero*

This is what he wanted to give to me that night. The gift was in his hand when he took my wrists, and I demanded he show me his face. But the words are the same ones Reid said the night at the hotel. He must have switched or whatever.

It doesn't matter to me because I love the good and the crazy. The sane and insane parts.

"You're a Riordan now."

I jump when I hear Veronica's voice and almost drop the paper and the box in my arms.

"You scared me."

"I didn't mean to. You know he's dead right?"

I nod and watch as she swipes her finger like she is checking for dust on the empty desk.

"How do you know I'm legally a Riordan."

She smiles, her red lipstick so perfectly applied that you wonder if she has it tattooed across her lips.

"Everyone in the Order knows of his choice, and they blessed whatever that choice was, including taking out your problem. They send the officiate to the next meeting after you sign. I came to say congratulations. You're a very lucky woman but I honestly think it is the other way around. He's the lucky one."

"Thank you, I think. What about you? Who do you have to marry or whatever."

She places her blonde hair over her shoulder. "I'm tarnished. I'm whatever they think I am."

"There must be someone you might consider. You have to, or they will get rid of you."

Veronica is no saint, but she isn't all that bad. She attempts to smile but fails miserably. If she doesn't marry before graduation as the rule states, Gia told me they will get rid of her by marrying her off to a monster that needs a wife.

"I have dealt with worse." She sighs. "There was someone once that now judges me like everyone else. He isn't fond of me anymore. After Alicia died, I wasn't the same person. I lost my best friend. We were never after power, even though we had it as the only women of the Order that would take over as head of our respective families."

"Who?" I ask curiously.

"You would think I was crazy if I told you. I respect your husband, even though he doesn't understand me. He is as ruthless as he is dangerous. He loves watching me suffer for what I have done to save others from the same fate as Alicia. They misunderstand my motives. They don't know what I know and they don't see what I see."

"He can't be that bad. You're...you. And you are beautiful. You can change his mind. There is still time left."

She shakes her head. "No, Jess. There isn't time for someone like me. I ask that you forgive me for what I did to you freshman year, but you now understand why I did it. I promised Alicia I would make sure her brother was happy if something happened to her. But then I saw how he looked at you and it reminded me of how someone looked at me once."

"I forgive you, Veronica."

"He's waiting outside for you. Please, don't tell him I was here."

"Okay, I won't. Will I see you around?"

She shrugs. "Yes, until my father marries me off to a monster."

"Who was he?" She knows I'm asking her who her mystery man was. but she looks away.

I watch her leave, noticing for the first time, the sadness she carries in her eyes. I can recognize a tortured soul when I see one. She pauses at the threshold and turns. "His name is Alaric Riordan, and he was my first love. I thought he loved me but it was all a lie."

I HOPE you liked Gia and Jess's story. Thank you for reading. The Prey series will continue with Veronica's story in Forgive Me For I have Sinned coming 9/28/2023.

Pre order Forgive Me For I Have Sinned (Standalone) on my website at www.carmenrosales.com or on Amazon and B&N.

Did you know I have specially priced signed copies of all my books on my website in my bookshop? I will also have book boxes available real soon for all my bookish readers that love extra goodies.

Scan the QR code to Preorder Forgive For I Have Sinned and for all links.

Carmen Rosales is an emerging Latinx author of Steamy, and Dark Romance. She loves spending time with her family. When she is not writing, she is reading. She is an Army veteran and is currently completing her Doctorate Degree in Business and has the love and support of her husband and five children. She also writes under Delilah Croww for her DARK romance horror stories with really dark themes that is coming out soon.

Join her VIP list- www.carmenrosales.com

She loves to see a review and interact with her readers.

Scan the QR code to follow her on Social Media and sign up for her Newsletter: